Ghosts of Rheynia

TIM FACCIOLA

FIRST
TORCH

Publishing Services provided by Paper Raven Books LLC
Cover Art by Lunaris Falcon Studio
Printed in the United States of America
First Printing, 2025

ISBN:
Paperback: 979-8-9862855-8-0
Hardback: 979-8-9862855-9-7

More by Tim Facciola:

A VENGEFUL REALM

Book 1: The Scales of Balance

Book 2: The Breaker of Chains

Book 3: The Age of the End

Scan below for more information.

For those with heavy hearts and unrelenting spirits.

PURE

TRUE

The Sisters

Nort

Gai

Drake Point

Sentellion

Avengard

Drakhardt

The Wing

THE
GROTT

Belgrave

Elyngro

THE GROVE

The Nest

Saltsp

Bheric's Hollow

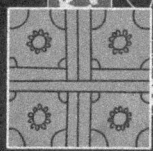

A WORD FROM THE AUTHOR:

If we fail to address our traumas, we're more likely to pass them, spreading the pain like a virus to the people we love most—whether we will it or not. In this story, a generational curse is given shape, physical form; it corrupts whoever it touches, forever staining their souls.

If you fear you might have been the victim of a generational curse, are at risk of passing one to someone you care for, or have already accidentally passed one onto someone you love—this curse doesn't have to stain you. Speak with a licensed therapist who specializes in generational trauma, legacy burdens and/or carried emotions and begin your healing journey today.

FOREWORD

BY CHRISTIE HEBERT-ASHBECK, MS, LPC, NCC

The unspoken tragedy of early life trauma is the inability for the victim to become the fully realized Self due to the difficulty of splitting from those created to protect and support their evolution. As a result, once the child has split from their perceived protector, the child is forced to adapt to a very curious environment, never sure of their place, perception, relationships, their purpose, or their own identity. This dynamic unfolds throughout this story in both individual and shared challenges, sorrows, and victories, yet always with the presence of an underlying and unsettling question that accompanies their eternal aloneness: what is missing?

Unless already consumed with a debilitating level of shame and depression, there will become an urgent "call to action" in order to find what is missing. Most generally, the search to fill the void will include abusing alcohol and drugs, eating disorders, chronic people-pleasing, compulsive sex, shopping, gambling, over-working, the next relationship and the rest of the mood-altering behaviors humans reach for in order to feel "whole." Unfortunately, these things only tend to expand "what is missing," as these behaviors will push the seeker further away from their True Selves, creating an even higher level of despair and suffering and debilitating depression.

Working with a trauma-informed therapist versed in these losses of Self, the seeker is strategically guided back to the point in their lives where they "lost" themselves—the point in which they were forced to detach (mentally or physically) from their harmful caregivers while also abandoning and disowning their own perceived "unworthy" Selves. "What is missing" has always been the True Self, the Self that comes with all of the imperfect and incredibly perfect pieces; the part that was created to thrive and evolve in the presence of nurturing and patient caregivers, the Self that does have a purpose.

PROLOGUE

Dracus

"*To dream is to die. To hope is to lie. To live is to...*" Dracus didn't remember the rest. His aunt had sung it to him when he was a boy. He remembered her voice better than her face. It was soft. Deep, but warm. She held him, his back against her chest as she'd sing. She was too sweet for this world. But then again, she wasn't long for it. Times like this, he wished he'd turned around. Looked her in the eye as she sang those sad lullabies. Then, maybe he would remember her and not the monster death turned her into.

But time for that was gone. He doubted he'd live long enough to recall any of her songs. The only music left was that of the Order's drums, the echoing shouts of their marching legions, and the moans of the poor undying souls who would remain trapped in their failing bodies after they left.

Dracus shuffled his feet, still clad in the Order-issued boots he wore the day he deserted. Standing in the valley of the Cut, side by side with *soldiers* who didn't want to be there any more than he did, he knew all too well what awaited the rest of the Underground. But also what awaited him: the Final Demise. Hollowing by a hundred cuts, one for each man in the cohort, a fate reserved for deserters. Dracus's own Vendetta dagger, *Fang*, rested on his hip.

Chewing on his mustache and not wanting to think about that, he considered how many of the *brave* souls beside him would be wailing the dirge of undeath once the battle concluded.

It wasn't fair. Wasn't right. How many laurels had he secured for King Bohen in his Order blacks? How many shrieking hollowed begged to be released from their undying bodies on the grounds of his victories? How many spectral shades fled their flesh to wander the battlefield, void of any recollections that made them human? He knew how many darklings were trapped in the soul jar on his hip. 804 tortured souls, denied their bodies and the release of not knowing what they'd lost, eternally searching to *live* once again by overtaking a host.

Those were his potential fates, and he wouldn't have a choice when the time came: hollow and suffer for eternity, become a shade and wander aimlessly forever, or become a darkling and end up in a soul jar as some low-level Justicus's trophy. If he was lucky, he'd be irradiated, and then he'd be done with this world.

"To dream is to die."

He shouldn't have been here. Most of them weren't supposed to be. They should've been on a ship far from Rheynia and its undying curse—he, Fawkes, and the boy, Canton. The first settlement in Sansia had disappeared without a trace—so what? Dracus welcomed that darkling over the darkling he knew. Welcomed the newness over the monster that still haunted Canton's dreams. The three of them, together, they would have made it. Found land, people, civilization—lived lives of meaning.

Those dreams died. Burned and went up in smoke along with *Resilience* and the rest of the Underground's fleet. Now they were here, fighting for a cause only less than a quarter of them believed in.

"Divided, ruin will reign," Arilette had said, standing before the burning ships and the scorched and still-screaming remains of her father. The same credo the Skeleton King had used in an attempt to reunite Rheynia in the Dominion of Neutreen's Holy Order was now the basis of Arilette's rebellion.

Dracus ran his palm over his shaved head, moisture coating both surfaces. The woman beside him practically shook, holding her soul-scorching irradiator in both hands as the Order's legions marched nearer, their voices growing louder. Swallowing, Dracus put his hand atop hers. Graeva, he thought her name was, but wasn't sure enough to risk the mistake.

Dracus forced a tight-lipped grin. "Too far out to fire. Set that down. Before ya hurt someone."

Graeva, or whatever her name was, nodded. She lowered the handheld arcanatek and put it in the holster at her belt. Flicking her black hair over her shoulder, she wafted the scent of burnt wood and human flesh to his nostrils.

Dracus cleared his throat, not wanting to swallow the acrid scent, or the ashes from the friend they came from. Arenius, Arilette's father and the founder of the Underground—but above all, a good man—was gone. Burned alive and thereafter.

Arenius's hope was to bring as many people beyond the curse and as far away from Bohen, the Order, and the hollowed as possible. His dream—ruined. Sabotaged by his own daughter. Her fires, birthed from the darkness of the Underground's past, brought death to his dreams, and from their ashes, she sold the second-greatest lie in Rheynia; King Bohen, the Skeleton King, was weak. Defeatable.

"To hope is to lie."

Graeva glanced in Dracus's direction, eyes wet, cheeks and nose blushed a rosy pink. She nodded, subtly at first, but then with more assertion. "We can do it, right?"

"Course we can," Dracus lied. Wasn't his first. If he somehow managed to escape this deathless massacre unhollowed with his soul still in his body, it wouldn't be his last either. Lying kept him living. Living through the War of the Seers, the Artificer's War, coming face to face with the single greatest lie in Rheynia, and now this? He lied again. "Just stay close, eh? I'll keep an eye out."

Graeva's lip appeared ready to warble like a charged irradiator.

"No more cryin'," Dracus said. "Time enough for that later."

Graeva nodded, sniffled, and tucked her lower lip like a right and proper legionary. Dracus would look after her. If he could. But he had a lot of people to keep an eye on, and Graeva wasn't particularly high on that list.

Keep livin'. Return to Canton and Fawkes. We'll find our own way off this rock, and gory ghostin' Arilette can count on that.

"To live is to…"

Dracus released his breath from his nostrils. *Blood and bone, what is the next word?*

"That's a good thing you did," Theodyn said, leaning close from Dracus's opposite side. He nodded at Graeva. "You've always done that."

The war drums neared, bellowing deeper with each successive beat. The high walls of the Cut reverberated the sound, making the valley tremble worse than Graeva's knees now that she'd buttoned up her lip.

"Wish I could've been more like you," Theodyn said.

Dracus turned to Theodyn. The familiarity of his tone rang oddly *unfamiliar*. "How you mean?"

Theodyn pushed a loose strand of silver-blond hair behind his ear, towards his messy bun. The muscles of his jaw clenched. Still staring straight ahead, he closed his eyes for a long moment. "I remember the day they brought you in after the fall of Cybellica. Couldn't've been more than five."

Dracus grunted. Cybellica wasn't a name mentioned often. The last stronghold of Cadrow Wing's band of Seers and murderers fell like every army did before the Skeleton King. A rush of muddy memories served as a temporary distraction from the army marching toward them now. But not enough to fool Dracus into believing there was any way Theodyn could have known him from back then.

Shaking his head, Dracus examined Theodyn. "Whatchu talkin' about?"

Theodyn lifted his gaze to the gray clouds forever shrouded over Rheynia. A gentle drizzle fell, undeterred by the notion of spitting in their faces. "I know what you lost, Dracus. In the days before you arrived, on the eve you were born—if the stories tell it true." Theodyn scoffed. "Difficult to tell. You're more myth than man these days." He grinned, shaking his head as if lost in memories he shouldn't have had. "You continually outdid the others. Plenty of boys were bigger, stronger, faster, smarter. You always found a way to win."

Dracus pursed his lips, trying to piece together how he knew anything about his Order past. Waiting for the eventual punchline to the old man's musings, Dracus said, "I never found a way to win. Winning's for stories with heroes, and this one don't have any. If ya can't win, just gotta find ways to keep playin'."

Theodyn chuckled. "Keep playing." He rubbed the back of his neck and took a deep breath. "Do you believe in the Purge?"

Dracus's mustache bristled in the wind of his flustered exhale. "Theodyn, this ain't the time for theology an—"

"You know as well as I what awaits us," Theodyn whispered, quiet enough that no one else could hear. "If not now, never."

Dracus snorted. If the Four Tenets of Elysianism ever stood, they fell long ago. Faytemarked be damned, Neutreen was long gone. He wished he was wrong, but after the things he'd seen, there was no Goddess of Justice. No deity waiting beyond the curse to grant the pious wings to fly to the divine realm. It was all a lie—perhaps the third greatest lie ever told—to get people up in the morning. There was no afterlife—only life, death, and the corruption between them.

The Tellers believed in the Purge—the lie that if all the hollowed were vanquished and every shade and darkling irradiated, Neutreen would return to Rheynia. Even before being indoctrinated into the Order's propagative education, no hellhound would have sold him on that crock. If Dracus was going to buy any of the pedantic divergences of Elysianism, it was that the One True God had infiltrated Neutreen's temples and needed to be struck down for the Goddess of Justice to return to her rightful reign. But Dracus had seen the One with his own eyes, and he was no God.

"Nah," Dracus said. "The Purge won't fix nothin'."

Theodyn put his hand to the fatekeeper hanging around his neck. The octagonal arcanatek customarily held prayers to be read and burned for Neutreen. Parents generally wrote them for their children, to be opened upon their deaths. No one who'd lived long enough to have seen the Disasters had any business wearing one, but come to think of it, Dracus had never seen Theodyn without it.

Dracus put his hand on the man's shoulder as the Order's legions encroached, their drums growing louder. He gestured to Graeva trembling beside him. "Brave face, eh, Theodyn? For the rest of 'em."

Theodyn turned to Dracus, a forlorn darkness in his blue eyes. "That's not my name."

Dracus searched the man's face. The sunken eyes. The elegant cheekbones. The strong jaw. Piecing Theodyn's ramblings together, he realized why the old man always seemed too familiar. The silver-blond hair should have given him away but hid within his age. The same hair of Belrich Fayte, the Legatus of the Order, the son of Bohen—Bherus, Prince of Rheynia.

A shiver rattled down Dracus's spine and coiled around his ribs. "Hmm. Seems I've found the long-lost prince, eh?" He put his hands on his hips and stared at his Order boots. "All this time, Bherus ghostin' Fayte right under my nose."

"I've gone by many names—Bherus, Dreyus, Theodyn. Lived many lives, as have you. But this has to be the end. A Teller told me once it was up to me to stop my father. Stop my brother. Save Rheynia."

Dracus couldn't help himself. What began as a smirk turned into a sarcastic chuckle that drew the attention of those looking for a distraction from the piss in their boots and the army marching towards them. But said chuckle also attracted the eyes of Arilette's Arch Premius, Lorath.

"Something funny, Dray?" Lorath asked, his thin lips parting in a snarl that made his default-darkling-stare seem like a smile. Shoulders too broad for his narrow mug, he stalked between the rows of Underground soldiers to the middle of the formation where those who didn't want to be there were shackled into obedience.

"No, Premius," Dracus said, standing to mock-attention. He pinched his thumb and index finger together, splaying the other three in the stocks.

Lorath stopped before Dracus, staring at the stocks.

Nearly a head and a half taller than Dracus, Lorath glanced down his crooked nose and cleft chin at him. "You're lucky Neutreen's no longer here. Do you honestly believe you'd measure up if you were in the stocks before her?"

Dracus shrugged. "Depends who's beside me." He pointed at Theodyn, or Bherus—whatever he wanted to be called. "Him? Nah, she wouldn't like me much." He jabbed his thumb toward Graeva. "Her? Psh, not a chance. She's gotta lotta wings to pass out before I get mine. But you?" He snorted. "Yeah, I reckon she'd turn me into a dove next to you."

If not for the slow patter of passing midday rains, the Order legionaries' shouting, and the bellowing war drums marching their way, silence would have stretched across the Cut.

Dracus smiled. Lorath didn't.

"Theodyn," Lorath said, "you've chosen poor company."

Theodyn cocked his head in the Arch Premius's direction. "I preferred to be with Arenius."

The bite in each of his words wasn't how one typically spoke to a commanding officer in the moments before battle. But when that battle occurred shortly after a coup that the commanding officer partook in, well… typical took a swim in the Grotto and never came back.

Lorath's nose wrinkled before turning on his heel and stalking to the frontlines to join Arilette and her mutineers.

Once he was gone, Theodyn lifted the fatekeeper from his neck and extended it toward Dracus. Dracus stared at it but didn't accept the arcanatek.

His mother never had the chance to write him prayers. Died in the Disasters the day he was born. His father didn't know how to write. Even if he did, he never bothered to hold Dracus before he marched off to join the War of the Seers. Odds were his father was still out there, somewhere. A wandering shade. A snarling hollowed. Or maybe trapped in the very soul jar on his hip. It didn't matter.

"Ain't those supposed to be personal?" Dracus asked of the pendant.

"Very," Theodyn said, staring at the Order's advance. "You might not believe in the Purge. You might not believe this story has a hero. But I need that Teller to have been right. I need the Purge to be true. We need a hero so my girls can live in peace."

He turned to face Dracus, his expression as hard as the Spine and as twisted as the Gullies. "If I fail, should I suffer and the Skeleton King live—if the Order is still in power, you must open this. You must do what I could not. Finish this. My father. My brother. All of it."

Fearing what it held, Dracus shook his head, thrusting the arcanatek back to Theodyn.

Theodyn persisted, shoving it towards Dracus. The Order's war drums were now close enough to resonate with the dissonance between them.

"I can't," Dracus said.

"For my girls. Please."

Dracus examined the black pendant.

Arilette's shouts and Lorath's echoes roared against the Order's approach, each as insistent as Theodyn's outstretched hand. Dracus had no idea what Theodyn was thinking or planning, but if he held what Dracus thought he held, he wanted nothing to do with it.

"If not for me," Theodyn said, "for your boy, Canton."

Dracus swallowed the knot in his throat, hoping Fawkes and Canton were as far from here as possible. But unless Theodyn's fatekeeper held another ship that they could sail away from Rheynia, it couldn't help them. Fleeing Arilette wouldn't go unpunished. Hiding from the Order was their only hope until another escape attempt revealed itself.

"I'm gonna suffer the same fate as you do here," Dracus said. "If you wanted to keep that safe, you shouldn't have brought it."

Theodyn took Dracus's hand in his. His touch, warm despite the chill of the falling rain, sent a hum up his arm. Pressing the arcanatek into his palm, Theodyn leaned close. Against the thrashing war drums, the shouting legionaries, and Arilette's attempts to rouse the Underground's fighting spirit, Theodyn's whisper drowned out all else.

"Find a way. Keep playing." He closed Dracus's fingers around the fatekeeper.

Light as it was, whatever it housed weighed him down. The soul jar on his hip contained 804 souls, but its heft was nothing compared to the fatekeeper. A darkness. A dread. A sentience denied of the hollowed and shades. Yet a power, far beyond that of any darkling, lived within the arcanatek.

Dracus met Theodyn's eyes. Suspicions confirmed, he knew now what was inside, but he didn't want to believe it.

Crestfallen, Theodyn nodded. A heart-rending tear trickled from the corner of his eye to conceal itself in the raindrops. The burden of his name, the weight of his self-imposed fate—they buried the man in shadows.

Dark veins sprouted up Theodyn's chest and erupted through the blue of his irises.

Dracus balked. *Blood magic…*

"For Threyna and Laela," Theodyn said.

Then the horns erupted. The battle for the Cut began. And everything went to gory ghosting ruin.

PART I

CHAPTER 1

UNTIL THE CUT

Threyna
Ten Years Later...

Threyna's boots sank into the murky silt of the Cut despite following in the footsteps before her. Lit by a dim illuminator, her squadron traversed the infamous valley, irradiators drawn and charged in the event that the quiet graveyard still held secrets to share. Shrugging the strap of her pack higher on her shoulder, Threyna surveyed the gloom ahead, not willing to take any chances.

The mission had been a success. Each of her squadron, five in all, hauled packs of their own, filled with enough stolen power coils to create an arcanatek large enough to vortex half the hollowed in the Gullies and irradiate whatever shades and darklings it drew out. Now they just had to return to Octarius. Once they were through the Cut, they'd be home free.

Though they had slipped past the Order's Justicus, infiltrated the silo, and navigated around Saltspire without incident, people didn't say, *"Don't thank Neutreen till after the Cut,"* for the fun of it.

Few places in Rheynia held positive memories. Anyone who had been in the Underground long enough knew there were few victories worth celebrating. But the scars of defeats suffered at the Order's hands abounded, none worse than the Battle of the Cut. Not one of Threyna's squadron escaped the ordeal unscathed, and the moment they entered into the valley for the last stretch of their return home, the typical banter between her crew hollowed, leaving them to pass through the haunted gorge like silent shades.

Threyna regripped her irradiator, fending off thoughts of the night she lost her father in this very valley. The night her mother and sister fled north. The way the hellhounds came for her from the shadows.

Stifling a shudder, Threyna peered past the arcanatek's glow to the night beyond. "Stay sharp. Stick to protocol." She nodded to Ebrus, the solemn, sensitive boy who lost as much as she had that night. "We'll be back in the hold in no time."

Ebrus's lip quivered more than any Centuriot of the Underground's should. As if realizing Threyna had noticed, he tossed the flop of his black comb-over to the opposite side of his head.

"Ay, that's what I like to hear," Yevon said, his ever-present grin dimpling his boyish cheeks. "The Legatus and Arch Premius get their power coils, Ebrus gets his poetry, Rivich the opportunity to salute some more, and Aylenia… hey, what are you doing once we get back?"

Aylenia, leading the way, whipped around as she continued to stalk forward. The white light of the illuminator did little to soften the sharpness of her high cheekbones or the glare of her dark green eyes. "If that's an invite to your bunk, you'd have better luck with the Legatus than me."

Rivich elbowed Aylenia. "Don't encourage him. Focus on the mission."

Yevon mocked Rivich the moment he turned his back.

Before Yevon could continue, Threyna tapped his shoulder and offered him a chiding shrug. Rivich was right, as he usually was, but despite all the darkness in the world, Yevon still found the light in it. His gentle teasing of Ebrus lightened the mood without attacking him, his levity softened Rivich's sternness, and his continued attempts to lure Aylenia's affections were one of the few forms of entertainment to be found within the Underground. This was not the time nor the place to become distracted, but better to be distracted by light conversation than the thoughts of their parents hollowing on the muck they walked upon.

"Keep it caged, Yevon," Threyna said. "Besides, you couldn't handle Aylenia. Once we make it back, a round of Valefyre on me. Perhaps then she'll give you a shot."

Aylenia scoffed. "I'd rather cozy up with Lorath. No offense, kid."

Yevon groaned in mock insult. "His hellhounds don't even bark anymore."

"That's the idea," Aylenia said.

Rivich grabbed the strap of Aylenia's pack and spun her around, glaring at Yevon. "Blood and bone. The mission." He bared his teeth at Threyna as if demanding her to discipline them. Though the glow from Aylenia's illuminator cast half his stone-chiseled jaw in shadow, it couldn't conceal the dark scar rising from his collar to slash across his throat.

A scar Threyna knew he still blamed her for.

Rivich wished he was Premius. Oftentimes, Threyna did too. She didn't enjoy leadership. She didn't want to be responsible for making the tough call when others' lives hung in the balance. But Arilette chose her. Not him.

Threyna returned his harsh gaze and lowered Rivich's irradiator until it pointed to the ground. "You are the only one slowing the progress of this mission, Centuriot." She seized his pack and yanked him forward despite the breadth of his shoulders.

He released his grip on Aylenia and allowed Threyna to draw his face close to hers. His furrowed brow and clenched jaw retained their tension, but he held her gaze.

He hated her. She saw it whenever he looked at her. Not out of jealousy. Not because Arilette favored her. Not even because he believed he would be a better Premius than she was, even though it was true. He hated her for the same reason she hated herself. But she couldn't let him know that.

She snarled, blocking out the screams in the back of her mind. "Move out. Or the Legatus will hear about this."

Rivich maintained his unyielding brown-eyed stare. "Yes, Premius."

Threyna didn't release him. Holding his stern gaze, she wished his grieving soul could recognize the same in her. That a look could speak in the space where no words could. But that was the point. She couldn't give him that. Not through words, looks, or any other form of communication.

I did what I had to. But that doesn't mean it doesn't haunt me...

Her grip slackened on his shoulder strap, but she didn't let go. The moment stretched too long. The sullen stillness swirled with the eerie quiet in the absence of their squelching footsteps and hushed banter.

Threyna forced herself to let go. Rivich stood to his full height, the stone in his throat bobbing with swallowed words. As he turned, something else moved in the distance. A pebble rattled down the wall of the southern lip of the Cut ahead of them.

Threyna motioned to Aylenia, closing her fingers into a fist.

Aylenia dutifully powered down her illuminator, cloaking them in darkness.

As Threyna's vision adapted to the absence of light, she tapped Ebrus beside her. Two gentle beats, a pause, another beat, then two more. Threyna drummed the same cadence on Rivich's shoulder, then Ebrus to Yevon, until all five knew the order. Taking care not to make noise, the five moved into formation. Rivich and Yevon took the front while Threyna and Ebrus turned to face their flank, each leveling their irradiators at the surrounding dark. Aylenia took center, readying to charge whichever arcanatek would best help once the threat was identified.

The wind picked up to conceal whatever had stirred in the night. It could be a hellhound, a single hollowed, or an entire horde. Worse yet, if confronted by a cohort of patrolling Justicus, they'd find themselves in a firefight. She knew better than to pray to Neutreen that it was just a falling rock; no amount of matches lit to the Goddess of Justice would see those prayers answered.

Threyna chewed the inside of her lip, scanning the southern ridgeline. As the wind softened to a whisper, she still couldn't hear anything. No voices. No footsteps.

Shoulder to shoulder with Ebrus, she felt the tremor of his arms, the slight rattle to his uneven breaths.

Gory ghosts, Ebrus. Not now.

Holding her irradiator steady and never averting her gaze from the horizon, she reached her left hand across her body to gently grip Ebrus's arm. His quivering posture settled and his breath found a steady rhythm.

The aura of a shade approached, growing brighter as it neared the ridgeline's edge, but this was coming from behind their position. Shades didn't disturb the environment around them; they only cast a ghastly visage of the people they were in life. There was no way this shade kicked the stone ahead of them, but where there were shades, there were hollowed. And once within the Cut, there were only two ways out: back the way they had come, or through.

Threyna hurriedly tapped Aylenia with three quick beats. She relayed the message to Rivich, and together, they stalked forward in formation. Continuing to watch their flank, Threyna sidestepped behind Aylenia and Rivich, irradiator aimed at the shade's growing aura.

A sharp inhale from Rivich's positioning stopped their progress.

Three more taps.

Another shade.

Threyna responded with one tap. They quickened their pace. Feet squishing through the muck, they traded silence for speed.

"Multiple," Rivich whispered, barely audible over the jostling of their packs and the shuffling of their feet.

Heart hammering, Threyna inclined her head to the glowing ridgeline. It didn't make sense. No arcanatek could cast that much light. There would need to be dozens of shades to even come close, but shades didn't travel in packs.

A low groaning breath droned behind her. Threyna looked over her shoulder just as a shade floated over the ridgeline to traverse the Cut. Behind it, a hollowed lunged for it. Its withered flesh passed through the incorporeal shade and plummeted down the valley's wall. Before it could hit the ground, half a dozen others followed it off the ledge.

"Run," Threyna hissed.

Weighed down by power-coil-ladened packs, they charged through the valley as more and more shades passed overhead, and more and more hollowed mindlessly pursued. The groans of the horde filled the Cut as decomposing bodies slammed into the ground and one another in their fruitless pursuit of the shades.

Threyna returned her gaze forward, feet sliding through the clay-like soot on the valley floor. As long as the hollowed were behind them, they'd be able to outpace them. If they were lucky, the shades would continue to occupy their attention and they'd never give chase. But it wasn't the shades behind them that made Threyna's chest tighten beneath the fatekeeper tucked against her breastbone; it was the ever-brightening aura of encroaching shades ahead that would bar their path and trap them.

"Dawnshards at the ready," Threyna said, as quietly as she could over their ragged breaths and trampling feet. "Once the first shade crests the ridge." The handheld light bombs wouldn't distract every hollowed, but one less hollowed in their path could make the difference between returning home and wandering Rheynia for eternity.

Threyna unhooked a Dawnshard from her belt and looped her finger through the ring atop the arcanatek. Ebrus did the same beside her. One moment, he was reaching for his belt; the next, he was gone from sight. He fell, face first into the wet clay along the valley floor.

Threyna inhaled sharply. Sliding to a halt, she turned back for Ebrus.

"Threyna!" Aylenia hissed.

"Keep going," Threyna called over her shoulder. She wouldn't let another member of her team hollow. Especially not Ebrus.

She charged back as he struggled to regain his feet. But the ticking of a live Dawnshard drew her attention.

Blood and bone.

Threyna scanned the ground for the black arcanatek. If it detonated, not only would she and Ebrus be blinded, but the radiant flash would draw every hollowed directly toward them. Feeling for the Dawnshard through the depressions of their footprints, Threyna's time slipped away, faster and faster with each passing moment. Hands caked in muck, Threyna scrambled, following the sound.

Ebrus crawled towards her, doing the same.

Threyna's hand closed around the octagonal shape absent its loop just as its ticking reached its crescendo. From her knees, Threyna closed her eyes and reared back to hurl the Dawnshard over Ebrus's head, back the way they had come.

Not a half a moment after it left her hand, it exploded. White radiant light blazed through her closed eyelids. Stumbling back, she called for Ebrus.

"I can't see!" he shouted.

Too ghosting loud. Eyes still closed, Threyna reached for him, sliding in the clay. Her muddy hands closed around his arm. Unable to see, she yanked him towards her, but he slipped, his weight dragging her off-balance.

The snarls of hollowed filled the valley. They were coming. Fast.

Threyna hauled Ebrus to his feet, sliding her shoulder under his arm. Charging back toward the others as quickly as she could, absent sight on the slippery surface, Threyna attempted to open her eyes. Flashes spotted across her vision. Darting halos swerved in the distance. Another blast of white light exploded in the sky to the shrieks of more hollowed.

Another Dawnshard. We'll be surrounded by a horde if we don't clear the Cut. "Come on," Threyna said. "We have to catch up."

"Threy," Ebrus said, "I can't see!"

"I'm here, but we need to move!"

The hollowed gained on them. Their decomposing maws gnashed, ready to tear them to pieces. Threyna kept her sparking vision ahead. In the distance, a vortexer warbled to life and released its charge, ejecting a new white aura into their path. Swords hacked into undead flesh, releasing fresh gales of haunted shrieks.

Swords wouldn't stop a hollowed in their pursuit of clawing their way through a living body, but severed limbs, clipped tendons, and broken bones certainly slowed them down.

Still, hollowed closed the distance on their flank.

"Can you see yet?" Threyna asked Ebrus, doing her best to keep the fear from her tone. Now was not the time to trigger one of Ebrus's episodes.

"No!" The panic in his voice tightened across her chest.

Blood and bone. With her own vision readjusting, she seized her blaster with her free hand. She pressed the button, switching it from irradiator to vortexer. The range on the vortexer wasn't nearly as far as the irradiator's radiant energy, but hitting a hollowed, even at its highest output, would only stun it. Meant for shades and darklings, shooting a body with an irradiator was a wasted charge. But if she could vortex a hollowed, the freed shade might distract the others long enough for her and Ebrus to get away.

A growling hollowed reached for them from its belly, its severed legs and mutilated arm slowing it down. Appreciating Rivich's handiwork, Threyna steered Ebrus beyond its reach. A pair of severed heads snapped their jaws as they strode past, their decapitated bodies wandering like Order legionaries lost in the Gullies.

At the end of the Cut, white blasts of irradiator fire erupted from her squadron's arcanatek, streaking through the air or stunning the few hollowed still ahead of Threyna and Ebrus. Threyna's own blaster, set to vortex, warbled in her hand, nearing its max output.

Just as she was about to turn to fire, Ebrus cried out as he was torn from her grip. A hollowed crawled from the muck to wrap its arms around Ebrus's leg. Its jaw hung slack, the muscles severed. Though it couldn't bite him, it clawed through his britches.

Threyna passed her blaster to her left hand to draw her short sword. She slashed down at the hollowed's outstretched arm, dislodging its grip from Ebrus. Sheathing her sword, she hauled a hyperventilating Ebrus from the hollowed's clutches. Its silent attack was just what the other pursuing hollowed needed to catch up.

A hollowed reached for her, close enough for her to feel the wind. Shoving Ebrus aside, Threyna lurched out of its immediate grasp.

A bright white rail fired past her and struck the hollowed in the chest, giving her breathing room. Leveling her blaster at the dozens closing in behind them, Threyna aimed at the stunned hollowed. With no time to wonder if her father was one of these tortured souls giving chase, she swallowed the grief left unresolved after he never returned from the Cut and pulled the trigger.

Air distorted between her and the stunned hollowed. The white luminescent soul of a man who once feared the very thing he became ripped from his body. The shade hung suspended in the air even as his body's momentum carried him through the incorporeal specter to fall motionless to the ground.

"Come on," Threyna said, holstering her blaster and spiriting Ebrus forward as the remaining hollowed surrounded the shade.

His arm shook in hers, his fingers bent at odd angles with the awkward cramping his episodes imposed.

"It's okay, Eb. I'm here."

Ebrus didn't respond. His blank, sightless eyes stared straight ahead, tears trickling down his cheeks. Following the path the others carved for them, Threyna led Ebrus beyond the Cut's mouth and into the trees lining Cybel's Tears where Aylenia, Rivich, and Yevon waited.

"Nice work," Threyna said, not slowing down from her charge out of the Cut. "Good shooting, whoever took the shot."

Aylenia bowed her head, falling in beside Threyna at a trot. "Is he prime?"

"He's fine," Threyna said.

"He'll need to go to the medicus once we get back," Aylenia said, gesturing to his lower left leg. "Those abrasions get infected, he'll get dewskull."

Yevon flinched at the mention of the disease.

"Yeah," Threyna said. "Then he'll be fine."

"Fine," Rivich scoffed. "Look at him. How can you say he'll be fine? What is this—three of the last four missions?"

Threyna bared her teeth, giving Ebrus a defensive squeeze. "Enough, Rivich."

"Oh, so this you'll shut down." Rivich snorted. "Anything goes when Yevon wants to shoot his mouth off mid-mission. You don't say gore when Aylenia's gotta be a know-it-all or when Ebrus hollows his eyes out to get you to notice him. But when I say he's going to get one of us killed—I'm the one waking the hellhound."

Heat rose to Threyna's cheeks. *Gory ghosting dammit, Rivich. Not now.*

She could feel Yevon's and Aylenia's eyes wandering between her and Rivich as they passed the remains of Fort Cybel to ford the bridge over the Tears. Gritting her teeth, knowing he was right—again—she couldn't even meet his eyes. "I said *enough,* Centuriot. That's an order."

Rivich scoffed, muttering under his breath.

An uncomfortable silence followed. Threyna exchanged a sidelong glance with Aylenia over Ebrus's shoulder. Aylenia's lip contorted. She alone knew how Threyna felt about Ebrus. Holding him now, he felt as frail as he had ten years ago after his parents never returned from the Battle of the Cut. It wasn't just his parents. Fawkes and Canton had fled. Threyna's mother and sister, Laela, too. Arenius was burned, vortexed, and irradiated. After just one night, his whole life fell to pieces, and all he had left was her. She'd lost everything that night too, but where it only hardened her, it broke Ebrus. He wasn't like her. He was too sweet for this world. Too kind for those left in it.

They walked in uneasy silence through the haunting woods along Cybel's Tears.

"Race ya back?" Yevon said to Rivich once they broke through the tree line and Octarius's ruins came into sight.

Rivich grunted. "Do we have your leave, *Premius*?"

Threyna pursed her lips. She didn't want to leave it like this. The gaping fissure between them was spreading faster than the Grotto during the Disasters, but she didn't know what she could say to mend the divide. This wasn't the first time she'd felt this way with someone she'd cared about, and it had been ten years since she last saw or spoke to her mother or sister.

"Go," she said, soft as a shade.

Rivich took off, his long legs building to a sprint despite the pack on his back. Yevon followed in his wake but never caught up. None of them could keep up with Rivich when he was of a mood, and Threyna had no doubt she had triggered just such a mood.

Watching them run away, she felt like she was watching her father march off to join the Underground in the Battle of the Cut. Like she was watching her mother and sister evacuate Octarius to head north through the tunnels with the others who abandoned Arilette.

They all leave. They all run away.

"Always another fight," Aylenia said.

Threyna was supposed to respond with, *"Always another victory,"* but the sentiment felt hollow. No victory was truly a victory; there was always a cost, and the price was always greater than what they'd traded for. Remaining silent and sighing through her teeth, Threyna, along with Aylenia, helped Ebrus the final distance to Octarius's underground entrance.

CHAPTER 2

TEST OF LOYALTY

Threyna II

With the choir of hollowed groaning in the distance, Threyna and Aylenia led Ebrus to the arcanatek-powered entryway that connected the ruins of what was once Victaryen Kaine's castle. Now, it was the Underground's subterranean bastion. Aylenia seized hold of the hidden spatial distorter. Disguised as a metallic hinge in what was once a doorway, the arcanatek was perfectly hidden in plain view. Aylenia pressed the buttons along the arcanatek's rectangular spine in the proper order and walked through the crumpled remains of the doorway.

There one moment, gone the next, Aylenia passed through the spatial distorter. Similar to the fatekeeper technology that housed the gifts parents left to their children, the arcanatek of the doorway served as a portal, a ripple in time and space.

"In you go," Threyna said, helping Ebrus through.

Together, they walked through the entryway. Like becoming a shade, their bodies glowed silver. But unlike the eternity of the shades' demise, Threyna and Ebrus's time in the strange ethereal plane faded. Over the course of a few steps, the dark gloom of Octarius's ruins became the illuminator-lit halls of the Underground's top level.

Aylenia greeted them with a grin. "Thank the Savior."

Threyna snorted. "If only she'd brought us an arcanatek that allowed us to bypass the Cut." She passed Ebrus off to Aylenia. "Get him to the medicus. Probably need a few hours in the warp to allow those hellscars to heal up."

"I'm right here," Ebrus said, as Threyna took his power-coil-filled pack from his back.

Threyna ignored him, continuing to speak to Aylenia as she slung Ebrus's pack over her shoulder. "Oh, and make sure he takes the rads. We don't need another dewskull outbreak."

"Prime," Aylenia said. "The others?"

Threyna hmphed, holding out her hand to take Aylenia's pack and sling it over her other shoulder. "Leave them be." She had no doubt Rivich delivered his pack to the quartermaster and made sure Yevon did the same. The last thing she wanted was to have to get between Rivich and Aylenia if he still had more venom to spit.

Aylenia nodded. "I'll take care of Ebrus and meet you back at the bunk."

"Still right here," Ebrus said, misery in his pale blue eyes.

Threyna finally met his gaze, unsure if she was disappointed in him, afraid that Rivich was right about him, or angry with herself for not being able to turn him into a Centuriot she didn't have to worry about.

His cheeks pale, face drawn, he gazed at the ground. "Apologies. Erm. Apologies, Premius." He let out an exasperated breath. "Gratitude. For saving me."

Threyna pursed her lips and nodded. She'd never look at him the way he looked at her. She knew that hollowed whatever small part of him still yearned for her to love him the way he did her. She wouldn't, as sure as the daily rains.

Breaking under the weight of the extra packs and Ebrus's hopes, she forced herself to smile. "Rest up, Eb." She inclined her chin to Aylenia, and the two left her for the medicus's quarters.

Waiting for their footsteps to recede down the south stairwell, Threyna sighed. *Gory ghosts, what am I going to do about him?* Setting off down the long corridor toward the armory, Threyna replayed the mission over and over again in her mind, knowing Arilette would expect details once she delivered their haul to the quartermaster.

Always the Cut. Everything goes wrong at the Cut.

She'd paced this very hall that morning after the battle ten years ago. Dracus had delivered her to the medicus after saving her from a pack of hellhounds. She'd asked where her father was, but Dracus said he didn't know.

"Is he gone?" she had asked.

Dracus had rubbed his blood-speckled hand over his bald scalp, chewing his mustache. *"He called you Little Dove, eh?"* He took a deep breath. *"I don't know, Little Dove. But you're here. You're still kicking. That'll have to do."*

The fatekeeper Dracus gave to her that night hung heavy on her chest, his words heavier yet. *"This was your father's, Little Dove. He said if he didn't make it, if he were gone and the Order still in power, you must open this,"* Dracus had said, quoting her father's last words.

She didn't believe he was gone. Not when Dracus said he didn't know. Not when Arilette told her the Skeleton King *got him.* Not even after she'd paced these halls, step by agonizing step, clutching his fatekeeper, waiting for him to return for a full day and night. And still, not ten years later, did she believe he was lost. Shade, hollowed, darkling, or still alive in Saltspire's *farm*—each was just as likely as the last.

Threyna trudged to the end of the hall and turned into the armory to find Old Man Marius sitting behind the table and reinforced cage. His bushy black brow inclined, and a toothy grin cracked his weathered face.

"If it ain't Lady Darkling herself," Marius said. "Ain't ya gotta crew to turn in your haul? Are we supposed to drink this Valefyre by ourselves?" He lifted the bottle of grog.

Too tired to tell him not to call her that, she pushed past pleasantries and set Ebrus's pack on Marius's neat and orderly table. "Did Yevon and Rivich—"

"Yeah, yeah." Marius waved his hand flippantly, setting the bottle down. "All these young Centuriots never care to swap stories. Not even over a few fingers of Valefyre. Dropped the power coils and stormed out all ghosting miffed. 'Specially that big one."

Threyna hmphed, shoving the first pack across the table to make room for Aylenia's.

Marius's broad hands dragged the first pack through the window in the cage and set it on the floor beside him with a whistle. "These are heavy. You lot did good work, Premius. Good work!" He greedily took the second pack, making room for Threyna to set hers down.

"All went well until the Cut."

Marius chuckled. "Doesn't it always?"

Unburdened by the weight of the power coils, Threyna's other concerns felt heavier. Ebrus. Rivich. The fatekeeper on her chest.

Threyna patted the table. "Always does, Mar. I'll see you later." She turned to go.

The big man grumbled. "Later? You just got here. What about swappin' stories, Valefyre?"

Walking backwards, Threyna shrugged. "Do you want to explain to the Legatus what kept me from delivering my report?"

Marius huffed, setting the last of the packs down inside the armory. "Just countin' and stackin' power coils for me then, eh?"

"Count 'em and stack 'em," Threyna said as she exited the quartermaster's chambers.

Setting back down the hall, her posture slumped. Though the mission had been successful, it left her exhausted. Halos encroached into her peripheral vision, her sight still distorted from Ebrus's Dawnshard.

"He's going to get one of us hollowed..." Rivich had said.

He still blamed her for Daeton's suffering. Maybe she should have aborted the mission as he had asked. Perhaps she should have gone herself instead of giving the order. Maybe then, Daeton would still be Rivich's bunkmate. Rivich would still smile. He wouldn't be so angry.

She'd made a call. It was the wrong one. There were a dozen ifs and maybes that could have been different. And though Arilette told her there was no room for a Premius to consider maybes and perhapses, it was all she thought about.

Returning to the entrance, she headed down the north stairwell and trotted level by level through the switchbacks, passing the long halls of barracks to the Legatus's chambers in the belly of Octarius's subterranean fortress. Momentum aided her fatigue and beat back her dark thoughts.

Will Ebrus ever forgive me if I have him taken off the strike team? Will I ever forgive myself if my hesitancy to do so got Aylenia, Rivich, or Yevon hollowed?

She took a deep breath. Rivich was right. But Threyna knew all too well how Arilette Desius felt about those who lacked the mettle to survive this cursed world. Divided, ruin would reign, and nothing divided a people faster than those who couldn't pull their weight. Even the safe jobs Marius and the quartermaster's staff served were earned through hard years in the field. No one got a free pass. If Arilette had her way, she would have cut Ebrus loose and fed him to the hellhounds years ago.

"I need him," she had said. *"He was here for me after the Battle of the Cut."*

It wasn't true. She didn't need Ebrus. He wasn't there for her. Arilette was. After her mother and sister left, Arilette took her in. After her father didn't come back, Arilette taught her what she needed to survive. She didn't need Ebrus. He needed her. But still, she couldn't let Arilette dispose of him.

Arriving at the base level of the Underground's barracks, Threyna stood before the wooden door taken from Arilette's ancestral home. The butterfly crest of House Desius, the once-stalwart defenders of the royal Faytes of Elyngrove, was burned into the panels of the door. The stretched wings of the carnivorous moth revealed the pattern of a ferocious beast's fangs.

Arilette was the inverse of the butterfly sigil. Where the butterfly's outward appearances presented a harrowing predator to protect its frailty, Arilette was as delicate as a flower. And as venomous as its thorns. Though

Threyna knew full well what her mentor was capable of, she had never been on the receiving end of the Legatus's wrath, and she wanted to keep it that way.

Threyna drummed her knuckles on the door to her tablinum.

"Enter," Arilette called from within.

Threyna pushed the door open and stepped inside. Arilette's placid expression softened at seeing her. She folded a parchment in half, then half again before reaching for a match. Striking it, she angled the ember to the folded parchment until its edges blackened and curled. She flicked the match and the burning parchment to the stone floor before tossing her straight black hair over her shoulders to lean back in her chair and set her feet on the desk.

"You're late," Arilette said. Her dark green eyes glanced toward two empty glasses on her desk. "I figured you would be successful. Don't mind me starting without you." She beckoned Threyna in.

Candles lit Arilette's tablinum, casting the room in a dim but warm orange hue. She had said something about how the candles reminded her of the old days, before illuminators. How her mother liked them. Others speculated she just had a fascination with fire, given her history. The lighting suited her, bathing her pale skin without revealing the wrinkles framing her eyes or the scars on her hands.

Threyna strode forward along the dark stone taken from Octarius's foundation several stories above. Her boots, still caked in the Cut's silt, managed to echo in the mostly empty stone room.

She saluted, lifting her fist to her chin. "Divided, ruin will reign."

Arilette nodded, gesturing for Threyna to take a seat.

Threyna sat on the cold stone stool across from Arilette and the solid wooden desk between them.

In a land of eternal undeath, blanketed by clouds and rain, few trees received the sunlight required to survive. At least according to the Order, only in the arcanatek farms outside of Bheric's Hollow could trees worth harvesting for timber grow. Without the aid of illuminators and time distorters, cultivating or sustaining vegetative life was a difficult task, making strong timber a rare commodity. A commodity rarely spared on something as trivial as a desk, yet it was the one luxury Arilette afforded herself.

Sitting, Threyna waited to be addressed.

Arilette eyed her, a playful grin tugging at the corner of her lip. "Report, Premius?"

"A solid haul, Legatus," Threyna said. "Marius is counting the coils as we speak."

"Any trouble?"

Threyna contorted her lip, debating if she should raise the question of Ebrus's reliability in the field or share Rivich's all-too-warranted outburst. It was another tough call, and indecision won out. "A little slippery in the Cut. Ebrus is in the warp, but otherwise—" She shrugged, her mind returning to the strange behavior of the shades. "Have our Artificers found a way to control shades?"

Arilette narrowed her eyes. "Not to my knowledge, and if they did, they'd best tell me about it. Right now, the focus is on the reaping arcanatek."

The new technology would revolutionize not just warfare but how the hollowed were dealt with too. Whether in the form of the reaping spears or the Reaper's Landmine, the arcanatek had the ability to vortex a soul and irradiate it in one fell swoop.

Threyna hmphed. "Any reports on the Order's ability to do so?"

Arilette sat back, eyeing the empty glasses before her, a stoppered bottle of liquor in hand. "Decimus, that old bastard—he's always looking for new ways to torture us, but controlling shades? Not that I've heard of. And you've got better luck getting me to believe there are still sea monsters swimming in Aeritan Bay."

Threyna forced a poor excuse for a chuckle. She knew what she saw, and this wasn't a story about carnivorous, humanoid sea turtles used to scare Order Boys at the Nest. "There were dozens, a horde in their wake." Threyna shook her head. "Strange."

"Indeed. But you made it back in one piece." Arilette nodded at the empty glasses. "Valefyre all around." She unstoppered the fermented swill. "You're going to want a double."

"A celebratory drink?" Threyna asked. "Or to deal with whatever news just came through?" She nodded at the charred remains of the parchment Arilette had lit aflame.

Filling both glasses to the brim, Arilette shrugged. "Bit of blood, bit of bone." She slid one glass to Threyna and lifted her own in toast. "For the celebratory drink, cheers to enough power coils to blast half the Order to oblivion."

Threyna stood to raise her glass. Together, they downed their drinks. Thick, bitter, and warm, the Valefyre burned from her nostrils to her guts. Wrinkling her nose and exhaling through her lips, Threyna set the glass back down. "And for the second drink?"

Arilette tilted the empty glass, rolling its edge to follow the contour of the knotted rings in the wooden desk. Resting her other hand on the table, she took Threyna's empty glass, filling it with another three fingers of Valefyre. "You may want to sit for this one." She passed the drink back to Threyna.

Arilette's generosity with her pours didn't come freely. Something had happened. Or something would happen. Yet the Legatus seemed content to hold the mystery captive a few moments longer.

With the buzz of the first drink flitting around her temples, Threyna took the second and tossed it back. The second always went down smoother, and that remained true for both bad drinks and feelings of abandonment. Inhaling through her teeth, Threyna set the glass down and slid it across the desk to rest beside Arilette's still-full glass.

Threyna reclaimed her seat on the dark stone, resting her hands atop her knees, her feet beneath her. "Must be good for you to share from your private stores."

Arilette smirked as she stalked around the desk to lean against it. Dancing shadows flickered across the walls, following in her wake. She sipped the Valefyre and licked her lips, as if she actually enjoyed the taste. "It's... shall we say... heavy." She took another sip.

Threyna tapped her thumb against her knee, attempting to wait patiently. If the drink was meant to dampen her nerves, Arilette's performance was having the opposite effect.

Arilette sighed. "The Order is expanding their Dominion."

Threyna raised an eyebrow. "Avengard?"

Arilette nodded.

Avengard had been vying for Order aid since Victarius Kaine lost the Artificer's War almost twenty years back. Though this was certainly drink-worthy news to the people of Northvale, even if they didn't fully know what they were agreeing to by entering into the Dominion, it didn't change much for the Underground.

Threyna scoffed. "Finally getting what they always wanted. Good for the ghosting fools. That can't be your big news, though."

"Far from it," Arilette said. "The Wraith, in the next of their unending schemes, is planning to utilize Avengard's feast to stage a mass exodus."

Threyna shook her head. *The Wraith...* Her jaw clamped down at the mention of them. "My mother and sister at it again, eh?"

Arilette snorted. "Not to worry." She sauntered over to the nearest candle and lifted it from its sconce. "Their escape plans will end as they always have." She tilted the candle and her glass of Valefyre until the flame touched the liquid, igniting the surface of her drink. Holding the glass up before her, her eyes reflected the licking tongues. "Fire. Smoke. Ash."

Threyna had seen that look in Arilette's eyes before. She was too young to remember when Arilette's father burned her lover, Aarkos, in the fires he'd set to the Underground's escape vessel, but she had witnessed Arilette's retribution. She burned *Resilience* and its fleet. She watched her father Arenius hollow in the flames while his dreams of leading the Underground to freedom beyond the curse went up in smoke.

Ten years to the day.

That was the night Arilette took command of the Underground and led the Battle of the Cut. That was the night her mother and sister left to found the Wraith. The night her father never returned from.

If they had stayed—if they had fought—maybe we would have defeated the Order and stopped the Skeleton King.

Heat rose to her ears. "They still haven't learned."

Arilette shook her head as the fire of her glass extinguished, leaving the room a candle darker than a moment before. "Divided, ruin will reign."

"So what's the mission?" Threyna asked. "How will we stop them?"

"Don't worry about that, Threyna. Taken care of. But there is something we must discuss."

Threyna swallowed, her mouth still stained with the Valefyre's spit. "I won't hesitate if I see either of them."

Arilette set the empty glass down and waved her hand. "I know, love. It's not that." She closed the short distance between them, kneeling down until she was of a height with Threyna. She scooped her hand under Threyna's fatekeeper pendant, rolling it between her fingers. "You still believe your father is alive—out there, somewhere?"

Threyna balked, her mouth suddenly dry. She nodded.

Arilette's dark green eyes met her own. "Applications to enter the Dominion are measured with a test of loyalty. The Order will give them one of ours. To be tortured. Hollowed. Vortexed and irradiated from the world. All to see if they are as committed to the Purge as the Order's Justicus."

Threyna nodded, warmth flushing her cheeks. *The drinks, Arilette's hesitancy, her line of questioning… followed by this.* The Valefyre made her vision swim, or perhaps tears were welling in her eyes.

"He's alive, Threyna," Arilette whispered. "Your father is alive."

Arilette placed a hand on her cheek, her touch soft, and loving in ways Threyna's own mother never was. Her thumb traced the corner of Threyna's eyes, dabbing the tears before they could roll down her cheeks.

"He will be Avengard's test of loyalty," Arilette said, softly.

Threyna's lip quivered. Her ribs rattled. But words wouldn't come. She fell into Arilette's arms as sobs tore loose. Sinking to the floor in Arilette's embrace, her cries echoed off the stone walls. The reverberations created a chorus as if the whole world cried for her and her father.

Arilette held her, rocking her back and forth. "Shh, shh, shh. It will all be prime. We're going to get him back."

CHAPTER 3

THE SUN'S WARMTH

Laela

Laela should have suffered six times by now. The first after her parents spirited her from the Roost before what would become the final battle of the Artificer's War. The second when her father slashed her across the chest while teaching her how to wield a sword. The third when hellhounds set on her while chasing after her half-sister, Threyna, on her way back to Octarius the night Arilette Desius burned their fleets. The fourth after the tunnels the Wraith began digging from Avengard to Beak's Bay collapsed in on her. The fifth when Tarus nearly killed her during the tournament to become the First Sword of the Wraith. And the sixth when Aedile Rance told her that this would be the day they would leave Rheynia and its curse behind. Forever.

Watching the Order legions march through Avengard toward Valefort, Laela only hoped this plan wouldn't be the seventh. She crossed her hands over the hilt of the bastard sword holstered at her hip, shifting her weight towards her mother as they stood on the ramparts.

Her mother looked older than her fifty-five years. Thinner and frailer after years of forgoing meals for the sake of others, her generosity had caught up with her. Crow's feet creased her pale green eyes, and her hair was more gray than black now.

Laela wanted to tell her all would be well. That soon they'd be aboard *The Relentless* and on their way to join the others preparing *The Dauntless* and *The Adamant* for their journey south. Soon enough, they'd all be beyond Rheynia, the Order, and the curse. But saying so again wouldn't change the doubt wrinkling her mother's forehead or the lines of worry framing her lips.

"What did you always tell me?" Laela asked, adjusting her Avengard city-watch cloak. "When I was a girl and Father was in a mood?"

Her mother's chest heaved, the exhale deflating her shoulders, but she kept her eyes trained on the Order legionaries. She forced what she likely assumed to be a smile but looked more like a wince. "Be strong. Be courageous."

Laela nodded. "This will be the last time. I know we've been down this length of the Spine before, but it will be different this time. Rance will see us from this place. The Order will be here, feasting. We've taken every possible precaution. No one will know. Not even the Aeritans will stop us. So be strong. Be courageous."

Her mother turned from the ramparts and the encroaching black-and-green banners of the Order to look at her. "I just wish we could have left with them."

Laela placed her hand on her mother's shoulder. "And leave Olerus in charge? The feast would be over and Belrich's legions would depart before nightfall. No. We need to be here, Mother. Trust the plan. Trust Rance."

After ten years of careful planning and living double lives as citizens of Avengard and leaders of the Wraith, now was not the time to doubt. They'd rebuilt Avengard's relationship with Aranoc through careful politics and gaining the Order-appointed Governors' trust. With prudent resource management and a fair amount of quota forging, they had gradually pilfered enough of Aranoc's supplies to inflate Avengard's potential in the eyes of the Order. For those citizens who believed the Order was still led by Neutreen, their lives would improve under the Dominion. Their walls would be rebuilt, their food supply would be bolstered by the Order's arcanatek, and the hordes of hollowed surrounding the Sisters would be culled, making all of Northvale safer. After Avengard, Aranoc would be soon to follow, and no one would miss the Wraith once they snuck beyond the curse. Other than Arilette, in her twisted sense of unity.

"I do trust Rance." Her mother sighed. "I just… I wish…"

Laela grit her teeth, stepping away from her mother. She knew what was coming. Ten years had passed. Hundreds of letters had gone unanswered. Laela had been by her through it all, but she wasn't the daughter her mother wanted. Ever since Threyna eluded Laela that night, her mother had never looked at her the same way again. She had never said it, but Laela knew her mother blamed her.

"Threyna can't come with us, Mother." Her tone came out blunt and unforgiving.

"But I dreamed of her. Just last night, after burning matches to Neutreen."

Blood and bone, I should have earned my wings by now, listening to you. Suppressing her frustration, Laela shrugged. "You always dream of her when you're nervous. You're scared, but Neutreen awaits beyond the curse."

"This dream was different; I saw her. She was old. Older than I am now." She shook her head. "I feared she'd never make it to old age, but there she was, sitting on a cliffside. With a man." She smiled to herself as if it was the most pleasant of memories. "There was a golden sun, setting over the ocean. You wouldn't believe the beauty."

Laela swallowed. There was enough to worry about today. Between distracting the Order, organizing the Wraith, and making sure the Underground didn't screw anything up, the last thing Laela needed was her mother becoming part of the problem.

"Maybe she'll find her own way out of Rheynia," Laela said. *I'll believe that when I see it.* "But we need to focus on leaving with the people who *want* to escape."

Her mother's smile faltered, then wilted, somber. "That's what I fear, Laela. What if… what if we're not supposed to leave? What if Threyna grew old to overlook the cliffs *because* she stayed and fought?" She reached for Laela's feather pendant hanging beside the fatekeeper her mother gave her as a child.

Laela's fingers twitched at her side. It didn't matter how many times she'd read through Faytemarked, praying that her mother would stop blaming her or herself for what became of Threyna. It didn't matter how many matches she'd burned to Neutreen; the outcome remained the same. But for her mother to doubt the very mission they fled the Underground for in the first place…

She seethed, letting the anger dispel before it could be shaped into hurtful words. Composing herself, she set her gaze on the front of the Order's procession where Aedile Rance, Governor Olerus, and the rest of Valefort's greeting party escorted Prince Belrich through Avengard toward the remains of the old Helixus fortress.

"It was just a dream, Mother. Trust in Rance. Keep faith in the Tenets. By moderation, modesty, measure, and merit, we will earn our wings and fly to Valencia with Neutreen. We just need to get beyond the curse."

Her mother looked up at her, slight and frail, yet somehow still talking down to her. "If she came, would you even let her leave with us?"

Laela closed her eyes. Her mother wanted her to say, *"Yes, of course!"* but Laela wouldn't. Tossing her hands into the air, she turned from her. "It doesn't matter." She couldn't keep the bite from her tone. "She's not coming. Because she doesn't know we're leaving."

Then it dawned on her. The hopeful staring at the horizon. The nervous energy. *She's not nervous about the Order. Gory ghosts, she's not even worried about the escape. This is about Threyna.* She seized her mother by her bony shoulders. "Mother. You didn't. Please tell me you didn't tell Threyna we're leaving."

Her mother's gaze fell.

The laughter of Laela's father rang in her ears, cold and cruel. *"Stupid. Weak."*

Heat rose to Laela's cheeks as she attempted to block him out. Her eyes blinked while her mind attempted to process what this could mean. Every precaution. Everything they'd done. It was all for nothing.

They coordinated Aranoc's city-watch shifts to make certain only their most trusted people were on duty. They'd worked around Aedile Verinius's fearmongering and met every one of Prince Belrich's ridiculous demands to avoid suspicion. They even hid the details of their plans from the majority of the Wraith to prevent a catastrophe if the Underground had a snitch inside the Wraith. Yet, careful plans be damned, her mother had told Threyna, a Premius within Arilette's Underground, that they were leaving.

Laela shook her mother and leaned close. "Gory ghosting dammit. What did you say? What did you tell her?"

"I couldn't leave her again," her mother said.

Ten years of frustration bubbled under her cuirass, making the scar across her chest burn. The sword at her belt, the daggers on her hip, in her vambrace, and in her boot weren't enough to win this battle. First Sword of the Wraith or not, this was one fight she'd never been able to win.

"You didn't leave her," she said through her teeth. "She left *us*." She shook her head. "And now you've betrayed us. For her."

Her mother, for all her talk of strength and courage, was weak. Brittle. Soft in a hard world, just as her father had said. Yet she stared at Laela, disappointment wrinkling the crow's feet at the corners of her eyes. As if reading her mind, her mother said, "I know your father was a bastard. I know he hurt you. I know I *let* him hurt you. But there is strength in knowing when to drop your guard and courage in actually doing so. Must you always be so—"

Laela stormed off, unable to even look at her mother. The scar across Laela's chest burned, and, despite her armor, she felt suddenly vulnerable. Now was not the time to drop her guard. Dropping her guard, like inviting an Undergrounder to an Order's Dominion feast, was a quick way to an eternity of suffering.

She retreated into her Center of Silence—the place of calm and focus from which her father, for all his flaws, taught her to fight. It made her the First Sword of the Wraith. It kept her alive. It made her fierce in ways her mother could only talk about. *Lower my ghosting guard. She's going to get us all hollowed.*

She needed to warn Rance, but not yet. First, Dracus, Canton, and Fawkes needed to know the new situation. Then she'd have to prepare the rest of the Avengard city watch for the Underground's attempt to interfere with their entry into the Dominion. Laela had known this was a possibility. Luckily, she'd even managed to convince Rance not to share everything with her mother. Still, she knew too much. And now the Underground would too.

Laela descended the stairs from the ramparts two at a time, her fists still coiled at her sides. Once upon the parapet-walk that led to the chapel where Canton and Fawkes would be standing by, she forced herself to slow down. It would not do well to arouse suspicion. Below, Governor Olerus, tall and thin, wearing his best green cloak to appeal to Prince Belrich and the colors of the Fayte banner, ushered the Legatus of the Order and his elite guard of Inquisitors through the courtyard.

Prince Belrich's curling silver-blond hair accented his high-cheeked grin as he passed his spiked helm to an Inquisitor. Belrich Fayte was the worst kind of handsome: eloquent, charming, hateful. The kind of man who would impale a supposed traitor and expect him to feel honored that it was he who gave the order. He was the son of the Skeleton King after all.

Neutreen's blessings, at least he's gone.

Avoiding the gaze of the Inquisitors' skeletal masks, Laela opened the door that descended the stairs that led to the chapel. Twisting the knob and shoving her shoulder through the rotten wood of the old door, she entered the side door to the chapel.

Making her way to the nave, she passed the termite-ridden pews, eying the crumbling statue of Neutreen at the altar. Wings spread wide with her head inclined, she gazed through her blindfold to stare out at the empty chapel, judging all. With her left arm outstretched, holding a single feather, and her right, broken at the wrist, she—like much of Rheynia—had seen better days. Before Laela, but with his back to the statue, Fawkes nodded, his thick arms crossed over his chest. Beside him, Canton knelt before the statue, burning prayers.

Laela approached, holding the stocks with both hands, head bowed as she waited for Canton to finish his prayers.

"See me and what I share with your children," Canton whispered, his breath causing the match before him to flicker. "For what is mine in this life is nothing like what awaits in Valencia. Keep me on bended knee when the One tempts me with false wings. Keep me vigilant when the Tellers attempt to burn me in their reckless Purge. Show me how I measure so that I might better serve and earn my merits. Above all, forgive me, for I have not yet earned my wings, but until then, I abide in the Four."

The match burned out, its smoke and his prayers lifting to Valencia. As Canton stood, Fawkes patted him on the shoulder, gesturing toward Laela.

"Ay, Lae," Fawkes said, his mouth hidden in his reddish-brown beard. "Everything prime?"

Canton spun toward her. His narrow face flushed beneath the fuzz on his cheeks and chin as they always did upon seeing her. "Laela, I didn't hear you enter."

Laela gave him a half-smile, hoping it wouldn't go to his head and make him think she saw him any differently than she had since Dracus brought him to the Underground as a child. "It's all blood and bone," Laela said to Fawkes. "Order's here, and you can bet the last darkling in the soul jar that the Underground will be too."

Fawkes grunted. "Yer mother?"

"Yeah." Laela scoffed. "Ghosting knew it. She had a *dream.*"

The moment the words passed her lips, she regretted them. Canton, prone to nightmares ever since the Tellers burned his village, hung his head, his cheeks a deeper shade of scarlet.

Cursing herself for her even mentioning it, she changed the subject. "Fawkes, go tell Dracus to be on the lookout for any Undergrounders. Canton, keep an eye on Erynia; she's a nervous wreck every time she sees a legionary."

"We should have sent her with Verinius," Canton said as if trying to prove her comment hadn't embarrassed him. "Then she'd be safe, and she wouldn't be the Dreadroot wrapping around our ankles."

"She's Rance's daughter," Laela said, putting her hand on his shoulder—half as an apology, half as a means of keeping Canton measured before Neutreen. "She comes with us. She'll be fine if you stay close to her. Lend her your strength. And don't let Gatius rile her up."

Canton's cheeks remained red, but at least they formed a grin at her encouragement.

"Stick to the plan," Laela said. "We'll be watching the sunrise from Sansia soon enough."

As Canton and Fawkes left the chapel to follow their orders, Laela lingered. Eyeing the feather in Neutreen's outstretched hand, she brushed her finger over her own feather pendant, thinking of her mother's dream.

The sun's warmth isn't for Threyna. It's for me. It's for us, Mother.

She told herself it was possible. She said it aloud, hoping that she could speak life into the words and make them come true. Yet she'd spared the last of her optimism on Fawkes and Canton, and all that was left for her was the darklings.

She had no more time to wallow. She had the Order to impress, Undergrounders to stop, and the Wraith to spirit to safety beyond the Curse.

Neutreen, watch over us all.

CHAPTER 4

FOR ALL THE DARKLINGS

Threyna III

Her boots didn't fit. Neither did the britches or the leather armor of the Avengard city-watch uniform the Underground had in the armory. Too snug in the toes, too long through the inseam, and too broad at the shoulders, the ill-fitting uniform was a pleasant distraction to the more pressing concerns of her mission.

Walking alongside Aylenia through the overcrowded streets of Avengard, Threyna eyed each lingering gaze.

"What if it's a trap," she'd asked Arilette, *"a lie to draw us out?"*

Arilette only shrugged. *"Then we'll show those ghosting bastards they're not the only hellhounds with fangs."*

Perhaps if Rivich had accompanied them, she wouldn't have felt the need to question authority, but in his absence, she couldn't help but fill the role. It hurt that he had met with Arch Premius Lorath, requesting a transfer to another strike team. It hurt worse that he didn't even blame her for his reason for seeking another Premius to serve. When asked about why, he only said that he didn't believe he was measuring up to the rest of Threyna's team. That he didn't deserve the merit associated with being in her squadron.

Quoting the Four Tenets might have appealed to Lorath's faith in the Faytemarked, but it didn't work on Threyna. She knew Rivich didn't believe in Neutreen, Elysianism, the Tenets, the Purge—any of it.

He just realized he was fed up with me.

Aylenia elbowed her in the ribs as they made their way through the crowded streets of Avengard. "You prime?" Only her eyes were visible through the plumed helm and the gray scarf helping to conceal her Palogian heritage.

Threyna nodded. "Making hordes out of a single hollowed. Just worried about Ebrus." It was only half a lie. Yes, she was busying herself with thoughts of Rivich so as not to consume herself with the spiraling thoughts of what would happen to her father should they fail, but that didn't mean she wasn't concerned with Ebrus.

"Did you speak to the Legatus?" Aylenia asked.

Threyna adjusted her oversized pauldron. She considered it, and would have after she'd finally worked up the courage, but that was when Arilette informed her that Rivich had requested a transfer. No, she couldn't afford to do this mission with only two of her squad, and she didn't trust the notion of adding two new people to the mix at the last moment.

"No," Threyna said. "One more mission. Then I will."

Aylenia nodded. "He'll be fine. And we'll finish this, just like any other extraction."

Threyna smirked, wishing she shared Aylenia's optimism. This wasn't just any extraction. They weren't here for power coils, arcanatek, or food. Their target was her father—a man the world thought lost. Arilette long believed he was dead and gone. Dracus wasn't even certain he survived the Battle of the Cut. Threyna was the only one who held out hope that somehow, somewhere, he was still alive. It took all her will to resist the urge to reach for the fatekeeper beneath her leather cuirass.

As they continued through the streets of Avengard, it was no wonder why the people were so eager to come under the Order's Dominion. Threyna had nearly rolled her ankle walking on the uneven street of broken cobbles. Yet people cheered from the windows of their crumbling stone homes. Children weaved through the rotting wooden structures lining the ravaged streets to wave at the procession of heroes who'd come to save them.

Soon, you'll have what you want, and I'll have what I want.

As the arched gateway of Valefort neared, Threyna wondered if her mother and sister waited within. Whether they were part of the distraction to host the Order or leading the escape plan out of Aranoc, it made no matter. She wasn't here for them.

After Arilette's deep-cover spy snuck them through the Wraith's tunnel into Avengard, Threyna became more keenly aware that she might run into them. She hoped she wouldn't, but she'd long learned wishes, wants, prayers, and the like had little bearing on outcomes.

Do they know that Father is the one they're to hollow? Could Mother watch as he's impaled and flayed? Could Laela? They had different fathers, but her father treated Laela more like a daughter than her own ever did. Still, she couldn't put trust in either of them; they'd already abandoned her once before, and she wasn't going to give them another opportunity to disappoint.

Threyna would not stand by while her father's soul went mad, unable to flee its tortured shell. She wouldn't watch as the Justicus vortexed his soul from his flesh or turn and run away as their irradiators charged.

As they passed through the gate, Threyna pinched the interlayer embedded on her earlobe. She whispered into the spatial arcanatek. "Yevon, Ebrus, you prime?" Like speaking into a void, her voice disappeared into the warper and reappeared in her strike team's ears.

"Prime as an Order boy at the Nest," Yevon said. After entering the city, Yevon and Ebrus, disguised as servants, infiltrated Valefort to get eyes on her father.

Tension gripped the back of Threyna's neck, making her shoulders creep up to her ears in her bulky cuirass.

Perhaps sensing Threyna's unease, Aylenia hissed into the interlayer. "Just say prime."

Yevon sniggered. "Prime as a hollowed in the Gullies."

Aylenia turned off her connection and spoke aloud to Threyna. "By Neutreen's nads and Drake's Six, I'm going to ghosting hollow him."

"I heard that," Yevon said in Threyna's ear.

"Where's Ebrus?" Threyna asked, doing her best to keep her body language as inconspicuous as possible. "We're through the gate."

"Might be outta range for you," Yevon said. "Says he's prime as a darkling in a soul jar."

Aylenia huffed. "No he didn't."

"You don't know," Yevon said. "He's inside Valefort. Got eyes on the package."

Threyna's throat constricted. She closed her eyes. *Please, let it be him.* Taking a slow, steadying breath, she asked for confirmation.

The interlayer went silent.

Aylenia and Threyna funneled into Valefort's courtyard. At the center was a row of oubliettes where Avengard's worst prisoners were once held. The subterranean cells allowed the prisoners to be ridiculed by all who passed over them. Though they were empty now, Threyna had little doubt that her father would be placed in one soon enough.

On either side of the oubliettes, several rickety, makeshift tables were arranged in rows—two on either side. The four long lines ran the length of the courtyard, one for each of Neutreen's Tenets. Order legionaries sat on benches that looked as old as Neutreen herself, while at the back of the courtyard, the high table of Avengard's esteemed guests joined tall and thin Governor Olerus and shorter and thinner Aedile Rance.

As they entered, Aylenia went left, Threyna right, each joining the Avengard city watchmen on the outskirts of what was to be the greatest feast in Avengard since before Damascus Drake led the Great Abdication.

Yevon's silence stretched.

Taking position, Threyna scanned the courtyard. The bishop of Neutreen's temple, his four priests, and each of their four deacons stood, head bowed, holding the stocks on the stairs of the chapel as their guests settled themselves. Beside Olerus, the Order weasel charged with governing Avengard's backwater populace, sat Erynia—Rance's daughter. Her painted smile never reached her dull gray eyes. Despite being the aedile's daughter, her pale complexion and sullen cheeks didn't foretell that she had received extra rations.

Threyna couldn't help but respect Aedile Rance for that. Many in his position took advantage of overseeing supplies, making sure their bellies were the first to be filled and their supplies the last to be donated to the Order's Collectors.

Beside Erynia sat a thinner and frailer woman. Threyna blinked, barely recognizing her.

Mother?

The black hair of her youth had fallen to ash. The full cheeks she had passed to Laela were gaunt. Sickly. In the Underground's care, Threyna had never gone hungry. *Gory ghosts, you left me for this?*

She forced herself to look away. *Focus.*

Still waiting for Yevon or Ebrus to answer, Threyna had nothing to draw her attention. *If Mother is here, that means Laela is too.* She searched for Laela, but she wasn't in Olerus's or Rance's retinue. Threyna bit her lip, memories of old wounds and petty arguments resurfacing to knot in her throat.

The smell of burned wood, the screams of Arenius Desius, a firm grip on her wrist.

"I see him," Ebrus said in her ear through the interlayer, shaking her from her thoughts.

Threyna swallowed the knot. She slunk away from the other city watchmen to inspect a corridor that led to what were once the stables.

"Is it him?" Threyna whispered into the interlayer.

Silence. For several agonizing moments.

"Dunno," Ebrus said. "He's got a sack over his head. They're bringing him to the oubliettes now."

Threyna closed her eyes, retrieving her fatekeeper from beneath her cuirass to clutch it in her palm. *Please, let it be him. Let it be my father.* She shoved the fatekeeper beneath her leather armor. "Aylenia, signal the

Legatus and the Arch Premius to be ready. Everyone else, to position. When they set the distraction, we need to be sharp. This is for all the darklings in the soul jar."

CHAPTER 5

THE UNWELCOME POET

Laela II

The feast had begun. Though the trays servants brought from the kitchens were likely as unimpressive to the Order legionaries as they were decadent to the men and women carrying them, this was the best Avengard had to offer. While the servers eyed the food with watering mouths and growling stomachs, most of the legionaries turned their attention to the wine they'd brought with them from the arcanatek-produced vineyards of the Grove.

Lord Premius Decimus, the Order's second-in-command behind Prince Belrich, at least had the decency to taste what the Valefort staff had provided. His stern gray eyes narrowed, inspecting the potato-and-onion stew, smoked mutton, and the few shriveled tomatoes before him.

Laela diverted her gaze from Decimus, not wanting to attract his attention. The aged Lord Premius had been pivotal in both the War of the Seers and the Artificer's War. Though time grayed his close-cropped hair and neatly trimmed goatee, he was still broad of shoulder. Had it not been for him and Dracus, in the time before he rescued Canton to join the Underground, perhaps Victarius Kaine and the Tellers would have prevailed over the Order. Perhaps the Skeleton King would have been defeated long before the Battle of the Cut. Perhaps her parents wouldn't have fled the Roost, seeking asylum from the Order's wrath in the Underground.

Things could have been different, but the Order would never be defeated. It was foolish to try. Neutreen wasn't coming back. Their only hope for salvation was to make it to her.

We'll be on the coast of Sansia by morning.

Laela circled the outskirts of the courtyard, searching for any sign of the Underground. Still furious with her mother, she couldn't even look at her sitting at the high table beside her husband, Rance. Olerus let out a forced, weaselly laugh at something Prince Belrich said. He wasn't involved in the Wraith. He had no idea what was truly going on below ground, but even appointed by Belrich to govern Avengard, he was still nervous around the Order blacks.

Laela turned from the high table to traverse the rows between the long tables. She knew the Underground's tactics. They wouldn't storm Valefort. They wouldn't attack Avengard. They'd incept themselves within, hiding in plain view until their moment arrived. Laela wouldn't let that happen.

Inspecting the face of every servant and guard, Laela felt a growing dread as time spilled like sand through the hourglass. With her tattered Avengard city-watch cloak flowing in her wake, she quickened her pace. She'd warned the other watchmen to be on high alert, but she couldn't even trust them. Olerus had doubled the guard, adding new names and faces she couldn't keep straight. Not to mention, her mother had expanded the kitchen staff to meet Belrich's demands for the feast.

I don't even know what I'm looking for. Arilette could have easily slipped someone into the kitchens or the city watch.

She spotted a servant she didn't recognize, for all the good that did her. Pale of skin, with a coiffure of dark brown hair, a young man with a crescent grin and dimpling cheeks refilled an Inquisitor's cup. By contrast, the expressions on the other servers' faces were grim, worried, or at best—stoic. He wasn't Wraith, but that didn't mean he was Underground. Still, his comfort around Prince Belrich's Inquisitors gave her pause.

She continued pacing between the rows of tables, never letting Dimples, the all-too-cheery server, leave her eye for too long. Passing over the oubliettes at the center of the courtyard, Laela took care to avoid the grates into the underground prison cells. She didn't know which held the Underground prisoner of war.

What if it's Threyna?

The thought made the scar across her chest burn and the scent of ash to fill her nostrils. She didn't want to imagine what her mother would do. *She'd attempt to stop it. She'd ruin everything to protect her, even though the only thing she'd accomplish is getting herself impaled and flayed.*

Laela wouldn't let that happen.

Spotting Canton, she made her way to him.

"See anything?" Canton asked.

She nodded in the direction of Dimples. "Keep an eye on him."

"What's the matter?"

Laela narrowed her eyes. "How many people do you know with something to smile about around Inquisitors? Don't make any moves yet. Await my signal." Slinking away before Canton could latch onto her, she returned to pacing the outskirts of the courtyard.

Behind the high table, Prince Belrich stood, raising his goblet.

Unable to continue inspecting the servers and watchmen without drawing attention, she stopped to hear his address.

"Dear, dear friends," Belrich said, his curling hair bouncing behind his ears as he stood. His high cheekbones framed a wide smile. "Look at where we find ourselves. Valefort. Avengard. Northvale. My brothers in black, when was the last time we came here in such numbers absent steel in hand or blood on our minds?"

The circlet atop his head sat crooked in a near-playful casualness. He turned to Governor Olerus. "It lifts the heart to be welcomed back—to welcome *you* back to the Dominion of Neutreen's Holy Order. For it is only together that we may rise to defeat the One and complete the Purge that stains these lands so that, one day, we might welcome Neutreen back to us."

The legionaries lifted their goblets and in unison shouted, "Neutreen is watching!"

Laela maintained a placid expression, but her insides twisted. The way in which they *used* her Goddess to propagate their power and justify their rule was sickening. They didn't want to defeat the One. If rumors were true, some believed the Skeleton King and his followers worshiped the One; others went as far to say that the Skeleton King himself was the One. Either way, though they said Neutreen was watching, it wasn't their good deeds and valor she observed, but their vile treachery.

She gripped the belt at her waist with white knuckles. *They will be judged.*

"Aye," Belrich continued. "Neutreen is watching. And she will lift us to Valencia on golden wings once the hollowed, shades, and darklings of our realm are expunged. But as you know, we can only do that together. Divided, ruin will reign."

Again, the Order Justicus, Inquisitors, and Premiuses echoed the call. "Divided, ruin will reign."

Laela stifled the desire to cringe at the mantra. The Underground had adopted the same ideology to justify the forced unification they wished to impose on the Wraith. As diametrically opposed as the two might be, the Underground and the Order had more in common than either liked to admit. A tyrannical ruler, an army of blind imbeciles, and enough arcanatek to usher in more destruction than the Disasters.

Belrich strode around his chair "These lands fell to treachery long ago. First when Helixus followed Drake away from Neutreen, then when he forsook his responsibility as your liege to chase the Chimera across the sea in the Great Abdication. After years of strife that brought suffering to your families, insurrections that saw your loved ones hollowed, and decades of poverty that allowed your walls to crumple and your crops to wither, it is my honor—no, my privilege—to bestow my sincerest gratitude upon Governor Olerus for making this possible."

Olerus stood to cheers, bowing to Prince Belrich.

Across the courtyard, a server clapped, but the joy of the sentiment never reached his eyes. His black hair parted, draping over the side of his head with the opposite side shorn short. Laela didn't recognize him, but there was something *familiar* about him. Too familiar.

"Oh, come now," her father teased. *"You don't remember? This is what happens when you—"*

Laela retreated to her Center of Silence to focus on the server. His features were soft amidst his contemplative stare. As if he felt her eyes on him, he met her gaze before stiffening and turning away.

The scar across Laela's chest constricted. She reached her hand for the feather pendant at her neck, recalling a time back at the Underground when Canton was pining after her, his little friend following in his wake. After Canton spouted a line about how pretty she was, his sad friend had taken her feather pendant in his hand and recited a poem—not about how she looked, but something about how Neutreen loved her.

Laela's fist curled at her side. She couldn't remember his name, but the sad poet was no longer a boy. Thin and undersized as he was, he was still an Undergrounder. An infiltrator. A saboteur who came to see Laela's mission—her life's work—burned to ash.

She remained still, not wanting to let the unwelcome poet know she was onto him. As Olerus spoke on behalf of Avengard, Laela slid behind the row of city watchmen to creep along the outskirts of the courtyard and close in on the Undergrounder. Whatever his mission, whatever his purpose, he would fail. She would stop him before he did whatever he was sent here to do.

CHAPTER 6

A GHOST FROM THE PAST

Threyna IV

Threyna's heart quickened, its beats coming short and sharp. Blood pumping in her ears, she descended the stairs that led to the subterranean dungeons beneath the courtyard. She stalked slowly down the corridor, clinging to the shadows between the torches.

More accustomed to the brighter, even hue of the arcanatek illuminators, Threyna strained her eyes to focus past the flickering flames. The long corridor ended at an intersection. To the right, stairs would lead into Valefort's barracks. To the left, the oubliettes and the precious cargo it held.

Voices ahead. Shuffling feet.

Threyna slipped into the dark recesses of the crackling torchlight's reach, breath held.

"He's already more hollowed than man," said a husky voice. "This'll be a kindness."

"Ghostin' right," replied a pinched companion. "At least the poor bastard knows he'll get a vortex and an irradiator. Better than either of us, eh?"

Two men, dressed in the same garb as she, strode from the cells, past her corridor, and toward the stairs into the barracks.

"An Inquisitor told me he's been in Saltspire's cells for the better part of a decade." The man with the husky voice had the frame to match. His profile masked the other guard entirely.

"A decade?" the guard with the pinched voice asked. "Neutreen's nads."

Threyna pressed her back into the wall as they passed. Her held breath released. *A decade.* It had been ten years since the Battle of the Cut. *It's him. It has to be.*

Their voices faded as their footsteps climbed the stairs. A lock clicked. Rusty hinges creaked. They were gone.

Threyna had no doubt there would be other guards. The Order delivered their Underground prisoner to them. Now it was their job to protect him until they completed their cruel test to enter the Dominion.

Likely two. I can take two.

Threyna pinched the interlayer earring. "I'm nearly in position."

Something stirred behind her, prompting her to look over her shoulder. Aylenia answered in a hushed voice. "Charges in place."

Their plan was reliant on Lorath's First Centuriots setting the explosives along Valefort's western walls. Without their distraction, even after she broke her father free, it'd be impossible to escort him through the Wraith's tunnels to the Cylian River outside of Avengard.

"Signal when you're ready," Yevon whispered.

"Ebrus, everything prime?" Threyna asked.

No answer.

Threyna's throat constricted. The longer she took the more she left up to chance. Quickening her pace down the corridor, she turned left toward the cells. With her stolen city-watch cloak draped behind her and a reunion with her father just ahead, her path was blocked by two men in Avengard's city-watch uniforms.

Threyna made a show of being out of breath as they noticed her. "Help. Underground. They're in the tunnels!"

"What!" A guard, as young and fit as Avengard was likely to possess, strode forward. "Knew those bastards would interfere." He drew his steel.

"Veryn, what about the prisoner?" the other guard asked, glancing back and forth between the cell they protected and his partner striding away.

Veryn ignored him.

Threyna waved him forward. "This way. We hafta stop them before they get too close. They'll ruin everything."

"C'mon, Davius," Veryn said, waving his compatriot onward. "For Avengard!"

Threyna rounded the corner, drawing a dagger from her belt. Once around the corner, she tucked herself into the shadows. Not knowing how closely Davius was following behind, she needed to take Veryn down quickly.

Veryn turned the corner. Threyna reared back and struck. Lashing out with a vicious backhand, Threyna's pommel crashed into Veryn's helm at the temple. The big man took two more steps before his knees realized he had passed out. He crashed into the far wall of the corridor and clattered to the ground.

"Help!" Threyna shouted. "They're here!"

Poor, sweet, dutiful Davius followed Veryn around the corner. The stocky guard lumbered past Threyna and came to halt before an unconscious Veryn and the otherwise empty corridor.

"Blood and bo—"

Threyna scooped the back of Davius's pale city-watch cloak and draped it over his head and around his neck. Slipping the cloth through to cinch like a noose, she kicked the guard's knee out and yanked upwards on the cloak. He gasped for breath, clawing at his neck with one hand while swatting at Threyna with the other. She wrenched to the side, out of his reach, and slammed him into the wall opposite Veryn. He toppled forward, but Threyna didn't let go. Driving her foot into his back, she strained, strangling the man with his own cloak.

His choked desperation slowed. His grasping hands faltered. The thick-necked man slackened to the floor beside his brother-in-arms. Panting, Threyna loosened the chokehold to admire her handiwork. Davius wouldn't hollow. Neither would Veryn.

She patted down Davius until she found the keyring on his belt. Yanking it free, she backed away and turned down the hall of cells. She pinched the interlayer. "Stand by. Almost there."

Threyna quickened her pace, passing empty cells on her right. Sound from the feast above filtered through the grates of the oubliettes, echoing in the dingy cells and out into the corridor. With each passing cell, Threyna's heartbeat quickened.

I'm coming, Father. I'm getting you out.

She stopped before a cell in the middle of the hall, her heart plummeting to her too-tight boots. A figure with a bag over his head slunk in the corner of the cell. Wearing soiled britches and no shirt, the man didn't look like her father. Black veins slithered down his torso, creating a cage around his heart. Sections of fair skin stuck out between the dark corrupting vines. Scarred, burned, and wrinkled by age, his arms, manacled behind his back, didn't appear like they belonged to her father.

As if hearing her breath, the figure drew closer to the bars separating them. Back hunched, he spoke as if through a gag, but the noises were indiscernible if he were trying to form words.

Threyna clenched her teeth to still her trembling lip. "Are you Theodyn?" Her voice quavered, fearing the answer.

The prisoner mumbled frantically, his body shaking.

Ghosts, what does it matter? Her fumbling fingers reached for the iron key on her ring.

"Threyna—" The urgency in Aylenia's voice sent a shiver down her spine. "People moving in on Ebrus."

"Give the sig—" Threyna cut off as cold steel pressed against the side of her neck.

A hand held hers, slipping the interlayer off of her earlobe. "Not another word, darkling," a voice said, slow and raspy behind her. "Sorry, lass, nothin' personal, but can't let ya do that. Drop the keys. Turn 'round."

Threyna's breath hissed between her teeth. So close. So far. But something about the voice rang with familiarity.

The flat of the blade pressed into her skin. "C'mon. Nothin' stupid. I don't wanna hurt you, but believe me, I will if ya make me."

The prisoner—her father or whoever he was—mumbled with greater desperation.

Threyna dropped the keyring. The keys clattered to the stone floor as she lifted her hands toward the low ceiling. Slowly, she turned to find a ghost of her past staring back.

Ten years had come and gone. For ten years, ruin's steady creep and death's slow consumption had imposed their undeniable will on the living and hollowed alike. Only the shades were immune. The shades… and Dracus ghosting Alius.

CHAPTER 7

DESIRE FOR DEATH

Dracus II

If his heart still beat, it would have exploded in his chest. If he could still sweat, his palms would have moistened. With such responses reserved for the living, Dracus sniffed, bristling his mustache.

He knew it was her before she turned. Before she fixed those sapphire eyes on him. Maybe it was the silver-blonde braid he knew all too well. Maybe it was the fact that that was just Dracus's luck. If she'd been some Teller troublemaker, an Order deserter like he was, or, ghosts, even if she was just any other Undergrounder, he'd have put her down first and asked questions after.

But no. She wasn't just anyone. She was Bherus Fayte's ghosting daughter. The reason why he fought. The reason why he wanted Dracus to fight in his stead, should he fail.

Time had melted the softness of her girlish cheeks. No longer was she a teen. Angular features, from the cut of her brow to her tight-lipped scowl, made Threyna appear related to a spear tip. His gaze followed down her neck to the black leather strap of the fatekeeper pendant her father had given him, and he had given her.

Don't suppose I deserve to escape my past, eh?

Today was the day he was supposed to finally die. A true death. After all the wrong he'd done, the pain he'd caused, it'd all finally be over. The ache of his joints, the nagging discomfort of his unhealed nicks and bruises, the itch of the half-healed wounds he'd suffered a decade ago that he'd never been able to scratch. It was all supposed to end. Once he got Canton off this cursed island. After this one last mission, his desire for death would be granted.

If it'd been up to him, all three of them would have been aboard *The Dauntless*, traveling south to Sansia. Far from here. Far from the Order, the Underground, the curse, and every darkling that haunted him. Fawkes and Canton would go on to live full lives, and he'd finally stop ruining others'. That was the plan. That should have been the plan. But no. Canton had to play at being hero.

Same as his father—reckless idealist.

He shook his head at Threyna. "You shouldn't be here. Your mother—"

"Save it," Threyna snapped. "I know why you're here. What you're trying to do."

"Then you know I can't let you ruin our chance of gettin' outta here," Dracus said, his blade still pressed to her neck. "C'mon, Threy. Old time's sake." He nodded at the prisoner. "Let us have this one. And spare me the 'Divided, ruin will reign' bit, eh?" He gestured his head to the tunnels. "You and yours—" He shook the interlayer, a woman's voice still speaking in a hushed voice on the other end. "—cut your losses and go."

Threyna shook her head. "Ten years I've waited. You, my *mother*, my *sister*—you might be content to let them impale him. But I won't let you have him."

Dracus chewed his mustache, flicking his eyes toward the prisoner. Hands shackled, head bagged, and wearing a soiled tunic, he groaned through a gag in unintelligible pleas. He was old enough to have witnessed the Disasters and watched the Great Abdication's fleet sail west from Drake Point. Whoever he was, he'd endured enough.

"He's had his time, Threy," Dracus said. "Don't trade your life for his. Let the Order have him. You come with us." He shrugged. "I know there are darklings to deal with between you and yer mother, you and Laela, but—"

"I'm not going anywhere," Threyna said, her lips peeling back in a snarl. "Not without my father."

Dracus's blade fell away from Threyna's neck. If blood pumped through his veins, it would have drained from his face. But it didn't. So it couldn't. He only managed to trip over his tongue, attempting to process what she'd said.

"Not without my father." He repeated her line again and again in his head.

Slowly, he turned to the prisoner. In the dim torchlight, Dracus squinted, taking a better look at the man. *Bherus? Impossible.*

But was it? He'd been with the Order long enough. He'd walked the black cells of Saltspire's dungeons. Blood and bone, he and Decimus were half the reason why they were never vacant. He was one of the few people to have seen the Skeleton King's *farm* and walk out alive. They'd keep prisoners alive, barely—regenerating blood bags for the Skeleton King to consume.

Dracus examined him. What he had thought was a soiled tunic was not. Black veins, thick with rot, stretched across his flesh, leaving only pockets of the fair skin beneath.

Bherus... He reached for the sack covering his friend's face. "Gory ghosting dam—"

Thunder exploded. The ground began to shake as if the Disasters had come again. Screams filled the night air.

Dracus fell away from Bherus's cell. Threyna, holding onto the cell bars, kept herself steady, and drew a short sword.

She pointed it at the stone in Dracus's throat. "Apologies, Dracus."

CHAPTER 8

TRAITORS

Laela III

Laela focused within her Center of Silence as she moved through the crowd toward the familiar Undergrounder. Fists clenched, teeth grinding, hate coursed through her veins. Hate for the Underground, the selfishness of its people, the cruelty of their leader, Arilette.

She's just as bad as the Skeleton King was. Just as bad as Belrich is now. Why must she always try to take from us?

The quiet poet knew she was coming for him. Head down, eyes darting, he tried to slink away, but he was in her territory. This wasn't Octaven; this was the home she had made for herself after everything was taken from her. She'd shepherded the meager flock of sheep across all of Northvale in search of living grass, fended off hellhounds and hollowed, defended Avengard's walls from the Tellers' raiders, and dug the tunnels that led to Aranoc's Gullies with her own hands. All for another chance to escape. Her father ruined the first opportunity. Arilette ruined her second. She'd be damned if she let this foolish boy stop her plans this time.

Laela quickened her pace to close the distance between her and the poet. Most didn't notice her movement, their attention fixed on Olerus's droning speech, but the poet began to slip away, shoving his way toward the stables.

Making eye contact with Fawkes, Laela gave him a hand signal to cut the poet off. Fawkes lurched into motion, but another servant seized the poet by the wrist, halting his flight. Laela couldn't see the other servant clearly enough to make out his features. Whether the other servant was another Undergrounder or one of the servants her mother had hired for the feast, Laela wasn't going to wait around and find out. The poet was speaking frantically. Then he turned and pointed at her.

Before they could turn and run, Fawkes caught them, putting a hand on each of their shoulders. Canton stood at his side, his hand on the hilt of his short sword.

No. Don't make a scene.

Just as Laela closed in on the four men in the corridor to the old stables, another woman in a city-watch uniform arrived.

"These the Undergrounders?" the woman asked Fawkes. Though she attempted to soften her consonants, her Palogian accent bled through. Her face was hidden behind a plumed helm and a gray scarf. It was possible she was a new recruit to the city watch. It wasn't entirely uncommon for a Palogian to hide their features and attempt to blend in, but they were rare enough that people took notice. It was just as likely that she was an Undergrounder disguised in an Avengardian's uniform.

"We're 'bout to find out," Fawkes said, eyeing Laela.

"What?" the servant asked. "Us? Undergrounders?" His cheeks parted in a smile as if the indictment was preposterous. With his charming grin and dimpled cheeks, he might have gotten away with it if the poet's quivering lip hadn't given him away.

They were Undergrounders; Laela was sure of that much. *But who else? And what about the woman?* She nodded at the Avengard city watchwoman. "Escort them inside. Lock them in the storage closet in the undercroft."

The woman seized both of the disguised servants by the elbows. "At once."

Fawkes let her take them from his grasp, but Laela drew a dagger from her vambrace and held it to the woman's face. The word *True* was embossed into the hilt, but the woman before her was a lie. *One woman to escort two men. How foolish do you believe we are?* She flicked her head towards Fawkes and Canton. "I was talking to them. The three of you will come with us. Quietly. You'll wait in the undercroft until the Dominion feast is over. And then, maybe then, we'll let you scurry back to your hole in the ground."

The woman stiffened.

"Canton," the poet said, attempting to face him. "Don't do this. Please."

Laela grabbed him by the collar of his servant's robes and bore into him. He didn't wilt beneath her stare as she expected. He barely even looked at her. He stared beyond, even through her. Behind his eyes, horror, pain, fear, and something deeper. Something darker. Knowledge.

"Ebrus?" Canton asked. "Gory ghosts... Ebrus?"

Ebrus. The poet. Canton's friend. An Undergrounder—here to destroy her dream of a life beyond the curse.

Laela angled the blade from the woman's face to his. "Don't do this? You come here, to our home, knowing our plans. And you have the gall to beg?"

The stone in Ebrus's throat bobbed. "If Theodyn falls... we all die."

Laela blinked. Her mind slowed, attempting to process. *Theodyn.* A name she hadn't heard in nearly a decade. Threyna's father. But that wasn't the worst part. She repeated his words again in her mind. *"If Theodyn falls... we all die."*

She inhaled sharply. "What under Neutreen's wings are you talk—"

Thunder tore the world apart. The ground quaked. The dilapidated stone of Valefort's west wall crumbled. Screams filled the night air as watchmen fell from the ramparts and crashed to the courtyard.

Before anyone could react, crossbow bolts flew through the breach, striking unsuspecting Order legionaries and Avengard citizens alike. More screams. More panic. Men and women wailed, bellowing the cries of the undying.

"Traitors!" Belrich shouted, wheeling on Olerus and Rance.

"It's not us!" Rance cried. "The Underground."

If anyone heard, if anyone cared, it didn't matter. Legionaries flipped feast tables to take cover behind. Drawing their steel and charging their blasters as shades and darklings fled from corpses, the Order directed their weapons not at the Underground. Not at the people responsible. But the people too stupid to hope for something more than death and curses.

Before Laela's eyes, dreams burned to ash. The scent of smoke filled her nostrils all over again as fighting erupted within the courtyard. Within moments, the feast had become a graveyard as bad as the Battle of the Cut.

Ebrus tore free of Laela's grip. He and his Underground companions charged into the fray. Laela couldn't let them leave. If this could be stopped, if Avengard's entry into the Dominion could be salvaged, it began with the impaled corpses of those three Undergrounders.

"We can't let them leave these walls!" Laela passed *True* to the other hand and drew her bastard sword. Fixed within her Center of Silence, Laela led Fawkes and Canton into the fray.

CHAPTER 9

Choose Your Battles

Threyna V

Screams filled the bailey as fighting erupted overhead. Threyna's father fell into the bars of his cell, slumping to the corner and groaning through his gag. Above, a legionary fell atop the grate of his oubliette, blood leaking from his trembling lips to drip onto the cell's floor. The crossbow bolt in his neck should have killed him, but he only wheezed, thrashing as if reaching for aid that wouldn't come. Nothing could help him now. Trapped within his undying corpse, the legionary's agonizing last breaths would only keep coming.

Threyna wouldn't let this be her father's fate. Keeping her blade leveled at Dracus's chest, Threyna knelt to retrieve the keys. As she stooped, the fatekeeper pendant dangled from her neck. The explosions in the half-trenched tunnels along the west walls and the cover fire from Lorath's cohorts were only diversions. If she didn't get her father and leave now, neither of them would make it out of Valefort alive.

"We're leaving. Don't make me hollow you."

Dracus didn't look at the blade. Didn't look at her. Not truly. His gaze fixed on the fatekeeper before flicking to her father. "Theodyn, is that really you?"

Her father strained through his gag.

Threyna fumbled with the keys in one hand, keeping her sword between her and Dracus. He'd saved her life once before. But that was ten years ago. And Threyna knew better than most, time changed people, and she wasn't about to take a chance on Dracus being the man she once knew.

Through the oubliette's grate, the fighting intensified. More arcanatek blasts. Dawnshards exploded and cries resounded as people hollowed and darklings shrieked as they tore from their torturous flesh.

She shoved a key from the ring into the lock, but it didn't turn. She glanced at Dracus.

"Canton and Fawkes are up there. If ya don't care about yer mother and Laela, fine. But I won't leave mine to hollow up there while you run off. "

Threyna snorted, trying a second key. "That's the thing with you Wraith. You think you can pick and choose your battles. You won't leave them to hollow, but you'll leave the Underground to save yourself."

Dracus shook his head. "C'mon, Threy. That's Arilette talkin'."

The second key didn't turn. Clenching her teeth, she struggled to seize a third. "If you hadn't fled, the Order might never have taken him. He wouldn't be here."

"Neither would you," Dracus said, his voice cold.

Another gale of screams tore through the courtyard. She was running out of time, but she glared at Dracus, trying to accept that the same man who saved her life from the hellhounds was the one who abandoned her father at the Cut. Who condemned him to this fate.

"You take him, Belrich will impale everyone up there," Dracus said as Threyna inserted the third key into the lock. "Everyone in Valefort. Blood and bone, maybe everyone in Avengard."

Threyna growled. "Better than joining the Dominion." Twisting the key, the lock *clicked*. She lowered her sword to undo the latch, but in the next moment, her arm was wrenched behind her back. Her sword clattered to the ground.

Dracus shoved her cheek into the cell bars. "Sorry, kid. Can't let y—"

Grunting, Threyna shoved off the cell bars, launching her and Dracus backwards. Dracus's back slammed into the opposite wall. Pain lanced through her arm and up her shoulder, but she was free of him. Arm limp, she spun and threw her opposite elbow at his jaw. He blocked with his forearm and chopped down between her neck and shoulder. The pain faded, replaced by numbness. Her arm hung at her side as she stumbled back.

He kicked the outside of her shin, buckling her knee, then lowered his shoulder into her sternum, dropping her to her back. Her head hit the metal bars of her father's cell. Ringing filled her ears to replace the screams of the fearful and undying above. Her vision blurred, but she threaded her foot between Dracus's legs. Coiling around his ankle, she twisted. Her world toppled, but Dracus slammed into the ground beside her. Head swimming, she pushed herself to her unsteady feet. Before she could ready an attack, Dracus speared her into the cell bars.

Holding her wrist with one hand and seizing her neck with the other, he held her against the cell. His flinty gray eyes glared. His mustache bristled through his snorted exhales.

"We surrender!" a voice shouted from above. "It's done! We surrender."

CHAPTER 10

PENANCE

Dracus III

Dracus would recognize that voice anywhere. Rance. The one voice of truth and reason in a world built on lies and propaganda. The one hope of the Wraith ever leaving Rheynia and creating a new life somewhere beyond the curse.

"To hope is to lie. To live is to..."

"On your knees," Belrich said.

Another voice Dracus would know anywhere. If a sound could send chills down his spine, Belrich's voice still would.

"All of you!" Belrich shouted. "If you wish to live to see the next Bheric's Day, each and every one of you will do exactly as I say." Groaning hollowed were his only answer. "Vortex and irradiate the fallen."

Whirring arcanatek replaced the sounds of the battle above. Still, Dracus didn't move. He held Threyna—firm, not tight—yet her glare might as well have strangled him. Her hellhound scowl didn't beg, didn't give up.

She's searching for a way out.

But Dracus needed to search for a way in. Canton and Fawkes were up there. He didn't know if they were alive or hollowed. If it were their souls being vortexed and irradiated, or if they were on their knees, watching as the legionaries did so to the people they'd come to know over these past ten years. He would have prayed to Neutreen, but if she existed, if she *ever* existed, she'd never answered him before.

Whether Canton was alive or hollowed, a shade or darkling, Dracus wasn't leaving without him. If things went how he assumed they would, the trembling man behind Threyna might be his only hope. He couldn't let him leave, and she wouldn't leave without him.

The stillness and their proximity only embellished the sounds of their labored breaths. Eyeing the fatekeeper pendant about her neck, and hoping against hope that she wouldn't do anything rash, he removed his hand from her throat to lift his index finger to his lips.

Her harsh stare refused to relent, but she didn't attempt to strike him either. He released her wrist, and the two leaned their faces against the bars of Theodyn's cell to glimpse what was going on in the courtyard beyond the grate.

As the last arcanatek warbled to a stop, Belrich's voice rang throughout Valefort. "Governor Olerus. My, my. You have some explaining to do."

Olerus whimpered loud enough that wherever he was, his blubbering reached the oubliette's listeners.

"I pray on every feather of Neutreen's wings that you will tell me the truth," Belrich said. "Trust in the Tenets will set you free, for only on the truth shall you fly from penance."

Dracus knew all too well of Belrich's brand of penance. It was his *mercy* that saw Canton's village burned. His mercy that impaled Canton's parents and flayed the flesh from their bones. He only hoped Rance could avert a disaster, or Dracus would have to cause one.

He exchanged a glance with Threyna, then held out his hand, nodding at the dagger at her hip. Hesitantly, she handed it to him. Reaching through the bars, Dracus took hold of the sack over the prisoner's head. He knew it was Theodyn, Bherus—whatever name he wanted to go by. He knew it. But as he cut through the sack to free his head from its veil, it wasn't the face of the man he remembered.

It was Theodyn. But the man he fought beside at the Battle of the Cut was gone. Black veins enveloped his face. His nose was carved off. Both his ears were missing. A scar slashed across one of his eyes, replacing its blue with a milky fog. Gone was the twinkle in his remaining eye.

Beside Dracus, Threyna began to tremble. She didn't know who he was. What he was. What he was capable of. To her, the walking corpse before them was a stranger wearing the tortured skin of a man she'd idolized. A man she'd abandoned her mother and sister to wait for. This was all that was left of him.

This was Belrich's brand of penance.

Theodyn's remaining eye found his daughter.

"For Threyna," he had said that day in the mouth of the Cut. Dracus knew this wasn't what he wanted for his little girl, same as Dracus never wanted Canton to grow, survive, and hollow in this cursed country. But here they were, and here they'd all suffer if they remained.

Threyna reached through the bars for her father's face, a tear trickling from her eye.

It would have been a beautiful moment if the whole world hadn't fallen to blood and bone.

Theodyn's gaze fell to the fatekeeper about her neck, the one he had given to Dracus. Standing at the Cut, prepared to suffer so that others could live, he'd said, *"If I fail... You must do what I could not. Finish this."*

Dracus had told him he couldn't. Wouldn't. He had his own battles to fight. But he had taken the fatekeeper, and worse, he'd given it to his daughter, knowing the terrible evil it housed inside. The same evil he'd likely earned those scars attempting to protect.

Theodyn forgot his daughter then, turning instead towards Dracus. He mumbled something incoherent, rage coursing through his black-veined eyes.

It was then Dracus realized that Theodyn hadn't been gagged. He didn't need to be. He didn't have a tongue.

CHAPTER 11

DISLOYALTY OR INCOMPETENCE

Laela IV

With *True* in one hand, bastard sword in the other, Laela charged into the courtyard. The feast was now a battleground. Darklings screeched as they tore from their failing bodies. Shades floated by, unaware and unconcerned of the scene unfolding around them. Hollowed howled in legionary blacks and Avengardian ivory, attacking anything still lucky enough to be amongst the living.

Crossbows thrummed as bolts flew through the night over the rubble of the west wall. Already, bodies littered the ground or were strewn across overturned tables from the Underground's attack, but it would only get worse.

While Belrich argued with Rance and Olerus on whether they betrayed him or not, their men, without commands, squared off with one another. All the while, the Underground's bolts and arcanatek fired indiscriminately.

Soon they would leave as they always did. There was no winning against the Order—the Underground just made sure everyone else lost, leaving everything in ashes.

She didn't have time to figure out what Ebrus was doing here. But if there was any hope of salvaging Avengard's admittance to the Dominion, of proving their innocence in the eyes of Belrich, it hinged solely on capturing the Underground saboteurs.

Laela leapt over a fallen legionary, chasing after Ebrus, the other servant, and the Undergrounder who disguised herself in the garb of the Avengard city watch. A crossbow bolt whisked past her face. She ducked as another zipped overhead, narrowly missing Fawkes.

The Undergrounders ran for the cover of the fallen walls, keeping low to avoid the spray of bolts. Staying focused within her Center of Silence, Laela skirted past a watchman dragging an injured servant from the fray. She passed the high table where her mother and Olerus cowered beneath. Belrich shouted orders to his Premiuses from behind the tight formation of his Inquisitors while Rance did the same behind the Swords of the Wraith. She should have been beside him. But she would have to trust Gatius and the others to see him protected.

A hollowed servant reached for Laela, a crossbow bolt through its chest. Laela sidestepped and slashed her sword across the hollowed's lower leg. It fell to the ground, separated from its limb. She forged forward, with no time to turn back. Ahead, Ebrus and his servant-disguised companion followed behind the Avengard city-watch-clad woman as she cleaved through hollowed with her stolen blade.

"They're going to get away." Laela's father's voice invaded her Center of Silence.

Heart pumping, legs churning, Laela ignored her father and closed the distance. The Underground strike team was retreating; she just needed to make sure the saboteurs didn't escape with them. Only a few strides behind Ebrus, she leapt. She buried *True* into Ebrus's hamstring and swiped her bastard sword across his ankles. She tackled him to the ground in a tangle of limbs and curses.

With Laela's momentum, they rolled until she sat atop him, *True* still embedded in the meat of his thigh. She ripped her dagger free, tearing a yelp from the prone poet's mouth. With his face in the dirt, Laela drove her knee into his spine and pressed the flat of her blade to his cheek.

"Don't ghosting move!" Laela spat.

Ebrus whimpered, but didn't resist. A few paces ahead, Fawkes wrestled with the grinning pretty-boy, attempting to avoid his dagger while Canton squared off with the woman.

They're not going anywhere. They won't get away with this.

Her father's laughter echoed in her mind. *"You always celebrate too early. Never count the darklings until they're in the jar."*

Laela walled him off, returning to her Center of Silence. But Rance's voice cut through.

"We surrender!" Rance shouted. "It's done! We surrender."

The Underground had stopped firing, already taking to the wind even before their own soldiers inside the walls had a chance to get free. Order legionaries, city watchmen, and servers alike all paused at Rance's words. Only the undead continued to move throughout the courtyard.

Laela wiped the blood from *True* on Ebrus's servant disguise and sheathed it in her vambrace, but dropped her bastard sword. With her hands free, she displayed the stocks.

Belrich emerged from behind his wall of Inquisitors. "That was unpleasant. Now, if you wish to live to see the next Bheric's Day, each and every one of you will do *exactly* as I say."

Like bodies before a vortexer, the wind was robbed of every person in Valefort, and everyone not clad in Order black fatigues dropped to their knees. Every person except the Palogian woman clad in the pale uniform of the Avengard city watch. She held a short sword against Canton's neck as she held him from behind.

A knot tangled in Laela's throat. Ebrus shook beneath her, or did she tremble atop him? *How did everything go so wrong?*

Slowly, all eyes turned on the woman. Fawkes knelt, the grinning Undergrounder in hand. He spared Laela a panicked glance. Not knowing what to do, Laela searched for Rance between the Inquisitors surrounding him, but couldn't locate him.

Belrich stared in her direction, not at Laela, but through her—toward Canton and the woman with the blade to his throat. He raised a silver-blond brow, a grin splitting his lips.

"Vortex and irradiate the fallen," Belrich said. He gestured towards two men, one tall and broad despite his graying hair, the other, a stout boulder of a man by comparison. Green pauldrons marked their shoulders—Premiuses.

"Decimus, Nerus—with me." Belrich waved them forward, a handful of Inquisitors in their skeletal masks followed close behind.

The scar across Laela's chest tightened. *Put me in the stocks, Nerus?* Laela had only heard the name from Dracus and Fawkes. She didn't know much of him; Dracus wasn't one for talk. But she knew what Nerus had done, and what evils Decimus was capable of. She didn't dare glance back at Canton.

As arcanatek whirred into motion all around them to contend with the grumbling hollowed and silent shades, Belrich and his escort approached the woman still standing.

"Do you not wish to see Bheric's Day?" Belrich asked, coming to a stop a few strides from where Laela had tackled Ebrus. "I'm partial to Cybel's Eve myself, but I wouldn't say that is worth being flayed over, hmm?" His expression darkened. His brows creased to a predatory angle. "I said kneel. Yet you stand. Speak or I'll have my Inquisitors help you find a stick to be impaled upon."

"He's an Undergrounder," the woman said, her tone even-keeled. "I caught him trying to rejoin their ranks."

Laela lurched from Ebrus's back. "Lia—"

The tall, broad Premius had a blade to her collarbone before she could blink. Inquisitors leveled their whirring arcanatek irradiators on her.

Struggling to swallow the knot in her throat, Laela pointed at the true Undergrounder. Anger constricted her vocal cords, making her unsteady voice quaver. "Prince Belrich, if I may?"

Belrich examined her, brow cocked with an air of interest rather than offense. He rolled his hand forward with a flourish only Saltspire could cultivate.

"I am Laela." She forced herself to work through the tension robbing her of voice and sense. "Laela Huron."

She used her mother's maiden name in place of the name she wore. Her father's name. The lost name of Velar still held weight amongst the Wraith, but it also held bad blood with the Order. She'd be branded a traitor and suffer the same fate as every Kaine and those who aligned with him during the Artificer's War if she wasn't careful.

Laela ignored the scar burning across her chest, the ghoulish grin painted on Belrich's too-young face, and the weapons trained on her. "I have lived in Avengard ten years. Ten years I've served. I've culled hollowed, shepherded flocks, and hauled crops with nearly everyone in this city. I have served in Neutreen's temple and can tell you something about every Deacon who has ever lit a match by the Valefort hearth." Hands still raised, she nodded at the woman holding Canton. "He is not the Undergrounder. She is." She gestured toward Ebrus and the other server, still in Fawkes's grasp. "They are."

Belrich chuckled. A flippant, unapologetic snicker that either lacked awareness of the bodies littering the ground around him, or possessed a callousness that rivaled the Skeleton King's himself. As the arcanateks' warbling ceased, Belrich's voice replaced it to echo off the crumbling walls of Valefort. "Governor Olerus. My, my. You have some explaining to do."

He turned his back to her to direct his scorn at the high table, but the arcanatek and the sword tickling the torn seams of Laela's city-watch collar remained. "I pray on every feather of Neutreen's wings that you will speak the truth. Trust in the Tenets will set you free, for only on the truth shall you fly from penance."

Olerus trembled beside Rance.

Belrich's singsong and playful tone rotted. "Bring him here."

Rough hands ripped Olerus from his cowering and dragged him before Belrich. The Inquisitors shoved the governor to his knees. Denied his height, the thin man looked small, but he shrank further beneath the stare of the Legatus of the Order. He wrinkled his hooked nose beneath bleary eyes as he groveled at Belrich's boots.

"My prince, this was not us. The Underground…"

Belrich squatted beside the governor, an exaggerated smile bunching his cheeks. "Yes, the Underground." He nodded in the direction of the Underground woman and Canton. "Can you tell me which of them should be impaled as a traitor—definitively?"

Olerus searched Canton's face looking for recognition, but found none. The woman holding Canton, keeping her blade at his throat, removed her shawl and plumed helm.

With the tanned skin, strong cheekbones, and dark features from the distant isles of Palogia, the woman's face wasn't one people would forget once they saw. Laela certainly hadn't.

Aylenia.

Though she remembered her from before the Underground, when they were both young girls in the followers camp of Victarius Kaine's Artificers, she didn't remember her like this. The skinny, quiet girl was replaced by a woman. As captivating as stained glass and just as sharp, Aylenia stared back at Olerus as if daring him to oust her as a traitor.

There was no way Olerus had ever lain eyes on her. Laela had. She knew she was an Undergrounder, but if she shared how she came by that knowledge, she'd be sharing the neighboring pike.

Belrich snapped his fingers. "The truth. Unless you truly cannot discern friend from foe?"

Olerus's eyes seemed to shake in their sockets as he glanced between Aylenia and Canton.

"My prince," Rance said from the high table. "If I may—"

"You may not," Belrich said playfully as if he were speaking to a child and not Avengard's aedile. "Olerus, you are governor of this city. I chose *you* to lead. Though I'm not certain which would be more disconcerting: your disloyalty, or your incompetence."

Olerus turned on his knees and held the stocks to Belrich. "My prince, I swear by the Tenets, upon every feather of Neutreen's wings, I am faithfully your man."

Belrich hmphed. "Incompetent then?"

"No, my prince, I—"

Belrich put a hand on Olerus's shoulder, still squatting beside the kneeling man. "Then tell me, why should I trust you if you don't even know which of your servants wishes to enter our Holy Dominion, and which seeks to tear it down, hmm? You see, loyalty can be bought. But competence—" Belrich wagged a finger before Olerus's hooked nose. "—competence can't be bought. Can't be scared straight or whipped into shape. No, there is only one way to deal with incompetence."

Belrich stood "Nerus, escort Olerus to his tower. Let him think upon his grievances and ponder the *gravity* of his circumstances."

"At once, Legatus," the squat Premius said as he hauled a trembling Olerus to his feet.

"Decimus," Belrich said to the tall, broad, older Premius holding his blade to Laela's throat. "I don't know who we can trust. So I suppose we can't trust anyone, can we?"

"No, Legatus," Decimus said.

Belrich hmphed, a self-satisfied smirk tugging on the corner of his lip. "In that case, I want every man, woman, and child within Valefort's walls to be detained, questioned. Provide them an opportunity to prove their innocence."

Laela pursed her lips. This wouldn't end well. Sentillion applied for entry into the Dominion. After a group of Tellers led a peaceful protest outside the walls, Belrich ordered Sentillion's lands salted. *What would he do if he blamed Avengard for the Underground's attack?*

She knew of the Order's form of questions. The Justicus had ways of making people talk. Even outside of the interrogations, the Doves, the

Order's spy network, would be all over Valefort. Not a single word could be uttered without Belrich's discovery.

Erynia will crack. Gatius will speak out of turn.

The scent of ashes filled her nostrils. She closed her eyes, searching for any possible way out of this. *Neutreen, if you have any power here, please. We need you.*

Without matches to light, a hearth to ignite, or a pyre to burn, there was no chance Neutreen would hear her prayers. She met Rance's eyes, hoping against hope that he would have something—anything—up his sleeve.

Rance stroked his gray goatee. Nearly imperceptibly, he shook his head at her.

"Take them to the cells," Belrich said.

CHAPTER 12

VILLAINS AND MONSTERS

Dracus IV

Dracus was hollowed, but Bherus was a horror. Death would have been a kindness compared to the fate the former prince had suffered. Bherus hissed out of the hole where his nose used to be. Spittle flew from his lips as his severed tongue attempted to form words against Dracus.

Bherus didn't need a tongue to give voice to the poison on his mind; Dracus knew his fury. He understood.

Ten years in the black cells. Torture. All the while taking peace knowing his failure didn't mean the end of the war.

He gave Dracus access to *the Blessing*, the cursed blood artifact that gifted the control of blood, bone, and soul. He wanted Dracus to defeat the Skeleton King, stop the Order, and find a way to *"keep playing."*

He hadn't. Instead, he'd lied to Bherus's daughter and passed the burden onto her.

The black veins in Bherus's face pulsed as if, even now, he wanted to conjure bloody arms and tear Dracus to pieces. If Canton and Fawkes were safe, if they weren't under attack in Avengard's courtyard or held prisoner to Belrich's brand of justice, perhaps it wouldn't have been the worst fate he could suffer. But no true death awaited him here. *If Canton and Fawkes are still alive, there's only one way of getting them outta here.*

Dracus held his hands up. "I'm sorry, Theodyn. I mean it. But this ain't the time." *Blood and bone, I hope the time never comes.* "I reckon ya feel like ya failed at the Cut. But ya didn't. Skeleton King hasn't been seen since."

Bherus thrashed within his bindings. Snarling and grunting, he shook his head.

If Dracus's flesh still lived, the reaction might have sent a chill down his spine. Whether Threyna noticed or not, Dracus didn't know.

After all this time, the monster still lives? You poor bastard, he's been living off of you.

Dracus swallowed. The Skeleton King wouldn't be his problem if he got Canton and Fawkes out of this. They could still meet *The Relentless* on the north shore and be in Sansia by tomorrow. Dracus would have his true death, and Canton would have a chance at life.

Asserting himself, Dracus pointed through the grate of Bherus's oubliette. "Listen to me. Lotta decent people are gonna suffer up there. You know Belrich. You know what he'll do. You might be the only one with the power to do somethin' 'bout it."

Threyna shoved Dracus's shoulder, twisting him to face her. "Are you insane? You want him to fight? Look at him. He's in no state to—"

Dracus shoved her off, returning his focus to Bherus. "You want to finish this? You stopped your father. Now stop your brother. End this."

Threyna grabbed Dracus by the collar with one fist. "What are you talking about? We can't win this fight. This is an extraction. We need to leave."

"Your people are up there too," Dracus said, gambling. He didn't mean the girl's mother or sister. He knew they wouldn't get through to her. But he didn't believe Arilette sent her here alone, and he understood the battle she'd been fighting for the last ten years; after what she'd been through, she wouldn't leave her team behind so easily.

Threyna glared at him, not knowing even half of the situation at play.

Belrich's voice carried through the courtyard and bounced off the walls of Bherus's cell. "I want every man, woman, and child within Valefort's walls to be detained, questioned. Provide them an opportunity to prove their innocence."

Dracus met Bherus's harrowing gaze. "You know what that means, eh? Everyone will suffer. Only you can stop this. Only you can save us."

"Do you believe in the Purge?" Theodyn had asked him that fateful day before the Battle of the Cut. He had said no. Truth be told, he still didn't believe it, but he needed Bherus to believe that he believed it.

"You were right," Dracus said. "This story has a hero. That Teller was right. But it's gotta be you. And it's gotta be now."

Dracus grabbed the soul jar from his hip.

"What are you doing?" Threyna asked. "You can't—"

He pressed the button, releasing the lid, and held the arcanatek to Bherus's tortured face. 804 darklings, procured from a lifetime spent fighting in the Order's wars and vortexing hollowed, flooded into Bherus's cage.

Threyna cried, but Bherus inhaled. The tormented souls imprisoned in his soul jar rushed into the tortured victim confined in the oubliette. As each darkened soul crashed into Bherus, the rot corrupting his veins began to recede. It wasn't until he'd consumed the last of them that he somewhat resembled the man who had handed Dracus the cursed fatekeeper ten years back.

Bherus convulsed, struggling against the darklings vying for control over his body.

"Father?" Threyna attempted to open the door to his cell, but Dracus held her back, pulling her away.

"Let me go! Let me—"

Tendrils of blood spawned out of Bherus's back. The manacles binding his wrists and ankles creaked. Fresh vines of rot snaked through his veins at the cost of his conjuring, stretching up his neck and encircling it like a corruptive noose.

There were no heroes to this story. Only villains. Only monsters. But the only way to defeat a monster was to make another one.

CHAPTER 13

A FEAST FOR HELLHOUNDS

Laela V

Decimus, the Lord Premius of the Order, took Laela by the shoulder, steering her towards Valefort's front doors. Behind her, Inquisitors disarmed Aylenia, Ebrus, and the other Undergrounder, as well as Fawkes and Canton. Guilty and innocent alike, all would suffer. All around her, the Order's legionaries corralled everyone from Aedile Rance all the way down to the youngest of serving girls. The city watchmen were rounded up like sheep. The only difference was that when a shepherd led their flock, they sought only to provide, protect, and guide. In this case, the shepherd might as well have been a group of black-clad hellhounds.

"Only on Neutreen's truth shall you fly free," Belrich said, standing on the front stairs leading into Valefort's foyer. "Speak true and pure. Cooperate and you shall be protected."

Laela didn't trust the lie. She still had a hidden blade in her boot and another in her vambrace, yet she followed the rest of the herd into the paddock and the slaughter awaiting inside. At least if she were a sheep, she would still have claws. She'd forge a way out.

Rance, ever the pillar of poise, stroked his gray goatee, smoothed back his hair in its horsetail, and encouraged Gatius to hand over his sword. *He'll find us a way out. I just need to be ready for his signal.*

Laela met her mother's eyes. Her mother averted her gaze, dropping her chin to her chest.

She sent the letter to Threyna. She told the Underground. Her mother's words returned to her. *"There is strength in knowing when to drop your guard."*

If there was strength in that, her mother didn't have it. She'd lowered her guard at the worst possible time, and now many would pay with their souls. The scar across her chest burned. The fatekeeper on her neck threatened to weigh her down. Noxious smoke filled her nostrils as if she were back in Octarius, watching her father burn. Watching the fleet burn.

Be strong. Be courageous. We'll find a way out of this.

Chewing her lip, she followed the crowd.

"Be warned," Belrich said. "Those who speak falsely... will suffer." He pointed to the tower overlooking the courtyard.

In the window, silhouetted shapes struggled in the torchlight of the tower.

"No. No, please. No!"

Gasps flooded the courtyard, followed by screams. A body fell from the tower window, arms and legs flailing within a green cloak. Olerus's body hit the crumbling stone steps of Valefort's front entrance with a sickening crunch. Dead on impact, Olerus still screamed, his broken remains mere strides from Belrich.

Laela's stomach twisted in knots. Her chest tightened, unable to draw breath. The thin veil that held back her father's commentary about this being her fault, her failure, her weakness—began to erode.

Olerus's skull was caved in. His ribs protruded through his skin. Blood overwhelmed the green cloak and leaked down the front steps, cascading into a puddle. He continued to cry, to groan. His arms, bent at awful angles, still moved, reaching for aid. Hollowed.

Belrich didn't spare him a glance. He raised his hand to still the horrified onlookers. "Be calm, good citizens of Avengard." A cruel grin slashed across his face. "You will not share poor Olerus's fate. Neutreen has judged him. In his pursuits of moderation, he fared well. But I fear in modesty, in merit, he did not quite measure up."

Belrich strode down the steps to Olerus's hollowed form. "Now I hope you all can appreciate the… *gravity*… of the situation. Or would it be gravitas?" He hmphed with a shrug.

"You murderer," Cyb, a veteran city watchman, said from beside Rance at the front of the procession. He strode toward Belrich. "You are not Neutreen. You do not get to ju—"

Belrich didn't even move. The nearest Inquisitor drew a sword and stabbed the unarmed man through the heart.

Cyb stumbled backwards. His hands grasped at his chest, trying to keep the blood inside, where it belonged. It spilled between his fingers. His legs gave out, and he fell into Rance's outstretched arms before he could hit the stairs.

Laela's world tore in two, not because she couldn't believe this was happening, but because this *shouldn't* have been happening. This should have been a celebration. Now it was only a feast for hellhounds.

"Still, you stay silent," her father said. *"Still, you do nothing."*

Laela didn't know what she could do if she didn't want to end up like Olerus and Cyb.

Cyb wasn't in the Wraith, but he was a good man. She'd served with him for the better part of the last three years. He'd lost his wife to dewskull, his daughter to a hollowed attack. All he wanted was to join the Dominion so others could live and grow under the Order's protection. Before he could ever see that dream come to pass, he learned the truth of the Order's lies.

"It seems your people are still not getting the *point* of this lesson, Rance," Belrich said.

Cyb's face went white as the purest shade. His blood drenched Rance's cloak as he held the suffering man.

"We submit," Rance said. He addressed the crowd behind him. "*Everyone* will submit."

Cyb, still suffering despite there being more blood outside his body than in, reached for Rance. Life, what was left of it, fled his eyes. He slackened in Rance's embrace, his Avengard city-watch uniform a crimson smear on the stairs of Valefort. A gray luminescent shade emerged from Cyb's fallen form.

He wasn't the purest soul Laela had ever seen, but he didn't deserve this. Everyone had their inner darklings, their moments of weakness, their failures to measure up to the Tenets—but Neutreen was merciful. She wouldn't have condemned him.

"Will you at least grant him release?" Rance asked Belrich.

That was what the Order's so-called job was—the Justicus culled the hollowed to purge Rheynia of its undeath, and the legionaries protected the Dominion from the Tellers and the Undergrounders. Despite their propaganda for the sheep they ruled over, they didn't care for the Purge. They didn't protect anyone. They preyed upon everyone else while worshiping the *One True God*. They didn't keep the Tenets. They didn't light matches, hearths, or pyres to whisper prayers on the rising smoke. They didn't long for Neutreen to grant them wings to fly to Valencia. All they wanted was power. Control. Dominion.

A smile split Belrich's lips. Not one of pleasure, but one of genuine pity. "A unified Rheynia—that's all I've ever wanted. Ever since I crawled from my mother's womb as she hollowed, all I've wanted was peace. Fifty-seven long years. Fifty-seven years of undeath, decay, dissent, and war. My entire life, these lands have been cursed. Not Rheynia, but here." He lifted his arms to Valefort behind him. "Valefort, Avengard, all of Northvale—you are nothing but traitors. Rheynia is not cursed. You are. Cursed to fight, to lie, to ruin everything. You conspired with the Underground to see the Dominion fall."

"We did not," Laela shouted, still in Decimus's clutches. Whether due to her father's prodding or her own anguish, Laela hadn't been able to contain herself any longer. She'd waited for Rance to object, but he remained silent. They needed to do something, or Avengard would become the new Sentillion; the lands within the valley of the Sisters would be set to flame and salted, never to rise again.

Decimus tightened his grip on her. Belrich fixed her with his ghoulish gaze, but she needed to appeal to him, or they were all doomed.

"My prince," Laela began, "Legatus of the Order, Neutreen's chosen to rule the land of the living, we are not the enemy. We did not attack. We have no reason to try. We have struggled these past ten years to prove ourselves a productive and contributing asset to the Dominion. What have we to gain from siding with the Underground when we were so close to receiving your absolution? Please, my prince. Isn't this exactly what the Underground wants?"

Belrich examined her, stroking his cleft chin with a gloved hand as if considering how to dispose of her.

"Ooh," her father mocked. *"Shouldn't have done that. Now you're in for it."*

Belrich strode towards her. "The Underground does seek to divide us, yes. Perhaps there is still a chance for unity." He nodded to one of his Inquisitors. "Irradiate the shade."

Laela let out a trembling breath. She could do no right in her father's eyes, but Rance gave her an appreciative nod.

As the Inquisitor charged his irradiator to end Cyb's eternal wandering, Belrich addressed the rest of the gathered Avengardians. "We shall continue as planned. You shall be questioned, but speak true and pure, and together we shall overcome the Underground and their treach—"

A shrill cry cut off Belrich's declaration. Not the whine of a shade, the screech of a darkling, or the groan of a hollowed, but the terrible sound of twisting metal. People at the back of the crowd, more to the center of the courtyard, gasped, backing away. The iron grate of one of the oubliettes flew into the air to crash down on an overturned table.

Gasps became screams. Out of the darkness, from one of the subterranean cells, giant scarlet legs like that of a gargantuan spider hoisted a bare-chested monstrosity of a man. Nose cut off, ears clipped, and covered with scars and black veins, this monster could only be one thing.

The Skeleton King...

CHAPTER 14

HEART OF STONE

Threyna VI

Memories of her father brushing back her hair and kissing her forehead goodbye, dreams of finally reuniting with him after all of her time alone, they both felt as pointless as prayers to Neutreen. His face mutilated, his body tortured, he was unrecognizable. Gone was the man she remembered. Gone were the dreams she foolishly allowed herself to envision for their future. All that remained was the weight of the fatekeeper around her neck, the knot in her throat, and the weakness in her knees.

Standing in the cell meant to hold her father until his execution, she stared out the destroyed ceiling at the creature her father had become. And what he was capable of.

Blood magic...

Suspended on blood-conjured spider's legs that lifted him to the height of three times of any man, he towered above her. Blood materialized in his hands—a shield in his left, a scythe in his right.

Shouts filled the courtyard. Arcanatek whirred into motion. Irradiators fired at him, but he blocked with his shield. Those he couldn't block himself were absorbed by conjured shields that bloomed to life only to fall to ashes moments later. The ashes rained down upon her, but as her father shifted from defense to offense, the shouting commands became wails.

Her father charged ahead, out of Threyna's view. Blood sprayed. Darklings ripped into the sky. The light of shades filled the courtyard. But the screams.

It was horrible. Threyna had only ever heard of the Skeleton King's blood magic. Never had she seen it. *But Father? How?*

Tears stung her eyes. She spun on Dracus. "What did you do to him?"

Dracus took her by the shoulders. "I gave 'em the power to see us from this place." His gaze fell to her fatekeeper. He pursed his lips. "I'm goin' up there. Gettin' Canton and Fawkes. Wait here. I'll explain, I promise."

Threyna tore from his grasp. Her head swam, but she knew Dracus's plan. Get the people he cared about and run. Threyna wouldn't leave her father. She wouldn't abandon the mission, or her strike team. Shoving Dracus away, she leapt onto the wall with her left foot, planted her right foot into the adjacent wall, and reached for the lip of the oubliette. Seizing the metal edge, she hauled herself up and into the courtyard.

Bodies littered the ground around her. Darklings swirled overhead, and shades ambled between the living and the fallen.

Inquisitors, legionaries, and Justicus threw themselves at her father. His scythe carved through crowds, cleaving men in two and spewing limbs to the ground. It wasn't just Order men who fell. Avengardians caught in the line of destruction suffered the same fate. Blood on the ground congealed into rows of blood-spawned pikes that rose from the ground, impaling all in their path. A rain of scarlet arrows appeared before her father before zipping into the people surrounding him.

The carnage, the destruction a single man could cause… It was no wonder how the Skeleton King remained in power. Her father was an army.

Black veins stretched along his flesh as it had before he consumed the darklings in Dracus's soul jar, but with each fallen body, he summoned more souls into him to abate the spread of the rot.

He will be fine. But Ebrus, Aylenia, Yevon… She needed to get them out. Her father slaughtered indiscriminately. Dracus had unleashed a monster. A weapon. One that wouldn't just turn the tables on the Order, but had the potential to obliterate them.

Dracus climbed out of the oubliette behind her. "Meet me back here. Please."

When she didn't respond, he charged into the fray in search of Canton and Fawkes. As if immune to the clamor of battle all around him, he sprinted into the onslaught.

Threyna took a more cautious approach. She couldn't afford to run in the wrong direction. She had few allies here. Threyna ducked an irradiator blast aimed at her father. Scanning the battleground for any of the gray-robed servants, she couldn't spot Ebrus or Yevon. That could have been a good sign.

Maybe they got out?

The west wall of Valefort's courtyard was a pile of rubble. It was possible between Lorath's distraction and her father's assault that Aylenia, Ebrus, and Yevon were able to take advantage. She cursed Dracus for taking her interlayer. Right before he took it, Aylenia had warned that people were moving in on Ebrus. Threyna couldn't take shelter until she knew for sure. She couldn't lose another of her squad.

Threyna skirted a flying sword, a severed arm still holding the blade. Crouching, she again surveyed the battleground for the servants. Most retreated towards the cover of the outer walls of the courtyard, but they were actual servants. Ebrus and Yevon were not.

Unable to stay by the oubliette, Threyna scampered across the field of slaughter. She came across a servant lying prone. The gray robes drank enough blood to dye the fabric in death. Whoever it was, their soul had departed, their corpse as still as the doomed.

Biting back her fear of seeing Ebrus or Yevon's face, she shoved the servant onto his back. Green eyes stared blankly to the clouds overhead. His slack-jaw fell agape. The torn flesh in the side of his neck where a crossbow bolt likely ripped through allowed a river to flow, draining all the color—all the life—from his face.

Threyna shuddered, releasing a trembling exhale.

Whatever soul inhabited this body once, it was not Ebrus or Yevon. Just some other poor sop struggling to survive in this cursed world. Not a fighter of the Underground, not a dreamer of the Wraith, just someone who believed the lie that everything would be better once they joined the Dominion.

Threyna left the dead man and continued her search.

Ebrus, where are you? She never wanted to take him. She knew this would happen. She knew, one day, she wouldn't be able to protect him. *Did he have another episode? Did he panic?*

In the torchlight lining the front steps of Valefort, between the lines of legionaries, before the skeletal Inquisitors defending Belrich, a shade, as silver as steel, spun to face her.

Tension denied breath from her chest and dread stole the thoughts from her head as she stared into the face of a boy she'd known her whole life.

No. Gory ghosting blood and bone, no...

The ghastly visage of Ebrus floated towards her. Threyna stood motionless in a courtyard of cataclysm. Time slowed. Consequences ceased to exist. Ebrus was gone.

A single tear slipped from her fluttering eyelashes. Her teeth clenched together as she shook her head, denying what her eyes told her.

No. No. No.

She took a single step towards Ebrus as he continued to float towards her.

It was said that shades lost sentience. They lost who they were, what they'd done, everyone they'd loved—everything. Threyna always believed that to be true. She had no reason to believe otherwise. But the way the shade of her friend looked at her now, she knew the truth: he remembered her. He remembered every poem he'd ever written her but never shared. If not for Daeton's teasing and Rivich finding where Ebrus kept his secret stash, she never would have learned of the love he had for her. Staring into the light of his soul, she knew he still felt every bit of love for her. But now he'd never be able to speak it.

Threyna reached for him. She didn't know what happened to him, where his body had fallen, or if Yevon and Aylenia were with him when he died.

"Ebrus, I…"

The sadness in his stare mirrored the same he shared in life. His phantom arm reached for her. Threyna extended for him, but as she did, she felt a draw upon her, as if a vortex attempted to suck her soul from her body.

Ebrus's form rippled. His face distorted like in the reflection of a trickling stream. As the current carried him away, Threyna reached out to grab him, but his spectral form slipped through her. A wave of cold washed over her hand. She spun, following his trajectory.

Ebrus's shade disappeared into her father marching overhead on the massive legs of a gargantuan spider. He slashed at the legionaries around her with a scythe.

Threyna stumbled, falling backwards between her father's spider legs. A groaning hollowed, severed at the waist, reached for her with both arms. Blinking away tears, Threyna scooted backwards on her backside. She gained her feet, but a path opened. Threyna located Aylenia. *She's alive!*

Alive, but cornered. She traded blows with two men. Two ghosts of her past. A lanky boy who grew into a lanky young man, Canton struck with his short sword alongside Fawkes who blocked Aylenia's riposte. Dracus was closing in on them.

Aylenia blocked Canton's short sword, slipping between him and Fawkes. Her arcanatek whirred as it charged in her opposite hand, but it wouldn't be enough against the three of them once Dracus arrived.

Threyna charged after them. Keeping low, evading bloody scythes that seemed to congeal out of the gore covering the ground, she weaved between the Order's lines. They took no notice of her, their focus fixated on the black-veined blood-wielding monster above her. At some point, her father's spider legs transformed into wings.

He soared overhead, consuming darklings and shades between conjuring death devices.

Threyna leapt over a downed legionary, his shade prying its way from his corpse. She landed in a crouch only for a dropped Dawnshard to land before her.

Inhaling sharply, Threyna lurched for it. With its ticking signaling its impending release, Threyna closed her eyes and tossed it behind her. It must have unleashed its radiant energy the moment she released it because a gale of disoriented shouts erupted behind her.

Threyna staggered in Dracus's wake. He was nearly on them. She wasn't going to make it in time.

Ghost dammit, where is Yevon?

Threyna drew her short sword as Dracus approached Canton's and Fawkes's backs. Just as Fawkes opened Aylenia's guard, Canton prepared the thrust that would take Aylenia through the ribs. Threyna's heart seized in her chest. She inhaled to shout, but it never came.

Neither did the strike.

Dracus seized Canton by the back of his collar, yanking him away. Canton's strike missed by half a blade's length. Spinning, Dracus hurled Canton behind him. "The oubliette. Now!"

Fawkes backed away from Aylenia, his guard still raised. Aylenia let him retreat, even as her arcanatek reached its crescendo.

Threyna continued towards Aylenia, but Canton stopped upon seeing her.

"You…"

Dracus again took a handful of Canton's tunic and shoved him past Threyna. "Yeah, her. Move!" Shoving Canton, he met Threyna's eyes. "Come with us, Threy."

Another Dawnshard exploded overhead.

If it distracted her father from his massacre, it didn't show. All around the courtyard, men fell, wailing even after they died. Shades tore from flesh, ambling through living and hollowed alike. Darklings ripped through the sky, charging into unsuspecting victims in search of a body to overtake.

"I can't go," Threyna said. "Not without my father."

"He won't leave," Dracus said. "He'll suffer here. Everyone who stays will. Don't be one of them." Once Fawkes caught up to him, the two ran for the oubliette.

Hissing through her teeth, Threyna let them flee. *Cowards. Always running.*

Arcanatek fired all around her. Wishing she had her interlayer, she ran toward Aylenia.

Aylenia aimed her arcanatek at a hollowed grasping at her ankles.

Not an irradiator. A vortex.

A gash across the cheek cut through where his grinning dimples should have been.

Yevon, so warm in life, was equally as cold in death. Not laughing. Not joking. He reached for Aylenia with a stump of an arm. A trail of blood followed in his wake, just as death had followed him everywhere he went.

First Ebrus. Now Yevon.

He'd joined the Underground after his sister hollowed from dewskull. On every mission, he never fired his last charge of his vortexer or his irradiator on the off-chance he ever found the hollowed remains of his sister to put her out of her misery. Now he never would.

Threyna came on this mission to save her father, but what was left of the man who hugged her tight and kissed her forehead? In coming to retrieve him, she'd lost two of her closest companions. Her friends.

Aylenia whimpered as she pulled the trigger.

Yevon's soul tore free from his hollowed body, but a shade of their fallen friend didn't come out. A darkling did. Before Aylenia could flip the switch of her arcanatek to irradiate him, the dark spirit dove into Threyna's chest.

The world around her fell away as Yevon drove her into the deepest darkness of her soul. Though she'd never fended off a darkling before, Arilette had trained her for what to expect.

The Heart of Stone, she had called it, the last bastion of one's sense of self. The deepest part of one's soul where the battle for control over her body began.

The walls of Valefort were replaced by the lowest level of Octarius—Arilette's tablinum. Yevon's darkling thrashed at her, but bounced off, careening off the stone walls only to attack again. Threyna cast Yevon's panicked soul away. She could feel his emotions pouring down on her, as tangible as if she were standing in the daily rains. His thoughts rattled around her, echoing off the walls of Arilette's stone chambers, but they sought—no, they needed—to entwine with hers. The malevolence, the fear, the hate was unlike anything Yevon demonstrated in life.

His spirit charged into her within her Inner Underground, but Threyna rebuffed him again. He bounced off Arilette's wooden table, crashed into the ground, and then rebounded off of the wooden door of House Desius.

"Stop!" Threyna cried to Yevon.

He didn't.

He charged again with the vigor of having not been fended off thrice already. If anything, his desperation only grew. His thoughts and memories bled into her mind as she felt him searching to gain access to her own.

Threyna spun, hurling Yevon's darkling into the far wall. Through Yevon's memories, she watched his sister, Kyra, hollow from dewskull. She felt his tears sting her own cheeks. She experienced his rage at the Order for having the cure, but not sharing it. Helplessly, she lived through Yevon's last moments, watching as he struck at Canton's back while he attacked Aylenia. Fawkes deflected the blade. Canton spun and slashed.

The first cut severed his forearm. The second cleaved a gash through his thigh that cut to the bone. But the third stabbed Yevon—stabbed Threyna—through the gut.

"We were only here because of you!" Yevon shouted with a voice void of all that made him human. *"You did this. This is your fault. Your fault!"*

Threyna flinched, but Yevon charged again. This time, Threyna didn't toss him off. She grabbed him by his spectral wisp of a throat, pulling his last modicum of humanity as close to her essence as possible. His soul, a swirl of deep purple, gray, and black, remained suspended within her grasp. Her hand glowed a bright evergreen within her Inner Underground, but holding him, wishing her friend would stop attacking her, she realized he wouldn't stop. He couldn't, even if he wanted to.

This close, she felt his torment—the endless physical pain of being a hollowed and the spiritually harrowing experience of being a darkling.

Yevon's thoughts bled through. *I can't go back out there. I can't. I won't. This is her fault! She owes me her body. She doesn't deserve it. I do. I've suffered enough. Blood and bone, Kyra, forgive me!*

Tears streamed down Threyna's cheeks. *Every moment he's outside of a host body, he feels like he's burning alive.* She couldn't give him what he longed for. No one who could would. But she had a mission to finish, and there was no place left for Yevon in those plans.

"I'm so sorry, Yev."

Threyna ejected her friend from her Inner Underground. The stone walls of Arilette's subterranean fortress fell away, and the calamity of the Valefort courtyard returned in a rush.

"Bherus!" Belrich shouted.

A vortex drew on Threyna's soul. Though she could resist it, Yevon could not. His darkling surged away, caught in the current that led directly into her father. Just like that, Yevon was gone.

"Threy!" Aylenia cried, taking her by the wrist. Her panicked eyes searched Threyna's. "Is that you in there?"

"Yeah, I'm fine," Threyna said. "We gotta—"

"Don't you ghosting move!"

The tip of a blade pressed against Threyna's back.

Threyna's nostrils flared. Her heartbeat, already a whirring irradiator, reached its crescendo. She recognized the voice. Hated it and she who wielded it, just as she knew it hated her.

"Drop it," Laela said. "Or I swear to Neutreen I'll cut you down and burn your corpse."

CHAPTER 15

True Scars

Laela VI

A monster climbed out of the oubliette. A horror. Worse than Laela's nightmares of her father's hollowed corpse burning on the pyre. Worse than the smell of fumes in her nostrils after another failed escape attempt.

Before her, in the flesh, a mangled monstrosity of tortured muscle and bone suspended itself on blood-conjured limbs. Black veins streaked down a scarred torso. His face was even worse. A milky, sightless eye. A snipped nose. Clipped ears. Yet despite his apparent torture, Laela recognized the man at once. Not the Skeleton King. The Undergrounder, the prisoner of war the Order demanded they execute to enter the Dominion—Threyna's father, Theodyn. The man her mother loved more than she ever did Laela's father towered over Valefort's courtyard.

"Hollow him!" Belrich shouted.

Olerus—forgotten. Cyb—a distant memory. Peace, unity, and the prospect of escaping this cursed island withered to ash. Likewise, Lord Premius Decimus's hand left Laela's shoulder. Laela found her mother's eyes through the crowd that separated them. Irradiators, set to stun, fired upon Theodyn, the man she loved, but there was nothing anyone could do to stop them.

Sinking into her Center of Silence, Laela ducked as an arcanatek warbled past her ear. She staggered, fumbling through the crowd of legionaries, attempting to close the distance between her and her mother.

Blood-conjured destruction rained from the sky or sprouted from the earth to rend flesh, bone, and soul.

A spearpoint jutted from the ground, skewering a legionary from groin to throat just beside Laela. She lurched out of the way, falling to the ground. The man didn't even have a moment to scream. A darkling screeched into the air, tearing free of its body before the blood-spawned spear could even fall to ash.

Another legionary stepped on Laela to shoot his charged irradiator. Before he could pull the trigger, a bloody knife dove like a haunted hawk and cleaved his hand off. The finger still pulled the trigger. The shot burst directly into the neighboring legionary, sending him seizing.

Screams and the constant fire of irradiators overcame orders and commands. In the chaos, Laela crawled towards the front stairs of Valefort. Between legionaries and beneath the screeching wails of darklings, she made her way to her mother and Rance, but as she stood, a hand closed around her wrist with iron strength.

"You did this!" Belrich's ghoulish eyes glared daggers into her. "You knew who the prisoner would be. You fed him the souls he'd need."

"Please, we had nothing to—"

Behind Belrich, Gatius drew his blade. Taking advantage of the distracted Inquisitors, Gatius made for Belrich's back.

It was never supposed to be this way. It never should have come to this. But the dead walked, and the living hid in underground tunnels. Neutreen was gone and not returning. Nothing was as it was supposed to be, but if Gatius did what Laela expected, Valefort would fall. Avengard would be burned, her lands salted, just like Sentillion. Belrich didn't deserve to be spared, but if she let Gatius attack him, there would be no way of blaming this entire episode on the Underground. Everyone in Avengard would be impaled.

"Watch out!" Laela wrenched her wrist toward her, pulling Belrich in her direction.

Gatius thrust, but an Inquisitor deflected his strike. Two others pounced on him, stabbing their short swords into the gaps of his city-watch armor. Blood spurted through the segments of leather, drenching the pale surcoat in moments.

Erynia screamed.

Laela tried to locate her through the fray, knowing that Rance and her mother wouldn't be far from her side, but before she could find her, Belrich spun on her.

"You try to murder me!" Spittle flew from Belrich's mouth.

"No! I saved y—" Laela's pleas cut off again as a swooping scythe forced them to duck. One Inquisitor didn't react fast enough. His head rolled from his shoulders to bounce across Valefort's front steps. His skeletal mask clanged even after his decapitated body fell to the ground.

Belrich's glare intensified, but he didn't release Laela's wrist. She stood, twisting to wrench free, but another Inquisitor seized her by the arm, his blade drawn.

Laela's hopes of peaceful de-escalation went up in prayerless smoke. If she didn't fight, she would hollow, and Belrich would salt all of Northvale anyway. She drew *True* from her vambrace and spun. Ripping away from the Inquisitor's grip, she stomped on Belrich's foot, threw an elbow into his chin, and caught the Inquisitor's pommel as he chopped down at her.

Laela drove her dagger into the eye slit of the Inquisitor's skeletal mask. His body went limp in her grasp, and a shade slipped out of him before his body could fall to the ground.

She turned on Belrich, but before he could shout another order, a bloody scythe cleaved through two legionaries coming to his aid. Gore sprayed across Belrich's Order blacks and splattered his face.

Laela didn't give him a chance to command more Order attention to her. Luckily, the threat of Theodyn's cursed blood magic drew more attention, allowing her to retreat into the mess of bodies in the courtyard. Servants and guards attempting to escape the abomination clashed with the Order Justicus attempting to defeat it. The living flailed and shrieked with eerie similarity to the hollowed.

Through the crowd, running from the collapsed west wall, Dracus shoved Canton past…

Threyna…

Heat seared across the scar traversing Laela's chest. The betrayal stung as hot as it had when her father's blade nearly hollowed her. Canton continued toward the open oubliette, Dracus and Fawkes behind.

Would they leave without us?

Dracus made a habit of running when convenient, and she didn't want to wait around to see if he would include her, her mother, or Rance in his inner circle. No time for her rage toward Threyna, confusion as to why Gatius would attack Belrich, or her distrust of Dracus, Laela spun, searching for Rance and her mother.

Just as she spotted Rance on the opposite side of Valefort's front stairs, a ticking Dawnshard exploded overhead. Laela closed her eyes, but not soon enough. Blinding light spotted her vision, even through her eyelids. Disoriented, Laela tripped over something writhing on the ground. She stumbled, landing hard on her back. The back of her head bounced off something metallic.

The spotted lights of her vision soared, her ears rang, and the wind was knocked from her lungs. Something crawled atop her. Unable to see, barely able to feel, Laela held *True* before her.

Pressure pawed at her thighs, climbing up to her torso. Before sight returned, Laela drove the tip of her dagger into flesh. Her attacker roared, but continued to rake its nails at her torso, clawing for her flesh but only finding armor.

Hollowed.

Feeling more than seeing, Laela drove *True* into flesh again and again, but it did little to stop the monster. Teeth sank into her hand. Biting back a scream, she clubbed the hollowed in the side of the skull. The vise-gripping maw released its hold, but pain lanced up her hand. She reached until she found purchase on what she assumed was its leg. Remaining in contact, she crawled up the hollowed's back, driving *True* with quick punches. It thrashed, wrenching the blade free from her bloody grasp.

Not bothering to search for the knife in her blindness, she pinned it prone by driving her knee into its spine. She wrapped her left arm under its snapping jaw, and her right on the back of its skull. With a grunt, she twisted.

The hollowed's spine snapped with a sickening crunch. Its body went limp, but its teeth continued to gnash.

Panting, Laela rolled off the monster to stare at the clouds overhead. Ears ringing, her vision returned; blurry silhouettes gave way to colors, shapes, and more horror. Part of her wished she was still blinded, but then she'd never get her mother or Rance out of this mess.

Retrieving *True* and gaining her feet, Laela scanned the battleground. Shades floated past. Darklings swirled overhead, entering into Theodyn's vortexing presence. Legionaries fired off round after round of irradiator blasts. Those who got close enough attempted to slash at his spider legs, but they were as fruitless as Avengard's crops.

Find Mother. Find Rance. Move.

Amidst the turmoil, she located Dracus. Half in and half out of the oubliette, he waved towards the eastern side of Valefort's front stairs where Rance and Laela's mother were running from Nerus. The Premius who shoved Olerus from the tower window bore down on Rance from behind. Despite already bleeding from a stab wound to the gut, Rance bowled towards Dracus and the oubliette.

He's not going to make it.

Laela, the First Sword of the Wraith, the Mistress of Blades, pulled another knife from her boot and charged toward them. Rance held her mother's wrist in one hand, and a discarded blade in the other. But Rance wasn't a fighter. He would be cut to ribbons if Nerus got to him before he reached the oubliette.

Nerus closed the distance, his short sword a hair's breadth from her mother's back. But Nerus was focused on Rance. Three paces away. Two.

Blood pumping in her ears, Laela vaulted over an overturned table and leapt at Nerus just as he reared to strike. She crashed into her mother, Rance, and Nerus.

The four of them tumbled to the ground just before the oubliette's busted grate.

Laela landed on her shoulder. Somewhere in her fall, either her blade, Rance's, or Nerus's slashed across her cheek. Blood dribbled down her face like tears, but Nerus gained his feet first.

He stood over Laela. "You gory ghosting traitors." He reared back his sword, ready to stab her through the gut.

With only two daggers to defend herself, Laela searched for a means of escape, but red blocked out the sky beyond Nerus. Bloody wings stretched from Theodyn's black-veined torso, and a tail-like projection coiled around Nerus, yanking him into the air.

Saved from Nerus, Laela crawled on hands and knees. Her mother was already up, but Rance was still on his back. Dracus attempted to haul him towards the oubliette.

Daggers in hand, Laela moved to aid Rance toward the oubliette's entrance. "Rance!"

"I'm fine," Rance said, though his thin, hard face was twisted in pain and his close-cropped goatee was stained bloody. "Your mother—"

"Threyna..." her mother said.

Laela followed her gaze as she lowered Rance down to Dracus in the oubliette. Threyna stood across from Aylenia, fending off a hollowed atop the rubble of the collapsed west wall.

"C'mon," Dracus shouted. "No time."

"My girl..."

Laela reached to stop her mother, but with *True* in hand, she couldn't secure her before she ran towards Threyna.

"Gory ghosting dammit," Laela spat. Her mother was going to get them killed. All for Threyna, who didn't care about anyone but herself. She looked into the oubliette. "Get him out of here."

Dracus nodded. "Hurry."

"Erynia," Rance said. "Find her."

"I will!" Laela glanced around the courtyard for any sign of Rance's daughter but found none.

"Aranoc," Rance said, sputtering blood. "Meet us at Aranoc."

Without another word, Dracus hauled Rance from the cell. Sparing no more time, Laela ran across the blood-soaked courtyard towards her mother.

Mother first. Then Erynia.

Her bloody hand from where the hollowed bit her throbbed, and her head pulsed in time with each beat of her heart, but the scar across her chest burned worst of all. Nothing good would come from this. They needed to run.

Aylenia fired a vortex into a hollowed, and a darkling tore free.

"No!" shouted Laela's mother, slowing a few paces ahead of Laela.

Too late. The darkling dove into Threyna's chest, and she froze.

"She's gone," Laela said. "We need to go."

She hoped her mother would finally see reason. The feast, Avengard's failed application into the Dominion, their escape to Sansia—everything was ruined. The massacre around them, the salting of Avengard that would follow—it was all Threyna's fault.

She was of half a mind to scoop her mother from her feet and carry her back to the oubliette against her will. But first she had to catch her.

"She's not gone. I won't lose her again. Not my baby." Her mother continued running towards the darkling-possessed Threyna.

She's going to get us all hollowed.

Just as Laela overtook her mother a few paces behind Threyna, the darkling ejected. Theodyn swept by on terrible wings, the wind of which dragged on Laela's soul. He consumed the darkling before circling back to slash his scythe at the gathered legionaries.

Laela squeezed the hilts of her daggers and stepped in front of her mother.

"Threyna?" her mother asked, her voice barely a whisper.

"Threy!" Aylenia cried, taking Threyna by the wrist. "Is that you in there?"

"Yeah, I'm fine," Threyna said, still holding a sword. "We gotta—"

Laela pressed the edge of *True* to her half-sister's back. "Don't you ghosting move. Drop it, or I swear to Neutreen I'll cut you down and burn your corpse."

Threyna raised her hands, but she didn't release her short sword.

Her mother stepped forward, but Laela held out a shielding arm.

"Threyna, you came…"

Laela hissed in her mother's direction, unable and unwilling to take her eyes off her half-sister. *She ruined everything. Again.* Staring at Threyna's back, it took all of her restraint not to hollow her, here and now. They needed to leave, but she knew that her mother wouldn't leave without Threyna, and Laela wouldn't leave without her mother.

"You're coming with us," Laela said. "One way or another. Don't make me say it again."

Her mother tugged on her arm, but something struck Laela in the back. Something cold. Cruel. The walls of Valefort fell away. The Order's battle against the blight of what Theodyn had become disappeared. All sight, sound, and sense faded in the presence of the darkling that dove into her and thrust her from the world and into the bowels of Octarius.

Fires burned all around her. Their ships, their means of escape, scorched black, filling the tunnels with acrid smoke. The screams of her father, burning and hollowed, wailed in the distance, but before her, the darkling stood.

Angry. Jealous. Hateful.

Gatius.

He charged.

Though Laela was armed in the physical world, she wasn't within this inner hellscape. The spectral wisp of Gatius throttled into her. He thrust his forearm into her throat and drove her backwards, slamming her into the burning hull of a ship.

"We could have killed him!" Gatius shouted. *"You saved him. You ruined it."*

Flames licked at the top of Laela's head, but Gatius's forearm crushing her windpipe presented a more immediate threat.

Laela couldn't find her Center of Silence in this place. Her father's ever-demanding and never-appreciating voice wormed its way into her mind. Focus overcoming panic, she shoved Gatius's elbow up with one hand, then wrenched his wrist down with her other. She twisted his arm, yanking it behind his back. Pivoting, she slammed Gatius, face first, into the ship's hull.

"Why!" Laela asked. *"We could have talked him down. We could have proved the Underground was behind this."*

Gatius's thoughts and emotions bled into hers until it was difficult to discern which were his versus hers.

Hopeless idiot, she still believes Neutreen is waiting for her, Gatius thought. *She probably still believes in Aeritans too.*

Laela didn't understand. He'd burned prayers before Neutreen's altar as much as anyone. Before Laela could question Gatius's thoughts, he kicked at her instep and spun into her. His elbow connected with her temple and sent her sprawling.

Her vision should have swam; her ears should have rung. But this wasn't the physical plane. Replacing pain, Gatius's thoughts—his desperate need for a host body—invaded her soul.

"Weakling." Gatius spat on the ground. *"Coward."*

She could feel him ripping control of her body away from her. Weaving through her thoughts and memories, he brought her most painful memories to the surface. They crashed over her, threatening to drown her.

Her father shoved her down again. *This is why we must run.* He stalked around her, circling her, his short sword jabbing at her to drive each barbed word home. *What hope do we have of defeating the Skeleton King if you can't even defend yourself from me?* His disappointment was as real and raw in memory as it was in life.

"Aarkos," her mother said, *"please. Leave her alone."*

He wheeled on her mother. *"I'm training her!"*

"You're hurting her!"

Her father snorted. *"You'd have our daughter as helpless as you."*

Laela closed her eyes, attempting to block out the memory Gatius threw at her, but as soon as she fended off the first, another, just as painful, raced through her mind as vicious as her father's steel carving the scar across her chest.

Laela felt weak, small, helpless. *Be strong. Be courageous.* But Gatius had already taken control. Through her eyes, Gatius glared at Threyna. Laela's disdain for her sister melted into Gatius's.

"She always favored you," Gatius thought. *"You got to be by her side while she sent me to live with the ghost damned Wraith. Not anymore. Not after this."*

Gatius strangled the hilt of Laela's dagger.

No… Laela didn't understand what Gatius was thinking, but she felt his wrath, his violence. She attempted to wrest back control, but Gatius had ascended the tunnel of her Inner Octarius, leaving her with the burning ships. Somewhere, far away from the smoke and ash within her mind, her mother screamed.

Laela could only watch as Gatius thrust Laela's dagger at Threyna's gut.

CHAPTER 16

BLOODY GRUDGES

Threyna VII

"Laela? Laela!"

The franticness of her mother's voice sent Threyna reeling. She spun and crouched, poised to strike. Laela's stern expression contorted. Her eyes darkened as her full cheeks practically chewed on all the hateful words she had yet to say even as blood dripped down from an open gash.

Aylenia grabbed her by the shoulder, yanking her backwards. "Darkling."

"Laela, fight it!" her mother pleaded.

"Threy, we need to go," Aylenia said.

Threyna's father flew overhead on blood-conjured wings, slaying legionaries at will. Nearly half the gathered legionaries were cut to ribbons. Their soulless bodies littered the courtyard while their hollowed brethren tore at the living. *We can win this.*

Threyna shrugged Aylenia off. "Not without my father."

Without warning, Laela struck, stabbing at Threyna.

Threyna's eyes widened, and her mother screamed. After freeing herself from Aylenia, Threyna wasn't positioned to defend herself. She flailed, but Laela's blade clipped her rib. Pain lanced through her side and radiated towards both her sternum and her spine. She recoiled, but before she could counter, Laela struck again, this time attempting to cut out Threyna's throat.

Aylenia caught Laela's dagger on her short sword.

Laela shrugged off their mother, spilling her to the ground. Without needing to reposition herself, she kicked Threyna in the chest and hacked at Aylenia with quick slices and stabs.

The kick stole the air from Threyna's lungs. She caved, stumbling backwards and cradling her ribs with her sword arm.

"Stop!" her mother screamed.

Laela, or the darkling controlling her, didn't. She slashed across Aylenia's borrowed armor, and though the blade didn't bite, the heavy strikes caused Aylenia's shoulder to slump. With Aylenia's guard broken and unable to defend herself, Threyna charged at her sister.

She had the advantage of reach—her short sword against Laela's dual daggers—yet whatever benefit it provided was soon nullified.

Laela dodged a thrust and a slash before lurching into range. Threyna narrowly avoided a pair of slashes that would have spilt her guts on the ground. Aylenia filled the space, stabbing at Laela's torso, more to keep her at bay than to strike.

Like a storm, Laela turned Aylenia's blade aside, shoved her away, and attacked Threyna. Her mother screamed for Laela to stop, but neither Laela nor the darkling inside her listened. Threyna dodged a stab, deflected a slash with both daggers, and ducked under a horizontal blow that sought to slit her throat.

Threyna was skilled with a blade, but she felt like a child against Laela. She was a nightmare of sharp edges, brutal strength, and bloody grudges. With nowhere to run and no place to hide in a battlefield she couldn't leave without abandoning her father, Threyna jabbed at Laela's midsection. At the same time, Aylenia chopped at Laela's backside. Just as Threyna thought they had her, Laela deflected Threyna's thrust, spun under Aylenia's chop, and sliced across Aylenia's thigh.

Aylenia fell back, tripping over Yevon's corpse to fall to the ground with a heavy thud.

Threyna felt her own breath depart. She'd already lost Ebrus and Yevon. She couldn't lose Aylenia too. As Laela launched herself at Aylenia to finish her off, Threyna jumped in front of her, sword leveled at Laela's nose.

The two glared at each other.

"You don't deserve her," Laela said. "She's mine now."

Threyna didn't understand, but she didn't want Laela to step any further forward.

"Laela, please," her mother shouted. "She's your sister!"

Hatred flooded Laela's eyes and flushed her cheeks. It was worse than the night of the Battle of the Cut after Threyna ran from Laela to return to Octarius. Threyna thought she was the only one harboring bitterness, but from Laela's contemptuous stare, the resentment was more than mutual. Worse, the darkling wasn't in control; Laela, her anger, her hatred, was.

Laela shoved Threyna's blade away, casting her aside to turn on Aylenia as she attempted to regain her feet. With Threyna's own frustration and disdain mounting, she lowered her shoulder and charged into Laela's side. Laela shrugged her off, barely moved by Threyna's attack. With a pivot, she used Threyna's momentum against her, and tossed her to the ground on the opposite side of Aylenia.

Laela shoved their pleading mother away, and advanced on Threyna and Aylenia.

CHAPTER 17

A DARKLING'S HATRED

Laela VII

Gatius's reasons for hating Threyna were petty—selfishness, jealousy. She could feel his emotions swirling with her own as Gatius leveled Laela's blade at Threyna's face.

He was an Undergrounder. Undercover. Assigned to assassinate Belrich if he got the chance during the distraction or the ensuing extraction of the prisoner. All Arilette's schemes.

The Underground never cared how many suffered in the collateral damages of their plots. It was one thing to extract one of their own; it was another thing entirely to attempt to assassinate the Prince of Rheynia. Had it just been an extraction, maybe—just maybe—they could have convinced Belrich that this was all a misunderstanding, an Underground ploy to divide the growing Dominion. But an assassination attempt... by one of Rance's own supposed men... there was no explaining that. All of Avengard, the entirety of the Sisters' Valley, would have suffered. But that didn't matter to the Underground. It never did.

Laela hadn't given up on regaining control over her body, but there was a part of her that accepted the relinquishing of power. A part of her that wanted Gatius to slay Threyna.

Mother would blame me, but it wasn't me. It was Gatius. The darkling did it.

Her guilt mixed with Gatius's darkling-magnified anger.

"Laela," Mother cried. "Fight it. Please."

Laela was glad she only had to endure Gatius's pain, and not her mother's. *Eventually, she'll see this is the best thing for her.* Threyna wouldn't come with them. She wouldn't become the daughter her mother wished her to be. She'd always be the same willful darkling that thought she knew best.

Gatius strode closer in Laela's body, blade leading the way toward Threyna's black heart. As they stepped in range for the kill, more of his mind opened itself to her. Every mission of the Underground, every dream of defeating the Order, every shared smile—everything was tinged with the same dark signature. Laela searched through the memories, seeing the glimpses of Gatius's past and the emotions that accompanied them.

Gatius was in the Order before the Underground. He, like Dracus before him, deserted after something happened. The frightful memory hid in a dark corner of Gatius's mind, but it was there—alive, hungry, and contaminating everything it touched. All the joy that might have ever been inside of him was stained rotten by this single memory.

Laela sank deeper into Gatius's mind, wading through the fear that encapsulated this memory.

A monster's heavy breathing. The coppery scent of blood mixed with the foul fragrance of death. Corpses, piled on the floor. There was barely anything left of them, as if they'd been drained of blood, leaving only a husk of skin and dried bones.

The walls of fire within Laela's Inner Octarius turned to blood, but the screams of her father only grew louder.

Fear gripped Laela, as if it were dragging her deeper into the harrowing hall of Gatius's worst memory. She drew nearer to the monster breathing heavily beside the pile of desiccated corpses. Through the shadows, the bent shape of slouched shoulders and a hung head loomed over her.

As Gatius drew nearer to Threyna, Laela crept closer to the slumbering monster. A cold swept across her like the howling winds along the Spine. Shivers raced through her essence until cold, dead eyes opened from the shadow before her.

In a deep whisper, the voice said, *"Bring me the next."*

Gatius forced a boy with more fingers to his hand than years to his life forward. The boy trembled, and Gatius flinched, but Laela crumbled.

Gatius extended *True* to Threyna's throat in the physical plane, just as a bloody nail extended from a long, slender, black-veined finger in Gatius's memory. The fingernail lanced forward, piercing the boy's throat.

Laela, unable to take it anymore, ejected Gatius from the depths of her soul. Not even her father objected to Gatius's removal. The chaos of the courtyard replaced the agony of her Inner Octarius, and instead of standing before the Skeleton King, Laela was looming over her sister.

Laela recoiled backwards, pulling her blade away from Threyna's throat with a gasp. Gatius's darkling swirled overhead, but Aylenia leveled her irradiator and pulled the trigger. With a shriek and a flash of white light, the darkling disintegrated into nothingness.

"Neutreen, Bheric, and Cybel be praised," her mother said, helping Threyna to her feet.

Aylenia holstered her irradiator and staggered on her injured thigh. She came to Threyna's side and whispered something, pinching a black earring on her lobe.

Threyna didn't break her stare from Laela. "I'm not leaving. Not without my father."

A scream tore through the air as Theodyn flew overhead on bloodborne wings rapidly deteriorating to ash. He bled from a dozen different wounds, black veins stretched along his torso and down his arms. The thick tendrils climbed his neck and framed his tortured face.

Despite all the carnage he had levied, there were still too many legionaries. The Order reformed its ranks. More reinforcements were pouring through the front gates of the courtyard.

We have to leave now.

Nerus jumped down the oubliette, after Dracus and Rance.

Another irradiator burned through the air. This time, Theodyn couldn't conjure a shield to absorb it. The blast hit him right in the chest. Seizing, his wings dissipated, raining ashes from the sky. He crashed to the ground in a dust storm of black-veined limbs.

"No!" Threyna cried.

Aylenia wrapped her arm around Threyna's shoulders. "We need to leave. We have orders."

As much as it pained Laela, she needed Threyna to come with her if she wanted her mother to come willingly. "Follow your people—" She nodded towards the opening in the west wall. "—and you'll run straight into more legionaries. If you want to get out, come with us."

"Go then," Threyna said to Aylenia, ignoring Laela. "I'm not leaving."

Aylenia glanced at Laela.

Laela sheathed a dagger in her vambrace and extended her free hand to Threyna. "Stay, and you'll lose two parents today. Leave, and you'll spare one. Come with us. Last time I'm asking."

Threyna wasn't even looking at her. Behind Laela, the legionaries surrounded Theodyn. With their blades drawn, arcanatek whirring, there was no hope of victory. There never was. But Laela wouldn't let Theodyn's defeat or Threyna's stubbornness mean her demise.

Having had no time to search for Erynia, she scoured the courtyard for Rance's daughter, hoping against hope that she wasn't already hollowed.

She spotted the young woman. Absent her guards, Erynia cowered in the corner by the steps to the main entry of Valefort. With her hands over her head and her focus drawn to the Order as they surrounded Theodyn, there was no way Laela could signal to her or manage to extract her. Not without announcing their position and condemning them all.

Failure gripped the back of her neck like her father's firm hand.

They'll question her. She'll crack. Then the Order will know all about the escape. All about Aranoc.

Cursing to herself, Laela seized Threyna by the collar. Either too transfixed to fight, or finally realizing the truth, Threyna didn't protest as Laela dragged her with their mother and Aylenia in tow towards the side door of the chapel.

Her mother opened the old, rickety wooden door, and she and Aylenia slipped inside.

"Where?" Belrich shouted over the wails of hollowed. A new scream filled the air. "Where is it? Tell me. Tell me!"

The lone scream grew louder.

Threyna didn't enter the chapel. She stared past Laela, past the corner of Neutreen's temple, past the ravaged courtyard to the men in black standing over the fallen form of her father. Laela kept a hold of Threyna's stolen Avengardian uniform, but she didn't wrench her away from what she knew was coming. She knew how it felt to watch a father die.

Tears had stung her eyes the same way they now did Threyna's. The heat of fire and smell of smoke overwhelmed her senses the same way the hollowed's groans and her father's screams did now.

"Will you weep for him too?" her father teased. *"Will he join me in here, laughing every time you—"*

Laela closed her heart to him. Though Theodyn wasn't her father, he'd been a better parent to her than Aarkos Velar ever was. *True,* the dagger he'd gifted her, remained clutched in the hand that wasn't restraining Threyna. His suffering would grieve her, as it would her mother, but there was nothing more they could do.

"You have failed us for the last time," Belrich said. "Goodbye, brother." Belrich stabbed his sword through Theodyn's hands and feet. His elbows and knees. Shoulders and hips. Each time, Threyna sobbed through clenched teeth, struggling against Laela's grip. Each time, Theodyn's shrill cries echoed weaker, losing his resolve to exist.

Laela prayed that this would be the moment Threyna realized the error of her ways, rejected the side she fought for and the fruitless war they waged. She wished this would be the beginning of something new. That perhaps, maybe this could be the catalyst she needed to come with her and her mother to escape this awful place.

But even as Belrich drove his sword through Theodyn's gut... his chest... his throat... Laela knew this wouldn't be the end of Threyna's delusions. In fact, it would only motivate her to fight harder. She could feel it through Threyna's stifled sobs, the tension held in her jaw—this was not the end of her fight, but the beginning of something worse; now it was personal. She'd seen it with her own eyes. And she would not leave this island while the Order still ruled and Belrich drew breath.

"We need to leave," Mother said.

Laela pursed her lips. Her mother was right. But she had failed Rance and left his daughter in the Order's hands. And to make matters worse, now that they had reunited with Threyna, her mother would never leave her again. Even if Threyna and the Underground allowed them to escape Rheynia, her mother wouldn't leave.

It had all gone so wrong.

"Meet us at Aranoc," Rance had said, even as blood dribbled down his graying beard.

Hopefully you have a plan, Rance. A frown tugged on the corners of her lips. *Hopefully you're still alive… and you can forgive me.*

"C'mon," Laela said, dragging Threyna away from the carnage of what was once her father. Like a shade of her former self, Threyna no longer resisted Laela's insistence as she led her into the chapel.

PART II

CHAPTER 18

A HOLLOW EMBRACE

Threyna VIII

One foot in front of the other. One shallow breath after another. Numb. Had she not seen the life in the eyes of Ebrus's shade, she might have said she felt like a shade, but he had more life in him than she did in her now. As they walked the Wraith's tunnels beneath Valefort and beyond Avengard's walls, she didn't have the ear for Aylenia's whispers of missions. She didn't have the care for her mother's fawning, nor the patience to oppose Laela's demands of silence as they traveled. All she felt was the overwhelming weight of loss and the incomprehensible emptiness that followed the question: *what now?*

There were too many questions stabbing at her mind to allow herself to feel anything. *How did Father learn blood magic? What happened to him over the last decade?*

She replayed the moments in the dungeons before Dracus released the darklings of his soul jar into her father. *"Skeleton King hasn't been seen since,"* Dracus had said in reference to the Battle of the Cut. *"You stopped your father. Now stop your brother."*

Threyna didn't understand. *Belrich called him Bherus, brother? Is it true? If it is, that makes Belrich my uncle, and the Skeleton King my...*

It was impossible. She rejected the idea, refusing to grant such vile thoughts access to her mind. But as Threyna's feet squished through the soft earth of the tilled tunnels beneath Avengard, the fatekeeper around her neck hung heavily. The contents inside likely held the truth, and it threatened to drag her into the ground.

Father's name is Theodyn. He named me after him. Yet Dracus's and Belrich's words mixed, combining into a poison that seeped into her bones. She gripped the fatekeeper Dracus had given her, the one her father wanted her to have in the event of his death. She recalled how her father's eye fell upon it, the wrath in his tortured face.

Why?

Just as the air was feeling too thin to breathe, either due to the Wraith's shoddy ventilation or the tension in Threyna's chest, Laela led them out of the tunnels into a murky forest. Climbing out from between the rotted roots of a thick tree stump, Threyna took in her surroundings. The Cylian River babbled past, running east.

"We continue through Caius's Bog," Laela said. "Legionaries will be inspecting every one of our tunnels. We can't risk it. Going will be slow, but we can follow the river through Caius's to Aranoc."

Threyna wanted to disagree, to tell Laela she was being stupid, wasting time. But it was a sound plan. If she *wanted* to go to Aranoc.

"Good luck," Threyna said.

Her mother blinked at her, the crow's feet over her gaunt cheeks creasing deeper. She reached her hands for Threyna's. "You're coming with us, aren't you."

Aylenia cleared her throat, placing her hand on Threyna's shoulder. "A word?"

Threyna shrugged Aylenia's hand away. "Escaping?" She scoffed. "No. We're not coming with you."

Laela's grim expression hardened, but her mother's blanched, taken aback.

"But, Threyna, you came—"

"I came to free my father," Threyna said through her teeth. "I failed. But I suppose you Wraith know a thing or two about failure."

"What's that supposed to mean?" Laela hissed.

Aylenia again reached for Threyna's arm. "Threyna, please…"

Threyna ignored her. "What were you going to do?" Threyna asked her mother. "Did you know it was him?"

"No," her mother said, placing her hand to her chest. "Of course not."

"Would you have gone through with it?" Threyna asked. "Would you have hollowed my father to treat with the Order?"

"That's enough," Laela said, coming to their mother's side. "This isn't on us. This is on you." She jabbed her index finger at Threyna, stabbing it as if it were a sword to cut her with. "Every life cut short, every tortured soul—your recklessness caused that."

Threyna shook her head. "Of course you would have done it." She smiled in disbelief, ashamed to have hoped for any other answer. "You left him once before. What's a second time? All for your—"

"Threyna!" Aylenia barked, louder than she should have. Once all eyes were on her, she took a steadying breath. "A word. Please."

Wanting to argue, but knowing better than to press Aylenia, she allowed herself to be dragged away despite the throbbing in her ribs from Laela's glancing blow. Once they were a handful of paces away with enough distance for whispered words to dissipate on the wind, Aylenia released her grasp to fix Threyna with a serious stare.

"New orders from the Legatus. We have to go with them." She glanced over Threyna's shoulder to where Laela and their mother were locked in a hushed argument of hand gestures and disagreeable postures.

Threyna didn't want a new mission. She wanted to be in her bunk. To sit in the dim illuminator's gloom and read whatever secrets were held in the ever-strangling fatekeeper around her neck. She'd failed enough for one day, lost enough for a lifetime.

Aylenia leaned closer. "The saboteurs within the Wraith successfully crippled the escape attempt. Now it's up to us to deliver the Wraith to Octarius. Not just them—" She nodded in Laela and her mother's direction. "—all of the Wraith."

Threyna lacked the heart to scoff. Blinking, she attempted to imagine a situation in which Laela listened to anything she said, let alone agreed to escort the Wraith back to Octaven. *Better luck putting the darklings back in the soul jar.* She turned her palms to the cloudy night sky. "They'll never follow us."

Aylenia pointed to her interlayer. "Arilette says they may just be desperate enough. Besides, orders are orders. Always another fight, right?"

Always another victory. Threyna couldn't bring herself to say the words. How could she? Every fight ended in failure. Loss. Daeton screamed. Ebrus became a shade. Yevon hollowed. Now her father was gone. Again, she considered all the maybes and perhaps a Premius shouldn't concern themselves with. Each hurt worse than the other. Each weighed her down to the depths of the Grotto.

She swallowed the knot in her throat, blinked away the tears stinging her eyes, and attempted to block out her failures. *Divided, ruin will reign.* She couldn't let her troubled thoughts rule her. She needed to focus, or she'd lose Aylenia too.

She wouldn't let that happen. Pursing her lips, she nodded. "Orders are orders."

Aylenia patted Threyna's shoulder, waiting for her to say her part of the mantra. When Threyna didn't, Aylenia forced a smile. "Smooth things over and let's go. We need to outpace the Order, and they will be following."

Returning to Laela and her mother, Threyna did her best to issue as close to an authentic apology as she could manage. "Apologies." She gripped the fatekeeper hanging from her neck. "I didn't come to Avengard to flee. I didn't come to fight either. I just wanted to…" Her voice choked off.

He's really gone this time.

She couldn't dismiss it as she had the night of the Battle of the Cut. Then, there was reasonable doubt; no one saw him hollow. No one witnessed a shade or darkling tear free from his flesh. There was a chance he could still be alive, and he was. But now…

Threyna took a deep breath. "I failed. Father's gone, and I can't bring him back, but you're right, Laela." She nodded at her sister, even though the tension in her neck barely allowed her to complete the action. "I won't lose my mother today too. And if that means coming with you…" She shrugged looking at Aylenia. "Would the Underground even take us back?"

Aylenia contorted her lip. "Not in any way we'd want to be welcomed."

Feigning to resign herself, Threyna hung her head. "Point is, regardless of what I want, I don't have anywhere else to go."

Threyna's mother reached for her; the wrinkles framing her smile crossed the frown lines that had taken residence there. "You always have a place with us." She embraced Threyna, squeezing her as tightly as her frailty allowed.

Threyna hugged her mother back despite the hollowness of the gesture.

She would have let them kill him. Then she would have left Rheynia on her boats without even a goodbye.

Suffering the indignity of the empty embrace, Threyna couldn't help but notice the bones of her mother's ribs jutting through her dress, the ridges as deep as the ravaged limestone of the Gullies after the Disasters.

Threyna retreated from her mother's arms. "We should get going." Behind her mother, Laela fixed Threyna with a discerning glare.

She didn't care if Laela believed her lie or not. She had orders, and no matter what, the Wraith wouldn't be leaving Rheynia this night or any night thereafter.

"Right," Laela said. "Let's go. Caius's Bog is up ahead."

CHAPTER 19

Two Kinds of Liars

Dracus V

"To dream is to die. To hope is to lie. To live is to…"
Dammit. Dracus couldn't remember, but with Rance leaving a trail of blood with every hobbled step and legionaries giving chase, even if he remembered, it might be his last thought.

Already, the injured tissues from his scrape with Threyna were adding their complaints to the choir. His forearm ached from where he blocked her elbow, and the blade of his hand prickled where he struck her between her neck and shoulder. They would be the least of his concerns if Decimus or Nerus got a hold of him. If looks could kill, Decimus's would have speared him through the chest. But if they were going to be caught, Dracus preferred to be caught by Decimus as opposed to Nerus.

Bastard would love to add my soul to his collection. But it wasn't his soul he was concerned for. Canton and Fawkes led the way through the tunnels, but they'd never reach Aranoc at this pace.

Grunting, with one arm under Rance's shoulder, he hurried to keep pace. "Gimme a hand, would ya?"

Fawkes took Rance under his other arm, drawing a hissing wince from their injured leader. Glancing at the wound before retuning his gaze to Dracus, Fawkes's cheeks paled beneath his beard.

He saw what Dracus knew, but couldn't allow himself to admit. *He ain't gonna make it.*

Voices echoed in the maze of tunnels behind them. The Order was coming, and though some paths were longer than others, all roads led to Aranoc. It was only a matter of time, and at Rance's current pace, it wouldn't be long.

"We can head for the north shore," Canton said. "If we can slip past them, we—"

"We won't," Rance croaked. "Aranoc. Must get to Aranoc."

He was so pale, his cheeks the color of the white hairs of his light gray goatee. Dracus didn't want to think what would be left for them at Aranoc. Aid? Protection? Sanctuary? If Verinius had done as he was supposed to, there wouldn't be much left. Sure, perhaps once the others arrived in Sansia and realized Rance wasn't with them, maybe they'd send an escort. Even if they did, that would take a night and a day. By then, if Rance even made it that long, all of Aranoc would be swarming with legionaries, Justicus, and Doves.

The Order's pursuit grew louder.

"*You* have to make it to Aranoc," Rance said.

Canton turned. "You're coming with us. We'll get you out of here."

Noble, honorable corpse. No chance. The wound was worse than Dracus had originally thought. Otherwise, he would have left him in the courtyard.

"No." Rance lifted his arm from Dracus's shoulder, but couldn't free himself from Fawkes's. "You go. I'll hold them off as long as I can." He held out a hand, asking for a sword.

Dracus hesitated. He respected the man sacrificing himself for the lives of others. But with or without a sword, Rance wasn't going to slow down Decimus or Nerus, even if he hadn't already been stabbed.

"Here." Fawkes let Rance's arm down and handed him his sword.

Canton shook his head. "We can't just—"

"We can," Dracus said. "And we gotta."

"He's right," Rance said, leaning on Dracus to support himself. "I've gotten us this far. Wish I could have made it beyond the curse. But you still can. Get to Aranoc. Escape with Verinius. Go to Sansia." He pointed at Canton. "Turn it into a place of hope. You're the future."

The Order's pursuit grew louder. Footsteps accompanied the shouts.

No time for sentiment, Dracus took Canton by the arm and beckoned Fawkes to follow. "You heard 'em."

They hurried down the tunnel, leaving Rance in their wake. If Dracus was a good man, maybe he would have looked back. Maybe he would have felt something, anything. But all he felt was relief. Relief that Rance didn't make Dracus have to be the one to decide to leave him behind, relief that he didn't ask Dracus to expend his limited charges to vortex and irradiate him. But like anything good in Rheynia, that relief was fleeting. It lay down and hollowed as sure as Rance would in the coming moments. In place of relief, dread spread through his still heart.

"To dream is to die. To hope is to lie. To live is to..."

Even as he repeated the lyrics in his head as they charged through the tunnels toward Aranoc, the lyrics for his aunt's song didn't come to him. Nor did they bring him comfort. Because just like the song reminded him, hope didn't wait for them at Aranoc. If Verinius was still there, something went wrong. And if something went wrong, there was no way they were figuring it out.

Not without Rance.

Canton continued to ask questions as they ran. About the blood magic, about Bherus, the Skeleton King, and a hundred other things that didn't matter. "That must be what Belrich is searching for—the Blessing. That's where the blood magic comes from, isn't it? *'Where is it?'* That's what he asked Bherus in the courtyard. So it must still be out there somewhere."

Dracus bristled, chewing on his mustache as he struggled to keep up with Canton and Fawkes. "Yeah. Somewhere."

Hanging from Threyna's neck was the most powerful weapon in the world. A cursed weapon, but a weapon that turned a man into an army, a war into a graveyard, and a kingdom into ashes. Dracus didn't know what fate was worse: if the Order defeated Bherus, and Threyna—unbeknownst to her—opened the fatekeeper Dracus had passed off to her, or if Threyna didn't make it out, and Belrich took it from her corpse.

Even if Belrich doesn't suspect the Blessing, if he learns that Threyna is his niece, he'll wanna read whatever Bherus left for her in the fatekeeper.

Either way, Dracus couldn't see a way in which another Skeleton King wasn't created. His feet hurt, his legs ached, and Canton's questioning only brought up old concerns.

"Where do you think it is?" Canton asked.

"Wherever it is," Fawkes said, "it ain't our concern. First Aranoc, then Sansia, eh?"

Canton opened his mouth to speak again, but Dracus cut him off. "Less talkin', more runnin'."

Glancing over his shoulder, he identified the split—a section of the tunnels where three converged to one. He slowed to a stop, putting his hands on his knees. Ahead, Canton and Fawkes stopped to look back at him in the dimly lit glow of waning illuminators.

"What's the matter?" Fawkes asked.

"Cant, if ya got all that wind in your lungs, run ahead and make sure the way is clear. Get as far as the north bend then turn back, ya hear?"

Canton said something under his breath, but did as he was told.

As his footfalls receded ahead, Fawkes leaned in to Dracus. "You alright?"

Dracus hadn't been alright since the Disasters, since his mother birthed him into this dying world. He thought he was doing well with the Order, but everything was based on a lie. "Yeah, Old Boy, I'm alright. Just gotta get him outta here."

Through labored breath, Fawkes said, "Ya think they're still there— Verinius, the others?"

Dracus would have chewed his mustache if he could spare the breath, but his dead lungs somehow required more air. "If they are, somethin' went wrong, and we're walkin' into trouble. If they ain't, we needa find another way off this rock."

Fawkes approached, rubbing the back of his neck. Beside Dracus, he rested his forehead against the crown of Dracus's. "We'll find a way. We'll get outta here."

Dracus grumbled. "All this talk of the Blessing and blood magic, Canton ain't gonna wanna leave. He'll wanna stay and fight."

They were so close. If only the Underground hadn't interfered, they'd be on a boat bound to Sansia by now. Canton and Fawkes would start a new life, and Dracus could die a true death knowing he did at least one thing right. But now, all that felt like an impossibility.

Fawkes rubbed circles between Dracus's shoulder blades as he struggled to breathe deeply. "And if he does?"

Not this again. Dracus pulled away and glared. "Then we talk 'em out of it. End of discussion."

A pregnant pause suspended in the thin air between them.

"How do you think he's gonna feel, Dray? How ya think I'm gonna feel?"

"Ghostin' grateful."

Fawkes's cheeks flushed beneath his beard. His dark eyes drank in the illuminator's light. "If you told him—"

"If I told him, he'd pull what you pull and make the same excuses not to go."

Dracus raised his fist to his mouth. His tone too dark, his words too forceful. "We don't have time to get into this again. We needa get outta these tunnels and make sure no one's followin' us." He nodded at Fawkes's belt. "Ya got any explosives?"

Fawkes inhaled sharply and exhaled slowly, letting go of the oppositional words Dracus knew he wanted to speak. But like any good soldier, Fawkes swallowed it. "Some small ones. Why?"

Jabbing his thumb over his shoulder, pointing to the split, he said, "Think ya got enough to collapse the tunnels?"

"Ya can't be ser—"

"We ain't comin' back, Old Boy," Dracus said. "And the only people following us through these tunnels are legionaries."

Fawkes put his hands on his hips. "Can't promise this won't collapse the whole system. Even if we're a league away, which we won't be, there's no telling we won't get caught in the rubble."

"Even better." He patted Fawkes's shoulder. "We'll head topside, follow the river the rest of the way. Gotta lose 'em one way or another. Otherwise, we end up like Rance."

Fawkes shook his head before letting out a deep sigh. "That why you sent Canton ahead—so I could set the charges, and you wouldn't have to explain to him that us getting out is more important than the others we'd be screwin' over?"

Dracus grabbed Fawkes by the chin and kissed him. "You know me too damn well."

Fawkes grumbled as he worked but rigged a trip wire that connected the three converging tunnels. Once set, he killed the illuminators leading up to the split. One misstep coming from any of the three tunnels and ten years of the Wraith's work would come crashing down. But if for whatever reason Verinius hadn't left yet and the Order showed up in Aranoc, they'd lose a lot more than wasted time.

Once Fawkes had finished, and after Dracus had recovered enough to continue, they resumed their run toward the north bend. Canton was on his way back by the time they met up.

"What took you so long?" Canton asked, only slightly out of breath.

Dracus snorted. "Hit fifty-some odd years, then come talk to me. Callin' me slow." He scoffed. The misdirection came easy.

There are two types of liars. For some, the more one lies, the harder it gets. The lies pile up and become difficult to keep straight. They get twisted and twist the liar's insides. Dracus knew their type; he'd caught hundreds of them in his soul jar.

Lucky I'm the second kinda liar.

Without breaking stride and ignoring Fawkes's side-eyed glance, Dracus continued. "Clear up ahead?"

Canton nodded.

"Alright then, c'mon," Dracus said. "Let's get topside."

CHAPTER 20

FOLLOW THE LEADER

Laela VIII

Laela's boots squished through the muck of Caius's Bog. 300 years of neglect soured the lands of what was once the palace of Caius Draakard. Following Bheric and Cybel's victory for Neutreen over the sea-monster-worshiping emperor, the land was burned, salted, and flooded to serve as a reminder of what became of corrupt rulers.

Irony.

But the bog was no longer some hallowed ground of victory over oppression. Now it was home to the lowest of the oppressed. Hollowed and hellhounds roamed this marsh, and one wrong step could mean joining them in their eternal undeath. With each stride she took, the impressions from Gatius's darkling weighed her down, threatening to sink her into the murky waters.

Gatius—Erynia's guard, a high-ranking member of the Wraith—had been with them since the beginning. He didn't flee the Underground the night of the Battle of the Cut with the rest of them, but he'd arrived shortly thereafter. Assigned by Arilette to infiltrate the Wraith. All these years he'd lain in wait. He'd been assigned to kill Belrich should the opportunity present itself. It had. Laela stopped him.

She hoped she didn't come to one day regret that choice. But long before Gatius was Arilette's hidden knife, he was an Order deserter.

He was only the second such deserter she'd heard of. Dracus had told her that few were willing to risk the Final Demise—the gruesome punishment doled out to anyone who forsook the black: death by a hundred cuts. No vortex. No irradiator. Just torment.

Laela's skin crawled. Less because of the eerie wind through the dead tree branches and more because of Gatius's memory that made him willing to risk such a fate.

The Skeleton King killed that boy. But that was before the Battle of the Cut. The Skeleton King is gone now. And so is Gatius.

It brought her little comfort. Belrich would question Erynia, discover their plans, and come for them. Additionally, for all she knew, there could be more Undergrounders within the Wraith. If that wasn't bad enough, Laela had a worse and more immediate threat to contend with.

Threyna kept to the back of their formation, only making it more difficult for Laela to keep an eye on her. She was lying. Laela knew it. She didn't know what about or what for, but she had no doubt that she had an ulterior motive.

Not knowing what they'd find when they arrived at Aranoc, if Rance was still alive, or if Tarus—the Second Sword of the Wraith—would be all-ghosting-over her if she arrived without him, Laela trudged through the bog. Sticking to the higher slopes and collapsed pillars of the fallen palace, the dark water's depth varied from her ankles to her thighs. Holding a spare sword Aylenia had taken in their flight from Avengard, Laela led their silent procession through the gloom. She ignored the pain from the gash across her cheek and where the hollowed bit her hand, but every huff or grumble from Threyna was enough to drive her mad.

Inevitably, Threyna finally said what was on her mind. "Did you know too, Mother?"

"Know what, my dear?"

"About the blood magic?" Threyna asked, more bite in her tone. "That he was Bherus-ghosting-Fayte? That I am…"

Laela stopped, inspecting her half-sister, then her mother. Aylenia did the same, equally as confused. Mother balked, opening her mouth and shrugging her shoulders, but no words came out.

"I didn't," her mother stuttered. "I didn't know."

Laela grit her teeth. *Too loud.* "Not now, Threyna. Voices down, eyes up—"

Threyna scoffed. "You didn't know? All this time Dracus just kept it to himself?"

"Shut her up," her father said. *"She'll get you all hollowed."*

Laela stepped between Threyna and her mother. Half a hand taller than Threyna, she glared down at her. "Not. Now. Aren't you some soldier? I don't know how that darkling tends to her hearth, but here, you answer to *me*. You follow *me*. And by every feather of Neutreen's wings, you will shut your ghosting mouth, or, so help me, I'll leave you here."

Threyna's sapphire eyes darkened as her brow pinched atop them. Her lips pursed, angular features sharpening to a dagger's point. If she feared Laela, she showed no sign of it, but Laela wasn't afraid of her either.

"Laela, Threyna," her mother said, stepping between them. "Please, sto—"

A gust of wind. A snapping twig.

Her mother cut off, and Laela and Threyna separated, each scanning the bog. Searching for any sign of hollowed or hellhounds, Laela slowed her breathing. She willed her racing heart to obey, but it continued to run wild as the wind rustled the branches and the surface of the water.

Was it just the wind... or something worse?

Gatius's memory wormed its way into her mind. The pile of corpses. The black-veined monster. The blood-red fingernail that pierced the boy's throat.

She shook herself, attempting to eject the memory from her mind. *Be strong. Be courageous.* Regripping her sword, she waved the others forward. "Come on. Just the wind. No more talking. Move."

Just as Laela was about to continue trekking through the bog, Threyna interrupted. "Over there."

Following her index finger, Laela spotted what drew Threyna's attention. A shade floated out of a thicket of brambles and into a clearing to glide over the water on false steps.

"Leave it," Laela said.

Threyna drew an arcanatek from her belt.

"It's just a shade," Laela said. "Leave it. If the Order managed to get ahead of us and you release a charge, it will bring an entire legion down on us."

"Where there are shades, there are hollowed. That one's far enough away not to be a threat, but the next one might not be so kind as to keep its distance. Now, I don't know how you *tend to your hearth*, but where I'm from—" She held up her arcanatek. "—we don't let the grunts do the thinking, so—" Threyna moved to step ahead of Laela, but Laela grabbed her by the collar and wrenched her close until they were nose to nose again.

"Call me a grunt again. See what happens."

But out of the corner of her eye, something glimmered. Turning towards the light, Laela spotted another shade. Then another.

Threyna inhaled sharply and turned to Aylenia. "Just like at the Cut… they're controlling the shades. Leading the hollowed."

"Blood and bone," Aylenia said.

CHAPTER 21

DARK DAWN

Threyna IX

"What are you talking about?" Laela asked, tone serious. "Who?"

"The Order," Threyna said, warmth draining from her face. "It's a trap."

Shades never traveled together. Threyna knew something was off about the shades at the Cut, but this couldn't be a coincidence; they had to be under control. That meant they had precious little time to get out of here, or they'd fall with the Draakard Empire.

"Orders?" Aylenia asked.

Threyna's mind went blank. In her hesitation, she watched Daeton hollow again. *My plan. My failure.* She opened her mouth to speak, but no words came.

"How many Dawnshards?" Aylenia asked Threyna. "I have one left."

Threyna stammered, taking one from her belt, leaving her with two. *Aylenia can take the north. I'll head south. We set off the Dawnshards, and maybe Laela and Mother can slip between. We meet at Aranoc.* It was a sound plan, as sound as any in the ghosting bogs, yet all she heard were Daeton's screams. She'd already lost Daeton, Ebrus, and Yevon. She couldn't send Aylenia to her death too. "I'll make a distraction. Take them to Aranoc. I'll meet you there."

"Are you out of your ripping mind?" Aylenia leaned closer to whisper. "Hollow that, you don't have an interlayer. I'll go. If need be, I'll relay to the Arch Premius for reinforcements."

Aylenia had never questioned an order before, only driving more doubt into her mind. Threyna's palms were sweating. *Ghosts...* "Fine." She shoved a Dawnshard into Aylenia's hands. "You take the north. I'll take the south. Meet at Aranoc."

"Prime." Aylenia splashed away.

Already, hollowed were filtering through the trees and trudging through the water. Voices followed behind. Legionaries' voices.

Hoping this wouldn't be the last time she saw Aylenia, Threyna grabbed her mother and Laela by the arm. "We're going to make a distraction." She pointed into the depths of the bog ahead, where, as of yet, there wasn't a wall of hollowed. "Head east. Fast. We'll meet at Ara—"

Laela wrenched free of Threyna's grip, but before she could object, Threyna stabbed her finger at Laela's chin.

"Do as I say, or you and Mother will never leave this bog alive."

Laela seethed, but held her tongue.

"No," her mother said. "I can't—I *won't* leave you again." She wrapped her arms around Threyna's waist and whispered in her ear. "You're sisters. Divided, ruin will reign, but united..."

Something unhooked from Threyna's belt.

"I love you," her mother whispered. She released Threyna and pulled the last two Dawnshards from her belt. "Be strong. Be courageous!" she cried to Laela as she leapt into the bog, opposite of Aylenia.

"Mother, no!" Laela shouted after her.

Threyna stood, dumbstruck. *Gory ghosts, what is she doing?* Her body disobeyed her as if a darkling had taken control.

"Run!" her mother yelled, charging at the shades and hollowed. Her frail frame struggled through the water.

Helpless, powerless, Threyna stared, unable to move or cry out.

Time stood still, and Threyna was transported back to the night of the Battle of the Cut. Only this time, instead of her running away from her mother and sister to go retrieve her father, her mother was running away from her.

She's going to get herself hollowed. Worse.

Simultaneously, Threyna and Laela charged after their mother into the wash. In their haste, they bumped into one another. Laela slipped, reflexively grabbing for Threyna to steady herself. Under Laela's weight, Threyna's footing slid out from under her.

Murky water invaded her mouth and surged up her nostrils. Her hands found the bottom of the shallows, and she pushed herself above the surface. Gagging out water and shaking the mud and rotten reeds from her hands, she chased after her mother, but Laela pushed her out of the way.

"Mothe—"

Laela's cry cut short as the world flashed a bright white. Blinking away spots, Threyna couldn't find her mother. Laela, ahead of Threyna, screamed, covering her eyes with both hands.

The legionaries, somehow corralling the shades, would have them surrounded in no time. Already, the light of shades and the shadows of hollowed closed in. Their mother was nowhere to be seen.

She shouted into the void, but the bog itself bellowed an answer. The ground shook with the force of the Disasters. Laela, unable to see, succumbed to the quake, falling into the shallows again. Threyna grabbed Laela by the arm, hauling her from the water, but a rift opened in the still marsh, creating a current.

The sudden tide ripped at her ankles, attempting to sweep her into the growing fissure, bisecting the bog. Another Dawnshard exploded behind her to the north, then another to the south.

Threyna shielded her eyes, but more spots blotted out her vision.

"Mother!" Laela shouted, her eyes wild and unseeing.

The ground's rumbling stopped, but the current created in the tremor's wake threatened to drag them under.

Threyna struggled against the growing current, searching through her distorted vision for any sign of her mother. Threyna was supposed to be the distraction. Laela and her mother were supposed to escape. Now the bog had become a cesspit surrounded by hollowed. She grabbed Laela and pulled her against the tide. "We have to get out of here!"

"I'm not leaving without her!"

"Then you'll die here with her." Part of Threyna felt inclined to leave her, to run north and find Aylenia. But her mother's words and Arilette's assignment clashed in her mind. Grunting, Threyna wrenched Laela to the east.

Whether because Laela couldn't see after the Dawnshard erupted or because she knew Threyna was right, Laela allowed Threyna to steer her away.

Trudging against the surf, Threyna headed for a fallen statue half-submerged in the wasteland, but coming from the north, a wall of hollowed chased a shade in their direction. *They're going to cut us off.* If they could climb the statue and run on solid ground to the bog's edge, they could escape. They'd have to fight their way free, but there was a chance.

"Can you see?"

Laela blinked, her hand still half-shielding her eyes. Tears streamed down her cheeks.

"Can you see, dammit?" Threyna snapped as they approached the submerged statue.

"Barely."

Threyna shoved Laela ahead of her, against the knee-high rush of the bog attempting to drag them backwards. "Climb."

Laela clumsily climbed the statue of the Draakard sea-god. Unsteady on her feet, she crested the top.

Threyna vaulted up in front of her. There were more hollowed than she expected. It wasn't just one line she'd have to cut past, but several, all while leading a blinded Laela through. But it was that or wait to be surrounded.

"Grab on." Threyna took Laela's hand and placed it on her belt. "Stay close, and whatever you do, don't let go."

Threyna drew her sword, trotting atop the fallen statue. Another Dawnshard went off in the distance. *Perhaps they can still make it out...*

She couldn't worry about them now, though, or she and Laela wouldn't make it to Aranoc.

As they drew nearer to the hollowed, the horrid creatures lost interest in the shades they chased. The nearest, impossible to tell if it were a man or woman due to its decay, swiped at Threyna's ankle. With a quick flick of her sword, Threyna severed the limb and continued forward. The hollowed wailed, attracting the attention of others nearby.

Another hollowed climbed the statue ahead of her. Larger and not quite as decrepit as the one before, it staggered towards her, arms reaching to tear the flesh from her bones.

"Slow down," Threyna said to Laela.

The hollowed lurched towards her, but Threyna waited. In its lunge, Threyna steered it aside with a back slash that flung it to the swampy tides.

"Come on." Threyna quickened her pace. More hollowed closed in on the embankment they needed to escape. "Can you see yet?"

"Shapes."

She groaned. "Get ready to jump."

Closing in from the south, behind the rows of hollowed, legionaries drove the last row of hollowed, impaled by pikes, forward. *That's how they're doing it. The front follows the shades; the rear is driven from behind. But how are they organizing the shades?*

"Over there!" a legionary shouted. "Don't let them get away!"

"Blood and bone," Threyna said. "Jump in three, two, one—"

Threyna leapt for the embankment. Laela landed hard, shoving Threyna forward into the first row of hollowed. Threyna ducked an openhanded swipe. She cut through an arm, slashed down at a leg, kicked another hollowed in the knee, buckling it backwards. She forged forward. Too fast and she'd risk exposing Laela, too slow and they'd both be caught by the Order.

Pain gripped her sword, loss drove her blade, and fear licked at her heels, but she fought through.

Threyna stabbed a hollowed through the neck and tore its throat in half. Black ichor drained down its gullet. It attempted to scream, but continued to reach for her. She slashed at one arm, then chopped down between its neck and shoulder on the other side, but more were encroaching.

There are too many.

She didn't have any Dawnshards left. A Nightfall would do her no good. And one charge of an irradiator wouldn't create the opening they needed. She needed Laela, even blinded as she was, if they were going to make it out of this before the legionaries caught them.

"Laela, sword!"

"I can barely see!"

"Anything that moves." Threyna lurched forward, sweeping her blade in a wide arc. Her blade tore through the rotten flesh of the undying, spraying black blood and gore across the cursed bog.

Laela's blade rang as she drew steel from scabbard. With a war cry, she cleaved through a shoulder, decapitated another hollowed, and wheeled on a third with a diagonal slice that carved the tortured ghoul into two.

Threyna, now free of Laela slowing her down, dodged a grasp and slipped behind the hollowed. She cut down on the hollowed's ankles, felling it to its knees. Dipping beneath another swipe and evading a third's chomping jaw, Threyna spun between two others. Limbs fell to the ground, but the Order's shouts drew nearer.

A path opened. One hollowed remained between her and the open woods.

She leapt, thrusting her steel at the creature's face. The blade took the hollowed in the eye socket. Brittle bones broke beneath the force. It fell to the ground, writhing—not dead, but so far from living. She ripped her blade free to attack another charging at her back. She hacked into its ribs, kicked it away, then stabbed it through the thigh to stop it from being able to chase her.

Wind rushed by her side and Threyna raised her blade just in time to catch Laela's.

The clang of steel startled Laela's tear-streaked, unseeing eyes.

"It's me," Threyna said, taking her by the hand with her free arm. "We need to run."

They took off running, and hand in hand, Threyna led her sister through the woods of Caius's Bog.

CHAPTER 22

A SOLDIER, A DREAMER

Laela IX

Feet racing, heart hammering, tears streaked down Laela's cheeks. Guided by Threyna's hand, they fled from the Order, their shades, and their horde of hollowed, but Laela left part of herself in the bog.

Mother… why? Of all the times to be brave, why now?

Not once had she truly stood up against her father. Not when he talked down to her. Not when he fought against Laela, trying to turn a child into a soldier. Not when she discovered he was sleeping with Arilette. But now.

She could have let Threyna be the distraction as she intended. She could have followed Rance and Dracus down the oubliette and never stepped foot near the bog.

Laela's hopes soured. Her frustration boiled. And the mere touch of Threyna's hand holding hers made her bloody cheek twitch.

If Threyna had just come with us ten years ago, if she hadn't returned to Octarius to become Arilette's pet, what could she have become? What could we have become?

Maybe childish insecurities and juvenile jealousies would have softened, and the shared suffering of both having lost their fathers would have brought them closer together. Perhaps together, they would have been a fearsome tandem, one which Tarus wouldn't have dared cross. Together they could have guarded Rance. Together they could have left for Sansia. Together they could have had a mother, a future, a hope.

But the future was stabbed in the stomach; she didn't even know if Rance survived. Her hope crumbled with Valefort's western wall, and her mother...

Laela reached for the fatekeeper pendant at her chest, but found Neutreen's feather instead. New tears leaked from her blurry eyes.

Neutreen, can't you feel our yearning? Do you have any idea of our pain without you?

Neutreen didn't answer. Threyna did.

"We're almost there," Threyna said. "The edge of the woods is just ahead."

Laela didn't know what to say or how to feel. *Am I supposed to be grateful that she got me out when I'm in this mess because of her?* Her fingers found the fatekeeper holding the prayers her mother wrote for her at birth. *Maybe she's still alive. Maybe she got out?*

The blurry shapes of trees rushing past opened to an empty gray sky. In the distance through the fog, the torches lining Aranoc's city walls burned, daring to be visible in such a dark world. Her vision improved just enough to make out the spires that rose above the shroud of fog.

"We made it," Threyna said, panting slightly. She released Laela's hand and took her arm instead. "You prime?"

Laela shook Threyna's hand from her arm, stepping forward to hide her face. The emptiness beside her, the void where her mother should have been, burned a hole through her heart, letting her blood drain like the tears down her cheeks. Silent sobs trembled through the tension of attempting to contain her emotions because deep down, she knew; she would never see her mother again.

She clutched the fatekeeper about her neck. On the edge of her Center of Silence, she felt her father's prodding. Despite how poorly he treated her mother, she felt his anger at her loss. He blamed Threyna. And for perhaps the first time in his miserable existence, he wasn't wrong.

"Laela..."

Laela's fist tightened about the octagonal pendant. "She's gone…" She wanted to say it was all Threyna's fault, but she couldn't bring herself to say it. For all her flaws, despite the role she played in causing all of this, Threyna had volunteered herself to be the distraction. Despite her swirling emotions, that wasn't lost on Laela. *She didn't want this any more than I did.*

A tentative hand slid up Laela's back. "I thought my father was gone. Blood and bone, for ten years, that's all anyone ever told me. I never believed them, and I was right. But now…"

Laela swallowed the knot in her throat. Her vision focused on her sister, the angular lines of her face, the sharp blue of her eyes. She too thumbed the fatekeeper about her neck. "She was always telling me, *'Be strong. Be courageous.'* But I never believed she had any in her. She did. She sacrificed herself… for you."

She meant to say, *"for us."* She'd intended the words to be tender, loving, sisterly. But even as they left her lips, the subconscious poison she injected into the sentiment soured, making it come out more as a condemnation.

Threyna's scowl deepened.

"Apologies," Laela said quickly. "That's not how I meant—"

"Open your fatekeeper and let's keep moving," Threyna said, her voice as cold as steel and just as sharp. "Or don't. I don't care. But I'm opening mine." She shoved past Laela, shouldering her as she strode down the hill.

Laela closed her eyes and clenched her teeth. *Ghost dammit.* Her mother's words from earlier that evening came back to her. *"Must you always be so—"* She hadn't let her finish, but Laela knew what she was going to say, or at least something like it. So intense. So stubborn. So unforgiving.

"There is strength in knowing when to drop your guard and courage in actually doing so." Now was the time. She couldn't let it serve as a wedge to deepen the divide between them.

"Threyna," Laela said to Threyna's retreating back. "I didn't mean it like that."

"Save it." She continued marching down the hill toward Aranoc.

"We both lost her," Laela said. Bitterness rotted her from within. Vexed by Threyna but also frustrated with herself, she attempted to narrow the gap. "She wouldn't want us to be like this. We should open them together."

Threyna stopped her descent down the slope and glanced over her shoulder. "This isn't Mother's fatekeeper. This is my father's. I opened hers years ago."

Whatever warmth she had tried to kindle for Threyna for her mother's sake burned to ash. Laela's fists clenched at her side. "You what? How could you open it before she was gone? The bad luck—"

"Don't give me that ghosting superstitious nonsense," Threyna spat. "She was gone. She never came back for me. Never even tried. No attempt, not a single letter or—"

"Not a letter?" Laela snapped. "Not a letter!" She marched down the slope, her finger aimed at Threyna's nose until she was close enough to jab her in the shoulder. "She wrote letters every. Single. Week." Her index finger stabbed into Threyna's shoulder with enough force to shove her backwards. "She lived and died for you. Not for me, the daughter who loved her, who comforted her when you never returned a single one of those letters. For *you*. She became a shade of herself without you. And you…" She shook her head. "Gory ghosts, you didn't deserve a mother like her."

Threyna's lips twitched as if she were about to spit venom. "Letters or not, a mother who forces her daughter to abandon her father is no mother. Now open your mother's fatekeeper, I'll open my father's, and then we continue onto Aranoc before it's too late."

Laela shook her head, unable to cope with Threyna's lies a moment longer. "Enough. Tell me the truth. You don't want to escape, so what do you really want, hmm? What's at Aranoc that you need so badly?"

She extended her arms out to either side, holding the stocks. "You're right. I don't want to escape. And you won't either once we arrive at Aranoc. We have orders to escort you and your people to Octarius."

Laela's mind raced, but she wouldn't give Threyna the satisfaction of seeing her doubt.

"I know what you're thinking," Threyna continued. "But this is the only way. Mother, for all her shortcomings, she's right about this; we are sisters, and if we remain divided, ruin will reign. We'll end up just like our parents."

Laela shook her head. "We took every precaution. We knew you Undergrounders would try something, but whatever it is, I promise you, it didn't work. Arilette didn't burn our ships this time."

Threyna smiled. "I wouldn't be so sure."

"Well, I am sure of what happened to Mother's letters," Laela spat. "When you return to Octarius—without the Wraith—ask Arilette about it?" She brushed past Threyna, continuing down the hill.

Spinning, she aimed her finger at Threyna. "And if you think there is any chance I'm *ever* returning to Octarius, you better hope you have me locked in a soul jar. Because that's the only way you'll put me back in that hole in the ground."

Threyna scoffed, lifting her blaster and leveling it at Laela. "Don't tempt me."

Laela drew her sword and in two steps had it leveled against Threyna's neck. Breath heaved hot and heavy from her nostrils. Her head ached from the combination of crying and scowling, but finally, her vision had returned to normal after the Dawnshard's explosion.

She would have cleaved Threyna's head from her shoulders and let her decapitated, hollowed form attempt to bring her back to Octarius, but as she stared at her sister, all she saw was her mother staring back. Her lips, her cheekbones, the shape of her ears, the unrelenting stubbornness.

"You're too weak," her father said. *"You won't do it."*

Laela wanted to prove him wrong, but she couldn't. She lowered her sword. "You're lucky *our* mother raised one good daughter," she said through bared teeth. She turned her back on Threyna. "Go hollow out."

Storming down the hill, Laela lifted the fatekeeper from her neck. It fit in the palm of her hand, but it threatened to sink her to the depths of the bogs.

Her feet squished within her muck-soaked boots. The pale Avengardian garb was stained with grime and ichor from the hollowed that stood in their way, but her soul felt dirtier yet. Ruined by hate, soured by guilt, sullied by failure.

She held the fatekeeper to her lips, wishing she had a match for the smoke to deliver her prayers to Neutreen. "Neutreen, if you can hear me, please guide me. Have I not lived by your Tenets? Have I not sought forgiveness at your altar? Wherever I fall short—in modesty, moderation, measure, or merit—guide me that I might one day earn my wings."

Only the sound of her own breathing, the wet squish of water through her toes, and the jostle of her mismatched leather armor answered her.

Laela closed her eyes, new tears slipping out from the corners. "Is she gone? Should I open this, or do you still have a purpose for her in this world?"

Squish. Scrape. Sniffle.

She needed something. A word of encouragement, a dream of something more than the horror behind her and the dread lurking in the shadows of her future. Squeezing the release triggers on either side of the octagonal arcanatek, she prayed her mother had more to offer than Neutreen.

The smooth black sides of the arcanatek clicked open, and a tightly rolled scroll emerged from within, larger than the device that housed it. Laela pinched it between her fingers and pulled the scroll free. Unraveling it, she blinked away tears to read the words in the dim light.

My dearest Laela,

You are the daughter of a soldier and a dreamer. You are the strength the world needs, the courage we all depend on, but in a bleak land, you are also the wings on which others will rise. It will not be easy, but Neutreen has given you life against all odds. Neither of us should be here. Neither of us should have survived your birth, but we did. She has chosen you, but don't let the weight of purpose burden you, my love. Never stop searching for wholeness. Never let anyone keep you hurting—not because it is bad to be hurt, but because there is nothing that can't be healed. One day, whether we defeat the One and Neutreen is restored or if we escape beyond the curse of this land, you will live a life of peaceful meaning. You are a soldier, but that is not all you are. Be strong. Be courageous, but fight for more. Dream for more.

I love you with every feather in Neutreen's wings,

Your mother

Laela didn't realize, but she had fallen to her knees. Her tears fell, staining the parchment. She dried her eyes and rerolled the scroll. Hugging herself, she knew her mother was wrong.

Nothing will heal this wound. This loss. This emptiness. Nothing. Ever.

CHAPTER 23

IT WILL ONLY HURT A BIT

Threyna X

She wanted to cry, but she couldn't. Not for her mother, not for her father, not for Ebrus, Yevon, or fear for Aylenia's wellbeing. Stone hardened around her heart. Darkness devoured the light in the world, draining even the brightness stored in the Viridite glowstones of the Gullies. A hollow numbness stomped the feelings from her soul until only logic remained.

As Laela stormed off down the hill ahead of her, Threyna remained fixed. Overwhelmed, confused, hurt, her mind raced to make sense of what had just happened.

Mother sent letters?

"Ask Arilette about it," Laela had said.

After a decade of thinking her mother had given up on her, the thought tore into Threyna's stomach. At first, her mother's sacrifice seemed a foolish gambit to make up for her failures, but now it seemed brave, loving. Maternal. But if that were true, if Laela was right...

Everything else was a lie.

The last hours rattled around in her head like darklings in a soul jar, trying to escape. Her father—not Theodyn, but Bherus. Bherus Fayte. Son of King Bohen, the Skeleton King. Brother to Belrich, the Legatus of the Order.

Dracus knew. How many others did? How many others lied to my face?

Anger replaced sorrow, but loneliness trumped all. Her bog-soaked clothes sent a shiver down her spine as the wind whistled through the trees and careened down the hill into the valley. She stifled a shiver that exacerbated the pain along her ribs.

I just need to get back home. I need to get the Wraith home. Focus on the mission.

Fidgeting with her father's fatekeeper around her neck, she tried reminding herself that nothing had changed. Up until the other day, Threyna's father was gone. Instead of speculating about it, now she knew it. Up until today, Threyna's mother had left her. Now she knew she wouldn't be coming back. She'd get home, and everything would be as it was.

But that wasn't true either.

Rivich had left her strike team. Yevon hollowed and became a darkling. Ebrus became a shade, consumed by her father's blood magic. Now Aylenia was out there, all by herself. Ghosts only knew if she was still alive. And to top it all off, now Threyna didn't even know if she could trust Arilette.

She released the fatekeeper to run her hands over her braid. She wanted to scream, but she wouldn't give Laela the satisfaction.

With her past in question and the future bleak, Threyna sat down on the hill. She stripped off the Avengardian leather armor to her clothes beneath—a sleeveless pale gray tunic and britches tucked into her boots. Soiled with a combination of blood and filth from the bog, Threyna wanted to be free from the garments and the memories they carried.

She pinched the octagonal sides of the fatekeeper, hoping against hope it held some long-lost truth that would pull her through the depths of her despair. She had always thought it strange that her father had left her a second fatekeeper. Back at Octarius, she still had the ones left to her by her parents. Her mother's, scrawled with the feather of Neutreen, rested in the footlocker along with the note she left and her father's unopened fatekeeper. He'd painted a small white dove on one of the eight sides.

She'd always thought he called her Little Dove because of their gentle beauty, but now she realized the truth. *I'm a dove of House Fayte.* Her stomach twisted in knots as she turned the octahedron in her fingers.

What did he feel the need to tell me after he left for the Battle of the Cut? If he thought he wasn't coming back, he could have told her before he left; he could have given her the second fatekeeper then. *So why give it to Dracus to deliver to me?*

There were already enough mysteries in the world. Some would never be answered, but the question of what her father left her was only a button away.

"This was your father's, Little Dove," Dracus had said. *"He said if he didn't make it, if he were gone and the Order still in power, you must open this."*

Knowing this time her father was truly gone, she swallowed. "Apologies, Father. I couldn't save you." Threyna pinched the release triggers, and the fatekeeper opened.

Expecting a tightly rolled scroll to protrude from the arcanatek, Threyna hmphed. She shook it upside down, but no scroll loosed itself from within. Instead, a glowing red liquid emerged from the fatekeeper's opening.

It didn't fall downward, or drip as she expected. Instead, it almost slithered out and up her fingers. Threyna gasped. Extending like a ribbon, it practically floated as it wound its way between her knuckles, around her wrist, and up her arm. Like a living thing, the red liquid inspected her, searching for something. Forked with ever-moving black veins that crackled like a lightning storm, the creature circled her arm, wrapped around her neck, and tickled her ear as it passed to descend her left arm.

Gooseflesh pimpled her flesh in the wake of the mysterious entity. Watching it with fascination, Threyna reached for it with her right hand, but true to its purpose, it wriggled away from her touch. It traced down her arm, wrapping around her wrist and fingers again before pausing, coiling. The red liquid blackened as the dark veins within expanded.

Fascination forgotten, Threyna's breath caught in her throat. Before she could react, the *thing* pounced. Threyna grunted as the liquid ribbon wrapped around her upper arm. She tried to pry it off, but tighter and tighter it wound. No longer a gentle energy of red liquid that wriggled away from her touch, it solidified—hardening, constricting, strangling.

Panicked, Threyna clawed at it, but it didn't relent. She wanted to cry out for help, but who would hear? Who would help? She grit her teeth, fighting the beast that had invaded her father's fatekeeper.

Fangs sank into her arm, tearing a reluctant wince from her lungs. Down the hill, Laela turned towards her, her face drawn, eyes wide.

Horror rippled through Threyna's veins as black vines snaked from the solidifying cursed bangle embedded into her upper arm. Stretching down her arm and into her fingers, up her neck and across her cheek, and down into her torso, corruption burrowed its way into her.

Worse than being invaded by a darkling, worse than suffering a steel stab to the gut—hopelessness wormed around her heart and squeezed.

Threyna's vision faded. She saw—no, she *felt* her father. Not kinship and familiarity, but the weight of purpose, the burden of responsibility, and fear. Terrible, crippling fear.

Loneliness circled her throat like a noose. Memories, flashes, glimpses of an isolated journey across the Scorch Lands flooded her mind. Hollowed were nailed to the mighty Pythwood trees. Their massive trunks smoked and popped as the hollowed screamed before submitting to the Purge. Then, a familiar face. Arenius, Arilette's father, stared back at her, wide-eyed.

A wave of guilt, a wash of denial, a lifetime of bitterness. Then something worse. In the dark recesses of whatever this corrupted artifact constituted for a mind, another memory rose to the surface.

A gaunt man sat alone at the end of a long, dark, cavernous room. Rain pattered down on the roof. The stench of death clung to the air, thick like the humidity after the daily rains. Her footsteps passed over the cracked stone floors and around the rubble of collapsed pillars. Another walked beside her, a boy, smaller than her, barely old enough to walk. With silver-blond hair and high cheekbones, he turned to her, a deep dimple in his chin despite his youth.

Belrich.

Belrich smiled. *"I'll go first this time. First is always the worst."*

Tears stung her cheeks—her father's cheeks.

At the end of the long throne room, heavy labored breaths awaited them from the shadows of the throne. Threyna's heart rattled against her ribs; her breath trembled through every fiber of her being, growing more erratic the nearer she drew to the throne.

A gaunt man inclined his head. Black veins drained down from the obsidian crown atop his silver-blond hair. *"I need you again, my sons."*

As her gaze fell upon the black crown atop his head and the dark pain in his sunken eyes, a new wave of emotions overwhelmed her. *His* spirit connected to hers through the artifact, the *Blessing*. A harrowing resentment, a wounded pride, an indignant wrath, all coming from her grandfather, Bohen Fayte—the Skeleton King.

The fangs of the red-and-black creature that spawned from her father's fatekeeper sank deeper into her arm, but deeper than the Blessing's prongs, something within her grew. She recognized it wasn't hers, and it wasn't her father's, but her grandfather's—an undeniable, unbridled, deep-seated fear of the One True God.

It wasn't an old emotion. It wasn't a distant memory.

This is here—now. The Skeleton King is still alive!

"It will only hurt a bit," the Skeleton King said to the two boys before him. He drew in breath and siphoned vitality from Bherus and Belrich to sustain himself.

The patter of rain and the walls of the throne room fell away, replaced by the sound of her own screaming.

CHAPTER 24

THE INNER THRONE

Threyna XI

"Threyna! Threyna!" Laela stood over her, shaking her by the shoulders.

Gasping, Threyna pulled free of Laela's grip. Rolling onto her belly, she crawled away from her sister, breaths coming in short, ragged spurts. The black-and-red bangle clung to her upper arm. Constructed of sharp angular lines, the bangle appeared like jewelry. But it was alive.

A stampede of hoofbeats like racing horses echoed in her head, but it was only her and Laela in the empty valley. *The Order is coming to finish us off.*

She hoped it was a dream. All of it. That she would wake in her bunk within Octarius. Aylenia would explain some new discovery in artifacy. Ebrus would poke his head into their room with some obscure comment comparing their discourse to the wind. Yevon would tease Ebrus with a grin on his face. And Rivich would roll his eyes, but steal himself a quiet smile after he passed.

Oh how she wished that was the world she'd woken to—one in which they never left for Avengard or learned of the Wraith's plans for her father's execution. A world in which her friends were still alive, still together, and she could live in the blissful ignorance that somewhere, somehow, her father was still alive.

Face-down in the soggy field of dead grass with Laela kneeling over her, a cursed bangle gouging into her arm, and a group of screaming Order horses charging through the murky woods to find and finish them, Threyna had woken to an entirely different reality.

"What happened?" Laela asked.

Threyna didn't know how to answer. She didn't know if she could. The pounding hoofbeats seemed to surround her. She wanted to retreat, to go to her Inner Underground as she had when Yevon's darkling invaded her, but when she did, she was back in the Skeleton King's throne room.

Yet, upon reentry, it wasn't as it was even moments before. The shattered windows were replaced with stained glass. The crumpled pillars were re-erected and the stone floor replaced. The throne called to her.

Within her Inner Throne, she strode forward and climbed the dais to sit in the high-backed chair overlooking the long hall. Princess of New Rheynia, Heiress of Saltspire.

Father wanted this.

Dracus's words returned to her. *"...if he's gone and the Order is still in power, you must open this."*

A sense of poise overtook her, settling her panic. The stampede of hooves were not hooves at all. They weren't even horses, but the beating of frightened heartbeats.

Not the Order then...

She could hear, even feel Laela's beating heart just outside the walls of her Inner Throne. Fear coupled with loss. Genuine care—for Threyna's or her own wellbeing, she didn't know, but the physical response was real.

A well of power called to her from just beyond her fingertips, but when she reached for it, it eluded her.

Is this how Father wielded the blood magic... from here in this seat of power?

The prospect didn't scare her as it had her father. She saw what her father was capable of, what blood magic could do to turn the tides of war. *This is the Blessing Belrich has been searching for. This could change everything.*

"Threyna!" Laela's shout ripped Threyna from her Inner Throne. She had flipped Threyna onto her back and was kneeling over her, attempting to pull the bangle from her arm.

Pain lanced from where the prongs sank into her flesh. She felt its panic. Something within her poised to strike at Laela. "Stop it." Threyna shoved Laela away. "Get off." Threyna turned her back to Laela, hugging her bangled arm, half horrified, half protective. Whatever defensive mechanism Laela had awoken within the bangle seemed to quiet.

"Blood and bone, what is wrong with you?" Laela snapped.

She didn't know how to respond—where to even begin. "It... It would have..."

"What are you talking about?"

"It!" Threyna gestured to her arm. "It was in my father's fatekeeper. It... the Blessing."

Laela's grim expression darkened. "He... cursed you." Her fingers reached out to brush Threyna's arm.

"He didn't curse me!" But before she could explain, the thundering heartbeats approaching from the woods beyond the bog drew nearer. Turning away from Laela, Threyna propped herself to her feet. "There are people in the woods."

"How can you tell?"

Threyna swallowed, understanding the burden her father carried, the responsibility that came with it. "No time to explain." She reached for her Inner Throne again, trying to discern how near the heartbeats were and just how many were coming. They pounded on the front doors to her throne room. "We need to get moving befo—"

"Hey!" a figure shouted, emerging from the tree line.

Another figure, cloaked in shadows, followed behind. Through the gloom, Threyna picked out Canton, Fawkes, and Dracus bringing up the rear. Still tapped into her Inner Throne, Threyna picked out the individual heartbeats. *Three...* Yet, behind them, something stirred, rustling the underbrush of the dead forest.

"Canton?" Laela stepped in front of Threyna. "Is that you?"

"Blood and bone," Fawkes said. "Ya alright? We heard screams."

Questions raced through Threyna's mind, unsure of what Dracus knew when he gave her the fatekeeper, but now was not the time. *Once we get to Aranoc. Better yet, once I get them back to Octarius. Then there will be answers, and an army to finish this war with the Order once and for all.*

"We're..." Laela glanced at Threyna.

"Fine," Threyna said. "But we need to keep mov—"

"Where's Rance?" Laela asked.

Fawkes and Dracus glanced at one another. Canton hung his head.

Laela shook her head. "Neutreen, how can anyone earn their wings?"

"He wasn't gonna make it," Dracus said. "Bleedin' out. Sacrificed himself so we could get to Aranoc."

"Barely made it as it was," Fawkes said. "Hadda collapse the tunnels and follow the Cylian to avoid the Order, and still had to fend off a pack of hellhounds."

"The quake..." Laela said. "We barely made it through Caius's Bog."

"Ay, we heard." Dracus gestured behind him as another figure, caked in the bog's murk, descended the hill.

"Mother?" Laela asked.

From behind Dracus, Aylenia strode forward, holding her arm at her side. Blood stained the pale cloak of the Avengardian garb, but relief flooded through Threyna.

She ascended the hill to embrace Aylenia in a one-armed hug. "You made it."

Aylenia sank into Threyna's embrace. "Good to see you too."

"We hoped she was with you," Dracus said to Laela.

"Ghosts," Fawkes said, rubbing the back of his neck and gazing at the ground. "Apologies, Lae."

"What about Erynia?" Canton asked.

Laela shook her head. "I couldn't get her out. She's still alive, so it's only a matter of time before Aranoc is crawling with legionaries. We need to go. *Us.*" She pointed to Dracus, Fawkes and Canton. "Not you."

"What do you mean, not us?" Aylenia asked, separating from Threyna. "We're comi—"

Dracus grabbed a hold of Threyna's shoulders. "Before we go anywhere, give it here, 'fore ya do somethin' stupid." He inspected her, undoubtedly searching for her fatekeeper. "Where is it?"

"This?" Threyna held up the empty fatekeeper by the leather strap.

His eyes examined it before falling to the bangle.

Threyna wrenched free of Dracus's grip.

Stepping backwards, Dracus shook his head.

"What did you think would happen," Threyna asked, "when you gave it to a ten-year-old girl who'd just supposedly lost her father? Did you know then, or just figure it out now?"

"Know what?" Canton asked, eyes passing back and forth between them.

"What's going on?" Aylenia asked.

Dracus chewed his mustache as Fawkes came alongside him.

Mixed emotions blurred in Threyna. He had lied to her. Kept the truth from her about who her father really was. And though now he wanted to stop her from opening the fatekeeper, she had no doubt it wasn't to protect her from the curse.

Threyna snorted. "Dracus knew. He knew who my father was and what he'd left me."

All eyes drifted to the bangle.

Canton gasped. "That's the Blessing."

"You had it around your neck all this time?" Aylenia asked. "Ghosts."

Dracus cursed to himself. He turned his palms to the cloudy sky, then rested his hands on his hips. Staring at her, he shrugged, resigning himself to what he was about to say. "Yer right. And ya can hate me all ya want. But what's done is done. And nothin's changed. We're going to Aranoc and you can run back to Octar—"

"You knew about the Blessing?" Canton asked. "What do you mean nothing's changed? Everything's changed."

Dracus winced, glancing at Fawkes.

Aylenia stepped forward. "We're not going back to Octarius. We're coming with you."

Laela cast Threyna a hellhound's side eye before setting in on Aylenia. "Spare us the act. I know about your *assignment*. You don't want to escape, and we don't want to fight, Blessing or not."

"You won't even consider it?" Canton asked.

Dracus growled. "Gory ghosting dammit. We're not doin' this."

Fawkes stepped ahead of Dracus, hand raised. "What do you mean—*assignment?*"

Laela fixed Threyna with a glare reserved for the most treacherous of darklings. "Why don't you tell them what you told me?"

"You told her?" Aylenia asked.

Threyna rubbed her temples with her hands, wishing she'd bit back her words earlier. *No chance of getting the darklings back into the soul jar.* She sighed. "You can go to Aranoc, but you won't escape. You have no way to leave. One of your people has likely spilled all of Aranoc's secrets, and when the Order comes, without us, you have nowhere to go." Threyna put her hands on her hips. "The way I see it, we're your best chance at surviving the night. So you can send us away, but it won't be long before you're marching for Octarius."

Dracus and Fawkes exchanged frowns. Laela glared.

"So it's settled?" Canton asked.

"We're going to Aranoc," Laela spat, staring at Threyna. "You better hope you're right—that *we* need *you*. Because if you're wrong, if we don't need you, I'll hollow you myself for even trying to stop us."

Feeling the untapped potential of the power at the armrests of her Inner Throne, Threyna half hoped Laela would try. She forced a smile. "Fine then. Let's go."

CHAPTER 25

LIVING AND SURVIVING

Dracus V

Dracus lagged behind the others. Not because of the aching in his foot or the throbbing in the back of his head from when Threyna shoved him into the wall in Valefort's dungeons, but because there was no point of going forward.

Rance—hollowed or worse. The Wraith—long gone, if Verinius hadn't mucked it up. If he hadn't, and Threyna told it true, then things were even worse, and no one had managed to escape. But that only meant the best path forward was *not* Aranoc. Threyna was right; if the Order had Erynia, they knew everything they needed to know about the tunnels, Aranoc, the escape—everything. Pair that with even the talk of sabotage? Nothing good awaited them at Aranoc. Only more death. More legionaries. Nerus, Decimus, Belrich and worse would be coming to the labyrinth beneath the city, and Dracus didn't want to be there when they arrived.

Laela led the way to the crumpled walls of Aranoc. Threyna and Aylenia trailed behind, with Canton following Threyna like a hollowed to a shade.

Dracus couldn't believe she'd opened the fatekeeper. He supposed this was always inevitable, but he figured he'd have died a true death long before it came to this. Now, Canton had everything he needed to object to leaving. He'd want to stay and fight. He'd make it sound all high and noble, a song for the ages, history in the making—some such ghosting nonsense.

Just like his damn father.

"You prime?" Fawkes asked, putting his hand on Dracus's shoulder as they followed several paces back.

Dracus snorted. "Lost the battle, losing the war, outta charges, and darklings are everywhere, but yeah—I'm prime."

The hill began to flatten, but the pain in his foot didn't abate. He trudged downhill one miserable step at a time, all the while considering how he was going to talk Canton out of his foolishness.

"You're not," Fawkes said. "I know what you're thinking, and this reunion ain't doing anyone any favors." He gestured to Threyna and Aylenia. Whether he was referring to Threyna and the Palogian girl who'd lost her mother in the first expedition to Sansia, or Viesa's daughters, it didn't matter—these reunions weren't good for Canton.

Viesa's daughters had grown in the decade since they'd last exchanged a glance, but despite how much had changed, some things were exactly the same.

"Ya ain't kidding," Dracus said. "Don't help none that Threyna threw me to the hellhounds back there."

"You knew?" Fawkes asked. "About the Blessing? About Theodyn?" He toyed with the fatekeeper about his neck. It wasn't one from his parents, but one Fawkes had written for Dracus. Dracus hoped he'd never need to read it.

Dracus wrinkled his nose, rustling his mustache. "Yeah. All of it."

"Blood and bone," Fawkes said. He didn't ask why Dracus didn't confide in him. He didn't stoop to petty arguments or lecture him on the importance of sharing his burdens. Dracus would have if their roles had been reversed—bet every soul in the soul jar, Dracus knew he would. But Fawkes had better tact in terms of how and when to broach such subjects.

"Needa convince Canton this ain't a fight we can win," Dracus said. "More than that, gotta convince him that we needa leave. Now. No Aranoc. No Wraith. We gotta find our own way off this rock."

Fawkes grumbled, rubbing his cheek. A slight bruise had formed. Whether he'd been struck during the fray in the courtyard or sometime in their flight from the hellhounds, it was starting to swell now.

Dracus caressed Fawkes's cheek.

Fawkes took Dracus by the wrist. "I'm fine. I heal, remember?"

Dracus grumbled. "None of us will if we get impaled by the Order. Nerus gets his hands on me—forget it—he'll make sure I get every slash of the Final Demise even if I invoke a Blood Trial."

Dracus had only seen the *traitor's punishment* doled out once despite the fact that every legion carried the wooden beams on every expedition. There were few enough deserters—only a handful in all his time with the Order. Occasionally, people managed to get away, start new lives. Gatius, one of Rance's men, had managed a fresh start after leaving the Order—first with the Underground, and then in the Wraith. But most ended up like Lacius. Every legionary carried a Vendetta dagger, reserved specifically for traitors and deserters. Death by a hundred cuts, every blade tasted Lacius's blood.

Dracus remembered the way Lacius screamed, the look in his eyes. He'd been a quota boy, same as Dracus. They'd climbed the ranks together, excelled together. He was one of Dracus's best Tribunii before everything hollowed out.

"I've heard rumors," Lacius had said.

Dracus hadn't listened. If he had, maybe he wouldn't have given the order. Maybe he wouldn't have slashed his own Vendetta dagger, *Fang,* across his chest. Perhaps they would have deserted the Order together.

Dracus swallowed, blocking out Lacius's hollowed-out eyes. "We can't go to Aranoc."

"We're on our way," Fawkes said. "Where else if not Aranoc? Besides, ya think Canton's gonna let you walk away from the people he's spent the last ten years with? Ya gotta shade's chance of that. And if what Threyna says is true, what choice do we have other than Octarius?"

Dracus's throat burned. It was the last time he tasted anything. He recalled the last living breaths he'd drawn. "I ain't goin' back there."

"What if that's where Canton wants to be?" Fawkes asked. "Will you let him choose?"

"I'll convince him," Dracus said. "I have to."

Fawkes shook his head. "You know, *we* can just leave. The two of us. If he wants to stay, he can stay. He's not a kid anymore, Dray."

Dracus scoffed. Fawkes was a good soldier, a better man, but he was wrong.

"Ya can't keep ignoring me on this," Fawkes said. "Canton's a man now."

Dracus bit his lip. "I'm not ignorin' nothing. Yeah, he's a man? Boy still has nightmares. Sees Tellers in every shadow."

Fawkes put a hand on Dracus's arm, stopping him to let the others continue on ahead. With both hands on his shoulders, he stared into Dracus's eyes. He bit his lip, thoughts churning behind his dark blue eyes.

"I know what yer gonna say," Dracus said.

"You can tell the truth…" Fawkes said.

Dracus waved him away. That ship had burned to ashes a decade ago. It was too late to come clean after all this time. Canton would never forgive him. Never listen to him. Then he'd die on this cursed island out of spite.

"You still blame yourself," Fawkes said. "It wasn't your fault. You don't have to stay any longer." He lowered his hand to Dracus's still and silent heart. "How much longer do ya think you can deal with it? The pain."

"As long as it takes," Dracus said. He brushed his thumb down the contour of Fawkes's bruised cheek. *The Old Boy's seen better days. Ghosts, I guess we both have.* Fawkes's face was marred by scars old and new. Crow's feet peeked out from beneath his bushy brows, but the same glimmer of hope he'd always had was still alive and dancing within his gaze. *Somehow, after all that those eyes have seen, Old Boy still has his soul.*

"Ya don't owe him anything," Fawkes said. "Not anymore. Whatever debt ya feel you owe him, it's paid. You've been a father to him longer than his own da. You've given him options, choices. Ya can't control him. It's his life. Ya gotta let him live it. Let him choose."

Fawkes saw everything so clearly and always cut to the heart of any situation. But not this time. *This isn't life. This isn't living. This is surviving.* "I gotta at least try. I won't leave him." *But that doesn't mean you have to stay and suffer, Old Boy.*

"It's not. Your. Fault. You didn't kill his parents. Belrich did. Nerus did. Not you."

Fawkes had said the words before. Dracus had heard them. Didn't make it true.

"You've done everything for that boy." Fawkes pointed towards Canton's back. "You're a good man. You've done so much good."

Dracus scoffed. "Not enough to make a difference."

Fawkes inhaled slowly through his teeth. "You've made a difference to him. What if we did stay? What if this could actually work?"

"Fightin' the Order?" Dracus couldn't believe his ears. He tried to shake free of Fawkes's grip on his shoulders, but the larger man held him. "If you think we're fightin', you're losin' it, Old Boy." Dracus gently tugged on the beard of Fawkes's cheek before brushing a few wild strands of reddish-brown hair behind his ear. "If he won't come with us, you should still go."

The words hurt to say. He couldn't imagine Fawkes not being by his side, but if he didn't say anything, Fawkes would stay with Dracus until the end, the same as he would with Canton. And the end was coming.

Fawkes pushed past Dracus to continue following the others. "How can you say that to me?"

"Because you can still live," Dracus said, following after him. "This curse is the only thing keeping me upright. When I leave...." *It'll be over. No more pain. No more worry. No more.*

Fawkes spun on Dracus. "When you leave, you're gonna die, and that boy is gonna lose the only father he's like to remember." He shrugged. "Are you doing this for him? Or for you?"

Dracus leveled his index finger at Fawkes. "You know the answer to that."

"Not sure I do." There was no malice in his tone. "But I do know one thing: if we leave, we leave together. If we stay, then we fight together, but don't think you're sending me away."

Dracus groaned, bristling his mustache. *How'd I manage to surround myself with such stubborn bastards?*

In contemplative silence, the two followed after Laela and the others, doing their best to regain ground before they arrived at the labyrinth beneath the city.

Aranoc was once a hub for trade, back before the Disasters. During the Artificer's War, it became a distribution center for arcanatek, but after the Order won and outlawed arcanatek, Arenius led the Underground to steal Aranoc's supplies. It was then that Decimus suggested placing the arcanatek under heavy protection at Order outposts throughout Rheynia. Although the product was gone, the infrastructure remained and the tunnels beneath had served as the Wraith's base of operations these past ten years. Entering now, Dracus only hoped they weren't marching to the same end as the Artificers.

As they neared the city, there seemed to be a commotion coming from within the walls. Despite the apparent turmoil, Laela and the others disappeared through the narrow gap in the gnarled roots and brambles that replaced the dried-up moat surrounding the city. Not too far behind, Dracus and Fawkes followed, lowering themselves through the gap and into the slender tunnel that would lead to the atrium and main cavern.

Once inside, the sounds from within were too loud for Verinius to have led the Wraith to the ships. Dracus and Fawkes exchanged a nervous glance before quickening their pace.

Don't tell me the damned Underground did it again. Dracus charged through the atrium to the landing that overlooked the main cavern where Laela, Canton, Threyna and Aylenia stood. Coming up alongside them,

Dracus saw what stopped the others in their tracks. If Dracus's heart could still beat, it would have stopped. "Gory ghosting dammit…"

"How?" Fawkes asked in disbelief.

Laela balked.

Rubble filled the tunnels that led under the city to the cove where the ships waiting to spirit them beyond the curse to Sansia were docked. The tunnels to their salvation had collapsed. Along with their hopes.

CHAPTER 26

A WOLF IN WOOL

Laela X

Laela's eyes watered. The cavern wasn't filled with smoke as it had the night her father burned the Underground's ships or when Arilette did the same when she executed her own father, but Laela felt like she was choking on acrid fumes all the same.

The scar across her chest burned hot. Her father's screams filled her ears as real as the arguments happening on the cavern floor.

No Rance. No Mother. Gory ghosts, where is Verinius?

Her shoulders sagged, slumping forward to wrap around herself, but there was no comfort to be found. Not here. Not anywhere. The weight of failed expectations threatened to bury her beneath Aranoc as the losses piled higher.

The tunnels had collapsed. Even if their escape vessels were still intact, without the tunnels to get to them, they'd have to navigate through the Gullies. Over the past decade, they'd done well to cleanse the limestone crags of the hollowed that infested them, but still—there was no way they'd get hundreds of people through unmolested. It would be slow going at best, a slaughter at worst. And that would be before the Order arrived.

"This is all her fault," her father said.

She glared at Threyna.

It was only fitting; she was the granddaughter of Bohen, Princess of Rheynia—was it any wonder she was such a darkling?

Beside her, Dracus stroked his black mustache with his thumb and forefinger as if he could pull from it the answers to all their problems—or at least some justification as to why Rheynia was so cruel.

"Ya can stop lookin' at her." Dracus nodded towards Threyna. "This wasn't her doin'."

"She is with the Underground; this *is* her doing."

Dracus leaned close, speaking conspiratorially. "Rance took every precaution. No one coulda known. Yer smart. Tell me—how many of us knew the ships were moved? Us, Verinius, the Second Sword, a handful of others?"

Laela bit her lip. It was true; everyone outside of their inner circle would have believed they'd leave using the south tunnels that passed through the underbelly of the Spine and out to Cybel's Tears. It was the easiest route of escape, but also the one Rance suspected the Underground would assume. Those who knew that the ships were moved to Beak's Bay through the east tunnel were few.

"One of our own did this?"

Dracus raised a brow, glancing down at the chaos below.

Some were trying to move the rubble blocking the tunnel, but for every stone removed, two more fell to replace it. Laela winced. Remove the wrong stone and the entire cavern could come crashing down.

"So what do we do now?" Laela asked. "Where is Verinius?"

Dracus hmphed. "Forget Verinius. What do we do now? Blood and bone, we get outta here 'fore anyone realizes we're here. We go now, just us and we can still make it through the Gullies. Get a ship, get the ghost outta here."

Laela couldn't hide her bewilderment. Stammering, she asked, "What about the others? You'd just leave them?"

Dracus grit his teeth and grabbed her by the collar. "Haven't you heard anything I said? *'The others?'* Someone, in this room, someone *among us,* did this."

She'd been the one to fall into Caius's Bog, but at this distance, Dracus smelled of death—rotten and rancid—yet his words carried truth. *What would Rance do?* She wished her mother was here. She always knew who to look to in a pinch, but without Rance, with Verinius seemingly invisible, and Dracus only concerned for himself, who was left?

"We need a leader, Dracus. People will listen to you. People will follow."

Dracus shook his head. "There's no leading this disaster. Too much division. Best chance we have is—"

"I'm not abandoning everyone to save myself," Laela snapped. "We can still do this."

Dracus growled. "They sabotaged this escape, and now ya wanna shepherd this flock? There's a wolf in wool here, ready to strike when we least expect."

Heat rose to her cheeks, and a knot balled in her throat. She shoved Dracus away. "Neutreen would burn our wings to ash if we abandoned these people—*our* people—for one traitor. You can leave if you want. Run away like you always do, but don't you dare take our ships. This isn't over."

She shoved past him and the others to descend the carved stairs down to the pandemonium of the cavern floor. She needed to find Verinius and tell him to take control. The Order was coming. They couldn't stay here.

Verinius was nowhere to be found amidst the men and women tending to the injured in the tunnel's collapse. Supplies were limited, but at least they were trying to do something productive; those with idle hands were at each others' throats. Without leadership, without hope, they might as well have dissolved into hollowed.

Perhaps the living and the undead are not so dissimilar.

As she descended the stairs, the closest thing she found to a leader amongst the chaos was a tall man with broad shoulders. Though Laela didn't know him personally, she recognized him in passing. There were few enough Rheynians with the tan skin and prominent features of the Palogian Isles for Laela to forget him.

"Stop moving the rubble," he shouted to people pawing at the tunnel entrance. After addressing a man and woman in a softer tone, he sent them away and ran over to the base of the tunnel. "We need to reinforce these walls before we remove any more stones."

Whoever he was, the others, the laborers—shipbuilders, tunnel diggers, and supply runners—did as they were told, absent questions.

Descending the last of the stairs, Laela jogged towards him, scanning the cavern in search of Verinius. Coming up empty amidst the squabbling Wraith, Laela approached the Palogian man and the laborers before the tunnel entrance.

"We're not getting out of here tonight," he said, his hands out in front of him in an attempt to placate the others' concern. "We'll find another way. Soon. But we can't panic now."

If Belrich didn't have Erynia, if the Order wasn't already on their way here, it would have been sage advice. But that wasn't the case.

As Laela approached, focus shifted towards her, and murmurs spread.

"Rance's First Sword," a man said.

"Thank Neutreen," another said. "Rance is here."

"Where is Rance?"

Gone. Laela couldn't bring herself to say it, but she needed to. Their leader was dead. He wasn't coming back.

"Rance is gone," Laela said. "I must speak with Verinius."

Eyes blinked. Stern jaws unhinged, and silent lips parted absent words as the myriad of worst-case scenarios ran through the laborers' minds.

Laela swallowed. "The leaders must discuss plans of recourse. Where is Verinius?"

The Palogian man's shaved head and finely plucked brows attempted to conceal the typical curls and dark complexion of his ancestry, but nothing could hide his disdain. "Verinius... you'd have better luck speaking with a shade."

Now was Laela's turn to blink. *Did he suffer in the collapse? Is he gone too?* While she took a steadying breath, searching for the words to speak, someone else beat her to the glowstone.

"He's over here," a quiet, breathy voice said behind her.

Stifling a twitch of her eye, Laela turned to the familiar voice.

Tarus, the Second Sword of the Wraith, glared up at her from beneath his black hood. Half a head shorter than her, two stone lighter, and ten times as stubborn, Verinius's protector pursed his lips, narrowing his already pinched face. "Follow me." With a swish of his cloak, he spun on his heel, quieter than a hellhound.

Before following him, Laela met the Palogian man's grim gaze. "What's your name?"

"Redge."

"Redge," Laela said, knowing it likely wasn't his given name but some Rheynianized subversion of the truth. Probably more like Redggar Breakspear or Redgeforth Swordsoul or some such. "Forget the tunnels. Divide everyone into groups—no larger than a dozen. Take only the vital supplies. Prepare to leave Aranoc and never return."

Redge stammered to phrase a retort, but Laela didn't give him the opportunity, already attempting to find and follow Tarus to Verinius. She spotted him just before his black cloak disappeared behind a stack of crates of arcanatek scraps. Hurrying to keep up with the agile Second Sword, Laela wished Rance and her mother were here. That Threyna and Aylenia weren't. That the Order wasn't on their way. And a thousand other things that could have made this situation more tenable.

Navigating the injured and the strewn supplies, Laela located Tarus again as he approached Verinius sitting in a shadowy corner of the cavern. The Aedile of Aranoc, already small of stature, huddled close to himself, hugging his knees and pulling them into his body. He rocked forward and back, muttering to himself.

Her father's laughter shattered her Center of Silence.

"Blood and bone," Laela said, stopping before Verinius. If the aedile identified her presence, he made no sign of it, continuing to blink, murmur, and coddle himself. "What happened to him?"

"The Tellers call it *shadeshock*," Tarus said, hands resting on two of the many daggers holstered on his belt. "Believe the Order calls is *head-hollowed*. Underground would just call it cowardice."

Laela palmed her forehead. "How long has he been like this?"

"Since the tunnels collapsed. Hasn't said a word of meaning. Keeps saying, 'The Seers were right,' over and over again."

"What Seers?" Laela asked.

Tarus shrugged, then nodded at Verinius. "Ask him."

Laela stooped closer to Verinius. Sweat beaded on his scalp. The wrinkles of his forehead crinkled and stretched as his graying brows raised and contorted, his lips mumbling continuously.

Laela put a hand on Verinius's forearm. "Verinius, we need your help."

He didn't even look at her. "The Seers were right..."

"See?" Tarus said.

"What were the Seers right about?" Laela asked.

Verinius continued to stare sightlessly, rocking back and forth as he held himself. "The crown passes. Passes. Passes. The flood of blood is coming. No escape. No escape!"

Losing patience, needing a leader, Laela shook the aedile. "Snap out of it. We need to leave."

"The crown passes, passes, passes."

Tarus grunted. "Shadeshocked, head-hollowed, whatever you wanna call it. Like it or not, we're the closest thing to leaders we got left, so tell me—what happened?"

Sensing his *"if I were the First Sword, this never would have happened"* bit, Laela powered past. "We don't have time for this. Rance is gone."

"Obviously. What now?"

Ready to defend herself, Laela was caught off guard by Tarus's pragmatism. She looked past Tarus to the Wraith behind him, fist clenched over the stolen short sword at her waist. "We need to leave. Immediately. The Order is coming."

"Blood and bone…"

"The ghosting Underground…"

Tarus shook his head. "Nah, no way. Tunnel just collapsed. No explosion, nothing. Just bad luck—a coincidence."

"Tell that to my sister," Laela said. She nodded in the direction of the overlook from the atrium, but Threyna was no longer there.

"She's here?" Tarus asked, dark eyes widening.

"She sabotaged the Dominion ceremony. Got Rance hollowed, Erynia caught." She shook her head. "Doesn't matter. She said this was Arilette's plan. They're here now to escort us to Octarius."

Tarus ran his fingers through his short black hair, pulling back his hood. "Options?"

"The tunnel collapsed. The boats didn't burn."

Tarus licked his lip and pinched his brow. "What you thinkin'?"

"We're *not* going back to Octarius," Laela said. "Arilette can hollow. We're getting out of here."

Scoffing, Tarus tossed his hands in the air. "How? We'll never make it through the Gullies, and if the Order is on their way, how long before Aranoc is crawling with Skulls and Doves?"

Laela considered, twisting her tongue against the inside of her cheek. The Skulls—Belrich's Inquisitors—would be out for vengeance. The Doves—the Order's spy network—would be looking for anyone they could lay blame on; people would disappear, be interrogated. If they were lucky, they'd be sent to the stocks. Unlucky, and they'd be sent to the fighting pits scattered throughout the Dominion where they would fight to earn Neutreen's wings of freedom to return to society, or hollow and be the next training exercise for new Order recruits. Either way, no one was safe here—Wraith or otherwise.

"Hours if Erynia holds out and they come in force," Laela said. "Moments if she caves and they only send a single legion. Either way, we need to act fast. If we send a small group, just enough people to man the ships, they may be able to navigate the Gullies."

Tarus nodded. "I don't see how that helps everyone else."

"We need to get everyone out of here quickly. Then the ships just need to meet us. We can travel north, to the Roost."

"You've been spendin' too much time in Avengard," Tarus said. "Justicus set up an outpost to mine Viridite from the Gullies. We'll never make it past them."

Laela grit her teeth. *Then there's only one other option.* "We can follow Cybel's Tears to Talon's Grip."

"Talon's Grip?" Tarus scoffed. "We'll be going straight through Octaven. Underground won't just let us pass."

It was all coming together. Threyna and Aylenia's mission—Laela could use it to her advantage. "We just need to play along with Arilette's game—let them *think* we're heading south to seek shelter at Octarius. Then, once we pass Fort Cybel, we make a mad dash for Talon's Grip."

"Won't be easy," Tarus said.

"Is anything?"

He hmphed. "I'll take twenty? Should be enough to get all three ships beyond the bay… factoring in a few casualties." He tilted his head. "Guess I'll see ya at the Grip."

Laela gripped Tarus's arm, stopping his progress. It wasn't a bad plan, but she didn't know the Aranoc people as well as he did. He was right; she'd spent too much time at Avengard these past moons. Part of her feared that she wouldn't be able to shepherd the flock without his aid. Another part, despite their rivalry, wanted him around to watch her back if Threyna was going to be coming with her. But something else prickled the hair on the back of her neck.

"There's a wolf in wool here," Dracus had said, *"ready to strike when we least expect."*

She thought of Gatius's treachery. Erynia's guard—an Undergrounder. But he wasn't the only one. There was no way the tunnel's collapse was a coincidence. She couldn't tell if she wanted Tarus close because she could trust him, or because she couldn't, but she couldn't let him leave.

"No," Laela said. "There's something else. Gatius was Underground. I don't think he was working alone. We need to stick together, watch each other's backs."

Tarus's mysteriously stoic demeanor cracked. "Gatius?" Again, he ran his hands through his hair. "Gory ghosting dammit."

There were few Laela could trust beyond reproach, but if she managed to lead the Wraith past the Underground to the Grip and there were no ships waiting for them, all of this would be for nothing.

"Send Rosler," Laela said. "Him and Taggart."

"The builder and the admiral?" Tarus asked. "You can't be serious."

"Rosler and his crew put too much of their heart and souls into building those ships to not wish them to reach Sansia. And Taggart loves the sea too much to wish to stay here."

More importantly, Rosler, Taggart, and their men were not partial to the change in plans. So if one of them wished to sabotage the escape, they would have collapsed the tunnels through the Spine, not toward Beak's Bay.

"Set them to purpose," Laela said, turning to the chaotic cavern. "I'll tend to the sheep."

CHAPTER 27

TO LIVE IS TO LOSE

Dracus VII

Canton stared at Threyna with two very different forms of desire—each more dangerous than the other. Whether he was lusting after the corrupted bangle injecting her with the Blessing's malice or the girl who wore it, nothing good would come from it. Only an eternity of suffering.

With a grunt, Dracus strode past Fawkes to grab a fistful of Canton's tunic.

"Dracus, what the—"

"Over here," Dracus said through his teeth. Pulling Canton away from Threyna, Fawkes, and the commotion within the cavern, Dracus leveled his finger at the boy's nose. "Answer is no. Not up for discussion. Not a debate or negotiation. We leave—now."

Canton swatted Dracus's finger away. "And leave everyone else?"

"Who else?" Dracus asked. "Who down there can we trust after this, eh?"

"You're the only one you trust." Canton scoffed. "You might be able to run away from everyone—everything—but I can't. I won't."

Dracus's lip twitched, but he swallowed the indictment. It wasn't fair. Dracus running from the Order was the only reason Canton wasn't a husk. If anything, he should have left the Underground sooner. Had he gone north with Fawkes and Canton the night of the Battle of the Cut, he never would have been there for Bherus to give him the fatekeeper. Never would have fled the lost battle to find Threyna fending off hellhounds on her return to Octarius. If he had just turned the other way, he never would have given her the cursed fatekeeper, never would have gone back to Octarius and shared that last farewell drink with Arilette. The only regret Dracus had from running away was not leaving soon enough.

Dracus exhaled, bristling his mustache. "Ain't no way we coordinate an escape of a group this size without Rance. You might think that pretty armband means somethin', but if it wasn't enough for Bherus ghostin' Fayte, what makes you think she'll be any different? There ain't a shade's chance of beatin' the Order. Wasn't when the Seers tried, nor the Artificers, and definitely not at the Cut—this is no different."

Canton scowled, his narrow face darkening just like his father's did after Dracus caught him stealing from the Order outpost outside of Salingard. He looked more like his father every day. Same shaggy brown hair, heroic jawline, and martyr's stubbornness. No matter how hard Dracus tried to steer Canton away from becoming just like his father, darklings would never be shades and Canton would never change.

Dracus remembered it like it was yesterday. Cavus Kruso was silent when they held him in the stocks for public humiliation. Not a shade's murmur passed his lips when he fought waves of hollowed on the sands of the gladiatorial arenas of Belgrave. It wasn't until they readied the pike that would impale him that he finally raised his voice for Elyngrove's masses.

"I'm not the villain they've made me. But if my suffering serves as the spark that wakes the sleepers from their slumbers, if my hollowing calls the courageous from their cowardice—so be it. Neutreen sees. Neutreen knows."

That was when Canton, Cavus's son, climbed the dais and stood before his father, arms wide. Dracus didn't know where any of them would be if he hadn't counseled Belrich to bestow mercy on the father and his son. So much would be different. Yet so much remained the same.

"Rance told us to get to Sansia," Canton said. "Turn it into a place of hope. That we were the future."

Still the martyr's son. Dracus chewed his mustache. "Yeah. Rance said *you* were the future. That don't mean everyone."

Canton tossed his hands to the atrium's ceiling. "You put me on a pedestal. Like I matter more than anyone else. 'No, Cant, that's too dangerous for you.' 'Not this time, kid. You'd have better luck in the fighting pits.' 'Don't be a hero, Canton.' 'Someone else's problem, Canton.' When does it stop?"

His cheeks flushed pink. A vein in his temple throbbed. Breath steamed from his nostrils.

The gifted curse of being alive. Every *"No"* Dracus had put in Canton's path ensured he could still feel the thrill of his blood running hot; everything he'd done kept Canton alive in spite of the boy's affinity for wanting to be the one to jump on the Dawnshard.

Dracus didn't flinch. "It stops when you get beyond the curse. Then if you wanna go kill yerself, be my guest. At least you won't be stuck dealin' with it for eternity. You'll die a true death and be done."

Canton said something under his breath that sounded an awful lot like the word *coward.*

"Call me a coward if you like, but it ain't cowardice if it keeps ya alive."

Canton's eyes widened. He slapped his palm with an open-fisted backhand. "Yes. It. Is. Yes it is!"

Dracus took a steadying breath and put his hands on Canton's shoulders. Not with force, but with pleading. "I know you think that maybe this time'll be different. That the Wraith, the Tellers, the Underground—everyone with an irradiator to charge against the Order will join together. That we'll unite behind a weapon like the Blessing and take the Order down for good. Believe me, kid, I wish it were true. But it ain't. Near sixty years I walked this forsaken place, and time and time again I've been where you are now. Hoping."

Dracus shook his head. "Ya gotta noble heart. It's good. Better than anythin' I could give ya. But that hope, that future where that noble heart of yours can do some good—it's beyond this place. It ain't here. So the best I can give ya is life. A chance, a hope for somethin' better. But trust me when I say, it ain't here. There's no Rance. If Verinius is here, he ain't getting us to Sansia; guy could barely find a hollowed in the Gullies. Nah. There's no plan to escape. There's no unity to fight for."

He allowed himself a sad smile. Straightening Canton's tunic, he gave the boy a playful clap on the cheek. "Wish it weren't so. Really, I do. But if we're gettin' outta here, it's you, me, and Old Boy. Can't save everyone, ya hear? I need ya to trust me on this. We'll find a way."

Canton's ire smoldered, then softened, crackling like the embers left after a bonfire. He nodded, dropping his eyes to the floor.

Dracus pulled him into a hug. *Thank Neutreen, the One, Bheric, Cybel, Draakard—whoever still gives a ghost about us... Thank you.*

He patted Canton on the back. "Let's go get Old Boy and get on outta here, eh?"

"Yeah," Canton said, slipping away from his embrace.

But as Dracus dared to hope he'd actually be able to get Canton beyond the curse, his aunt's haunting lullaby returned. *"To dream is to die. To hope is to lie. To live is to..."*

The next words returned to him as he watched Canton walk away. With Canton's footsteps fading into the din of the cavern's chaos, Dracus wished so too did the memory.

"To live is to lose," Dracus said aloud to the empty atrium. He sniffed, kicking a loose stone along the floor. "Good thing I ain't alive." He followed after Canton, eager to prove his aunt and her grim song wrong.

CHAPTER 28

INCOMING DARKLINGS

Threyna XII

Threyna clutched the rail of the overlook atop the cavern with one hand and held her stomach with the other. The scars she'd received from the hellhound attack the night of the Battle of the Cut seemed to burn, just as fresh as the prongs embedded by the Skeleton King's Blessing in her arm. She found no humor in the irony that she had Dracus to thank for both. If not for him, the hellhounds would have finished her. He never would have given her the fatekeeper. He never would have lied to her face about what it held.

There was no changing the past. *Father, gone. Mother, gone. Ebrus, gone. Yevon, gone.* Nothing was bringing them back. Pointless to try. The only path was forward, and she would need every cursed blessing she could get to walk it.

Threyna inhaled the thick air of the poorly ventilated subterranean cavern. Difficult to breathe and in pain, her other senses flared with unwanted life. Absent arcanatek illuminators, the cavern was still too bright, the noise within the cave too loud. Worst of all, like waking from a nightmare only to remember it in glimpses throughout the day, Threyna felt a shadow over her Inner Throne. She could sense the Skeleton King's presence, feel him in a way that stained her soul rotten the way the blood artifact embedded into her arm.

Aylenia put a hand on her arm, just below the bangle. "Legatus was right. It worked."

Whatever it was, whoever was behind it, they'd made sure no one was escaping through that tunnel. Even if the Order wasn't breathing down their necks like hollowed to a shade, it would have taken until Bheric's Day to clear the debris. But they didn't have weeks—they had hours at the most, and the time warp was against them.

Threyna nodded, attempting to block out the Skeleton King sitting in her Inner Throne. "Arilette or Lorath share who we have to thank?"

Aylenia grimaced. "She wouldn't say. Said it's better we didn't know until everyone was back in Octarius." She took a deep breath. "Do you think they'll agree to come?"

"Agree? Laela won't come easy." She gestured in Dracus's direction. "And you can bet the last darkling in the soul jar he won't wait around."

Aylenia tossed her black curls over her shoulder with resignation. "Divided, ruin will reign."

"Divided, ruin will reign," Threyna agreed.

"So what if they don't comply?"

Threyna glanced over at Canton. He hadn't taken his eyes off of her since he emerged from the woods. She didn't want his attention, but perhaps he wasn't the only one who would be curious about what she could do. She could use that if she needed to.

"They will," Threyna said. "They have to. Or we've failed again."

Leaning on the rail overlooking the cavern floor, Aylenia shifted her weight from hip to hip. "Times like this we could really use Yevon's levity, eh?"

Threyna snorted. "Or one of Ebrus's poems. Something like a ray of sunlight to burn off the fog?"

Aylenia chuckled. Threyna could sense from her Inner Throne the warmth resonating within Aylenia's heart, but as quickly as it came on, it fizzled. The memory of their lost friends only highlighted the weight of what was lost.

Aylenia's gaze fell to the bangle about Threyna's arm. "Threyna, your arm…" She reached for it, but as if she were afraid to touch it, she came up short.

Black veins spread up and down her arm from the bangle like dark worms burrowing into a rotten onion. Threyna pursed her lips, remembering the corruption that scarred her father and the torture he'd endured to keep this very artifact from falling into the Order's hands. *That won't be my fate.* She wanted to believe it. Maybe one day she would, but now, all she could think about was failure. Loss. Anger.

"I'm prime," Threyna said, turning away from Aylenia as Dracus dragged Canton off. Deflecting her dark thoughts, she nodded after Dracus. "See, what did I tell you? Already running."

Aylenia fixed Threyna with a leveling stare, clearly seeing through the diversion, but also knowing better than to push it. "Should we stop them?"

Threyna shrugged. "As fun as this little reunion has been, I'm ready for it to be over. There are plenty of others here. We don't need all of them. After the hurt my father put on the Order, if we can get back to Octarius and mount an attack, who knows… we might just be able to win."

Aylenia nodded, but then gestured to the stairs where Laela was bounding up, two at a time. "Incoming darkling."

Breaths only slightly labored, Laela came to a stop before Threyna. She tossed her raven-colored braid over her shoulder and placed her hands on her hips. "Offer still stand?"

Threyna cocked a brow. "It was never an offer."

Laela glared. "Will you help us make it to Octaven?"

Threyna listened to her sister's heartbeat. Heightened by the exertion from the stairs, the stress of the moment, or the duress they'd been through to get here, Laela's heart throbbed—not with the irregularity of a lie, but the dishonest composure of a half-truth.

Not trusting Laela, Threyna bowed her head. "Of course. Divided, ruin will—"

"Blood and bone, we know," Laela snapped. "We need to evacuate. I'm dividing the people into small groups to misdirect the Order through the Spine. We'll regroup at Cybel's Tears and follow the river to Fort Cybel, then cross toward Octarius."

The pressure of Laela's heart spiked as she said Octarius. *Is it because she's afraid to return, or something else—a deception?*

Before Threyna could respond, Laela's green eyes, the eyes their mother had given her, fell upon the dark vines snaking from the bangle on Threyna's arm.

"Good plan," Threyna said, pulling her arm behind her. "See it done. Quickly."

Laela hmphed, and Threyna didn't need her Inner Throne's aid to identify that Laela hadn't taken kindly to being ordered by her. "I'll address my people. Just… stay out of my way."

She shoved between Threyna and Aylenia.

Aylenia's eyes followed her as she stormed away like Rivich from a good time. "I don't remember her always being—"

"Such a ghosting hellhound?" Threyna finished.

Aylenia smirked. "I was going to say something else, but you are definitely related."

Threyna shook her head. If her mother's last words to her weren't saying exactly that, she might have denied it. "We take after our fathers. Regardless… she's lying. Or at least she's not telling the whole truth."

Aylenia cocked her brow, then tossed her head back and forth as if considering. "Does anyone ever?"

"No one with sense, I reckon."

Aylenia put her hand on Threyna's arm, the one without the bangle. "I'm gonna keep an eye on her, see who she talks to."

Threyna nodded. "Good idea. I'm just behind you."

"You prime?" Aylenia asked, examining her as if she too had an Inner Throne to hear heartbeats.

"Yeah, just need a moment."

Aylenia gave her arm a squeeze before following after Laela, leaving Threyna alone on the cavern's overlook. She didn't know where Dracus, Fawkes, or Canton went. Frankly, she didn't care. Good fighters they might be, but good soldiers don't desert. As far as she was concerned, they were more trouble than they were worth. Not to mention seeing their faces brought back too many painful memories of the past.

Forward. Only forward.

Tapping into her Inner Throne, she attuned to the different heartbeats around her. The rest of her physical sensations seemed to dull as she focused on this other sense. At first, the sheer volume of people in the Wraith's hovel beneath Aranoc overwhelmed her, but quickly, she was able to separate the individual beats. Each one had its own unique tenor and tone. As she became more acquainted with each one, connecting its sound to its owner, she expanded her reach.

The city above the surface buzzed despite the time of night, but something else came with it. A dull hum, a background noise, faint and faraway, but present. The more Threyna focused on it, the more she couldn't unhear it.

Sinking deeper into her seat of power, she gripped the arms of her Inner Throne. The black veins wormed down her arm, reaching for her elbow, but she pushed further until she identified the source of the sound.

She snapped back to the cavern, having been so separated she hadn't realized Dracus and Canton were standing only a few paces away, and all eyes were fixed on Laela addressing the entirety of the Wraith from the opposite end of the overlook.

Threyna breathed heavily. *The Order. They're in the tunnels.*

CHAPTER 29

STRENGTH, COURAGE, AND LIES

Laela XI

L aela gripped the rail of the cavern's overlook. "Be strong. Be courageous."

Tarus set Rosler, the lead shipbuilder, and Taggart, the admiral of the small fleet, to purpose. They would lead their crews through the Gullies to the ships and prepare to rendezvous at Talon's Grip. Now it was up to Laela and Tarus to get these people to those ships. If all went according to plan, even if Rance was gone, his dream could still live—they could make it to Sansia. They could have the fresh start they all wanted under Neutreen's providence, beyond the curse and the Order's reach.

But making that happen was easier said than done.

Threyna and Aylenia thought that Laela would be leading the Wraith south to Octarius, so she needed to keep up that illusion lest she create more strife for herself later. But her people would not take lightly the suggestion of returning to the Underground and Arilette's rule. If anything, she expected backlash, but they didn't have time for that. The Order was coming, and they needed to leave. Now.

Below, as Laela had ordered, Redge and Tarus had taken the responsibility of organizing people into small groups, but as of yet, the Wraith didn't know why. Now was her turn to explain.

"This should be entertaining," her father teased.

Laela closed her father out, solidifying her Center of Silence. But even still, her palms moistened, her throat constricted, and her mother's words of affirmation were not enough to calm her mind or organize her thoughts. Prayers to Neutreen didn't yield any better results, but time was of the essence.

Laela cleared her throat and took a deep breath. Her chest quivered, her lip trembled, and her hands rattled, but a leader could show no fear. She straightened her tunic beneath the Avengardian armor and raised her arms to the cavern ceiling.

"People of Aranoc." Her voice boomed louder than she knew it could, echoing throughout the cavern and cutting through the chatter. Shouting was replaced by muttering as heads and pointing fingers turned towards her.

"We have been betrayed. But the time for arguing ends now. Though the tunnels have collapsed, there is worse news you must know." She paused, knowing what she was about to say could leave the others in despair. By now, rumors had likely spread about Verinius's shadeshock and Rance's demise, but they needed to know the truth and they needed to hear it from her.

They need a new leader.

"Rance is dead." Saying the words aloud hurt. Rance, who had given her hope, given her purpose, named her the First Sword of the Wraith… was gone.

Gasps answered her. People turned towards one another, palms lifted skyward, lips turned down. Mutters spread like a plague. Laela held up her hands to quiet the noise and recapture their attention.

"I know you're scared, but we must prepare to leave Aranoc. Our enemy marches towards us. Belrich, his Inquisitors, and far worse horrors will enter our tunnels." She gestured to the rubble blocking their escape. "Our plans have been sabotaged, but we are the Wraith. We do not give up. Grab only what you can carry. Prepare to leave and never return."

Redge's broad shoulders and chiseled face pressed through the crowd to stand at the front of them. "And go where?"

"South," Laela said. "We spread out, navigate the Spine in the small parties you've been grouped into. We'll follow the Tears and reunite at Fort Cybel."

"We'll be walking right into the Underground's trap for us!" Redge spat. Many others shared his concern.

Laela feared this. She couldn't tell them the whole truth, not without openly defying Threyna, Aylenia, and the Underground. *Can't afford to risk that. All it would take is one whisper on Aylenia's arcanatek communicator and the Underground would come in force to collect us. They must believe we are desperate enough to cooperate.*

"No," Laela said. "We do not need to worry about the Underground, because we are going to Octarius. They have offered us sanctuary."

If Rance's death brought despair and news of traveling south brought outrage, this was enough to start a riot. Screaming voices shouted over one another in cacophony. Laela held her arms up for silence, but it was Redge who regained the crowd's composure.

"Who are you to lead us?" Redge asked. "You are not Rance. You are not Verinius. You're just a Sword."

Redge was right. She wasn't a leader. But she'd been around leaders since she could speak. First Victarius Kaine and Aarkos Velar. Then Arenius Desius and Theodyn Perill—or at least who she thought was Theodyn—before being First Sword to Rance himself. She'd been a part of strategic meetings, served in crucial operations, and been on the front lines for the Wraith. *Were there better potential leaders?* Laela certainly hoped so. But right now, someone, *anyone,* was better than no one, and they didn't have the time to debate who should lead. She'd given them a piece of truth; now she would give them hope.

"You're right," Laela said. "I am not Rance, nor am I anything like him. Ghosts, we may never see his like again. And by every feather of Neutreen's wings, you better believe I do not wish to stay and fight alongside the Underground for this cursed and forsaken land, but I will not let Rance's dream die because we are unable to accept aid when we are in desperate need. We go to Octarius, but we will carry on what Rance rebirthed, what the Undergrounders were meant to provide to the people of Rheynia—a hope. A future. A kingdom beyond the curse.

"Today we have suffered many losses, but we *are not* defeated. We march for Octaven. We leave now. But believe you me, that is not where our story ends. We will not join the Underground's war. We will escape Rheynia—but this night, we must only escape Aranoc and our pursuers."

Redge clenched his muscled jaw, his dark brows pinched visibly even from this distance, but he offered no refute. Laela's words were enough. At least for now. The Wraith wouldn't be happy. Neither would Threyna and the Underground with her declaration to eventually escape. But for now, it would have to be enough.

"Get ready," Laela said. "Take only what you must. We leave at once."

As people began to move to purpose in disgruntled fear, Laela allowed herself a shaky breath. She felt naked absent her customary blades. With only the stolen short sword, a knife in her vambrace, and *True* in her boot, she needed to replenish before the long march. The way would be treacherous. With hollowed and hellhounds in their path, legionaries chasing them from behind, and the Underground lying in wait, she did not want to be caught empty-handed.

On her way, Canton intercepted her with Dracus pawing at him from behind.

"Tell me the plan," Canton said.

Laela gestured to the rail overlooking the cavern where she'd just made her speech. "You heard me. I just told everyone."

"See," Dracus said. "There *is* no plan."

"No," Canton said, shaking Dracus's grip from his arm. "Tell me the truth."

Laela glared from the boy who had followed her around since their time at the Underground to the man she once idolized. "Fine. But tell Threyna, and so help me, I'll hollow you myself." She leaned close, glancing around to make certain no one was listening. She'd noticed Aylenia skulking earlier, but now she was nowhere to be seen.

"I sent Rosler and Taggart through the Gullies," Laela whispered. "We'll make our escape from the Underground's escort, and meet them at Talon's Grip. Then the only ones left to stop us will be the Aeritans."

A grin slashed across Canton's slender face. "We're with you, then."

Dracus tossed his head back, muttering under his breath.

Laela scoffed. "Prime news. If that'll be all…" Turning from them to go see what was left in stock in the armory, Laela caught Threyna making her way towards them. With black rot stretching down her arm and the color drained from her cheeks. she looked as if she'd seen the Skeleton King himself.

Whatever courage she'd managed and composure she'd mustered for her speech—her foundation cracked. Before Threyna could open her mouth, Laela knew.

They're here…

CHAPTER 30

DEWSKULLED

Dracus VIII

He hadn't expected the elated relief he held in Canton's embrace moments ago to last long, but he hoped it would last longer than a few breaths. The only things Laela's address did was give Canton hope, and worse—options. Her plans to travel south to accept the Underground's offer of sanctuary with thoughts of a future escape were preposterous. He knew better than anyone—Arilette didn't *let* people leave. Not without paying a price. But this admission, the truth beneath her poorly veiled lies, was worse.

Escape the Underground's escort? Make it past Octarius to the Grip? Even *if* the ships were still floating in the cove, even *if* the Underground hadn't created some sort of blockade, Rosler and Taggart still had to make it through the Gullies. Too many ifs on both sides of the Spine. The chances of success were shades to a corpse, and now Canton had taken the bait of Laela's false hope. To make matters worse, even if all went as planned, Canton could decide once they reached Octaven that Threyna and the Underground were worth fighting alongside.

Threyna shoved past Dracus and Canton, making for Laela.

Ay, watch it," Dracus called after her, but she didn't acknowledge him.

Laela stopped, noticing her sister.

"They're here," Threyna said. "The Order. Hundreds of them."

"Where?" Laela looked over Threyna's shoulder as if she were half-expecting to see a legion charge in from the atrium.

"The tunnels to the west."

Laela shook her head. "How can you tell?"

"I just can!" Threyna reached for the cursed Blessing on her arm.

Fawkes emerged from the stairway on the opposite end of the overlook from behind Laela, an armful of swords in his grasp. Aylenia followed not too far behind.

"Got swords from the armory," Fawkes said. "Wanted to grab a few 'fore everyone else got their hands on 'em." Seeing the long faces, he paused. "What's wrong?"

"Order," Canton said.

"How much time?" Laela asked.

"Not enough," Threyna said. "Did you mean what you said… about going to Octarius?"

Laela's steely gaze met Threyna's. "Every word."

Threyna inhaled sharply. "Fine. Aylenia, stick with Laela. Make sure she keeps her word."

Aylenia jutted her head forward, cocking her brow. "Where are you going?"

"The tunnels," Threyna said. "I'll hold them off. You make sure everyone gets out."

Dracus scoffed. *Bad to ghosting worse. We need to get out of here and far away from these two hellhounds.* He didn't know which sister was worse—Threyna for believing she could take down the Order, or Laela for thinking she could outwit Arilette.

"By yourself?" Aylenia asked. "Blood magic or not, you can't hold back an entire legion alone."

Just as Dracus was about to grab Canton and pull him away from this ever-hollowing situation, Canton spoke up. "She won't be alone. We'll help."

Fawkes blinked at Dracus, his arms full of swords.

Dracus stammered. "You lot must have dewskull. What darkling put this into yer head?" He dragged his hand down his face. "Nah. You're on your own there. We're—"

"We've already left Rance to die on his own," Canton said. "We're not letting Threyna do the same."

"We can collapse the tunnels," Fawkes said, meeting Dracus's eyes. "I can collapse the tunnels."

Dracus could only stare. *Fawkes, what are you doin'?*

Fawkes shrugged. "Like ya said, we ain't coming back, and it's kinda late to run away. If we're gonna do this, we'll need to do it together. Ya know; divided, ruin will reign—all that blood and bone." He dumped the sheathed swords into Laela's arms, keeping two for himself. "Gonna need more than one sword if yer gonna keep bein' Mistress of Blades."

Laela hmphed. "Fine, then. Blow the tunnels." She nodded at Threyna. "Fort Cybel."

"Fort Cybel." Threyna turned to go.

Fawkes shoved a sword into Canton's hands as the two made to follow. Laela strapped a long sword onto her back and another short sword onto her hip. Aylenia did the same.

"Looks like you're in this now too," Laela said.

Dracus growled. "For now." He glared, chewing his mustache as Laela and Aylenia went the opposite way of Threyna, Canton, and Fawkes. He felt cursed. Hopeless.

Is there any way to stop this?

"Divided, ruin will reign," he said aloud, repeating Fawkes's words. He stroked his mustache. "I don't reckon forced unity's any better."

Without another choice, he hobbled—sore foot, head aching, and hollowed to the core—after Canton and Fawkes, hoping against hope that this wouldn't be their last mistake.

CHAPTER 31

THE STONE GOLEM

Threyna XIII

The hum grew to a buzz as if a whirring arcanatek were strapped to her hip. There wasn't. She'd lost it and all of her Dawnshards in the bog. All she had left was a Nightfall, and in a narrow tunnel packed wall to wall with legionaries, that was about as useful in a fight as a Teller. She was out of useful arcanatek, but she had a power much stronger. If she could harness it.

But blood magic or not, that wasn't why she volunteered to collapse the tunnels by herself. She couldn't risk sending another of her friends to their demise, but perhaps even more so than that, the prospect of facing down an entire Order legion was preferable over traveling all the way to Octarius with Laela.

Aylenia will get the Wraith there. I'll catch up. One darkling at a time.

"We got some scraps tucked away," Fawkes said, hurrying to catch up. "Get me a short fuse and a trip wire, and we'll bury some skulls."

Threyna hmphed. "I didn't ask you to come."

"Didn't need to." Fawkes winked. "Yer helpin' our people escape. That ain't lost on me."

His grin was contagious. Once she had thought of him as an uncle, and he hadn't changed a bit in ten years—quick to smile and calm while the world was burning. Not in a numb or disconnected way, but a wise, contemplative fashion. Like a less-literate Ebrus, he was too kind for this fallen world. But as the shade of a smile tugged at her lips, her sentiment soured.

Push comes to shove, he'll leave me again. Everyone leaves.

"We want to help," Canton chimed in.

Threyna quickened her pace, wishing they had just let her go alone. Unable to outrun them, she hid in her Inner Throne, but the Skeleton King sat in her chair. Threyna startled, but red lightning flickered outside the stained-glass windows, and in an instant, her grandfather was gone, replaced by her father. Another bolt of lightning struck, and she was back in power.

She shuddered before gritting her teeth. This connection, this kinship she had with the Skeleton King, made the hairs on the back of her neck stand. *If I must deal with his presence, he could at least show me how to use the ghosting magic.* But even after thinking it, cold sweat trickled down her spine. She shook the notion away as Fawkes jogged ahead.

"This way." The big man waved over his shoulder as he bounded down the stairs.

Threyna stopped at the top of the flight. "They're this way." She jabbed her thumb in the direction of the approaching legionaries she could feel beyond the walls of her Inner Throne.

"Arcanatek stores are down here," Fawkes said. He nodded at Canton. "You go with Threy. I'll be back in a spell."

As Fawkes charged down the stairs, Canton turned towards Threyna, his face split by a toothy grin. "A spell? Blood and bone, who talks like that?"

Threyna inhaled sharply. The mannerisms and timing reminded her altogether too much of someone else, but Yevon was gone. Hollowed and vortexed until his darkling attempted to take Threyna's body for his own. *All because Canton killed him.*

It wasn't fair to judge him for it, but when her mind melded with Yevon's, she saw his last moments… and Canton's slash that ended him.

With a grunt, she spun from Canton and set off down the hall towards the marching legions. The heartbeats echoed through the narrow tunnels, but there were others above as well. Enough arcanatek-wielding Justicus to pursue every last refugee who escaped Aranoc.

That'll be Laela's problem. For now, I just need to buy them time.

"Hey," Dracus shouted down the tunnel.

Threyna and Canton stopped.

"Ya wanna stop them from gettin' in, here's where ya gotta wall it off. They'll have to backtrack halfway to the bog before they can turn back."

Threyna scoffed. *Spoken like a true runner.* All the Wraith were the same, looking for the easy way instead of the most effective. She had expected better of Dracus, but his time in the Wraith had dulled what made him formidable in the Order and what made him useful in the Underground.

"I'm not trying to block them," Threyna said, continuing on her path. "I'm trying to bury as many legionaries as I can."

Canton guffawed. "Gory ghosts, yes!"

As Threyna charged forward, she realized the Order was closer than she had originally thought. The heartbeats thundered outside the walls of her Inner Throne as she neared a section where two tunnels converged into one.

"Here," Threyna said through labored breath.

Canton came up beside her and put his hands on his knees. "Which way?"

"Both."

Before Canton could catch his breath or return his eyes to the appropriate level of openness, Dracus approached.

"Of all the bad ideas, this one's gotta be the worst."

"You don't have to be here," Threyna snarled. "You can run. I know that's your specialty."

Dracus grunted. "Can't win 'em all so don't make much sense fightin' every ghost damned chance ya get."

"Spoken like a true turn-cloak," Threyna spat back.

"Stop," Canton said. "We're all here. Might as well work together. Now what's the plan?"

Threyna's glare softened, drifting towards Canton. She shrugged. "See if I can do half of what my father did in Valefort. Buy Fawkes time to rig the explosives."

"See *if...*" Dracus threw his hands up. "Gonna get us all hollowed."

Threyna ignored him. The Order's legionaries were close enough that their footsteps echoed through the tunnel. Fawkes approached from behind, his arms full with an assortment of mismatched incendiary devices and a stretch of crimped trip wire.

"I'm here," Fawkes said through labored breaths. He examined the convergence point before them, inspecting the stone framework and the rotting wooden support beams reinforced with iron. "This can work." He gazed down the tunnel to the army of arcanatek-wielding men ready to hollow any who stood in their way.

"How long will you need?" Threyna asked, feeling the gale of heartbeats howling against the walls of her Inner Throne.

Fawkes shook his head. "Longer than we got."

"Get to work then," Threyna said. "I'll hold them off."

Fawkes began rigging the explosives. Dracus swore at how stupid this was. Canton bickered with him to be more helpful, but Threyna blocked them all out, tapping deeper into her Inner Throne.

Sitting alone, enthroned, she felt power at her fingertips, but it lay dormant beyond a veil she couldn't see past.

How did Father do it?

She recalled the spider legs that stretched from his back, the wings that carried him above the courtyard, the shields he conjured as the Order attacked, and the weapons he forged out of nowhere in the blink of an eye.

I can too.

She imagined blood bowing to her will. Though she could sense the well of power prickling at her insistence, the approaching footfalls beyond the walls of her Inner Throne made her stomach churn. Panic flitted through her, but panic wouldn't collapse the tunnels, wouldn't stop the Order, wouldn't allow the Wraith to escape and make it to the Underground.

Focus!

Sinking deeper into her Inner Throne, she blocked out the encroaching tide of soldiers threatening to drown her. She drew in breath, deep and slow, calming her mind. Red lightning sparked again beyond the stained glass, but this time, Threyna didn't shudder. She allowed the energy outside to flow into her, coursing through her veins.

No longer was she sitting upon her Inner Throne, but standing on the dais. The magic the Skeleton King wielded to forge a tyrannical empire was the very weapon she'd use to tear it down. Rage for her father's mistreatment throbbed in her heart. A gnawing guilt bit at her conscience for her mother's demise. But strongest of all, a fury for the Wraith stirred within her like a tempest.

If they hadn't run ten years ago, if they weren't always trying to run now, we could have destroyed the Order a long time ago.

Her parents would still be alive. Maybe they'd still be together had they all stayed and fought at the Battle of the Cut. No more Order. No more Dominion. No more quotas or collections. She and Laela could have actually been like sisters. But no. Instead she only had lost parents, dead friends, and a sister already planning to betray her.

Threyna screamed down the tunnels at the charging legionaries, their arcanatek illuminators bouncing as they ran. Those approaching from the left came faster than the legion in the adjacent tunnel.

"Need more time," Fawkes said as he ran the trip wire from the outermost wall of the left tunnel to the opposite side. "Get out ahead of me. Here." He handed Threyna a handheld crossbow with a line of half a dozen small bolts mounted to the handle.

Threyna stepped over the trip wire, fitting one of the short bolts to the bow.

"Careful," Canton said, fixing a bolt to his own crossbow as he followed Threyna into the tunnel. "They're laced with Dreadroot oil."

Threyna grimaced. Not exactly the arcanatek bolts she was used to. These might slow an attacker, cause a limb to go limp, but they wouldn't blow a hole through armor and scorch the man inside it.

"This ain't gonna work," Dracus said, drawing his own crossbow.

The legionaries were close enough now that they weren't just bobbing lights in the distance, but a jumble of arms and legs churning forward.

"Blasters ready!" a legionary shouted.

Arcanatek whirred to a charge, but Threyna struck first. She pulled the trigger. A grunt, a falling illuminator, and the yelp of others tripping over the downed legionary accompanied her reloading. Kneeling beside her, Canton and Dracus's bowstrings *thrummed* into the crowd of incoming legionaries, but for every one that fell, three more charged over them. Ruthless, relentless—like hollowed after a shade, they kept coming.

"Shields!" a legionary cried.

The illuminators were near enough to cast the walls of the tunnels around them in an eerie glow. Threyna fired, wound the crank, and fired again, but her shots clanged off shields as the arcanateks' buzz grew louder.

Threyna dropped to her belly and aimed lower, hoping to hit a leg below the shield wall. "Down." Threyna yanked Canton to the ground as Dracus rolled onto his back to wind the crank of his crossbow.

Several stunning blasts of irradiator fire flew overhead, but none found targets.

"How much longer?" Dracus shouted to Fawkes, flipping onto his stomach to fire another bolt into the charging legion.

"Almost there!" Fawkes cried. "Company down the other tunnel."

"Gory ghosts."

Threyna unloaded another bolt from her belly. Her target fell forward with a cry, his shield clattering to the ground. More bolts snapped from bowstrings, but no matter how many legionaries fell, there was always another to replace the fallen.

Threyna reloaded her crossbow. *Last one.* Taking aim, she squeezed the trigger. They were nearly upon them now. Another wave of irradiator blasts fired through the tunnel, but this time, they aimed at the ground. The radiant energy scarred the ground only an arm's reach from Threyna's head. Another streaked the wall beside Dracus, and several others burned just overhead.

"Outta time, Fawkes!" Dracus shouted as the Order closed in.

"We have to retreat," Canton said.

As the last blasters sizzled past, Threyna gained her feet and released Fawkes's crossbow in exchange for her short sword. There was a time and place for retreat. She would—they would have to—but not yet. Not until she taught the Wraith that the Order could bleed.

"No!" Threyna said. "We stand."

Only a few paces away, legionaries drew their steel. With five abreast, the Order's formation was packed too tightly to allow movement. Their restriction was Threyna's opening.

Sinking deeper into her Inner Throne, she felt their heartbeats hammering, the bloodlust that drove them, and the accolades they'd receive for victory. Threyna would be their denier.

Shoulder to shoulder with Canton and Dracus, Threyna stabbed over an advancing shield. The legionary attempted to block, but his shield arm got caught on his neighbor. Her steel slashed through the side of the legionary's neck. The wounded man staggered, creating an opening. Dracus thrust into the opening, striking a Justicus through the ribs. Canton slammed his short sword into the approaching shields—once, twice—but they continued to advance, pushing Canton back.

Threyna and Dracus backpedaled with him, keeping in formation despite losing ground. Deflecting a thrust, Threyna countered with a downward hack of her own that glanced off a shoulder. More blood filled the air, calling to her, pulsing with a life all its own. It begged her to use it. To harness it. To give it purpose and shape. Black veins snaked down her arm toward her elbow with the strain of obeying its call, but no blood weapons took shape at her command.

"Fawkes!" Dracus shouted. He kicked a knee, buckling it backwards, and slammed his short sword down, lowering the shield in his path. With a horizontal hack, he slashed across the legionary's throat. Blood spouted from the gash, spraying Dracus before the hollowed man fell, gurgling.

"Got it!" Fawkes said.

But before they could retreat, Canton cried out. A crimson crescent followed the legionary's steel across Canton's arm.

"Canton!" Dracus slid behind Threyna, abandoning her right flank to yank Canton backwards. Dracus stabbed Canton's attacker through the shoulder, then shoved the shield back. Instead of following up with a hollowing blow, Dracus retreated, shoving Canton towards the convergence of the tunnels.

With no one else to divert their defenses, all five legionaries collapsed in around Threyna. Before she could scold Dracus or cry out for aid, steel raced across her right arm. Blood dribbled down the wound as black veins slithered up from the bangle to her left shoulder.

She blocked a downward chop, but as the impact vibrated down her sword, pain sliced across her hip. Threyna backpedaled, but the legionaries corralled her, charging forward like juggernauts.

Blood filled the tight confines of the tunnel. The metallic scent of it flooded her nostrils. The intangible vitality called to her, begging her to command it.

Threyna sank into her Inner Throne, but within, she was drowning. Blood poured from the ceiling like the midday rains, rippling the surface as the gore climbed the walls to paint her Inner Throne scarlet. A force dragged her beneath the surface. But when she feared she wouldn't be able to breathe, she realized she'd never drawn breath before. Every waking moment of her life to this point, she had been drowning, dying a slow, inevitable death. But now... now, she was alive.

She drank the blood within her Inner Throne, and without. She swung her unarmed left hand at the nearest legionary. Unthreatened by the unarmed strike, he barely reacted, but before her eyes, a bloody blade spawned in her closed fist. The bloodborne sword cleaved through the wide-eyed legionary's neck.

A resounding *click* rang through the tunnel, but Threyna didn't concern herself with it. More blood, more life flooded the tunnel. She roared, slashing with blood and steel. Bodies fell around her. No longer retreating, she took the offensive as legionaries, recognizing the blood magic, screamed in fear.

They were right to fear her.

But as she swung again with her blood-forged blade, she noticed the rot stretching down her arm to blacken her knuckles. Gasping, Threyna hesitated. Her bloodborne sword fell to ash.

A firm jerk on the back of her tunic sent her stumbling backwards. "C'mon, dammit!" Dracus hauled her away from the legionaries with one hand while he hurled a beeping Nightfall into their frontlines. The arcanatek exploded in darkness, blotting out the legionaries' illuminators.

"This way!" Fawkes waved them down the tunnel where Canton nursed a bloody slash across his forearm.

As they neared the trip wire, Dracus pointed it out, and together they vaulted over it as the legionaries resumed their pursuit. Once past the convergence, Fawkes hurled another Nightfall into the tunnel.

"Run!" Fawkes shouted.

Panting, arms aching with fatigue, and wounds stinging with the memory of steel, Threyna retreated. Black veins devoured the entirety of her left arm. A hollow numbness throbbed within her chest.

"How much of the tunnel will collapse?" Canton asked, leading the way back to the cavern.

"Dunno," Fawkes said. "Don't wanna find out eith—"

The ground shook. The walls around them threatened to cave. Screams reverberated throughout the tunnel. A swell of heat roared at her back before the ceiling crumbled, devouring the heat like a stone golem. Yet it wasn't satisfied. The snapping jaws of the collapsing tunnel nipped at their heels, threatening to bury them all.

A fault line rippled through the ceiling above their heads.

The exit to the overlook atop the main cavern was just ahead. The orange glow of torchlights illuminated their escape. Threyna pumped her arms and legs, pulling ahead of the others.

She wanted to run to the light, to make sure after all this, she survived to finish what her father started, but she retreated inward to the darkness of her Inner Throne to find she wasn't alone.

Sitting in a puddle of blood on the tile floor before her dais, Threyna inclined her gaze to her throne. The Skeleton King leaned forward within her chair, his face gaunt, his eyes sunken. Weary as the old man appeared, his eyes, the same shade of blue as hers, rippled with recognition.

Dread ensnared Threyna's heart like Dreadroot. Close enough to hear his breathing, smell the scent of death that clung to him, she couldn't look away from the monster.

He took measure of her, inclining his head before standing to his feet. He towered over her, yet the amused expression splitting his pale, thin lips was practically inviting. As if he welcomed her to try, like every other who sought to take his claim before her.

He hmphed, turning his back on her.

Then the light of her Inner Throne winked out, and all went black.

CHAPTER 32

A DEAL WITH DARKLINGS

Laela XII

Tarus waved another group through the southern tunnels. "Go!" Disgruntled, another band of confused and concerned members of Aranoc's Wraith relented their arguments and demands for answers to obey Tarus's orders.

A young girl, overburdened with a stack of blankets taller than she could see over, wobbled, dropping two onto the hard-packed ground. Laela bent down to pick them up, smiling at the girl with brown braids hanging behind her shoulder.

As if a smile could bring courage...

The girl was no older than she had been when she and her parents fled the Artificers after the fall of Victarius Kaine. She remembered how scared she was, and rightfully so. Nothing had gone right since. She'd been on the run or hiding her entire life. Sansia was supposed to be the hope for little girls like her. Rance had given them that hope. But now that hope was buried beneath a pile of rubble.

There's still a chance. Be strong. Be courageous.

Laela stood, tucking the blankets under her arm. "I'll take these. You need to watch where you're going."

"Are you coming?" the little girl asked, cocking her head. She too had a feather pendant next to her fatekeeper. Golden, and as beautiful as she was.

A knot formed in her throat. *I'm going to get you to Sansia...* She swallowed and nodded into the tunnel. "Right behind you. Run along now."

Tarus growled at the stragglers of another group. "Hurry up. Order's comin', didn't ya hear?"

"We should go too," Aylenia said from beside Laela.

Laela gestured to the tunnel's mouth. "No one's stopping you."

Aylenia smirked. Her thick, dark brow cocked, and she bit her lower lip as if something Laela said gave her pleasure. "Nice try, but you won't get rid of me that easily."

Laela rolled her eyes, waving another group into the tunnel. "You've already seen to it that we can't escape. Where else would we go? You've got us trapped in the soul jar, so for Neutreen's sake, give it a rest."

Aylenia crossed her arms over her chest, shifting her weight into one hip. "You heard your sister. I go with you. I make sure you keep your promises."

Laela pursed her lips and leaned in until she was practically nose to nose with the Undergrounder. "Oh, believe me, I keep my promises."

If Aylenia was intimidated, she gave no sign. Being so close to her, Laela recalled when they were girls back in Octarius's depths. She never backed down then either. Even after her mother never returned from Sansia's lost settlement, Aylenia never lost heart. *If only she'd come north instead of staying with Arilette... Instead, now I have a keeper.*

Still smirking through her bit lip, Aylenia backed away, not letting Laela out of her sight.

"This is taking too long," Redge said to Tarus, glancing up at the overlook as if the Order were going to charge in at any moment.

He was right, but she had already done everything she could think of. While most were funneled out the southern tunnels to the Spine, she'd sent Rosler, Taggart, and their company through the Gullies towards the fleet, and even sent a handful of groups up to the city for those who elected to hide rather than engage in the mad dash to Octarius. Short of sending more people through the Gullies, which was as enticing a prospect as volunteering to host a darkling, there weren't any alternatives.

Redge had dragged Verinius from the corner to sit him by the tunnel, but he assumed the same position she'd found him in. Despite the change of scenery from the north wall to the southern exit, he offered no insight or ideas on how to expedite their exodus. Cross-legged, hugging his knees, and rocking back and forth, the aedile continued to mumble incoherent drivel.

Laela didn't know what to do about him. Rance's motto was, *"no one left behind,"* but at what cost? They'd emptied half of the cavern so far, but if Threyna was right and the Order was as close as she feared, then dead weight would have to be cut loose.

"Open to suggestions," Tarus said to Redge. "Otherwise keep it shut."

Redge grunted, but said nothing. As the crowd began to realize the same thing, people began shoving and arguing.

"Break that up," Laela said to Aylenia. "Make yourself useful. Keep everyone calm."

Aylenia narrowed her eyes.

"I'm not going to run away," Laela said through her teeth.

Aylenia gave a mocking bow. "At once, Premius."

Laela scowled.

"What's her deal?" Redge asked. "Clearly, she's not an Avengardian."

Tarus scoffed, hustling people along. "What, 'cause she's Palogian? Sorry, you're not the only one."

Redge's finely plucked brows narrowed to daggers atop his dark eyes. "My family has been here since before the Disasters. We burned prayers on Bheric's Day and made offerings in the Grotto on Cybel's Eve just like everyone else. I'm Rheynian."

For a moment, Laela thought she was going to have to break up a fight herself.

Tarus, considerably smaller than Redge, only grinned from beneath his hood, and good thing too. He didn't become the Second Sword without the skill to back up his mouth. She had no doubt Redge wouldn't be the first to mistake that size and strength could overcome skill.

Tarus shrugged. "Whatever you say."

Just as Redge readied a reply, the entire cavern trembled. Loose stone vibrated, and whatever stalactites hadn't fallen during the collapse of the east tunnel rained down on the gathered Wraith as the west tunnel collapsed.

"Stay calm!" Laela shouted, attempting to steady herself. But there was no hope in staying calm. The steady stream of small groups they'd allowed out to ensure they didn't trample each other in their escape erupted into a flood. Flowing like the Bherian River after the midday rains, people charged into the tunnels and away from the falling debris.

Before Laela could stop them, she was swept up into the tide of screaming people shoving their way into the narrow passage.

She called for the people behind her to stop, but she might as well have been yelling for the cavern's ceiling not to fall. Glancing over her shoulder, she spotted Tarus before he too got lost in the dark tangle of screams and flailing limbs. Shoved into the back of the people before her, she never saw the body she trampled over.

Sorrow knotted in her throat, but though it was the first body she was forced to step over in the manic flight from the tunnels, it wasn't the last. As the tunnels separated, diverging into different paths along the Spine, the pace slowed as the pressure dissipated.

She slunk off to the side of the tunnel, out of the way of everyone's escape. Balling her fist, she rested her forehead against the stone, staring down at her boots. Even in the dim light, she could see the bloodstains on the leather.

Squeezing her eyes shut, she tore herself away from the wall. She wanted to blame Threyna. She collapsed the tunnel. She was the reason they were in this mess in the first place. But she couldn't. She knew this wasn't Threyna's fault. Neither was what happened to her mother. But this *was* the Underground's fault. And Threyna *was* an Undergrounder.

Fist still clenched, she started down the least traveled of the tunnels. She was a leader now, whether she liked it or not. She'd never seen Rance become so emotional, and it would not do her well to allow the others to see her in such a state. Not if she wanted the Wraith to follow her out of the hellscape Threyna and the Underground had put them in.

Be strong. Be courageous.

Putting up her boundaries, she followed the tunnel, hand tracing the stone wall as her feet dragged. There were people ahead of her, people behind, but not close enough to hear her prayers.

"Neutreen, get us through this. Guide me so that I might guide them back to your embrace beyond the curse. Do not forsake us. Do not let us fall into the hands of the Order or the Underground. Please. Please?"

Doubt drowned strength and strangled courage.

Laela's nerves were frayed, yet her journey hadn't even begun. It was a hard day of travel to Fort Cybel, then the better part of another to Talon's Grip. *How many of us will make it? How many have I already lost?* She fought off the urge to look back, denied the desire to stare down at the blood on her boots. They wouldn't serve her.

"No one left behind," Rance had said. But he was gone now, and there was no way everyone could have survived this venture, yet she didn't believe she would lose people within her own tunnels. Beneath her own feet.

Her stomach churned. Her back ached. She didn't know if those who had perished could be restored by Neutreen, nor was she sure the goddess wouldn't count their losses against her, but there was only one way forward.

She stared straight ahead, rubbing at her hand where the hollowed had bitten her. Drawing nearer to an exit into the mountain pass of the Spine, she didn't know if she should hurry forward to join one of the small groups she'd sent ahead, or hang back to join the next. But as she neared the exit to the tunnel, faraway screams filtered into the passageway.

Underground... or Order?

Laela was already running, sword drawn. The tunnel became a jagged set of short but steep switchbacks to the surface. Her legs, stiff and achy, forgot their misgivings and propelled her toward the screams.

Not knowing what she would find when she emerged from the tunnels to the crags, she crouched, surveying her surroundings. Arcanatek whirred and fired. Shadows ran. Exposed steel caught the glints of moonlight that fought through the fog's shroud. The scent of blood tinged the air, proving this wasn't the Underground's doing, but the Order's.

Threyna said they were coming through the tunnels! They couldn't turn back. They couldn't wait them out. Their only option was to run, and hope to be amongst the lucky few to escape the Order's justice.

Below her, a handful of shapes descended the stony crags. Pursued by a group of sword and arcanatek-wielding Justicus, they'd never make it out.

"Hide if you know what's good for you," her father's voice said, taunting her from the past. *"That's all you're good for."*

Ignoring him, she grit her teeth, and leapt from the ledge. Wind rushed past until she landed atop the back of the rear-most legionary.

In a flail of steel and limb, the man crumbled beneath Laela's gravity-aided attack. She flung off his plumed helm, grabbed the hair on the back of his head, and slammed his face into the stone path. Shoving herself off of him, she slashed twice at the backs of his legs, severing his tendons. A blood-curdling scream tore from him as she kicked the arcanatek free from his hand and ripped the sword from his grasp.

Two other legionaries turned to face her, standing shoulder to shoulder with warbling blasters trained on her, but three more pursued the Wraith refugees. Silent as a shade, deadly as a hellhound, Laela charged at the men taking aim, swords in either hand. The first fired. Bright radiant energy spotted the dark horizon, but Laela lurched left.

The blast sizzled past.

The second fired, but Laela spun, slicing through the air to close the distance. She backslashed with her stolen left sword, swiping the nearest blaster away, then followed with a diagonal chopping forehand. Her blade carved down atop his shoulder, cracking bone. As he fell to her blade, Laela torqued, ducking and thrusting to stab her left sword into the second legionary's gut.

They fell like leaves of a tree withering in a Dreadroot's grasp, but Laela didn't stop to survey her carnage. Neither wound would hollow quickly;

that meant no immediate risk of adding a hollowed or a darkling to the mix, allowing her to cleave a path for her people's escape.

The fallen's screams would alert the Order that not all of the Wraith's flock were sheep.

"Don't get ahead of yourself, girl." Her father's voice grated her nerves.

Sidestepping a large rock and leaping over the trunk of a rotten tree, Laela ran, hoping to make up the distance. The Order gained on the party of Wraith refugees faster than she could catch up.

"Hey!" she shouted after them, hoping to distract them from their prize, but these weren't the poor farmers or shepherds who'd taken up weapons to join the Underground's hopeless war. These were trained soldiers, true fighters.

The first arcanatek blast hit a woman in the back. Her scream ripped through the night worse than any shrieking darkling. Something flew from her arms as she toppled to the ground. Two other shapes turned to help, but the legionaries' steel cut them down for the attempt. They stabbed repeatedly, making sure if they hollowed, they wouldn't be able to move, while the other charged an irradiator in the event of a darkling.

A little girl screamed.

No… Laela watched her father burn, Rance get stabbed through the gut, and her mother run into the darkness only to vanish in an explosion of light. She would not let this little girl suffer too.

Laela let out a battle cry, demanding any brave enough to stand against her. All three legionaries turned towards Laela. Slowing to face them, Laela began to pace left and right, pointing her sword at them. "Fight me." She glanced past the men in Order blacks to the little girl behind them shaking her mother. Alive, but stunned from the irradiator's blast, she wouldn't be able to run yet.

Go… Run. Leave her.

Even as she thought the words, she knew the little girl wouldn't. Just as Laela never would have left her mother if it were up to her.

"Leave them," Laela spat at the legionaries, buying time. "Fight me. Unless you're too afraid to fight someone who isn't running away."

Her father tsked at her, but Laela ignored him and the burning scar across her chest.

Two legionaries charged toward her while the third recharged his blaster. Their swords were wet with the blood of two men who only ever wanted to live and die with Neutreen's love. Laela would make sure they paid.

One legionary grinned, a snaggletooth jutting beyond his lip. The other, as stoic as a carving of Neutreen, advanced more hesitantly. Before they could make their move, Laela lunged between them, aiming her first thrust for Snaggletooth's thigh, and her second swipe at Statue's torso. Caught off guard by her aggression, they both blocked, assuming defensive positions, but Laela slipped between them and closed the distance on the legionary with the blaster.

Before he could pull the warbling trigger, Laela hacked the arcanatek in two. Her backslash opened his throat. Praying his darkling would stay trapped in his prison of a body forever, Laela planted her foot and lunged at Statue. To his credit, he parried and countered with a thrust aimed at her head, but Laela was better.

She ducked beneath the thrust, blocked a trio of Snaggletooth's cuts, and riposted with a glancing blow to his sword arm. As the limb went limp, Laela lurched forward, stomping her heel into his toes and driving her shoulder into his chest.

Snaggletooth fell. Before he could hit the ground, Laela repositioned herself to face Statue. She blocked his overhead charge with both blades, and kicked him in the stomach. Then, before Snaggletooth could regain his feet, Laela thrust her sword into his chest. Statue stood, witnessing the carnage she'd dealt with as much expression as his namesake.

Behind Statue, the little girl helped the woman who'd been shot by the blaster to her feet. Laela breathed heavily through her teeth. It wasn't enough. All throughout these wooded mountains, legionaries would be cutting down her people. She was only one soldier in a war against an undefeated army.

If the Underground fought with us to help us flee, then—maybe then—we could make it.

"*If the Wraith quit trying to run and actually learned to fight back—*" Laela walled off her father before he could finish. Yet in the absence of his heckling, hope dwindled. Doubt ensnared her.

Rage replacing her helplessness, she charged at the remaining legionary. Her first strike opened his guard; her second sent him off-balance. She leaned back to avoid his poor excuse at a defensive strike. Then she made her move. She struck him first in the thigh, next in the shoulder, and lastly through his heart.

Skewered on her blade, Statue finally proved he wasn't a face carved from stone. His eyes welled as he opened his mouth to speak his last words. Blood dribbled down his lips as he fell to his knees, releasing his sword.

"Neutreen watches," he said, an affront to everything Neutreen flew for. He interlocked his fingers together, leaving them extended. "But the One knows."

Laela snarled. "You will be judged." She ripped her blade free and slashed across his throat. Blood sprayed from the opened gash, showering her in viscera. Breathing heavily, she stepped backwards as a shade climbed from his body.

Behind her a slow, steady clap resonated off the mountainside.

"Splendid. Truly magnificent," Belrich said, continuing his mock applause. "I must say I am impressed. Now that's not to suggest that you haven't been—hmm, how to put this—quite the Dreadroot in the garden? No, that's not it. Hmm, quite the...oh yes, the dagger in the heart."

Belrich stopped clapping. His gray-green eyes hardened to a ghoulish glare, but he continued to smile.. "Your mother put up quite the fight."

Mother...

"My men managed to save her from the hollowed, but... I put a blade through her heart." He pointed to the dead legionary at her feet. "Just like you did."

If he wanted a reaction, Laela didn't give him one. Not out of strength of will, but out of sheer shock. She felt rooted to the spot. Screams shrieked in the distance. Shades wandered in her peripheral vision, and a semicircle of Inquisitors and legionaries spread out around her.

Mother's gone? She wanted to ask, to know the fate of her mother's soul. She wanted to cry and mourn her suffering, but at the same time, she didn't trust one hollowed word that came from Belrich's mouth.

"And your stepfather," Belrich shook his head, advancing. "Can I call him your stepfather?" Not waiting for a response, he shrugged, drawing nearer. "He put up less of a fight, but entertaining all the same. See, you never quite appreciate privacy until you've had a darkling worm through your thoughts, do you, Laela Velar?"

Laela swallowed. Somehow, he'd learned her name—her true name. Not Huron, her mother's maiden name that she went by. The bloody swords in her hands wouldn't win her this battle. *Can the Order control darklings?* If that was true and Belrich had sent darklings into her mother and Theodyn, there wasn't a single secret she could keep from him.

"You have broken every law of our land, spat on each of Neutreen's Tenets, and betrayed your guests—your prince. You should be impaled. Flayed. And still your punishment would not be enough. Every one of your Wraith renegades should be put in the stocks in the Gullies and left for the hollowed."

His ghoulish grin flattened, becoming a hard line. "That can be your fate if you wish it, but I will offer you this alternative, once and once only. Refuse me and I will make you watch as I impale everyone you've ever known, but work with me..." He held his palms to the shroud of clouds smothering Rheynia and tilted his head. "Work with me and I'll let you leave. All of you."

Laela took a cautionary step backwards as he continued to draw nearer, but the rest of his henchmen surrounded her. The threats entwined with the offer, but she couldn't take one without the other. *Trust Belrich? Believe the Order?* Yet even still, what other options were there? She tried to speak, but her voice croaked. She cleared her throat. "What do you want?"

Belrich's smile returned. The stuff of hellhounds and nightmares. "It is quite a small thing, really. Of inconsequence as far as you and your people are concerned."

A scream tore through the wooded mountains that even gave Belrich pause.

"See, this is the sort of travesty I would like to avoid. I don't want you, Laela. I don't even want your people. If you don't wish to be in the Holy Dominion of Neutreen, don't. If you don't wish to stay here in Rheynia, leave. I know what you think of me—" He held his arms out to gesture towards his Inquisitors. "—of us. But I also know that we are not your enemy." Belrich pointed south. The direction she and her people were heading. "They are. Your sister is."

Equally as entwined as Belrich's threats and promises of passage, Laela's emotions warred. She knew her father had an opinion on the subject, but she kept him walled off. She despised Belrich, hated the Order, and, though he wasn't wrong, agreeing with him made Laela's stomach turn.

The cries of her people running from the Order sent chills down her spine. *We're only running because of the Underground.* She gripped the hilts of her swords. "You still haven't said what you want."

Belrich's grin spread, sharpening the cleft in his chin. "Just like your mother, to the point. I like that, but it is important to me that I make myself as transparent as a shade. In times such as these, all it takes is a little misunderstanding to set the world aflame."

His eye twinkled as if searching to get a rise from her. The scar across her chest burned, but she wouldn't let him see that he was getting to her. Every word he said was a carefully crafted tactic, and though he liked to hear himself speak, there was an intention. *He's stalling...*

"See, I know *you* didn't want to attempt to kill me. It was…Gatius? Yes, Gatius." He shivered. "Heinous name. Seems he should be grateful we put him from his misery. But the truth remains—though he shared your standard, he wasn't with you." He referenced Laela's Avengardian attire.

"He was an Undergrounder." Belrich began to circle her. "Just like your sister. Half-sister. I suppose she never was much of a sister to you, though, was she? Truly a Dreadroot in the garden—see, now that works! She ruins anything she touches. Always has. Always will. Your mother knew it. Your stepfather feared. I know it. You know it."

"You want the Blessing," Laela said. "You think she has it?"

Belrich wagged his finger at her. "Laela, Laela, Laela. Don't play coy." His expression darkened. "I *know* she has it. And so do you. Maybe she has figured it out as well."

Laela pursed her lips, recalling Threyna's ear-piercing scream as the cursed artifact coiled around her.

"We know she's here," Belrich said. "Give her to me. We let the rest of you go."

Laela's fragile façade threatened to fracture. If it were such an easy trade, she'd be a fool not to take it. Her mother would never forgive her for giving Threyna up. *How many lives would be saved by giving her to Belrich? Wouldn't Mother care about the rest of us, about me?* She knew the answer. But even still, her mother was gone. The Order stood in her way, and eventually, Laela planned on leaving Threyna anyway.

"No one left behind." Rance's words might as well have been a blight on her soul as bad as the Blessing was on Threyna's.

Belrich stepped closer. "What will it be, Laela?"

Another harrowing cry erupted along the Spine, sending shivers down her neck.

Laela grit her teeth. *Can I trust Belrich? Could I live with myself if I gave Threyna up?* She imagined escaping Rheynia, arriving in Sansia to be greeted by Neutreen. *Would she deny me my wings even if I brought so many back to her?* But if she refused, there was no escape. She couldn't fight Belrich, half a dozen Inquisitors, and just as many legionaries at the same time.

"Time is of the essence, Lady of Blades," Belrich said. "Choose. Your sister or your freedom?"

Her father was inexplicably silent. She didn't like making a deal with such a darkling either, but it was the hard choice leaders needed to make.

Laela opened her mouth to speak, but stammered. A shrill beeping replaced her words.

Suddenly, the void opened, swallowing everything in pitch black. Darkness devoured Belrich and his men, the rocky crags of the mountains and the safety of the dying woods beyond. Belrich shouted commands, and arcanatek whirred to motion, but something—someone—grabbed Laela around the arm and wheeled her around. Caught off guard, Laela couldn't have resisted if she wanted to.

She was dragged away from Belrich. The wind of grasping hands, lunging blindly, rushed by her. Somehow, she managed to slip between them. Before she could question what was happening, the darkness abated, and the cloudy scene of the Spine returned.

"Run!" Aylenia released Laela's arm.

Bewildered, Laela followed, glancing over her shoulder at the sphere of darkness left behind by the Nightfall.

"You prime?" Aylenia asked.

But still, Laela didn't have words. Unsure if she'd lost the best opportunity she would ever receive, or spared an impossible decision with damning consequences, Laela did the only thing she could; she put one foot in front of the other.

CHAPTER 33

HOLLOWED OUT

Dracus IX

D racus coughed, ejecting dust from his lungs as he dragged himself along the wall of the tunnel. The rumble of the collapsing stone still rattled his chest. One step at a time, he hauled himself out of the tunnel and onto the overlook of the main cavern. He fell to his knees, crawling, coughing, hollowing further.

His shoulder ached from where a falling stone hit him. His throat screamed, stripped raw from breathing in debris. He'd feel like this for the rest of his miserable existence, which was only growing longer by the moment, and would stretch longer yet if Canton and Fawkes kept electing to try to hollow them all.

On all fours, he shuddered out trembling breaths as Fawkes and Canton carried Threyna beyond the tunnel's mouth.

"Wake up, Threy," Fawkes said once they set her down. "C'mon now, yer alright."

No response.

Dracus hoped she was dead, but that's not how it worked. No shade, no darkling, and she wasn't trying to claw at the nearest breathing thing? Still alive.

"She's fine," Canton said. "She has to be."

"She's breathing," Fawkes said, "but that rock hit her good."

Dracus shook his head. "Don't worry 'bout me. I'm gory ghostin' fine." He shoved himself to his feet, wincing. Clouds of dust descended around him as he brushed himself off.

Fawkes tilted his head at Dracus. "You prime?"

"No," Dracus said. "I ain't ghostin' prime. Now let's get outta here before they try findin' another way in."

Canton bent down to pick Threyna up.

"No." Dracus shook his head. "Leave her."

"Leave her?" Canton's eyes practically jutted from their sockets. "Did you not see what she did?"

"I did. And now look at her." Dracus pointed to the black veins snaking up and down her arm from the cursed bangle. "Look at you!" He referenced the slash across Canton's forearm. "If I didn't pull her out when I did, she'd still be in there fightin' and you'd be daydreamin' your trouser fantasies, wondering how best to ask her to join ya on Cybel's Eve."

Canton balked.

Dracus continued in a lower voice. "I know ya think she can make a difference. That maybe, if we band together, we can win... we can't. We won't. We never have, and we never will. Her father wasn't enough, and she won't be either. And now that *that*—" he pointed to the bangle around Threyna's arm. "—has resurfaced, the Skeleton King will make sure—"

"The Skeleton King hasn't been seen since the Battle of the Cut," Canton said.

Dracus scoffed. *Like that means he's gone.* "Neither has the Blessing. Mark me. It's back. He'll come lookin'. Worse, so will Belrich, the Tellers, and anyone else senseless enough to try to wield it. So unless you want to stay here and hollow, our best bet is to leave now. Mark me—anyone found here will go straight to the black cells for the Skeleton King to farm."

Fawkes stepped beside Canton. "Dray, Skeleton King and Underground aside, we can't leave her here. The Order—"

"Yer damn right, the Order. Which is exactly why *we* gotta get outta here. If we quit jawin' and get a move on, we might catch Rosler and Taggart. We get on those ships and get off this rock."

Canton shoved past Fawkes to level his finger at Dracus. "You're not just talking about getting on the ships. You're talking about stealing one, aren't you?"

The condemnation in his voice would have hurt, but Dracus had enough other hurts to distract him. He rolled his eyes, tossing his hands to the cavern ceiling. "You'd rather go to the Grip and watch Laela try to lead the Wraith away from Octarius? Do you not remember what Arilette's capable of? Ya think she'll let us leave after all the work she did to make sure we'd end up on this path? Blood and bone, Cant, she burned her own father alive. She poisoned—"

Dracus cut himself off, tasting the Valefyre all over again. He stammered, unsure how to continue without telling Canton the truth.

Behind Canton, Fawkes nodded, encouraging him as he had time and time again to do exactly that. But he couldn't. Armed with the truth, Canton would use it as an argument to stay and fight. *I can't, Old Boy. I won't.*

"I knew it." Threyna sputtered, rolling onto her side.

Dracus groaned. As much as she'd spared him from having to answer, her being awake presented a wealth of new issues.

"You're all liars," Threyna said, staggering to her feet. "Every last one of you. *'You have my word.'* I should've known better."

Threyna made for the stairs on wobbly knees. Canton followed after her.

Dracus hung his head.

"Tell him," Fawkes whispered. "Tell him the truth. Trust him to make his own decision."

Just like that, Dracus was transported back to Salingard a lifetime ago. The Artificers' thief had taken power coils from three of the biggest depots from Drake Point to Bheric's Hollow, hoping to reignite the Artificer's War after the fall of Victarius Kaine. Dracus had caught him. Not Nerus, not Decimus—Dracus. Another stripe on his pauldron. Another chapter in his storied career. Cavus Kruso would finally meet his end.

Dracus shook the thoughts away, pushing past Fawkes to follow Canton and Threyna down the stairs to the cavern floor, Fawkes on his heels.

"Threyna, where are you going?" Canton attempted to help her down the stairs, but she shrugged away from his touch. "Slow down."

"Slow down? Slow down! You have slowed us down for ten years. Ten years we could have stood together, worked together, fought *together*. Blood and bone, we could have won this war by now, but you've wasted a decade trying to run away instead—"

Dracus grabbed Threyna by the back of her tunic and spun her around to jab his finger into her collarbone. "*You* wasted a decade of our hard work. *You* didn't just slow us down—you *stopped* us."

"I wish we wouldn't have," Threyna said. "Truly. Because what good is an army that won't fight? What good are soldiers who turn and run when blood comes to bone? You say Canton was trapped in his trouser fantasies, but what about you, Dracus? You're the one who pulled him back. You're the reason I had to fight them all by myself, so don't you dare think for a single moment that I owe you a hollowed's shriveled—"

Dracus held the flat of his index finger against her cheek. "You don't owe me? Let's ask the hellhounds I saved you from, eh?"

Threyna wrenched free of him. "Go hollow out, Dracus. Oh…" She cupped her hand to her ear and leaned toward his chest where his silent heart refused to beat. "What's that? Sounds like you—"

Dracus grabbed Threyna by the collar. "Don't. Say. Another word."

Threyna drove her elbow through Dracus's wrist, tearing herself free of his grasp. Without a second glance, she spun on her heel and stalked away, leaving Dracus to clutch his forearm as pain stretched up his wrist. Had he been amongst the living, it wouldn't have bothered him. He would have shaken it off; it might have ached for a bit, but it wouldn't throb for the rest of time. But that wasn't the case. He wasn't living, and he would feel it for the rest of his miserable existence..

Gripping his wrist, Dracus could only snarl at Threyna's back as she descended the stairs.

Canton sucked his teeth at Dracus before grumbling and chasing after her. "Wait, where are you going?"

"I'm going south," Threyna yelled, her voice echoing throughout the cavern. "Like I said I would. Because unlike the Wraith, the Underground keeps its promises."

Canton chased Threyna down the stairs and across the cavern to the southern tunnels. As Dracus and Fawkes reached the cavern floor, Dracus grabbed Fawkes's shoulder.

"She's gonna lead us all to a tragedy," Dracus said. He chewed his mustache. "I know you want me to tell 'em the truth. I know it don't seem right to take the ship for ourselves. I know it ain't fair. But I know how this ends, Old Boy, and it ain't good for any of us."

Fawkes scrunched his bearded face. He took a deep breath, but his eyes flicked toward Canton and Threyna, marching back towards them.

"Order's crawling all over the southern pass," Threyna said as she stormed ahead of Canton towards them. "Where's the entrance to the Gullies?"

"Does that mean you'll come with us?" Canton asked.

"No," Dracus and Threyna said simultaneously before exchanging a heated glance.

"I'm going to work around the Order and find my ghosting sister," Threyna said. "You can get your precious boat and sail away for all I care."

"Fine," Dracus said.

"Fine," Threyna sneered. "Lead the way. And for all our sakes, how about we keep our mouths shut?"

CHAPTER 34

PRISONER OF PROMISE

Laela XIII

They ran. Laela struggled to keep up with Aylenia's long legs though she was taller than her. Weaving through the dying woods, climbing over and through crags, they avoided the Order when they could, and cut through them where they had to. Together, they'd seemingly outrun the legionaries. For now.

Panting, Laela sheathed the sword she'd held onto after letting her other sword go. Not having a second scabbard to holster it, she wasn't willing to let it slow her down. She hoped another of the Wraith would pick it up in her wake; Neutreen knew they'd need steel if they were to make the journey south. Order and Underground aside, there were more terrors in this countryside than any were likely prepared for.

It had been ten years since she'd traveled above ground for any length. Only the Justicus were equipped to handle the hollowed and hellhounds roaming the countryside, and only the Tellers were foolish enough to try doing so without arcanatek. Now, she wished they hadn't collapsed the Underground's tunnel through the Spine nearly a decade ago; it made sense at the time, but the Underground still managed to learn their secrets and plant a saboteur within their ranks anyway. Now she was stuck in the middle of nowhere, sucking down air on her hands on her knees, while Aylenia stood over her.

To make matters worse, Aylenia was barely breathing heavily. Hands on her hips, and looking as if she'd just climbed a set of stairs rather than running for her life up and down a mountain, she made Laela feel like a child. Sweat dampened her brow, making her dark green eyes glisten.

"Now that's a soldier," her father said, looking for any opportunity to put her down. She quickly resealed her Center of Silence, closing him out. Yet she found herself admiring Aylenia anyway.

"How?" Laela said through labored breath. "How are you not…"

One of Aylenia's dark brows dipped until there was no space between it and her eyelashes while the other raised halfway up her forehead. "If this is the setup for some Palogian Islander joke, spare me. How? Because I train."

Laela wasn't trying to make a joke about Aylenia's heritage, but she took an affront to Aylenia's insinuation. "You saying I don't?"

Aylenia shook her head. "You're not this ignorant, are you? Hmm, maybe you are. You were considering making a deal with Belrich Fayte after all."

"I—"

Aylenia held her hand up. "What—were you looking for an escape?" She snorted. "If that were true, you would have seen me trying to get your attention. Certainly would have made my part easier, but you were too busy trading Threyna for a lie."

Laela growled, but there was truth in Aylenia's condemnations.

"Wouldn't have worked," Aylenia said with a shrug. "You saw what her father did with the blood magic. If you think Belrich and a few Inquisitors will be able to take her now, then you don't know ripping anything about her."

Laela hmphed, but again, Aylenia was probably right. Either way, she didn't need a lecture from an Undergrounder. Finally catching her breath, Laela stood to scour the woods. There should have been more Wraith ahead, or bringing up the rear, but the only movement through the fog was the gentle sway of dying branches in the breeze.

"Will you admit it?" Aylenia asked. "About Threyna."

Laela bit her lip, but stepped up to Aylenia to gaze down at her. "I was weighing my options, yes. That's what leaders must do."

Aylenia smirked in self-righteous indignation. "Your own sister." She shook her head. "She figured you'd try to sell her out, but you barely made it ten steps outside of Aranoc. I thought you'd at least make it to Octaven before having second thoughts."

Laela's lips curled back in a snarl, but before she could tell Aylenia off, someone squealed in the distance. Their cry cut short. Barely a breath's span passed before Laela and Aylenia were shoulder to shoulder with swords drawn, staring into the fog.

Without speaking, Laela nudged Aylenia's elbow and nodded in the direction of a thick tree trunk. Together, they sidestepped towards the tree and out of the center of the clearing.

Dead leaves and rotten branches crunched underfoot. A dozen footsteps drew closer. Laela gestured her head to the south, suggesting they run, but Aylenia shook her head.

Laela clenched her teeth. The scar across her chest burned. Her father screamed while he burned alive. Her mother disappeared into the bog, only to be caught and stabbed in the heart by Belrich. She gripped her sword. *Be strong. Be courageous.*

"Watch out, more Dreadroot there," one said.

"Keep your ghostin' voice down," another hissed.

Laela recognized those voices. Stepping beyond the tree, she called out, "Redge, Tarus?"

Emerging from the fog with blades drawn—Redge, Tarus, and a group of refugees from Aranoc strode forward. Some limped. Others clutched themselves, still on high alert from the tunnel's collapse and the Order's attack. Aside from Redge and Tarus, those who held weapons didn't appear like they knew how to use them. Faulty grips, awkward postures, and quivering lips didn't typically translate to sound soldiers.

Laela let out a relieved sigh. "You made it."

"Some of us," Tarus said. "More ahead, more behind, but we can't wait."

Redge stepped ahead of the rest of the group, curved daggers in each hand. "I won't take another step until you tell us the actual plan. The real one."

Laela wrinkled her nose. Maybe he'd heard about her intention to break from the Underground's tether once they reached Fort Cybel, maybe he hadn't, and that was his problem, but speaking of it in front of Aylenia wasn't going to happen. "As I said, we're going south. We can discuss the details on the way, but—"

"No," Redge said. "Now. Not another step. This whole situation has the Underground scribed all over it. Convince me this isn't the Underground's plan. Convince me you're not their puppet."

Laela had enough to worry about without anyone questioning her authority. Yet those standing behind Redge and Tarus seemed curious enough to follow his line of questioning. Though she'd lowered her sword, she squeezed the hilt.

"We don't have time for this," Aylenia said. "You don't want to take another step, fine, wait for the Order to come."

"Spoken like a true Undergrounder." Redge eyed Aylenia up and down, his lip contorted in apparent disgust. He stalked toward her, daggers pawing forward like razor-sharp claws. "I don't know you. Does anyone? Course not. Who wouldn't recognize a—"

Aylenia leveled the tip of her sword between Redge's carefully plucked brows. "Choose your next words carefully, *Redge*."

"Enough." Laela lowered Aylenia's blade and inserted herself between the two. "We're going south."

Redge inhaled sharply. "To our ships or Octarius? What about Rosler and Taggart?" He jutted his chin forward as if to assess whether the names meant anything to Laela. "You sent them east. I need to know—*we* deserve to know; are we heading towards salvation or destruction?"

Flustered, Laela tried to search for a means of shutting Redge up while still assuaging his concerns. Before she could, Aylenia chortled, biting her lower lip.

"Blood and bone, you really are a darkling," Aylenia said to Laela. "Threyna was right not to trust you." She shook her head. "Shame on me for actually believing in you."

"See?" Redge said, jabbing his dagger in Aylenia's direction. "Undergrounder! What's the truth, Laela? We deserve to know."

Seeing no other option, and having already wasted too much time as it was, Laela relented. "Fine. It's true. The Underground planned to trap us, to give us no alternative other than going to them for protection."

Aylenia threw her head back.

"I agreed to their plans," Laela said. "But I arranged for an escape."

Redge nodded, and others began to murmur amongst themselves. As always, Tarus's mysteriously blank expression provided no inkling as to his inward thoughts.

"That's just gory ghosting perfect," Aylenia said. She reached for the arcanatek on her ear, but before she lifted her arm half way, Laela positioned her blade in Aylenia's path.

"Take off the arcanatek," Laela said. "Take it off and give it to me, or lose your hand. Try anything, and it'll be your head."

Aylenia smiled. Her amusement took Laela aback, but she hoped Aylenia wouldn't be foolish enough to test her. Slowly, Aylenia removed the cuff from her earlobe and tossed it to Laela.

Laela caught it. Part of her wanted to keep it. It was unbelievable technology that could revolutionize the world, but she didn't know what it was capable of. *Would the Underground be able to track it? Would the Order?* She couldn't take the chance.

Between her thumb and forefinger, Laela squeezed, bending the soft metal until it snapped. Aylenia winced, but could only seethe through her teeth.

Redge glared at her before turning his attention back to Laela. "You think she'll let us leave?"

Laela bit her lip and gripped her sword. "She won't be able to stop us."

"I mean Arilette," Redge said.

Tarus, typically stoic, practically flinched at her name.

Laela understood. Ten years ago, she'd ruined their lives. And every day between the Battle of the Cut and today's sabotage of their escape, she'd made everything harder than it needed to be.

"No," Laela said. "No, she won't let us leave. But we won't let that stop us."

Laela gazed at Aylenia. The shape of her eyes, the disbelief in her grin, how the curve of her cheek flattened into the trim line of her jaw… Laela wished Aylenia glared back at her. Her hatred would have been more palatable than her betrayed disappointment. But like so many things in this cursed world, she would have to bear the burden of it.

Laela nodded at Redge and Tarus. "We're getting off this cursed island. One way or another. And you…" She fixed Aylenia with a hellhound's stare. "You are not the Wraith's guide. You are our prisoner."

CHAPTER 35

A HILL TO HOLLOW ON

Threyna XIV

Threyna's blood thundered in her ears and flushed her cheeks, but black veins stretched like rotten vines out of the bangle. Up and down her left arm, the corruption snaked. She hoped with time it would dissipate, but even after they'd spent hours worming their way through the Gullies, the rot had only managed to stretch further.

The green glow of the Viridite walls along the Gullies illuminated their path, but it cast her in a ghoulish hue that only made the black rot stand in starker contrast. She examined the bangle. It had *clicked* after she had conjured the blood blade. She'd done something, released something. But whether that was a good thing or not, she didn't know, and she didn't have time to worry about it.

They'd already found trails of fresh blood left in the wake of the shipbound party Laela had deceptively sent ahead. Severed limbs, the black blood of the hollowed, and discarded weapons littered their path. There was no telling how many of the Wraith had left on Laela's mission, or how many were still pursuing it. Hollowed tended not to stay in one place too long, but one thing was clear; not everyone Laela sent was still alive.

Ahead, Canton dragged his feet. Fawkes's gait lilted to the left, his broad shoulder occasionally brushing against the Viridite crags. Despite the length of the day, the emotional tax she'd had to pay, and the scars left behind by the battle in Avengard, the bog, or Aranoc, she didn't feel tired.

That must be the blood magic too.

There was so much she didn't know about her abilities. The Blessing seemed to have a mind of its own. She'd felt it stir when Laela attempted to pry it off her arm. If she hadn't shoved her away when she did, there was no telling what it would have done. But one thing was certain; she could not let Laela lead the Wraith away. Her father had fought and nearly won all by himself, but he wasn't enough to defeat the Order. If she wanted a different outcome, she needed help. As much as she hated to admit it, Laela and the Wraith were the Underground's best hope and she couldn't let them abandon rank just because Laela didn't trust Arilette.

"You're sisters…" her mother had said. Threyna only wished that counted for something.

Fawkes stumbled. Canton caught him, keeping him upright.

"We should rest," Canton said, looking back at Dracus and Threyna. "Been too long on our feet."

"The ships," Fawkes said. "We need to catch up before they leave without us."

"Do you think Rosler and Taggart are making better time?" Canton asked.

Dracus grumbled. "Yeah, you wouldn't mind if they left without us, though, eh? Then we can stay and fight a losing battle, right?"

"Dracus," Fawkes said. The two exchanged weary expressions.

Threyna didn't have time to stop. Canton might not have cared if they got on the ships or not, but she did. If she was going to have any way of catching up to the Wraith and stopping Laela from betraying the Underground, she'd need to get out ahead of them. The only way she could ensure those ships didn't carry the Wraith away from Rheynian soil was to make sure she was on one.

"Stop if you want," Threyna said, "but those ships aren't leaving without me." She shoved past Canton and Fawkes to continue through the Gullies.

Dracus scoffed. "You don't even know where you're going."

"I just need a moment," Fawkes said, leaning against the walls glowing with the sun's stored rays.

Threyna didn't look back. "I can hear heartbeats now. I've got a better chance of finding your people than you do."

Dracus grumbled something to Canton and Fawkes before he came hobbling and wincing after her.

Threyna rolled her eyes at his approach, but didn't slow. "Don't worry. I'm not going to burn your ships, and I don't care if you leave."

Dracus hmphed. "You don't care? And you call Laela the liar. If that ain't the shade calling the darkling dead, I don't know what is."

"No, I don't care," Threyna said, increasing her pace so that Dracus struggled to keep up. "You're three people—two if we're only counting the living ones."

Dracus growled. "Keep yer ghostin' voice down."

"...and if Arilette let you go the first time, then I'm not about to try convincing you to stay," Threyna continued, ignoring Dracus. "Better luck putting darklings back into a broken soul jar then getting Dracus Alius not to turn cloak."

"Me the turn-cloak?" Dracus guffawed. "That the story she's tellin'? She let me go? Ha!"

Threyna didn't want to hear it. She approached a fork in the crags and turned left.

"Wrong way," Dracus said.

"Like you'd tell me the truth anyway," Threyna snapped, continuing down the leftward path. She held up her bangled left arm. "Just like you told me the truth about this? Or about my father?"

Dracus hustled to get close, then grabbed her by the blackened wrist and whipped her around. "I know yer ghostin' mad. Ya even got the right to be. Hate me if ya want, but I haven't lied about everythin'. And I'm not the worst of the liars in your life."

"What's that supposed to mean?"

Dracus took a deep breath. "Your mother wrote letters. She loved you, Threy, whether you wanna believe it or not. She'd stamp the wax with a little dove, even though she never knew why yer father called ya that in the first place."

Threyna bristled. *A dove of House Fayte.* Though the truth of her ancestry stung, it hurt half as bad as the knowledge that she'd never hear her father call her that again.

"I'm tellin' ya, letters were sent," Dracus continued. "So if you never received 'em, who did? Who told ya that I *left* the Underground?" He spat on the ground and cleared his throat as if he'd swallowed a weevil in his bread. "Arilette didn't *let* me leave." He pointed to his chest. "How ya think I hollowed?"

Threyna chewed the inside of her cheek but remained as silent as the still heart in Dracus's chest.

"All I'm sayin' is—what are you fightin' for?" Dracus asked. There was an honesty in his dark eyes, a solemnity in his sullen expression, but he wouldn't understand. How could he?

Her father had left the fatekeeper, the source of the blood magic, to her. Even her mother had said with her last words, *"Divided, ruin will reign, but united…"*

Threyna pursed her lips. "I'm fighting to defeat the Order, the Skeleton King, and any other tyrant who'd enslave the world under their dominion. And I can't do it alone. No one can. United—"

Dracus tossed his hands in the air. "There's no winnin' this. Even if ya could, you'd just put another tyrant in Saltspire. Please, Threy, forget this war. Join us. Leave with us."

"Why do you care what I do?" Threyna asked. "I already said I don't care if you stay or leave." She narrowed her eyes. "Wait, what will happen to you if you go beyond the curse?"

Dracus chewed his mustache. "I'll die. A true death. Dead and gone… I hope. But this ain't about me. Canton'll follow you… wherever you go. You fight, he'll fight. You leave, he'll leave."

Threyna hmphed. "Strange hill to hollow on…"

"It's the best I got," Dracus said. "I got my darklings, you got yers. So I'll ask ya one last time; for Canton's future, for your mother's and father's sake, will you leave with us?"

Threyna didn't want the blood magic. By fate, chance, or because everything in Rheynia was cursed, it came to her and dug its fangs into her arm. But now that it had, she'd be damned not to use it to defeat the Order. "My father wanted this."

"Don't give me that. He wanted *me* to have it. He wanted *me* to fight."

Threyna took a deep breath. "I suppose we're all fortunate he didn't get what he wanted then. No. I won't leave with you. I'll stay. I'll fight. And if the Skeleton King comes for me, I'll fight him and kill him."

Dracus shook his head. "It won't be enough."

"You're right. I'll need help. But I don't need *your* help."

Dracus sniffed, nodding past her. "Fine. Go. But leave now. I'll say you went scoutin' ahead. Blood and bone, if there's any ghostin' god that'll listen, may our paths never cross again."

Threyna shook her head. Without another word, she spun and left the coward in her wake. The fabled Dracus Alius, the youngest Premius in the Order, the battle-hardened commander who'd collected the most souls of any Justicus and single-handedly closed out the Artificer's War, was nothing more than a coward.

She didn't need him or his lies.

She'd make sure the Wraith couldn't escape Rheynia. She'd deliver them to Octarius. They would stay and fight with the Underground as they should have during the Battle of the Cut. United, they would win, cleanse the curse, and together they'd usher in a new regime.

She set off into the Gullies alone, sinking into her Inner Throne and listening for heartbeats. But as she advanced further, questions arose about her mother's letters, Arilette's version of the truth, and whether or not the Wraith's help would even be enough to clear the stocks against the Order. She clenched her fists at her side, one blackened by rot.

Can't trust a darkling, can't trust Dracus. "Go hollow out," she said to the narrow crags.

A reverberation echoed faintly in her Inner Throne. Heartbeats. She could sense them, but they weren't heading east as she expected. They were around her. Above her.

Threyna peered upwards through the gaps in the crags to the gray clouds above. Though the green glow of the Viridite shone eerily off the shroud of clouds overhead, something else illuminated the sky.

Shades. Lots of them.

Knowing what followed behind them, Threyna ran.

CHAPTER 36

REST IS FOR CORPSES

Laela XIV

One step at a time. Laela trudged forward, her feet dragging, but onward nonetheless. They hadn't slept. With Belrich tailing her and the woods crawling with hollowed, staying still was a death sentence—only worse. After a short rest, Laela, Redge, and Tarus led the others on their journey south. They had found other groups of refugees along the way until their numbers were over fifty. Laela tried to learn the names of those who followed her.

Freyan, who'd joined the Wraith after she'd lost three children to dewskull. Landus, who'd once served as a medicus in the Underground before defecting to the Wraith. Taylas, whose last surviving son was taken by the Order collectors and never saw or heard from him again. They each had a reason to want a new start. They all had dreams of a future far from the pain they'd endured. She wanted to hold a special place for them in her heart, but by the time they'd found the fourth group, the names and faces began to blur together. In her exhaustion, she couldn't commit any to memory.

Laela held the lead bound to Aylenia's wrists, but despite appearances, she wasn't a prisoner. Bound by thin straps of torn fabric that would struggle to keep a paddock door closed on a windy day, Aylenia walked in silence. If she wanted out, she would have little trouble, but for some reason, the Palogian woman Laela had known as a child went along with the farce. Though it gave Redge and the other Wraith who feared traveling to Octaven hope, Laela knew Aylenia was only biding her time.

We still have to bypass Octarius. Whether we're in bindings or she is, we're going in the same direction.

"Maybe you should quit running and fight," her father said.

Laela ignored him and tugged the lead around Aylenia's wrists. Aylenia scowled.

"Who is your mole?" Laela asked for the tenth time. She couldn't conceal the fatigue in her voice any longer.

"Don't know," Aylenia said. "Can't liars always tell when someone else is lying?"

Laela might have taken the bait if she had the energy, but she pushed past it. "You knew we wouldn't be escaping."

"Because that's what we were told."

Same question. Different answers, same result. *"There's a wolf in wool here,"* Dracus had said. On the run from the Order with the Underground likely waiting for them ahead, now she needed to concern herself with the notion that Aylenia wasn't the only one in their group who didn't want to flee Rheynia.

Their procession stopped as a groan resonated down the line.

What now? While Laela elected to bring up the rear of their procession, she sent Tarus and Redge to lead from the front. People identified Tarus as Verinius's Sword, and others seemed to appreciate Redge's outspoken demeanor, but by the reaction to this latest stop, they might as well have been the Order's Collectors coming to take their boys, crops, and supplies.

"Come on," Laela said, tugging Aylenia forward to see why they'd stopped. Aylenia didn't grumble half as much as those they passed.

Hope was an ephemeral flame. It sparked to life with each group they found, but was quickly doused by the impossible march they continued upon. These frequent stops didn't help.

Through the night, they'd trekked along the Spine, nearing the Cut, many with arms full of food, clothing, or various other supplies. Although she had instructed people to take only what they could carry, some goods—specifically arcanatek, low on charges or broken as they were—were still too valuable to leave behind. Loaded onto carts and sent with the first groups to depart Aranoc, the arcanatek likely wouldn't make a difference if it came to a fight, but it gave people hope. Hope that if they encountered hollowed, Order, or Undergrounders, they could defend themselves. Hope that if they made it beyond the curse, they would have the means to aid their new beginnings. Yet that hope came at a cost.

Sure enough, while Laela and Aylenia neared the front of the procession, a group of men were assisting Redge in shoving a cart that had gotten stuck on a rock back onto all four wheels.

"Leave your scraps," Aylenia said. "It won't be worth it where we're going."

Laela inhaled through her teeth, but she couldn't argue. If they made it beyond the curse to Neutreen, she would provide them with everything they needed. They wouldn't require the Savior's gifts to fend off hollowed or grow crops. They could live off the land as Neutreen intended. However, that wasn't what Aylenia meant. "We're *not* going to Octarius. So keep your mouth shut before I have you gagged."

"Gag me then," Aylenia said. "Because someone should be telling the truth around here."

Laela seized Aylenia by the arm and dragged her forward.

"Can't we just leave it?" a man asked through labored breath as he and the others attempted to free the cart. His messy gray hair clung to his sweaty brow.

"And let the Order have it?" a younger man asked, attempting to tow the cart. Laela couldn't remember either of their names, and she was too tired to try.

"Better that than our lives," Elisara said. *Or is that Onaren?*

Arguing broke out. Tired, frightened, and overwhelmed, tensions were too high to ignore.

Redge released the cart with a growl that caused everyone to go silent. His too-neat brows pinched in a scowl as he strode towards her. "We need to rest."

She wanted to. *Ghosts,* she'd have traded a ship for an hour of sleep, but every moment they rested, Belrich gained on them. Every step they didn't take separated them from Sansia. She looked up to the overcast sky. Surrounded by tall dead oaks that refused to fall, this was as good a time as any to rest.

"Rest is for the corpses," her father said.

"Why won't you leave me alone, then?" Before he could respond to her, she put up her walls, blocking him out.

"Fine," Laela said. "We'll rest, but don't let anyone get comfortable." She turned to the train of refugees behind them. "Give the order, but assign watchers for our flank."

Redge nodded and addressed the refugees. The groans of relief waved through their party at Redge's words, but like any bit of joy in Rheynia, it wouldn't last—it never did.

"We shouldn't stop." Tarus appeared at Laela's side like a hollowed in the Gullies, seemingly spawning from the shadows of the woods.

"Blood and bone," Aylenia said. "Where did you come from?"

Laela stifled her own surprise. She didn't want to stop, but Redge was right.

"Leave the scrap, but we needa keep moving," Tarus said, not even acknowledging Aylenia's existence.

"We need rest," Laela said. "But then we'll need to make up ground before the midday rains. We'll take only what we can carry. Travel light."

Aylenia scoffed. "You'll listen to him…"

Now was Laela's turn to ignore her. "Short rest." She nodded at Tarus. "Can you watch her?" She handed Tarus the lead to Aylenia's bindings. She mumbled something under her breath, but Laela was too tired, too heartbroken to care.

Laela separated herself from the group, returning to their flank. She needed quiet. She needed to pray. After finding a wedge between two gnarled roots with a thick trunk to lean against, she squatted down. Her legs ached as she nestled between the exposed roots, but she was relieved to have pressure off of her feet. Lying back against the trunk, she gazed at the clouds over Rheynia, lightening with the dawn of a new day.

We should have been in Sansia by now.

The knowledge pained her. They should have been free. Safe. But they weren't, and they wouldn't be. *How many have we lost to even get this far? How many more will we lose before we reach the Grip?*

This was Threyna's doing. All because she didn't want to accept that her father was gone.

Laela had lost her own father. She'd watched as Arenius had him staked to the hull of the ship he had burned. Her father wasn't a good man. Perhaps not a bad man, but certainly not a good one. He deserved his punishment. He had earned it. It hurt to watch, but she owed it to him. She didn't throw herself on the pyre just because he was willing to die for what he believed in. No, she wanted to *live* for what she believed in.

Threyna's father wasn't like her own. She recalled Theodyn giving her *True*, one of the two twin daggers he had made when Threyna was born. It was still tucked in her boot, and had saved her on more occasions than she could count. *"You're as much a daughter to me as she is,"* he'd said. She'd never believed it. He might have loved her as his own, but she never wanted another father.

As different as the two men were, they were both willing to die for what they believed in. They died wanting to fight a losing war.

How different would things have been had he not agreed to fight at the Battle of the Cut? Threyna never would have run away. Maybe in time, we would have actually become like sisters.

The thought soured in the space between her mind and her heart, because where Laela listened to her father's screams as he hollowed in the fires he started, Threyna refused to let her father go to his end. Instead, she'd condemned hundreds of people to a terrible fate…

"Fight for more. Dream for more." The prayers of her mother's fatekeeper kept her from sinking into despair.

Reaching into a pocket within her britches, she pulled out a match. Unsure if she'd be able to get it to light after her voyage through the bogs, she needed to try. She grabbed the feather pendant beside the empty fatekeeper and held its flinted edge to the match's head. After a few failed strikes, the match lit.

Puny really, the small flame did little to fend off the gloom of the dying forest or the dark thoughts swirling around her, but tendrils of smoke rose from the flickering light to carry her words to Neutreen—wherever she was. With the match in one hand, she held the stocks with the other.

"Neutreen, judge me. Have I not languished in your name? Have I not shared your blessings with all who abide in your Tenets? If you find me a glutton where you've called me to practice moderation, deny me my wings. If you find me prideful where you've called me to practice modesty, deny me my wings. If I have overstepped my place within your measure, deny me my wings. If I have not provided to your people and have failed to earn my merit, deny me my wings. But if I have been faithful, answer my prayers.

"See Rosler, Taggart, and the others safely through the Gullies. Shelter them beneath your wings and defend their mission to help deliver your flock back to you. See the rest of us safely beyond the Order's grasp, past the Underground's clutches, and deliver us to Sansia. Please, Neutr—"

The match blew out. The fog devoured the smoke, denying it from carrying her words to Neutreen's ears. Dejected, she turned her attention back to the camp. Already, their relief had dissolved into muttered complaints. She supposed she should be grateful they weren't bickering. Give people any amount of idle time and they'd soon find a commonality to grumble about. Oddly enough, at least they were united—even if it was in lamentation.

Something stirred towards the camp's flank.

Laela stood to gain a better perspective, but the fog was too thick. Heading back toward the others, she stopped as the crowd parted, moving out of the way of a lone shade. As mutters grew, so too did the swell of light emerging through the fog.

Another shade entered their camp. Then another. More shapeless motes of light approached through the fog in the distance.

The scar across her chest burned. She inhaled sharply, but all she smelled was charring flesh. She shouted, but all she heard was her father's taunting voice.

The Order...

"Run!" Laela shouted. "Leave everything and run!"

CHAPTER 37

OUT OF THE SOUL JAR

Dracus X

D racus dragged his feet back toward where he'd left Fawkes and Canton, partially because it alleviated the impact on his aching soles and partially because if he showed up without Threyna looking as chipper as he felt having sent her away, he'd catch an earful worse than Decimus ever gave him.

He rubbed the back of his neck. *At least then Decimus and I were on the same side.* Dracus couldn't imagine leaving Rheynia without Canton. He'd sworn he'd get Canton off of this rock. Swore it to the ashes of Canton's old man, to Arenius before he burned, to Fawkes, Theodyn—anyone who would listen. But now they were all hollowed or worse; only Fawkes remained, and he actively tried to convince him to let it go.

"To dream is to die. To hope is to lie. To live is to lose all we've come by…"

"Stupid song. What kinda lullaby is that anyway?" But he knew the answer to that. *The kinda lullaby to prepare a kid born into a haunted world that he'd have a haunted life.*

Dracus quickened his uneven gait, motivated to get back to the others and make sure their hellish existence at least had a happy ending. But as he neared where he'd left them, they weren't there.

A nearby hollowed growled.

Eyes wide, Dracus crouched, surveying the diverging paths through the Gullies. He cursed to himself, knowing he never should have split from them, but it was too late for that. Drawing his short sword as silently as he could, he crept along the wall's shadows.

Couldn't've gone far. He peeked down one crevice then another. A loose stone skidded down the crags, descending from above. Each bounce of the pebble might as well have been a warbling blaster. Dracus held his breath, waiting for a horde of hollowed to come out of nowhere to chase the rock, but the Viridite walls' glow was enough to keep their attention. Not wanting to know where the stone had come from, he glanced between the gaps in the limestone-green walls that led to the gray shroud over Rheynia.

Straining his ears, he listened for any sign of motion above. When he heard none, he continued moving down one of the branching paths Fawkes and Canton could have taken.

They'd have come lookin' for me… unless somethin' got in their way.

A gurgle coming down an adjacent path stopped Dracus midstride. He pulled up just in time to put his back to a rocky outcropping as half a dozen hollowed staggered past. If they saw Dracus, they gave no indication, but more were coming from the same direction.

Backtracking, he slid between a tight crevice just as several snarling hollowed turned down his path. Not having time to hope they didn't see him, he wriggled his way through the crag. As he emerged on the other side, there were more roamers stumbling down another path and heading northeast as if intentionally cutting them off from their ships. Their limbs were bent at odd angles—not enough to stop them from ambulating, but enough to slow them down.

Another group of about half a dozen.

Dracus held his breath and waited for them to pass before he returned to the shadows. Taking care to be as silent as his dead heart, he advanced, heading east towards the shore and hoping Fawkes had the sense to do the same.

A flare from above, the sound of dragging feet and droning drivel. The shade passed over the crevice overhead, but the hollowed chasing after it dropped right into Dracus's path. It bounced off each of the walls before landing with a sickening crunch on the ground. Bone broke through decrepit flesh. Black ichor oozed thick and viscous from around the wound. The hollowed screamed, but already, another was falling on top of it. Then another.

Blood and bone. Sword in hand, Dracus cut south. He didn't have time to fight his way through a horde in the narrow passes, not while Canton and Fawkes were—

A scream tore through the Gullies, reverberating off the walls to tear the night asunder.

Canton?

Dracus spun towards the cry from the east. Not bothering to look up, he charged toward the yelling. It didn't stop. It wasn't the short, sharp burst of surprise or the roaring shout of a battle cry—this was the sound a man made as he watched his intestines get ripped from his gut.

Three hollowed blocked his path, but they were stumbling toward the sound of the screams too. They didn't even notice Dracus. Not when he slashed across the back of the first one's ankles, the second one's knees, or even when he rammed his sword through the back of the third, shoving it to the ground as he trampled over it.

Dracus didn't have a heart, but he could have sworn it was pounding in his ears. *Not Canton. Not Fawkes. Not Canton. Not Fawkes.* He charged through an intersection, his caution thrown to the Grotto, and turned northward in the direction of the growing shrieks. He didn't know how much of whoever it was would be left, but Dracus needed to know either way who owned those hollowing screams.

A pair of fresher hollowed emerged just ahead of Dracus. Originally intent on following the excitement, the hollowed took notice of Dracus and sought to add screams of their own making to the Gullies' haunting choir. Teeth grit, hilt choked, Dracus charged between the two. When one reached for him, he cleaved through the arm, dropping the severed limb to the ground. The hollowed, fresh enough to still bleed, screamed. Dracus followed the downward chop with a slice across its face. With a pivot, he thrust his steel through the second hollowed's chest, kicked her away, and then spun, slashing at the first hollowed's head. The poor bastard must have had dewskull, because Dracus's blade cleaved through it in one fell swoop.

The half-headless hollowed crashed into the wall. The one he kicked buckled to the ground, but they'd both be back up. With the screams growing louder, Dracus didn't bother to clip their ankles. He ran toward the cries, fearing what he might find. As he rounded the corner, he screeched to a halt.

A dozen hollowed climbed over one another to tear at a screaming red splotch between them. Blood painted the Viridite walls crimson. The hollowed themselves were drenched in gore. Dracus's lower lip trembled. There was no way of telling who the poor soul was.

A firm hand gripped Dracus's shoulder. He spun around, sword poised, but Fawkes stood opposite him. Face pale aside from the blood spatter freckling his cheeks, Fawkes managed a nod and gestured with his head to follow. Canton stood behind Fawkes.

No words were needed. The hollowed weren't tearing through flesh to get to Canton's soul. Whoever it was, Dracus thanked him. Before he could let out a sigh of relief, Canton whispered.

"Where's Threyna?"

Unable to consider a reply, Dracus was spared when a group of hollowed fell into the Gullies from above, crashing to the ground and blocking their path east.

Fawkes waved him south. Dracus chewed his mustache, contemplating if they could fight their way through. He didn't want to run south. Without a ship, they'd be stuck traveling through Octaven and hoping Laela managed to outmaneuver Arilette. He'd be stuck trying to convince Canton that fighting wasn't an option.

As if Rheynia wasn't cursed enough, more hollowed seemingly fell from the sky, landing atop one another in a mess of snapping jaws and flailing limbs. With a grunt, Dracus abandoned the eastward path and followed Fawkes and Canton south.

⚖

After navigating the narrow crevices and steep crags, it turned out escaping the Gullies was the easy part. The Order patrolled the Spine. Legionaries armed with short swords, Justicus equipped with arcanatek—it seemed all were assigned to make certain the Wraith did not escape.

The fog that cloaked them offered little comfort. Though it concealed their slinking, it also prevented them from seeing those searching for them.

"Stay close," Dracus said to the others. "If we get split, head for Fort Cybel." He didn't want to go to Fort Cybel. Didn't want to join with Laela, the rest of the Wraith, or their Underground escorts, but after being cut off from the ships, that was their best chance for survival. He only hoped Rosler and Taggart managed to slip through to the ships. Otherwise, getting to Fort Cybel would only bring them out of the soul jar and into the irradiator's blast.

Hiding behind a bramble of dead Dreadroot, Dracus waited until a group of legionaries, wearing the badge of the Second Legion, passed before waving Canton and Fawkes westward.

The Second Legion was once his. Now they were hunting him.

Ghosting Nerus, that bastard.

Had he known the Order's numbers would be so thick through the Spine, he would have taken his chances with the hollowed. He understood the hollowed. But monsters like Nerus were another story entirely.

As they went the opposite way as the legionaries, the ground became softer the further they snuck from the limestone of the Gullies, but it only served to slow them down. Over fallen trees, under hanging vines, and around Dreadroot brambles, they crept through the forest in silence.

Hellhounds howled in the distance. Arcanatek warbled, but whether they were aimed at fleeing Wraith or the undead, it was impossible to tell.

Once seemingly away from immediate Order threats, Canton grabbed Dracus's arm. "Where's Threyna?" The cut of his brow and the scowl he wore did little to distinguish him from the hellhounds.

Dracus's nostrils flared. "Not now, Cant."

"Not now—when? Did you just leave her?"

Dracus glanced at Fawkes, but Old Boy wasn't coming to his defense. He scoffed. "Ya think I'm some kinda hellhound? She left us. I was tryna stop her."

Canton grunted. "Bet you tried real hard."

Dracus prepared a rebuttal, but a twig snapped, too close for comfort. Spinning in the direction of the sound, he positioned himself between it and Canton.

Green slits for eyes floated through the fog, drawing nearer. Several others encroached in a semicircular pattern around them. *Hellhounds.*

Moving slowly, Dracus reached for the hilt of his sword. Canton and Fawkes did the same, but before any of them could draw, the first hellhound pounced. Bared fangs launched at Dracus's throat. Unsheathing his sword and striking in one fluid slash, Dracus's blade sliced across the ghoulish predator's neck before it crashed into him. With a grunt, he threw the mangy beast aside just in time to skewer a second attacker through its open snout.

Fawkes finished stabbing one hellhound and flung a meaty backhanded fist at another attempting to take him from the side. Canton hacked at another's ribs until it was as unrecognizable as the screamer in the Gullies.

Only one more remained, snarling at them, preparing to strike as the rest of its pack struggled to get up. Areas of matted fur exposed the corrupted flesh beneath. The rotting husk of what was once a small wolf or a large coyote snapped its teeth.

Don't do it, ya ghoulish mutt. Don't—

It did. Extending its bloodied claws and opening its maw of rotten teeth, it leapt at Canton's back. Dracus gripped his sword with two hands and spun. With a grunt, steel met rotten flesh. Bone and cartilage crunched beneath the force of his blade, diverting the hellhound's attack. It hit the ground with a thud a sword-length from Canton's back.

"Oy! Over there!"

An illuminator cleaved through the fog, revealing the green pauldrons of a Tribunus in Nerus's legion. Behind him, a wall of legionaries in their Order blacks snapped to attention.

"Blood and bone," Dracus said. "Run!"

Caution to the wind, mutilated hellhounds in their wake, and a wave of warbling arcanatek chasing after them, they ran. Dracus led the way, legs churning, feet squishing through the murky lowlands at the base of the Spine. Despite the poor footing, Canton's long legs soon overtook him. In a footrace, the kid could outrun anyone, but he just needed the sense to run and not to fight.

He looked over his shoulder. Fawkes was lagging behind. The Order was gaining on him. Dracus cursed to himself. *They'll let them go if they get their hands on me...* It wasn't a perfect plan; Canton might not listen long enough to let him stay behind. If he were caught, there was no way Canton and Fawkes wouldn't come back for him. But those circumstances were better than this one.

"Canton, hold up."

Canton slowed, and Dracus grabbed him by the collar.

"Don't argue. Don't question. You and Fawkes. Fort Cybel. Trust me."

"What are you gon—"

"No questions!" Dracus shoved Canton as Fawkes caught up to them. "Go!"

Fawkes looked back at him but knew better than to argue. He and Canton disappeared into the fog, the Order closing in from behind. Scanning his limited visibility, Dracus charged up the hill, heading south east making as much noise as he could.

C'mon. Follow me, ya bastards. Willing himself onward through the pain of his affliction and past the dark thoughts swarming like darklings, Dracus shouted over his shoulder. "You know who I am? I'm Dracus ghostin' Alius. Ya hear me?"

His whole life, he'd resolved not to wake sleeping hellhounds, not to poke the distracted hollowed. But in eternal undeath, he'd do just that to keep the living alive and well.

His legs burned as he summited the hill and continued further south. The Order gained on him, shouting at his back, charging their arcanatek as if the rumors they'd made about him were true.

He entered a clearing and stopped short. He'd been here before. Dracus, Arenius, and Theodyn had pillaged a Viridite caravan heading from the Gullies to Saltspire. He scanned the surrounding trees, searching for the entrance they'd taken back into the Underground's southbound tunnel.

Past the trunk of a fallen tree, a wide stump with a gap between the roots called to him with the promise of succor. He could run, hide, and wait out the Order. They'd never find him, and it would be too late for them to resume their pursuit of Canton and Fawkes.

With the clamor of the Order closing in on him, he crept toward the entrance to the tunnel. But as he took his next step, his shin brushed up on something that didn't belong there. Stopping in his tracks, he bent down to find the trip wire with his finger.

He blinked, not knowing if stepping away would cause whatever was rigged to blow. Taking a deep breath, he stepped backwards, releasing his finger. Nothing happened.

Blood and gory bone. That was close.

"Don't move!" a legionary shouted behind him.

Dracus chewed his mustache. *Out of the soul jar, into the ghostin' irradiator.*

CHAPTER 38

THE BLESSING'S IRE

Threyna XV

Chased. Cornered. Trapped. Threyna's path east was cut off by hollowed falling into the Gullies from above. Turning northward, she hoped to circumvent them, but she only found more and had to retreat west. Now she had been turned around more times than she could count, and her sense of direction had corroded, as rotten as her blackened veins and as desperate as the screams that tore through the crags.

Part of her hoped it wasn't Canton, Fawkes, or Dracus. Another part of her couldn't afford to care. Despite the rot spreading up and down her arm, she decided she'd spent enough time in these cursed Gullies. Visualizing the conjurations she wanted to create, claws formed from her fingers and toes. She kicked into the Viridite walls, searching for purchase. As her claws took anchor, she climbed the smooth stone, hand over hand, toward the surface.

Once she was outside the maze and atop the mountains, she could conjure wings as her father had. She could fly to Beak's Bay and intercept the ships, making sure none reached Talon's Grip to lead the Wraith away from the Underground. Ignoring the fatigue in her arms and the heavy throb in her chest, Threyna crested the vertical Viridite climb and spun to orient herself.

A dense fog had settled over the Gullies. The shroud practically reflected the green glow of the Viridite as opposed to illuminating it, limiting her visibility to only a few paces before her. Letting her claws crumble to ash, she listened from within her Inner Throne.

Heartbeats deadened the silence around her, not exactly close, but their vibrations reverberated in the inky black vines that snaked around the pillars of her Inner Throne. Yet something else was there. Closer. Not quite a heartbeat, but the absence of one. She'd felt the same strangeness near Dracus, similar to the sensation of knowing you're being watched without seeing anyone.

Her natural senses filled in the blanks of what her Inner Throne offered. The scent of rotting flesh, the low growl of ruined vocal cords—hollowed. Hollowed everywhere.

If they knew she was there, they gave no sign, but she didn't see how she'd be able to navigate out of this. Sinking deeper into her Inner Throne, Threyna imagined the wings that sprouted from her father's back, the depiction of Neutreen's feathers that every good Elysian prayed for.

Dark capillaries weaved through her hand, blackening her fingertips, but the wings of a great bird emerged from her back. Amazed at what she was capable of, Threyna flapped her newly formed wings and jumped into the air. Ignoring a growing ache in her chest, she took flight.

Wind and fog rushed past as she climbed higher and higher into the sky. Then, through the veil of fog and the shroud of clouds over Rheynia, she ascended to the heavens. Thousands of stars stared back at her. A moon she'd only seen the light of glowed brighter than any arcanatek illuminator she'd ever seen.

She felt like she'd left the dead and undying world behind and transcended life itself to the world beyond the curse. Suspended in the cool night air, flapping her wings, she wished the moment could last forever.

But nothing in Rheynia lasted. Only the dead.

The ache in her chest constricted like Dreadroot around her heart. She grabbed at her chest, but she was already falling. Her wings began to disintegrate, trailing ashes behind her. The moon's beauty died as she plummeted down into the shroud of fog.

Threyna drew in a choked-off breath and willed her body to move. Her fading wings flapped, attempting to slow her fall. But they continued to melt away as her descent, more gliding than flying, carried her back towards the hollowed wishing to devour her and the Order looking to capture her.

The pain in her chest gripped harder, crumbling the walls of her Inner Throne until Threyna couldn't take it any longer. She released her Inner Throne and her hopes of being able to slow herself down.

The ground fast approached. Trees whizzed by. Brambles reached their greedy limbs for her feet. Wings all but gone, she was a slave to momentum.

Unable to stop, unable to move, Threyna hit the ground hard. Impact slammed into her shoulder. Her world spun. Pain lanced from her back around to her sternum. Her leg struck something hard and unforgiving, sending her toppling in a new direction. Brush scratched at her exposed skin until momentum's abuse relented, leaving her face-down, still in the mud.

Afraid to move, daring to draw breath, Threyna attempted to steady her swimming vision. She rolled onto her back, still clutching her chest. Her peripheral vision narrowed. If the moon existed, if the stars were ever real, they denied her now. Tall figures loomed over her, but as her consciousness waned, she couldn't tell if they were trees blackened by undeath or men in Order blacks.

CHAPTER 39

LUCKY

Dracus XI

The Order came with the steady march of assured victory. Any man still clinging to life should have run, but Dracus retained nothing so precious. *The longer they spend on me, the more time Canton and Fawkes have to escape.*

He smirked, standing before the trip wire. "Took ya long enough." Dracus raised his hands in surrender, taking care not to glance at the entrance to the old Underground tunnel in the knotted tree roots. "Ain't easy runnin' on these old knees. Coulda done me the favor of chasin' me down before I climbed the damn hill."

Turning around slowly, he met the face of the man who ruined him. The one who, in many ways, set him on this doomed path. He might not have been sustained by the blood of children, and he might not have given the command to have Canton's village burned, but he was the one who hollowed Canton's parents. Perhaps if they were still alive, Dracus could have dumped the kid on them and been on his way. Maybe then he coulda been the weapon Arilette wanted instead of the protector Canton needed. Then he never would have threatened to leave the Underground. She never would have poisoned him. He'd still be able to taste the sweetness of food, sleep like he needed to, and, by Neutreen's nads, he'd even be able to heal the minor bruises and scrapes that now plagued his existence.

The aches and pains he'd accumulated faded to a dull din once Dracus laid his eyes on the villain. The former Third Premius—now the Second,

265

behind only Decimus—strode between his men to the front of the Order's lines. His grin spread above his square jaw as if he and Dracus shared a past of more than blood, bone, and ruined souls.

"Darkling Dray," Nerus mused. "I always knew we would meet again, but my, my, you've seen better days, old frie—"

"Spare me." Dracus glared. The First Cohort of the Second Legion fanned out around him, trapping him. They drew closer, but not close enough. He resisted the urge to glance at the trip wire. *Not yet.*

"Do any of ya know the truth 'bout me?" Dracus asked, stalling. "Don't tell me ya actually believe this '*possessed by a darkling*' bit?" He scoffed.

Arcanatek and swords drawn, they advanced on Dracus and the Underground's trip wire.

Almost there…

"Ya think I got taken over by the darkling of Victarius Kaine?" He forced a laugh. "Why else would anyone possibly wanna leave the Order? Surely no one of their own volition, eh?"

"Drop the act," Nerus said, his grin from moments ago crushed between his flat lips. "Sure, that was the story told to the hamlets, but we know the truth. Everyone knows the truth. You couldn't handle it. So you ran."

Dracus blinked. His breath, still tight from his attempt to outrun the legionaries, withered in his chest like hollowed's flesh. *Everyone knows…* He shook his head. "Yet ya stay?" He glanced from Nerus to his Tribunus, then to the rest of the First Cohort.

Some had the grace to at least avert their eyes. Some swallowed their shame out of either their fear of reprisal or their misguided belief that perhaps the Skeleton King was a necessary evil to maintain the civility of Rheynia's chaos. But most only stared. Blank. Emotionless. Soulless, as if they'd been vortexed and were just empty shells of humans.

They all know. And yet they still follow. Dracus shook his head. "Then I'm afraid I got no choice." He pulled *Fang*, his Vendetta dagger, from his belt. "You're all gonna have to die."

Nerus and his men shared a laugh, closing the distance on Dracus. Dracus supposed it was funny and let out a chuckle himself. Nerus was only a few strides away from the trip wire.

"Not this time, old friend," Nerus said as he and his men advanced. "It's the Final Demise for you. Then we'll find your lover. We'll find your boy. And they'll get it the same as you."

Dracus snarled. Taking care to step over the trip wire without making it obvious, he backed away from the encroaching legionaries. "Come and try."

If he turned and ran and the arcanatek's blast wasn't overly large, he might just be able to jump clear of the cliff. He'd have to be careful not to break every bone in his body in the fall down the hillside, but if he was lucky... *Lucky?*

"To dream is to die. To hope is to lie. To live is to lose all we've come by. The lucky, we fall. And the misfortuned, we cry, but forever and ever, it is we who survive."

Dracus seethed through his teeth, wishing he'd stop trying to remember this cursed song, but hoping the lyrics held enough truth to see him from this fate. *Fang* in hand, he backed away, glancing to the hillside and a potential escape from Nerus and his legionaries.

"You might take out a few of us, but you won't win, Dracus." Nerus stopped before the trip wire. He held out his hand to signal his men. At once they halted, and Dracus's still heart lost whatever hope he'd clung to.

"Certainly not to our own trap." Nerus let out an amused sigh. "You didn't really think that would work di—"

Dracus hurled *Fang* end over end at the trip wire. A low beep indicated he hit his mark. Spinning, he ran for the cliff, trying to put as much distance between him and the whirring arcanatek.

"Ghosts!" Nerus shouted. "Take co—"

Light exploded behind him. A concussive blast hurdled him through the air. Trunks cracked, branches splintered, and Dracus hit the ground. Covering his head with his hands, he didn't bother to look in the direction of the shrill shrieks piercing the air behind him. A gust of wind too powerful to be anything but an arcanatek dried out his eyes. Even still, he couldn't do anything but stare at the cliffside he didn't make it to, hoping it wouldn't be his last failure. The trees not obliterated by the blast and illuminated by the radiant light cast their ghoulish shadows around him. They reached for him, threatening to pull him into whatever underdark was worse than the curse of Rheynia.

Finally, the light winked out. The rush of wind faded. Somehow, only silence was left in its wake.

Disbelieving he'd managed to escape unscathed, Dracus patted himself down. No blood. No exposed bone. Somehow, the blast had missed him completely. He turned back to the trip wire and surveyed the scene.

Bodies lay silent. Still. Eviscerated by the radiant energy of the arcanatek's explosion, the bodies offered no shades, no darklings. Yet they remained motionless. Not hollowed. Gone.

A reaping bomb.

The perfect one-two punch—a vortexer and irradiator blast within a singular device of desolation. Dracus couldn't believe his eyes at the destruction one mine could do. Decimus had been experimenting with such technology years ago, back when Dracus wore the green pauldrons of office. Once, it wouldn't even work on a single target, but now, two dozen legionaries were dead. Gone with the severing of a trip wire.

Dracus's empty stomach churned at the thought of what Belrich could do with such technology. *Underground doesn't stand a chance. Do they even know about this?*

Just another tally in the long list of reasons why they couldn't take this fight. Threyna's blood magic and Canton's defiance be damned, there was no winning against the Order even *if* the Skeleton King was gone.

For better or worse, the blast fired in the opposite direction of him. Dracus was still alive, still fighting, still playing this cursed game. He pushed himself to his feet, eager to put as much distance between him and the death he left in his wake, but he couldn't leave yet.

He stalked back to the trip wire and pulled *Fang* from the ground. Resheathing it, he stared at the wide-eyed expression of Nerus's corpse. It didn't feel fair—for Nerus to be gone and at peace while Dracus was still here, suffering in undeath. "Ya don't deserve it. Ya got off easy, ya twisted bastard."

He spat on Nerus's face. "That's for Canton."

He stomped his heel down on Nerus's nose. Bone crunched and blood leaked, but his surprised expression remained the same. "That's for his da." He stomped down again. "His ma!" He stomped down again and again, no longer taking the time to dedicate each strike.

Eventually, breathless, Dracus stopped. He smoothed out his mustache with his thumb and forefinger, then straightened his tunic. He didn't bother to look at what was left of Nerus's broken face. He didn't glance back as he stalked off, dragging his right heel to get Nerus's brains off his sole. He marched forward. To Canton, to Fawkes, to Sansia and the sweet embrace of a true death. He'd survived. He'd move forward. He was *lucky*.

CHAPTER 40

How It Ends

Laela XV

Tarus had warned her. She hadn't listened. Laela cursed herself for stopping to rest. Behind her, shades seemed to emerge from all directions. If she bothered to stop and managed to ignore the pumping of her heart in her ears, she could probably hear the guttural groans of the hollowed following not too far behind. Fearing another trap like the one the Order had set at Caius's Bog, Laela tore between the dying trees and bound over the decomposing brambles, shouting for her camp to leave everything and run.

Most people didn't bother to look and see what Laela was screaming about. A lifetime in Rheynia hadn't conditioned them to ask questions. The fatigue that made them stop to rest in the first place evaporated, replaced by a flood of adrenaline. Panic gripped the entire encampment in a chokehold. Spurred into motion by Laela's shouting, people ran.

The carts that had slowed them were left, forgotten. Abandoned. Supplies littered the ground before her, creating stumbling blocks that threatened to trip her flight to safety and cast her to the hollowed's snapping maws. Weapons, arcanatek, blankets—everything was left in lieu of retaining the most important thing in Rheynia: life.

Laela's warning reached the front of the encampment. Praying that Redge or Tarus took the lead so they wouldn't just run into a dead end in the Spine, Laela also worried that the Order would be waiting for them at any possible escape. With no time for such thoughts, Laela, bringing up the rear of the procession, glanced over her shoulder.

The encroaching shades were everywhere.

"This is how it ends?" her father's voice asked, tinged with cruel laughter.

Laela swallowed the knot in her throat. *Be strong. Be courageous.* She shut her father out. "Stay together. Help each other."

Her cry fell on deaf ears. Their tight formation began to spread as runners attempted to circumvent the people in front of them. Pushing and shoving to stay ahead of their pursuers, regardless of whether they had to climb over their brethren, the Wraith weaved through the craggy woods at a grueling pace. Yet still, they couldn't create any separation between them and the growing number of shades that followed.

A terrible howl pierced the woods, signaling that the glowing harbingers had delivered their promise—hollowed were close, and drawing nearer. The shades were moving faster than Laela had ever seen; it was as if they were spirited by the wind in coordinated flight.

Sweat clung to Laela's brow. Her chest tightened with a mixture of physical exertion and the strangling grasp of fear. Her calves protested the effort of traversing the growing incline, but up ahead, a valley cleaved east through the Spine. The width of their party reconverged into the confines of the narrowing pass. The combination of their merger and the steep incline slowed their party and allowed the shades and hollowed to gain ground.

Fearing a trap, Laela scanned the peaks overlooking the mountain pass. Half-expecting an ambush, her relief that nothing was there was cut short as a shrill cry split the din of trembling breaths and pounding feet.

Up ahead, the crowd divided like a stream around a boulder.

"Help! Please!"

A dozen paces in front of her, a woman clutched her lower leg with one hand while reaching for the people moving past her, asking for help. No hand took hers. No one offered help. They ran. Too scared to stop. Too focused on survival to offer aid.

With the scar across her chest burning as it did every time it felt like the world was going to blood and bone, Laela hustled over to the downed woman. She yanked her to her feet, but the woman collapsed, wincing with pain.

"My ankle," she cried. Her strawberry-blonde hair clung to her cheeks, wet from tears. In her eyes was a wild fear that made Laela wonder how she'd found herself involved with the Wraith in the first place.

Laela glanced down the incline she'd just climbed. From the gained elevation, the horde of hollowed were visible beyond the shades. The slope would slow the failing tissues of the hollowed, but eventually, they would ignore self-preservation, climbing tooth and nail until they caught the shades or found something more interesting to sink their teeth into. If Laela left, this woman was as good as hollowed.

Grunting, Laela lifted the woman and slung her over her shoulder. She was lighter than she should have been, likely underfed for most of her life. She clutched to Laela, determined not to be cast off. *No one left behind.* She tried to convince herself that Neutreen was watching, that her valor would earn her merit in the goddess's judgement, but all she could think about was the horde of hollowed stripping her flesh from her bones.

She climbed, losing pace with the Wraith ahead. The woman praised her, thanked her, but Laela wouldn't accept her gratitude—not until they were out. Not until they were safe in Sansia. The ascent into the pass only seemed to stretch longer, growing in steepness, and degrading in footing.

Ignoring her aching back and the cramping in her calves and thighs, Laela drove one foot in front of the other. Ahead, again the narrowing procession of running Wraith split. This time, instead of them moving out of the way of a fallen woman, Redge charged back the opposite direction.

"Move!" Redge shouted, waving his arms to separate the herd. He spotted Laela, his dark brows rising as he took in the scene of the injured woman on her back and the encroaching threat behind them.

Beyond him, Aylenia, no longer bound, followed close behind.

With no time to concern herself with Aylenia's freedom, Laela beckoned for Redge to help. He glanced between her and the pleading woman, examining the way she favored her ankle.

"We can't take her," Redge said.

"No, please!" The woman's tear-streaked face stretched long at the prospect of being left.

"We can't leave her," Laela grunted.

"I can make it," the woman cried. "Don't leave me. I just need help."

"She'll get us all hollowed," Redge said. "The hollowed won't tire."

Laela was done leaving people behind. "Help me and no one will hollow."

"Come on," Aylenia said, scooping her shoulder underneath the woman's arm. "You take that side." Redge grunted, glaring at his fellow Palogian, but he did as he was told.

Happy that Aylenia took her side and Redge acquiesced, Laela trudged up the incline absent the woman's weight. Despite her attempt, she was unable to regain her former pace. Breathing heavily, she nodded at Redge. "Who's leading?"

Redge's lips were pulled back as he breathed through his teeth. "Tarus."

If he did in the beginning, Tarus handed off his duty to someone else. As they summited the incline to the flattened mountain pass, Tarus knelt beside a man and a woman fiddling with an arcanatek as if telling them what to do. Sparing a glance at Laela and Redge, he quickly returned to his work.

"Outta the way," Tarus said, snatching something out of the man's hand. "I'll do it myself, or you'll get us all hollowed."

"What in all the blood and bone are you doing?" Redge asked, snarling.

Laela didn't need to ask. They'd wedged an explosive into a crevice at the base of the taller northern peak. A fuse extended from it all the way to the detonator in Tarus's hand.

"You wanna get outta here?" Tarus asked Redge, nodding at the wounded woman. "You wanna pick up every straggler? Sometimes ya gotta fight if you want a chance to flee." He examined Laela, as if awaiting her approval even as he lectured her.

She balked. *He could collapse the whole mountain pass. Even if we didn't hollow, we'd be buried in stone. Not to mention, this would alert every cohort from Drakhardt to Octaven of our location.* But behind, the hollowed grew louder. Nearer. Climbing the hill behind them with unrelenting ire, the hollowed would not give up once they traversed the pass.

Tired of waiting, Tarus struck a match and lit the fuse. "Move."

Panic surging through each beat of her heart, Laela and the others chased after the Wraith ahead and the promise of safety that waited on the opposite side of the pass. With stone underfoot, clouds overhead, and the echo of the hollowed's haunting howls resonating behind them, Laela pumped her tired arms and legs.

She could practically hear the fuse burning as the sand of the time-turner slipped through the neck, counting away her final moments. She ran harder, praying that saving this one woman wouldn't lead to each of their deaths.

For Mother. For Rance. For—

Thunder erupted through the mountain. The ground quaked. Stone screamed. And the world began to collapse all around her.

CHAPTER 41

ROT AND RUIN

Threyna XVI

Threyna woke in a coughing fit. Her body jerked, but as she attempted to raise her hands to her mouth, she couldn't. Blood flew from her mouth to land on a rug of swirling green and silver. Her chin fell to her chest and lolled side to side as the room spun around her. There were figures in the room. They spoke, but she couldn't understand them as if her head was held underwater. Again, she tried to move, but to no avail. No stranger to pain, she groaned as nausea entwined with agony, unlike anything she'd experienced before. Her head throbbed, her ribs ached, and something awful burned along her arm.

Turning towards it, she found the skeletal mask of an Inquisitor staring back. The eyes, devoid of a soul, were fixated on something else. He jerked on her arm, sending spasms of short, sharp stabs into her shoulder to wrap around her ribs. She tried to tap into her Inner Throne, but a stabbing pain lanced from her fingertips to the center of her breastbone. Again, a storm of coughs rattled her body; blood and mucus climbed her throat with a fury that burned worse than Valefyre.

She spat, and though she aimed for the Inquisitor's faceplate, her accuracy was limited by her vertigo's inability to steady the room. Her head hung, too heavy to hold. Her eyes fell upon the stain she'd left on the green-and-silver carpet.

Black.

As rotten as the hollowed's ichor was, what came from her was worse. The memory of how she'd arrived here returned in a rush. Her escape from the Gullies, the wings she'd conjured... the rot reaching her heart.

"Ugh. Vile."

The voice, still distorted from when she'd slammed her head into the ground, came from behind her.

"Gag her. Or get it off before she completely ruins my rug."

The voice became more defined, easier to recognize. Belrich strode out from behind her.

Agony, fear, shame, and guilt swirled like a tempest within her. But absent her Inner Throne and secured to a vertical post with ropes wrapping around her legs and torso while binding her hands behind her back, she was helpless. She was in a tent—large and spacious, with lavish silver-and-green tapestries and rugs with the dove of House Fayte at its center.

Threyna fumed, angry with herself for not listening to the signs of her limitations. She finally understood where she was, what was happening, and why the Inquisitor was tugging on her arm.

The Blessing.

She glared at Belrich, though her vision hadn't quite settled. Despite his smile, the sharp line of his cheeks and the cut of his brow foretold of his true feelings. He pinched his chin, creasing its cleft as he paced the tent, circling around her like a hellhound.

"Do you need to be gagged?" Belrich asked. "Or can you do me the pleasure of not spitting on my rug?"

Threyna hocked and spat—not on Belrich's carpet—but directly at him. It spattered on his chest, glistening wet and gooey on his black Order uniform. He narrowed his gray-green eyes. Crow's feet creased at the corners, but his smile remained.

"Hard to believe we share blood," Belrich said. "Then again, your father did his fair share of spitting... before I took his tongue. Wasn't much of a spitter after that. Or a talker, I suppose."

Heat burned up Threyna's neck to her ears. Anger sobered her vision and cleared her mind, but before she could speak, the Inquisitor yanked again on the bangle, attempting to pry its prongs from her arm. Threyna winced.

Belrich tsked. "What a waste. He could have saved himself a lot of pain. An eye, a nose. Fingers and toes. Oh, the fingers and toes. You wouldn't imagine the songs one could sing once they have their toes tickled by my Inquisitors. I've heard just about every song there is to sing, but not a single one from old Bherus."

He shook his head, still grinning as if the thought warmed his heart like Cybel's Eve memories. "Pity, though. All that tickling, not a single song, and yet here you are. I don't know if it's better to say you *handed* it to me or you fell right into my lap. Flew too high, did you?" He wagged a finger in her direction. "I suppose Neutreen didn't feel as if you'd quite earned your wings." He pouted his lower lip. "Poor Threyna."

Threyna shook with rage. "If you think you'll get a song out of me, you're sorely mistaken."

Belrich guffawed. "A song... from you? Gory ghosts, no. I have no questions for you, and I care not for any song you'd sing. Songs are for the pretty birds, niece, not for the hellhounds. No, no. We have everything we need." He gestured to the pointed bangle on her arm. "However, if you wouldn't terribly mind, could you tell us how to remo—"

"I'm not telling you anything." Threyna snarled. Though she couldn't connect to her Inner Throne, the Blessing also seemed to be on the verge of snapping. She could feel it preparing to strike like a hellhound sinking into its haunches, but it was chained to a tree.

Belrich's smile flickered like the brazier in the corner of the tent. "I was going to ask if you'd be so kind as to take your bangle off. It's not quite my style. I'd prefer something more regal. Stately. Not something so haughty. So... boorish. But I'll take it as is. I'd hate for my Inquisitor to have to cut your entire arm off."

The Inquisitor grunted, getting up from where he knelt at her side. He stalked over to a bag of what looked like silver surgical tools, searching for something he could use to separate the cursed bangle from her flesh.

Threyna's nostrils flared as she attempted to think of some way out of this mess. Her father had consumed blood, absorbed souls. If she could too, she'd have Belrich on a spit over a fire before a vortexer could charge. But absent her Inner Throne, she'd be limbless. Again, she tried to sneak into her throne room, but pain gripped her chest.

Helpless, she needed to buy herself time. Threyna glared at the Inquisitor as he returned with what appeared to be a file and a pair of tongs.

"You even spill one drop of my blood and I'll shape it into a needle," Threyna said. "I'll sew your lips shut so I don't have to listen to you scream. Then I'll pluck out your eyes one by one. As you bleed, I'll turn that needle into a dagger and make snacks out of your fingers and toes. Then, once you're a right and bloody mess, I'll turn my dagger into a sword and cleave your—"

"Gory ghosts," Belrich said, appalled. "Your father's daughter indeed. How, under Neutreen's gaze, could we ever share blood?"

Threyna snapped her attention to her uncle. "Don't you mean the One's gaze?"

Belrich's smile returned. "Oh, pardon me. How well informed you are. I suppose we're no longer in mixed company. We can speak freely. Why don't I tell you about the One and, while I have you here, why don't you tell me about your plan with the Wraith? Clever plan of yours, sabotaging their escape, but it seems that half-sister of yours isn't entirely hollowed in the head either. What will happen next, I wonder? Who will outwit whom?" He clapped his hands together. "What a fun little diversion." Belrich's grin only spread, more evil than the rot in her veins or the artifact embedded in her flesh.

The Inquisitor pinched her with the tongs before getting a grip on the Blessing. He pulled, creating separation, and slid the file between her skin and the inside of the bangle. The cursed artifact sensed it was being threatened, similar to when Laela tried to pull it off, but this time, the chained hellhound within promised that something bad was about to happen.

Threyna hissed through her teeth, returning her gaze to her uncle. "What do you want, Belrich? Yeah, you want this—" She jerked her head in the direction of the bangle and the Inquisitor attempting to pry it from her flesh. "—but why not hollow me? Why not vortex me and be done with it?"

Belrich let out several gales of laughter before dropping his hands to his knees to support himself. After slowing to a hearty chuckle and flicking a tear from his cheek, he put his hands on his hips and shook his head. "Oh, Threyna. Dear, insufferable, Threyna. One day I pray you outgrow this recklessness. Well, I suppose you probably don't have much time left... But there are too many uncertainties. What if the Blessing dies as you do? What if it lashes out to protect you?"

He shrugged. "I can't take such chances. This isn't the Underground where we can rest on the laurels of our mere lack of extinction. This isn't the Wraith where failure is a necessary part of life. No. I am the Order. I am the future of Rheynia. I have waited nearly six decades for my time. If you believe I will grow hasty just because the summit is in sight, you are terribly, terribly mistaken."

The Inquisitor attempted to lever the bangle away with his file. The prongs pulled, but their anchors held fast to her muscle.

"It is securely bound, Legatus," the Inquisitor said.

Belrich's grin returned. The sly twinkle in his eye caught the glowing brazier. "Take your time. We'll be on the road to Saltspire by morning. Then, back at home, we can be more... diligent in our experimentations. We'll show my niece here to the black cells and... I'm sure she'll enjoy the farm, don't you think?" He strode towards the flap and threw it open.

The soft patter of the midday rains began to fall atop the tent. Threyna cursed herself. She'd lost too much time. There was no telling where the Wraith was now. She hoped Aylenia had managed to lead them to Octarius, or at least communicate with Arilette. Maybe, if all hadn't hollowed out, Aylenia and Arilette were looking for her right now, but she knew that was a fool's hope.

"Tribunus," Belrich called out into the rain. "Assemble ten Centuriots, fully equipped. No one goes in or out of this tent without my leave."

He turned back to face Threyna. "Oh, darling, don't look so glum."

"Ten won't be enough," Threyna said, smothering her fear. "And call me darling again and I'll—"

"Oh!" Belrich's grin flashed. "Would you prefer I call you Lady Darkling like your Underground minions? Or, hmm… how about *Little Dove*?"

Heat rose to Threyna's cheeks. She wanted to scream, but she didn't trust herself not to cry. She could only glower. Scared. Helpless. Alone. She'd heard of the black cells and the Skeleton King's *farm*. If she didn't get out, she would end up like her father, or worse.

Belrich's cruel grin softened into something that could almost be considered genuine. "I would say rest well, niece, but I'm afraid you will not."

As a group of Centuriots filed into the tent, Belrich addressed them. "I'm inclined to warn you to be on the lookout for any Wraith, but…" He shrugged, glancing at Threyna. "Something tells me the First Sword has more pressing priorities than a sister she never wanted."

Belrich exited the tent, calling for another of his men to bring him a fresh uniform as his had become, in his words, "*soiled.*"

Panic rising, Threyna eyed the new Centuriots and their commanding Tribunus, searching for any sign of open wounds she could draw blood from. If they had injuries, they were hidden behind their black uniforms, and, unable to tap into her Inner Throne without afflicting herself with more pain, she couldn't risk searching for one.

With Belrich a safe distance away, the Inquisitor's experimentations became less cautious. Squeezing the tongs, he yanked, attempting to dislodge the prongs from her arm. The chained hellhound within the

Blessing howled, but it did not strike out. Blood bubbled down her arm. Black blood. Seeing an opportunity to help herself, she sank into her Inner Throne, calling to the blood. Just as it began to congeal into an arrowhead, pain throttled her. The rotten noose around her heart constricted. Ejected from her Inner Throne, she vomited, her body betraying her.

Tired, wounded, and powerless, she'd hoped this was the opportunity she was waiting for. For all of her earlier threatening bravado, there was nothing she could do to stop the Inquisitor from his experiments.

Laela's not coming for me. Dracus isn't coming for me. I sent Aylenia away. I let Rivich quit. Yevon hollowed. Ebrus is gone. No one is coming for me.

Isolation would kill her faster than the cursed magic that blackened her soul.

The Inquisitor pulled harder, levering the file against her skin. The gentle patter of the rain outside began to fall faster. Harder. Winds whipped the tent's flaps, but the tempest within the cursed artifact thrashed. Like a hellhound, it raked its claws against the inside of her ribs, crying, fighting—not to be let free, but to be left in peace.

Threyna screamed in place of the spirit that had dug its prongs into her arm. Tears streamed down her face. "Stop! Stop!"

He didn't. He wouldn't. Her father had suffered in the Order's care because he wouldn't tell them where the Blessing was. Now they had it in their sights, and they wouldn't stop until it was theirs.

Thunder rolled in with the midday storms, heading west, but the hellhound within the artifact howled louder. The Inquisitor levered the file harder. Pressure built in Threyna's arm where the prong threatened to tear free of her flesh.

"Silence," the Inquisitor said, straining from beneath his skeletal mask.

Threyna bared her teeth. A primal, savage energy rose from deep within her—a concoction of desperation, fear, and a longing to complete a task left unfinished. The chain holding back the hellhound yanked taut, but it would not give. Neither would the hellhound.

"Please. Stop. Please."

The pain that coursed through her body when she had opened the arcanatek pendant Dracus had given to her so many years ago returned with a vengeance. The cursed and bloody artifact didn't want to be taken. Clinging to her flesh, it refused to be removed.

The Inquisitor didn't care.

Thunder boomed beyond the tent's walls. Rain poured down.

The Inquisitor put his full weight behind the file, and something bent. Something snapped. Not the bangle. Not the file. Not the chain holding back the hellhound, but the tree it was attached to.

Blood spurted from both eyeholes of the Inquisitor's skeletal mask.

Before Threyna could understand what was happening, she was falling. The Inquisitor fell as she did, and the surrounding Centuriots released panicked exclamations. She fell to the floor, unable to break her fall with her hands tied behind her back. She spun so her shoulder took the brunt of the collision instead of falling face first. Rolling to her back, the sky fell atop her.

Blackness surrounded her. The beam that she was bound to had cracked, dropping her and the tent's ceiling to the ground, but while the legionaries struggled to free themselves from the tent's fabric, Threyna crawled free of her wooden bindings. Her wrists, still secured behind her back by rope, couldn't aid her escape. Squirming like a snake, she kicked her legs in an attempt to propel herself away from the legionaries and toward the tent flap Belrich had exited.

Half-expecting a full cohort of arcanatek-wielding Justicus to come storming toward the fallen tent, Threyna was surprised when she crawled from beneath the tent's flap to find the rest of the encampment in complete chaos.

Rain poured. Thunder roared. Lightning pierced the dark veil of clouds to illuminate the camp. The legionaries were preoccupied. Darklings swarmed overhead. Irradiators whirred to charge, but darklings dove on viable hosts, eager to reclaim living flesh.

Absent the Inquisitor's prodding, the bangle seemed content to rest; the hellhound within went dormant, returning to hibernation now that the immediate threat had been dealt with. Threyna attempted to tap into her Inner Throne. Be it adrenaline, the darklings flying over the camp, or the prospect of escaping a terrible fate, Threyna focused through the pain that came with returning to her Inner Throne and seized control.

Enthroned upon her seat of power, Threyna drew in breath as her father had. The sharp inhale wrenched a nearby darkling off its course and pulled it towards her like a soul to a vortex. The darkling left the physical world and entered her Inner Throne.

The stained-glass windows of her seat of power were sullied black. The torches in her court smoldered and smoked, but cast no light in her Inner Throne. Through the shadows, a dark wisp stalked toward her, preparing to strike.

Similar to when Yevon's darkling had attacked her in Avengard, she felt the soul's thoughts, feelings, memories, and emotions. Likewise, it attempted to weasel its way into her own past. Determined to keep it out, she resisted its prying. She stood from her Inner Throne and let the darkling charge. Just as it was about to collide with her, she sidestepped out of the way. Grabbing hold of it as if it had corporeal form, she threw the darkling into the back of her seat of power.

The darkling crashed into the stone seat and crumpled, falling to the floor. Threyna stomped on it. Once. Twice. A third time. It cried out. But it was not welcome here. She needed it to abate the rot in her veins, not to challenge her for superiority within her seat of power. Lifting it from the floor, the dark wisp held a face from deep within its smoky façade. A child's face.

Pressure built around her as their thoughts entwined. The darkling was just a girl. A sad, scared girl. As Threyna sifted through the child's memories, the emotions she'd died with magnified into something savage. Sadness because her father had hollowed in an attempt to protect the Roost, the last bastion of the Artificers' rebellion. Fear because Dracus

Alius would come again to hollow the rest of them. Together, the two morphed into jealous hatred.

Sad or not, scared or not, child or not—Threyna needed to remove the rot so she could fight her way out of here. It wasn't fair. But nothing was. Neutreen be damned; justice didn't exist. She drew in breath as she had in the world beyond her Inner Throne. The child's darkling faded into a mist. As she inhaled, the darkling vanished; its dreams disappeared, its fears evaporated, and the soul dissolved to nothingness.

She didn't know what to think. What to feel. But in the absence of such, all she felt was the child's jealous hatred. Not for the living as the child had, but for the Order. Belrich. Dracus. Laela. Everyone who'd abandoned her.

The inky black staining the painted glass of her Inner Throne melted away, letting light into the gloomy court and flooding her once more with the abilities gifted by the cursed blood magic.

A resounding *click* accompanied her return to the real world beyond her seat of power. Barely a moment had passed, but the rot had retreated down her neck and up from her wrist, back towards her bangle. Somewhat restored but still thirsting, Threyna conjured a dagger into her hand and tore through the rope that bound her.

Now freed from her bindings, she searched for another soul to consume. Not seeing a darkling, she conjured a whip and snagged the leg of a nearby legionary. With a yank, she ripped him from his feet and spilled him to the mud. Unraveling her whip and shaping it into an axe, she gripped it with two hands and brought it down on the fallen legionary's neck. His head rolled through the mud. Blood spurted past the severed vertebrae to pool in the ground.

As a shade emerged from the headless corpse, Threyna drew in breath. Unlike when drawing upon the darkling, the shade passed easier, dispelling more rot and purging her Inner Throne from the black ink that covered her walls.

Behind her, legionaries scurried from beneath the fabric of their fallen tent. Empowered, Threyna converted her axe into a scythe. In a wide sweeping arc, she cleaved across the bellies of the three legionaries in front. As they dropped to their knees, attempting to prevent their guts from spilling between their fingers, Threyna allowed the momentum of her slash to sweep over and around her head. Following the momentum and lurching forward, she sliced horizontally again. The two unsuspecting legionaries in her way didn't have time to widen their eyes before their heads were tumbling through the air.

With five bodies around her and another five Centuriots and their Tribunus in front of her, she charged. Morphing her scythe into a curved blade more suited to the closer quarters, she hacked off a hand as it drew a blaster. Both fell to the bloody, rain-soaked earth. Before the neighboring legionary could defend his brother-in-arms, Threyna clipped the handless legionary at the knee and conjured a second blade in her off-hand. With a thrust, she speared the collapsing legionary through the chest.

She drew in breath to claim his escaping shade, blocked a thrust of another legionary's short sword, and countered with a vertical swing. The bloody blade split his chin and divided his lower jaw in half. He fell to her like a sapling ensnared in Dreadroot. Conjuring and consuming as she was, the rot danced up and down her arm, ebbing and flowing like the tides.

The marriage of power and corruption embraced within her veins. The shades sacrificed themselves to her on the dais of her Inner Throne. All around her, the Order's men fell one by one, and whether she had to rip their essences from their hollowed forms or bend their darklings to her will, all bowed. All submitted.

The Tribunus stood before her, the last of the men Belrich ordered to watch her. His vortexer warbled in his shaky hands. Within her Inner Throne, she sensed his heart beating rapidly. She felt it. Seized it. Staring down the barrel of the blaster, she dared him to pull the trigger. Just as he gathered the nerve, Threyna squeezed from within her Inner Throne.

Blood dripped from his nose. Then his eyes. And his ears. The Tribunus's blaster slipped from limp fingers. He staggered, swayed, and fell—hollowed before he hit the ground, his heart a mess of pulp within his chest.

Thunder echoed off the Spine as the winds carried the storm wall west, but lightning continued to strike. In the wake of nature's power, Threyna once felt small. But now, with blood, bone, and soul bowing to her on her Inner Throne, she felt like a queen of cataclysm. A harbinger of death. A weapon to end the Order. And Belrich was near.

The Tribunus's soul remained entombed in his body, but it didn't take much effort on Threyna's behalf to coax him out. As his essence wiped away the majority of the black rot staining her arm, she let her blood-spawned swords fall to ashes and sank deeper into her Inner Throne, searching for Belrich.

The camp was a horror—at least it would have been had she not received the gift her father never wanted for her. Here, surrounded by souls and mere mortals, she was the weapon the Underground needed. The difference-maker that could have finished off the Order years ago was now hers to wield.

She attuned to Belrich's heartbeat amidst the chaotic, soul-swirling encampment. Just as she found him, he disappeared—not entirely, but as if he was hiding in the shadows. She sank deeper into her Inner Throne.

More legionaries approached in formation from the direction Belrich disappeared in. She wanted to chase. She could, now that she'd learned to consume. She could kill and consume her way through the entire legion. Part of her prompted caution, but another part—a deeper, darker aspect of her soul—yearned to continue the slaughter.

Arcanatek warbled as darklings were irradiated from the sky or vortexed into soul jars. Her fuel was being spoiled. She would have to take more. Make more. Kill more.

A voice shouted her name. It seemed far away beyond the storm, as if it were a memory calling from the past. A dark tunnel. Ragged panting. Leather soles squished through the soft, muddy earth.

"Threyna, come back!"

It was Laela's voice. Then her mother's. But they faded, swallowed by the underground tunnel's darkness and the bodies, distance, and time between them. The darker part of her whispered that if they wanted her to come back, they would have chased her. They would have come for her. Even if Dracus told the truth about her mother writing letters, it wasn't enough, and she couldn't trust Dracus besides.

Forward. Kill Belrich. Defeat the Order.

She started marching toward the Order's reinforcements, but something snagged her arm.

"Threyna!"

She spun to find Fawkes, his cheeks flushed beneath his beard, his eyes bleary.

"Threy, come on!" Fawkes said, tugging her to follow him away from the advancing legionaries. "Blood and gory ghosting bone, I'm all outta soul jars. I been yellin' attcha long enough. We gotta get."

She wrenched free. "I'm not going anywhere. I can finish this."

Fawkes took her shoulders in his hands with a gentle kindness despite his burly bulk. His eyes searched hers—milky, scared. "Yeah, ya might be able to take em'. But not on yer own. Ya got caught on yer own. But I came raisin' death to get you out."

Threyna glowered, but a part of her softened. *You came… for me?* She swallowed, not sure if she believed him, not understanding why he cared.

He glanced over her shoulder. "Threy, please. Let's get outta here. Live to fight another day and all that, eh?"

Threyna growled. Still searching for Belrich from upon her Inner Throne, she couldn't find him beneath the encroaching shadow. She didn't understand how or why. Under Fawkes's pleading stare, the dark hunger in her began to subside. The rot stretched up toward her neck and down towards her wrist.

Maybe he's right. Live to fight another day.

She was a weapon. She had an army. Together, she and the Underground—with or without the Wraith—could bring the Order to ruin. Yevon and Ebrus were gone, but perhaps Rivich and Aylenia would rejoin her. With the combination of Arilette and Lorath's strategic prowess and her new abilities, perhaps the war of attrition they'd been suffering through for over a decade could be brought to a decisive victory. It was possible, but not if she risked herself now.

"Fine." Threyna glanced over her shoulder at the disarray of the Order's camp and the wall of encroaching legionaries. "Lead the way."

Fawkes nodded with relief. "Aye. Fort Cybel. Let's go."

CHAPTER 42

ONE OPTION

Laela XVI

Before the Suffering, people once said phrases like *"dead man walking."* Having seen dead men walk, run, and attack the living all her life, Laela never fully understood the concept. But now, as she and her beleaguered group descended the eastern slope of the Spine with the ruins of Fort Cybel ahead to the south, she understood all too well. Heavy fell the feet of the hopeless. And with the Order flag flying above the decrepit ramparts of where they planned to rest, whatever hope they had after outrunning the hollowed and narrowly escaping the collapsing rubble of the mountain pass was gone.

The dark skies of the midday rains began with a drizzle, and at first, Laela thought perhaps it would be light today. But as thunder rolled in from the east and lightning illuminated the sky like Dawnshards, she knew she was only lying to herself again.

Laela's shoulders sagged as if Tarus's explosion brought the entire length of the Spine down on her. They'd emerged with their lives, but left behind were their weapons and supplies, which only made the prospect of circumventing the Underground more implausible.

She couldn't help but tense her jaw whenever she glanced at Aylenia. Freed from her bondage by Tarus in their flight from the shades and hollowed, she'd yet to be put back in bindings. That only made Laela feel all the more like she—they—were the ones being led by the manacles. Now in Octaven, only separated from the Underground base beneath the foundations of Octarius by Fort Cybel and the Tears, Laela was running out of time.

Trudging along at the back of their procession—one tired stride at a time—she wondered if Rosler and Taggart managed to make it through the Gullies and secure the ships. Her head hung low at the thought that, even if they managed to bypass the Order and the Underground, there was still the chance that the ships wouldn't be there when they arrived at the Grip. Not wanting to think about that, she put one foot in front of the other.

"Sent scouts ahead," Tarus said, nodding at the front of their procession where Redge took the lead.

Laela startled. She hadn't even realized he'd slipped back in their caravan to enter the shadow beside her. Composing herself and attempting not to appear as caught off guard as she was, she adjusted her sword belt. "East or south?"

"Neither." Tarus nodded at Fort Cybel in the distance.

Laela shook her head. "The smoke of their fires was visible ten steps from the pass, the Order's standards are visible from here—we can't rest there. We can't go near there. We should have sent scouts south if we wanted to follow the Tears to the Grip, or north if we needed to cross to the east side of the river. Nothing good will come back from Fort Cybel."

If Tarus took any insult to Laela's criticism, he showed no sign. Stoic as ever, the Second Sword of the Wraith didn't even blink. "We weren't the only ones to escape Aranoc. Could be more of us. Could be they found 'em before we did. Can't hurt to check."

Laela ground her teeth. He should have checked with her before giving orders. He never would have done so if Rance or Verinius were here. "We should have discussed it before you sent scouts ahead."

"Should we have discussed me collapsing the pass too?" No malice. No arrogance. Just words uttered as simply as if he were asking about supper. "Or should I have waited for you to hollow?"

There's the sarcasm. Heat rushed to her cheeks, and despite her fatigue, she found she had energy to put Tarus back in his place. She rounded on him. Resisting the urge to disrupt their caravan to scold him, she exhaled through her nostrils, and kept her voice low. "I saved someone's life."

"Right. 'No one left behind,' eh?" Tarus said. "My point exactly."

"This is different." But Laela wasn't even sure if she believed that. It was one thing to abandon a woman pleading for help. It was another entirely to risk open conflict with the Order. "Whether we have people there or not, what are we going to do about it? We can't fight the Order." She lowered her voice, making certain only he could hear. "It is our duty to get as many people to the Grip as possible. That's all we can do. The rest is up to Rosler and Taggart."

"Ya might be right," Tarus conceded. "But, the scouts will return with word of how many legionaries they got, and how many of ours they've captured. If it's our duty to get as many people to the Grip as possible, ya can't argue if they've got a horde full of Wraith and a paltry resistance."

Laela shook her head. "Even *if*, and that's a big *if*, we're not fighters. Look around."

The men, women, and children who had fled Aranoc and escaped the Order and the hollowed marched onward in sullen silence. Hoods pulled low to protect against the rain did little to conceal their drawn expressions. Who could blame them after their bleak trek across the cursed island?

Tarus shrugged. "Let's see what the scouts say."

"It won't matter." She quickened her pace, passing others to get to the front of the procession to make sure Redge too wasn't taking Aylenia's counsel. *Of course she wants us to fight. She never wants us to leave.* Pulling ahead of Tarus, she hissed over her shoulder. "If you think that's going to convince me, you must follow the One."

By the time she made it to the front, Laela had stewed herself into a rage. Luckily, her fears that Aylenia was in Redge's ear too were assuaged by the fact that the two may as well have been walking on opposite sides of the Tears. Though both led at the front, Redge remained in the Spine's shadows, while Aylenia clung to the brambles along the river valley to the east as if she were considering making a run for it.

Part of Laela wondered what was more dangerous—letting her leave so close to Octarius where she could summon Underground reinforcements, or forcing her to stay where she could convince the Second Sword of the Wraith that fighting was a viable option.

Laela approached Redge first. His finely groomed brow raised as she neared.

"Aren't you supposed to be watching the flank?" Redge asked.

"I was." She shot Tarus a disdainful glare. "But I grew concerned with how we were being led."

Thunder rumbled overhead, echoing off the Spine as the rains picked up. Wind whipped through the river valley. It was no wonder why the Order had stopped to take shelter in the ruins. Though it meant they wouldn't be able to rest at Fort Cybel, the midday rains also offered cover by which they could circumvent the Order altogether. If they were lucky, they could sneak by and continue toward the Grip.

"We're heading south," Redge said, more obvious than the Tenets of Faytemarked. He told her that they'd sent scouts ahead that should be returning soon. She hoped he was right, because if they weren't coming back, that meant the Order had already found them.

Laela grit her teeth, sparing a glance to Aylenia to make sure she wasn't eavesdropping. The more she thought about it, the more she realized Aylenia was likely just playing one of Arilette's games.

If she suggests fighting the Order to Tarus, knowing I would refuse, would she counter with heading east? If the Underground had managed to infiltrate their ranks and sabotage their plans of escape, it wasn't impossible to think that they could be preparing to seize their beleaguered party by force. The closer they drew to Octarius, the greater the chance that they were stumbling into another trap.

She dropped her chin and whispered to Redge. "To what end? We can't stop at Fort Cybel with legionaries crawling all over. Unless the Undergrounder got to you too?" She scowled in Aylenia's direction.

Redge's dark eyes narrowed like crossed swords. Their time on the run hadn't allowed him his typical grooming routine. The dark hair of his Palogian heritage began to prickle his shaved scalp and shadow his cheeks. "I don't care if we have to tunnel beneath Fort Cybel. We are *not* fighting the Order."

Laela nodded. "What other options do we have? Because we're running out of time, and I believe the Undergrounder's suggestion to take Cybel by force is a false one."

Redge raised a brow, not following her meaning.

"She suggests we take Fort Cybel, knowing we'll deny it. But when the time arrives, she'll suggest a second option. A *safer* option. Head east. But we are not taking a single step east. She knows we're trying to make it to the Grip. We know Arilette won't let us leave. The moment we cross Cybel's Tears, the moment we come within Octarius's reach, they'll have us just where they want us. They'll never let us leave, Redge. So before we get to Fort Cybel, we need a plan."

"Ghosts." Redge took a deep breath as he massaged his scalp. He opened his mouth to speak but closed it, looking towards the gloomy horizon in the east. "I'd rather take my chances out there than fight the Order. There at least we have a chance to run. Here…" He nodded at Fort Cybel's haunted remains. "No choice but to fight. They'll catch us if we try to sneak past."

Laela grumbled, fearing the same. "There must be another option. Think!"

"Incoming," Redge whispered.

Laela didn't need to turn to know Aylenia had cut across the procession, no doubt to attempt to bend Laela's ear to whatever poison Arilette had injected into Aylenia's head. Before Aylenia could speak or make her presence known, Laela spun on her. "Speak not a word, or I swear by Neutreen, I'll hollow you out and send you into the Order camp on your own."

To her credit, Aylenia did not back away; she barely seemed fazed by Laela's sharpness. Without a word, she raised her finger to the figures trotting through the darkness heading in their direction.

The scouts.

Laela scowled.

Tarus placed his hand on the small of Laela's back. "Let's hear what they gotta say."

His touch sent a shiver up her spine. His words made her heart sink. She knew what the scouts would say. She knew what Aylenia would suggest, how Tarus would respond, how Redge would fall right into whatever trap Arilette and the Underground had waiting for them.

"You thought I was a bad leader," her father said. *"Not so easy, eh? Don't have all the answers after all, hmm? There's a reason I taught you to fight. Runnin' ain't an option."*

Laela closed her eyes, shutting out his taunts, but darkness closed around her all the same. *There is no escape. Neutreen, you've left us. You've abandoned us in a rotting world.* The Goddess of Justice might have sent the Savior to deliver them arcanatek to combat Rheynia's curse, but what good was any of it when the Order and the Underground only used the power to wage war against each other?

After instructing their procession to take rest in the undying forests along the river, Laela joined Tarus, Redge, and Aylenia in meeting the scouts who'd returned from Fort Cybel. Not knowing who Tarus had sent ahead, Laela was at least relieved to find familiar faces would be giving the report and not some potential Underground mole.

Asla, a girl who'd served as a messenger between Verinius and Rance, pulled back her hooded cloak. She had overcome the scratch marks that scarred her cheek after a scrape with the hollowed, but the loss of her brother to dewskull the previous winter left a sullen sadness behind her eyes. Now, after losing Verinius, Rance, and Erynia in a single day, hopelessness softened her brow as if she'd given up.

Bhen, a veteran in Aranoc's city watch, crossed his arms over his chest beside Asla. His grim expression flattened his already grizzled features. Stern at the best of times, even at the feet of Neutreen's shrine, Bhen's disposition displayed dissension between him and Asla.

Today was supposed to have been their escape. Their triumph over the Order, the Underground, and the undying. The new hope of Sansia wasn't far away. But now, at least by the look in Asla's dewy-brown eyes and the set of Bhen's clenched jaw, those hopes were crushed.

"A score of legionaries," Asla said. "They got a dozen of our own, looks like. Least as far as I can count."

Bhen bristled. "There could be a hundred Wraith in their clutches. It shouldn't make no difference. Them in there are of the Eighth Legion. They're not Order boys just flown the Nest; they've got arcanatek, defendable positioning, and—blood and bone—stop looking at me like that."

Asla's defeated expression hardened to hateful. "So you're just gonna let them rot here—with them? While we scurry off? Whatever happened to 'No one left behind,' eh?"

Bhen tossed his hands in the air. "Here we go."

Laela held up a silencing hand. She already knew Asla's take on the matter. Maybe that's why Tarus sent her, because he knew she'd side with him. Laela snuck a glance at Aylenia to see how she felt about the matter, but the Palogian woman's face was a mask of hard lines and soft lips— impossible to read. She nodded at the former city watchman. "Could we sneak around, continue south?"

Bhen grunted. "They'd spot us. Trees are sparse. Brambles would barely cover us if we crawled on our bellies."

Laela examined the dark clouds, wondering how long they'd last for. "They could move off once the rains pass. If they found us on our bellies, we'd be impaled and flayed long before we saw the Grip." The scent of ashes filled her nostrils as every viable option brought her closer to the flames. "What do you suggest, Bhen?"

"Go north until we find a crossing. Follow the Tears down to the Grip. Even if the Order sees us, we'll have a head start with the river between us."

Asla bit her lip, clearly frustrated with the idea. Her scowl met Laela's gaze, as if waiting for the answer she'd been fearing.

Laela snuck another glance at Aylenia. *You'd love that, wouldn't you? How far out are your reinforcements?* After Laela had destroyed Aylenia's interlayer arcanatek, there was no telling how Arilette would respond, but their goal never changed: don't let the Wraith leave. *We can't go east.*

Redge nodded at Bhen. "He's right. No one left behind is a nice thought. But that's all it is. We'd lose more than we'd gain attempting to take the fort. Crossing the river gives us the best chance of getting the most people to the Grip."

Asla scoffed.

"Go on," her father said. *"Run away. Cry to your mother."*

Laela didn't like the prospect. Waiting for Aylenia to weigh in and add a third voice assenting to head east, Laela found herself agreeing with Asla and Tarus. If these truly were their only two options, Laela would rather take the fight on her terms.

"Is there another option?" Laela asked. "Besides fighting or backtracking to head east?"

Silence.

Aylenia snorted. "There is only one option. There has only ever been *one* option."

"We're not joining you," Laela snapped. "We're not serving as fodder in your war against the Order. We will escape this ghosting curse."

Aylenia's nose wrinkled, her brow cocked. "Not what I was going to suggest." She shook her head. "You fight. I've seen you fight. But you fight *in order* to flee. You're not an army. I get that. But you have the numbers, the advantage of surprise, and with a decent plan, you could save your people."

Redge scoffed. "At what cost?"

"Does it matter?" Aylenia asked, never looking at Redge. Her eyes glittered, a pleading in them as if she wanted so badly for Laela to see the world the way she did. "If you're talking about lives, yes, odds are you'll lose more than you reclaim if you try. But if you don't…" She shook her head. "Then the cost is hope. And without that… what does the Wraith even stand for?"

Laela found herself without a response. She knew what the Wraith stood for, but Aylenia's indictment sent the scar across Laela's chest aflame. *"No one left behind."* To Rance it meant something. It was an ideal, not an absolute, but the burdens of leadership required sacrifices, even for symbolic victories. It was one thing to go back to Aranoc and pick up every straggler along the way. But they were right here, in need of saving.

Laela pursed her lips, searching for Aylenia's ulterior motive, but found none. *Does she actually want us to fight in order to flee? Or is she trying to prove that if we fight and win here, we can defeat the Order if we join together?*

"I know you're afraid of losing more people," Aylenia said, glancing between them. "Rance, right? And Verinius? Your mother."

Laela swallowed, the wounds of their losses still too sore to pick at.

"We lost them because of you!" Redge snapped, taking full advantage of the roaring storm.

Laela held up a silencing hand.

Aylenia sighed. "I could say I lost people because of you too. But where would that get us? We've all lost people. We all will continue to lose people. So it's what we do about it that matters."

Laela didn't trust Aylenia. She didn't need to burn a match to divine Neutreen's will on the matter, but still, she had a point. "What say you of Bhen's plan, then? Go north, ford the Tears, then travel down the east side of the river?"

Aylenia shook her head. "You risk too much for not enough. Return north, through these forests, only to come back down the other side of the river? Yeah, you might evade the Order, but the hellhounds and hollowed will have twice as long to find you. Might as well do what you did in escaping Aranoc and send small groups south attempting to sneak past Fort Cybel at that point and hope the rains last long enough to keep the Order inside." She shrugged. "But we can win this fight here and now. Take the camp. Rest a while. Then go from there."

"Go?" Tarus asked. "Don't you mean return with you to Octarius? Wasn't that yer plan?"

Aylenia exhaled through her nostrils. "Me and what army? Divided, ruin will reign, but you're not soldiers." She waved her hand back at their resting procession. "Sure, we could use the help, but if all your efforts would be to escape from us, what good would it serve?"

Laela scoffed. "So you don't want us to go east?"

Aylenia scowled. "When have I said go east?" She pointed at the shadow of Fort Cybel. "I already told you; there is one option. South. Whether you try to sneak past and leave your people or stay and fight to free them, that's up to you. But if it were my people in there, my family… I know what I would do."

Shame crept into Laela's cuirass, making her fidget in an attempt to dissipate it. *Am I so concerned with saving myself? How many am I comfortable leaving behind?*

"Same as your mother," her father said. *"Run away. It's all you're good f—"*

Encasing herself in her Center of Silence, she glanced from Aylenia to Asla. The scout nodded vigorously as if she were ready to join the Underground after Aylenia's speech. Though Bhen's frown remained firm, his crossed arms had settled on his sword hilt as if resolved to the inevitable fight. Tarus too, despite not needing any convincing, appeared ready to draw steel. Of their group, only Redge remained unconvinced.

Redge spat on the ground between them, closer to Aylenia's feet than anyone else's. "You say you lost people. Yeah. That's what happens in war. That's what happens when you pick a fight with a tyrant—you lose people." He snorted, stalking closer to Aylenia, his index finger leading the way. "You enlisted. We didn't. We just wanted to leave this cursed place. Don't compare your losses to ours. Don't act like you stand atop the Spine while we're down in the Gullies just because we don't take fights we can't win."

Laela put a hand on his arm, half to make certain Redge didn't continue to attempt to lord over Aylenia to keep his ego intact, half because he wasn't entirely right. Stepping into the center of their small circle, she nodded at Redge. "You're right. We didn't pick this fight. It hasn't been fair, and it never will be. Reality is, whether we enlisted or not, we are up against a tyrant and a curse."

Redge's expression darkened once he realized she wasn't on his side. "You too? You realize this is the first step, eh? First we fight for our own. Then we fight because we've proven we can. Next thing you know we'll be wearing Underground whites and marching in Arilette's legions."

"No." Laela met Aylenia's eyes, thinking of her mother. "There is strength in being able to fight and courage knowing when to do so. We fight today and seek Neutreen beyond the curse tomorrow. We are not Undergrounders. We will not go with you to Octarius. We are not part of Arilette's war. We do this. Then we go our separate ways."

Aylenia held Laela's gaze, not averting when Redge asked why Laela would let Aylenia go when she could warn the Underground of their location; not when Tarus asked about tactics or how they'd go about liberating Fort Cybel from Order control; not when Redge stormed off, muttering curses in a Palogian dialect she couldn't understand.

Aylenia's stare unnerved her at first, as if she'd played right into the Underground's plan, but with each passing moment, Laela found the look in her eyes strangely comforting.

"We do this together," Laela said. She broke from Aylenia's gaze to take Asla's tattered scarf between her thumb and forefinger. "I have a plan. Tarus, Bhen, gather those who can fight and whatever weapons we can muster. We have a fort to take."

CHAPTER 43

SHADOWS OF UNDERSTANDING

Threyna XVII

The threat of Belrich's Inquisitors, the Order, and the darklings were gone, but despite the relative safety of the woods, Threyna's fingers began to tremble. Surrounded by legionaries and the tempest of souls wishing to overtake her flesh, she'd been fine. Composed. Present in mind and body. But now, as she strode with Fawkes through the dead forests beyond the Gullies and along the Tears with the midday rains storming down on them, all she wanted was to hide in her bunk.

With Octarius too far away, she sank into the solitude of her Inner Throne. She breathed deeply, gazing out the stained-glass windows. There was a storm gathering in the distance—a circling black cloud, emitting forks of red lightning. Whatever it was, it was coming her way.

Fawkes placed his hand on her elbow. Startled, Threyna reared to strike.

"Gory ghosts, Threy." Fawkes retreated his splayed hands. "Just wanted to check on ya."

Threyna took a deep breath, lowering her fist. "Apologies, I—" She didn't know what to say. She didn't know what to feel or think. The thought of the Inquisitor's hands poking and prodding her arm while his eyes hid behind his skeletal mask sent shivers down her spine.

"What happened to ya in there?" Fawkes gestured his head back the way they'd come.

Threyna swallowed a knot in her throat. Subconsciously, she reached for the bangle embedded into her arm. They resumed trudging through the mud. "They tried to take it."

Unable to tap into her Inner Throne within Belrich's tent, the bangle had reacted on its own accord to make certain it was not taken from her... with bloody results. It wasn't exactly protective, but possessive, which only scared her more. There was no kinship between her and the artifact, no relational responsibility to care for her. Only an adamant and unyielding desire to finish its task with her. Whatever that was.

Another prong had released from her arm when she consumed the first darkling's soul. Two down—the first when she'd conjured a bloody sword in the tunnels beneath Aranoc, and now again at consuming a soul. Two more prongs remained deeply entrenched in her flesh, but what it would take to unlock them remained to be seen. Whatever needed to happen, Threyna had no doubt that it would not part with her before it was finished.

Trudging through the puddles from the midday rains, Fawkes examined her arm. Aside from the black veins pulsing above and below the onyx-and-crimson artifact, she was marred with bruises and scrapes from when she'd fallen through the trees on the ashes of her failing wings. Her entire body ached, but she didn't want Fawkes's sympathy or his concern.

"I'm prime."

Fawkes bristled. "Prime? Ya look like ya been spat outta a Dreadroot's arse."

Heat rose to Threyna's cheeks. "What do you want, Fawkes? Why are you here?"

If before he bristled, now he outright blubbered. "What'dya think? Heard legionaries settin' up camp. Saw they had an unconscious prisoner. Figured you were someone important when Belrich went into the tent with ya. What else was I supposed to do?"

Threyna scoffed, quickening her pace and stomping through puddles. "Someone important? Sorry to disappoint."

"C'mon," Fawkes called from behind. "It's not like that."

Threyna spun in the mud. "What's it like then, hmm?" She made a mockery of looking behind him. "You can't find Dracus or Canton to pick up after, so you assume I'm someone in need of saving—is that it?"

Fawkes furrowed his brow. "Dracus created a distraction so Cant and I could get away from the Order. Then Cant and I got separated by a horde."

Threyna couldn't help but chuckle. "So you thought I was one of them. Now it makes sense."

"What are you on about? *Someone* needed help. Course I didn't think you were Canton."

"But maybe Dracus." Threyna fixed him with a glare. "Who else would you waste an entire soul jar on?"

Fawkes tossed his hands in the air. "Threyna—girl, listen to me. Did I think ya might be Dray, yeah—it was possible. But ya don't see me disappointed in findin' ya. I didn't waste no soul jar. I'm damn glad ya got out. So why are you layin' this on me?"

A storm of memories poured down on her, heavier than the rains. Mornings spent in Octarius's bunks not wanting to get up if her father wasn't going to return home. Evenings before the last light fled the horizon spent staring north, waiting to see if her mother would come back for her. Long days and longer nights wondering if anyone even cared. They felt childish. They were childish. She'd sound ridiculous if she gave them voice, yet still, she wouldn't release the anger that clung to the memories, or exonerate Fawkes from his association with them.

"Forget it." Threyna whirled, unable and unwilling to give Fawkes an explanation he wouldn't even begin to understand. She charged into the night. Away from Fawkes. Away from the Order. Away from her past and towards the future—the only thing that mattered.

"Where ya goin'?"

Threyna wheeled on him again. "Home. I'm going *home*. All you care about is escaping. So go. Run away with Dracus. Run away with Canton. Blood and bone, I don't care. But stop pretending you give a ghosting damn about me."

Thunder roared overhead, and lightning struck nearby.

Fawkes shook his head and took a deep breath. "None of that's true." He held up a finger. "One, Octarius ain't your home. Two—" He held up a second finger. "Escaping don't mean nothin' without the people ya get to start anew with. There's a time to fight. There's a time to flee. I fought to free ya so we could run. Not to fight a whole ghostin' legion. But if ya won't even try to see the difference, then you're not worth the charge."

They stared at each other for a long moment, falling rain and dead foliage all that lay between them.

"Yer mad," Fawkes said, holding up his hands. "I get that. I'd be mad as a hellhound too if I was you. Ya want us to fight. Ya want the lot of us to join you and Arilette cause you believe it'll bring ya life. 'Divided, ruin will reign,' and all that. But Arilette ain't who ya think she is. She believes that mantra to a fault, killin' any who threaten division." He stalked closer, hands up as if he were approaching a rabbit ready to bolt.

"There's truth in the words," Fawkes continued. "We gotta unite, or we will fail. But yer someone who people will follow—who people'll listen to." He pointed to the bangle on her arm. "If ya told the Underground that we had the ships, that we could get everyone outta here, we could unite—in freedom."

She bit back the pain of Laela's betrayal again, focusing on the argument worth having. "In Sansia." Her thoughts drifted to Aylenia. Her mother had gone on that voyage with dreams of establishing a new settlement for the rest of the Wraith's refugees to come to. To *start anew.* Her mother, nor anyone else in the camp, was ever seen or heard from again.

"Yeah. Sansia." Fawkes drew nearer with the careful caution of a hunter.

Threyna pointed to the dying earth beneath her feet. "Everyone disappeared the last time you went to Sansia. It's either the darklings you know or the darklings you don't. We don't need to run to start anew. We can start anew *here*. If we join together, we can defeat the Order. We can make a new home here!"

The desperation in Fawkes's eyes threatened to overflow. "Even if ya did defeat the Order…" He squeezed his fists before him as if holding onto a terrible truth. "Dracus believes the Skeleton King is still out there. Waitin', storin' up souls, preparin' himself for someone like you to threaten his reign. I'm tellin' ya, Threy, if we don't leave now…" He shook his head. "Even if you could defeat the Order, ya won't beat him. He's got limitless souls at his disposal, a farm of blood bags to siphon vitality from. This ain't a battle that can end in victory."

Frustration pulsed in her ears, in her fists, and behind her eyes. Hot breath seethed out from between her teeth. She considered her mantra with Aylenia. Always another fight, but victory had become elusive. She wanted to believe it was possible. She needed to believe it could be done.

She closed her eyes, blocking out images of Daeton's death, Ebrus's shade, and Yevon's darkling. *There will be victory. There has to be, or it was all for nothing.* She fixed Fawkes with a darkling's stare. "You only say that because it hasn't happened before. You only say that because the last time someone tried—my father tried—you, my mother, Laela, and everyone else who could have made a difference ran away! Chasing their *new start*. Blood and bone—when will you learn from your mistakes?"

Fawkes inhaled sharply, wrinkled his nose, and spat off to the side of the path between them. He held her in his gaze, no longer attempting to get closer, no longer holding his hands out innocently. He only stood— resolved. Defeated.

"Dracus fought beside yer father. He woulda died beside him."

"He didn't," Threyna hissed. "He ran away. Like he always does."

Fawkes shook his head. "Ghosts, Threy. He only left 'cause yer father told him to." He pointed at the bangle on her arm. "So that wouldn't fall back into the Skeleton King's hands." He inclined his gaze to the clouds overhead and scratched his beard in consternation as if deliberating whether he should say what was truly on his mind. "He found ya. Right around these here woods, aye? He didn't run away then, did he?"

Threyna narrowed her eyes, not appreciating the darkening tone of Fawkes's words.

"No. He didn't run. Not even when yer wounds were dire. He coulda ran. He coulda returned to me and Canton. *Alive.*" Fawkes sniffed. If he hadn't rubbed his face with the back of his hand, Threyna might not have even noticed the tears streaming silently into his beard. "He brought you back to Octarius because you wouldn'ta made it up north. He took ya down into that hole in the ground to the warps. He saved yer life, but he never came back."

Threyna didn't understand. Of course he came back.

"Ya can hear heartbeats, eh?" Fawkes asked. "But ya can't hear Dray's. Ever wonder why?" He pointed his finger at her, leveling it like a dagger's tip. "She poisoned him. Said he was done after what she did to those ships, what she did to her own father… so she poisoned him."

Threyna's mind slogged through Fawkes's words, attempting to deconstruct them and piece it all back together. *No. Arilette wouldn't. She couldn't have…* But it was true; she couldn't hear Dracus's heartbeat. He was hollowed, somehow managing the pain of death while clinging to sentience. She grasped for words, but her dry mouth and her addled mind formed none.

"So you ask if we'll learn from our mistakes? Aye. We learned we can't trust Arilette. So go back to Octarius. Convince the Wraith to join you if ya want, but understand this: forced unity will only build a fractured army. And we won't be a part of it. Not Dracus. Not Canton. Not me."

Threyna pursed her lips. She asserted herself onto her Inner Throne and listened to Fawkes's heartbeats: deep, impassioned, but even. Honest. True.

"So I'll ask ya one last time," Fawkes said. "Come with us."

Threyna released her grasp of her Inner Throne. She didn't need it to determine the genuine desire in his voice. He wanted her to go with him and join them in their flight from Rheynia. But she couldn't.

She afforded him a sad smile. "What is it you Wraith say? 'No one left behind.' We both know this will only end one way. I won't live my life on the run. You won't spend your life fighting for a cause you don't believe in." She shrugged, all anger towards him gone. The resentment she'd held all these years washed away, leaving only the stain of memory.

Fawkes nodded. He approached at a normal gait to place his hand on her shoulder. Behind his beard and tangled hair, beneath the hardened exterior of a man who'd lived a life of war and survival, a tenderhearted soul stared back at her. "Divided, ruin will reign. May we all escape its shadow." He gave her shoulder a squeeze and disappeared into the rain, heading toward Fort Cybel, his partner, and the boy they'd raised as a son.

Threyna watched him go, hoping they'd find what they were looking for. She understood why their journeys couldn't continue together. Like a hollowed, some wounds would never heal. Threyna could forgive Arilette, if what Dracus, Laela, and Fawkes said of her lies was true. She could forgive Laela for not believing victory was possible.

If the Wraith see what I'm capable of, if I convince Laela to join with me, Belrich, the Order, and the Skeleton King—none of them would stand a chance.

She'd sent Aylenia with Laela to lead the Wraith south, but now it was up to Threyna to convince them to come to Octarius and join the Underground. *Always another fight. I need this one to end in victory.*

With her rot well abated, she tapped into her Inner Throne and conjured wings. Resolving herself to listen to the artifact and not repeat her own mistakes, she took flight, determined to find the Wraith and defeat the Order.

CHAPTER 44

TRUE JUSTICE

Laela XVII

Laela felt naked. No sword at her waist or strapped to her back. No dagger on her belt, no knife concealed in a vambrace. Only *True* was safely hidden in her boot. Otherwise, nothing. She couldn't remember a time when the Mistress of Blades was so deprived, but it was necessary for her plan to work.

Tarus and Bhen hated the plan. Redge would have protested even worse had he not already stormed off. Though Laela had come up with it, she wasn't even sure how she felt about it. It didn't feel like something Rance or her mother would have considered, let alone allowed. Neither Asla's staunch support nor Aylenia's unreadable silence provided any confidence, but if they were to escape the Order's stranglehold over Rheynia, it would not be without risks.

Yet as Laela, Aylenia, and Asla approached the front gates of the fallen fort, Laela began to wonder if the risks were too great. Unarmed, hands raised in surrender, they trudged through the rain toward the two legionary lookouts.

"Oi!" called one of the sentries over his shoulder. Three more legionaries hustled out through the broken portcullis followed by two additional stragglers.

"Play the part," Aylenia whispered, as tears began to well in her eyes. "Don't let them see the soldier." Letting out a cry, she ran towards the legionaries.

Swords drew from five scabbards. "Halt!"

Aylenia collapsed to the muddy ground. "Thank Neutreen. Thank Neutreen!" Unleashing full sobs between each shout, Aylenia put on a performance that would make the mummers from the days before the Disasters quake with envy. She wailed as if attempting to rival the midday storms.

Despite the legionaries slackening at her supplication, they did not sheath their steel.

Following Aylenia's lead, Asla collapsed to the ground a stride behind her. "Please, we're sorry. We'll never do it again. Mercy. Mercy!"

Laela knew what she was supposed to do. It was her plan after all. But bowing to the Order, even in a farcical manner, felt like a betrayal of everything she was. And just like that, she was a girl again. A scared girl gripping the hilt of a quivering sword with a dulled blade. Her father stared down his nose as if he were examining the underside of his boot after stepping in something foul. His lips moved. His head shook. He turned away. Anger burned within her. She wanted to use the sword in her hand. She wanted to stab him in the back. She wanted to prove him wrong.

Laela felt his voice at the edge of her Center of Silence, but she shielded her mind from him, returning to the present moment.

"What about you?" said a legionary with a fat lip and a bruised cheek. He jutted his double chin at her, scratching his stubbly beard. "Your turn to cry?"

Heat flushed Laela's cheeks despite the cool rain.

"Run while you still can," her father said. *"Neutreen knows you're no use in a fight."*

He was wrong. She'd proven him wrong time and time again. She was the First Sword of the Wraith. He was just a soldier in Victarius Kaine's army—a bitter, selfish deserter and betrayer. He might as well have been standing before her because all Laela wanted to do was fight to prove him wrong. She could take all five if she'd brought her blades.

But he wasn't there. Even his voice wasn't real. He only existed because she refused to let go of him. As horrible as he was, he was still her father. He had left his mark on her and she had the scars to prove it, but she was tired of holding onto him. Especially when he only baited her into trouble.

Fists clenched, jaw tight, she forced herself to breathe. *I fight to flee. Neutreen is watching.* She swallowed her rage, ignoring the fire coursing through the scar on her chest.

"We just wanted to leave," Laela said, her voice small. "We never wanted to fight. We just wanted to leave, but they wouldn't let us." She cowered. "My turn to cry? I have cried every moment since the Underground ruined our escape. I have left a trail of tears with every step from Aranoc's safety. I have lost…"

"Rance sacrificed himself so we could get to Aranoc," Dracus had said.

"Be strong. Be courageous!" her mother had cried before running into a horde of hollowed only to be stabbed in the heart by Belrich. She'd spent her last words—not on her—but on Threyna. All Laela had received was a shout over her shoulder and a fatekeeper that told her not to let anyone keep her hurting. She was injured beyond repair. Beyond time's healing capabilities. She'd carry this pain for the rest of her days.

Bitterness knotted in her throat. "I've lost everyone… Neutreen knows we're guilty. But guilty of wanting to run from this curse, not of opposing you. The Underground…" She feigned looking over her shoulder at the supposed legion on their tails. "They're trying to drag us back to their stronghold in Octarius."

The legionary with the purple bruise and split lip appraised her, searching her from head to toe in a way that made her skin crawl.

Stomaching his *inspection*, Laela pushed through her disgust. "You ask if I will cry; that depends on your next words. You can help. You can protect us from the Underground. We wanted to head west toward the Wing, but they collapsed the mountain pass with arcanatek!"

"That's what that was?" one of the other legionaries asked. "Ghosts."

"They're coming," Laela said, looking over her shoulder again. "Please. Defend us."

"Don't let them take us," Aylenia said.

Asla crawled through the mud to the feet of the nearest legionary with a beaked nose and skittish eyes. "We beg you."

The legionary shoved her with his boot. "What do we do?"

"Gotta tell Calyx," a short, stout ham of a man said over the storm.

"We must help them. We can put them with the others," a younger man said, his wet blond hair clinging to his forehead. Still green with the propagandic do-goodery instilled at the Nest, his noble nature reminded her of Canton's idealistic foolishness, but if he led them to the other captives, he might as well have been one of Neutreen's angels.

The bruised leader bit his fat lip and grunted. He seemed to shrink at the mention of Calyx. He bent to grab Aylenia by her upper arm, hoisting her from the mud to yank her close. "How many?"

Aylenia's tear-streaked cheeks quivered. "I don't... I don't know. 100. 200."

The color of his cheeks surrounding his bruise paled. "From where? How far behind?"

Laela looked over her shoulder. "They're here!" Torches flickered in the distance, barely burning through the rain. Dozens from the east, and even more from the north.

"Blood, bone, and black death." The legionary shoved Aylenia toward the blond-haired boy. "Put them with the others. And hurry." He advanced on Laela.

It took every fiber of her being not to grab him by his thumb and wrench his arm behind his back until he squealed. Chewing the inside of her cheek, she let him seize her by the arm and haul her through Fort Cybel's dilapidated entrance.

"To arms! Underground—from the Spine and to the north!"

The camp, a cohort of closer to fifty legionaries, scrambled. The initial fumbling of men turned to straight rank and file. The discipline and the speed of their response sent a chill down Laela's spine as doubt ate away at the foundations of her plan.

Be strong. Be courageous. This has to work.

The Premius, Calyx, strode from a tent at the center of the camp, sword drawn and arcanatek charging. "Report!"

Before Laela could assess their strategy for defense, she, Aylenia, and Asla were dragged deeper into the courtyard of the fallen fort. They passed crumbling structures where rotten wood collapsed upon fractured stone, ruins of what was once a chapel, and an old forge long past the state of repair on the way to the remains of horse stables. Once inside, a score of long faces looked up at them over their bound wrists.

"Bind them!" the split-lipped legionary said, shoving Laela to his blond-haired compatriot escorting Aylenia. Laela feigned weakness, allowing his push to send her sprawling. His heavy footsteps squished away to join the ranks with the rest of the Order's Eighth Legion.

The beaked legionary's flighty eyes darted between Laela, Asla, and the rest of the Wraith. Laela had already spotted familiar faces within their captives. She only hoped they wouldn't do or say anything to give her away.

Beak beckoned for the younger soldier to pass Aylenia to him. "Give her here. I'll hold these two. You tie her up first."

Laela, prone in the mud, examined the Order boy playing at being an honorable servant of the realm, inspecting him for any signs of weakness. A droop in the shoulder, a shift in his hips that might have suggested a potential injury. The picture of health, he gave her no easy opportunities. The short sword in its scabbard, the arcanatek strapped to his hip, and the dagger in his boot only made her feel more vulnerable before him.

If there was any hesitation in him, it lasted but a moment before the Nest's brainwashing tactics took hold. He passed Aylenia to Beak. "This is for your protection, my ladies. Stay here. We will protect you." As he stepped close to help Laela to her feet, she eyed the dagger in his boot.

While Premius Calyx shouted orders, directing his men against the torches lit by the weak and infirm of their number, Bhen and Tarus would be leading any who could fight around to flank the fort's weaker walls.

"Where there is order, there is justice!" Calyx shouted, rallying his legionaries.

Two men stand between twenty refugees and freedom. They will not stop us.

Laela felt his hand scoop under her arm to hoist her up. She pushed into the ground, snapping her head back. The back of her skull collided with the soft cartilage of his nose. Bone crunched as he yelped, but before he could step back, Laela ripped his dagger from his boot.

Simultaneously, Asla stomped on Beak's foot, then kneed him in the groin. Aylenia elbowed him in the gut before drawing his short sword and plunging it into his lower stomach.

Laela continued her own assault. Grabbing at his nose, the legionary was in no position to defend her first stab. The dagger bit deep, chewing through the leather armor and into his shoulder. She tore it free and stabbed it into his other shoulder, rendering both arms useless. She kicked his leg out from under him and dropped her knee into his spine. With two quick slashes, she severed the tendons behind his knees and ankles. He cried out, not dead, not even dying, but incapacitated to the point that he wouldn't be able to hinder their escape. Luckily, the rain, thunder, and wind prevented his voice from attracting others.

As Asla took Beak's dagger and began cutting refugees free, Aylenia held her stolen short sword to Beak's unfortunate nose as he attempted to hold his intestines in place.

Laela yanked the legionary up by his blond hair, exposing his throat to his own steel. "Keep silent and you will survive this. Scream and it will be the last thing you do."

He whimpered, helpless as she stripped him of his arcanatek.

"Head to the river," Asla said to those she liberated. "There's a hole in the curtain wall."

"Oi!" Beak screamed. "Hel—"

Aylenia slashed across Beak's skinny neck, cutting short his shout. His skittish eyes went wide and still as she opened his throat. Despite his thin frame, dark blood gushed from the gash and bubbled from his open mouth.

Ghosts. Laela fumbled with the arcanatek. She'd held the magical tools provided by the Savior before, but the one in her hands wasn't the same device as those she'd practiced with in Octarius's underdark. She flipped the switch, and it began to warble, but whether it was set to vortex or irradiate, she couldn't be sure.

Beak was fading fast. His gasps for air came shorter and sharper as blood filled his lungs. It wouldn't be long before either his hollowed form tried to tear the life from Aylenia's body or his soul departed his ravaged flesh.

Aylenia ripped Beak's arcanatek from his belt and flipped the switch. "He hollows, you fire. He goes dark, let me handle it."

Laela nodded, gripping the arcanatek tighter as the warbling's charge reached its crescendo. Asla continued to cut through the bindings of the Order's captives. One by one, they took flight, running east towards their flanking force and the succor of reuniting with the rest of the Wraith. Yet as the first of Tarus's force scaled the rubble on the northeastern edge of the fort, the Order boy at Laela's feet whimpered.

"Liars," he said, his gaze fixed on the shapes drawing crossbows. "Traitors. Murderers." He took a deep breath, preparing to shout.

Laela dropped to a knee and plunged her stolen dagger into the back of his skull. Not a heartbeat had passed before Tarus's volley of not nearly enough bolts collided with the backs of the unsuspecting legionaries. As screams erupted, so too did the Order boy's darkling. It screeched as it leapt from his body into the air.

"Darkling!" Aylenia aimed her arcanatek and squeezed the trigger.

Radiant light exploded. Laela shielded her eyes, but glowing auras filled her vision, blinding her to anything and everything else. She blinked, falling onto her back to leave the dagger planted in the back of the legionary's skull, the vibrating arcanatek still whirring in her hand.

More screams filled the night as a Dawnshard exploded elsewhere. The calamity of battle collided with the storm's wrath to swallow Fort Cybel in cacophony.

Laela forced herself upright as her vision began to return. Aylenia tore another Dawnshard from Beak's belt and hurled it at the legionaries attempting to reconfigure to defend their flank. Aylenia reached down to take another Dawnshard just as the light faded from Beak's eyes. No longer dying, but fully hollowed, he seized her by the wrist and attempted to bite at her exposed neck.

Laela pulled the trigger.

Aylenia reared back just as a bluish-white shade was drawn from Beak's body. He crumpled, absent a soul to keep him upright. Laela blinked, unable to look away from the ghastly visage of what was once a man. He appeared very much like he did in life. Poor bastard was cursed for eternity with his horrid nose.

"Come on," Aylenia said, helping Laela to her feet.

"That's the last of them." Asla cut the last of the refugee captives free.

The Order had reformed and began their counterattack. Out of arrows, the Wraith charged with whatever weapons they had.

Laela drew the short sword from the fallen legionary's scabbard. She pointed at Asla and Aylenia. "Run. Get to cover."

Asla took off, following the path of those she freed.

Aylenia stalked past Laela in the other direction, toward the developing melee. "Let's go, Mistress of Blades. We don't run." She flashed Laela a grin that made her appear half-mad. The other half tightened Laela's throat and flushed her cheeks.

"You'd fight with us?" Laela asked.

Aylenia smirked. "We fight to flee, right?"

A mad smile stretched across Laela's lips too. And when she expected her father's commentary, nothing came. She drew *True* from her boot. "Let's give the Order some true justice."

Together, they charged in just as Tarus and Bhen led the assault on the Order front. With steel in one hand and an arcanatek in the other, Laela entered the fray, ready to finish what she'd started.

Bhen reached the legionaries first at the center of their triangular formation. The clash rippled down the line, but with the legion's focus on the Wraith, Laela and Aylenia came in from the side. No battle cries. No flash or pomp. Just the swing of steel, the scent of blood, and the wails of the forsaken.

Closing in, Laela found her mark. The nearest legionary was engaged with an overmatched and undersized Wraith refugee, overextending from the formation. Laela struck at his neighbor, swatting his sword aside to stab through the back of the overzealous legionary's shoulder. Thrown off-balance, the legionary's parry missed. The refugee's blade punched through the leather armor, but Laela was already onto the next.

She blocked. Kicked the back of a knee. Shoved her shoulder into one legionary while striking at another. Aylenia was right behind her, her short sword already stained scarlet. While Bhen's long sword swiped the Order's shorter gladii aside, he made room for Tarus's dual daggers to punch holes in the leather. Decent enough as a duelist to be the Second Sword of the Wraith, Tarus was an absolute terror on the battlefield.

Shades and darklings rose from falling bodies on both sides. Those who were hollowed were eviscerated with multiple stab wounds to make certain they never regained their feet. Even still, groaning forms of the undying sprawled on the ground, grasping at ankles. Arcanatek whirred and fired all around her.

They were winning. Their numbers and the element of surprise overwhelmed the Order. But Laela fought from the silent sanctuary within her mind that earned her the title of Mistress of Blades and the First Sword of the Wraith. The battlefield melted away to reveal only the most immediate threat to her. Everything else was just a detail, a distraction that didn't require her attention.

A sword swung for her. Laela blocked, slid down the blade, and thrust. Fresh blood dripped from her sword's tip. Her opponent fell from sight, someone else's problem now. Another blade came for her, swiping at her lower leg. She high-stepped over it and took a diagonal position to press her new target.

Not faces. Not people. Bodies and blades. They're just bodies and blades.

Stab. Diagonal slash downward. Upward lashing backhand.

She closed the distance, driving *True* through a legionary's wrist. He attempted to strike her with his unarmed fist, but she got there first. Steel bit through leather, flesh, and bone. His fist connected with her cheek, but it lost whatever force it began with. She shook off the blow and stabbed again. Again. Again.

Wind rushed beside her in the dark abyss of her Center of Silence. Before she could react, steel raked across her back. Pain streaked along her ribs like a hellhound's howl through the Cut. She spun to the source but had to fend off a flurry of attacks. She blocked the first, but it threw her off-balance. The heavy hack sent vibrations down her arm. She repositioned her feet to steady herself, but she stepped on something in the slippery mud.

No. Not something.

Fingers curled around her shin. Sharp, cruel, hateful. They scratched at her britches, searching for purchase.

"Focus!" her father shouted, breaking through her Center of Silence.

Reckless strength sought to tear the stitches from her clothes and the flesh from her bones. All the while, the legionary's blade darted for her with an insatiable thirst for her blood. She stomped, attempting to kick free from the hollowed crawling up her leg, just as a horizontal slash aimed to part her head from her shoulders.

Unable to bring her sword around in time, she raised *True.* Though it didn't block the strike, it bought her a precious moment to duck beneath it. She stabbed at the hollowed clawing at her, then kicked the beast in its snapping jaws. She froze. She'd assumed it was someone from the Order.

Someone without a name. Without a face. But they weren't in Belrich's legions. They'd followed her from Aranoc, and she'd led them here.

Elisara? Onaren? She still didn't know what name the woman had in life, but she was gone now.

"Gonna cry?" her father taunted. *" This is war, girl. Life is war."*

A flash of green. The swish of steel through the air. Laela reared. Her foot didn't move with her. She fell back, tripping over the hollowed's severed arm. The green returned, the pauldrons of an Order Premius. Calyx, leader of the Eighth. His face, hard and unforgiving, appeared through her Center of Silence. He roared as he stabbed down at her.

She slapped the strike aside and rolled in the mud. Caked in grime, the slash across the back of her ribs screamed, but she shoved herself to her feet and launched at Calyx. Her shoulder took him in the belly, forcing him backwards. Despite the effort she put into the attack, he barely moved aside from the rain-slick ground. Without reprieve, he struck with a quick combination of three light strikes. Laela met each, deflecting them aside. She countered with a quick jab, but Calyx deflected and began a new assault, this time of four cuts.

Calyx overextended. Opportunity presented, Laela lunged. Calyx turned at the last moment. Her blade glanced off his pauldron, but she brought it around to hack down, batting his sword away before stabbing him in the gut with *True*. As she went to wrench her dagger free, he shoved her away. Rain-slick and bloodied, the dagger's hilt slipped from her grasp.

His sword came for her neck, but she caught his pommel in her free hand. She attempted to hack with her short sword, but he caught her by the wrist. She strained against him, but his strength was gradually overcoming hers.

Laela attempted to knee him in the groin.

"Don't leave your feet!"

Her father's shout came too late. Just as she drove her knee up, Calyx brought the crown of his head down on the bridge of Laela's nose. Her Center of Silence fractured. Lightning split across her face, branching through her entire body. Tears exploded from her eyes, blurring her vision. The ground seemed to sway before punching her in the back.

"Your sword!" her father yelled. *"Ugh! Just like your mother. Useless."*

Calyx stood over her, sword raised. *True's* embossed hilt protruded from his stomach, but his grim expression and hate-filled eyes gave no indication of keeling over and hollowing.

"I told you to run while you could."

Calyx began to swing down at her, intending to split her in half. Laela reared back her heel and kicked *True's* hilt, still embedded in Calyx's gut. His strike faltered, giving Laela just enough space to roll out of the way. She pressed herself to her feet, but Calyx shoved her down with one arm. He seized her by the collar of her tunic, blade poised to strike. Blood drained from his face. Sweat trickled down his brow. *True* struck deeply, likely clipping something vital. He would hollow from the wound eventually, but not before he made sure she suffered.

The blade's tip came for her chest. Laela threw herself backwards, yanking Calyx with her. Using his momentum, she rolled onto her back and kicked up, launching him over her. Cold steel sliced between her ribs, robbing her of breath. Clutching her side, she wheeled. Calyx was on his back. His own sword had disappeared in the fray of bodies all around them.

He groaned, his exposed teeth painted red. Laela crawled through the mud to get to him first and finish the fight. Hands covered in muck, she tore her dagger from Calyx's belly and plunged it back in. She reared back and punched the tip home again. Unable to breathe, barely able to see, she stabbed down again and again.

Warm blood spattered across her face as Calyx gasped. She continued to sink steel into the black leather armor until her arms gave out and she was drowned in white light.

A shade rose around her. Cold as the blade that pierced her, Calyx's shade passed through her, uninterested. Dead. Gone.

The raging battle had faded into a dull din of warbling arcanatek and groaning hollowed. Faraway shouts calling for mercy were soon extinguished. So many bodies lay around her, so many shades drifted into the night, she couldn't even tell who had won. Dark blood made everyone appear to be wearing Order blacks.

The scent of rain and eviscerated organs stained the air. Nausea rose, burning her throat. *Why did we fight? Everyone loses. Everyone.* Laela lowered her gaze, angry with herself for letting this be her end. This *"No one left behind,"* mantra, this notion—it was a lie. A black-and-white ideology just as bad as the Underground's credo. *Divided, ruin will reign. As if everyone could possibly work together. I should have run. I should have saved who I could. I'm no better than you, Father.* She sank into the mud. Defeated.

Footsteps squished over to her, ready to finish her off. A figure knelt down beside her. The fight had left her. She didn't want to look at her killer, not knowing whether their face would be etched into her mind for eternity if she did. A hand on her shoulder turned her.

Despite wanting to look away, Laela's gaze fell upon Aylenia and she was the most beautiful thing Laela had ever laid eyes on.

Aylenia gave her shoulder a squeeze. "We did it. We did it."

CHAPTER 45

LET GO, MY LOVE

Dracus XII

Dracus's footfalls squished deeply despite his best efforts not to sink into the sodden earth. As the worst of the midday rains stormed past, Fort Cybel lay ahead, and within, he would either find a hope to cling to, or an emptiness that would kill him as sure as the poison in his veins.

"To dream is to die," Dracus said to the wind. "To hope is to lie."

Fawkes and Canton could handle themselves; there was a chance they made it to Cybel's without him. There was a damn good chance, but Dracus's life had taught him not to trust the odds—not when they were in his favor.

He sighed, sinking deeper into the earth and his grief with each step. "To live is to lose all we've come by." He wished his aunt had suffered sooner. Maybe then he wouldn't be cursed with this half-hollowed rhyme that he couldn't fully remember.

He closed his eyes, blocking out the thought of how Nerus razed Salingard. How Canton's parents were scorched, not by the Tellers as he led him to believe, but by the Order. All because Dracus counseled Belrich to stay the mighty hand of the Order. Belrich had, but as Belrich did, it was only long enough to turn that hand into a fist. Cavus, Canton's father, was right in stealing from the Order. Right in attempting to rise up against the Skeleton King's tyranny. If only Dracus had realized that same truth sooner, seen through the lie the Order was built on. He'd failed time and time again. Yet now, he couldn't help but hold out foolish hope.

They hafta be here. They're waitin'. Just like I told 'em to.

"The lucky, we fall. And the misfortuned, we cry, but forever and ever, it is we who survive." Dracus neared the dilapidated fort, remembering the days when it stood triumphant. Now the ramparts were more rubble than anything else. He just wanted to believe they could still protect the last two souls he cared about on this forsaken island.

"Let go, my love," Dracus said, remembering the chorus. "Let go and see. Let go the woes and sing high for me." He hmphed before spitting out the sour words. He wouldn't let go. He couldn't let go. When Victarius held the Roost and full legions had fallen to his defenses, Dracus didn't let go. He didn't give up. When Arilette poured poison into his Valefyre and told him to hollow out, he didn't let go. He made a vow, and by Neutreen, the One, or whatever other cosmic darkling, he was going to keep good on his word and get Canton out.

The foul stench of death tinged his nostrils before he was even in an irradiator's range. By the time his eyes could make out the shapes on the ground, the scent of death was strong enough to choke on. Bodies—undying or void of their souls—marred Fort Cybel's courtyard. Dracus's stomach tightened, twisting in knots.

He drew his sword with one hand and lifted his tunic over his nose and mouth with the other, praying to anyone who'd listen that Canton and Fawkes would not be found amongst Cybel's rubble. The bodies were fresh. Wearing Order blacks or the odds and ends the Wraith managed to assemble, they suffered together. And on both sides of the fight, Dracus found familiar faces caked in mud as he ventured toward the center of the courtyard.

Calyx, the Premius of the Eighth, had once been one of Dracus's Centuriots. A good soldier if not a good lad, but it was hard to blame him; good lads tended not to survive in the Order. Calyx had afforded himself well in the legions—Premius of the Eighth—but he wore death in silence, his soul either wandering this Neutreen-neglected isle as a shade or a darkling.

Beside Calyx was his dutiful Tribunus. Wearing the striped pauldron that marked his office was Conorus, his black fatigues stained bloody as he sightlessly stared at the clouds overhead. Dracus had been with the collectors at Belgrave when Conorus had been recruited. Dracus could still hear the boy's mother crying if he wanted to subject himself to the torment. Now her son lay dead.

As if wandering the graveyard of his own past deeds, Dracus found Niallus next. At least what was left of him. His torso was ravaged, nearly torn in half from shoulder to navel. His joints must have been ruined too. By the book, Calyx's legionaries followed protocol; stab wounds to the knees and shoulders wouldn't allow Niallus to walk or even crawl again, whether in life or undeath. He groaned as Dracus neared. He'd been a darkling to him the moment Dracus had arrived at the Underground with Canton. He'd wanted him flayed and burned. Nothing he did changed Niallus's opinion of him—not after he fought at the Battle of the Cut, not after he'd joined the Wraith. Couldn't even say he was wrong about him. But now here they were.

Dracus patted his arcanatek. *Two charges left...* "Sorry, Niallus. Ya weren't worth the charge on the best of days." He turned from him, scouring the battlefield, hoping he wouldn't find someone who was.

Off to the outskirts of the courtyard, in the shadows of what might have once served as stables, a body—about Canton's build—lay face-down. A dagger protruded from the back of his skull. Dracus's heart might have skipped a beat if it bothered to beat at all. Instead, he just felt his guts twist.

What was Canton wearing? He racked his mind, trying to recall. From this distance and with minimal lighting, Dracus couldn't tell if he wore black fatigues or a dark brown tunic. He   hurried closer and flipped the body over.

Mouth agape, face pale, eyes wide—the face looked eerily like Canton's. But traces of blond hair stuck out from the rest of the bloodstained mop to catch the light of a flickering torch. Dracus allowed himself a deep sigh. *Blood, bone, and gore. Just another Order boy.*

Before he could celebrate the fact that it wasn't Canton, another hollowed hauled itself towards Dracus. Even in death, he recognized her immediately. A woman whose kindness many within the Wraith thought wasted on Dracus—Liss.

Hollowed, she hauled herself towards him. One of her arms was cut short halfway up the forearm. The other was clipped at the wrist. Her face, a wash of agony, yawned open to let out a droning groan as she neared. She had a hole in her back that trailed blood. A stab wound to the spine that rendered her legs useless.

Why would the Wraith take this ghostin' fight?

It didn't make sense. It was insane. But for the Wraith to have less losses and emerge victorious, they'd have to have been the ones to initiate. For whatever reason they'd fought, the Wraith had done well. However, they were not without casualties, and unfortunately, Liss, among others, lay in defeat.

Guilt gnawed at him. *Two charges left...* He chewed his mustache. "Sorry, Elisara. Wish I could ease this pain. Wish I coulda been here to talk whoever thought this was a good idea outta their stupidity." He shrugged. "Not that anyone ghostin' listens to me." He kicked the Order boy's body.

He knelt down, inspecting the legionary for his arcanatek. Missing. Dracus moved onto the next body and the next, searching for a working arcanatek, but the bodies were picked clean. The only one he found was practically cleaved in half, and, as if Neutreen really wanted to punch him in the gut, the power coils that could have given him the charges to vortex and irradiate Elisara were taken too.

Dracus slammed the broken arcanatek into the mud. "Blood and bone! Mus—"

Something creaked. Dracus tensed. Whether it was the rusty hinge of a door or the whining of a hollowed, he couldn't be sure. He spun toward the sound to find a figure cloaked in shadow.

"What took you so long?" the shadow said.

The stress held in his shoulders softened. His knees threatened to give out like Elisara's. Canton stepped from the gloom, but it stained his expression.

Dracus snorted. "Took me so long? I got 'ere first." He stared past Canton expectantly, but Fawkes didn't follow in his wake. The tension he'd released returned with dread.

Old Boy's fine. He's gotta be.

Composing himself, Dracus nodded behind Canton. "Where's Fawkes? How'd you two get separated?" He shook his head, advancing on Canton. "How'd I beat ya here?"

"You didn't." Canton pointed west. "I just came from the Cut—"

"The Cut? Blood and bone, what're you doin' there?"

"I think they have Fawkes."

Dracus's eye twitched. His lip bristled. His mind buzzed, weighing the possibilities, but it couldn't be true. The aches and pains he'd accumulated since his untimely death refused to quiet, denying him the ability to think. He swallowed, shaking his head again. "Nah, slow down. Why d'ya think that? First off, how'd ya get separated?"

"Hollowed. He went west. I ran south." The words spilled out too quickly for his lips to form the proper sounds. Dracus held his hands out to slow him down, but Canton continued, barely comprehensible. "Figured he crossed the Tears, so I doubled back for him, but had to hide as legionaries marched past flying the dove standard. I retreated to the eastern bank just in case more came. Then I came here, hoping you'd be here so we could go after them. But you weren't and I couldn't stay here with all this—" He waved at the dead and undying that littered the courtyard. "So I went west. The Order's in the Cut. I came back here to find you because we need to hurry. So let's go!"

Dracus raised his hands to his temples. "Kid, yer not makin' sense."

There was only one reason Belrich would return to Saltspire. If he managed to get his hands on Threyna and the Blessing, Rheynia would fall into greater calamity. Though her loss would make it much easier to convince Canton to give up on this reckless dream of fighting alongside her, it brought Dracus no pleasure to think of what Belrich would do to her.

Hopefully, he puts her outta her misery sooner than he did her father.

Dracus twisted his heel in the mud. A wave of guilt washed over him at the relief that it was her and not Fawkes they'd taken, but he'd trade a thousand Threynas for his Old Boy.

"If they're in the Cut, where ya think they're goin'?" Dracus asked. "They're headin' to Elyngrove. Saltspire. Sounds like they nabbed her. Not Fawkes."

"Her? You mean Threyna." Canton shook his head. "No. I—"

"Yeah, yeah, yeah. I know. 'Can't be her. She wields blood magic.' Listen, I'm sorry, kid. Really, I am. But why else would they be headin' west? Which means we gotta get as far south as we can bef—"

"They're not *heading* west." Canton's fists were curled at his sides. "If you'd ghosting listen to me for once, you'd hear me. They're *camped* in the Cut. They're not going to Saltspire. They're not going anywhere. They've got Fawkes, and they're setting a trap."

Dracus blinked, but Canton's stern glare didn't soften.

Camped. Trap? It didn't make sense. And it certainly wasn't enough to determine that it was Fawkes they had. It could just as easily have been Threyna or Laela. They could be setting a trap for the Underground or the Wraith. But a gnawing disquiet ate at the back of his mind.

His foot screamed. The back of his head howled. He ignored the pain, pushing past it as the realization that they very well could have had Fawkes began to sink in. *Is the trap for me?* There was no telling what they'd do to him in order to get to Dracus. They'd torture him, use him as bait—a combination of both. They would give Fawkes the Final Demise that Dracus deserved.

He inadvertently reached for *Fang* and closed his eyes, but that only made it easier for him to picture the last time someone had earned the Final Demise. The traitor's death. The reason why every legionary carried a

Vendetta dagger. Not the standard-issue short sword given upon graduation of the Nest, but their own personal blade only forged for the purpose of punishing a fellow legionary. Some chose serrated edges. Others selected dull ones that could barely cut through moldy bread. One didn't just betray the Skeleton King or Belrich when they deserted. They betrayed the entirety of the legions. Flayed, piece by piece, cut by cut, the traitor hollowed a slow and agonizing death.

Dracus stammered. "How do you know it's Fawkes? It could be Threyna. Laela even."

Canton pursed his lips in a way that made him look like his father. "I don't. But Fawkes went west. And never came south. If they don't have him... what else would stop him from getting to Fort Cybel?"

Dracus swallowed and wrinkled his nose. He hated himself for thinking it. He knew Canton would hate him more for saying it. But it was what Fawkes would want. "If they have Fawkes. If they're waitin' for us, setting a trap as you said... we can't fall for it, Cant. We gotta—"

Canton held a finger up before him, advancing on Dracus. "Don't you dare say it. Don't you ghosting dare. We can't leave him. You know what they'll do to him."

Dracus swatted Canton's finger out of his face. "Course I know. Blood and bone, I know better than any. But ask yerself this: what would he want, eh? What would Fawkes have us do?"

Canton backed away, tossing his hands into the air. He turned, taking in the ravaged remains of the battle that had befallen Fort Cybel. "Unbelievable. It's unbelievable. First you want us to take the ships meant to save everyone else so *we* can save ourselves. So *we* can have a new life. *We*, Dracus. You're fine leaving the entire Wraith behind. You're fine leaving Fawkes behind. What is it all for?"

Dracus chewed his mustache. His foot throbbed. His shoulder ached. The back of his head felt like it was splitting in two.

"Just tell 'em." Fawkes's voice filled Dracus's head. *"He deserves to know."*

Dracus didn't even know which secret Fawkes was referring to. Why he wouldn't fight for Arilette after she'd poisoned him? That the very curse they were trying to escape was the only reason Dracus was still somewhat alive? Or why, after all this time, Dracus felt responsible for making sure Canton escaped? Maybe Fawkes didn't need to specify.

Dracus nodded. "All right. Fine. What's it all for? Ya really wanna know?" He buried his index finger in Canton's chest. "Hope. The hope that you get to live a full life. To die a true death. The hope that there's more to this existence than just wanderin' around this hellscape. The hope that there's something more than just death and an eternity of suffering. You say I'm selfish. Fine, call me selfish. Maybe I am, cause yer right; I don't care how many I leave behind. I care 'bout you. Care 'bout Fawkes. But if I gotta choose—and ghost dammit, seems like I gotta—it's you kid."

Canton's brow formed a wedge, his glare as unyielding as the worst sort of darkling. "You always do this. You act as if my life is worth more than anyone else's. Why? Ghost dammit, why!"

"Tell him the truth," Fawkes insisted.

Dracus released his breath, deflating until every ache and pain in his body threatened to hollow him completely. "You're not gonna listen to me. Ya haven't for years now, and maybe that's on me. Neutreen knows I ain't been the most honest."

"Tell him."

Dracus swallowed. Belrich's mercy was always a twisted thing. After he'd let Cavus walk, Belrich said his boy would be raised in Elyngrove, trained at the Nest, and given the very best Rheynia had to offer. All to make the *"much-needed changes Rheynia needed to thrive until Neutreen's return."* Neutreen was never coming back. No changes would be made. But to the masses, Cavus was set free. Dracus escorted Canton to Bheric's Hollow to meet King Bohen in honor of his courage. No one knew that Nerus was sent to follow Cavus home and burn the entire village of Salingard to make it look like a ritual of the Tellers.

His head hung heavy, weighed down by the burden of unspoken words. "Remember the day Salingard burned?"

Canton paled. Scratching his neck, he backed away. "We don't talk about that."

Years gone. Nightmares plagued him ever since that day. But Dracus had been content to let him believe it was because his home and everyone he'd ever known had burned in the Tellers' purifying fires. That was only part of it.

Dracus inhaled through his teeth, cursing to himself. "I know, kid. But ya asked, 'Why you?' Truth is, Tellers ain't the ones who burned Salingard."

Canton blinked. "What do you mean?"

Dracus didn't set the village to the torch, but he might as well have. After all, it was he who warned Belrich about the Artificers' Revival. He who feared making Cavus Kruso into a martyr. He who suggested a different end to the thief's life. Dracus thought it would be cleaner, but nothing ever was.

"It was my fault, all right?" Dracus said. "Blood and bone. I told Belrich to spare your father to prevent incitin' a riot. No way he was gonna let him walk away, though. So while I brought ya to Bheric's Hollow, Nerus burned Salingard. Not the Tellers."

Silence tore between them like the Disasters that formed the Gullies.

"You knew that was going to happen?" The words came forth expressionless. Not angry. Not even hurt. Just duteous. Data gathering.

"Nah. Not for certain. Figured it." Shame constricted across his chest like a belt. Guilt stooped his shoulders.

Canton thumbed his nose, stoic as the statues of Neutreen. "And me?"

"Thought I'd take ya to the king, then drop ya off at the Nest. Never see you again."

Canton advanced, his brown eyes black in Fort Cybel's gloom. "But then Bheric's Hollow…" His lip twitched.

Dracus knew he wanted to ask but wasn't sure if he actually wanted the truth. Ghosts knew Dracus didn't want to tell it, but if he was going to make Canton see—if he was going to convince Canton to abandon Fawkes, Threyna, Laela, and the Underground—he needed to tell the whole truth.

"What happened in Bheric's Hollow?" Canton asked, the rain obscuring whether or not tears were welling in his eyes. "All these years. The nightmares. You said you'd be honest."

Dracus hadn't said anything of the sort. Just that he *hadn't* been honest. But he'd run out of time and room to run. "I brought ya to the Bheric's Hollow. To meet King Bohen. But what was left of the King of Rheynia was gone. Only thing left was his rotting flesh and his pursuit of power."

When he closed his eyes, he could remember the stench of the atrium. The slickness along the floor. The darkness of the hall. The pile of desiccated bodies beside the hunched form of King Bohen, the Skeleton King.

"Bring me the boy," Bohen had said.

Dracus only stared at the remains—withered flesh atop a puddle of blood. Canton clung to Dracus's leg, petrified. He was just a boy; Dracus was a survivor of the Disasters, the top of his class at the Nest, the Second Premius behind only Decimus. He couldn't be scared stiff; he was the hero of the Artificers' War. But he was terrified.

"Premius. Bring me the boy." Bohen's skeletal hand extended from the arm of his throne.

He'd relived this moment a hundred times before. A thousand. He'd thought about what he could have done instead. He should have drawn his sword and stabbed Bohen until he'd run out of souls to consume. He should have ended the monster's reign and damned the consequences. But he didn't. He only looked down at the very boy standing before him now.

Dracus had taken his life away from him. He'd taken his father who was only guilty of wanting to stop this monster from ruling and condemned him to a fate worse than death. He'd hoped the kid would get a new start at the Nest, just as he had—an opportunity to make something of the pain he'd endured. But that future wasn't an option. He was a sacrifice.

In the presence of the desiccated corpses beside the Skeleton King, all of Dracus's achievements burned to ashes. *This is where all those boys ended up. This is what the Order has become.*

Honor, duty, pride, peace—everything he'd fought and risked his life for was a lie. He wasn't a soldier in the Order of Neutreen's Holy Dominion. He was a hellhound on the leash of a bloodsucking tyrant. With his future flashing before his eyes, he considered the two paths. Both felt like death.

"Premius!" Bohen stood from his chair on shaking legs.

Dracus covered Canton's eyes, lifted him from his feet and cradled him in his arms. He ran as fast as he could, ignoring Bohen's shouts and praying he was too weak to conjure bloody daggers to shred his back. Pushing past the confused guards, Dracus descended the stairs of Bheric's Keep and fled into the Hollow. The next day, they'd stolen a horse. Two days later, they were in Arenius's tablinum in the hovel below Octarius. Seven years later, Arenius was dead—burned alive by his daughter, Arilette.

Now, standing before Canton, after Dracus had recounted the memories that the boy's mind had done its very best to try and forget, Dracus felt only shame.

"That's why," Dracus said. "That's why I put you on a pedestal. That's why *you* gotta get outta here, 'fore it's too late. Because I messed up. Ghosts know, I messed up good. But I've made it this long 'cause I wanted to give you a new life, a better one. So let me, kid. Let me get ya beyond this curse." He eyed Canton, pleadingly. "You get out and it'll all have been worth it."

Canton's lip curled back before he pursed them again, averting his gaze to the mud and blood puddled on the ground between them. "This new life..." His voice was barely a whisper. "You'll come with me?" He inclined his eyes to meet Dracus's.

Dracus met the boy's glossy stare. The hollowed seemed to still for a moment allowing only the falling rain to disturb the silence. He knew what he was asking of Canton: to walk away from Fawkes—a second father to him. It would be a loss they'd both have to grieve. Albeit Canton would have to shoulder the burden for a few ages longer than Dracus would, but that didn't matter. This time, Dracus was sure even Fawkes would have agreed with not telling Canton the truth.

"Yeah," Dracus said. "You and me. Sansia and the rest of the wide world. Just not here." He forced a smile, but Canton didn't share in it.

He sniffed, staring into the abyss of the surrounding remains of a battlefield. He said something under his breath that Dracus couldn't catch.

"What's that, now?"

Canton snapped his attention back to Dracus, the sheen of water on his eyes gone. Replaced by a dark determination. "You might be content to trade your guilt for Fawkes's life. But I am not." He marched past Dracus.

Dracus grabbed his wrist, stopping his westbound movement. "Canton, ya can't mean to—"

Canton shook free of Dracus's grasp. "You go to Sansia. Go on. Run away from your guilt, but I'm going to the Cut." He held up a finger before Dracus could interject. "And ghost dammit, if you ever actually cared about me—about either of us—you'll come with me."

Canton stormed off, making his way across the dead and undying courtyard of the fallen fort. Dracus put his hands on his hips and shifted his weight. His foot throbbed. His head ached. His back whined. He looked to the rainclouds sailing overhead on the gentle breeze. Every once in a while, a glimmer of sunlight managed to poke through the shroud, a glimmer of hope in a dark world.

"Let go, my love," Dracus whispered to the star, repeating the chorus to the rhyme. "Let go and see. Let go the woes and sing high for me." He hung his head.

So close... Thought I had 'em. But he'd never had anything. Only delusions. And one by one, they had all fallen. *Only one path left to take.*

He took a deep inhale, hardly believing it had come to this. "Cant?"

"Are you coming or not?" Canton asked from the other side of the courtyard.

Dracus turned to face him. "I'm goin', but I need ya to do somethin' for me."

Canton narrowed his gaze, the distrust visible despite the low light.

"Ya remember the way to Octarius?" Dracus asked.

Canton stalked closer as if not believing his ears.

"If we're doin' this," Dracus said, "we're gonna need help."

CHAPTER 46

TWO PATHS

Laela XVIII

In a perfect world, Laela and the surviving Wraith could have rested in Fort Cybel. Even a few hours to patch wounds and mourn those who'd suffered in the liberation of those held captive would have been enough. Yet this was far from a perfect world.

A handful of legionaries ran in defeat, but their escape meant the Wraith would not be safe. There was no telling how soon they could arrive with reinforcements or in what numbers. Fort Cybel wasn't worth holding; by Laela's estimation, it was barely worth taking. They'd lost a handful less than they'd freed, but despite the transactional vantage point, morale was high on their trek south. If only Laela shared in the sentiment.

Though the slash across her back was but a flesh wound, the stab she'd taken from Calyx's blade bit deep, and his headbutt made everything from her nose to her teeth hurt. Each step and every breath was agony. After stripping her armor and letting the rain wash away most of the mud, she'd been bandaged up enough to stop the bleeding. But all she wanted was sleep. Sleep, however, would not deliver them to Sansia, and, if Neutreen had any sway on this cursed island, Rosler and Taggart would be waiting for them at Talon's Grip. There was no telling how long they'd wait. If they'd even made it there at all.

"Don't look good," Tarus said, having snuck up beside her.

Laela groaned. "Must you keep doing that?"

"Pointin' out the obvious?"

"Showing up." Laela's terseness wasn't personal, but Tarus wasn't exactly the bearer of bright news, and she didn't trust that the next words out of his mouth wouldn't take things from bad to worse. "What?"

"Blood and bone," Tarus said. "Go hollow out, then. I was just checkin' on you."

Laela winced, grabbing her bandaged ribs. They were Aylenia's bandages. Aylenia's antiseptic. Aylenia had even been the one to apply them and Laela wasn't sure how she felt about it. It wasn't the first time Aylenia had cared for her. It was Aylenia who sat with her after her father had beaten her. It was Aylenia who gave her a lap to cry on when she felt like she'd never be enough. It made her feel like she was a kid again. A sad, scared, helpless kid forever doomed to live in her father's shadow in Octarius's depths. Part of her wanted to thank her for taking care of her. The other part wanted to throttle her for making her feel like she needed to be taken care of.

"Apologies, Tarus. You're not exactly known for presenting people with Neutreen's wings. Please, tell me you have good news."

Tarus shrugged. "Your Undergrounder tells me you won't make it to the Grip, let alone Sansia."

Laela exhaled through her teeth.

"Spare me the, *'What's she know?'* bit, eh? She dressed your wounds."

"What's she know?" Laela said darkly, tasting bile in the back of her throat. "Let me guess. She's suggesting we head east? Walk straight into Arilette's outstretched arms—something like that?"

"Somethin' like that," Tarus said.

"We're *not* stepping foot past the Tears. We haven't come this far only to become kindling for her pyres."

Tarus shrugged. "They got warps. Wouldn't mind a little attention myself" He examined a gash along his forearm.

Like he needs healing arcanatek for that. Laela shook her head, but regretted the movement as vertigo distorted her vision. Tarus stabilized her, taking her by the arm with a raised eyebrow.

"I'm not going to Octarius," Laela said. "And neither are you. I'll gladly trade a warp and an eternity beneath the Order's rule for some sore ribs and the promise of freedom. I'm fine, Tarus."

Tarus snorted. "Said the hollowed to the hellhound. I'll be up ahead if ya need. Gotta make sure this craven doesn't lead us to our doom."

As Tarus stalked off, Laela couldn't help but notice that ever since Fort Cybel, he hadn't referred to Redge by name, electing instead to call him *the Palogian* or *craven*. After their spirited victory over the Order, many who had taken heed of Redge's leadership seemed to shy away, choosing instead to follow more closely to Bhen, Asla, and—to Laela's growing concern—Aylenia.

Staring at the back of Aylenia's head as she strode a few people ahead of her, Laela clutched her ribs and hurried to catch up with the woman. Each step sent a sharp stab along her spine, and each deep breath felt like Calyx was standing over her all over again, but she persevered as she always had.

Be strong. Be courageous.

Rance and her mother had sacrificed too much for her to fail in achieving their dream of delivering the Wraith beyond the curse, and she wasn't about to let Aylenia threaten that.

As she attempted to walk past Aylenia, she said, "A word?" Though she tried to quicken her stride to force Aylenia to follow to keep up, she barely kept pace ahead of her. Reluctantly, she settled back, falling into step with the girl from her childhood.

"How're you feeling?" Aylenia asked, nodding at Laela's dressings.

With light rain falling, it was difficult to tell if it was rain or a cold sweat clinging to her brow. *One foot in front of the other. Show no weakness.* "Never better. Why'd I hear tell that you're suggesting we make for Octarius?"

Aylenia cocked a thick black brow that seemed to connect to the corner of her lip. "Where'd you hear that? I didn't say anything of the sort."

"You implied, then," Laela said. "How many times do I have to tell you? I'm not—*we're not*—going to Octarius. You helped at Fort Cybel, and for that, I'm grateful. But you are my prisoner. Not the other way around."

TIM FACCIOLA

The words sounded weaker than they felt coming out of her mouth, but anticipating anger, she was surprised to find Aylenia's smile spreading.

"What?" Laela asked, like she'd been made the brunt of a joke she didn't understand.

Aylenia snorted. "Two things: one, if I was your prisoner, how long do you think you could actually keep me here against my will? And two, if you are my prisoner, why am I back here with you and not leading from the front?" She glanced at the mountains. "We're south of Octarius by now. We're not far from the Grip. Did you ever think that maybe... just maybe... I might actually want to be here with you?"

Laela stammered. While attempting to clear her throat, the pressure of the action throttled her ribs, resulting in a groan she couldn't contain. Aylenia extended her arm to help, but Laela waved her away. "I don't understand you. What do you want?"

Aylenia took a deep breath, examining the horizon where the clouds met the land ahead. "Do you remember—back before the Wraith even existed—the *Resilience*?"

Smoke filled her nostrils and watered her eyes, but it was all in her mind. Laela remembered *Resilience*. All too well. The ship was built in the aftermath of her father's last act of defiance. He had set *Curse Breaker* aflame, burning the Wraith's hope of escape. "What of it?"

Aylenia's smile turned solemn. "I thought it was named just for me. Most beautiful thing I'd ever seen. My grandfather came here on a ship from Palogia before the Disasters. Never thought I'd see one myself, you know?" She snorted, shaking her head and tossing her curly hair. "He hollowed in the War of the Seers. My father and brothers suffered in the Artificers' War. If not for my mother, taking me and leaving when we did, I might have too. Took a few years, but then we found the Underground. We found hope."

She remembered. Her stomach had fluttered the first time she'd laid eyes on Aylenia. While *Resilience* might have been the most beautiful thing Aylenia had ever beheld, for Laela, after growing up in a tunnel of dirt and dust, fighting for her father's love, Aylenia was the most beautiful thing she'd seen. Laela swallowed uncomfortably.

"I remember begging my mûnta to take me with her when she first went to Sansia," Aylenia said, lost in a painful past. "Sansia sounded like such a beautiful place, cloudless days under a blue sky and bright sun, just like her mother had described in the Palogian Isles. Nightly rainstorms with light that streaked across the sky. And after the storms passed, the stars would shine down from the Exalted Halls and the Corners would come together to reveal their majesty."

Laela hummed. She didn't know much about the Palogian Gods, the Corners of Kataan. She'd heard of them in passing, but if they existed, they were much further away than Neutreen. It was interesting to consider the world beyond Rheynia—Palogia to the east, Sansia to the south, and wherever Damascus Drake and Harrow Helixus led the rest of the abdicators.

Listening to the wonder in Aylenia's voice, Laela imagined such sights. A blue sky. A starry night. It seemed so close, but so far away. "It does sound beautiful." But Laela knew how Aylenia's story ended; her mother never came back from Sansia. No one who'd settled over the course of the dozens of excursions Arenius had organized was there when *Resilience* returned. There was no sign of them, as if they'd never even stepped foot upon the sandy shores.

"I wonder where I would be now," Aylenia said, staring at the cloudy sky. "If I had gone with her, I wonder who I'd be..." She turned to Laela. "I know you don't trust me, the Legatus, the Underground—but trust this. Whatever happened to my mûnta, to Sansia—one day, I will go, and I will either find her or discover what happened to her." She shrugged. "This isn't how I thought I'd go to Sansia, but... I can either fight to avenge my father and brothers here, or I can see if perhaps my mother's still out there, still alive somehow."

For a moment, Laela forgot the pain in her ribs, feeling instead Aylenia's heartbreak. *By Neutreen's wings, she's telling the truth.* She swallowed a gulp of guilt for misjudging Aylenia, but the guilt was quickly overcome by a new sensation. Absent the enemy's veil, she felt like she was seeing Aylenia for the first time. Laela had been so focused on fleeing Rheynia, she'd never considered—outside of surviving Sansia and setting up a new home—the possibility of a future.

"That sounds like quite the adventure," Laela said, her lips spreading in an unfamiliar smile that reminded her of the cut across her cheek. "Searching for your mûnta." The Palogian word felt strange on her tongue, and didn't come out quite right, but it drew a smile from Aylenia that returned heat to Laela's cheeks.

Momentarily embarrassed, Laela averted her gaze, but that left her dizzy. Holding her head in her hollowed-bitten hand, she steadied herself. "Did you ever tell Threyna about this?" She didn't intend for her half-sister's name to leave her lips with such distaste, but it did, and Aylenia's grin flattened.

Aylenia stared at her feet as her long legs took shorter strides to match Laela's slowed gait. "Of course. There's little we don't know about each other."

Laela had to consciously will herself to relax the tension held between her teeth.

"We shared a bunk for the past..." Aylenia tossed her head back and forth as if considering the arithmetic. "Ten years?" She hmphed. "I remember the day the Legatus told me to take her under my wing. She was just a kid after all. She was a mess after you and your mother left. Fawkes and Canton were gone, and her father... well, I suppose you know what became of him." Aylenia took a deep breath. "I know you hate to hear it, but she became the spitting image of Arilette—the good and the bad. It wasn't long before I was under her wing. Ripping Corners, we all were."

Laela's emotions conflicted. She couldn't help but take Aylenia's words with a degree of indictment, that she was somehow to blame for Threyna's predicament in the Underground. But at the same time, she pitied the little girl Threyna had been—alone, scared, angry.

"Makes sense," Aylenia said. "Bherus Fayte's ghosting daughter and all." She shrugged. "But yeah, we talked about Sansia. About me wanting to find my mûnta."

That still hadn't quite settled in. Theodyn wasn't Theodyn. The man who'd been a better parent to her than her own father was the son of the Skeleton King. And his blood ran through Threyna's veins. *As well as the curse.*

"And what did she have to say about that?" Laela asked. "An Undergrounder leaving for Sansia? Sounds like a deserter."

Aylenia allowed herself to grin again. "Another truth you won't like to hear, but you two are a lot more alike than you're different."

Aylenia was correct. Laela did *not* like to hear that. "What makes you say that?"

"Gory ghosting dammit," Aylenia teased. "It's not a bad thing. Don't forget. There's no one I trust or care for more in this world. But tell me this—if you'd been left behind instead of Threyna, or you were raised in the Underground while she was with the Wraith, would you still be at odds with one another?"

Laela chose to ignore the phrase concerning Threyna having been *left behind*, and opted instead to consider the question.

"You're as good a fighter as any I've ever seen," Aylenia said. "And Threy, you put something in her head, and she won't stop until she's the best at it. All I'm saying is if you two swapped places, you'd probably be a Premius in the Underground's legions, and she'd be First Sword of the Wraith. And if either of you would let your guard down for a warp and let someone else in, you might see that vulnerability doesn't mean weakness."

Though the words rang familiar to something her mother had said within Avengard, the word *weakness* made the scar across Laela's chest tingle. *"There is strength in knowing when to drop your guard and courage in actually doing so."*

Laela didn't know how to respond. Feeling her father's presence on the edge of her Center of Silence, her reflexive reaction was to deny—to cite how every time she had been vulnerable, it resulted in dire consequences. Yet with each passing moment, she struggled to remember ever allowing herself to be vulnerable since childhood.

Is Aylenia right? Her entire life, she'd been jealous of Threyna—the love she received from her father, the attention she received from their mother, the way people seemed to notice her while Laela faded into the background. She thought they were just different, each taking more from their fathers than the mother they shared. And although there was truth in that, were they all that different? She knew she put walls up, but they were to defend herself. *But maybe Threyna only saw that as a means of blocking her out.*

"Must you always be so—"

Laela wondered what her mother would have said if she had allowed her to finish. She imagined it was probably something similar to what Aylenia was saying now. Vulnerability didn't necessarily mean weakness, as much as her father beat the contrary into her.

The storm clouds disappeared beyond the Spine, leaving the river valley cloaked in Rheynia's typical gray shroud. Yet in certain patches where the clouds were thinnest, the sun's light illuminated the sky just enough to make Laela believe hope still existed beyond the curse.

Aylenia chuckled, following Laela's gaze as she admired the sky. "Threyna would do the same—silent contemplation as a response. Like I said, more alike than different. Aside from maybe one or two things."

Laela, still digesting Aylenia's last words, paused before responding. "Yeah, what's that?"

Aylenia cast Laela a darkling's grin and brushed the back of her hand along that of Laela's. "I'm just saying, if you and I shared a bunk…"

Laela's mouth went dry. Her stomach flipped, and it had nothing to do with the abrupt halt their procession came to.

"What's going on?" Aylenia asked. The softness in her cheek from a moment ago instantly fell as she reached for the blade at her hip.

The stalled crowd parted as Redge pushed his way through. He spotted Laela with wide eyes, but they narrowed as they flicked to Aylenia. He advanced, continuing to shove his way through the crowd until he was toe to toe with Laela.

"Underground up ahead," he whispered so only she could hear, glaring at Aylenia beside her.

Bile returned to Laela's throat. *We're so close...* She set her jaw, but it sent blinding pain up to her temples. "How many?"

Redge shook his head. "Only have eyes on a few, but there's no telling with the Underground. Could be a patrol. Could be a trap meant to look like a patrol. I don't know where their tunnels are. Do you?"

Laela turned to Aylenia, feeling more dizzy by the moment. "She does."

Redge backed away as Laela leaned closer to Aylenia. All around them, hushed murmurs began to rise until Redge, Tarus, Bhen, and other leaders settled them.

"Does the Underground know where we are?" Laela asked, practically leaning on Aylenia.

Aylenia examined Laela, but steadied her. "I'm not sure. I've been out of contact since you took my interlayer back at Aranoc."

Laela winced as the pain in her ribs began to demand more of her attention. Her heart hammered louder in her chest, but she ignored it, attempting to focus. "Who would be out here? Why would they be out here?"

Again, Aylenia turned her palms skyward. "I don't know. Could be scouts. Could be a strike team returning from the east and wanting to bypass the Cut."

Vision swimming, Laela peered into Aylenia's eyes, longing to know if she was being honest. *Was any of this true? Was Aylenia trying to distract me so I wouldn't notice the Underground's ambush?*

She rubbed the back of her hand where Aylenia had brushed her. The electricity coursing through it nullified as she curled her fingers into a fist. She didn't know what to believe.

Not for the first time, she wished Rance was here. She wished her mother was. They always seemed to know what to do. Laela was a soldier. A bodyguard. Not a leader. She was meant to follow orders, not give them. Yet here they were, so close to Talon's Grip and the possibility of rescue, but with the Underground between them and salvation, they might as well have been back in Avengard. Only now, Laela could feel her body fading, her mind losing focus with each passing moment.

She examined Aylenia. She wanted to trust her, to believe that she'd been earnest. About everything. But fear clawed at her ankles and crawled up her legs. *Am I willing to bet the fate of the Wraith on it? On her?* She steadied her breathing, slowed her heartbeat, and attempted to search Aylenia's soul as a darkling would.

Be strong. Be courageous.

She chose to trust Aylenia. "Which do you believe it to be?"

Before Aylenia could answer, Tarus and Redge approached with Bhen and Asla in their wake. They distanced themselves from the rest of the crowd for more privacy.

Once away from the others, Asla spoke first. "We just took down Fort Cybel. We're so close to the Grip. If it's just a few Undergrounders, what are we even considering?"

"We had more numbers and the element of surprise," Redge said. "And it might *not* be just a few Undergrounders. For all we know, an entire legion could be waiting for us around the bend. And don't think I haven't noticed, but this is the second time you've seemed eager for a fight."

"And this is the second time you've wanted to delay us leavin' this Neutreen-forsaken place," Tarus hissed in Asla's defense.

Laela held her hand up, but the action of summoning silence made her ribs flare with pain. Sucking air between her teeth, she grimaced at the pain in her nose and jaw. "Let's ask someone who might know whether it's just a few Undergrounders or an ambush."

Aylenia stared back at her, undoubtedly taking note of all her physical tells that she was struggling. "It could be an ambush—there are enough crags and tunnel exits along the Spine to hide half a legion—but I don't know."

"Like we can trust her," Redge said, not even bothering to address Aylenia.

Tarus glared at Redge. "Like we can trust you." He scoffed then spoke more to himself. "Wantin' to turn back…"

Asla held pinched fingers before Laela. "We're this close. If not forwards, where are we supposed to go? The boats are that way!" She pointed south and east toward the sea.

Bhen only crossed his arms, declaring his stance of not taking a stance.

Laela wanted someone else to take the lead. Her mind felt like it was slowly sinking into the Grotto as pain overcame logic. She imagined another fight and didn't believe she could make it. Conversely, what were their alternatives?

"There is a lowland gap in the Cut," Aylenia said. "We'd have to backtrack, but they wouldn't block both sides of the Spine. They'd expect you to follow the Tears, and they'd wait at the bend, not further south."

Tarus rolled his eyes and tossed his hands in the air. "Ya can't be serious."

"We could follow the west side of the Spine like we're heading toward Aeritan Bay," Aylenia said, ignoring Tarus. "Then cut back just south of the Grip. They'd never expect us to come from the south."

Laela's ribs screamed. She wanted so desperately for this to be the end of their journey. She was hungry and exhausted, but if Aylenia was right—if she was telling the truth as Laela believed she was—then the path forward, the easy path, was reckless.

She looked over her shoulder, back the way they had come. There was a chance the Order would come south. They could be trapped between the Order and the Underground with nowhere to run and no place to hide. Both paths presented risk.

Tarus crossed his arms, facing south. Redge tapped his foot, ready to trek back the way they had come. Asla turned her feet parallel with the Tears until she was facing the Grip to further indicate her thoughts. Meanwhile, Bhen remained silently noncommittal.

Aylenia held Laela's gaze. She suggested going back. Laela didn't want to. She wanted to rest, but rest was for the corpses. Ignoring the pain and protest in her wounds, she turned to face north. *I can do this. I can survive. Just breathe.* Steadying her swimming vision, she took a deep breath. "We can't afford to be reckless just because we're close. We go back."

CHAPTER 47

UNTIL THE CUT

Dracus XIII, Laela XIX, Threyna XVIII

Dracus

D read accompanied each of Dracus's agonizing steps. Worse than the pain in his withering flesh and bones, worse than the anguish of letting Canton return to Octarius—the knot in his throat at the prospect of what he might find threatened to hollow him here and now.

The Order camped in the middle of the Cut. The legionaries' hoots and howls echoing off the high walls of the canyon rattled through his head like darklings in a soul jar. They were exactly where Canton said they would be with enough numbers to ensure victory against whoever their noise attracted. The fact that they were making a concerted effort to let every hollowed and hellhound from Bheric's Hollow to the Roost know their whereabouts confirmed his suspicions too; this was unequivocally a trap.

Could be Threyna, a ploy to lure out Arilette. Ghosts, could be Laela. If Belrich found out her father was Aarkos Velar, he'd throw a festival to rival Cybel's Eve.

Another gale of laughter rose from the fire at the center of their camp, but Dracus couldn't see what instigated it. Walking along the southern rim of the valley, both buying time for Canton to reach Octarius and for him to formulate a plan that didn't involve approaching Belrich head-on, Dracus attempted to count their numbers. Though it was difficult to discern shadows from legionaries in Order blacks, the banners waving in the gentle breeze rippled taut enough to see clearly.

If Belrich was with them earlier, he wasn't any longer. Though the black dove flew on the green flag—the Order's standard—the green dove atop a black backdrop was missing.

A spark of hope ignited in his chest. *They might not have anyone. Just an empty trap!*

Beside the black dove was the headless horse of Jagras's Fourth Legion and the slain chimera of Artanius's Ninth. Neither were at their full strength, which prompted Dracus to wonder if the remainder had accompanied Belrich back to Saltspire along with the First. To do so either meant he had the Blessing he'd long coveted, or he was afraid enough of the one who did that he wasn't leaving anything to chance.

The encampment was two rings of tents in concentric circles around each of the Premiuses' pavilions. Unable to count the men, Dracus settled for counting the tents, just high enough for a single legionary to crawl into. Counting twice, he tallied 108 tents. While not a full regiment of either legion, they had enough men to fend off any who took their bait. Whatever their goal, they were committed to it, but the more Dracus observed, the less confident he felt that they actually had a prisoner. If they had someone, they'd be torturing them. And torture was never silent.

With half a mind of turning back to chase Canton down before he could ask Arilette and the Underground for aid, Dracus stopped his westbound trek atop the Cut's rim. Dropping to his belly, he crept closer to the edge. Crippled hollowed groaned on the outskirts of the camp, which only made his reconnaissance more difficult.

Just as he was about to turn back, cheers resounded, echoing off the wet walls of the Cut. The spark of hope he dared to dream of died as nothing in Rheynia did.

Out from the pavilion marked with the slain chimera, a figure with a shroud over their head was escorted in manacles toward the eastern end of their encampment. Dracus scuttled along the southern ledge, attempting to see who they held captive, who they were jeering at.

There was only one man Dracus knew who, even staring down the wrong end of an irradiator's sight, could strike such an imposing figure. His throat constricted. His lip curled, making the bristles of his mustache tickle his nose.

No. Not my Fawkes. Don't touch him, you bastards…

"Daggers out, boys!" Artanius cried, punching a green-pauldroned arm to the sky.

The shout sent a wave of exuberance through the black-clad legions and made Dracus's still heart consider beating again. His mind raced as it became clear that Fawkes wouldn't have enough time for him to do as he and Canton had discussed. By the time he stalked to the western entrance of the Cut to draw the Order's attention with the hopes that the Underground would come to his aid and attack from behind, Fawkes would be a goner. But to engage them now, Dracus would only ensure that they had two to torture instead of one.

Wishing he had a soul jar, a Dawnshard, or anything else that could create a distraction, Dracus stood to his feet. As legionaries led Fawkes to the edge of their encampment, another pair began shoveling a hole with spades. Bringing up the rear, another pair of legionaries carried the pavilion pole that Fawkes would be bound to.

Not happenin', Old Boy.

Dracus had already failed. Canton wasn't leaving; he'd all but ensured that by sending him to Octarius. If not for that boy, he would have hollowed a long time ago. Now, he had nothing but Fawkes. If the legionaries believed the lies that he'd been overtaken by Victarius Kaine's darkling, then he'd show them the darker truth.

We'll take down half this camp. Then when Canton and the Underground come and finish 'em off, they'll write songs about us, Old Boy. You and me. 'The Love That Conquered The Cut.' Wouldn't that be somethin'? And maybe our song can torture some other poor bastard who can't remember the words.

As for him, he was done trying to remember. *Let go.* That was the theme of his aunt's rhyme. Let go of your hopes, your dreams, anything and everything you've ever loved because you'll lose it anyway. Let go and persevere; learn to *live* without. Learn to survive. If that's all life was supposed to be, Dracus was done with it, but he wouldn't go down without a fight.

The legionaries hoisted the pavilion pole upright and positioned it in the hole they'd dug in the soft silt of the Cut. A handful of others restrained Fawkes, as if he needed restraining. He stood stock-still, quiet as a lamb and just as docile as he awaited his fate.

He probably thought they were long gone. That's what they'd always discussed. *"Whatever happens, get Canton off the island."* That's how it should have gone. But Canton had other plans, and now, so did Dracus.

While they cut Fawkes's clothes from his body and undid his manacles, the rest of the legionaries prepared for the ritual. Regardless of cohort, the legionaries arranged in a single file line by rank. One by one, the Premiuses, Tribuni, and high-ranking Centuriots dug the edge of their Vendetta daggers into the pole and left it there until the column was lined, from head to heel, with the Order's vindictive fury. All the while, the lower-ranking men drew their own blades, preparing to take their pound of flesh from the body that had dishonored their oaths. Only Fawkes was never a soldier of the Order—Dracus was. His was a punishment Dracus would have gladly let any other man take in his place, but not Fawkes. Never Fawkes.

Threyna

The rush of wind and the thud of blood pumping in her ears drowned out the wailing of the souls she'd taken into her Inner Throne but had yet to consume. On her journey south over the Rheynian countryside in search of the Wraith, all she found was the Order. Pockets of them were scattered about the Spine in groups anywhere from a dozen to a score.

Each might have rounded up a handful of Wraith refugees in their flight from Aranoc, but none had Laela. None had Aylenia. And none had the numbers that would make any difference, but as she continued, she began to wonder if she even needed them at all.

She'd encountered three groups thus far and didn't hesitate to make use of her rage and newfound powers. Thrice now she had exterminated the legionaries like the vermin they were. She didn't need a blade to make them suffer or an arcanatek to vortex the hollowed or irradiate the darklings. She, by herself, was the perfect weapon, and she would continue to sharpen her edge on the whetstone of the Order's division until she defeated all of them.

Divided, ruin will reign. They had separated their forces to cover more ground, capture more Wraith, but that was their mistake. If she had to face a full legion, she could be overwhelmed, become overtaken by her rot, and not have the time to consume. Divided, however, they were her prey. And she was becoming a better hunter after each engagement. Consuming souls became easier, more natural, and took less expenditure to achieve. The result—a surplus of souls that she could consume as she needed. The only problem was that she had to listen to them.

Her conjured wings flapped against the dying rains as the winds carried the storm west. The rhythmic flap added another percussive distraction to the voices and the growing rot that stretched up and down her left arm. She didn't need to consume yet, but she knew who she would select when the time came.

Devult. A legionary in the Order's Eighth, Devult had been the first to turn and run after their camp was assailed, by the Wraith of all people. Threyna had sifted through his memories and searched his thoughts for any sign of why the Wraith actually fought. She didn't think them capable. She dared to hope that perhaps Laela had started to see the light that there was no escape. Or maybe Aylenia had convinced her that they could actually win this if they joined together. She sought any memories of

Aylenia or Laela in Devult's soul, but all she found was absolute devotion to his One True God.

However, as she flew in search of the Wraith, she felt the presence of the swirling black storm of red lightning drawing nearer to her Inner Throne. Looming large and foreboding, it brought credence to Devult's faith. Even with the power she possessed, she couldn't lose sight of what she needed. She couldn't do this alone. She might not have needed Fawkes, Canton, and Dracus, but she did need Laela and the rest of the Wraith if they were going to succeed in beating back the dark.

She hoped Devult's memories of the Wraith storming Fort Cybel were the signs of change. It was possible. Perhaps after losing Rance and their mother, Laela finally snapped. Perhaps there were others in the Wraith who'd grown tired of running, tired of failing. Laela was one of—if not—the best fighter she'd crossed blades with. If she did wish to fight, she would be a force to be reckoned with.

"You're sisters," her mother had said. *"Divided, ruin will reign, but united…"*

To have her on their side, to have the Wraith in addition to Threyna's blood magic… victory was possible. But how many times had she hoped for the best and ended up in the stocks?

The memory of her brief reunion with what remained of her father flashed in her mind. His noseless, tongueless, milky-eyed face. The way he looked from her to Dracus. The way Belrich stood over him and stabbed down.

Pain. Frustration. Grief.

The souls in her Inner Throne began to clamor around her as if sensing her weakness. She could feel them attempting to gain access to the thoughts that brought them up in the first place. She tried fending them off, but like hollowed tearing the viscera from a fresh kill, they began strewing her memories all over.

Rivich's pleading eyes, begging her to abandon the mission. Daeton's ravaged form after her decision got him hollowed. The anger of Yevon's darkling. The pain on the face of Ebrus's shade as if he recognized her from beyond his flesh.

Too much pain. Too much loss.

"You're alone," Devult said. *"Let go. Join the One True God in eternal undeath."*

Outside her Inner Throne, Threyna's conjured wings began to falter. Within her seat of power, the dozen or so remaining souls encircled her.

As her wings began to dissolve to ash, Threyna sank deeper into her Inner Throne. This was *her* seat of power. *Hers.* She rebuffed them, shutting down her emotions and holding her thoughts captive. Walled off from their encroachment, she needed more space. She wanted to eject them, but, at the same time, she needed them, or at least eventually, she would. But they couldn't stay in her Inner Throne any longer.

The walls of her Inner Throne began to blur as the entire room began to change. A door led out of the throne room down a dark, narrow corridor, away from her seat of power. A spiral staircase descended into an abyss that wound down and down into a damp, hopeless, cold.

"Here!" Threyna commanded. She forced the souls inside, but seized hold of Devult. *"Not you."* She forged a stone wall across the cellar at the bottom of the spiral staircase, sealing the crying souls inside. But down here, she wouldn't be able to hear their screams. The silence brought peace to her soul, but the fear emanating from Devult gave her pleasure.

She drew in breath within her Inner Throne until there was nothing left of Devult. No vile retorts. No entitled bravado. No profession of faith in the One True God's salvation. Only silence.

Returning to her seat of power, she reconjured the feathers of her deteriorating wings. With her focus returned to the physical world around her, the scent of smoke stained the wind. Ahead, tendrils of a campfire rose from the Cut. Threyna sank deeper into her Inner Throne, attuning to heartbeats. There were a lot of them. Even more approached from the east. Order, Wraith, or both—she couldn't tell, but either way, the Battle of the Cut was about to have a second coming. She would redeem all that had been lost.

Dracus

There were some perks to being on the edge of becoming hollowed. For one, Dracus didn't feel the effects that came with fear. Though he was terrified of what he was about to suggest, his heart remained still, his fingers stayed relaxed. The living could become enslaved by their emotions, but to Dracus they were only the shadows of something he once remembered feeling.

He slid down the lip of the Cut's wall and advanced past the crippled hollowed on the outskirts of the Order's camp. At his approach, the slack-jawed legionaries standing watch balked.

Dracus stopped before them, and realizing they weren't about to introduce him, he announced himself. "Jagras, Artanius? Quota's due."

The legionaries forgot about Fawkes as all eyes in the encampment turned towards Dracus. The men parted as both Jagras and Artanius approached. Dracus didn't wait for them to come to him. Striding between the parted legionaries, Dracus closed the distance between him and Fawkes. *Hang in there, Old Boy.*

Dracus pasted on his fakest smile. "Ah, Jags, Arty, I'd say it's a pleasure, but…" He shrugged, continuing to saunter forward through the legionaries. "Never was, was it?"

Jagras, the longtime Premius of the Fourth, had more gray in his beard than brown, and more wrinkles framing his eyes than Dracus had souls in his old soul jars. Stern and stoic as ever, the near-perfect protégé of Lord Premius Decimus lowered his brow.

"Dracus Alius." Jagras pursed his lips.

Fawkes jostled beneath the shroud over his head.

I'm here, Old Boy.

"My, my," Jagras said. "I must be slipping. I never thought you would be foolish enough to show yourself. Let alone so… brazenly."

His eyes flicked in a near-imperceptible motion. Dracus could practically taste the perspiration bubbling on the bridge of Jagras's nose. After all, Dracus had made a name for himself over his storied career of tactical warfare. Surely he wouldn't be so foolish as to walk into an obvious trap. But he had, and he needed them to believe that too.

Dracus scoffed. "Ya throw a party for me, yet yer surprised when I show up? Come on, Jags. I see y'all got yer daggers out."

He drew his own. *Fang*. A simple name for a simple blade. Unlike many of the legionaries' Vendetta daggers, his lacked the ornate designs, intricate carvings, or embedded seals. Just cold steel. Simple. Straight. Sharp.

"They're for me, eh?" Dracus prodded, coming to a stop ten paces from Jagras and Artanius, and another twenty or so from where Fawkes was being held. "So what'dya say ya let him go, and we do this the right way. And shut yer mouth, Arty. Ya look like a hollowed, gaping like that. Blood and bone, Belrich must be slipping if he made you a Premius."

Younger, prouder, and packed full with all the ego Decimus had beaten out of Dracus, Artanius bristled, ready to defend his honor before his men. Jagras cast a fixing glare, preventing him from acting rashly.

"You will address Prince Belrich as his station demands," Jagras said. "Though you have lost your right to call him Legatus."

Dracus hmphed. "My right?" He shook his head, tossing *Fang* between his hands, feigning a clumsiness that didn't exist in his youth while attempting to stall without making it obvious. "Where there is order there is justice, eh? But I'm glad ya brought up rights, 'cause that's exactly what I wanna talk to ya about, Jags."

"You have no rights," Artanius snapped. "You're a disgrace to the Dove and all who ever wore the black."

Dracus tilted his head and cocked a brow as if scolding a petulant child. "Adults are talkin', Arty. Thought I told ya once already to keep your gab shut?" Not giving Artanius time to retort, Dracus nodded at Jagras.

"I'm accused of turnin' traitor. Punishment for any legionary is the Final Demise. As Second Premius, I ain't exempt. But like any legionary, I can invoke the right of the Blood Trials."

"Dracus, no!" Fawkes's words were barely muffled by the sack over his head. He wasn't the only one; men of the Fourth and Ninth, supposedly well-disciplined men, broke out in gasps or murmurs.

Dracus knew he had them. The Blood Trials had never been invoked, and for good reason; no one elected to fight to first blood blindfolded against the Legatus's Champion. The Final Demise at least guaranteed an end. Hollowed, shade, or darkling—whatever fate, they would all be irradiated. But to lose in the Blood Trials, one would suffer the Final Demise without its absolution. Flayed, imprisoned, left in the dark to heal, only to be flayed again. And again. And again. Then, once they eventually succumbed to their end, they would not receive the arcanatek's release.

Artanius gawked, his jaw unhinging at the prospect of a Blood Trial. Even Jagras raised his brows before flicking his eyes to the southern lip of the Cut as if expecting to see an army.

Dracus chuckled. "I see my reputation precedes me. What else they sayin' about good, old Darkling Dray? Don't tell me you believe the whole Victarius thing too? Ya think I conjure blood magic, command the hollowed? Betcha think I can fly too. Blood and bone, I expected it of Nerus, but not of you, Jags. Oh, speakin' of which, I hear there's an openin' to be Second Premius. Actually… quite a few openin's in the Second."

More muttering. Though Dracus couldn't feel the fear eating at him, he could sense it on the others as his legend grew and his mystery deepened. The word *How?* formed on the lips of dozens before him. Fawkes continued to protest, but Dracus only focused on the Premiuses.

Jagras's scowl deepened. Artanius's surprise turned predatory, and Dracus knew he had him, but there was one more thing he needed to ensure.

"One other thing." Dracus gestured to Fawkes. "I invoke a second Blood Trial for him. I'll serve as Champion for both."

Artanius opened his mouth to speak, but Dracus cut him short.

"Before you say anythin' stupid, me versus your two Champions. Same time." As Dracus expected, Artanius didn't bother to find his tongue—his query answered. "If I win, exonerated by Neutreen's judgement, we both go free."

More shock. More mutterings, louder this time.

"Dracus!" Fawkes shouted, but no one was listening.

While Artanius was ready to draw his Vendetta dagger, Jagras fixed Dracus with a darkling's glare. "You are requesting to fight two Champions, simultaneously, while blindfolded."

Dracus nodded. "I win, we walk, and you don't come after us. Ever."

"And when you lose," Artanius said, "we will skin you. *Both* of you. Then, just before you fade, you'll sit in the tombs of Saltspire and wait for us to do it again."

"Where there is order, there is justice," Dracus said.

"Dracus…" Fawkes was practically pleading. "What are you doin'?"

He didn't like gambling with Fawkes's fate. If he let them go through with the Final Demise, Fawkes would at least be irradiated. But if he lost, Fawkes would be condemned to a life of suffering followed by an eternity of more. *Good thing I don't plan on losin'…*

As the legionaries grew giddy, Jagras presented Dracus with a blindfold. Sparing one last glance at Fawkes and the eastern mouth of the Cut, Dracus tied the fabric tightly over his eyes, hoping the dark abyss wouldn't be the last thing he'd see. With *Fang* in hand and his and Fawkes's fates resting on the blade's edge, he refused to lose. Not to an upright Dreadroot like Artanius or a dull glowstone like Jagras.

Just draw first blood on each of 'em. We'll get outta here, Old Boy.

"Neutreen is watching," Jagras said.

The legionaries cheered. Fawkes pleaded to end this madness. Dracus blocked it all out, focusing only on the sound of Jagras's and Artanius's boots squelching through the muddy, clay-like floor of the Cut. Artanius charged at his right, coming in faster than Jagras and on an angle as if to take him from the side. Overeager, as upstart Order boys tended to be, Artanius reared back and slashed, evident by the disturbance on the wind. Dracus lurched to his left, spinning out of the way. He knew he'd be in the path of Jagras's slower, more direct approach, but he needed to bait the attack.

He won't slash. He'll thrust.

Dracus didn't attempt to stop his leftward momentum, allowing his spin away from Artanius and the slick ground to carry him past Jagras's thrust. He wheeled around, attempting to reorient himself. Artanius's overzealous swings came with a grunt born from low in his throat. Dracus evaded a savage slash that attempted to part his head from his shoulders, then dodged a thrust where his midsection had been a moment ago. Having evaded the joust, Dracus grabbed for Artanius's wrist, but found his forearm, just past the bracer, with his free hand. He drove *Fang* up and through.

Steel met flesh and tore loose a scream. Despite his focus, the wave of gasps and the silence that followed disturbed the din of the legionaries Dracus had drowned out. Unable to hear the squish of boots or the stroke of a sword, he wheeled. Steering Artanius's body around like an unruly horse with *Fang* serving as the reins, Dracus felt his blade slide along Artanius's bone. Artanius released his short sword, screaming.

"One down," Dracus said, tuning his ears for any sign of Jagras. "Let Fawkes go."

Jagras wasn't foolish enough to answer. Though Dracus managed to filter out the other legionaries again, Artanius's cries did more than enough to conceal Jagras's sneaking.

"Let him go!" Dracus shouted.

"Dracus!"

At Fawkes's shout, Dracus crumpled to the ground, kicking out Artanius's feet. On the ground, in the muck and entwined with Artanius, he released *Fang*. With both hands free, he grappled the young Premius and rolled. Relying on landmarks, Dracus slid his hands up Artanius's arm, over his shoulder, and around his neck. Artanius squirmed, but Dracus didn't need to see to fight this type of battle.

He could feel Jagras was close and searching for a clean attack. Dracus wouldn't give him one. With one arm around his neck and the other hand pressing the back of Artanius's head forward, Dracus secured the chokehold. Artanius's wounded limb flailed helplessly, attempting to break his bind.

"Let him go, Jagras." Dracus grabbed his own upper arm and squeezed, increasing the pressure on Artanius's windpipe. "Or he'll suffer, here and now."

Boots slid to his right, attempting not to make a sound. Dracus wrenched Artanius, positioning the Premius between him and Jagras. Steel punched through leather and met flesh. Artanius groaned, unable to breathe in Dracus's grasp. There was no way of telling if Jagras's strike was a killing blow, but if Artanius hollowed, Dracus didn't want to wait to find out. He shoved Artanius away and kicked at where he expected Jagras to be. His shin connected with something. Pain spread like fissures through his lower leg. Jagras attempted to reposition, but his foot slipped, and he fell to the ground beside Dracus and Artanius.

Unarmed, but desperate to draw first blood, Dracus rolled, climbing over Artanius to locate Jagras. With his shin screaming, he crawled atop the Fourth Premius, searching for landmarks. Dracus found Jagras's right wrist and pinned it. Jagras was face-down. Planting his knee in the Premius's spine, Dracus reared and slammed his fist into the back of Jagras's head.

Blind and covered in mud, unable to tell if he'd drawn blood, Dracus wailed on Jagras to ensure it. "Let!" Crunch. "Us!" Crunch. "Go!" He punched, sometimes connecting, and other times only half-hitting his target. Each missed punch hurt worse than the ones that landed. Still, he didn't stop until his knuckles felt like they'd shattered. Then he drove his forearm into the back of Jagras's skull, crushing the man into the mud that had already claimed so many lives. Finally, confident that he'd drawn enough blood to sate the trials' completion, he tore the blindfold off.

Heaving for breath, he stared down at the mess of the back of Jagras's skull. A ruin of mud and blood, the Premius twitched. If he was alive, he wasn't long for this world. Dracus spun, searching for Artanius.

Clutching his gut with his skewered right arm, Artanius gained his feet. His face was pale, but his eyes were black as the rot that turned Bohen into the Skeleton King.

"Let us go," Dracus said, his voice breathy. "Neutreen has made her judgement."

Jagras's shade rose from his body, passing through Dracus like a cold wind.

Artanius's gaze followed the shade. He nodded to a Tribunus, who flipped the switch on his arcanatek to irradiate. While the Tribunus prepared to end Jagras's existence, Artanius turned his attention to Dracus, breathing heavily.

"Neutreen may have found you innocent," Artanius said, clutching his arm. "But you fail to realize, Dracus—here, the One has final authority." He shook his head, grinning all the while. "You aren't going anywhere. Neither of you! Ready the Final Demise!"

Dracus's jaw unhinged. He'd done it. He'd survived the Blood Trials against not just one, but two men. There was no order. There was no justice. Only the promise of pain.

Dracus lurched to his feet, but before he could ready a defense, the legionaries swarmed him. Men grabbed him by the arms, dragging him away from Jagras's fallen form and towards the tent post lined with Vendetta daggers.

Fawkes resisted the men working against him, but there were too many. Dracus couldn't squirm away. His ankle felt numb from below where he'd kicked out Jagras's feet. His fingers couldn't even curl into a fist to strike or break free from their grasp as they dragged him closer to the dagger-lined post and the ensuing torment.

Though Fawkes had been closer to the Vendetta-daggered post, he had fought to get away from it, while Dracus could barely slow the men dragging him. His feet slid in the silt, providing no friction for his feeble resistance. He glanced over his shoulder to see how much room he had to mount an escape, but too late.

The legionaries threw him into the post. His upper back crashed into the daggers. Razors slashed sharper than any hellhound's teeth and with more malice than any hollowed's rotten fingernails. Fire lanced through him as he slid off the blades and fell sidelong to the ground. His consciousness waned. The call within, the desire to let go and hollow, rang like a bell on Bheric's Day.

"No!" Fawkes shouted. "Dracus!" He headbutted one legionary, elbowed another, then grabbed a third and hurled him over his shoulder, slamming him into the ground. Bruised eyes wild, beard a tangle, the scars across his bare chest stretched and contracted with each pump of his arms as he fought his way toward Dracus.

Don't. Let. Go.

Eyes on Fawkes, Dracus resisted the urge to succumb. *Not yet. Not while they have him.* This time, when the legionaries hoisted him up, readying to secure him to the daggered pole, Dracus channeled his pain into rage. Blocking out the bumps, bruises, and lacerations that coursed like an electric current, Dracus used the legionaries' support to stomp down on one's instep. Wrenching his arm from the legionary's grasp, Dracus shoved him, face first, into the pole of the Final Demise.

The legionary fell, screaming, his hands clutching his shredded face. As another went to replace him in securing Dracus's arm, the legionary on his opposite arm crumbled beneath the blow of a double-fisted overhead strike. Hand free, Dracus struck with the heel of his hand into the nose of the legionary on his left. Dracus's wounded fingers unsheathed the legionary's blade and resheathed it in his gut.

Fawkes secured the short sword of the legionary he'd struck and pushed his back against Dracus's. The contact drew attention to the injured tissues that would never heal, but simultaneously, the rise and fall of Fawkes's breath brought him peace.

"Never shoulda come 'ere," Fawkes said.

Dracus snorted, eyeing the surrounding legionaries too scared to make a move. "Cant's idea. I woulda left ya. Wonder where he got that ghostin' hero complex from."

Fawkes scoffed. "Not us, eh?"

"You never give up, do you?" Artanius shouted.

Dracus ignored him and the rest of the Order. There seemed to be screams all around them, chaos swirling within the Order's ranks. But he blocked it all out. It might as well have just been him and Fawkes from Elyngrove to Octaven. "Think we gone done run outta luck, Old Boy. Don't see us makin' it outta this mess."

Fawkes took a deep breath as if savoring every moment of it. "Whatever happens. This isn't the end, Dray. Hollowed, shade, darkling—don't matter; I'll find you. We'll find a way."

Dracus felt the darkness calling to him. He could just let go, and this suffering would be over. There was no telling what the next stage would bring, but at least this part would be at its end. Yet Fawkes's words granted a glimmer of hope. Since he'd hollowed, he'd never allowed himself to really think about what would happen next; it hadn't mattered. So concerned with getting Canton beyond the curse, he'd denied the possibilities. *Could Fawkes and I find each other, even on the other side of suffering?* It was a long shot. An implausibility. But a possibility. Like a lone glowstone in the depths of the Gullies, there was light left, even in this fallen world.

He would not let go. Not while there was still light to be had.

A shadow passed overhead, and all eyes drifted skyward.

Then Neutreen descended with the wrath reserved for the unjust.

Threyna

The Order formed a circle around two heartbeats at its center, but the spectacle distracted all from the approaching horde. Running as they were, the Wraith might have appeared as hollowed, but the blood pumping through their veins was unmistakable. On the opposite side of Cybel's Tears, the Underground marched, bathed in the glow of arcanatek illuminators.

It felt like the making of a song. An epic poem that would live on long after the Order was defeated, the curse was lifted, and Threyna and everyone else could die true deaths. She was back in the Cut, where her story truly began. Though the Wraith were not entering to fight the Order—but rather spurred by their fear of returning to Octarius—they were still here.

The Order can bleed. They'll all see that together, we can win!

Threyna dove on the outskirts of the circle of gathered legionaries. Barely hovering above the ground, she conjured a hooked blade and slashed at the lower legs of the clamoring men. Before the falling legionaries or their neighbors could locate what had attacked them, Threyna charged past. Her blade ripped through muscle and tendon like an irradiator through a darkling.

Their cries mixed with the shouts of their brothers-in-arms as the Wraith came into view in greater numbers and with more speed than even Threyna had given them credit for. But the legionaries' divided attention afforded her another pass. Sinking deeper into her Inner Throne and ignoring the black veins stretching from her bangle, Threyna drew upon the blood of the fallen and gave it shape. It congealed into several pikes. All at once, they shot up from the puddles of blood, skewering the legionaries attempting and failing to help their fellows up.

More screams echoed through the Cut. Some of the men hollowed. Other souls fled their pierced flesh in the form of shades. A few became darklings ready for her consumption. Kicking off the ground with a flap of her wings, Threyna took flight, this time drawing gasps and pointing fingers. Adding to her curved blade, the conjuration morphed into a scythe. With the Wraith approaching, it was time to showcase her abilities for all to see.

She drew in breath, taking the souls in with ease. Barely needing to focus on the task, she ushered them into her Inner Throne and assuaged the rot in her veins or escorted them to her Inner Dungeon for later consumption. As all eyes rose to find her flying atop them on blood-conjured wings, Threyna focused on those who didn't look up.

Dracus and Fawkes pressed their backs together at the center of the bloody circle, bodies in Order blacks around them. They hadn't noticed her. Neither had the men immediately before them. Threyna would show them the error of their ways.

She dove, rearing her scythe for another strike. Spreading her wings to control her descent, she slashed in a wide arc. Just as eyes widened and lower jaws unhinged, the curved edge of her bloody weapon cleaved through heads and necks alike.

She landed to the ground before Dracus, allowing her conjured wings to fall to ash. Glancing over her shoulder to Fawkes, she said, "Fight. Win."

With no time to address their shock or awe, she drew in breath, taking new souls into her Inner Throne. From her seat of power, she formed the blood at her feet into a wall of pikes. The newly forged weapons burst upward, impaling those nearest. More souls launched into the air as darklings, or seeped from their failing flesh as shades. Those condemned to their mortal form lost all sense of humanity and attacked whatever was closest—in this case, their Order brethren.

She allowed her conjured pikes to crumble to ashes, dropping the bodies of the departed to the ground and releasing the hollowed from their bindings. Darklings dove into other legionaries, beginning the contest of wills. Conjuring a double-bladed glaive, Threyna made quick work of their distractions.

Hack, slash, thrust. She skewered a legionary too stubborn to run. Retracting her glaive, she spun it over her head to chop horizontally across his face. Power surged. The blood all around called to her. Feeling invincible, Threyna leapt into the air, conjuring new wings. An angel of death, she wanted to be seen—by the Order, the Wraith, and the Underground reinforcements approaching from the east.

Divided, ruin will reign. I will unite.

She sank into her Inner Throne, deeper than she'd ever dared go before.

Dracus

The veil between life and death decayed—thin and fragile. Under the curse of Rheynia, it became difficult to discern the difference between the two. The long faces of the newly deceased held the expressions of their last moments, but those among the living were of equal torment.

Fear. Pain. Loss.

Dracus would not fall victim. Not here. Not now.

Grateful that Threyna had chosen this moment to return, Dracus had no qualms with cutting their reunion short. He searched for an escape between the ranks of the distracted legionaries. There wasn't a path, but that didn't mean they couldn't carve one.

"With me!" Dracus called to Fawkes.

Heading westward, he took advantage of the space created by Threyna's double-bladed glaive. Charging forward with Fawkes at his heels, he shoved a hollowed into a legionary, then hacked down on the pauldron of a legionary taking aim at Threyna with his vortex.

Dracus's wounds screamed from where the razor edges of the Vendetta daggers carved across his back. His shin felt like it wouldn't support another step. His knuckles could barely bend, swollen and numb. He could feel himself slipping into the night of death. But he knew the comfort it offered was a lie. He'd go mad, slaughtering everything in his path out of jealousy of the living—unable to tell friend from foe, Fawkes from a hellhound, or Canton from Belrich.

"Let go, my love. Let go and see. Let go the woes and sing high for me."

He wasn't ready to sing. He refused to. Guided by his blade, he hacked, stabbed, and slashed his way, attempting to carve a path through the Order.

"Dray!" Fawkes's voice seemed so far away, though he could feel his hand on his back.

Focus. Follow the blade. Just you and the blade, kid.

Fire coursed across his ribs. Roared along the back of his head. Scorched a hole through his shin. His body was failing; he could feel it with each stroke of his sword. It seemed as if between his mind and his body, he could only keep one working properly.

He deflected a thrust aimed for his midsection, blocked a second aimed at his shoulder, and countered with a jab of his half-closed fist. As the legionary stumbled back, Dracus slashed from neck to navel. His Order blacks split, divided by a bloody gash. He stumbled and fell. Behind the legionary, the walls of the Cut and the blackness beyond called to him. They could survive. They could escape. And once Fawkes was safe, then he would let go.

"Dray!"

Almost there, Old Boy. Just a little farther.

"Dracus!"

Fawkes's voice seemed even further away now. But his hand was no longer on his back. Dracus spun to find Fawkes engaged with two legionaries while fending off a hollowed.

Desperation gripped him like Dreadroot. Vision narrowing until only Fawkes was in view, Dracus abandoned the possibility of escape. There was no future. No hope of giving Canton the life he'd never had or the peace he'd only dreamed of. There was nothing. Thoughts vanished. Pain ceased to exist. Only Fawkes.

The distance that separated him from Fawkes and his assailants faded in a blink. With a lunging jump, he stabbed his short sword straight through the back of a rearing legionary. The hollowed was on Fawkes, barely held at bay with his free hand while he jostled with the other legionary.

Something burst from the ground beside Dracus, evoking a scream from another legionary. It barely registered. A single groan in a horde of hollowed, a pebble of Viridite amongst all the light of the Gullies' glowstones. Ignoring the distractions, he sliced through the lower leg of the legionary across from Fawkes. Fawkes shoved the hollowed away and buried his acquired sword through the legionary's open mouth.

"C'mon, we gotta go!" Dracus spun back to the path he'd carved for them, but it was closing. Not just by legionaries, but crimson walls that sprouted out of the ground behind them. As dark and deep as the blood coating his sword, a gory curtain closed in like the jaws of a giant beast.

"No..." Even if they made it past the last of the legionaries, they'd be trapped.

"Watch out!"

Something crashed into Dracus from behind. Wind rushed past his ear as his momentum carried him forward, and he fell to the bloodstained clay of the Cut's floor. The sound of colliding swords rang in his ears. Warbles of half-charged irradiators exploded all around him. The wall of blood closed, sealing him and Fawkes inside with the Order. He glanced to the sky above the encroaching blood wall, waiting for the Skeleton King to rise on draconic wings.

Before anything could come over the wall, it faltered, never reaching its full height, and crumbling to ashes. Dracus didn't understand what he was seeing, yet somehow, amidst the chaos of the fight, the soft squelch of steel sliding through flesh overcame all other sounds. Dracus looked over his shoulder.

Fawkes blinked. His face paled. Blood dribbled from the corner of his lip.

A sword point protruded through his stomach and out his back. Fawkes gripped the arm of the legionary who held the blade, staring at it as if unable to make sense of how it had gotten there.

Dracus opened his mouth to scream but found he had no voice. Ashes swept through the Cut. Unable to tell if they were real or if he'd been transported back to the pyre that burned Arenius's fleet, Dracus fought for lucidity. He tried to pry himself from the ground, to hurl himself at Fawkes's attacker, but he couldn't move. Pain worse than anything he'd ever experienced gouged through his stomach and erupted out his back as if he'd taken the blade to the gut himself. He couldn't blink. Couldn't breathe. He felt his lips move, mouthing Fawkes's name, but still, no sound came forth.

Fawkes roared. He reared back his head and brought the crown down on the legionary's brittle face. The first headbutt broke the legionary's nose. The second, his orbital bone. The third didn't connect because the legionary had already lost his grip on his sword and collapsed to the ground, seizing. Fawkes fell atop him, sword still embedded in his gut. He drove his own sword through the legionary's twitching chest.

His soul made no effort to stay; his shade slipped from his flesh as easily as Fawkes's blade slid from his belly. Then Fawkes staggered, falling to all fours. Inclining his head, he searched for Dracus.

Dracus's vision tunneled tighter than the entrances to Aranoc. The world might as well have been burning around them. Legionaries were screaming, backing away, even running past Dracus and Fawkes, but Dracus didn't care to know why. Both on their hands and knees, they crawled toward one another until Fawkes collapsed an arm's reach from Dracus.

Denial robbed Dracus of sense. He saw the angle of the thrust, knew the damage such a blow would do. As much blood drained from Fawkes's body to litter the ground around them, more was pooling within, leaking from his eviscerated intestines and his punctured lung. Yet he crawled the remaining distance to Fawkes as if he were slipping into their bed after a long, painful day.

He'll get up. He's gotta get up.

No fear. No sadness, disappointment, or regret. Those were for the dead. Fawkes would live. Dracus would hollow, but Fawkes would live. He fell prone beside Fawkes so they were facing one another.

Blood poured from a gash in his hairline and leaked from his too-red lips. "The boy…" Fawkes's voice came forced, weak. "Alive?"

Dracus nodded, grounding the side of his face into the mud, his throat too tight to speak.

Fawkes reached his hand for Dracus's face. The gentleness of his touch was ruined by the tremble in his hand as he attempted to caress Dracus's cheek. "Not here. True death. Out there. Together."

Dracus wanted to let go. He and Fawkes could hollow together. Maybe, just maybe, they could hold onto the piece of themselves that loved each other. Maybe they could hold onto that as they withered away, waiting for a Justicus to vortex and irradiate them, or a Teller to burn their bodies until their souls were released to Neutreen.

Delusion.

"Forever and ever it is we who survive."

The lullaby haunted him, taunting him for ever wanting more than just to endure this fate. But he was a survivor. Stubborn or stupid, he even believed he could do what Fawkes was asking of him. It didn't change his desire to let go, accept the pain, succumb to the hollowing. Yet how could he ignore Fawkes's last request?

The arcanatek on his belt weighed heavily on his right hip, as did the absence of his soul jar, but he knew what he needed to do. He placed his hand atop Fawkes's on his cheek. "I've gotcha, Old Boy. Beyond the curse, eh? We go together, right?"

Fawkes nodded, but his eyelids were drooping. Dracus flipped the switch on his blaster, setting it to vortex and allowing it to begin its warbling charge. Needing a new soul jar, he rolled onto his back in search of a fallen legionary. Wincing through the effort of moving, he dragged himself towards the nearest body as battle waged all around him. Screams filled the air. Shuffling feet stumbled over one another as bodies collided— hollowed and living warred while a goddess of death reigned overhead.

He rolled a legionary onto his side, searching for the soul jar at his belt. His hand, stained with Fawkes's blood, closed around the orb. Taking it from the legionary's possession, he opened it, releasing whatever foul souls it carried. Not caring who they sought to overtake, Dracus crawled back towards Fawkes, empty soul jar in hand.

Fawkes was fading fast. His eyes, so vibrant in life, were a dull, wandering gray as they searched for him. He reached for the fatekeeper at his chest. Too weak to pull it from his neck, Dracus took it himself, plucking the arcanatek from its leather strap.

"I... love... you," Fawkes said.

"This ain't the end." Dracus pocketed Fawkes's fatekeeper. "I'll see you again, Old Boy." The arcanatek hummed on his hip. He screwed the soul jar onto the back of the vortex despite the tremble of his hands. He aimed unsteadily at the man he loved.

"I love you, too, Fawkes."

No tears fell. Not because emotion wasn't welling up inside him, but because such gifts were reserved for the living. Fawkes wouldn't receive the proper send-off. There wasn't a proper send-off to give. He was supposed to live. Canton was supposed to flee. And Dracus was supposed to have died during the Disasters when the building collapsed on his mother. He never should have escaped Bheric's Hollow with Canton. He never should have survived the Battle of the Cut or been able to endure after Arilette poisoned him. But here he was, and everything was wrong.

His teeth clenched. His vision narrowed tighter until Fawkes was the only thing he could see. Smoke stained the air, ashes dried out his mouth, but they were just memories from back when he had dreams. Now he watched the life flee from his last dream yet to hope for.

Fawkes forced a smile, but his teeth were stained with blood. His eyes, barely open at this point, searched sadly as if to see where they had gone wrong. Nearly fifteen years ago, after arriving in Octarius and joining the Underground, Fawkes was the only one who welcomed him. Fawkes was the only one who treated him as a man and not a darkling warlord. They had dreamed of leaving together aboard Arenius's fleet and starting a new life together in Sansia, but that future was burned to ash when Arilette set *Resilience* aflame.

"Not the end," Fawkes said. "Just a new beginning. Beyond the curse."

"A new beginning… I won't fail you." Dracus closed his eyes, daring to believe it possible. He pulled the trigger. The vortex spun, drawing Fawkes's soul from his body and funneling his essence into the soul jar.

Dracus fell to the ground and rolled to his back. The pain persisted as if he'd just been thrown against the Vendetta daggers, but it paled in comparison to the loss he couldn't feel. He only felt cold, empty, alone.

Threyna

Spears rose from the ground, born of the blood of the fallen. Conjured arrows rained down, pelting legionaries as they tried to take aim at her. Flying upon blood-spawned wings with a double-bladed glaive in her hands, she swept over the distracted legions. They were no match for her. Like sheep to slaughter or crops before a scythe, they came and fell all while the running Wraith approached.

She could sense their terror in the beating of their hearts. They were afraid of the Underground, but their fear was misplaced. It was the Order they ran from and the failed Dominion they claimed to uphold. Their dream of a life beyond the curse could begin anew, here in Rheynia. The Order was the blight upon the land, and finally, the Wraith would see and they would not fear.

An irradiator fired. Radiant light flashed in her peripheral vision. Threyna opened her wings, slowing her momentum and swerving out of the way of the blast. She raked her glaive atop the shoulders of her enemies, sending more men in black uniforms to the ground and more shouts to the clouds overhead.

Another irradiator fired, forcing her to roll to the side. The bolt of energy sizzled past, but Threyna chased it, climbing higher into the sky and preparing to swoop down again. She drew in breath, calling upon the freshly departed souls, but another irradiator charge screamed past. Barely dodging out of the way, she lost control of the shades she'd called upon. Unable to abate the growing rot, she consumed a pair of souls from the dungeons beneath her Inner Throne.

Only half of the Order's number remained. With the Wraith nearing and her rot receding, Threyna prepared a statement she would make certain no one forgot. A flood of blood was available to her, asking—no, begging—to be used for her purposes. Threyna raised her arm, and with it, a circular wall, lined with pikes directed at the center, rose from the ground to encompass the legionaries.

"Bring me Belrich," Threyna shouted as her wall enclosed and began to constrict. "And I will bring you dea—"

A vortex's charge distorted the air around her. She inhaled, but reacted too late. Pressure pulled upon her. The walls of her Inner Throne quaked with a force that threatened to rip her from her seat of power altogether. The door of her subterranean dungeon shattered, allowing her kept souls to escape. Unable to restrain them amidst her own unsteadiness, she couldn't stop them from bursting free from her throne room and soaring into the night air.

Threyna's grip on her Inner Throne faltered. Her wings burned to ash. Though she wasn't as high as when she'd flown over the clouds above the Gullies, gravity opened its fragile arms to her again.

Panic seized her stomach, and her blood glaive disintegrated within her hands. Flailing, she crashed onto the legionaries. They broke her fall, but entangled in a mess of limbs, blades, and arcanatek amidst a tempest of shades and darklings, it took everything she had to emerge unscathed. She stomped on a fallen legionary, wrestled a short sword away from another, and stabbed a third through the shoulder.

Desperately, she tried to reclaim her Inner Throne. She could see her high-backed chair, the red cushion on the ivory stone, but it might as well have been across the sea. She charged for it, but outside the palace of her mind, the battle still raged. Absent her blood magic, she ripped her sword free to attack the man she'd taken it from.

Before she could finish her cut, something whined through the light armor of her fatigues. She sensed blood, but not its power, its warning.

Pain sparked up her spine and wrapped around her ribs. She spun to defend herself, but another blade punched her through the shoulder. Fire radiated along her collarbone and into her sternum. Smoke climbed through her neck and choked the breath from her lungs. Reeling, she swung at her attacker, but her edge merely slapped at the legionary's armor.

"Kill her!"

She shoved away from a counterattack, but she lost her footing in the fray of legionaries. Ash swept from her crumbling blood wall. Again, she reached for her Inner Throne. She was almost there.

Before she could gain access to her blood magic, rough hands yanked her braid from behind, jarring her head back.

"Die!"

Cold ripped across her throat. Blood sprayed before her eyes. She gasped for breath, but none came. Warmth flooded down her neck until she was drowning in it. Again she tried to breathe, but again she was denied.

She didn't know when she'd dropped her sword, but she must have, because both hands were wrapped around her throat, begging her blood to stay within the thin walls of flesh that kept her alive.

She fell before the seat of her Inner Throne. Crawling up the dais with her hand outstretched, reaching for the arm of the chair, she fell short, collapsing a handspan from her seat of power.

No. No. No! The bangle's panic melded with her own.

She willed her body, her mind—whatever kept her conscious—to work. Bloody hands grasped the arm of the chair, but it seemed closer somehow, as if the throne had leaned down to lift her up.

She hauled herself into her Inner Throne and pressed her back into the chair. Blood stained her ivory palace, but power and potential returned to her like a Legatus standing before their armed and ready legions. Instead of soldiers, she had bodies, blood, souls.

Bow. Bow to me.

Bodies of the deceased contorted. Shades and darklings alike stopped what they were doing to surge towards her.

Lying on her back on the floor of the Cut, bleeding out, she gripped her throat and stared at the sky. Red. Not gray. Red. Not clouds. Mist.

Instinctually, she drew in breath. Not through her nose and mouth, but directly into her Inner Throne. Blood, bone, and soul obliged, and she devoured them. Power unlike any she'd felt before pumped through her.

As a resounding *click* came from the bangle, blood reversed its flow, seeping back into her. Flesh restitched. Breath found its way back to her lungs, and rot retreated like darkness from the light. The legionaries that had stabbed her backed away, their mouths wide, eyes blinking.

She felt their fear—heard their short, rapid breaths, the immediacy of their racing hearts. From within her Inner Throne, she could identify each and every unique pattern of their individual pulses. And they were hers.

Rising to her feet as they continued to back away from her, she seized their frightened hearts and squeezed. Pressure throbbed, making the walls of her Inner Throne seem to pulsate. The tempo increased, the intensity grew. Their eyes bulged as veins dilated in their necks and along their foreheads. Blood began to drip from their noses first. Then their eyes and ears.

She squeezed harder until, all at once, the pressure burst. The nearest surrounding legionaries collapsed to the ground, their hearts nothing more than the remains of muscle that had torn itself asunder.

The legionaries surrounding them lost containment of their constitution. Backing away as five shades and one darkling rose from the deceased, some turned to run, but no one was going to get away.

Threyna drew in breath, consuming the souls and spiriting them to her Inner Dungeon while advancing on the retreating legionaries.

She felt her lips split in a grin. Hardly believing she had escaped death, feeling invincible, she rose into the air on a pillar of conjured blood. The

Wraith stood, dumbstruck, the Underground at their backs, watching and waiting.

This is it. This is how we unite.

Only a few dozen legionaries remained. Even outnumbered and ill-equipped, the Wraith could have finished them off. The Underground could have taken the whole of the hundred or so men who had been here prior to her arrival. But this wasn't their fight. This was hers.

Raising her arms, Threyna conjured a wall of blood from the north wall of the Cut to the south, blocking off the legionaries' westbound retreat. Some attempted to hack a hole through her blood wall. Others attempted to climb out of the Cut, but the walls were too slippery and too steep for any to have a chance. Those toward the back of their number knew the truth.

They were all going to die.

Threyna conjured a second wall, trapping the last of the Fourth and Ninth legions between them. Pressing her hands together, one black with rot, the other stained with her own blood, she drew the walls in towards one another. Panicked voices rose from between the walls. They grew louder, more desperate, but in the end, all were silent.

Threyna allowed her bloody walls to fall to ash around the remaining shades and darklings. If any were hollowed, there would be nothing left of them to worry about. Staring out over the length of the Cut, she didn't spot Dracus or Fawkes amongst the sea of bodies in Order blacks. She'd lost sight of them once the fighting had begun. She supposed they'd run away—climbed out of the Cut at one of the shallower areas. But she didn't need them. All she needed were those gathered behind her.

Still elevated on her bloodborne pedestal, she turned to face the gathered Wraith and the legions of the Underground. Swallowing, the effort of passing her saliva agitated the scar at her throat. She placed her fingers to where the legionary's blade had slit, wondering if she'd even be able to speak.

Unable to let the moment pass absent words, she lifted her black-veined fist to the sky and tried. "The Order's reign is at an end." Her voice came out hoarse, but it echoed off the Cut's walls either way. "As is our division. United, we will reclaim Rheynia. We will restore our home."

Laela

A cacophony of light and sound assaulted her senses; Her vision—a blur of spots and streaks. Her hearing—a flood of high-pitched and distorted voices. Lying flat on her back and staring at the sky, she tried to move but found herself restrained. The clouds overhead, typically stagnant, seemed to move in a chaotic rhythm.

The last thing Laela remembered, they were heading south along the Tears towards the Grip, where Rosler and Taggart would be waiting. She didn't know how she ended up here. She didn't know where *here* was. She recalled pain. Aylenia's hands stained with blood.

My blood.

They'd turned around, unable to continue fleeing south. She'd collapsed. And now…

Glimpses of faces flashed within her field of view, but it happened too fast to identify them. Voices spoke, but the distortion made them sound more like steel on a whetstone.

"Look what ya've gone and done now," her father chided. *"After all that runnin', you're right back where you started."*

Though she could understand her father, she didn't comprehend what he was saying.

One of the blurs of faces drew near and remained long enough to solidify. Aylenia loomed over her, examining her. Her head jerked and her mouth moved as if she were speaking to someone else, but it was so fast that it was incomprehensible.

Aylenia reached over her, and suddenly, as if time were slowing down, her movements and voice approached something close to understandable.

"Return her too fast and she could hollow," a voice said so quickly Laela could barely grasp. "Make her heart explode or her lungs collapse." The voice slowed as it continued speaking.

Laela attempted to turn toward the sound and found she was able. Carried in a stretcher with Aylenia and another figure walking beside her, Laela examined the silhouette of a man, backlit by a bright white light. Her eyes adjusted, taking in the gray-clad man.

An Undergrounder.

"See what I mean?" her father said. *"We shoulda just stayed at the Roost. All this runnin'... for nothing."*

"She's conscious," Aylenia said. "She needs to know, then we can slow her back down."

"Make it quick or she won't make it to the medicus. She needs the warps. The bad one. She's likely suffered a brain contusion, she's got a hollowed bite that could give her dewskull, and if that stab wound doesn't kill her the blood loss will."

Laela felt pressure from within her chest and a sudden rush of blood that nearly made her pass out. Pain twisted through her back and along her side. Blinking through it, she swallowed, but her tongue felt thick and dry in her mouth. Her eyes tracked lazily between the two before settling on Aylenia.

Aylenia touched Laela's cheek, her hand warm and wet. "You need to stay calm. Do you hear me? Calm. I need you to trust me, prime?"

Laela tried to speak, but her eyelids were drawing closed.

"We *have* to get you to Octarius. You'll hollow if—" Screams echoed in the distance, drawing Aylenia's attention.

Laela tried to make sense of Aylenia's words. *Octarius? No. We're going to Sansia. She said she wanted to find her mûnta.* Her heartbeat became shallow and rapid at the realization of Aylenia's betrayal and the meaning behind her father's jibes. "You..."

"I need to put you back under or—" Their caravan stopped short, cutting Aylenia off. She directed her attention to the horizon. "Corners… Neutreen… Is that… Threyna?"

The sound of her sister's name sent a pang of conflicted emotions through her. A concoction of anger, guilt, and loss overwhelmed her, but Aylenia's words entwined with her mother's sentiment to counsel vulnerability. Yet now, in the Underground's possession and with the Grip so close, she couldn't sit by and do nothing.

Riding the emotional spike of energy, she forced herself to sit up in her stretcher. At the foot of it, an unfamiliar arcanatek glowed green within its black casing.

The medicus held out an arm to block her. "Stay still or you'll—"

Laela waved the medicus out of her way, ignoring the pain and effort of sitting up. Her father had warnings of his own, but she was tired of listening to him. She walled him off and retreated to her Center of Silence as she followed Aylenia's gaze.

Standing atop a red pillar, covered in blood with black veins snaking up and down her arm, Threyna held up her fist. "The Order's reign is at an end. As is our division. United, we will reclaim Rheynia. We will restore our home."

Laela blinked, not believing her eyes or ears. Threyna was a horror. As grotesque as the creature that crawled out of Avengard's oubliette wearing Theodyn's skin was, Threyna was worse. And she was attempting to unite the Wraith and the Underground together, in the wrong mission. *I will not go back. I need to stop her.* Clutching her ribs, she swung her leg over the side of the stretcher.

"What in gory ghosting tarnation are you doing?" scolded one of the porters carrying her stretcher as her weight shift sent it off-balance.

Laela crashed to the ground, catching herself on a knee.

"Laela, no." Aylenia came around the other side of the stretcher to help her up, but Laela was already pushing herself to her feet.

Wincing and holding her ribs, she couldn't avert her gaze from Threyna. She shoved past Aylenia and limped her way through the gathered crowd. Undergrounders in gray, Wraith in mismatched travel garb—all so transfixed on Threyna they barely noticed Laela.

Aylenia called after her, following her, begging for her to return to the arcanatek that was keeping her alive, but Laela had no ear for it.

"The time is now," Threyna said, her voice echoing through the Cut. "Belrich ran, tail between his legs. The Order is weak, and they know it. Even if the Skeleton King lives, he hides—too old, too weak, to show himself. Now I wield the same magic that decimated the Seers and defeated the Artificers. No longer must we tunnel underground, surviving on scraps left after their collectors have taken their quotas. No longer will we let them take our boys and train them to fight against us."

She's going to send us to our deaths.

"Laela, please," Aylenia said, grasping for her.

Laela swatted her away, forging ahead. There were more Wraith than Undergrounders as she neared the front. Some turned to look at her as she shoved her way forward. She pointedly ignored Redge's sharp glare, Asla's slack-jawed expression, and the crushing realization that the Wraith would never escape painted across Bhen's faraway gaze.

They were doomed. They couldn't run. Couldn't fight. She searched her addled mind, looking for the words that might allow the Wraith to walk free. They'd come so far, tried so hard. She couldn't let it end like this. She couldn't return to Octarius. Smoke stung her eyes, and fire licked at her hope, but she couldn't let everything they'd worked toward for the last decade fall to ashes.

For Rance. For Mother.

"A new age is dawning in Rheynia," Threyna said. "And finally, *we* are in control. I know you don't want to fight, but there are other ways to serve. This war is not hopeless. We *can* win, but we must work together. We are here, not as your enemies, but as allies requesting your aid."

Laela didn't know how many of her people would believe Threyna's lies or how many would submit to the Underground out of fear of reprisal. But if she said nothing—if she did nothing—Rance's dream was dead. They'd never leave Rheynia, never see Sansia, and even if they did defeat the Order—regardless of how many lives it cost—they'd still be under the rule of a tyrant.

The Underground would become our new overlords. We'd still be living under a curse.

She'd watched Arenius burn. Then while she and the others ran north, Arilette led the Underground to the Cut and into ten years of torment. Laela couldn't do anything then, but if she did nothing now and allowed Threyna to follow in Arilette's footsteps, Neutreen would never grant her a single feather.

She pushed her way to the front, Aylenia trailing behind her. At the head of the gathered group, Canton, red-faced and panting, stared up at Threyna. Beside him, Arilette watched with a grin as sharp as the knife she'd stab into the back of anyone who dared cross her.

"Divided, ruin will reign," Threyna said. "But join us. Together, we will take back Rheynia!"

Laela wouldn't stand for it. This was not how it was supposed to be. Her father's taunts fought to enter her Center of Silence, but she kept her walls up.

"Fight for more. Dream for more," her mother had said.

Everything Aylenia had said about Laela and Threyna being more alike than dissimilar was a lie. Staring up at Threyna, she had nothing in common with her. Nothing but a mother. But their mother was gone, stabbed in the heart by Belrich.

"There is strength in knowing when to drop your guard and courage in actually doing so," her mother had said. Now was not the time. Vulnerability would not make her dreams of Sansia come true, regardless what Aylenia wanted her to believe.

If they were going to make it out of this, she needed to make her stand now. She couldn't let the Wraith return with the Undergrounders, because once they set foot inside Octarius's ruins, they were done for. As good as dead and gone.

Laela planted her unsteady feet and pointed at Threyna. "You!" All attention turned towards her. "You speak of division, but you are the divider. You speak of ruin, but you are the Disasters! Look at you… look at what you've done."

A graveyard of still and desiccated corpses surrounded Threyna. The mass of legionaries who tried to escape were a heap of twitching limbs in a pond of viscera. As horrific as the scene before her was, the sight of her sister was the worst of all; not even the mess of blood and gore covering her could hide the black veins slithering up her cheek.

"Look at what you've become," Laela spat, attempting to ignore her swimming vision and wobbly knees. "You've sold your soul to the One, and for what? Your father possessed blood magic; what good did it do him?"

Threyna's pedestal melted, lowering her to the floor of the Cut. She stalked towards Laela with a predatory angle to her eyes. "My father suffered. For ten years. Ten *years* of the Order's torture. *'What good did it do him?'* If we had joined together and fought ten years ago, it could have made all the difference."

Laela didn't back down. Hobbled as she was, she advanced on Threyna, clutching her ribs. Each step a labor. "If we had fled to Sansia—*together*—it could have made all the difference. You want to fight, but you don't care about the bodies you leave in your wake."

Only a few paces away now, Laela nodded over Threyna's shoulder to the massacre behind her. Something stirred—someone. Shoulders heavy, knees knocked, and gaze downcast, the figure hoisted a fallen form from the ground.

Dracus…

With Canton standing in the Underground's ranks behind her, there could only be one other person who Dracus would bother to treat with such reverence. Fawkes, still and bloody, weighed Dracus down—in body and in spirit—yet he trudged forward, towards them.

"Dracus!" Canton cried, breaking rank to charge towards Dracus and Fawkes.

Threyna's gaze followed Canton. Dracus collapsed to his knees before Canton, holding Fawkes in his arms.

Canton knelt before Dracus and Fawkes's body. "Fawkes… no. Blood and bone, no!"

Laela's heart broke for them, but not just for them—for everyone whose life was better because Fawkes was in it. He who had been there for her after her father died, he who had supported her mother after Threyna had run off.

For a long moment, Threyna stared at the two men crying over their loss. Her mouth opened and closed, but no words came forth.

A sad smile tugged at Laela's lips. "Do you even care who suffers for your *victory*?"

Threyna's brow hardened; her mouth formed a tight line. Laela could practically hear Threyna's teeth grinding behind her grim expression.

Laela shook her head at her sister, but with her vision waning and adrenaline fading, the movement made her stagger. Aylenia came up beside her, preventing her from falling over.

Threyna glanced between the two of them, bewilderment painted atop the gore and rot marring her face. She snorted, but still was unable to form words.

"You need to go back to the warp," Aylenia said. "You're going to bleed out."

Laela ignored Aylenia. She needed to prove to the Wraith that they couldn't return to Octarius. Leveling her index finger at Threyna, Laela stabbed the sword of truth into her sister's web of lies. "You act like you're our answer, the Savior come again." She wagged her finger instead of shaking her head, but even still, she was seeing double. *Be strong. Be courageous. Make them see, or we're all doomed.* "You're not the Savior. You claim you come to us as allies seeking aid, but only after *you* sabotaged our escape and forced us down this path. This is not unity. We are not allies. Even in victory, you're just another tyrant: a Skeleton Queen instead of a Skeleton King."

Her shouting left her exhausted. Her eyelids drooped. Her knees threatened to cave.

Threyna snarled, stalking close enough for the black veins in her eyes to become visible in Laela's swirling vision.

Despite her efforts to stand proud, Laela could barely remain upright even with Aylenia's aid. Yet she hadn't convinced anyone of anything yet.

"Shoulda stayed down," her father said. *"But you never learn, do ya?"*

Threyna stopped before Laela and leaned close so that only she could hear. "Make me the monster if you must, but the way I see it, you've run out of options. You're going back to Octarius. Rest, heal, and maybe you'll *finally* see reason."

Laela inhaled sharply to protest, but her knees gave out. Even in Aylenia's grasp, she nearly crumpled to the ground.

"Laela," Aylenia urged, though her voice felt faraway. "The warp."

Laela's eyelids drooped.

Threyna backed away, lifting her voice so all could hear. "Legions, escort the Wraith to the safety of Octarius. The Order will come, and battle will soon be upon us. We must prepare."

Smoke blinded her. Heat licked at her insides. Ashes rained down upon her.

"Weak," her father said. *"Just like your mother."*

No longer able to stand, not even Aylenia could prevent Laela from falling. Darkness devoured her, pain consumed her, and failure lulled her to unconsciousness.

Part III

CHAPTER 48

DREADROOT'S CARESS

Threyna XIX

"The world is cold and dark. Your father and I have seen and survived our fair share of it. Yet you, child, you are proof that beauty can still exist in such a fallen world…"

—an excerpt from a fatekeeper

Threyna crossed her arms over her chest, cupping the bangle protectively in her right hand. Only one prong remained, but the way Arilette and Lorath's eyes trained on it made her gut twist. Though back at Octarius, secreted deep within the bowels of the Underground's fortress in Arilette's tablinum—a place where Threyna once took comfort—she felt only disquiet.

Neither Arilette or Lorath had batted an eye when she'd told them about what had become of her father or what happened to Ebrus and Yevon. All they cared about was what they'd witnessed at the Cut. Arilette's pacing around the candlelit room only aggravated Threyna's unease.

"It is fortunate we intercepted the Wraith when we did," Arilette said. "Scouts reported a pair of ships—quite impressive ones actually—lurking off the coast south of the Grip. Had we not received word and arrived when we did, they could have been halfway to Sansia by now. You did well to lead them south."

Threyna bowed her head. Canton had been the one to find and direct the Underground to the Cut. She didn't have to imagine how desperate Dracus must have been to send Canton anywhere near Octarius, but he had.

"Centuriot Aylenia deserves the credit, Legatus. She remained with them after I got separated at Aranoc."

Arilette smirked. "A Centuriot's achievements rest with the Premius that gave the order. But now we have more pressing matters to discuss." She strode closer, her eyes on Threyna's bangle glowing with the candles scattered about the tablinum. "We have to find a way of leveraging this gift you've received. The Skeleton King didn't know what he had... or maybe he did, and didn't want the competition."

Lorath, the ever-grim Arch Premius of the Underground, stared down his crooked nose at Threyna from where he leaned against the back wall. "If the Skeleton King and Theodyn have set any precedent, then one doesn't need the Blessing to wield the blood magic. If we could pass it to another, we could build an army of blood mages."

The thought brought Laela's incriminating accusations to the forefront of her mind. *An army of blood mages...* She couldn't imagine. Yes, with such a force they would certainly defeat the Order, but at what cost? She wouldn't become the Skeleton King—at least that's not what she wanted to become, despite what Laela thought of her—but that didn't mean others wouldn't want to wield the same authority he did. The way Lorath fixated on the bangle, she didn't have to wonder what he would do with such abilities.

"Is that possible?" Arilette asked, drawing close. She moved Threyna's hand out of the way to inspect the blood artifact for herself.

Threyna acquiesced, but the essence of the Blessing seemed to clench like a fist at her touch. All she could think about was Belrich's Inquisitor trying to strip the bangle from her arm. She closed her eyes and swallowed the fear that crawled up her throat at the memory.

It's okay... we're safe here. She wasn't sure if she was saying it to herself, or the Blessing. In either case, even that felt like a lie. If Fawkes told it true,

Arilette hollowed Dracus. If Laela had been honest, Arilette had hid their mother's letters from her for years, letting her believe she was unwanted.

The seeds of doubt sprouted within, coiling around her like Dreadroot and strangling her. She'd worked so hard to return to Octarius, but now that she was here, nothing felt right.

"Maybe," Threyna said, fighting to stay present, "but is that what we want—an army of blood mages?"

"We will use every weapon in our arsenal," Arilette said. "Whatever it takes to win."

"This isn't *just* a weapon." Threyna turned her shoulder to hide the bangle from Arilette's inspection. "It's a curse." She pointed to the black veins stretching from the bangle. She'd consumed everything she could from the Cut, but after the darklings and shades wandered off, she only had the hollowed to draw upon. It abated the rot, but not completely. And she had no souls left in her Inner Dungeon to call upon. The more she used her blood magic, it seemed like the more souls she needed to consume just to return to her baseline.

Threyna hung her head. "I don't know what will happen to me. But the more I channel the blood magic, the more…"

"The more what?" Arilette asked, absent a mother's tenderness.

"I don't know," Threyna said. "The better I get, the more it wants. It takes more souls to recover. And besides, it's not just about winning the war, right? What would happen afterwards? We'd defeat the Order but what then? An army of blood mages could unleash a war worse than that of the Seers or the Artificers combined." She gripped the bangle.

"Those are problems for another day," Lorath said. "First, we must defeat the Order."

"Lorath is right," Arilette said. "Concern for the future is a luxury we can't afford. Rivich has reported that the Order's legions are returning to Elyngrove from all over Rheynia. Once they mobilize, they could be here within a day's march."

Threyna snapped her head up. *Rivich?* She had been wondering why he hadn't marched with the rest of the Underground and where he had been. He wasn't present to greet them upon their return. Part of her longed to see him. After Ebrus became a shade and Yevon hollowed, and considering Aylenia's disconcerting desire to remain at Laela's side in the medicus's chambers, a familiar face would have been most welcome. But even as she wished he were here and not out on a dangerous scouting mission, part of her feared their reunion.

He'll blame me for Ebrus and Yevon, same as Daeton.

Her shame and guilt disintegrated to ash like a conjuration she could no longer wield once Arilette continued.

"They've allowed us to be a thorn in their side. We make for an easy Dawnshard to take the blame. If they march with those kinds of numbers, they're coming not to put us in our place, but to grind us beneath their heels. Your success in leading the Wraith here will be important, but they won't be enough to put the darklings back in the soul jar. The Order is scared of you, Threyna. So when they come, we must be ready to fight, to win—regardless of the cost."

"The Blessing is the key," Lorath said, uncrossing his arms and abandoning the wall he was leaning against. "It's time you shared it. Let another stand beside you in wielding its power."

As he approached, Threyna had to resist the urge to tap into her Inner Throne. She took a stilling breath as the Blessing's essence recoiled defensively. *It's not a threat. Not yet, anyway.* Standing straighter, she glanced between Arilette and Lorath. "I can't just take it off and give it to someone else."

"Have you tried?" Lorath extended his hand as he neared.

Threyna sank into her Inner Throne and conjured a dagger before Lorath's throat, stopping him in his tracks. Rage pumping in his temples, his lips twitched with words yet to take shape. He glanced from her to the blade.

"Incredible," Arilette breathed.

"Belrich's Inquisitor *tried*," Threyna said, letting her blood-spawned dagger dissipate to ash. "*It* made blood erupt from his eye sockets. That's how I got out. That and…"

The thought of Fawkes's fallen form knotted her throat. If not for him coming back for her, even with the blood artifact's protection, there was no way she would have made it to the Cut, let alone back to Octarius.

"How?" Arilette asked. "How does it work?"

Threyna explained what she could—everything from the prongs and her Inner Throne to her abilities and what it took to sustain them. Recounting everything from the past few days made her realize all that had happened. She'd lost her father, her mother, and her closest friends. She'd narrowly escaped death in its many different forms on more occasions than she wanted to count, but they needed to know everything.

"So what must be done to make the last prong release?" Lorath asked, leaning too close for comfort.

Threyna shrugged. "I don't know. The first was conjuring. The second was consuming. The third was…" She touched the scar at her throat that should have killed her. She swallowed the tension in her neck, unwilling to display any vulnerability before Arilette. "Healing myself, when the legionaries tried to kill me." She shook her head. "There's no telling what will release the last prong."

"When it does release," Arilette began, "we give it to Laela."

Threyna and Lorath both balked.

"Her!" Lorath's crooked nose scrunched. "We can't trust her with such power."

Arilette placed her hand on Lorath's arm. "That is exactly why we must give it to her. It will force her to fight. She'll have to stay."

Threyna didn't understand. Her stomach twisted like a Dreadroot's vines, and for a moment, she thought she was going to be sick.

"With such power at their disposal, would the Wraith want to leave?" Arilette asked with a darkling's glimmer in her eyes. "The Wraith wish to leave because they have no control—too weak to stand up to the Order, too cowardly to carve a life for themselves here, they only want to run. But give them a taste of power, of control…" She made a fist. "They won't run. We give her the Blessing and she'll want to fight."

Threyna wanted Laela to stay and fight, despite the hatred her sister had for her, but she didn't believe Arilette was right about Laela. Laela had power and control. No part of her was weak. She had single-handedly bested Threyna and Aylenia together and defeated the Eighth legion at Fort Cybel with a ragged group of poorly trained and ill-equipped plebeians; cowardly was not a word she would use to describe Laela or the Wraith, and yet they still wished to flee. And though her mother had planted the idea in her mind that together—united—they could do anything, this felt wrong.

"Forced unity will only build a fractured army," Fawkes had said.

The Underground sabotaged the Wraith's escape, led them to Octaven, and literally escorted them back to Octarius against their will, but this wasn't just manipulating a situation. This was forcing a curse on someone who wouldn't want it.

The horrified look in her father's remaining eye when he saw the fatekeeper about Threyna's neck returned to her. He never wanted her to have it. He had asked Dracus to take it and bear its burden, not her.

He knew what it was: not just a weapon, but a curse.

"That is risky, Legatus," Lorath said. "That power should go to someone we trust. If we have another capable of wielding the blood magic, the Wraith are useless. If what Threyna says is true, we'd be better off using them—taking their souls, storing them in this *Inner Dungeon* so we can give ourselves every opportunity to defeat the Order."

Threyna scoffed, glancing between Lorath and Arilette. "You can't be serious. It's one thing to consume souls of the fallen, but these are still people. They're not our enemies."

"But they're not our allies." Lorath's voice came slow and stern.

Arilette framed her chin with her thumb and forefinger, tapping the side of her cheek in thought.

She's seriously considering this. Dracus's warnings, Fawkes's last words to her, everything her mother and Laela said about Arilette's recklessness—they all wormed inside Threyna like a darkling prying through her thoughts and memories.

"Manipulating the Wraith against fleeing," Threyna said, hoping Arilette would listen, "that's one thing. I understand not wanting them to run when we need all who are willing to stand against the Order's Dominion to stay and fight. But forcing a curse on someone, making them fight—that's not unity. And consuming their souls... that's worse!"

Lorath snarled like a hellhound. Arilette cocked her brow.

"What do you suggest then, Premius?" she asked Threyna. "The Order is coming. For all we know, the Skeleton King is leading them. If we fail, we lose, so now is not the time for you to develop a conscience. We must unite. Divided, ruin will reign, and *everything* we have worked for will burn."

Threyna chewed the inside of her cheek, fearing Arilette's capabilities. "I understand."

Lorath tapped his foot. "Then what do you suggest? Time is wasting."

Threyna had thought about this for the entirety of their journey from the Cut to Octarius. Walking alongside Aylenia as they stood over the stretcher carrying Laela, she realized what she needed to do. She'd taken offense at every turn, only escalating the tension between them. Aylenia had fought for common ground, earning perhaps the closest thing to Laela's trust as anyone was capable of receiving.

It had worked. Laela and the rest of the Wraith were here. Now, Threyna needed to do the same—swallow her pride, put on a brave face, and act the part of the apologetic sister and grieving daughter. Laela would be able to connect to that. Then and only then could they join together, stand united, and do what no other army had been able to do since the Disasters.

"There is no telling what will release the prong," Threyna said. "And even then, if it is anything like how it attached onto me, I won't be able to choose who receives the blood artifact next. But what we can do is convince the Wraith—not force them, but convince them—to stay and fight with us. They're worth more to us alive than as souls to spend."

Lorath threw his hands up to the stone ceiling. "They're only worth more alive if they fight. A decade's worth of talks have failed. What makes you think, now at this final hour, you'll be able to convince them?"

"I will speak to Laela," Threyna said, forcing calm into her tone. "The Wraith will listen to her. If I convince her, the rest will follow."

Arilette nodded slowly. She strode over to the wooden desk in the center of her tablinum and grabbed a time-turner and flipped it over. The sand began to run from the top of the glass to the bottom. Without a word, Arilette approached the door that once belonged to House Desius and swung it open. "You have until the last grain of sand. Understand that her choice will impact everyone in the Wraith. She will stay and fight and convince her people to do the same, or they will all be removed from the warps. We can't waste the power coils on those who won't join us."

Threyna nearly choked. "But she'll die."

"Precisely." Arilette didn't blink. Her face remained expressionless. "She'll die. You'll consume her. Either way, she will aid our war against the Order. And like I said, how she chooses to serve the Underground will determine the fate of the rest of the Wraith. As soldiers or as fuel—the choice is hers. Divided, ruin will reign."

"Divided, ruin will reign," Lorath echoed.

Threyna struggled to find her tongue. Under Lorath and Arilette's harsh glares, Threyna repeated the words.

Arilette's gaze flicked to the sand sliding from one glass to the other. "Time is of the essence, Premius. Do your duty."

Dreadroot caressed the scar on her throat, threatening to choke the life from her. Short of breath, stomach in knots, Threyna exited Arilette's tablinum with haste. *Please, Laela. Please see reason. For all our sakes.*

CHAPTER 49

No Choice

Threyna XX

The medicus's chambers were crowded. Warps hummed, speeding up the recovery times on the injured Wraith who managed to make it to Octarius. Though there were significantly fewer than those who were gathered beneath Aranoc, there were enough to pack Octarius wall to wall. It didn't help matters that for every Wraith jammed into the medicus's wing, there were two armed Centuriots to make sure nothing got out of hand.

After pulling back each curtain and investigating every pod, Threyna still could not find Laela. To her surprise, however, she did find Marius, the quartermaster.

A wide, toothy grin split across his wrinkled face as she approached. "Ah look who it is, Lady Darklin' herself!" He opened his arms to her, and she accepted his embrace. After a moment, Threyna released the old quartermaster. He looked over her shoulder. "Where's Ebrus? Yevon?"

Threyna blinked. The knowing expression on the face of Ebrus's shade stared into her soul. The haunting memory of Yevon attempting to tear through her mind as a darkling returned with a wave of emotion. She took a short, sharp breath, pushing past the pain. "Marius, what are you doing down here? Who's manning the armory?"

Marius grunted, wise enough to accept her omission as answer enough. He took a deep breath before moving on. "Arch Premius *requisitioned* control of the armory. Somethin' 'bout *urgent and imperative* business or some such." He rolled his eyes. "Ya know how he is. Sent me down 'ere to keep an extra eye on all the shades you dragged in. I don't ask questions."

He scanned the medicus's chambers. His smile from before melted into a frown. "Seems you lot been makin' some noise, eh? Word is every legion and all the boys at the Nest are flyin' 'ere." His eyes drifted to her bangle. "Suppose that's got somethin' to do with it."

Threyna scratched the back of her head. "Yeah. A bit." With no time for small talk, she changed the subject. "Have you seen Laela—half-sister, looks like my mother if she'd been raised on a diet of swords and shields?"

"Aye, never time for Valefyre and stories, eh?" Marius pointed toward a metal door at the back of the medicus's wing where a group of Wraith were trying to get past two armed Centuriots. "Hooked up to the bad one. Wasn't lookin' too good comin' down."

"Gratitude," Threyna said, hoping she wasn't too late. She patted his shoulder before making her way to the metal door.

"We deserve to know if she's going to make it," said a woman with claw marks across her cheek to a grim-faced veteran. "You can't keep us out."

"We have orders," the Centuriot said, not even looking at her. "One at a time, and one of yours is already back there. Wait your turn."

"Bring him out, then," said a broad-shouldered Palogian man attempting to hide his foreigner's features. "I trust him as much as I trust you."

That drew the Centuriots' attention. "Step back or—"

"Stand down, Centuriot," Threyna said. "I have business with the leader of the Wraith."

The Centuriots saluted. "Prime."

As they turned to open the door, Threyna addressed the Wraith. "I'll send out Laela's other visitor so each of you can have a turn." She forced a smile, fearing what each of them might think of her. There was no telling what Laela had filled their ears with.

The Palogian man grumbled. The woman with the scarred cheek turned to her stern-faced shadow. Though she looked as if she were about to claw Threyna's eyes out, the man holding her back nodded.

Threyna returned the gesture and strode past the Centuriots and through the opened door. The door closed behind her, muffling the clamor of Centuriots and injured Wraith beyond. Illuminators dimly lit the walkway between four rooms dedicated to patients in need of intensive care. While the warps in the main chamber of the medicus's wing had the ability to slow time down, allowing for medical attention to be administered, or speed time up to promote healing and recovery, the *bad one*, as it was called, referred to the high-powered warps with the ability to augment time locally.

After the Savior had gifted Rheynia with the abilities of arcanatek, too many lives were lost due to mundane starvation or dehydration, hooked into the warps for too long. For nonlethal injuries, a wound that might have taken a few days to heal could be mended within the hour. A patient might spend the rest of the day in their bunk eating and drinking anything they could get their hands on, but aside from feeling fatigued, they'd be fine. For more extreme injuries like broken bones or severe blood loss, one might have to spend multiple bouts in the warps with time in between to recover from them. But for those that had life-threatening injuries, too much time in a warp was a death sentence. The highly specific *bad ones* could localize the passage of time for individual tissues, allowing muscles and bones to heal while the body's other organ processes continued at a normal rate. The amount of power coils it took to run a *bad one* for a day was equivalent to powering every illuminator in Octarius for a moon's turn.

Threyna gulped. Arilette was content to let Laela suffer and watch as the Wraith's hope died with her.

"You're sisters," her mother had said. *"Divided, ruin will reign, but united…"*

She must join me. She has to. I will make her see.

The last door on her left was ajar. Beyond the din generated by the warp, the sound of voices and the illuminator's glow spilled out of the room and into the corridor.

"Perhaps we're where we belong," said Canton's familiar voice. "We've been running from it for so long, but maybe it's time."

"I don't see what choice we got," another man's voice said. "Regardless what ya want."

Threyna crossed her arms over her chest and shouldered through the half-opened door.

Aylenia stood from Laela's side. "Threy… ghosts, where have you been?"

 "Speaking with our Legatus and Arch Premius." She never met Aylenia's eyes, looking instead at Laela. Tubes connected Laela's midsection to the black-cased arcanatek beside her. The soft green glow of the Viridite power coils snuck out from between the cracks in the arcanatek's shell, painting Laela in a ghoulish light.

Her chest rose and fell in the gentle tides of breath. Her eyes wandered left and right beneath her closed lids. She was alive, but her skin was still sallow and covered in a sheen of sweat.

"How is she?" Threyna asked, ignoring Canton's awestruck stare.

"Halfway down the Grotto on Cybel's Eve," the man said, his dark-featured face narrow and grim. He rubbed the stubble on his cheeks.

"And you are?" Threyna asked, recognizing him from her childhood but not able to place him.

"Tarus."

Tarus didn't care to elaborate further and didn't bother to ask who Threyna was, which told her everything she needed to know about how he felt about her.

She cleared her throat. "I need to speak with Laela. Alone."

Aylenia's lip contorted. "You can't mean to wake her? The medicus just finished stitching her up."

Tarus guffawed. "If ya think I'm leavin' the First Sword alone with you, ya might wanna get checked for dewskull. Ain't happening."

Threyna rounded on Tarus. "You are here at the mercy of Legatus Arilette Desius. You follow orders. You don't give them."

That broke Canton's gushing gaze. Seeming to remember where he was, he carefully inspected the floor between his feet.

Laela stirred. Her eyes crept open, though they lacked any sense of lucidity.

"Ripping Corners." Aylenia glared at Threyna.

"This can't wait," Threyna said. "It's a matter of life and death. And not just for Laela. I must speak to my sister, alone."

"No," Laela croaked. Despite barely skirting death, her defiant stare remained more intact than ever. "Out with it."

Threyna pursed her lips, looking between Tarus and Aylenia. The sand through Arilette's time-turner slipped faster and faster, mocking her—threatening her. She took a deep breath. "Laela, I owe you... a hundred different apologies. But there isn't much time, so I'll stick to the biggest ones. You're right. I made my choice. I chose my father. I didn't know what it meant at the time. This isn't how I expected things to turn out, but I suppose neither did you. I've made mistakes. I've blamed you and other people for them. I know that now. And... I'm sorry. Truly."

Laela only blinked her heavily lidded eyes, seemingly disinterested, as if she could barely stay awake. When she didn't offer any form of communication, verbal or otherwise, Threyna drew closer, kneeling by Laela's side before continuing.

"I'm sorry you're here. I know it's not where you wanted to be." Threyna examined the bangle on her arm. "Not where I wanted to be either, for what it's worth. We've lost too much. I lost my father. You lost Rance. We both lost our mother."

A knot formed in her throat that she hadn't expected to feel. Planning on feigning emotion for the sake of connecting to Laela, she found she didn't have to.

"We lost two of our friends," Threyna said, glancing at Aylenia. "Maybe three. Even then, I know that's a lot less than your losses." She nodded at Canton. "Fawkes… he saved me. I was reckless. Got caught. If not for Fawkes, Belrich would have stripped this from my arm and done ghosts only know what."

The memory of the Inquisitor's eyes exploding from behind his mask tightened the scar across her throat and made the bangle itself seem to cling desperately to her arm.

"My point is," Threyna continued, "Mother, Fawkes—ghosts, even Arilette—everyone talks of unity, but no one is willing to sacrifice anything to make it happen. The Order is coming, and we *need* your help. I know what I'm asking of you, but if we don't make sacrifices now, no one wins. No one escapes. But if we band together—"

Laela snorted. "You ask for sacrifices but make none in return."

Now was Threyna's turn to blink.

"You want us to fight for you," Laela said, snarling as if she wasn't halfway to hollowing. "And then what?"

"Then, once we've won, I'll petition Arilette to let you go."

Laela's anger turned to laughter. Two gales in, the wounds in her midsection morphed her humor back to rage. Cheeks reddening, she bared her teeth. "So *we* fight for you. And in return, *once* we've won, you'll *petition* your Legatus to see if she'll *let* us go where we want?" She shook her head. "Seems like we're making all the sacrifices for your precious unity. What are you giving up?"

Threyna's ears flushed warm. She glanced at the rotting veins that marred her arm. She touched the scar at her throat. "What am I giving up?"

Threyna stood to her feet. She wanted to say that Arilette would let her die. That either way, regardless of what Laela said, Arilette would make sure the Wraith served in the battle to come—either as spears in the field or souls for her conjuring. She didn't realize that Threyna was trying to protect her. But if she told Laela the truth, it would only justify her rationale for not trusting Arilette or the Underground.

"I'm apologizing on my knees," Threyna said. "I'm asking you for help. Does that count for anything?"

"No."

Laela's answer, short and sharp enough to punch a hole through plate mail, suspended in the air between them. Threyna clenched her fists, attempting to hold back her rising anger. She needed Ebrus's way with words, her father's courage, and Fawkes's wisdom. But all she felt was a child's fear, a child's wrath.

"Laela," Canton said, "this isn't like the other times. This could be different."

"It won't be."

Tarus crossed his arms over his chest. "Might be worth hearin' her out. We don't even know if we got ships left to leave on." Laela cast Tarus a dark glare. "What? Don't act like she don't already know."

Laela's nostrils flared. "I have no ear for talk of a war I don't believe in."

As tension grew in her jaw, Threyna searched for the words to bend Laela away from the unnecessary demise she would surely suffer if she remained on this path. She understood Laela not wanting to listen to her or Canton, but she was surprised Tarus—seemingly one of her closest confidants—held no sway. More surprisingly, Aylenia said nothing.

Canton scratched the back of his neck. "I understand that—"

"You understand nothing," Laela snapped. "You look at her and see a hero, an answer to your prayers. She's not. You might think her abilities will be enough to defeat the Order. They won't be. What you don't understand, Cant, is that she doesn't understand." She pointed at Threyna. "She is the reason Rance is dead. The reason my mother is gone. By every feather of Neutreen's wings, how many names do you want to hear? Erynia, Olerus, Gatius, Verinius... Fawkes."

Canton hung his head, staring at the opposite corner of the room where the wall met the floor.

Laela returned her gaze to Threyna. "It's not your fault, Canton. It's hers. And she will never understand that."

The tension in Threyna's jaw exploded like the lid on a soul jar filled to the brim. "I understand that your people are hooked up to *our* warps." She jabbed her index finger at Laela so suddenly that Aylenia grabbed her by her fatigues to pull her back. "Your people will die without *our* help."

Laela surged with newfound energy, slapping Threyna's finger away from her. "We're only here because you sabotaged *our* escape."

"Stop this," Canton said, but no one was listening.

Tarus came to Laela's other side, opposite Threyna.

"We're here because *you* want us here," Laela spat. "That's not unity. That's not *sacrifice*. That's tyranny, and I would rather hollow than serve you—Skeleton Queen."

Threyna tore free of Aylenia's grasp and loomed over Laela. Glaring at her sister, her voice came out a whisper. "You might think me some kind of monster, but I'm trying to protect you. You will die if you don't listen to me."

The room fell silent.

Canton stammered. Aylenia gasped. Tarus widened his stance as if preparing for a fight.

Laela narrowed her brow. "What does that mean?"

Threyna exhaled, reluctant to let the breath go. "She'll remove you from the medicus's wing. You'll die without the warp."

Laela scoffed. "So be it. I'd rather die than—"

Threyna shook her head. "Not just you. All of the Wraith. She wants you to declare to fight so that everyone follows. Otherwise, she'll hollow all of your people—everyone from Aranoc and Avengard."

Aylenia's jaw dropped. "No… she wouldn't."

"She would," Threyna said. "The sand is slipping, Laela. I'm asking you—please, for your own good—join us."

Laela shook her head, settling back into her cot. The warp seemed to hum with an ominous rhythm that resembled the sound of marching soldiers. "There's never really a choice, is there?" Lying in the cot, she stared at the tubes connecting her body to the arcanatek that assured her survival.

Threyna found herself wondering the same. Ever since she'd run from Laela ten years ago during the Battle of the Cut, she'd never really had a choice in what to do next. Live, fight, survive, repeat. No options. No choices.

Laela glanced from Threyna to Aylenia and back, her brow softening, forehead wrinkling. "If our roles had been reversed—if I had been raised in the Underground and you'd gone with Mother... would I be asking the same of you as you now ask of me?"

Threyna inhaled sharply before letting her exhale seep out. "If I was with the Wraith and you were an Undergrounder? Blood and bone, Laela... I hope you would do the same." Part of her didn't believe Laela would. If their roles were reversed, Laela would probably consume Threyna and use her as fuel for her conjurations. But Threyna couldn't. Wouldn't.

Laela nodded, her faraway gaze staring into the abyss for a few long moments. When she spoke, her voice came weak and breathy. "Tell Legatus Desius I will report for duty as soon as the medicus gives me leave." She sank into the cot as if the effort of speaking spent whatever energy she had left.

Threyna took a deep breath. Canton did his best to hold back a relieved smile. Tarus folded his arms over his chest. Aylenia gave no reaction, but Threyna knew that when she turned to leave, Aylenia wouldn't follow.

Was she actually leading them here? Or was she trying to escape? Aylenia had talked of finding her mother one day, leaving Rheynia and searching Sansia. She'd never believed it, but now she did, and even though it wasn't fair to blame her, it still felt like a betrayal.

Threyna spun on her heel and made for the door. Halfway out, she stopped. "You have some friends out there wanting to check in on you. I'll make sure they are allowed in."

Laela grunted. Realizing that was the only response she was likely to receive, Threyna drummed her fingers on the door frame and let herself out.

CHAPTER 50

STORIES AND VALEFYRE

Dracus XIV

"*L*et go, my love. Let go and see. Let go the woes and sing high for me.*"

Dracus stared at the glass in his hands. He swirled the Valefyre within, wishing he could let go, wishing he could sing. But there were no melodies left in the world without Fawkes in it. The soul jar on his hip weighed heavily, but not quite as much as the fatekeeper in his pocket. He hadn't found the courage to open it or the desire to read its contents. It felt like once he did, it would be real; Fawkes would be dead, his soul crammed into a jar.

Dracus leaned back in Arilette's chair, attempting to ignore the injured flesh from the Vendetta daggers' fury. He sank into the pain. Became one with it. That was the only way to stay present. The call of hollowing felt so close, so welcoming, but he couldn't accept it. Not until he and Fawkes were united, beyond the curse.

Groaning, he put his feet up on Arilette's wooden desk as she eyed him with venomous disdain. He crossed his feet and lifted the Valefyre to his lips.

Arilette cocked her brow, but then smiled, taking a seat across from him on the opposite side of her desk. "Thought you were joking when you asked for a drink."

Dracus drank, focusing on the burn as it trickled down his throat. "Oh no. I was serious. Dead serious."

Arilette laughed. "Dark humor."

"Dark days," Dracus said, taking another drink.

"But a light is rising on the horizon," Arilette said, raising her glass to her lips. Settling in, she crossed her foot over her knee and slung her arm over the back of the chair. "It's almost as if we're right back where we were. Ten years. Blood and bone, so much has changed, but in many ways, it's like…" She shrugged. "Nothing's changed at all. Tell me, was it worth it—this past decade, running around, trying and failing to escape?"

Dracus grunted. "Canton got to grow up as a survivor instead of a child soldier. I'd say that's worth something."

"Yet he was the one who came to me," Arilette said, a darkling's grin painted across her face. "If not for him, we might not have found you in time."

Dracus drank again. "Ya weren't in time. You were late."

"Oh, poor Dracus." Arilette pouted her lips in mockery. "It's a shame what happened to… what's his name—Finks, Ficks?"

Dracus downed the rest of the Valefyre, letting the pain of the swill overshadow the ails of his failing body and the woes of his broken heart. "It's good ya don't remember his name. Means we weren't around long enough. But I guarantee yer father wouldn'ta forgot. Arenius wouldn'ta let us become divided in the first place. But you, you were the wedge of division. What's that say about you and yer funny little mantra?"

Arilette's grin never faded. She stood, grabbed the bottle of Valefyre and refilled Dracus's empty cup before sitting back down. "My father would have led us to our doom. Sansia—that desert wasteland—is not our home. Rheynia is. My father got discouraged by loss and dreamed of a life where victory wasn't required, because he lost sight of the war we needed to win. As a Premius of the Second, you can't tell me you knew every legionary's name. You couldn't. Because you knew that if you were going to stop Victarius, squash the Artificers, and unify Rheynia under the Order's Holy Dominion, they would have to suffer—to hollow, become shades, or live on as darklings. Names of legionaries, Centuriots, even

Tribunii—they are distractions. Distractions that made my father weak and would have led others to weakness. A good leader can't lose focus on the big picture; sacrifice is necessary to succeed."

"And that's you?" Dracus asked, drinking again to forget his other pains. "A good leader?"

"When we win—"

Dracus interrupted her with a laugh. "Win? Ten years and you still haven't learned, eh?" He shook his head, lifting his glass to empty its contents. Wiping his mouth with the back of his hand, he placed his feet on the floor and leaned forward to rest his forearm on the desk. "You're crazy, Arilette, if ya think you're gonna win this."

Arilette's smile never faltered. "But that's what it takes, darling Dray. Only an equal to Belrich can hope to defeat him. Aarkos, for all his many fine attributes, was not enough. My father—the tragic hero you make him out to be—was not enough. Neither was Bherus. Neither are you. But Threyna..." Arilette lifted her glass. "Threyna is everything and more. Because that is what I raised her to be."

"That poor girl." Dracus closed his eyes. "Never shoulda brought her back here. Never shoulda let you sink yer claws into her. You poisoned her worse than ya did me, and that's sayin' something."

Now was Arilette's turn to put her feet up on the desk. "Dracus, Dracus, Dracus... do you really believe us to be so different? You and I, we're the same—at least we used to be. Did you not do the same to Canton as I did to Threyna?"

"You hid Viesa's letters," Dracus snarled. "Ya let her grow up thinkin' her own mother didn't even care."

"And you hid the truth of Canton's parents from him," Arilette said, cocking her brow as if to say *"See, I told you so."* Her grin widened. "And you still lie to him. He doesn't know the truth of your... condition."

Dracus bit his lip. The truth in her words stung worse than the Valefyre. He snatched the bottle and poured himself another drink, wishing it would go to his head and numb the guilt.

"See?" Arilette taunted. "Not so different. Except I'm at least honest with myself. Yes, I burned the letters. Yes, I cultivated Threyna's disdain for her mother and Aarkos's daughter, but look at her now. I sharpened her edge to be a weapon capable of defeating the Order. And now, with the abilities of the Skeleton King, new reaping arcanatek, and the Wraith's numbers on our side, we will liberate Rheynia and reshape our home."

She tilted her cup back before slamming it down on the table and waiting for Dracus to top her off. Dracus only stared.

Arilette's grin grew gruesome, her eyes cold and calculating. "What of your pet? What good have you done for Canton? Oh, right. He wishes to fight... for me." Her smile spread again. "Make no mistake, Dracus. We will win."

She snatched the bottle from Dracus and refilled her glass. "Question is, where will you be when we do so? Will you right the wrongs of your cowardice? Will you do as Theodyn asked of you all those years ago? Or will you remain the craven?"

Dracus lowered his gaze to the soul jar at his hip. With a sigh, he slid his empty glass across the table to clink against the near-empty bottle of Valefyre. He wanted nothing more than to get Canton and go to the Grip. To see if Laela's plan could actually work, and together, they could set sail for Sansia and whatever the future held. Canton could go on to live a full life and die a true death. Dracus could release Fawkes from the soul jar just as he crossed the barrier of the curse, and together, they could venture forth into whatever the afterlife held beyond this eternal hellscape. But he knew he couldn't do that to Canton. Not anymore. In that regard, Arilette was right. He had dug his claws into the boy he'd intended to save; he'd ignored Fawkes's begging to let the boy decide for himself what he wanted to do. But no more.

Looks like it'll just be me and you, Old Boy.

Dracus met Arilette's eyes. "Call me craven, but I'm done. You think you got it won. But you don't. You think you can use Threyna, make her into the monster Bohen became, but you're wrong. She's conflicted, yeah, ya made sure of that, but she's more than just a weapon. Belrich ain't. Bohen had the magic, but Belrich's the real monster. And when shades turn to darklings, he'll have the upper hand. If ya think you got him dead to rights, he's got two more tricks up his sleeve. If ya cut his sleeves, he's got another stashed in his boot. And even if ya can see his bare soles, you better believe there's somethin' hidin' under his silver tongue."

Arilette stared at Dracus for a long moment. "All that worrying…" She shook her head. "It's enough to make a man crazy. Crazy enough to hollow out."

A bustle outside the door to Arilette's tablinum drew his attention. Muffled at first, the cries became clearer the nearer they got.

"Help! Dracus, help!"

Dracus bolted to his feet just as the wooden door burst open.

A frantic Canton, his narrow face long and pale, stood in the doorway. "The medicus's wing. We need your help!"

CHAPTER 51

THE BAD ONE

Laela XX

Laela's jaw clenched as Threyna paused in the doorframe. For the briefest of moments, Laela hoped Threyna was going to turn back and say something that would change things—that she would speak to Arilette, that she would give Laela time to decide—something, anything. But such hope was wasted on the Undergrounders, perhaps Threyna most of all.

"You have some friends out there wanting to check in on you," Threyna said. "I'll make sure they are allowed in."

Laela grunted. Aylenia had said they were alike, but she was wrong. She had said vulnerability wasn't a weakness, but she was wrong, at least in regards to Threyna. If she gave ground, Threyna would take it. If she lowered her guard, Threyna would punish her for it. The only thing Aylenia was right about was that Threyna had become everything Arilette was, and Laela had nothing left to say to her.

As if Threyna realized the same, she drummed her fingers on the doorframe before slipping out and closing the door behind her.

Laela took ten slow deep breaths, considering her options and plotting her next move. She glanced from the warp humming beside her to Canton chewing his tongue in the corner, then to Tarus as he returned to his pacing. She was too weak to fight, and hesitant if she could trust even the people in this room. It was Canton after all who summoned the Undergrounders to the Cut. Whether he believed he was doing so to save Fawkes or not, he still made a choice, and he chose Arilette, the Underground, and fighting in this losing war. She couldn't be sure where exactly he placed his loyalties.

Even Aylenia, for all her talk of going to Sansia, was now back in Octarius, surrounded by the people she'd grown with and fought beside. Such bonds were not easily broken. It was one thing to talk of escape while traversing the Rheynian countryside, surrounded by others wanting to do the same. *What if she changed her mind? What if she never truly wanted to escape and this was all a ploy to gain my trust?* She couldn't tell, and she didn't know how to tell.

Tarus was the only one she could trust. His wanting to stay was born of pragmatism, not true want. If she had a moment alone with him, she'd convince him of finding a way to escape Octarius and lead their people to the Grip. But first, she needed to make sure she healed from her injuries before Arilette had second thoughts of letting her live at all.

"Aylenia, is there a way of speeding up the warp?" Laela finally asked.

Aylenia, previously lost in thought, returned to the cramped corner of the private room within the medicus's wing. "Yes, I'll summon the medicus."

"No," Laela said, sharper than she intended. "No... if you wouldn't mind, just speed me up a little bit."

Aylenia nodded. Leaving the comfort of her corner, she approached the arcanatek and turned a knob on the back of it. The green hue illuminating the cracks in the black shell glowed brighter, but aside from a tickle where the tubes met her flesh, Laela didn't feel much different.

"More," Laela said. "It's fine. I can handle it."

"That's not how this works." Aylenia pursed her lips. "You suffered a lot of blood loss." She pointed to the tubes in her stomach. "This one is healing the injured tissues. This one is going to your liver. And the one in your leg is telling your body to replenish what makes your blood work in the first place. If we speed it up too fast, your blood will thicken; your heart could stop. You could clot." She shook her head. "No one is kicking you out of the medicus's wing. I promise."

Laela didn't understand this arcanatek. She didn't understand the body, how it worked, why it worked or what would make it fail, but she hated being reliant on Arilette's goodwill. "Fine." She took a deep breath. "Would you and Canton mind giving Tarus and I a moment to speak before the others come in?"

Aylenia nodded. "I'll get the others and be right back." She strode towards the door, and Canton absentmindedly followed. Tarus, however, stilled at the mention of his name. No longer pacing, he became as motionless as a charcoal drawing.

The door closed behind Canton.

"Want me to turn it up more?" Tarus asked.

"Neutreen's wings, yes. I want out of this place as fast as possible."

Tarus did as commanded, but glanced up from the arcanatek to examine her. "What you mean, 'this place?' Ya mean the medicus or—"

"Octarius," Laela finished, her voice but a whisper. "Rheynia. We can't stay here, Tarus."

Tarus hmphed. He turned the dial on the back of the arcanatek. The tickle that resulted from Aylenia's adjustment was more of a gut punch at Tarus's administration. It knocked the air from her lungs and sent her sputtering into a weak cough.

"Perhaps Aylenia was right," Laela said with a wince.

Tarus shrugged. "Like ya said. You can handle it." He grinned at her, and though Laela did her best to return the sentiment, something felt wrong, and not just with the warp.

"You don't think we should stay here, do you?" Laela asked. "Stay and fight? Arilette and Lorath were bad enough, but now with Threyna and what she's becom—" Tarus turned the knob on the warp further, making her body practically seize.

She felt like a warp was placed on her heart; each beat became a slow, thunderous clap that rattled her ribs. Pain spasmed across her back, arching it until she was driving the back of her head into the pillow of her cot.

Writhing, powerless, she tried to hold up a hand to tell Tarus to lower it, but she couldn't even do that much.

Even if she could, she didn't need to. Tarus knew what she wanted, but he didn't turn the knob down, nor did he show any interest in doing so. Sweat beaded on her brow; her muscles clenched from her toes to the base of her neck. Her body did its best to acclimate, but between her heavy breathing and tunneling vision, it took all of her might to hold Tarus's gaze.

"What are you doing?" Her voice barely carried the short distance between them.

"You're relentless, aren't ya?" Tarus scoffed. "Ya know how long it took me to gain Rance's trust, Verinius's?" He rolled his eyes. "This coulda been so much easier if I'd been the First Sword, ya know that right?"

Laela blinked. Beads of sweat became rivulets down her forehead.

She recalled Dracus's reaction after they had arrived to find Aranoc in disarray. *"Someone, in this room, someone among us did this."* She tried to make sense of it, but her tunneling vision was narrower than it had been when she was suffering in the Cut. Her addled mind struggled to fight for consciousness, let alone clairvoyance.

"You…"

"I'd have suffered Rance in his sleep," Tarus said, dusting his hands off as he stalked over to the door and slid the bar across it to ensure no one entered. "Woulda been easy. Never woulda had to build the tunnels west through Northvale, never woulda had to try farmin' along the Sisters, or slaved away strugglin' to fulfill the Order's quotas. Blood and bone, the number of nights wasted walkin' the tunnels back and forth between Aranoc and Octarius—you wouldn't believe. A decade dealin' with greedy governors and dewskulled aediles, and now—finally—you're here, the whole lot of you." Tarus shook his head. "Yet you can't give it up, can ya?"

Laela couldn't believe what she was hearing. A hundred different instances flooded her mind. Times in which Tarus's lingering stare remained on Rance during a meeting with Verinius. Every hushed word and stolen glance constructed a case in her head, but still, she couldn't understand.

"Traitor. Why?"

Tarus stalked over to her with a predatory hunger in his eyes. His narrow face shadowed by the black stubble on his cheeks made him look like a darkling given shape.

"I ain't the traitor." He pulled the pillow out from under her head, and she was powerless to stop him.

The door jostled. Someone tried to open it, but the bar held. "Hey. Open up."

Redge.

"Tarus? Laela? Laela!" Aylenia shouted, pounding her fist on the door.

Tarus ignored the door and the people behind it. "Traitor? I been loyal. True—always true. Arilette sent me with you and all the *real* traitors ten years ago when ya left right before the Battle of the Cut. 'Make sure they don't leave,' she told me. 'Make sure they never leave.' And you…" He strangled the corners of the pillow in his white-knuckled grip.

Her vision waned. The room spun. Her muscles spasmed. Bodies flew into the door, trying to break it down, only adding to the cacophony. But Tarus barely seemed to notice.

"Ten ghostin' years, I finally got ya here, and you want to leave—just like that?" He snapped his fingers before choking the pillow once again. "I thought—between me, Canton, the Palogian girl that's got ya twisted up like a Dreadroot—I thought maybe you'd listen to sense. Then ya pretend to listen to her." He nodded at the door. "And for a warp, I thought, 'There it is. Unity. Victory. An end to the Order's reign.' And the moment she turns her back, you… would ruin… everythin'."

The door rattled. Hinges creaked, but the bar held and Laela remained trapped in the room with the darkling she'd trusted most. Her heart thundered in her chest, echoed in her ears.

Not like this. I can't hollow like this.

Tarus glowered down at her. "You will serve the Underground—if not in life, then in death. You and everyone you thought you'd save." He pressed the pillow over her face.

She tried to fight, but her body was failing from the inside out. The warp meant to save her life would kill her if Tarus didn't, but he throttled her, wanting the kill for himself.

She slapped at his hands, fought to pry the pillow free from her face, but blind, weak, and fading fast, she knew this was the end.

CHAPTER 52

COMPRESS. RELEASE.

Threyna XX

"Love can still warm the cold and triumph over the dark even if all seems lost. And you, our little dove, you are loved. Loved by your mother, your father, and your sister, and nothing can take that away from you..."

—an excerpt from a fatekeeper

Threyna's shoulders hung heavy the moment she was beyond the door to the medicus's wing and back in the corridor. The brave face she put on for the Wraith and Underground alike softened once she was on her own. Weighed down by guilt, loss, and the fear that Laela was right, Threyna barely had it in her to put one foot in front of the other.

She needed to tell Arilette that Laela and the Wraith were with them, but all she wanted was her dark bunk in the quiet barracks. Aylenia wouldn't be there; she was with Laela. Ebrus and Yevon wouldn't be there either. Threyna didn't know what happened to the souls she'd consumed after she'd utilized them for her blood magic. Whether they disappeared as if they never existed at all, or they somehow made it to Neutreen, the One, or whatever other deity was too sadistic to show themselves to the mortals, Threyna couldn't be sure.

The only thing she could be sure of was that this didn't feel right.

Unable or unwilling to walk any further, she sank to the floor, sliding down the wall between illuminators. Knees bent, she hugged them to her chest, resting her cheek against her thigh. She felt alone, scared, and even though she was back in Octarius, she'd never felt so out of place.

This is my home. This is where I belong. I am a Premius of the Underground. If not here, where else?

To make matters worse, she didn't even believe her efforts accomplished anything. The Wraith and Underground were no more united than they had been before this all started. The Wraith who'd made it to Octarius, those lucky enough to survive the Order and the hollowed, were just that—lucky. They weren't fighters. And sure, there would be roles in which they could serve in the coming battle without fighting, but it was clear that they didn't want to be here.

"Forced unity will only build a fractured army," Fawkes had said.

Threyna closed her eyes, sinking into her own embrace as she clutched her knees. *Fractured unity is still division. Ruin will reign.*

"I would rather hollow than serve you—Skeleton Queen." Laela's words felt like a knife to her neck. She touched the scar at her throat. She never should have survived that, but she had. And then she'd slaughtered the rest of the Order as they retreated without even needing to engage with them.

Maybe I am ruin. Maybe this is what I am—the Skeleton Queen. There's only one place I can truly belong.

She retreated to her Inner Throne, seeking the comfort of its power in place of the support or approval she needed. Arilette hadn't said a single word about the loss of her father. Hadn't mentioned her mother. It was clear that she wasn't going to either.

"She poisoned him," Fawkes had said.

She hadn't believed it at the time, but upon returning with the power of the Skeleton King, Arilette looked at her differently—no longer a person or even a soldier, but a weapon. She'd suggested forcing the cursed blood artifact onto Laela as a way of making her comply. Then when Threyna had said such a thing was impossible, she wanted her to consume the Wraith to source her blood magic.

"She'll die," Arilette had said if Laela refused her. *"You'll consume her. Either way, she will aid our war against the Order."*

A thousand thoughts tore through her mind like a tempest of darklings. She sank deeper into her Inner Throne, trying to block them out, but they still found their way in.

"That woman wrote letters every. Single. Week." Laela wasn't the only one to have said so. Dracus and Fawkes had too.

Threyna approached the entrance within her seat of power and sealed the double doors shut. Breathing deeply, she held the doors closed, willing her mind to quiet. Once she protected herself from her dark thoughts, she turned her back on the door and sank into the same position she was in within the halls of Octarius. Hugging her knees, she stared out the stained-glass windows of her throne room, but even here, there was no comfort.

The dark cloud she'd felt encroaching on her Inner Throne along the Spine drew closer. A black mass with forking red lightning crept nearer and nearer with a hunger that could rival all the hellhounds in Rheynia. It could only mean one thing.

The Skeleton King is coming.

A door burst open—not within her Inner Throne, but in the physical realm—wrenching Threyna back to the present.

"Threyna! Help!"

Aylenia scanned the halls frantically, her knees bent, hips coiled as if ready to run. She was only about twenty paces away, but Threyna could feel Aylenia's heart hammering in her chest.

"I'm here," Threyna said, springing to her feet.

"Ripping Corners. It's Tarus. Come on!" Aylenia darted back into the medicus's wing.

Not understanding, Threyna charged after her, mind racing as fast as her feet. Skidding to a halt before changing directions, she follow Aylenia into the medicus's wing.

"Tarus locked Laela inside!" Aylenia shoved a Centuriot out of the way, shouting for others to clear aside. The Centuriots barring the way to the intensive recovery warps upon her first entrance weren't without, but within, trying to knock down the door to Laela's room.

Threyna didn't understand. *He's one of hers. Why would he—*

"Move!" Aylenia cried. "Clear the door."

The Centuriots and a broad-shouldered Palogian man stood aside. The door was dented, but unmoved. Threyna came to a stop before the door, her mind racing.

"He's going to kill her!" the Palogian man shouted. "Do something!"

Threyna attuned to the two heartbeats inside. One pounded, deep and punishing, the blood hot with wrath. The other barely beat at all. She could sense Laela's blood, but it was wrong. Thick and congealing faster by the moment, it was barely moving within her veins.

"He sped up the warp," Threyna said.

"She's going to hollow!" Aylenia cried. "Open it!"

There's no time to open it. She tried to reach for Laela's heart, the same way she had with the legionaries surrounding her in the Cut. She willed the blood to thin, for her heart to beat, but it wasn't working. She knew it was there, but as if she were searching for something under her bunk without the ability to see it, she was only feeling around.

I've never conjured absent sight.

Aylenia was yelling; the Palogian man shook her by the shoulders, screaming in her face. But they were just distractions. She sank deeper into her Inner Throne, blocking out the long faces of the Centuriots, the frightened gasps from the warps beyond, and the screaming all around her.

She was back in Avengard, watching from a distance as Belrich and his Inquisitors surrounded her father. She saw her mother's back as she ran deeper into Caius's Bog. She stood face to face with Ebrus's shade, felt the torment of Yevon's soul. *I will not lose Laela too. Not like this.*

Deeper.

Deeper.

Deeper.

Taking her place upon the seat of her Inner Throne, Threyna gripped the arms of the chair. She envisioned the room beyond the door blocking her path. The cot. The warp. The green hue of the Viridite. The gleam of the illuminators in the corners. She envisioned Laela in the cot. Tarus standing over her.

Laela's heart was no longer beating.

Threyna reached and found Tarus's thundering heart. She envisioned blood seeping from his eyes and ears, dribbling out of his nose and mouth and down his chin. She seized his heart, willing to make her vision a reality. She squeezed.

A thud beyond the door signaled Tarus's collapse to the floor. She hoped he'd become a shade, but Threyna couldn't worry about that yet. Even if Tarus was no longer a threat, the warp would hollow her if Threyna couldn't turn it off quickly. Simultaneously willing Laela's heart to beat while envisioning where the tubes would be connecting her to the warp, Threyna felt the rot slithering through her own veins.

Focus, ghost dammit.

She tried to conjure a dagger to sever the tubes to the warp, but absent sight, it fell to ashes before it could gain its edge. After a second failed attempt, she sought Tarus's blood. Sensing it as it spread along the floor, she tried to give it shape, but it was happening too slowly.

Though she was forcing the chambers of Laela's heart to pump, her blood was so thick that Threyna worried the pressure would do more harm than good. Abandoning Laela's heart, she focused solely on the dagger. She pictured the dagger her father had given her, kept safe in her lockbox. A simple blade, straight and narrow with a short crossguard, the word *Pure* embossed into the hilt.

It formed, and far away, something *clicked.* And though she felt clumsy wielding it, absent sight, she did her best to envision where Laela and the warp were, and where the tubes connecting them might be. Running out of time, she slashed with the dagger.

Laela's blood hadn't thinned, but the warp, which was actively thickening her blood, stopped. She felt her own blood thickening as the rot encroached on her heart. Ignoring it and trusting that she'd survive it as she had the last time, she sank even deeper into her Inner Throne, knowing that if she failed, Laela would hollow.

She could sense the viscosity of Laela's blood, but from this deep in her Inner Throne, blood, bone, and soul were hers to command. She dispelled that which thickened Laela's blood, but still, her heart did not pump.

Come on, Laela.

Trying again, Threyna squeezed Laela's heart, willing it to beat. In a rhythmic fashion, she compressed and released. Compressed. Released. Compressed. Released.

Within her Inner Throne, the black rot flooded the floors and climbed her chair. The dark tendrils wrapped around her legs like corrupted vines. They dragged her down, attempting to pull her beneath the acrid liquid. Threyna closed her eyes to it.

Just a little longer. Don't give up.

She didn't know if she was talking to herself or Laela, but she couldn't allow it to end like this.

Compress. Release.

Compress. Release.

Laela's heart thrummed to life with a beat of its own. The first few came slow, weak. But the subsequent pumps grew stronger, each echoing throughout Threyna's Inner Throne.

Gasping, she released her Inner Throne. Just as she returned to the present, the Palogian man charged through the door, snapping the bar that held it in place. He spilled into the room, tripping over Tarus's downed form on his way to Laela. Blood covered the floor around Tarus's fallen form. Despite the grisly scene before her, Threyna couldn't look away. Something was wrong. Tarus's wasn't moving. She saw no shade.

"Where is his darkli—" Before Threyna could finish, Tarus's darkling tore free of Laela's chest and dove straight for her. She fell back. Not into the wall of the corridor within the medicus's wing, but over the back of her chair and into the rising black ichor in her Inner Throne.

She fell beneath the surface of the corrupted liquid, wrestling with Tarus's soul. He shoved her down, preventing her from gaining her feet and holding her beneath the surface. Slick and putrid, the rot invaded her nose and mouth. She fought for leverage, but found none on the slippery tile floor.

The spectral wisp of Tarus wrenched her out of the rot. She drew in breath, attempting to regain her composure. She could feel him worming through her thoughts and memories, sifting through her emotions like old papers. She tried to rebuff him, but couldn't. His anger threatened to drown her more quickly than the ichor filling her throne room.

"She was going to betray us!" The darkling of what was once Tarus screamed in her face. His shadowy visage glared down at her with smoldering eyes. *"Blood and bone, do you have any idea what you've done?"*

She managed to take a short breath before he shoved her back beneath the surface. His shouts became muffled, but his thoughts bled into her mind.

Ten years I served from afar while you ate out of her hand. You ruined it. You ruined everything!

Threyna thrashed, trying to free herself from his grasp. She couldn't break his grip. Her lungs burned as he held her under. Her mouth opened, and a silent scream erupted from her, but the rot flooded in. Unable to push him off or disengage, she grabbed Tarus by the collar of his tunic and wrenched. Torquing her body, she dragged Tarus beneath the surface with a splash. Taking advantage of his momentary disorientation, Threyna broke free of his grasp and resurfaced.

She coughed, hacking out the rot that invaded her lungs as she stumbled away from him. The rot was rising. Tendrils of it snaked up the columns lining her throne room. The once-pristine walls of her Inner Throne were now a haunting even hollowed would run from.

Scrambling away from him, wading waist deep through the flood, she trudged to her seat of power.

"You think you saved her," Tarus shouted, emerging from the thick, black liquid. He appeared more like walking sludge than a shade or darkling. *"You've doomed us all."*

As their thoughts meshed, and with Threyna no longer fighting for air, she denied Tarus's access to her mind. Completing the reversal, she tore through his.

"When they abandon us, as I know they will," a young Arilette said, *"go with them. Make sure they never leave."*

"But we'll be apart," Tarus exclaimed. *"I should be with you for the battle. The Cut is dangerous—"*

Arilette put a finger to his lips. *"Don't tell me of the dangers. Tell me what we'll be when we defeat the Order and rule Rheynia ourselves."*

The happiest memory of Tarus's life became his curse. And now, seemingly so close to fulfilling that dream, Threyna had robbed him of it.

You were the mole within the Wraith. The one who sabotaged the tunnels to the ships.

Tarus put his spectral hands to his head. *"Get out!"*

Threyna's resolve grew. Her anger boiled over. Tarus was proof of the lengths Arilette was willing to go, the evidence of just how devious her mind was. *My mother did send me letters. How many? How many did Arilette keep from me over the years? How many times had I asked? She lied to my face. She let me believe I was abandoned, unwanted, rejected...*

Tarus marched towards her, slowed down by the rising rot. *"Laela will ruin us. All of us. Consume her—consume all of them!"*

He believed, even now, even in death, that Arilette would save him. She'd find him a host body she found pleasing and vortex whatever soul inhabited it. That he would live and Laela would die, and Arilette would love him for it. He thought himself her equal, but he was her puppet. She wouldn't care when he disappeared from existence. She wouldn't mention him at all, as she hadn't for the past decade. He was just her tool, her means to make sure that if Threyna failed, Laela wouldn't attempt to lead others in escape.

Threyna glared at him. *Laela would have hollowed in the warp, and if anyone spoke out against it, how long before a Centuriot's blade was through their gut?* Her fury mounted, but it paled in comparison to her resolve.

She grabbed the arm of her throne, pulling herself up to stand upon her seat of power and stare down at him as the rot climbed to his chest.

"Divided, ruin will reign," Tarus said, his voice quavering.

His confidence in his future waned. Fear wormed through his spectral body and infected his thoughts, but he could hide none of them from Threyna.

"Right you are," Threyna said. Ignoring the rot and fueled by all the lies that led to this moment, Threyna drew in breath.

Tarus screamed, attempting to resist her.

Slowly, his spectral body began to stretch towards her. She drew upon his soul, consuming him, until no trace of him remained.

Threyna released her grip on her Inner Throne and returned to the medicus's wing in Octarius. She could feel the rot constricting her heart retreat slightly at Tarus's consumption, but she felt exhausted. It took all of her effort to incline her head.

Two Centuriots craned over her, aiming a vortex and irradiator at her, unsure of who had won the contest of wills for control over her body. Behind them and the busted door, the Palogian man stood beside Aylenia as she held Laela's face in her hands. All eyes were upon her, including Laela's, though they were barely open. Her head sagged, unable to support its weight on her own absent Aylenia's aid, but she was alive.

Threyna wished she could have her mind enmeshed with Laela's so she could gain access to what she was feeling. *Does she know? Will she believe me if I tell her?*

Not wanting the Centuriots to get too excited with their fingers on the trigger, she raised a weak, black-veined hand. "It's me. He's gone." But just as she raised her arm, she realized the bangle was dematerializing. With the final prong released, it returned to its original state, a red-and-black sentient liquid of malice.

The Centuriots backed away, lowering their arcanateks, unsure what they were witnessing. The Centuriots and injured Wraith from the atrium of the medicus's wing filled the open doorway, their faces long and mouths agape.

Still in a heap on the floor, too tired to move, Threyna could only watch in horror as the blood artifact slithered down her arm before coiling on the ground like a serpent ready to strike.

"Move, move!" Canton pushed his way through the onlooking crowd and into the private quarters of the medicus's wing. Dracus and Arilette followed at his heels, all three of them panting. Canton halted, the blood artifact's crimson reflected in his dark eyes.

Dracus pulled him behind him. "Everyone back!" Reaching into his pocket, he lunged for the red-and-black liquid at the same time it launched itself toward Canton. Ripping his hand from his pocket, something within blurred, causing a distorted rippling effect that seemed to suck the snakelike curse into it. As it disappeared into the distortion, Dracus snapped the fatekeeper shut. Staring at the fatekeeper in his clenched palm, a wave of emotions warred along the lines of Dracus's face.

"Gory ghosts," Arilette said. "Was that—"

"No." The finality in Dracus's tone allowed no one to speak, and for a long moment, no one did. As if seeing the full scene for the first time now, eyes drifted from Threyna on the floor to the busted door, then inside to where Tarus's body lay in a pool of blood before Laela's cot.

"What happened here?" Arilette asked, her tone husky.

Threyna lay against the wall of the corridor, glowering at the woman who she'd often considered to be her true mother. She swallowed the bile in her throat, wishing she could spit it at her. "I need a soul jar, Legatus. Laela needs a new warp. Then we have a *lot* to discuss."

CHAPTER 53

A DARKLING'S DEAL

Threyna XXI

"If you are reading this, the One has tried to take that love away. Whether I have hollowed, become a shade or a darkling, that doesn't change that you are still loved…"

—an excerpt from a fatekeeper

A rilette's tablinum once felt like the safest place in all of Rheynia. How wrong she had been. Blind, naive, and utterly foolish, she had hinged on Arilette's every word, working tirelessly for her approval. All for nothing. All for lies. Even now, backed into a corner, Arilette refused to tell the truth that Threyna now knew to be fact.

"And who told you that?" Arilette snapped, both hands placed atop her wooden desk as she leaned over it. "Seems to me that her most trusted adviser lost faith in her, didn't want to leave the safety of our walls, and attempted to ensure that—even if she wanted to leave—the rest of the Wraith wouldn't be forced to."

Lorath nodded behind her. Canton huddled in the corner, unable to meet her eyes, but Dracus glared daggers at her. Aylenia hugged herself, clearly conflicted. But only Threyna knew the truth. Dracus might have suspected it, but he didn't have access to Tarus's mind as she had.

With her rot abated after consuming the darklings of a soul jar, Threyna was replenished, but still, she tired of playing games. She knocked a chair out of the way and placed her knuckles on Arilette's desk opposite her.

"No one told me. No one needed to. I had Tarus's darkling in my head. I saw his every memory, felt each of his emotions—I know *exactly* what he was doing, why, and who told him to do it."

To Arilette's credit, she didn't react. Her grim composure showed no sign of guilt, no glimpse of remorse.

Threyna's knuckles pressed into the tabletop. *She will never admit it.* Disappointment grew like the aura of glowstones soaking up sunlight. Every foothold she'd established, all the high ground she thought she'd secured— they were all built on lies. Laela's every feeling toward the Underground and Arilette would be vindicated with what she was about to say. And though she still felt Laela was wrong about the war, Threyna couldn't keep her or the Wraith here against their will. Not without hating herself. Her proposal would set the Wraith free and potentially doom the Underground, but the alternative—unity without choice—was still a pact doomed to hollow.

"We're focusing on the wrong things right now," Lorath said. "The Order is coming. Even the Skeleton King could be marching with them. We must—"

"The Skeleton King *is* coming," Threyna snapped. "Not *could be.* Is! He's coming, which makes this the best time to focus on the truth." Returning her snarl to Arilette, she pressed. "You ordered Tarus to go with the Wraith ten years ago. You sent him to ensure that they would never leave. You wanted him to be the First Sword, assassinate Rance and anyone else who showed the competency capable of delivering people beyond the curse. He sabotaged the escape from Aranoc. He ensured the Wraith made it to Octarius. And I can prove it."

Threyna opened her fist to hold up a small, flat, black disk on the tip of her index finger. "You gave him an interlayer. A new one, even smaller than the ones the strike teams use. I wouldn't have known to look if I hadn't gained access to his memories. I wouldn't have found it embedded in his hairline behind his ear if I didn't know exactly where to look for it. You gave it to him on the walk back from the Cut. You told him—even before bothering to speak to me—'If she speaks of escape, hollow her. Make it look *natural*.' Do you deny it?"

Aylenia fidgeted behind her. Despite how uncomfortable it made her feel, she needed to hear the truth.

Arilette fixed Threyna with a disappointed stare. With the barest shake of her head, she said, "I did what I had to. To bring us here, make us strong, give us a fighting chance!"

Threyna hung her head. "Say it." She didn't raise her voice as Arilette had; she didn't need to. Inclining her gaze to meet Arilette's eyes, she watched her childhood hero become a darkling.

Exasperated, Arilette tossed her hands and rolled her eyes. "Yes, *Premius*. Yes, I ordered him to ensure our unity."

Dracus scoffed. Aylenia's held breath released. Canton didn't make a sound.

"Divided, ruin will reign." Arilette emphasized each word as if none of them had ever heard them strung together before.

"And forced unity will only create a fractured army," Threyna quoted Fawkes's closing remarks to her along the Spine. "This is not the way to victory over the Skeleton King."

"What is it then, eh?" Lorath snapped. "Since you know everything now."

"Me." There was no pride or bravado in her tone. If anything, the word came out soft, weighed down with guilt and regret impressing upon her heart. It was a burden of responsibility she didn't wish to bear alone. But it was a curse she would take upon herself if it meant others didn't have to live beneath a tyrant's manipulations—Belrich's or Arilette's.

Arilette stalked around the table, coming nose to nose with Threyna. "You can do this, but not alone."

Her motherly tone that once made her feel loved only grated on her now. It wasn't love—never was. It was a depravity, a perversion of the notion of love for the means of control.

"There is one key to victory—" Arilette pointed at Dracus. "—and it's in *that* fatekeeper."

Dracus tensed, turning sideways as if to put his body between her and the fatekeeper in his pocket.

"Give it to me," Arilette said, extending her palm toward Dracus. "Let us wield it, defeat the Skeleton King, the Order, and anyone else who would stand in the way of peace."

Threyna lowered Arilette's outstretched arm. She stared into Arilette's eyes—a woman who murdered her own father. A woman she no longer trusted. But she was right; if even one other person possessed the blood magic and Threyna taught them the basics of what she had learned, they stood a much greater chance of winning. Yet she knew the taint the Blessing imposed on a soul. She wouldn't let Arilette force it upon anyone, absent choice, but neither could she let such a destructive power fall into the hands of someone who coveted power for the sake of it. *We'd only replace the Skeleton King's rule with a new tyrant.*

A knot formed behind the scar across her throat as she considered a way of determining if even a shred of humanity still lived within Arilette. *Last chance.* "Did my mother send me letters?"

The words barely carried the distance between them, yet despite how softly they were spoken, they hung in the air as thick as the clouds over Rheynia.

Arilette searched her. Her brow hardened, lips tightened. "No."

"A little dove stamped in wax," Threyna said softly. "Surely, you'd remember. There must have been…" She shrugged, turning to Dracus. "One, two, every few weeks?"

Dracus raised his index finger, indicating a higher sum. "More than that."

"More than that," Threyna said, tears welling in her eyes. Tears of wasted resentment on her mother, now lost to her. Tears of betrayal from Arilette's manipulations. She blinked them away. "I'll ask you again. Were there letters?"

Arilette grit her teeth, shaking her head. "You listen to him?" She cast Dracus a darkling's glare. "She left you. I raised you. I looked out for you."

"Ghost dammit, were there letters?" Threyna's back knotted. The tension in her body slackened. So badly did she wish Arilette would just admit it. To, for once, be honest with her.

Arilette seethed, her nostrils flaring. She took a composing breath before tilting her head to the side. "No."

Threyna swallowed the knot in her throat, her fists clenching as tension returned to her muscles. "No, then."

"No?" Lorath asked.

"You asked for the blood artifact," Threyna said, matter of factly. "I said, 'No.' Seems simple enough, Arch Premius."

Lorath's cheeks reddened. "What do you mean *no?*"

"I wasn't asking for it," Arilette sneered. "We must ensure—"

"We must ensure that when we win, another tyrant doesn't take the throne," Threyna finished, glaring at Arilette. "Here is what's going to happen." She glanced at Aylenia, resolving herself. It was the right thing to do, but she knew what it would cost. She'd be alone. She'd likely die alone. *Perhaps that's what I deserve...*

"Aylenia, should she accept, will lead the Wraith and anyone else who wants to flee to the ships waiting at the Grip. *Anyone.*"

Aylenia's mouth hung open and Arilette began to object, but Threyna cut them both off.

"Dracus will keep the blood artifact in the safety of his fatekeeper and make certain that it never afflicts anyone again."

Lorath raised his voice. "We can't afford to—"

"We can and we will," Threyna snapped. "Because if you don't let them leave, I leave. I'm the best chance we have at winning this. So if I leave, how many do you think will remain in Octarius?"

"You'd doom us all," Arilette said.

Threyna met Arilette's cold stare. "Everyone should have a choice." She couldn't back down. "Laela wants to leave. Her people want to leave.

You've tried to take their choices away, but now I'm giving you one: let them go and I'll stay and fight. Or force them to stay, and see what happens if you try to stop me from leaving."

"Threyna…" Canton emerged from the corner of the tablinum, his narrow face long. "You can't do this. We're so close. We might actually be able to do this, but only if we stay together."

Threyna scoffed. "We might be here together, reunited, but we have never been more divided." She returned her attention to Arilette and Lorath. "I will fight. I will try to defeat the Skeleton King and the Order, but only if you let them go."

Arilette hung her head. Lorath practically chewed through his teeth based on the sound of grinding coming from his direction.

On the opposite side of the tablinum, Dracus grinned. And though Aylenia remained at a loss for words, her posture had straightened, and a glimmer of hope flickered in her dark green eyes.

Threyna addressed the whole room. "So what will it be? Do we have a deal?"

CHAPTER 54

CHOICE AND CONSEQUENCE

Dracus XV

Once upon a time, before the Disasters, it was said that the sun would rise in the east. An orange mote of fire that illuminated the sky and bathed the shoreline in glittering gold. As it climbed higher to fly over Rheynia, it grew brighter than any illuminator. But the brighter it became, so too did it become smaller, as if it were sailing away like the Drakes and Helixuses on their western voyage. Nearing its zenith, clouds would roll in, blotting out the sun's light. But the rain and storms would always pass. And just as each day began, each day would end, only instead of the eastern shore basking in the sun's fiery glow, the west would receive its due. On and on it went, a daily miracle.

"A dawn for every day."

Dracus remembered those songs. People who lived in such times would sing them to children—joyous tunes with uplifting melodies. He imagined once that such songs, such words offered hope.

"There's always tomorrow."

"Tomorrow's a new day."

Tomorrow. Tomorrow. Tomorrow.

It made Dracus sick as a child. All his years, he'd never truly seen the sun. It hid beyond a gray veil holding back its warmth. The rains came each day, but that beautiful golden orb never rose or set on him. Not truly.

As he sat in the mess hall, ignoring the din of those likely eating their last meals, he couldn't help but wonder if such beauty existed beyond the curse. That's what they said—those who went to Sansia. Blue skies, purer than the sapphires mined along the Wing. Stars would come out at night, scattered across an endless black sea in the sky. And the sun's sister, the moon, would change its shape, waxing and waning from a sickle's curve to a buckler's round.

He patted the soul jar holding Fawkes's shade. *We'll see it together, Old Boy.*

Dracus hung his head, taking Fawkes's fatekeeper from his pocket. Its contents, the message Fawkes had written for him, were locked within. Trapped with the Blessing. He wished he'd opened it sooner, but he'd been afraid to; it would have made it real. The truth that Fawkes was nothing more than a silent, pale spectral visage of everything he'd been in life, sitting in a jar on his hip, was enough to make him want to hollow. But Fawkes was still gone. And now his last words were trapped in the same vessel as a near-sentient curse.

The blood artifact could never fall into another's hands. If Arilette or Lorath had gotten their wish, there was no telling what kind of hellscape Rheynia would have become. Threyna had prevented that ill fate.

Of all the people Dracus would have expected to be the voice of reason, Threyna was the last on his list, but because of her, he was taking Fawkes beyond the curse. The daughter of Bherus Fayte and Viesa Huron. A child of a prince and a rebel, a product of war in a world hellbent on devouring itself.

"It was Fawkes," Threyna had said after Dracus had asked what made her change her mind. *"Fawkes and… Tarus's darkling, Arilette's lies, the way Lorath coveted the Blessing. But it began with Fawkes."* That was something he could relate to. Now there was only one last thing to do before he left this place for good.

Seeing that Canton had finished his meal across the mess hall, Dracus pocketed the fatekeeper and rose to his feet. The bandaged wounds across his back screamed. The weakness in his ankle, the aching in his chin, the scrapes along his arms, and the swollen feeling of his knuckles had become his existence. The pain was the only thing that kept him present, kept him from hollowing.

Won't have to make it much longer. We march soon. Just keep it together.

Putting one foot in front of the other, he made his way to where Canton sat. Canton's back was to him; Marius the quartermaster and another Centuriot sat opposite. The Centuriot, a few years older than Canton, bore into Dracus at his approach. Dark eyes burned like coals beneath his coiffure of blond hair. A scar stretched diagonally along the side of his neck. His shoulders seemed to broaden as he stood, drawing Marius and Canton's attention.

"What do you want?" the Centuriot asked, an obvious grudge inflecting his every word.

Dracus didn't acknowledge him with a response. He nodded at Marius who returned the greeting. "Cant, ya mind a word before… before we get ready."

Canton bit his lower lip, swinging his leg over the bench. "Yeah."

"I asked you a question," the Centuriot said.

Marius held his arm out. "Easy, Rivich, he's—"

"I know who he is."

Dracus sank deeper into his bodily pains like armor, not allowing this new aggravation to penetrate. Rivich was a full head taller than he, as broad as Fawkes, and likely half his age. Clearly, he wanted trouble, but Dracus couldn't step in the Dreadroot's snare. *Not here, Old Boy. Out there. Together.* He pointedly ignored Rivich.

As Canton stood, Rivich strode around the table, inserting himself between him and Dracus. Inclining his gaze, Dracus met the Centuriot's glare.

"Maybe you forgot what it's like in here," Rivich said, "but here, when a commanding officer speaks to you, you—"

"I answered you, Centuriot." Dracus felt the call of the dying, willing him to hollow out here and now. He focused on the pains, reliving each and every one of them again in a fight to retain his humanity. He took a deep breath. "You asked what I wanted. I said I wanted a word. Canton?"

Canton placed a hand on Rivich's shoulder as if telling his hellhound to stand down. "It's fine. Won't be long."

With one last parting glare, Dracus led Canton away from Rivich's shadow and out of the mess hall. Every other step sent a new, compounding flash of pain into his shin from where he'd kicked Jagras's feet out from under him. Each stride told the bone to crack just a little bit more. Knowing his steps were numbered, hoping he wouldn't have to take them alone, he stopped in the quiet hall to speak with Canton.

He placed a hand on each of Canton's shoulders, looking him in the eye. He'd grown into the spitting image of his father, and try as Dracus might to knock the rebellious martyrdom out of him, nature defeated nurture. Despite his failure, Dracus found himself grinning. "Here we are. Not exactly how we wanted it, eh? But nevertheless…"

Canton nodded, but Dracus's grin never found its way to his lips. "I know what you want. I know what you're going to ask of me—"

Dracus shook his head and gave Canton's shoulders a squeeze. "Nah, kid. No ya don't. Cause I know what you want. For a long time, I thought, I dunno… I thought, if I did this one thing right, maybe I'd redeem myself. Give ya the life I'd never had. But that ain't it. Fawkes tried to get me to see, but you know me, kid—ain't exactly dewskulled, but not the brightest either." He took a deep breath. "I thought I needed to get you off this rock to redeem myself. Realize now, givin' you a choice is 'bout as good as I can do. Now, you got that; you got a choice."

"Dracus—"

"Lemme finish." He closed his eyes before glancing down at the soul jar on his hip. Gently, he touched it, wishing he could reach through the arcanatek's shell and feel Fawkes. "I gotta get Fawkes beyond the curse. True death and all."

Canton took a trembling breath. "The world is darker without him."

"Aye."

"Sansia?" Canton asked.

Dracus nodded. "At first."

It would be his last lie, his last stretch of the truth. Though that's where the boat would go, Dracus would never make it to land. If tales were true, the moment they were beyond the curse, he'd die a true death; his soul would leave his body and depart to whatever awaited him in the afterlife. Whether Neutreen would grant him wings to ascend to the heavens, or he'd just cease to exist as if he'd been irradiated, he didn't know. But it would be the end of this stretch of existence. If there was a new beginning, he and Fawkes would make the journey to whatever was next. Together.

Canton sniffed, thumbing his nose. "I know you want me to come with you, but I can't. Not yet. I must see this through."

It hurt Dracus, but he understood it. Worse, he accepted it. Perhaps it was the futility of trying to bend someone else's will to his own. Perhaps he'd finally learned to let go of things he couldn't change, but regardless of what happened next, he would have to make peace with it.

"That's yer choice, kid. I mean it."

"I'll come find you," Canton said. "Afterwards. After we win."

Dracus swallowed. *I hope not, kid. Not where I'm goin'. Not for a long while yet.*

"I'll help you protect that." He pointed at Fawkes's fatekeeper around his neck containing the Skeleton King's Blessing.

"Nah, Cant. This is it. I need to disappear. This—" He touched the fatekeeper around his neck. "—needs to disappear."

Canton narrowed his eyes and cocked his head. "What do you mean?"

"I can't protect this. No one can. Whether you defeat the Skeleton King or not, someone will come lookin' for it. So I can't tell ya where I'm goin'. No one can know. All it'd take is one darkling to get into yer mind, and there's no tellin' how many people would know the truth. They'd come searching for me. For it." He shook his head. "Ghosts, even in Sansia, someone'll talk. Word'll get out somehow, rumors will spread, and someone wantin' power will come lookin'."

Canton blinked. "So what does this mean?"

"This is goodbye, Cant." Dracus shrugged, hating that this was how it would end, but knowing there was no better option. In some ways, it was almost easier this way. If Canton came with him, believing they were going to spend the rest of their days protecting the Blessing from the Skeleton King and anyone else seeking its power, he'd be grievously disappointed. The moment they were far enough out at sea, Dracus was going to drop the fatekeeper into the abyss, pray it would never be found, and die a true death with Fawkes once they passed the edge of the curse.

Canton hung his head. "Always thought we'd have more time—you, me… Fawkes." His shoulders slumped at Fawkes's name. His feet shuffled. "Dracus, I… I've said some things—"

Dracus held up his hand. "Me too, kid. Ya don't gotta explain nothin'. I deserved it. Ya got courage. Shoulda known better than to get in the way of that."

Canton inclined his head. "I don't feel brave. I'm terrified."

Dracus didn't need to focus on the pain to stay present. He saw the boy in front of him, no longer a boy, but a man. No longer filled with the disillusionment of glory and battle, he was seeing war for what it really was: an ugly truth in this cursed land with its neglectful Gods. But Dracus understood his desire to fight. Like the rot in Threyna's veins, war was a corruption, ruining all it touched, but with it, it offered the opportunity to change everything. It offered hope for a new beginning. Canton still had hope, despite how long ago Dracus's was snuffed out.

How many times have I sought to extinguish Canton's flame? He pursed his lips. *Not this time.* "Let it in," he whispered. "That fear—that weakness in your knees, the moisture on your palms, the tension in the back of your throat… ya might think it's a bad thing. It ain't. Means ya got somethin' worth fightin' for. Somethin' worth losin'. Means you're alive." He gave Canton a squeeze and inhaled with the pain as Canton hugged him back.

"You go out there, you use that fear. That's what it means to be strong. Can't be brave if you're afraid of nothin'; it's when you stare it in the face and tell it go to the Gullies that you can be brave. So what's that thing Viesa always used to say to ya when you were a kid nippin' at Laela's heels?"

Canton snorted. "Be strong. Be courageous."

Dracus gestured with his hand. "See what I mean, kid? Woman was afraid of everything. Don't mean she wasn't brave. If anything, might make her the bravest of us all."

Canton's lip curved upwards in the barest hint of a smile, though it never reached his eyes. "She would've told me to go with you. Fawkes would have too."

Dracus nodded. "Yeah. Probably right. But at some point, ya gotta make yer own choices. Yer own mistakes. Ya learn to live with them. But if ya never get to make them for yerself... is yer life even yers?"

"Suppose not." Canton took a deep breath. "Gratitude, Dracus. For everything."

Dracus pulled Canton in close, embracing him in another hug. Holding him, he wanted to believe that Fawkes would've been proud of him, that all of this had a meaning and a purpose. That there was something greater at work than them just being the sorry sods that outlived their goddess to decay in a haunted land. He didn't know, but that's the difference between believing and knowing—he didn't need all the answers.

"You're gonna do what I couldn't, kid," Dracus said, separating himself from Canton to hold his gaze. "You and Threyna. I believe that. The Order, Belrich, the Skeleton King—they're gonna hit ya with all they got. But yer not alone. Ya ain't helpless. Arilette's gotta plan, Threyna's got the power, and you..." He shook his head and smiled earnestly. "You're too damn stubborn to fail."

He patted Canton's shoulder. "To full life... and a true death. Give my regards to Belrich."

Canton chuckled, though he lacked the conviction he typically displayed. "And mine to Fawkes."

Dracus released Canton's shoulder and nodded. Not knowing what else to say but not wanting this to be the end, he opened his mouth to speak, hoping the words would come. None did. Not the love of a father to his son. No words of encouragement to strengthen Canton's resolve. It felt wrong. It all felt wrong. Before doubt and hopelessness could drown him, he sank back into the pains of his failing body, spun on his heel, and stalked away.

CHAPTER 55

SEPARATE PATHS

Laela XXI & Threyna XXII

"May Neutreen give you the strength to win your battles, and the courage to choose which must be fought."
—an excerpt from a fatekeeper

Laela ignored her father's nagging and her own lethargy as she helped a young girl load up a pack that her brother wouldn't be able to carry after being taken off the warps too soon. "There you go." She forced a smile at the girl's brother. "Now you stay close to her; she'll protect you."

He returned her grin, beleaguered as it was. "Gratitude." He placed his hand on his sister's back, and together they strode out of the armory between where Redge and Bhen were standing guard.

"Next," Marius the quartermaster called from behind the counter, summoning another to step forward.

"Blood and bone," a burly Undergrounder said, folding his arms across his chest and not bothering to keep his voice low. "These Wraith rats are gonna clean us out."

Heat rose to Laela's cheeks, but Marius spoke first. "Easy, Rivich. They're not takin' anything we can't afford to give."

Rivich scoffed, continuing to speak under his breath as a woman approached the quartermaster's counter.

Marius slid a pack across the table. "Couple days' rations. A bent blaster, still got some charges, though. And, lucky you, the last Dawnshard."

The woman took the pack and slung it over her shoulder without a word, glaring at Laela as she passed.

Another of Tarus's followers.

Aylenia had been the one to tell her what had actually happened. How Threyna had fought with Tarus's darkling and gained access to the truth; all these years he'd been loyal to the Underground, to Arilette and her mad war against the Order. Laela had trusted him, and she'd been a fool. No one would have listened to Laela had she tried to explain what Tarus had tried to do. Ghosts, Laela didn't think for a warped moment that Threyna would bother listening, let alone that she'd make a deal with Arilette to set the Wraith free. But that's what happened.

"We're going to the Grip," Aylenia had said after Laela had woken from her recovery in the medicus's wing. *"Scouts saw ships along the coast. You, me—everyone who wants to leave this cursed place. It's actually happening."*

Laela had believed it a dream, but here they were, preparing to leave and never come back. That was the deal. There would be no return voyage to shepherd more people from Rheynia to Sansia. This would be the lone trip of Rance's fleet, but Rosler and Taggart had defied all odds and made it to the Grip. And with Threyna and Aylenia's help, the Wraith would be leaving Octarius never to return.

But that didn't mean everyone was happy about it.

"Get outta here," Rivich snapped as Asla approached the armory for a second time.

"You gave me a broken blaster." Asla flipped the switch to vortex and waved it in front of her. The arcanatek's warble whined into motion before sputtering to a hissing stop. "What good is having a full cartridge of charges if I can't use them?"

Rivich slammed his palm down on the table. "What good are people who run when they can fight?"

The warmth in Laela's cheeks became fire in her throat as a great and terrible guilt burned her from within at Rivich's words.

Threyna had fought for her. She could have let Tarus hollow her. She didn't. Despite how Laela had treated her, neglected her, then even most recently admonished her and called her a monster, Threyna had not only saved her from Tarus, but also stood up to Arilette. All so Laela could leave her once again.

Divided, ruin will reign. What would happen if we stood together?

On the precipice of delivering her people beyond the curse, she felt she owed it to Threyna to stay and find out. But her mother had sacrificed herself so that they could escape. These past ten years, everything they'd been through, it was all for this. She couldn't give up on it now out of some sense of obligation.

Her father impressed upon the walls of her Center of Silence, but she kept him out.

Marius extended an arm to stay Rivich's wrath. Asla didn't back down, but Laela came up beside her and took the blaster. She'd seldom held such arcanatek before, but she knew how they operated. She pulled the pin, removing the power coils that charged the weapon, and slid the broken arcanatek across the countertop toward Rivich.

"You're right. You need it more than we do." Laela patted Asla on the shoulder. "Take the charges to someone with a working blaster." Asla began to protest, but Laela gestured with her head toward the door. Asla grunted, but did as directed.

Rivich snatched the blaster from the countertop and muttered under his breath as he disappeared into the armory's shelves. Marius grumbled before summoning the next of the Wraith in line to receive the rations Aylenia had secured for them.

Eyes tired, heart heavy, Laela turned from the quartermaster and made for the exit.

"Where are you going?" Redge asked. He hadn't let her out of his sight since Tarus's betrayal, fearing that another attempt would be made on her life.

She needed to speak with Threyna. They had yet to break words despite the passage of time. Whether that was happenstance due to the Underground's preparations for the upcoming battle and the Wraith's arrangements to leave or her sister was intentionally avoiding her, Laela couldn't be sure. Though Aylenia had served as a messenger between them, Laela couldn't leave without speaking to Threyna.

"To find Threyna," Laela said, her tone of voice ladened by more fatigue than she'd realized.

"I'll come with you," Redge said, nodding towards Bhen.

"It's fine." Laela didn't need an escort. As far as she understood it, Threyna was more a threat to Arilette's plans of coerced unity than Laela was. "Once provisions are obtained, get everyone topside. We can't afford to be here when the Order arrives."

Redge and Bhen nodded, allowing her to pass, but then Redge grabbed her arm and lowered his head to speak softly so that only she could hear. "Gratitude. We'd never have made it this far without you." He gave her arm a squeeze.

Lips pursed, she bobbed her head, unsure if she deserved such praise. "By Neutreen's wings, we might yet reach safety." Staring at the floor, she strode between the two men and exited the armory.

The long corridor leading to the stairwell was busy. All of Octarius was. With no time to be wasted, Wraith and Undergrounder alike saw to their preparations wherever they could. Despite the dull hum of the illuminators and the light they cast, all Laela heard was the crackling of fire. All she saw was billowing smoke. All she tasted was ash.

She was glad she was not a Seer like Cybel—such premonitions would not bode well for either of their futures. But the Seers were wiped out. As were the Artificers. She told herself Threyna and the Underground would not suffer the same fate beneath the Skeleton King's magic and the Order's legions, but the fires of her past consumed her hopes for the future.

Attempting to suppress her dark thoughts as she searched Octarius's halls for her sister, she focused on what lay ahead: a sky beyond the clouds. Matches to burn to once again make communion with Neutreen beyond the One's curse. A life not ravaged by war, a life without Order collectors, hordes of hollowed, wandering shades, or the fear of darklings. A future. She imagined building a new home in Sansia, traveling with Aylenia in search of her mûnta, and using her hands for something other than wielding a sword. It sounded too good to be true. And with each step she took in search of her sister, she felt less and less deserving of it.

Threyna wasn't in the barracks, the mess hall, or Arilette's chambers, though she didn't dare to knock and find out. She'd found Canton, wearing the pale garb of the Underground's infantry as he was receiving instructions prior to the impending battle. He met her eyes for a brief moment as he listened to the Centuriot who would be commanding him in the coming hours. For so many years, he'd pined after her like a lovesick puppy. She'd never fancied his attention, but now, she wished he'd follow her this one last time. As they shoved a glowing white arcanatek-like spear into his hands, she knew that wouldn't come to pass.

She bumped into Dracus as he returned from the medicus's wing. His shoulders were more stooped than hers.

"Have you seen Threyna?" Laela asked.

"Nah." Dracus scratched the back of his neck.

She frowned, not knowing where else to look. She looked over his shoulder to the medicus's chambers. "All patched up?" Dracus looked like a hellhound ensnared in Dreadroot that had lost the will to live. Pale, with dark saddlebags under his eyes, he didn't bother to hide it either.

"Not quite." He'd been different since returning from the Cut. Maybe it was Fawkes's shade trapped within the soul jar on his hip, perhaps it was the blood artifact housed within the fatekeeper around his neck, or possibly it was just the burdens of the journey to make it to this point, but he wasn't the same man she'd known these past fifteen years. Gone was his assured swagger and bitter pugnacity, replaced instead by a sullen resolve. An accepted defeat.

Laela took a deep breath. "We'll all feel better once we reach Sansia."

Dracus snorted at that. "Yeah, 'bout that…" He glanced about conspiratorially to make certain no one was within earshot. "Once we leave, get beyond the curse, that's the end of the road for me."

Laela narrowed her eyes, not understanding.

He caressed the soul jar on his hip. "Need ya to know in case I screw it up. Not exactly sure how it'll happen, ya know?" He took a deep breath. "I been dead. Long time now. Ten years."

Laela's jaw unhinged. She stammered, unable to form words.

"Yeah, I dunno either. But I've held out this long." He sighed, stroking his mustache. "Just wanted to get Canton out, ya know? But here we are. Gotta let him make his own choices, I suppose."

"Dracus, I—"

He waved his hand dismissively. "I just need ya to know—I ain't makin' it to Sansia. Plan is to set Fawkes free beyond the curse. Dunno what Neutreen would want from me, but hopefully, she takes us both. But if I… ya know… before I let Fawkes out. Do me the honors, eh? Send us together."

Laela shuffled her feet, flabbergasted.

"Yes?" Dracus asked.

Laela nodded, barely able to process. "Dracus…"

"Keep it between us." He strode past her before calling over his shoulder, "I'd check the Artificers' workshop. They're up to something. I'd bet the last darkling in the soul jar she's in there with 'em."

Laela bit her lip, considering what Marius had said to Rivich earlier. *"They're not takin' anything we can't afford to give."* She thought he was saying it because of the meager supplies they were parting with, not because they were *"…up to something."*

Dracus's footsteps retreated, leaving her with the harrowing truth of his painful existence and the frightful prospect of whatever awaited her in the Artificers' workshop. Despite not having been in Octarius for ten years, she'd spent too much time in this hovel to ever forget her way around.

Returning to the stairwell to ascend another level, she wondered what the Underground had in store. The glowing white spears being distributed by Centuriots were one thing; she could only imagine what fresh horror they could cause. But what hid behind closed doors, that was something else entirely.

As she climbed the stairs, another pair of hurried footsteps descended.

"You should be at the armory." Aylenia's face was long, her voice breathy. She paused a few steps above where Laela stood.

Something was wrong. Laela paused, waiting for Aylenia to explain herself, but whatever plagued her, she gave it no voice. "I must speak with Threyna," Laela said, continuing her march up the stairs.

Aylenia gripped Laela's arm. "Make it quick. We need to leave now. We have less time than anticipated."

"Is she in there? The workshop?"

Aylenia swallowed, a visible knot tangled in her throat. "Yes. But so are Arilette and Lorath. They're not going to let her out of their sight."

Laela grit her teeth. "Then they'll hear what I have to say too." Aylenia opened her mouth to protest, but Laela cut her off. "I must speak with her."

Aylenia's lips contorted, but she nodded despite her obvious disagreement. "Make it quick. Prime? I'm going to summon everyone from the armory If you're not at top level in—"

"I'll be there," Laela said, giving Aylenia's arm a squeeze. She climbed the stairs two at a time.

Speaking to Threyna was never the easiest thing for her, and she wasn't keen on the idea of having to talk with Arilette and Lorath present, but if she didn't now, she'd never have another opportunity.

"Some things are better left unsaid," her father said, managing to disturb her within her Center of Silence.

"Yeah," Laela said. *"But not this."*

Sealing her father out, she approached the arcanatek-forged door of the Artificers' workshop. A smooth, inky-black surface sealed the way, conjured from the same shadows of a Nightfall mine. Muffled voices spoke harshly from within.

"If you're wrong, we could vortex and irradiate our own Centuriots," Threyna said. "Blood and bone, you could hit me."

Arilette's response was too quiet to hear. Laela crept closer to the door, searching the long hall to double-check that no passersby would catch her snooping. Laela put her ear to the shadows. Lorath was speaking.

"—defeats the Skeleton King, our Centuriots will gladly lay down body and soul to see it done. If you wanted to spare the lives of our Centuriots, you should have thought twice before sending off the Wraith."

Threyna scoffed. "You'd have sent them to their end."

"No," Arilette said, "we'd have sent them to their duty. The future of Rheynia will be bought in blood, bone, and soul. You, of all people, should understand that."

A pregnant pause on the other side of the shadowy door emphasized the volume of Laela's heavy breathing.

"Divided, ruin will reign," Arilette finally continued. "You've made it through the Cut. You've made your choice. Now own the consequences."

Another pause.

"I can't hear you, Premius." The bite in Lorath's tone chewed through the arcanatek door.

"Prime, Legatus."

At movement from within, Laela staggered back. Not wanting it to seem like she was eavesdropping, she pounded her fist on the smooth black doorframe. "Threyna? Are you in there?"

Silence.

"It's me. Laela."

"Leave, girl," Arilette said. "While I still allow it."

Laela's nostrils flared. "I'm not leaving until I speak with my sister. Threyna, please."

The moments stretched on. Too long, too sullen. Rejection's despair coiled around her heart like a Dreadroot's vines. Ten years of guilt compounded with the time spent before the Battle of the Cut. Every time she'd shunned Threyna's sisterly advances, each occurrence in which she'd dismissed Theodyn's fatherly love—they'd led to this. They'd taught Threyna *this*. All these years, she'd blamed Threyna for being difficult, or Arilette for manipulating her.

Would any of this have happened if I had just loved her?

Laela closed her eyes. She recalled the letter her mother had written her in her fatekeeper. Overwhelmed by grief, she wished she'd read it again. She wished she'd understood its meaning before they parted at Aranoc.

"Never let anyone keep you hurting," her mother had written, *"not because it is bad to be hurt, but because there is nothing that can't be healed."* All she'd focused on was being strong, being courageous, not letting anyone hurt her like her father had. But in doing so, she'd put up walls and become more attached to her duty than the people she was doing it for. She'd kept hurting, and hurt others in the process—none more so than Threyna.

"You two are a lot more alike than you're different," Aylenia had said, walking along the Tears. Considering that, Laela tried to piece together the words she would have wanted to hear from her father. She dropped to a knee and pulled *True* from her boot, the dagger Theodyn had given her. She examined the finely forged dagger, and fresh tears fell to the floor. Now, more than ever, she needed to be true, to herself and to her sister.

Vulnerability is not a weakness. Strength is knowing when to drop your guard. Courage is actually doing so.

Laela cleared her throat, hoping she could speak truth into the wounds she'd inadvertently caused. "I should have been there for you, Threyna. I was so wrapped up in myself, my anger, my hatred for my father that I was never a sister to you. I chose my jealousy of you for your father over our friendship. Maybe... maybe if I hadn't been so selfish, I would have realized, could have seen you—truly seen you." She rested her head against the shadows that separated them as the regrets piled between them mounted higher.

Tears dampened the corners of her eyes, threatening to spill down her cheeks. She squeezed her eyes shut and swallowed the knot in her throat. She opened them, allowing the tears to trickle. No longer would she close her eyes to the truth her mother had wanted her to see all these years. She thought Threyna was the monster, but Laela was. She could point the finger, blame her father for abusing her for his own shortcomings, blame her mother for allowing him to do so, but at the end of the Cut, the only one she could blame was herself for perpetuating that trauma onto her sister.

"Apologies, Threyna. Gratitude, for saving me, for saving the Wraith. Neutreen knows I don't deserve it. Moderation, Modesty, Measure, Merit—I failed in the Tenets, but I will not leave without telling you that I know I failed. I failed you. I should have loved you, and I didn't. That's my fault, and I know that now it's too little, too late, but I do love you, Threyna."

She took a deep breath, hoping against hope that Threyna might respond, walk through the shadowy door and embrace her. But again, heartbeats passed in silence. Part of her wanted to believe that, if she stayed and the Wraith fought, they could actually win and defeat the Skeleton King and his Order legions. But she didn't believe. And with the truth that Arilette would have sent them to die as a distraction for the future of Rheynia, she couldn't throw her life away or let any of the Wraith do so.

"Fight for more," her mother had written in her prayers for her. *"Dream for more."* She needed to leave, and Threyna needed to stay. She'd said her piece, she'd lowered her guard, and though she felt like that was all she could do, she still felt like leaving was a betrayal to her sister.

When it was clear that Threyna wasn't going to break the silence, Laela continued. "I like to think, in another life, at a different time, we truly could have been sisters, you and I. Though it seems, not in this one. Not now, not after all we've been through. I blame myself for that. But, Threyna, I pray that one day we can make it so." She wiped her eyes with the back of her hand. "Fight. Win. May we find each other again. May we earn another chance to be the sisters our mother wished us to be."

Another silence.

"She ain't gonna talk to you," her father said. *"Same way you don't talk to me."*

He was right. Laela ignored him. The silence stretched. The failure mounted.

Laela took a deep breath, resheathing *True* in her boot. She pressed herself to her feet despite the difficulty of standing under the weight of her emotions. "Goodbye, Threyna. Good fortune in the battle to come." She pried herself away from the Artificers' door and began the long, slow retreat down the hall.

Threyna

Sitting before a bench in the Artificers" workshop, Threyna avoided the heavy gazes of Arilette and Lorath. She held the dagger her father had given her beneath the table, rolling its embossed hilt in her hand. *Pure,* it read. But she didn't feel pure. Not after retrieving her mother's fatekeeper from the footlocker in her bunk and reading its contents. Not after hearing of Arilette's plans to sacrifice Centuriots in a gambit to kill the Skeleton King. And certainly not after leaving Laela's heartfelt words unanswered.

When she was born, her father had given Laela a similar dagger. Hers said *True.* Laela had been just that. True to herself, true to her heart. There were a great many things Threyna would never understand about Laela, but she understood this, which only made Threyna feel worse leaving such words unanswered.

She hung her head, not wanting Arilette or Lorath to see the tears welling in her eyes or the blush of weakness upon her cheeks. Her emotions warred within her, a tempest of a child's painful past and a soldier's callused stoicism. Overwhelmed, frantic, out of control but determined to be the hero this war needed, she felt disconnected from herself, and further yet from her sister.

She turned from the Legatus and Arch Premius towards the door that separated her from Laela. Worse than when Arilette had flipped the time-turner, time spilled, slipping away from her. With each passing moment, her opportunity—her final chance—to make things right between her and Laela began to fade. From her seat upon her Inner Throne, Threyna felt Laela walking away like a shade wandering into the distance.

"You're sisters…"

Threyna had dealt with enough blood to know that being family didn't mean much. Blood was water and iron—important to sustaining life, but not so important as to bind people together. Love did that. So often she'd confused love with companionship out of her fear of being alone. She'd confused Arilette's mentorship with love when really it was manipulation. Conversely, she'd viewed her mother's apparent rejection as neglect, when all this time she'd never stopped loving her. She didn't know if she'd ever truly gain the grasp of what love was, what it felt like, or how to tell its validity from its shadow, but in this case, she knew.

The prayers written in her mother's fatekeeper returned to her. *"May Neutreen give you the strength to win your battles, and the courage to choose which must be fought."* This was one fight that needed to be finished.

Threyna stood to her feet, sheathing *Pure* in her belt. Not for the blood she shared with Laela, but for the love with which she spoke. She strode around the workbench, shoved her way between Arilette and Lorath, and slammed the heel of her hand into the button that created the shadowy door.

Halfway down the corridor, Laela turned back to look at her.

Allowing her soldier's stoicism to depart, Threyna let the child's tears flow freely. Her first few steps toward her sister came slow, hesitant. But with each stride, she picked up speed. Now, Laela was moving towards her as well. The distance between them, the leagues, the years, the arguments and fights—all of it receded until they both stopped just beyond an arm's distance away.

Laela's cheeks were flushed, her eyes wet, and lower lip quivering.

Threyna's vision blurred with tears, but never before had she seen Laela so clearly. Forever at odds, she found herself not wanting Laela to leave, but knowing she couldn't stay. She searched for the words left unresolved between them, hoping to find something that could make up for the years lost. She shook her head, finding none that would suffice.

Gasping, she stepped forward, and Laela did the same, closing the remaining distance between them. Threyna wrapped her arms around Laela's neck and shoulders as Laela's encircled her waist. She sank into her sister's embrace, realizing after all this time, that was all she had ever wanted.

She held Laela, squeezing tightly, and where words failed, teary touch served.

"You fight," Laela sniffled into Threyna's shoulder. "You win."

"You go. Lead, live, and don't ever look back," Threyna said, not wanting to let go, but knowing the time had come. Their grip on each other slackened before the two separated and it was time for them to follow their divergent paths.

CHAPTER 56

ALWAYS ANOTHER FIGHT

Threyna XXIII

The reaping spear pulsed with power in her hand. Its radiant tip made the rest of the surrounding hall gloomy by comparison, but despite the power flowing through the Underground's newest arcanatek, Threyna had never felt more frail. Watching the Wraith leave made her feel like she was still just a girl on the eve of the Battle of the Cut. She hoped, however, she and Laela had done enough to ensure a different outcome.

Though they were parting on different terms than they had a decade ago, it took all of Threyna's focus not to feel abandoned again. Loneliness clawed at her like a ravenous hellhound. Dreadroot curled around her limbs, fixing her in place. And the fear of failure flashed in her mind between every blink of her eyes. Her father's scars, what Belrich's Inquisitors did to him, what they'd do to her if they lost…

"I guess this is it then," Aylenia said, watching the last of the Wraith ascend the stairs out of Octarius. A short distance away, Canton and Dracus exchanged another round of farewells. She gave Threyna a sad smile. Threyna couldn't return it.

Laela had been the first to lead the charge to the Grip. The rest of the Wraith followed in her wake, Canton being the only of their number electing to remain, while Aylenia was the only Undergrounder choosing to leave.

Threyna gripped the haft of the spear and chewed her tongue to still her trembling fingers and quivering lip. The arcanatek had the ability to irradiate a soul still within its body. A bane to the living and hollowed alike, the reaping spear would kill the Order's legionaries and leave nothing for the Skeleton King to consume. But nothing for her to consume either. Despite its power, Threyna felt weak before her friend.

"No. This isn't it—not the end, anyway." Threyna forced her lips to curl even though the effort formed a new knot in her throat. *I'm not a kid anymore. I'm not being abandoned. I chose this. We chose this.* She swallowed the wave of emotions. "Just a new beginning."

Aylenia's sad smile broke, leaving a genuine one in its place. Taking care to avoid the spear, she wrapped her arms around Threyna and held her close. "I wouldn't have survived this place without you. You know that, right?"

Threyna pressed the side of her head into Aylenia's like she had the night she realized her father was never coming back. Aylenia had been her strength then. Just as Threyna had been hers when her mother disappeared along with the Sansian settlement. "We survived here together. But you'll live out there. With Laela. With your mûnta."

Aylenia pulled away. She glanced over Threyna's shoulder to where Rivich and a handful of new Centuriots stood with arms crossed as if they needed to make sure the Wraith would be leaving. "Come with us," Aylenia whispered. "Leave with us. Think of the trouble the three of us could get up to."

Threyna allowed herself a chortle, but her eyes fell to the floor between them. They both knew she couldn't, not because anyone would be able to stop her, but because if she left, she was abandoning all of Rheynia. She was their one chance as her father was before her, as Dracus chose not to be. This fate was not meant for her, but its yoke fell upon her either way. This was her burden to bear, her enemy to defeat, and her country to save. It wasn't fair, but Threyna had given up on Neutreen's justice long ago.

"What will you do?" Aylenia asked. "When you win?"

Threyna grinned. She hadn't thought about it, hadn't dared to imagine. "Queen Threyna?" Aylenia teased. "Has a nice ring to it."

Threyna scoffed. She wasn't meant to rule. She didn't want to be queen. More than anything, she just wanted to see the sun rise and fall. She didn't know if Rheynia's curse would end with the Skeleton King's defeat, if it would live on because the same rot coursed through her veins, or if it would follow her wherever she went, but she knew rule wasn't something she cared for. She'd seen what it had done to her grandfather, Bohen. She knew firsthand how terrible Belrich was. Whether that corruption was borne from his position of power or if he was always such a darkling, there was no way of knowing. But Arilette was no better example despite the years Threyna had spent idolizing her. Threyna had enough power at her disposal; the last thing she needed was a crown.

"One day," Threyna said, "maybe when all this is over, I'll come find you in Sansia." She hoped it was true. That would mean that Laela and Aylenia had escaped the curse and established a new home, and that she'd managed to defeat the Skeleton King and his Order.

Aylenia took Threyna's free hand in her own. "Laela has already mentioned searching for a cure." She glanced down at the scars left behind by the bangle. Black veins snaked up and down from where the blood artifact's prongs bit into her flesh.

Threyna shook her head. "Find your mûnta. Make a home for yourselves. Don't worry about me."

"Better chance finding gold in the Gullies and Viridite in the Wing." Aylenia gave her hand a squeeze. "Oh, before I forget." She released Threyna's hand and untied a pouch from her belt. She extended the pouch to Threyna. "They're glowstones."

Threyna cocked her brow, not knowing what to say. Though they were valuable in their raw form for charging power coils that fueled arcanatek, the mined stones themselves were barely worth their weight. "Gratitude…"

Aylenia shrugged. "My mûnta said there was nothing like Viridite in Palogia, and Sansia was more sand than stone. Might not be worth much here, but stones that can absorb light in a world with a blue sky and a bright sun… might be worth hanging onto if you decide to come join us. You never know when you'll need a bit of light." She patted a similar pouch on her other hip. "I'm bringing some of my own."

Threyna smiled. "Thank you, Aylenia." Clutching the pouch in her fist, she gave her friend another one-armed hug, squeezing as tightly as she could. "Be safe out there."

"Always another fight," Aylenia said.

Threyna closed her eyes and forced a smile. *Always another victory…* It was on the tip of her tongue, but still, she couldn't bring herself to say it. "Not for you. Not anymore."

Aylenia gave her a sad smile. "I suppose not."

"Enough already!" Rivich said. "Get out. We have a war to fight."

Aylenia scowled at Rivich before taking Threyna's hand in her own and giving her one last squeeze. "Be safe. Win. I know you can."

Hating Rivich for depriving her of one more moment with Aylenia, Threyna let her go. "You be safe."

Aylenia turned away, strode up the stairs, and just like that, another friend was gone from her life. First her family, then Daeton. She lost Rivich that day too even though he was still warbling at her hip. Then Ebrus, Yevon—now Aylenia too.

Beside her, Dracus and Canton exchanged one more hug, a final pat on the shoulder, and the ultimate goodbye. Dracus nodded to her, patting the fatekeeper about his neck as he strode away. The hollowed man, Dracus Alius—Order legend, Underground rebel, and Wraith runner—walked past with the fate of the world around his neck.

No words needed to be said on the subject. He knew better than anyone, and she knew that he didn't need to hear it. As Dracus walked away, she wondered if Canton knew that this would be the last time he would ever see his protector. That soon after their ship left Rheynia's shores, his soul would leave his failing body, and the man who'd saved him and raised him as his own would cease to exist.

Whether Canton realized or not, his tears fell in Dracus's wake.

Threyna went to his side. "You prime?"

Canton nodded before meeting her gaze. "No. Not really."

Threyna inhaled sharply. "Yeah, me neither."

"You did a good thing, letting them go. I just hope it was the right thing."

She knew Canton's stance on the matter. He believed Arilette's mantra as she once had: that they needed everyone. Divided, ruin would reign, but Canton didn't see that keeping them here, trapping them... that wasn't unity. They would have been sent out on the front lines to serve as a distraction, a sacrifice.

Arilette and Lorath had filled her in. They'd tunneled underneath the grounds outside of Octarius's ruins where an approaching army would inevitably attack from. All the power coils the strike teams had stolen from Order supply depots around the Dominion these past years were constructed by the Artificers to forge one massive arcanatek. A landmine. One large enough to vortex a legion in one heartbeat and irradiate all the souls in the next. If the Wraith had stayed, they would have been bait to lure the Skeleton King into the blast radius.

Threyna closed her eyes and choked her reaping spear. "There are no good things, Cant. There are no right things either. Maybe out there, but not here. Just blood, bone, and eternal undeath."

She glanced at Rivich and his underlings watching them from a dozen paces away. He gripped his reaping spear like it was her neck and she'd just told him Daeton's death didn't matter to her. The newly graduated cadets, fresh out of Arilette and Lorath's brainwashing academy, stood sentry, arms crossed, glares stern. It was hard enough getting Canton to understand. It would be impossible to make them see reason. After all, no one had been more stubborn, more adamant than she had been.

She grabbed Canton by the sleeve of his tunic and pulled him close. "I need you to stay close to me once the battle begins."

Canton cocked his brow. "Legatus told me—"

463

"I don't care what she told you. Once the battle starts, you don't leave my side unless I tell you otherwise. Prime?"

Before Canton could answer, Rivich's footsteps came to a stop behind her. With one hand on his reaping spear and the other on his hip, he glowered, his lips a hard and unyielding line. "Enough of this. We've wasted enough time on deserters and traitors."

Threyna eyed him. They were never quite friends, but they'd fallen a long way to the hatred she felt from him now. "Leave us," she said to the Centuriots and nodded at Canton.

The Centuriots glanced at Rivich.

"Fall to command," Rivich said. "The Premius has spoken. Return to the war room, Legatus Arilette and Arch Premius Lorath will be addressing us shortly."

The Centuriots did as instructed. Canton hesitantly strode away, but he too left, falling in line with the rest of them. Once it was just the two of them, Rivich's propriety faded to reveal his true feelings. His tight lips curled back in a scowl. His brow hardened, wrinkling his nose.

"Hate me if you must," Threyna said. "But hate me for the right reas—"

"I don't hate you. I should hate you, because you've ruined us," Rivich snarled. "I should hate you for Daeton. I should hate you for Ebrus and Yevon. But I just don't understand you. You're cold. Selfish. With some distorted sort of honor code that will see us all hollowed."

Threyna felt Rivich's heartbeat from within her Inner Throne. Wrath rained down the stained-glass windows of her throne room in the form of black blood. She wanted to rage. To tell him he was wrong, that he didn't know anything about her, but what good would it do? *It's not true. He's wrong about me.* She let go of her desire to be seen, to be understood. She was alone. Even if she emerged from the impending battle victorious, she'd likely always be alone.

Threyna took a deep breath. "I won't ask you to try and understand. All I ask is that you fight with me. Help me win this, not just for us, but for all of Rheynia. For Daeton, Ebrus, Yevon—everyone we've lost. Please, just fight *with* me."

The lines in Rivich's face softened as he averted his gaze. "What choice do I have?" His voice came out breathy, tone riddled with pessimism.

Threyna grabbed Rivich's arm. "Rivich, we can do this. *I* can do this. Just promise me, once the battle starts, promise me you won't leave my side."

His defiance returned. "I'll follow my orders." He tried to pull away from her, but Threyna held fast.

"Do you know about the landmine?"

Rivich searched her. If he was looking for any deception, he wouldn't find it. Clearly, despite his apparent promotion to Tribunus, he had not been partial to Arilette and Lorath's plans.

She stepped in closer to whisper, despite the fact that they were alone. "The Artificers have developed a new arcanatek." She nodded at the reaping spears in their hands. "Like these, but a landmine fueled by all the power coils we've stolen. They're going to detonate it just beyond the fallen arches of Octarius's front entrance, where the battle will likely be thickest."

Rivich squinted, trying to reason it out. "But our own legions will be engaged."

Threyna nodded. "Please. I know you think I don't care, but I'm begging you; even if you're ordered to be there, don't be."

He blinked, worked his mouth in the shape of words, but none came forth.

A shrill whine echoed through the interlayers located on every floor of Octarius before Arilette's voice resounded off the stone walls. "Report to the war room. Our time is upon us."

Part IV

CHAPTER 57

BAIT

Threyna XXIV

Octarius was not the best place to stage a defense. Perhaps in the times before the Artificers' War tore it down, before the War of the Seers ravaged its walls, or the Disasters sent fissures through its foundations. But now it was just dilapidated walls and crumbling towers. It offered no defense, and though Arilette claimed this was a fight they were ready for, Threyna had lost faith in the Underground's Legatus. Arcanatek spears and the Reaper's Landmine aside, their numbers were not enough for the Order's legions, and as long as the Skeleton King continued to exist, the Underground was at the disadvantage.

Lorath's voice boomed throughout the ruins as he reiterated Arilette's war room speech, but standing at the front of the Underground's formation, staring out into the distance as the legions emerged from the tree line along Cybel's Tears, Threyna knew it would all come down to her. Soon, the full fury of the Order's might would be upon them. She could practically see Belrich's twisted grin, hear his haunting laugh as he stabbed his sword through her father's flesh. He would have done the same to her if not for his lust for the blood artifact, but now Dracus was well on his way with it in his possession. If she failed, the only thing that would stop Belrich from torturing her would be if the Skeleton King beat him to it.

Lorath continued to cry out with his motivational speech on the history that would be made this day, the valor that would be earned and remembered throughout all time, but he didn't sense the Skeleton King the way she could. Even now, even at this distance, she could feel his ever-looming presence within her Inner Throne. Black as the rot in her veins, corrupt as the taint on her soul, he was coming. Unlike the echo of a heartbeat or the sense of a hollowed being close by, his presence was that of a gathering storm.

Threyna took a deep breath as more and more men in black uniforms stalked from the trees, spreading out like a plague and promising just as much pain. The plan was simple, but that didn't mean she liked it. The Reaper's Landmine was meant for the Skeleton King. Arilette had said that every battle he'd been a part of, he'd always led at the front. The expectation was that Belrich would want frontline glory for himself as well, and so the Underground's vanguard would meet them in the open field atop the tunnels where the reaping mines were planted. The Artificers' calculations as to the radius of the blast, however, were estimations. A guessing game with the lives of their own people on the line. And all the while, Threyna would have to watch and wait for the blasts to go off. Then and only then could she enter the fight and finish off what the Reaper's Landmine left behind. If all went as planned, the Skeleton King, Belrich, and the Inquisitors would all be dead and gone. But so too would a portion of the people standing at her back.

"Are we clear as to our purpose?" Lorath cried.

"Prime!" shouted the men and women of the Underground's legions.

Threyna did not raise her voice. Did not punch her fist to the fading rain clouds overhead or shout in defiance at the encroaching horde. They were screaming into the void. Hollowed blindly following a shade into the Gullies. It would be one thing to fight and die, to suffer in pursuit of victory. But it was another thing entirely to be sent for slaughter as a diversion, as bait.

It wasn't personal with Arilette; it was tactics. But that was the problem; it was never personal. How many would have volunteered to lure the Skeleton King into the Reaper's Landmine if it meant defeating the Order once and for all? Once upon a time, Threyna would have without a second guess. For the future of Rheynia and justice for its people, Threyna would have gladly hollowed, wandered as a shade, or been irradiated as a darkling. To avenge her parents, to serve the Underground's cause, and gain Arilette's approval, she would have triggered the detonator herself if it meant the Order's end. But Arilette wasn't asking. She wasn't telling these brave fools what was coming. Whether because she didn't trust that they would do their duty or she didn't care that they didn't know what they were walking into, it made Threyna sick. Yet from cadet to Centuriot and Tribunus to Premius, all cheered at Lorath's call despite the fact that he held the detonator that would see their lives forfeit.

As the midday rains traveled from east to west, the Order advanced like a black cloud in the opposite direction, promising more than just rain. Every time she thought their force had fully crossed the Tears, new ranks formed. At the front, a long thin row of skirmishers led the march, spanning three times the width of the Cut. Behind them, the fresher cohorts were organized in columns with uniform gaps between them. Behind them and offset between the gaps of the leading formations, more columns took position, with more at their backs, and so on, and so on. Thousands of men to their hundreds.

The Undergrounders' cheering fell silent on the precipice of battle and the sheer numbers that stood against them. The Order's ranks formed a wedge intent on spearing their defense through the heart. Before them, the ruins of Octarius seemed a relic of ages past, proof of battles lost. But as the wedge encroached, neither the Skeleton King nor Belrich were visible at the front.

Arilette approached Threyna, her brow sharp, lips drawn. Pulling Threyna out of formation and ahead of the rest of the soldiers, she spoke quietly despite the iron in her tone. "Where is he? Can you sense him? They're nearing the dead zone, but we only have one shot at this. We can't waste it on their infantry."

Threyna blinked, examining the army in black before them. *They're supposed to be at the front. Where are they if not the front?*

"Premius!" Arilette snapped.

Threyna sank into her Inner Throne, searching for the Skeleton King's dark presence, but he was everywhere and nowhere all at once. She couldn't tell where within the formation he was, just that he was nearby. Trying to locate Belrich, she couldn't find the rhythm of his heartbeat amongst the legions.

"I don't know," Threyna said, attempting to keep the panic from her voice. "The Skeleton King is close... but that's all I can tell." Knowing that wouldn't be enough for Arilette, she tried again, sinking deeper into her seat of power. But *nothing*. She met Arilette's stern gaze, attempting to conceal the fear and doubts swirling in her mind. "I can't locate him."

"What about Belrich?" Arilette snapped.

It was like he wasn't even there. "I can't find him at all. Is there a new arcanatek? Something that could cloak him?"

Arilette growled. "With Decimus there's no telling what advancements they have." She swallowed. "Change of plans. You will accompany the vanguard's charge. You need to draw him out. Once you do, retreat, and we'll reap the bastard."

Threyna bit her lip. She was joining the bait with the rest of the vanguard. Unlike them however, she could sprout wings and at least attempt to escape the blast radius. She didn't like it, but she didn't see any other options at this point. "Prime, Legatus."

"Don't push too far into their lines," Arilette said. "We need to draw them into the dead zone. If you push beyond it, you're on your own."

Threyna nodded, but found herself shaking. Daeton's hollowed form reached for her. Ebrus's shade stared through her. Yevon's darkling blamed her for everything. Her father was gone because of her failure. Her mother, gone because of her hesitation. Everyone near her suffered. And now, once again, everyone was depending on her.

"Prime?" Arilette asked.

"Yes, Legatus." Threyna saluted, lifting her fist to her chin.

Arilette returned the salute before traversing the ranks to inform Lorath of the change in plans. Watching her go, tension coursed through Threyna's muscles. She returned to her position where both Canton and Rivich were waiting for her. As she neared, Canton's narrow cheeks became more drawn, and Rivich's stern brow creased deeper wrinkles in his forehead.

"Change of plan," Threyna said, attempting to keep the quiver from her voice. "I need to lure the Skeleton King into the dead zone. If Belrich is in the back of the formation, I need you to flank their wedge." *And I need you two as far away from me as possible. Or you'll end up hollowed too.* "It will give you the berth to avoid the blast radius, and if you can catch Belrich off guard, we may still take this day."

Rivich saluted, but Canton hesitated.

"Where is the dead zone?" Canton asked, conspiratorially.

"The front," Threyna said. "Where the vanguards will meet."

Canton shook his head. "Dracus always said the Skeleton King would come in at the end, clean up the mess after he and Decimus did the dirty work. Why would they plant the landmine at the front of the formation?"

Threyna leaned in. "What are you saying?"

Canton contorted his lip, glancing down the line at Arilette. "I don't know. Something feels… wrong."

The Order drew nearer, entering into stun-range for an irradiator. On cue, Lorath raised his arm.

"Vanguard, charge!"

Threyna was out of time. Thoughts swirling, trust teetering, she left Canton and Rivich to forge forward with the vanguard. War cries resounded from the men and women about to die as they charged with reaping spears at the ready. Threyna sank into her Inner Throne, conjuring bloodborne wings as she ran.

With a few mighty flaps of her wings, wind billowed beneath her, and she took flight. Reaping spears glowed white beneath her feet. Blasters warbled within the black-clad mass approaching from the west. Short swords screeched out of scabbards, battle screams ripped across the landscape, and in the space between the two charging armies, a sleeping giant of arcane technology waited to tear their souls from their bodies and scorch them to nothingness.

Ignoring the destruction lying in wait under the surface and the spread of rot in her veins, Threyna lost herself in the rush of wind and the light fall of rain. Reaping spear in one hand, she conjured a curved scimitar in the other. Flying faster than the Underground vanguard could run, she felt the Order's blasters train on her.

No longer responsible for leading others, fear melted away. She welcomed the Order's attention. Power pulsed in her veins and thundered from her Inner Throne to the tips of her fingers. She wanted them to try to defeat her as they had along the Spine and within the Cut. She would ravage the Skeleton King's legions until he had no choice but to show himself.

I will finish it, Father. I will finish him.

The arcanatek's warbles reached a crescendo, and short-range vortexes fired while longer-ranged irradiators attempted to stun her. Threyna conjured a floating kite shield before her that spanned from her ankles to her neckline. Radiant bolts fizzled into her bloodborne shield. Vortexers attempting to draw on her soul met resistance and lacked the strength to reach past the shield. Three flaps away. Two. One. Threyna swooped low, her shield burning to ash as she descended. She slashed with her scimitar at an upheld vortexer.

The scimitar cleaved through flesh and bone. The hand and blaster flew through the air. Threyna plunged her reaping spear into the chest of the neighbor to the handless legionary. Her flight's momentum carried her forward and drove the impaled legionary back.

Regaining altitude with another flap of her wings, her reaping spear dislodged from the leather armor. The legionary spilled to the ground between his brothers-in-arms, but he did not stir as a hollowed. No soul rose from his flesh as a shade or darkling. He simply was no more. Dead. Gone.

Rising into the sky above the Order, she summoned a storm of spears above their heads and let them fall with the rain. Spears fell, impaling the legionaries who stopped their charge to focus on her. Absent the momentum their formation required to be effective, the Order was defenseless against the Underground's charge.

Reaping spears plunged into flesh. Blood stained the air. Enough screams filled the river valley to make Cybel weep again. Steel and arcanatek chewed through the impaled vanguard of the Order, her Centuriots finishing what she started in heartbeats. But Threyna couldn't forge forward. She needed to draw the Skeleton King here. She couldn't locate him in her Inner Throne, everywhere and nowhere all at once, but the only way to summon him was through the blood of his men.

Threyna flapped her wings, building up speed, as she crossed the second line of the Order's wedge formation. Slashing her scimitar, stabbing with her reaping spear, she alternated between conjuring shields to defend herself and summoning projectiles to decimate the Order's lines.

Already, the Order's training adapted. The back lines of their wedge formation fanned out creating an umbrella to encompass the battlefield. In moments they'd have the Underground's vanguard trapped in a pincer formation. The Underground's seconds were already charging forward to support the vanguard and prevent the pincer, but there were too few, and they'd be too late. She needed to cleave at least one side of the Order's flank to give the vanguard a fighting chance. The Order's northern arm was closing in faster than its southern counterpart. She needed to prevent the vanguard's slaughter, but if she wanted to forge a path for Canton and Rivich to start a flank of their own, she'd need to make it to the southern flank as well.

Threyna dove for the legionaries spreading out to the north, hoping she'd have the time to do both. Three cohorts, 300 men, gathered along the expanse. She wouldn't be able to take down all of them, but she could delay them and even the odds for the Underground's lesser numbers.

Spear, sword, and conjurations at her disposal, Threyna called upon the spilled blood of the vanguards and coagulated it together. Like a bloody serpent coming to life, she stretched it along the northern arm of the Order's advance. Thinning as she flew, the blood-conjured serpent became a barely visible trip wire, hovering just above the ground before the Order's charging flankers. Just before they could close in and surround the northern aspect of the Underground's vanguard, the first line of legionaries tripped. A wave of black rolled as the Order's charge disintegrated into a maelstrom of sword and limb. While the legionaries fell over one another, the Underground's reinforcements swept over them like harbingers of death.

Stabbed by reaping spears, the Order's legions gave no deposit of souls for her to consume. Only the Underground's fallen, few as they were to this point, offered sustenance for Threyna's efforts. Doubling back to the dead zone, Threyna drew in breath, ushering the departed shades and darklings into her Inner Throne, consuming them as she went. The black rot ebbed and flowed, but the battle raged on, and still, no sign of the Skeleton King.

He's depleting me, waiting for me to tire. Coward.

She didn't need to be at full strength. She didn't need to fight him. She just needed to lure him to the dead zone and get out before Lorath detonated the Reaper's Landmine.

With black veins slithering up her shoulder and down past her elbow, she prepared another sweep across the Order's wedge. Despite their initial losses, the Order did not break rank and devolve into chaos. With their form and file retained, their superior numbers began to push back. Along the southern flank, they'd begun to enclose on the vanguard's side before the Underground's reinforcements could come to their aid.

Threyna swooped low again, slashing and stabbing with her spear as she tore through the wedge. The fallen blood at their feet, the bodies on the ground, they called to her, begging to be used in her fury. Threyna obeyed. Forming the spilled blood into a row of angled pikes, she impaled the Order's second wave, driving them backwards. But the moment she created the space, the Underground charged forward, filling the void.

Remembering Arilette's warning, Threyna cursed herself. *I can't push too far forward.* The Underground's vanguard didn't know of their inevitable sacrifice. Only she did. *But we're winning. We can do this. I can do this.*

Warring with herself as to whether or not to follow Arilette and Lorath's plans, the soldier within her won out. The Skeleton King would eventually show himself. She needed the Reaper's Landmine to ensure victory. If she pushed too far ahead, yes, she might be able to spare Underground lives, but if the Skeleton King wasn't vanquished, if she fought and lost, they'd suffer a fate worse than obliteration.

She sailed across the formation to aid the southern flank and carve a path for Rivich and Canton to reach the Order's backline. An arcanatek's warble distorted the air beneath her. Too late in sensing it, she rolled. The blaster fired. The irradiator's radiant bolt singed through the air, too close for her to conjure and moving too fast for her to dodge. It blew a hole in her blood-spawned wing. Threyna lost altitude. Buffeted by wind resistance and throttled by the inconsistency of flight granted by her wounded wing, she floundered just above the legionaries' heads. She attempted to conjure to fill in the hole in her wounded wing, but she was trailing ash faster than she was replacing it.

Something slashed at her as momentum carried her through the air. Fire sliced across her back and nicked the back of her elbow, sending tingling pain all the way down to the fingers of her right hand. Her conjured scimitar suddenly felt heavy within her grip. Pushing past the pain, she tried to flap her wings, but the effort only sent her spiraling. She lost altitude and crashed into the Order's line.

She slammed into a legionary's shoulder, spilling him, her, and everyone in her path to the ground. Her inertia carried her in a torrent of limb and steel. Even after she skidded to a stop, her vision swam. The ground around her tossed and turned like waves that crashed along the eastern shores. She tasted blood and ash. The scent of death overwhelmed her. Screams echoed all around, disorienting her.

She attempted to gain her feet, but she fell back to the sodden earth, her head throbbing, right arm tingling. A sharp pain ate at her back where a legionary's sword had raked across her shoulder blade. Her conjurations had dissipated, wings and scimitar alike. Somewhere in her crash, she'd lost her reaping spear.

She planted her left hand on the wet ground to steady herself, but an explosion of agony surged through her wrist and up her forearm.

I must heal.

Sinking into her Inner Throne, she called upon the blood and bone around her. She drew upon the fallen, Order and Undergrounder alike. She couldn't sense the difference. As legionaries gained their feet, she had no time to waste in discernment. Bodies desiccated, exposed blood crept towards her, and a rush of souls spirited her way, but too slowly.

A legionary staggered to his feet, using his short sword as a crutch. He stumbled the short distance towards her. Gripping his sword with bloodlust in his wide eyes, he reared, preparing to stab her through the chest.

Threyna rolled at the last second, barely dodging the off-balance thrust. The slash across her back screamed as it made contact with the ground. Vertigo attacked her, but though she didn't know which way was up, she drew in breath. A bloody mist flowed through her body and into her Inner Throne. Flesh restitched; balance returned. The tingling down her right arm faded into nothingness, and the displaced bones in her left hand realigned. The vitality of the living around her and shades, unbridled by attachment, flowed into her, abating the rot in her veins.

The legionary stood over her, preparing to thrust down. No longer disoriented, Threyna conjured a short sickle in one hand and slashed across his shin. In the other, a long, thin rapier thrust forth from her outstretched arm. The legionary buckled at her sickle's slice, his head keeling forward and straight into the path of her extended rapier. The narrow blade pierced his cheek and sank deep, through the roof of his mouth and into his brain. He crumbled atop her as a darkling rose from his failing body.

Threyna kicked him off of her and drew in breath, but the darkling did not obey her call. Suspended in the air above her, it seemed caught between two tides. Threyna sank deeper into her Inner Throne. The rot had spread more than it had receded in the efforts of healing herself. She needed that soul.

Come on, you stubborn bastard.

The more she sank into her Inner Throne, however, the more aware she became of the other draw upon the soul before her. Deep and dark yet practically emanating power, the Skeleton King's pull ripped the darkling away from her.

Growling, Threyna pushed herself upright. The soggy ground, slippery beneath her feet, wanted none of the falling rain or the wash of blood, but it would have its fill and more before the day was out. All around her, the Underground and the Order clashed.

An engagement away, Rivich rammed his reaping spear into the belly of a legionary. He ripped the glowing spearhead free and slammed the butt of the spear across the dead man's face, spilling him to the ground, a soulless body.

Beside him, Canton hurled his reaping spear into the leg of another legionary. It wasn't a killing blow, but the man staggered to the ground, his soul irradiated within his injured body. Another came for him, the pauldrons of a Tribunus on his shoulders. Canton ducked under a slash, drew his short sword, and exchanged a quick combination of thrusts and swipes.

Threyna moved like a darkling through the battlefield. Slashing with her conjured sickle and stabbing with her rapier, she slipped between displaced legionaries, knocked out of position by her fall. Bodies fell to her conjured weapons. Shades seeped out, darklings tore free, and hollowed continued to claw at her, but none heeded the call of her drawn breath.

One by one, all souls, regardless of their proximity to her, abandoned her for the Skeleton King. Yet still, there was no sign of him.

Canton deflected the Tribunus's thrust, but a kick to the chest sent his feet sliding out from under him. Canton fell backward. Before the Tribunus could follow up, Rivich swept his leg out from under him and jammed his spear through the leather armor and into the legionary's chest.

The Underground surged forward, reinforced by another garrison of Lorath's troops, allowing Threyna a moment's respite. Heaving deep breaths, Rivich nodded to her as he helped Canton up from the ground.

"I'll forge you a path," Threyna said. "Find Belrich."

"Where is the Skeleton King?" Canton asked, reclaiming his thrown reaping spear.

Threyna didn't answer. *"I'm not sure"* wouldn't suffice. She conjured new wings—smaller, less powerful, but also harder targets for errant irradiator blasts. Despite the simpler conjuration, the rot spreading down her forearm to her wrist and up her shoulder to twist around her collarbone was already entering dangerous territory. She needed to consume, but the Skeleton King was disallowing her.

I must draw him to the dead zone before it's too late.

The clang of steel rattled to the chorus of rolling thunder and the gentle patter of rain. Occasional bolts of lightning divided the sky in the distance as the storm traversed the countryside, but though the storm was passing, Threyna couldn't help but feel like the true tempest was about to begin.

Threyna took flight, her smaller wings flapping faster than her beating heart. She zipped over the advancing Underground, combining her sickle and rapier into a double-sided glaive. Staying low, flying fast, she sliced her glaive in a figure-eight-like pattern, shearing a line through the Order's southern flank. She hoped it would be enough to both keep Canton and Rivich out of the blast of the Reaper's Landmine and give them the opportunity to find where Belrich was hiding. Decimus, the First Premius of the Order was also nowhere to be found, which only made Threyna feel like tactically they were missing something.

Circling back toward the dead zone, a gap formed at the center of the Order's wedge formation. Threyna's heart raced, but her breath caught. A man a head and a half taller than the nearest legionary held his arms out to either side, but he wasn't facing the Underground's front. He faced her.

Clad in a black cloak with an obsidian crown atop his head, the Skeleton King eyed her. His silver-blond hair was so thin it might as well have not even been there. Sharp blue eyes stood stark against his sallow flesh. Dark veins stretched from his sunken eyes and down his gaunt cheeks—the stain of his prolonged use of blood magic.

Though the fight raged on along the frontlines across the river valley, all else seemed to stop as the Skeleton King made his presence known. The midday rains trickled to a stop, passing over the Tears and retreating westward beyond the Spine. Threyna paused in her flight, hovering before the Skeleton King on her conjured wings. The Order legionaries not engaged with the Underground only watched, no longer seeing her as a threat but an object of interest. Never had they borne witness to a battle of blood mages.

Threyna swallowed the fear at the prospect of giving them the show they desired. If his control over the darklings was any indicator as to how much more powerful than her he was, she didn't want to find out what else he was capable of.

He was too far from the dead zone, and standing between her and it besides. *I have to get past him. Draw him in.*

"We finally meet, in the flesh." The Skeleton King didn't open his mouth to speak, his voice echoed throughout her Inner Throne. He grinned, a haunting and horrific twist of his thin lips that made him appear more feral than regal. Yet even as she gazed upon him, she saw her father's visage in the shape of his jaw and the point of his nose... before Belrich had chopped it off. He was her grandfather. And he'd come to consume her.

"You say I have taken everything from you..." His voice was but a whisper, yet it thundered within her Inner Throne, louder and more

sinister with each passing word. *"Tell me, Granddaughter, do you recognize this woman?"*

Threyna hadn't even noticed the woman huddled on the ground at his feet. Caked in mud, disheveled and unkempt, the woman did not move, but she spoke in a rhythmic iteration, her voice growing louder with each pass.

"Please, no. Please, no. Please, please, Neutreen, no. No. No!"

The woman didn't move, but spindles of blood congealed around her, wrapping around her wrists and ankles and raising her from the ground and splaying her to face Threyna in bloodborne stocks.

"You know her, Granddaughter," the Skeleton King said within her mind.

Threyna couldn't breathe. She couldn't believe her eyes. She lowered to the ground in the clearing made by the Order's formation around the Skeleton King. Her tongue felt thick in her mouth, her throat tight.

Mother...

"I have taken nothing from you," the Skeleton King said softly, almost kindly. *"Not your father..."* A darkling slipped free from the Skeleton King's chest and flowed into her mother. Suspended in the bloodborne stocks, her body rippled as another soul joined hers. *"Not your friends, Ebrus or Yevon..."* Two more souls—one darkling, one shade—left the Skeleton King and flowed against their will into her mother.

Threyna trembled, paralyzed. Horrified. *Impossible.* She wanted it to stop. She wanted to stop it, but she didn't know how.

"If anything, Granddaughter..." The Skeleton King's tone turned bitter and belligerent. *"You were the one who robbed my men of their purpose when you collapsed the tunnels of Aranoc."* Dozens of shades and darklings swirled together, leaving him and flowing into her mother, who was now convulsing within her bindings. *"You were the one who attacked the Cut, leaving the souls of my followers ravaged."*

Even more souls flowed into her mother. Too many to count. Too many to conceive of. Outside the stained-glass windows of her Inner Throne, a black tower of tyranny rose to the clouds. Seemingly infinite souls swirled around its top. As many souls as he'd poured into her mother, robbing any chance of her being able to control her own body, he still possessed a well of power beyond anything she'd ever come close to touching.

"You say you want nothing but my demise." His piercing blue eyes examined her, taking in the rot in her veins and the emptiness of her Inner Dungeons. *"Prove it. Kill her. Consume their souls and let us make this a fair contest."*

Threyna's heart thudded in her chest. Her breath trembled through her lips. Fear knotted in her stomach and twisted until her entire body felt like it was crumbling in on itself.

The stocks holding her mother lowered to the ground and released her. The bindings themselves morphed, dividing and changing shape into two short swords that formed in her hands.

"Choose, Granddaughter. Or suffer where you stand."

Without warning, Threyna's mother screamed, charging at her with conjured swords held high. Threyna stumbled back, raising her double-bladed glaive just in time to block a heavy, overhead attack.

"Mother!" Threyna shouted. "Fight it! Take back control!"

Her mother's body, controlled by another, reared to strike again and again. Threyna defended, retreating in the muddy, dead grass.

"Please, stop!"

She didn't. If her mother was still in there, she was lost. And whoever had taken control wanted her dead.

CHAPTER 58

THE DAUNTLESS

Laela XXII

With each step closer to the Grip, Laela's fatigue began to wane. The stranglehold Octarius had on her lessened as the ruins faded into the distance; soon it would be nothing but a memory, as dark and twisted as it might be. The scent of smoke, the taste of ashes, the sound of screams—they would all fade with time. The years she'd lived in that underground hovel, the time she'd lost trying to rebuild what was taken from them at its depths, they would all mean something once she saw Rosler and Taggart and the ship that would spirit them into the future.

Leading the procession south, she raised her hand to the scar on her chest from where her father had slashed her. In recent days, she'd gained a web of new scars to accompany her first. They would come with her. She could leave the land and the people that inflicted them behind, but she would never be rid of her scars. No amount of time on the warp would see them healed, not truly. The unseen scars on her soul cut deeper than flesh, and they would remain no matter how far past the curse she traveled.

Badges of merit. Signs of strength and courage. That's what they are. That's what they must be.

Yet heavier than the scars she bore was the guilt of what she left behind. Despite all that Laela had done these past years in preparing the Wraith for their departure, all that she'd fought for these past days to bring them to this point, Threyna had done more. By defying Arilette, she'd all but secured the future for Laela and her people. *But at what cost?*

As they traveled south towards freedom, the Order marched east towards conquest. In that one act, whether Threyna believed it or not, she had likely earned enough feathers to fly up to Valencia and meet Neutreen herself.

A hand slipped into Laela's and squeezed. Aylenia gave her a timid smile as if she too were feeling the weight of what was left behind. "The skies are clearing. Should be smooth sailing all the way to Sansia."

Laela rubbed her thumb over Aylenia's, their fingers entwined. It was strange to share such intimacy. It felt like a luxury she'd never allowed herself. Though unfamiliar, it brought warmth to her cheeks and hope to her heart. Yet she couldn't help but think about Threyna and the encroaching Order legions.

"Can they do it?" Laela swallowed, but the knot forming in her throat remained trapped. "Can they survive?"

"Maybe they would have if you didn't run," her father said. *"Divided, ruin will—"*

Laela didn't care to hear her father's take on the matter. She walled him off before he could finish the mantra.

Aylenia's grin flattened into a firm line. She licked her lip thoughtfully, but instead wrapped her other hand around Laela's forearm, pulling her closer.

Seeing it for what it was—a consolation of comfort for what words could not offer—Laela sank into the embrace. "We'll have to live for them in that case…"

Aylenia nodded. "Remember the past. Live in the present. Dream for the future."

Laela swallowed the hard lump sitting at the top of her sternum and allowed herself a smile. "May we make the most of it."

"Look!" Asla, striding behind them, pointed to the horizon.

Following her outstretched finger past the decrepit tree line along the eastern shore of the Tears, a mast rose in the distance to the south.

"Gory ghosts," Bhen exclaimed. "We did it."

Cheers went up throughout their ranks as people quickened their pace to reach the ship first. After shouts of praise to Neutreen, tears of joy, and grateful embraces, people began to rush past Laela and Aylenia.

Redge clapped Laela on the opposite shoulder of Aylenia, grinning ear to ear. Laela had never seen Redge's face parted in such a way. It suited him better than his grim stringency. "You did this." Tears welled at the corners of his eyes. "You." He shook her, his smile spreading even wider to envelope his entire face. He slid behind her to sling his arm over Aylenia's shoulder. Despite his contempt for her throughout their journey, whatever disdain he'd held for her seemed to blow away in the sea breeze. "Ripping Corners, we did it, eh?"

Aylenia guffawed at the Palogian expression and returned his contagious smile.

With a squeeze of both of their shoulders, Redge ran ahead with the others.

At seeing them all so happy, Laela choked up. *"You did this,"* Redge had said. *But it wasn't just me.* Aylenia gave her a knowing nod, as if she were thinking the same thing. *Gratitude, Threyna. Mother. Rance. Everyone who gave us this hope, this dream for the future.*

All that was left was to descend the beach, climb aboard, and set sail.

Dracus came up alongside Laela.

"We did it," Laela said, barely believing it.

Dracus's face, contorted in a web of wrinkles undoubtedly from the pain of his condition, began to soften. He took a deep breath as if preparing to say something, but his gray eyes flicked to the tree line to the west.

Laela followed his gaze. She couldn't see anything through the foggy gloom that settled between the twisted trunks, but something seemed to move. A soft glow traversed the tree line.

"Shade," Dracus said, his voice but a whisper. "Just a shade…"

Before Laela could let out a sigh of relief, a scream tore through the air, coming from the Wraith ahead of them. They'd stopped at the precipice of the steppe before descending to the beach.

The scent of smoke filled Laela's nostrils, though no tendrils rose.

The scar across her chest burned with an intensity worse than when she'd initially received it. The knot she thought she'd swallowed sank like a stone into the pit of her stomach. Aylenia's hand fell from her grasp. Running now with Aylenia and Dracus falling in behind her, she drew her sword, determined to overcome whatever final obstacle stood between her and their freedom. Between her and the dream of their future.

Laela shoved her way through the Wraith to see what turned their tears of joy into cries of despair. Finally at the front, she saw what robbed her people of hope, and she too felt hers burn.

Decimus, the Lord Premius of the Order, stood before the First Legion, their backs to the watching Wraith. Ahead of them, six spears rose from the sands. On some of the spears, bodies writhed, their arms flailing, mouths gagged. The bodies on the other spears lay still, motionless, their souls already departed.

Laela's sword fell limp in her hand. Her jaw unhinged.

Taggart, the admiral of the fleet Rance had built, squirmed. Hollowed. Beside him, Rosler, the shipbuilder who had slaved for ten years to rebuild the Wraith's hope, hung limp. Dead and gone.

Aside from the gentle lap of the waves and the whistle of the sea breeze, the beach remained silent as the Wraith's hopes died.

A slow clap broke the quiet contemplation of their doom. Coming from behind them, Prince Belrich emerged from the treeline, applauding in mock ovation. Filing out of the woods, more legionaries took position behind him, walling off any chance at their retreat.

"Well done! Bravo!" Belrich cried over his own clapping. "You're just in time to see the finale to our grand spectacle."

An explosion detonated on the beach. Laela ducked, reflexively covering her head along with the rest of the Wraith. Turning, her worst fears came true again before her eyes. Rance's last ship, *The Dauntless,* Rosler and Taggart's daring mission through the Gullies to deliver it to the Grip in the hopes of still finding a way to escape the curse—it all went up in smoke. The explosion blew the hull to pieces that rained down on the beach. The mast cracked at its base, the sails already consumed by flames. Fire licked hungrily, devouring the deck.

Cries went up along the Wraith's line as they took in the devastation.

So close… We were so close. It took all Laela's strength to prevent her knees from buckling beneath the burden of despair, but she needed to use her sword as a crutch to keep herself upright.

Redge sank to his knees, the elation emanating from him moments ago all but evaporated. Bhen stared out to sea, as if imagining he were someplace else. Anywhere else. Asla shook her head, muttering to herself as tears streamed down her scarred cheeks.

The First Legion. Belrich and his Inquisitors. Surrounded. No way out. No hope of victory.

"No…" Aylenia whispered from beside her.

Dracus coddled the soul jar at his hip, Fawkes's soul trapped within.

Failure wormed up Laela's legs like Dreadroot, threatening to drag her underground, strangle the hope she'd dared to cling to. She felt the fight leaving her, the strength fleeing her body like shadows from a Dawnshard. *So close, yet so far away.*

She turned away from *The Dauntless* and collapsed to her hands and knees.

"Divided, ruin will reign," her father said, and for perhaps the first time, it sounded like he took no joy in her defeat. Yet the haunting words that had plagued her most of her life rang true.

I'm sorry, Threyna. I'm so sorry.

"Seize them," Belrich shouted. "Impale each and every one of them."

CHAPTER 59

OBLIVION

Threyna XXV

It took all of Threyna's physical might to meet the strength and speed of her mother's attacks. Despite the frailty of her body, empowered by the innumerable souls within, she hacked and slashed at Threyna with reckless abandon.

Threyna blocked with one side of her glaive, then flipped the other side around to steer another slice away. With a kick, she shoved her mother away, allowing for a moment's respite.

"Mother, please!" Threyna's words had no effect. Worse yet, a bloody circle formed around her like the gladiatorial arenas of old. She couldn't see the Skeleton King. As her mother prepared another savage swing of her dual swords, Threyna leapt into the air, attempting to leave the arena the Skeleton King intended for her. But just as she left the ground, the ring began to enclose in a dome. Before she could escape, the bloody barrier sealed shut, enclosing her inside.

"Fight!" her mother screamed in a voice not her own. "Win! Consume! Or die and join the One True God."

Hatred, purpose, and pain hid behind her eyes. A concoction of the Skeleton King's making. An oblivion that no soul could climb out of.

Wings useless, Threyna let them meld onto her shoulders, turning into pauldrons. She didn't know what to do. She didn't know how to defeat this, but every moment she was in here, the Skeleton King was out there, devastating the Underground.

491

Her mother stabbed, slashed, parried and thrust again. Threyna turned the first three strikes away, but the fourth sliced across her side. Pain raced across the top of her hip, but Threyna grit through it. With her mother overextended, Threyna pinched her mother's wrist between her underarm and her ribs. She let her glaive dissipate to ash just in time to catch her mother's follow-up chop at the hilt.

Threyna reared her head back and brought her crown down on her mother's nose. Bone crunched, cartilage caved, and her mother staggered within her grasp. Pain fissured outward from the impact site on her forehead, warm blood draining down her face. Ignoring the ringing in her ears, she kicked the inside of her mother's knee and wrestled her to the ground. Her mother struggled, blood spilling from her busted nose to flow around her mouth like a scarlet beard.

The darklings within fought with fury, but Threyna was still stronger. She twisted her mother's wrist, not enough to break it, but enough to disarm her of one of the Skeleton King's bloodborne swords. The moment it fell from her grasp, it dissipated to ashes. Her mother refused to let go of the other sword. With it wedged between Threyna's arm and ribs, and no longer fearing the threat of the other hand, Threyna rolled. The sword point stuck into the ground, and Threyna's momentum levered the hilt from her mother's hand. She continued to roll until she was on top of her mother once again.

Pinning her mother's thin wrist to the ground with one hand, pivoting her lower body to kneel across her other arm, she punched with her free hand. Her knuckles connected with her darkling-controlled-mother's forehead. The impact rattled up Threyna's forearm and sent tingling through her fingertips, but it had the desired effect. With her mother stunned but not gravely injured, Threyna attempted to siphon the souls out of her. As she drew in breath, however, the souls remained tethered to her mother's body.

Black veins slithered up Threyna's neck and down her left hand with the effort.

Her mother only laughed, her teeth awash with blood. "You must kill her!" a man's voice said from her mother's mouth, different from the previous speaker. "You can't have us if you won't kill her."

Threyna grunted. She was running out of time. Screams rang beyond the bloody dome the Skeleton King had trapped her in. She feared what carnage awaited on the other side, but she couldn't remain here.

She flipped her mother over, pinning her arms behind her back. She conjured bloody bindings around her wrists, then her ankles. Before the man's voice could speak with her mother's tongue again, Threyna conjured a gag as well.

The Reaper's Landmine hasn't gone off yet. There's still a chance.

Sinking deeper into her Inner Throne, Threyna called upon the exposed blood within the dome. The dome itself refused her summons, but between her and her mother, there was enough to forge a battering ram.

"I'll come back for you," Threyna said, hoping she wasn't lying. She left her bound mother writhing face-down on the ground and sent the battering ram through the walls meant to confine her. Her conjuration crashed through the arena's wall, and she followed behind it.

The ram and her pauldrons melted together, reforming her double-sided glaive. Gripping it in a blackened fist, she scoured the battlefield. But it was no longer a war zone. It was a massacre.

Bloody spires twisted into the sky, their limbs spearing Underground Centuriots through the chest. Discarded reaping spears littered the ground. A chorus of screams filled the air as a black cloud swept overhead.

Flying on draconic wings thrice as wide as he was tall, the Skeleton King conjured another distorted spire. Erupting from the center of the Underground's last line of defense, the spire's limbs exploded outwards, coiling around Arilette and Lorath.

Threyna's heart pounded in her chest. Her Inner Throne quaked with each explosive contraction. *The dead zone.* The Skeleton King was too high in the air. *I need to get him on the ground. Now!*

Out of time, rot encroaching on her heart, Threyna conjured wings and took flight. With each flap of her wings, she felt the corruption seeping deeper, but if she didn't stop him now, all was lost. Rising higher into the sky, she ascended past the Skeleton King as he circled before Octarius's ruins. More spires erupted from the ground, dividing the Underground's forces and disrupting their positional advantage. The Order's superior numbers closed in.

Everyone will suffer if I fail.

She couldn't let that happen. She wouldn't. Praying Lorath still had the sense to detonate the Reaping Landmine, Threyna dove. Rot coursing through her veins, blood rushing to her head, she prepared herself, knowing that there would be no returning from this gambit. The Underground could not win without her, but if she took the Skeleton King down with her, Rheynia could rise together—truly together—and take down the Order. Maybe not now. Maybe not in a year, or even ten. But without the Skeleton King, Rheynia could be free once again.

Committed, tears streaming from her eyes, Threyna closed in on the Skeleton King's back. Floating in lazy circles above the dead zone, he gave no sign of sensing her. She reared her glaive, preparing to thrust it through his back and drive him into the Reaper's Landmine.

We'll go down together, you ghosting bastard.

She was right on top of him. Three heartbeats until impact, two, one.

He spun at the last moment, deflecting Threyna's thrust with the blade of his scythe. She countered as they toppled towards the ground. The combination of his twist and her momentum nearly sent her sailing past him. She let her glaive disintegrate, using her hands instead to grapple with the haft of his scythe as they both wrenched and turned, entwined as they plummeted. He let his own scythe crumble to ashes, attempting to disengage with her, but she grabbed a fistful of his billowing cloak and seized *Pure* from her belt. He tried to shove her away, but Threyna slashed him across the cheek. Dark blood sprayed across his pale flesh. She reared to strike again, but the ground was fast approaching.

"Blow it!" Threyna screamed. "Blow it!"

Sound ceased. A blinding white explosion overtook her peripheral vision, but she kept her focus fixed on the Skeleton King. His blue eyes stretched wide, pupils shrinking in the erupting glow of radiant energy. Black veins bled out of the irises, corrupting the whites as the blood from his cheek left a trail in their wake.

She'd made him bleed. Now she'd end him. Even if it was the last thing she'd do.

The soundless white light swallowed them both.

CHAPTER 60

ALL THAT IS GOOD

Laela XXIII

Inquisitors advanced, arcanatek whirring, swords at the ready. They marched to her doom. The end of the Wraith. The end of hope itself.

Tears stung her eyes, rolled down her cheeks, and fell to the sodden ground. *Everything was for nothing.* Neutreen had abandoned her, forsaken her, and left her to hollow on this beach. To forever stare out at the open expanse of the ocean beyond and never know the freedom it offered. It was a cruel torment, one that would last for eternity if she hollowed. One that would be abundantly brief if she became a shade or darkling.

Still on all fours, sword hilt beneath her palm, she looked out over the First Legion on the shoreline, the impaled Wraith writhing on spears, and *The Dauntless* burning. But beyond the smoke and flames, just past the breakers in the distance, the clouds that enshrouded Rheynia burned away. The sky was a lighter gray, almost a pale blue.

"No running anymore," her father said. *"Ya can't win… but you still gotta sword."*

He was right. She averted her gaze from the future she'd nearly had and gripped the hilt of her sword to take hold of the only justice she could claim for herself. It wasn't fair. None of this was fair. Yet she'd spent years before Neutreen's shrine, kneeling in modesty, living in moderation, earning her merit. She knew where she measured up in society. She was a sword—a weapon forged to break the throne of tyranny. And not just any sword, but the First Sword of the Wraith.

I will not lie down for them. If they want me, if they want us, they will have to take us. I will be strong. I will be courageous. We will fight to flee.

Her heart hammered in her chest. Her tears burned away as rage warmed her cheeks. The Inquisitors' footfalls drew nearer, their arcanateks warbling louder. All around her, she felt the contagion of fear infecting her people. It clung to her as well, but she would not give it a foothold. She would not let it in. Not while she had a sword in her hand and fire in her heart.

The scent of smoke on the wind returned her father's screams to her ears. The ire of his voice, his condemnation had tempered her into hardened steel. Steel that would make the Order bleed before she met her end. She sank into her Center of Silence, allowing all else to fade away.

She glared up at the approaching Inquisitors in their skeletal masks. Only a few paces away, with more legionaries at their backs, they would be Laela's final offering to Neutreen. She launched forward with a bloodlusting cry.

The unsuspecting Inquisitors turned towards her, but too late. She slapped one blaster aside, deflected a sword thrust, and countered with a hack that cleaved into an Inquisitor's pauldron. The screech of metal on metal was the first in a chorus of clangs. Aylenia was beside her, skewering an Inquisitor through his plate mail. Dracus, adjacent to her, hacked and slashed as if he wasn't already hollowed.

Vortexers fired, dragging shades from their targets, but the Wraith's numbers overwhelmed the Inquisitors. Laela led the charge, pushing them back and carving her way into the legion's formation.

She slashed at the weak joints in the Inquisitors' armor—the backs of knees, the folds at the elbow. Legionaries closed in around her. She blocked a thrust, kicked another away, caught a chop at the hilt, and stabbed a legionary through the chest. Without wasting a moment to see if his soul would depart or he would hollow, she found her next target. First with a punch of her free hand, then with an up-cleaving swipe.

His head rocked back, and blood burst like a fountain from his mouth. Laela slashed horizontally across his chest, more to clear him out of the way of her warpath than to finish him. As he fell, three more filled his place, but they were no match for her.

In the years since the fall of Victarius Kaine, the Order had grown soft. Weak in their sense of security, brittle in their belief that no one would challenge them. Gone were the days of soldiers like Dracus Alius. These men were chaff, Dreadroots to her Pythwoods, kindling to her fire.

Laela carved across another legionary's throat, cutting him to the bone. Sensing someone behind her, she threw her elbow into where his nose ought to be. Though it connected, the contact was more jarring to her than she'd anticipated. Deflecting a weak chop with poor edge alignment, she parried with a thrust to the legionary's gut, sending him stumbling into his brothers. But the assailant behind her struck again.

She turned and stabbed, burying her blade between the segmented plates of his armor and deep into his belly. He seemed barely to have noticed. With her blade hilt-deep in his organs, he did not recoil. Did not pause in shock. Hollowed beyond any sense of humanity, the fallen Inquisitor reached for her face. A gauntleted hand clawed at her, attempting to tear her flesh from the bone. Laela took a step back to regain leverage, but another hollowed seized her ankle.

An arcanatek's warble resounded. The hollowed Inquisitor dropped as a shade tore free from his armor. Aylenia shoved him aside, stabbing her short sword past Laela into the legionary at her back. Bhen kneed a legionary in the groin, then pounded his pommel into the back of his head. Dracus swept in beside him, quicker than a hellhound and twice as fierce. Blaster in one hand, short sword in the other, he wove between legionaries. Stab, fire. Slash, charge. Thrust, fire. Slice, recharge. Not waiting for the vortex to fully prepare its charge, he didn't rip souls free from their bodies, but he spent the Undergrounders' power coils at will, doing just enough to stun his next target.

Vigor restored by the Wraith's surge, Laela stomped on the hollowed grasping at her ankle. Kicking it away, she wrenched her sword free from the Inquisitor Aylenia had vortexed to return to the fray. She drew *True* in her free hand. Thrusting, slashing, and stabbing her way forward, Laela carved a path through the Order's legion, searching for Belrich and vengeance. But there were too many.

No matter how many legionaries fell, more Wraith littered the ground. If it hadn't happened already, it wouldn't be long before Decimus's First Legion ascended the steppe and finished them off, but if that was to be their fate, they would suffer having exhausted all their hope.

Spattered in the blood of others, surrounded by the souls of the departed, Laela would fight until her last living breath. She backhanded one legionary across the side of his head, tearing his green-plumed helm from his head. She stabbed past the disoriented legionary, piercing his brethren between the nose guard and the faceplate, then jabbed *True* into the neck of her first target.

Blood spurted down her fingers and along *True's* hilt, but its blade was not buried in a man of the Order. Not a true soldier in the Holy Dominion's Legions. He was but a boy. A boy without even a wisp of hair on his chin. Greener than the Fayte banner, as young as the Wraith itself, he stared back at her, wide-eyed and terrified.

Laela hesitated. *Boys. Not soft, arrogant men. Boys.* She pulled *True* free, but the blood on her blades felt heavier. The white-and-gray tunic and britches she'd left Octarius in were stained a gory red and brown. The darklings overhead and the shades passing through the battlefield watched in judgement.

"Laela!" Aylenia shoved into her, knocking her aside. She chopped downward, cleaving a gash across the boy's face from his brow to his opposite lip. He twisted and fell, releasing his sword as he died. But not before he thrust his blade forward.

Aimed for Laela, but pushed aside by Aylenia, the legionary boy's steel took Aylenia in the gut.

Laela screamed within her Center of Silence until it shattered. Blood thundered behind her eyes until all she saw was red. Anger consumed morality. Hatred devoured humanity. The brutal beauty of battle bled out, and from the hollowing body of hope, a thrashing whirlwind of steel and fury emerged—a darkling dead set on destruction.

Screams cried from beyond the red veil. Voices called for Neutreen. Laela even thought she heard her own name. Steel licked at her skin, grazed on her flesh, but she ignored them. They were just distractions that sought to sever her from her vengeance.

Ships burned. Wraith trapped. Aylenia dying.

She would not be denied. But her sword swung wildly, *True's* thrusts came slowly, her feet staggered lazily, and eventually, the combination of the cuts she'd sustained and the exhaustion of her battle-born fury sank her to her knees.

Her vision returned as her rage faltered. There was a sword through her belly. She didn't remember it happening. Even now, staring at it, she barely felt it.

Legionaries stood over her, around her, yet they gave her a wide enough berth to see all that she had wrought. Dozens littered the ground. But not enough. Never enough.

"Laela!" Aylenia called. "Please!"

She was still alive, kneeling just a few paces away. A pair of legionaries grabbed her under each of her arms and hoisted her to her feet. Behind her, Lord Premius Decimus raised a spear.

Laela's jaw unhinged. Blood spilled out. *No. No.*

Decimus brought the spear down. Through the top of Aylenia's shoulder, down the length of her spine, and out through the front of her hip.

Aylenia's face contorted. Her body writhed, and though her mouth opened, no scream came forth.

Decimus drove the spear deeper until its tip pierced the wet ground. The legionaries hoisting Aylenia up released her. But there she stayed, fixed to the spear. Dying. Suffering.

Laela couldn't move. Couldn't breathe. She stared past Aylenia to the crashing waves beyond. Unable to watch Aylenia's torment, awaiting her own, she lowered her eyes. She clenched *True* in her fists, but nothing good was true in this world. Only pain. Only suffering. Only failure.

CHAPTER 61

THE FALL

Threyna XXVI

Crimson became her entire existence. Her whole world was awash with blood. Red clouds marred the sky. Red bodies littered the ground around her. Red spires held writhing red figures in its twisted limbs. Red. Red. Red.

Did I hollow? Am I a shade? A darkling?

Lying on her back, Threyna patted her torso. *I still have my body.* She attempted to roll to the side, but she felt like her soul would slip free of its mortal shell if she dared. Despite the risk, she forced herself up from her back to support herself with her hands. *Pure* rested in a pool of blood beside her.

Not knowing how she survived, she seized *Pure* and scoured the battlefield. Still corpses surrounded her—their souls vortexed and irradiated by the blast of the Reaper's Landmine. It was a mass grave rivaling the Tellers' burnt bodies throughout the Scorch Lands, but it wasn't spread throughout the countryside; it was all here, confined to one small plot of dead land. Order legionaries and Underground Centuriots alike were strewn about. Those who fell before the detonation left bloody puddles beneath them, but those who fell victim to the reaping bomb's explosion were bloodless, soulless—dead and gone.

The battle beyond the blast seemed to stop as all beheld the devastation.

Threyna shouldn't have been here. The fact that she was only made her gut twist in knots. *If I survived...*

The Skeleton King rose to his feet as the wall of blood he'd conjured around them dissipated to ashes.

He blocked the reaping bomb...

He saved her. She wished he hadn't. She wished they were splayed on the ground as soulless and empty as those around them, because then at least her life and death could have meant something. They could have ended the Skeleton King's tyranny. But no. She was alive. And so was he.

Towering above her, he glared—not in anger, not with malice, but with the condescension of a god unable to believe that a mere mortal would bother with such paltry attempts on his life. Black veins slithered up his neck, but slowly, they were receding. He had more souls in his Inner Dungeon than she'd ever consumed.

Laela was right. There's no beating him.

He held out his empty hand, his scythe reforming. "You are weak. Selfish." He stared out into the distance, not even deigning to look at her. "I gave you scores of souls. Power to try and defeat me. But you lack the spine to do that which must be done, as all others have before you." He shook his head, the rot in his veins retreating to nothingness, leaving only a black stain behind. "Divided, ruin will reign. You have spoken those words, believed in them, trusted in them—yet you, like everyone else, have failed to honor them."

Threyna didn't understand. She scuttled backwards in an attempt to put distance between her and him, but he advanced, negating her progress.

"I gave the Seers that credo," the Skeleton King said. "I gave the Artificers the same. It fell to you—the Underground—and again you have proven that axiom impossible to achieve." He loomed over her, clutching his bloodborne scythe in bony fingers. He drew in a short sharp breath, desiccating the bodies around them. The wound on his cheek from where she'd slashed him sealed shut until only a scar remained.

"I prayed the One True God could be proven wrong. That I could be defeated. That the whole world could live in peace and harmony absent this, this…" He inspected the sallow flesh of his free hand before curling it into a fist. He released a slow, defeated sigh, before refocusing his haunting gaze upon her. "This curse is the answer. The only answer. We will never unite. We will always be divided. Peace cannot reign without the One True God's unity."

Threyna trembled, unable to form words. *He wanted to be defeated. He wanted us to unite against him. And yet… still we failed.* She glanced around, looking for someone—anyone else. Arilette and Lorath were ensnared in a spire's grasp. Canton and Rivich were nowhere to be seen. *We are divided. I am alone.*

"And now, Granddaughter…" The Skeleton King took another step forward. "You must join the One True God." He lifted his scythe high overhead.

Arilette screamed in the distance, but even suspended in the spire's tendrils, she threw something.

The scythe came down, intending to cleave her in two. Sinking into her Inner Throne and grasping at the pools of blood nearest her, she raised a half-formed trident. She caught the scythe's shaft between her prongs, the tip of its blade stopping a hair's breadth from the top of her head.

Inexplicably, her trident began dematerializing. The ashes fell from the prongs first, then the length of her shaft.

"Blood and bone bow to me," the Skeleton King said, fighting against her last resistance.

Then something hit the ground and sank in. A Dawnshard. An arm's length away, it beeped rapidly, signaling it was about to blow. Threyna inhaled sharply and rolled away from it. Her conjuration failed. The scythe hit the ground where she had been a moment ago. Threyna closed her eyes as radiant light exploded at her back.

The Skeleton King wailed. Threyna took the opportunity. She crawled away from him, stumbling over fallen legionaries and Undergrounders in an attempt to reach safety. But there was no safety. Her spotted vision struggled to focus despite having had her eyes closed and her back to the Dawnshard's brilliance.

The Skeleton King's wail became a roar. The wind whisked above her as he swung his scythe in a wide arc. *He's blinded. Go. Run.* He wouldn't need his sight to kill her, and now that he was done toying with her, she wouldn't even be able to conjure a means of defending herself if he could disintegrate her blood spawns.

Something grabbed her by the arm, hauling her away.

"I've got you." Canton slung his arm under hers, leading her away from the Skeleton King. "We need to get out of here. To the Tears."

Black rot pumping in her veins, spots blinking across her vision, she skipped between bodies and leapt alongside Canton, attempting to keep pace.

The Skeleton King's laugh rattled the ruins behind her. "Run, Granddaughter! There is nowhere I won't find you. There is no succor. All will bow to the One True God!"

The spires that had risen into the sky erupted ever higher, carrying with them scores of Undergrounders. Then, all at once, they dissolved into ash, the empty air opening its arms to them. As high as Octarius's tallest towers at the peak of the Kaines' might, they fell. Arilette, Lorath, so many others. Their screams rose as their bodies plummeted.

Canton didn't give Threyna the chance to look. He dragged her away, carrying her over the bodies littering the ground. "This way!" As flanking legionaries charged in towards Octarius's remains and the last of the Underground's forces, Canton led her in the opposite direction.

Somehow, the main column of the Order's wedge formation was decimated. The Underground had taken down more of the Order than Threyna had realized. She didn't understand how, but as they trampled over the fallen, she noticed that the bodies beneath her feet all wore Order blacks.

"Into the river," Canton said as they neared the Tears. "It can carry us to the Grip. Maybe they haven't left yet. Maybe we can…"

Threyna wasn't listening. The Skeleton King's presence within her Inner Throne called to her, taunting her. *Don't leave without saying goodbye, Granddaughter.*

Threyna stopped before the Tears, her own sobs sending streaks down her cheeks as she turned to face the Skeleton King. Hovering high on draconic wings, he held someone by the throat.

Mother…

She struggled, attempting to free herself from the Skeleton King's chokehold.

Threyna felt as if she were being strangled. Failure denied the breath from her lungs. Loss flushed her cheeks. Rot thickened in her veins as it encroached on her heart and built pressure behind her eyes.

She retreated into her Inner Throne, but the Skeleton King's tower outside the windows of her throne room seemed to have grown—wider, taller, closer. It pulsed with power, making the walls of her mind palace tremble. A great wind shattered the stained glass, tearing the shingles from the roof of her seat of power and threatening to cave in the pillars that supported it. Threyna resisted the draw, but outside her Inner Throne, trapped in the Skeleton King's grasp, her mother could not. Shades and darklings left her mother's body, rushing back towards the Skeleton King as he drew in breath. Dozens, scores, until not one remained.

She no longer struggled against his grip. She dangled—thin, frail, limp. He let her go.

Unceremoniously, she fell. Far off, silently, she hit the ground. Dead. Gone.

"Fly, Little Dove," the Skeleton King said within her Inner Throne. *"When I finish here, I'll find you. The One True God will have his wish. Peace will reign."*

A tug pulled at Threyna's hand, attempting to drag her away. She didn't want to move. She didn't want to run, to prolong the agony. She wanted it to end.

The tug became a yank, and before she could catch herself, she was falling. Falling like Arilette. Like her mother. Cold washed over her. Darkness enveloped her.

CHAPTER 62

THE SPIRIT OF RESILIENCE

Threyna XXVII, Dracus XVI, Laela XXIV

Threyna

The river's chill sapped Threyna of whatever hope remained. It had washed them south to the bend before slowing to a trickle, forcing them to climb out and make the rest of the journey on foot. Not that it mattered. Everything was lost.

"There were two landmines," Canton had explained when Threyna asked about Rivich. *"The one we knew of, and… another at the back of their formation. Rivich was only a few paces ahead of me. If I—"*

"Did it get Belrich?" she'd asked despite already knowing the answer.

He wasn't there. Neither was Decimus. Yet Threyna had sent Canton and Rivich after them, hoping it would keep them clear of the Reaper's Landmine. *I sent him away to protect him, and yet I sent him to his end anyway. Just like Daeton. Just like Yevon and Ebrus.* Again, she'd made a call, and it got someone killed.

"I don't think Arilette intended for you to survive," Canton had said. *"She sent you in to lure him out. If you hadn't changed course to defend our flank, she may have tried to catch you both in the landmine."*

Threyna hadn't wanted to hear it. She didn't care about Canton's analysis. But trudging along the Tears and heading towards the Grip, Threyna couldn't help but see the validity of his argument. Arilette wouldn't have wanted a Skeleton Queen to deal with after they'd won. Whether it was her idea or Lorath's, it didn't matter. The results were the same, and this new betrayal didn't make her feel anything. She was already cold, empty, and defeated.

They walked in silence for a time, but Threyna's mind remained busy, trying and failing to conceive what she should have done differently, what could have tipped the scales in their favor. Nothing. Their defeat was inevitable.

All will join the One True God.

"Maybe they're still there," Canton said of the Wraith, ever the optimist.

They weren't. At least she hoped they wouldn't be. Even though it meant her demise, Threyna hoped he was wrong and they were long gone. Because if they were still there, that meant something went wrong. And that something had Belrich's cruel touch all over it. She didn't give such thoughts voice. If there was any justice in the world, they would arrive to find a beach of legionaries staring out at the departed ship bound for Sansia. Then at least the Skeleton King's cursed blood artifact would disappear, Dracus and Fawkes would receive what small measure of peace came with a true death, and Threyna could bow to the One True God knowing that Laela and Aylenia had at least made it out.

Please, just let me have that.

Perhaps she should have been angry with Laela. If they had fought together, perhaps they could have defeated the Skeleton King, as he had always wanted. She'd always thought it was Belrich who allowed the Underground to live on, a convenient sufferer in the stocks to blame for all that was wrong with the Order's Holy Dominion. But it was King Bohen. If he wanted to stamp them out, he could have at any point in time; he gave them opportunities to band together and try to stop him. But even if the Seers, Artificers, Tellers, Undergrounders, and Wraith had all rallied together, would it have made a difference?

"We were never going to be able to win this," Threyna said. "Laela and Dracus were right. We never should have stayed, Cant."

Canton didn't respond. He soldiered on in silence, trekking ahead at a grueling pace believing they could still catch up to the Wraith. Over time, however, his pace slowed, his head hung, and in their silence he too reasoned out what Threyna had already accepted; it was hopeless.

"We were so close," Canton finally said.

Threyna scoffed. *No we weren't.* Despite how many marched on Octarius, that wasn't even the entirety of the Skeleton King's force. Belrich, Decimus, the Inquisitors, the Doves who comprised his spy network, the boys who hadn't graduated the Nest yet—they weren't at Octarius. Which only begged the question of where they were.

Anywhere but the Grip. Please, just let Laela escape. Laela, Aylenia, Dracus, please...

"We were, Threyna," Canton said. "We had the technology. If we'd stayed together, if we'd recruited more to our cause, we would have had the numbers. And you..." He grinned.

His expression wasn't befitting of the dreary riverbed they walked, the decisive defeat they'd suffered, or the inevitable end they neared, yet it remained. Painted to his face, a mockery of all they'd lost, his smile only stretched longer.

"You were incredible," Canton said, gushing. "I know we didn't win, and this is likely the end for us. But you made him bleed, Threyna. That must count for something."

It didn't count to Threyna. Close didn't matter. They either won or lost, and they had lost. She snorted. "A feather short of Neutreen's wings—isn't that what the Elysians say? Might as well have spared the matches. We're not making it to Valencia either way."

"Not all losses are in vain. The same way not all victories get songs. The Skeleton King had to hide away for a decade, collecting souls and gathering his strength, and he still barely survived. There is hope for the future of Rheynia... if not for us. People will rise again, join together, and one day defeat him and his One True God… maybe not today or tomorrow, but one day. I believe that, Threyna. Even now."

Threyna wished she shared in his belief. But she didn't. Canton had probably convinced himself that Dracus would be proud of him for fighting the good fight. He probably believed her father would be proud of her too. A valiant effort. It was all a gory ghosting lie. There was no such thing as a moral victory.

As if the wind agreed with her sentiment, a gust carried not the scent of the salt sea, but the taint of defeat. *Smoke.* Threyna inclined her gaze to the horizon. Black tendrils climbed to the clouds that shrouded Rheynia in darkness.

Canton followed her gaze. "The ship…" He sank to his knees, finally coming to terms with what Threyna had already feared. They had reached the end of their journey. Ruin would continue its mighty reign.

But a silhouette stood before the windswept smoke—tall, thin… motionless. Before Threyna knew it, she was running. Heart heavy as it thudded in her chest to the rhythm of her footfalls, she feared what she would find on the beach. The smell of smoke grew stronger. The sound of screams rose above the crashing waves. The spilled blood called to her upon her Inner Throne.

Bodies of both legionaries and Wraith littered the way. Bounding over them as she had in her flight from Octarius, Threyna scanned their faces.

Please, no. Not Laela. Not Aylenia. Blood and bone, please.

Threyna didn't spot their faces as she leapt between the fallen, but she found a dagger plunged into the earth at the center of a group of corpses. *True* was engraved in the hilt.

No…

Threyna knelt down to pick it up, the twin to her dagger, *Pure.* The gift her father had given to Laela. Clutching it, she inclined her gaze to the figure overlooking the sea.

Pierced from neck to navel, a woman looked out to the smoky sky, impaled on a spear. Threyna attempted to speak, but the knot in her throat forbade it. The scent of death would have been strong enough to make her gag if she could manage to breathe. But she couldn't.

Aylenia turned her head at her approach, blood dribbling from her lips, eyes drooping in the fading moments of consciousness. "Threy…" she wheezed.

Threyna whimpered, falling to her knees behind the spear that impaled Aylenia. Beyond her, dozens of spears lined the shore, each erecting familiar faces. Some squirmed as they suffered. Others writhed, already hollowed. Others yet remained stock-still, their souls departed. But the army in black dominated the sands. There were still two for every Wraith left standing as they waited their turn to receive a spear of their own.

She searched for Laela among them, but found Dracus first, kneeling before Belrich and Decimus. A short distance from him, a woman sat in a puddle of blood with her back towards her. Her shoulders sagged. Her ribs rattled with silent sobs as new tears streamed down her face at the horror of it all.

Laela… they're making her watch.

It was horrible. Worse than the Battle of the Cut. More vile than the ruins of Octarius. More destructive than all of the Disasters combined. She couldn't think, couldn't move. Paralyzed by failure, overrun by loss, she wished she were standing on a Reaper's Landmine with the detonator in hand.

"Threy…" Aylenia groaned again. She extended a bloody, trembling hand. "Did you… do it?"

Threyna took her hand, wishing she could offer Aylenia the comfort of a lie to ease her passing. But she couldn't. The twitch in her clammy fingers, once so dexterous, made her want to vomit. The stickiness of the blood dripping down her arm made her want to scream. "We lost, Aylenia… it's over."

"No." Aylenia's quivering fingers found the strength to squeeze Threyna's hand. "Always another fight."

Threyna had no fight left in her. The rot in her veins sought to strangle the last of her humanity and leave her for the Skeleton King.

"Consume me…" Aylenia said. "Fight."

Dracus

"Look at what we have here," Belrich said as he sauntered over. His attention was divided between where Dracus was being held at sword point by two Inquisitors and a smidge of dirt beneath his fingernail. Flicking the refuse away, he regarded Dracus much the same.

Dracus struggled within the Inquisitor's grasp, but he'd sustained three fresh cuts in the battle, each luring him closer to the abyss of hollowing. A thrust that clipped the meat between his neck and shoulder, a diagonal slice across his bicep, and a stab wound to his thigh. Each should have been enough to hollow him in their own right, but with Fawkes's soul in a jar on Decimus's hip, he could not let go. Not when they were so close.

The Inquisitors shoved Dracus to his knees. The wet sand forgave his intrusion, squishing to accommodate his new posture before Belrich. Despite his predicament, his was a kindness compared to those erected on spears along the beach. Joining Rosler and Taggart, Redge, Bhen, and Asla were positioned before the burning ship, watching as their last hopes went up in smoke. All while Laela was forced to witness.

Bhen hollowed, limbs still grasping for any that came near. Redge struggled for a while, but eventually, his darkling tore free. Dracus wasn't sure if he was irradiated or trapped in a soul jar, but what did it matter? Asla, for all the fight she possessed in life, left the pain of her body as a shade, attempting to wander away. She didn't make it very far. Vortexed into a soul jar, she would soon be consumed. Even if Threyna managed to defeat the Skeleton King, someone on this beach would take the fatekeeper from around Dracus's neck, find the Blessing, and use it for the purposes of the One True God.

Dracus glanced from Belrich to Decimus, wondering whose hands it would be more dangerous in. Either way, the world was all blood and bone.

"Did you ever imagine the day, Decimus," Belrich began, "Dracus Alius—lounging on a beach?" His chuckle entwined with the screams—those of the dying, the hollowed, or the poor souls watching and waiting for their turn to do the same.

"No, Legatus," Decimus said, ever the paragon of duty. He failed to meet Dracus's eyes, but then again, Dracus could barely look upon him either.

It was difficult to reconcile how the man that had taught him everything could knowingly serve such a monster and call it honor, righteousness, fealty. Yet he imagined it was no easy draft of Valefyre for Decimus to swallow either for his esteemed protégé to fail in his duty and rebel against the very power that lifted him from the rubble in the wake of the War of the Seers.

Belrich smirked. "Dear, old Decimus, don't look so grim. You had to have known that Darkling Dray's days were numbered." Belrich leaned down, looming over him how a parent might an infant. "Ever since poor, poor Dracus ran from Bheric's Hollow."

Dracus spat a glob of bloody phlegm on Belrich's boot. To his chagrin, Belrich didn't even appear dismayed, his infuriating grin still plastered upon his face.

"Tell me, Dracus," Belrich said, softly, almost tenderly. "Why did you run? A storied career—every accolade as a Justicus, every victory as a Premius—why did you throw it all away?" He shook his head as if perplexed by the enigma that Dracus didn't want to sacrifice children to preserve the life of a tyrant king.

"Was it the child?" Belrich asked. "The boy you ran off with? If you wanted boys to spear, we could have given you boys."

Dracus snarled. "You're a gory ghostin' darkling."

Belrich raised his hands in mock surrender, erecting from his leaned posture. "Not that then. Apologies. Blood and bone, so easily offended. Forgive me. But… why?" He gestured his hands to the row of impaled

Wraith, growing longer down the coast with each passing moment. "Is he here—your boy?"

Dracus glared. The bristles of his mustache impressed upon his curled back upper lip. He wanted to hollow, throw caution to the wind, and maul Belrich. He imagined ripping free of the Inquisitors, pouncing on Belrich, and sinking his teeth into the soft flesh of his neck. But then Fawkes would suffer in Decimus's hands.

"No," Dracus said. "He ain't here. Hollowed got 'em."

Belrich pressed his lower lip forward, pouting at Dracus before turning to Decimus. "All these years—hiding with Tellers, sleeping in the Underground's hovel, dreaming of a daring escape with the Wraith… all for a boy. Was it worth it?"

Dracus snorted, recalling the endless questions the boy would ask. How quick he was to pick up a sword. How brave he'd been in the face of hollowed. In the beginning he'd found it tiresome, burdensome. Even after he'd grown to care for the boy, he only saw Canton's courage as a danger he and Fawkes had to overcome to keep him safe. Looking back at the last seventeen years—between surviving with the Tellers, fighting alongside the Undergrounders, and preparing with the Wraith—he couldn't help but smile. *Was it worth it?* He grinned at Belrich. "I'd trade a hundred lifetimes in the Order to do it all again."

Striking like a viper, Belrich grabbed Dracus by the collar of his tunic and twisted. His mocking tone became one of wrath and malice. "Why!"

Belrich's heated breaths filled Dracus's nostrils. His mercurial rage told of the frustration that this question had caused over the course of years.

Dracus continued to grin. He closed his eyes, sinking into his pain and taking joy in Belrich's, despite how he tried to hide it.

He met Belrich's harsh gaze. "Because I believed in the lie of the Order. Not the ghostin' propaganda of Neutreen, not the Purge. *'Where there's order, there's justice.'* Order after the Disasters ripped us apart. Order after wars devastated anything else left standin'. Order. Safety. Peace for the livin', in a world of the dead. Ya name me traitor. Ya call me the darkling, but I'm the only one who stayed true. So why, you ask? Because I fight for the livin'. And that boy, he lived! Not as long as he shoulda, not as well as he deserved, but I gave that boy a chance."

And a choice...

Whether due to his words, his thoughts, or the way Belrich twisted his collar, Dracus became keenly aware of the fatekeeper on his neck. *The fatekeeper... the Blessing.*

Before Threyna had given him charge of it, he had given it to her. It was never meant for her. Bherus had handed it to him ten years ago, before the Battle of the Cut. He wanted Dracus to finish his objective, should he fail. But Dracus made a choice. He declined Bherus's last request. Yet now he was presented with the same opportunity, the same mission.

"If I fail," Bherus had said, *"should I suffer and the Skeleton King live—if the Order is still in power, you must open this. You must do what I could not. Finish this."*

Dracus closed his eyes. *What d'ya say, Old Boy? Think I got one last trick up my sleeve? One more shot at this?*

Fawkes couldn't respond, but Dracus knew his answer. He shook his head, staring past Belrich to the sky beyond, preparing for how he was going to break free of Belrich and the Inquisitors to open the fatekeeper. But figures upon the steppe made him balk. Beside where Aylenia was impaled, Threyna and Canton came into view.

A wave of conflicting emotions and dark thoughts crashed into him. It took every fiber of his being not to react at the risk of drawing Belrich's attention. He didn't know what happened at Octarius. He didn't know if Threyna would be able to do anything that could put the darklings back in the soul jar, but if he took the curse upon himself—together, they might just be able to finish this.

A resolve returned to him. Not the desire to hollow and destroy, but hope. Hope that this wasn't the end. That everything that had led them to this point wasn't all in vain.

"Find a way," Bherus had said. *"Keep playing."*

This story wouldn't have any heroes, but it would have survivors.

He stared Belrich dead in the eye. "I gave that boy a chance and a choice," Dracus said again. "That's all any of us really deserve."

Before Belrich could respond, Dracus threw himself onto his back, staggering the Inquisitors and dragging Belrich atop him. The wounds from the Vendetta daggers screamed as he rolled, but he kicked Belrich over his shoulders and freed himself from the hands that bound him. Decimus drew his sword and advanced, but Dracus seized Fawkes's fatekeeper and squeezed the octagonal arcanatek's sides.

The Blessing tore free. Red, black, and slithering—the blood artifact wrapped around Dracus's wrist and slithered up his arm, searching for a place to bite. All eyes were on him, everything else on the beach forgotten.

"The Blessing!" Belrich shouted.

Laela

The stab wound in her gut throbbed as new screams joined the haunting choir. All she could do was watch as the legionaries went down the line, impaling her friends, her followers, and anyone brave enough to defy the Order. She wished she'd die faster. Hollow out. Become a darkling and haunt Belrich. Become a shade and be irradiated. Even if she was trapped in a soul jar, she wouldn't have to witness the suffering of everyone she'd failed.

She should have hollowed days ago on the Spine. Her life should have ended with Tarus's treachery. And now, bleeding from a dozen different wounds with a gaping hole in her gut, still she remained. But that seemed to be her fate; she wouldn't die until everything she'd cared for was ruined.

She wondered if Threyna, Canton, and the Undergrounders fared any better. After all, the Order too had divided its force to stop them from leaving. Maybe Threyna defeated the Skeleton King as she claimed she would. Maybe she was the fool to believe that he couldn't be defeated.

If we had stayed and fought together, would we have won? Would we have survived?

If they'd won, that didn't mean that they'd have had to stay forever. They could have built a new ship and left for Sansia. If they'd stayed and fought, Arilette might have allowed them to return as they pleased, ferrying all who desired to new lands. But they hadn't stayed. They hadn't fought. And now, Laela would never know.

Another spear. Another scream. Another life ruined by the Order's form of justice.

Her vision darkened at the corners as death's familiar approach closed in around her. The pain in her stomach rivaled that of her broken heart. She knew Aylenia was staring down at her, suffering and dying upon the steppe—if she hadn't already hollowed.

She should have stayed. She could have lived.

"Years," her father said. *"I been tellin' ya this for years. Now you'll die on your knees."*

She anchored herself in her Center of Silence to block him out, but the scar across her chest burned worse than the gash in her stomach. The guilt chewed a hole through her, body and soul. She looked at the smoke climbing into the sky. The ship's wood wasn't anointed with the proper prayers to carry its smoke to Neutreen's ears, but the Goddess of Justice likely wouldn't hear it in either case. Despite the futility and the hopelessness in her heart, she held the stocks and prayed.

"See me," Laela whispered to the rising smoke. "I have served at your altars on bended knee, stocks raised. I have given the shirt off my back despite winter's chill, offered food from my plate even as my stomach growled for more. I submitted when needed and rose when called upon everywhere you've seen fit to position me. Never did my supplications end without blessing your name. Not once have I questioned you. I have abided by the Four. Now see me for what I've become."

More screams rose as the fires consuming the ship roared, billowing more smoke to Valencia. Laela wanted to sink into the sand, bury herself and wait for the tides to roll in. *What good has any of it done?* She closed her eyes.

"I chased after you my entire life. Do you see what I have done? I forsook a sister in need chasing after you. I blamed a mother for her suffering because her pain wouldn't bring us closer to you. Tell me, what was it for?"

The question broke every principle of the Tenets. Modesty be damned, Moderation denied—Laela tired of measuring her life by the merits she'd earned for a faith that had failed her.

"I don't want my wings," Laela said, the realization welling new tears in her eyes. "I don't want to live for a life beyond this one if I must abandon everyone in it. But if you can hear me, if you still have power, if there is any point in any of this at all—please, Neutreen, see Threyna. Let her fight where I have run. Let her win where I have failed."

"Why!" Belrich snapped, breaking Laela from her prayers.

Tears rolled down her cheeks as she opened her eyes. Belrich loomed over Dracus. Held in place by two Inquisitors, hollowed and in pain that Laela couldn't begin to comprehend, a fire gleamed in Dracus's eyes brighter than that of the conflagration consuming their ship. He said something in response to Belrich's shout, but Laela couldn't hear it.

With a sudden jolt, Dracus threw himself backwards, toppling the Inquisitors and hurling Belrich to the sands over his shoulder. Dracus was up on his feet in the blink of an eye, Fawkes's fatekeeper held between his thumb and forefinger. The legionaries along the entire beach seemed to react at once as shouts resonated down the shore.

The two Inquisitors watching over Laela moved towards Dracus, as did Decimus and other nearby legionaries, but they all paused as a crimson creature blossomed forth from the fatekeeper. Red light flickered across Dracus's face and cast shadows behind the surrounding soldiers. The blood artifact elongated, circling his arm as it ascended his shoulder.

"The Blessing!" Belrich shouted. "Get him!"

Pain forgotten, fatigue thrown in the fire, Laela was on her feet before she could think about all the reasons why it wouldn't matter. Hobbled as she was, she didn't need an invitation to see what Dracus was trying to do.

If he becomes a blood mage, he can stop this. He can give us another chance.

Vision tunneled, heartbeat rapid and shallow, Laela lunged for one of the Inquisitors who'd abandoned her to advance on Dracus. His sword was drawn, but, more concerned with Dracus than her, he wasn't ready when she seized the hilt of his dagger in her left hand and shoved him forward with the right. As his neighbor wheeled on her, she jabbed with her reverse-grip and drove the dagger into the ear-hole of his helm. His shade left his body before his corpse hit the ground.

The sudden movement made her gut twist and her head spin, but she would not die on her knees. The Inquisitor she'd disarmed spun on her, short sword raised.

"The Blessing is mine!" Belrich charged at Dracus as the blood artifact continued to slither around him, searching for a place to attach.

The Inquisitor thrust. Laela barely managed to avoid his stab. Off-balance, she stumbled in the sands, tripping over the other downed Inquisitor. Her combatant swiped at her, but Laela grabbed his downed compatriot, bringing his armor between his blade and her flesh. The sword clanged off the skeletal mask of the helm. Reorienting herself, Laela took the discarded short sword from the dead Inquisitor and gained her feet.

Dagger in one hand, short sword in the other, Laela deflected a thrust, blocked a hack, and countered with her dagger. Splitting the segments of his cuirass, her blade found the flesh beneath. Ignoring the protest of her stomach, she twisted the blade. The Inquisitor fell back, holding his gut. Using the separation, Laela left him, closing the distance between her and Dracus as he backed away from Belrich, Decimus, and a combination of Inquisitors and legionaries. The blood artifact still circled his body, but had yet to attach.

What is taking so long?

"Don't let him take it!" Belrich launched himself at Dracus, slashing with his own sword. Rushed and clumsy, the strike went wide, and Dracus easily avoided it, but he was running out of room to evade.

Clutching her stomach with her forearm, bloody dagger still held in a reverse-grip, Laela staggered towards them. Decimus swung his short sword at Dracus. Dracus barely avoided the blow, reeling backwards, away from her.

The blood artifact snaked up to Dracus's neck, still unable to find purchase. It coiled, not in preparation to latch on, but to launch off and seek a new host.

It needs a host. Dracus is hollowed. It won't attach.

"You can do this, Laela," her father said. *"No more walls. No more half measures."*

Laela couldn't recall a time her father called her by name. But he was right; she couldn't let Belrich possess the Blessing. But more than that, she saw it for what it was—for what it could be. The blood artifact was the wings she'd always prayed for, a means to make the difference. A curse for her, but a path to freedom for everyone else. It was her means of fighting to flee, the Dawnshards her mother had charged into Caius's Bog with, her last chance to right the wrongs that would keep her and her people suffering in Rheynia for eternity. No longer walling herself off from her pain, she welcomed it, deriving from it the strength and courage to overcome.

Laela charged—not for Dracus, but the path between him and Belrich.

The red-and-black snakelike entity sprung from Dracus. Dracus shouted, reaching for it. Belrich and Decimus lurched towards it. But Laela wouldn't be denied. Finally understanding Threyna's sacrifice, she leapt to insert herself between Belrich and the blood artifact. She flew through the air, extending her sword arm as far forward as she could stretch. The Blessing continued to extend, uncoiling like a serpent, but too far out in front of her.

I'm not going to make it.

The blood artifact flew past. Close enough to feel its energy, to see the black lightning forking through its liquid body, but still too far. Her momentum died as gravity returned her to the sand. All she could do was watch as the red darkling collided with Belrich and began to wrap around him, searching for a place to attach to its new host.

Belrich's grin stretched from ear to ear as his eyes attempted to track the Blessing slithering up, down, and around him.

No.

It wasn't over. She wouldn't let it be over. Not once a glimmer of hope had returned. She wouldn't let its fickle spark fade. She pressed herself off of the sandy beach and threw herself at Belrich, forsaking her blades. Too entranced by the blood artifact, he never saw her coming. With one hand, she seized his wrist, controlling his sword arm. With the other, she attempted to grab the red serpent as it wrapped around his neck like a haunted pendant. Like trying to grasp the wind, it slipped through her fingers, around her wrist, and back around Belrich's neck.

As legionaries closed in on them, Laela wrestled him to the ground. Afraid of stabbing their Legatus, they hesitated to strike at her. She hooked her left leg around his and used her right leg to propel off the ground. Man, woman, and blood artifact rolled.

"Kill her!" Belrich shouted.

The Blessing ensnared both of them, never staying in one place too long. Belrich's forehead. Laela's neck. Belrich's shoulder. Laela's arm. Belrich's torso. Laela's hips. Entwined as they were, Laela couldn't determine if the blood artifact could tell them apart.

"It's mine!" Belrich screamed in her face.

She switched her legs and rolled back the opposite way, making sure she never left her back exposed to the legionaries' blades. Each movement lanced a spike of pain across her midsection, but she could not give up.

Please, choose me. Please.

The blood artifact wrapped around Belrich's throat again, as if it had searched all and finally made its decision.

No. No. Not him!

She pinned Belrich on his back and gripped his throat again as if attempting to choke the red liquid into choosing her instead. She knew she was exposed to the legionaries, but if the Blessing chose Belrich, all was lost. It coiled around Belrich's neck again, wrapping Laela's wrist in its bindings.

Please, choose me!

Wind rushed past her ear. The sound of a blade. The sound of death. She knew she was dead before she felt the pain. But still she didn't let go because the Blessing—this curse—was her only chance.

Threyna

"Always another fight," Aylenia said again. "Consume me. Fight."

Threyna cupped Aylenia's cheek in her hand. Aylenia didn't know what she was asking. She could consume her and put her out of her misery, but she couldn't use her soul. She wouldn't trade her for a few more moments with less rot in her veins. One soul wasn't enough to fight the legions, let alone to defeat the Skeleton King.

"I can't, Aylenia," Threyna said, sniffling. "But I won't let you suffer any longer."

"You can," Aylenia said, life fleeing from her eyes. "If anyone can change the tides, it's you." She closed her eyes. "Say it. Please. Always another fight."

She'd been unable to say it since Daeton's death. While there was always another fight, Threyna had lost the belief that she'd be able to win. *Always another victory.* They were just words, but she hadn't believed in them, not even enough to utter them. With all her losses piled before her, she didn't believe victory was possible. Yet Aylenia still squeezed her hand, still held out hope.

Is that all it takes? For so long now, she'd fought scared, so afraid of losing, that she'd given up trying to win. She'd taken a risk and lost Daeton, but it was the right decision gone wrong. Ever since, she'd been too hesitant to make the hard call. If she had stood up to Arilette, maybe she could have gotten Ebrus the help he needed, and he never would have been with her at Avengard. If she'd been more decisive in the bog, maybe she could have prevented her mother from taking charge and falling into the Skeleton King's hands. And if she'd fought the darklings controlling her mother outside Octarius, maybe she could have defeated the Skeleton King.

She was tired of *ifs* and *maybes*.

Father is gone. Mother is gone. Laela is gone. Ebrus, Yevon, Aylenia—all gone. She had nothing left to lose. In the wake of the realization, absolutism took root. Not like the dying roots of trees that twisted in Rheynia's mud, but like the towering Pythwoods that grew in Drakhardt before Damascus Drake chopped them down to build his fleet. Before the Disasters, before the Tellers burned them all down, they reigned on high and burrowed roots down deep—unyielding, unshakable.

She touched *Pure*'s hilt at her belt; *True* still in hand. The two were finally reunited. *Pure of thought. True in purpose.* Threyna was done fighting scared. She would fight with all she had and snatch victory from the skeletal grip of defeat. She would hope.

Threyna squeezed Aylenia's hand. "Always another victory."

Aylenia smiled. "Finish this. Prime?"

"Yes," Threyna said. But Aylenia's face contorted in pain.

Threyna couldn't let her suffer any longer. She drew in breath. Aylenia's soul came easily, leaving her body and entering her Inner Throne. Black vines slithered along the white marble, climbing the columns and snaking up the walls between the broken windows that were once so glorious. By comparison, Aylenia's spectral body wisped through the throne room like white smoke given shape. Compared to the darkness in and around her mind palace, Aylenia's light was practically blinding, a Dawnshard against the night.

Aylenia glanced at the door that led to Threyna's Inner Dungeon.

"No," Threyna said, feeling Aylenia's thoughts mesh with her own. *"You stay with me."*

Aylenia shook her head. *"You must fight, Threyna. Use me. Let me help."*

Threyna looked beyond her Inner Throne and out to the beach below. She knew how many legionaries lined the beach based on their heartbeats. She could sense the concentration of souls trapped within the soul jars on their hips. There were plenty of souls to fuel her conjurations, but not Aylenia.

She returned her attention back to the bloody tower just beyond the broken windows of her throne room. *"I won't use you, but you can still help me. Let me know if that tower gets closer."*

Aylenia followed her gaze. *"What is—"*

"The Skeleton King's coming." Threyna tallied how many souls were on the beach. *"I might not be able to defeat the Skeleton King, but I can fight these legionaries. I can consume enough of them to forge a bloodborne boat and carry the survivors to Sansia myself... I don't need to fight him."* She placed her hand on the shoulder of Aylenia's wispy form. *"Let me know when he draws near. I don't plan on being here when he does."*

She returned to the outside world. Canton watched in horror as Belrich stood over Dracus and Laela knelt before the line of skewered Wraith. Before the burning ship and down the coastline to the east, legionaries stood in pairs, holding the Wraith as they waited to be impaled. One by one. A long line of legionaries stood sentry, facing the grim scene, their backs toward her. There were enough legionaries and plenty of spears to end the Wraith's suffering quickly, but they wanted to draw out the dread. They wanted the anticipation of suffering to hollow them before their spears did. That cruel torture would be their undoing.

Threyna held *Pure* in one hand, *True* in the other. She nodded at Canton. "Steel yourself; we're not done here."

She didn't give Canton a moment to object. She slid down the dunes and onto the beach. The legionaries, too preoccupied with their victims, and the Wraith, too terrified of their immediate circumstances, didn't notice her. Neither did the sentries with their backs toward her. With her approach muffled by the lapping waves, the whip of the sea breeze, and the lash of the undying's screams, she neared the back of the closest legionary. The black rot pumping through her veins begged to be quenched, and she would provide it a feast.

She slashed at the exposed skin beneath the belted skirt of the nearest legionary, cleaving across the back of one knee, then sliced across the other before following up with a stab to his neck. Her blade tore through flesh. The neighboring legionaries reacted, but Canton took one unaware, jabbing his sword into his ribs and dropping him to the sands.

As the two bodies lost their hold on their souls, Threyna drew in breath, calling upon them. Both came willingly. She quickly spirited the shade and darkling into her Inner Throne, consuming them. The black vines snaking up the walls of her throne room began to erode.

Threyna parried a panicked thrust and spun to close the distance. Inside the legionary's reach, she slashed her twin daggers across his neck. His hand reached for his throat, but blood gushed between his fingers. Lurching out of the way of a stabbing spear, Threyna formed the fallen legionaries' blood into a web. Her conjured web ensnared the spear. With an opening to overcome his advantage of reach, Threyna planted *True* in the space between the spearman's plumed helm and green-trimmed pauldron. She drew in breath, calling upon two more souls.

The rot retreated as she feasted upon their vitality, allowing her the ability to conjure even more. Calling upon the exposed blood from the felled legionaries, she raised a series of spears from the sands, each stabbing up and out in a defensive perimeter. Her conjurations pierced through a handful of advancing legionaries' bellies, including one who was engaged with Canton. Canton took advantage, swiping across the impaled legionary's raised arm and stabbing him in the gap between his nose guard and face plate.

More souls. More power.

The rot ebbed away, allowing Threyna more conjurations. Daggers still in hand, she diverted a stab aside, and conjured a short spear before her. Following the spear like an army behind a battering ram, the bloodborne spear took a legionary through his leather cuirass, breaking ribs and puncturing his lung. Charging through him, she sliced and cleaved her daggers through the legionaries at his back. With quick thrusts and forceful punches, her steel found every gap in their armor. And every time she ripped *Pure* and *True* free, she called upon the exposed blood that sprayed forth and shaped it into a scythe. In a wide swinging arc, her conjured scythe obeyed her commands and slashed across three more legionaries' knees as they attempted to surround her.

Drawing in more souls and consuming them immediately, she forced them to bow to her will. They tried and failed to resist, each soul serving to strengthen her cause. But the legionaries holding the Wraith in preparation to impale them began to attack their captives, butchering them.

"The tower is drawing nearer!" Aylenia said from within Threyna's Inner Throne.

She needed to hurry if she was going to get people out of here.

Threyna conjured wings and called upon the spilled blood to form a layer of protective armor around Canton as he continued to fight. "Open their soul jars!" Threyna propelled into the air with a jump and a flap of her wings. Arcanatek whirred into motion, but she jettisoned away as they fired. Speeding towards the unarmed Wraith, Threyna sheathed her daggers. She conjured a scythe with greater reach to swipe at the Wraith's attackers. She couldn't save all of them, but she could help. Cleaving through legionaries as she passed, she drew upon the shades, darklings, and hollowed. Souls flowed into her, from the Order and Wraith alike.

"Aylenia, keep the Wraith in the throne room. Drive the legionaries into the dungeon!"

A score of souls filled her Inner Throne in moments, but with Aylenia's aid, the souls of the Wraith fell to command and those of the legionaries were forced through the door to her dungeons.

Threyna circled back towards Canton. Some of the Wraith had freed themselves and picked up the fallen legionaries' weapons to join the fight. A small group rushed to Canton's aid as he unleashed a soul jar.

An explosion of darklings and shades rose into the air. Threyna rushed in, drawing in breath. Power—greater than she'd ever experienced before—radiated within her. Empowered by the collaborative efforts of Aylenia and the Wraith working within her throne room, Threyna quickly ushered the darklings from the outside world into her Inner Dungeon. She was forced to consume some to continue her conjuring, but for every one she feasted upon, she sent three more into her dungeons for later use.

Canton, clad in the blood-forged armor, fought like a man possessed. It took a great deal of focus to maintain the conjuration, but it kept Canton alive. A spear thrust slid off his scarlet pauldron. A sword clanged off his bracer. He drove his short sword through the belly of another legionary as the Wraith charged up the beach to come to his aid.

Canton released another soul jar, directing the freed Wraith to do the same. While some darklings surged into nearby legionaries or Wraith, most swirled into the sky like rising smoke. Threyna drew in breath, consuming more and more until her dungeons were filled wall to wall with souls.

They wouldn't be enough to fight the Skeleton King, but they would be enough to help her conjure a ship that could carry the remaining Wraith beyond the island. The battle was quickly shifting as the Wraith took up arms against the legionaries, but something exploded to life within her Inner Throne. A dark cloud bursting with red lightning.

"Aylenia, what was that?"

"I was hoping you'd tell me!"

Even though she saw it inside her Inner Throne, she felt it on the opposite side of the beach by Laela and Dracus. "Canton, when you can, lead the Wraith upshore."

Canton hacked at a nearby legionary. "Where are you going?"

She didn't have time to explain. She dodged an irradiator's blast and swooped around the burning ship to take cover from other shots. Soaring upon a gust of wind, she banked a turn with speed, charging toward the explosion she'd sensed. As she neared, she saw its source.

On the beach, Dracus retreated from Inquisitors, Decimus, and Belrich. The red glowing blood artifact circled around him, searching for a place to inject its prongs.

Dracus opened it.

Pushing past the poetry of him taking on the mission her father had bestowed on him years ago, the possibility of victory blossomed within her. But just behind Dracus, Laela, bleeding from a dozen different wounds, stabbed a legionary in the ear and took up his sword. More were coming after her.

"Laela!" Aylenia cried within Threyna's Inner Throne. Her voice would never reach Laela's ears, but with their thoughts and emotions entwined in her mind palace, she felt the sentiment that accompanied her shout.

Determined, Threyna bent her scythe into a bow and drew back on the string. An arrow formed along the nock as she took aim and released. Attuned to the heartbeats of Laela's attackers, Threyna divided her single shaft into four needle-thin projectiles and guided them towards their own targets. Four legionaries fell behind Laela as she charged towards Dracus and Belrich.

Threyna drew again and released. Her arrows split and pierced the hearts of Inquisitors rushing to aid in Dracus's demise. But the blood artifact still hadn't attached to Dracus.

It won't. It wants a viable host. He's hollowed.

Suddenly, she understood why Laela was rushing toward him; she'd realized the same thing. *She's trying to become the next host.*

"Don't let him take it!" Belrich shouted.

The blood artifact coiled, preparing to forsake Dracus and find a new target. Belrich was closest. It couldn't be him. She flew in, firing more arrows as she neared, but despite her guidance, her arrows lodged into the backs of the Inquisitors following on Belrich's heels.

Cursing herself, Threyna swept in, but too late. The slithering red liquid abandoned Dracus and launched itself at Belrich. Laela dove, attempting to intercept it, but she fell just short.

The blood artifact wrapped around Belrich.

No! Threyna charged forward, flapping her conjured wings as hard as she could for Belrich. Before she could get there, Laela tackled him. She'd abandoned her sword and dagger, grappling Belrich and wrestling him to the ground. They entwined, and the blood artifact encircled both of them.

"The tower!" Aylenia shouted within Threyna's Inner Throne. *"It's coming closer. Quickly!"*

Threyna grit her teeth. She was running out of time if they were going to escape this beach. But if she let Belrich take the blood artifact, all would be lost.

"Kill her!" Belrich cried.

But his men were distracted. Decimus and a handful of other legionaries charged at Dracus as he picked up Laela's discarded weapons to defend himself. Others positioned themselves around Laela, but for the same reason Threyna couldn't afford to attack Belrich without the risk of hitting Laela, neither could the Inquisitors and legionaries attack Laela.

It will choose her. It has to.

Abandoning her attack on Belrich, trusting that the blood artifact would choose Laela, Threyna focused on the surrounding legionaries. Straightening her bow into her double-sided glaive, Threyna slashed and stabbed, cutting down every Inquisitor searching for an opportunity to stab at Laela. The blood artifact circled around Belrich's neck, but Laela seized him by the throat. The two continued to roll until Laela was on top, exposed. A pair of legionaries stepped in to stab her in the back.

Threyna landed on the sands behind them and slashed with one side of her glaive to part one's head from his shoulders. She pivoted and brought the other side of the glaive in an arcing uppercut that severed the arm holding the sword about to stab Laela.

The blood artifact's prongs bit deeply. A scream pierced the gloom, louder than all the others: Laela's. A red-and-black bracelet encircled her wrist. It chose her.

Dracus

Decimus slashed at Dracus's midsection as he advanced with three others. Dracus barely dodged out of the way. He deflected a legionary's thrust and backpedaled away from a second. Death rotted his flesh, and pain assumed dominion over his entire being, but sword in hand, surrounded by foes, Dracus felt alive.

He parried an overzealous lunge and countered with a disarming strike that crunched fingers between steel and hilt. The legionary cried out, dropping his sword to the sands. Dracus shoved past him, weaving between two other legionaries to keep Decimus at a distance. He sidestepped a vertical slash, ducked a horizontal chop, and stabbed a well-placed thrust into one of the legionary's shoulders. Taking what he could, Dracus withdrew, scampering away as his assailants reformed.

Threyna and Canton had come to their aid. The entire beach was in chaos. He didn't understand why the Blessing had rejected him. If he had known there was a chance of that, he never would have opened it. Hoping he didn't just make another Skeleton King by handing the blood artifact to Belrich, Dracus had more pressing concerns.

He ducked a swipe, high-stepped over a strike that intended to separate him from his foot, and parried Decimus's thrust. Dracus slashed across the nearest legionary's cuirass. His blade didn't find purchase through the armor, but it gave him the necessary space to step forward. The legionary with the wounded grip clutched his sword in his opposite hand. His attack, clumsy with poor edge alignment, slapped at him rather than cut. Dracus easily caught the sword on his own blade and drove Laela's discarded dagger into his neck.

The legionary with the weakened shoulder attempted to come to his aid, but Dracus met his steel. Overcoming his own pain as he'd grown accustomed to, he overpowered the legionary, using the leverage of his blade to slide down and thrust past his nose guard. Another fell. Another died.

Two remaining.

Decimus lurched forward, stabbing with his short sword as Dracus wrenched his blade free from the falling legionary's skull. He deflected just in time, but was poorly positioned to defend against the other legionary. Late in lowering his guard, the legionary's steel raked across Dracus's thigh.

The new cut's scream joined the horrid choir of his other injuries as the hollowing abyss called ever louder. But he would not hollow. Not with Fawkes's soul jar on Decimus's hip, Canton fighting for his life on the opposite end of the beach, and the barrier beyond the curse right before him.

Dracus dropped to a knee but raised his sword to catch a downward chop. He punched, dagger in hand, into the inside of the legionary's thigh, felling him like a Pythwood strangled by Dreadroot. As he fell, Dracus pushed off the sand to stab down, but his newly slashed thigh failed to obey. His attack missed, and new fire sliced across his back. Twisting away from Decimus's blade, Dracus fell to the ground, losing his grip on the dagger embedded in the legionary's thigh. Sand invaded his open wounds, only adding to the pain.

He could feel himself slipping away. Into the void. The chorus of agonizing injuries beckoned him to accept the darkness, to stop fighting the inevitable.

Focus on the pain. Stay. Fight.

Dracus refused to be dragged away from his pain. Not until it was his time, and now was certainly not.

He rolled towards the downed legionary, driving his forearm atop the flat of the blade to keep him from lifting it. With his free hand, he seized the legionary by his pauldron and reversed his momentum, dragging him atop him just as Decimus stabbed downward. The legionary gasped as Decimus's thrust took him in the back.

Not waiting to see what form the legionary's afterlife would take, Dracus shoved him off, taking his short sword. Decimus chopped down at him, but Dracus caught his strike between his blade and the legionary's discarded one.

"All these years," Decimus said, his eyes dark slits of disappointment. "All these years, this *chaos*, and still you fight."

Dracus slapped his sword aside and shoved himself to his feet, staggering away from Decimus. His back cried louder than the slash in his thigh. Decimus's slice had reopened the dressings that covered his injuries from the Vendetta daggers. Every movement offered a new wave of pain that made Dracus's vision tunnel until only he and Decimus remained on the beach.

He scoffed at his old mentor as the two circled one another. "I fight *because* of all these years. I'll make it mean something. All this suffering. All the ghost damned propaganda." He wiped his nose with the back of his hand. "I know what I'm fightin' for. What 'bout you, Dec?"

Decimus bristled. "My allegiances have not changed with the wind as yours have."

"Storms always seem ta be blowin' east to west. I just stopped lyin' to myself about which way was which."

The hollowed legionary that had been stabbed through the back gained his feet and staggered towards Decimus, limping heavily with his injured knee. Decimus swept the legionary's lead leg out from under him. As he fell prone, Decimus maimed him—stabbing him through the shoulders and hips and slicing across the back of his knees and ankles, ensuring that he would never rise again. Decimus barely averted his gaze from Dracus's through his grisly work.

"We could have talked about it," Decimus said, disgust plain upon his twisted face. "I could have explained where King Bohen and Prince

Belrich could not. You didn't need to betray us. You didn't need to run, to fight against us!"

Dracus turned his tunneled vision to where Laela sat atop Belrich, both of them glowing in the Blessing's red aura. Behind them, Threyna flew on conjured wings, slashing at legionaries and consuming the souls of fallen Inquisitors.

A runner. A fighter. In the end, we all gotta face our pains. Dracus was tired of ignoring his. The pain of guilt at what happened to Canton's family. The weight of regret that he hadn't been able to change things. The stain of failure to provide for a boy in this cursed world. If he'd confronted himself sooner, dealt with his issues, he could have actually listened to Canton.

How different could things have been?

There was no time to wonder. There was only Decimus and the soul jar on his hip.

"What could I have done?" Dracus asked. "I saw what Lacius saw before he deserted."

Decimus snarled. "You could have learned from his mistake. Where there is order, there is justice! Bohen is order. The Dominion is order. Yet look at what you have sown. And in the name of what? For what purpose?"

Choice. Dracus kept coming back to it, because that's all that mattered in a world without any. That simple, basic right in a Gods-forsaken world..

"We fight," Dracus said. "We run. Because if we don't, we *do* nothing. We endure only to serve. We bow only to scrape. We suffer only so that one tyrant can keep wearin' his gory ghostin' crown and call it peace." Dracus shook his head. "Nah, Decimus. I made my choice—now you gotta. Fight me or run. Do nothin' and I promise ya, I'll end you like I did Nerus, Jagras, and Artanius."

Decimus roared. He charged and Dracus met his ire. Their steels clashed, sending vibrations through Dracus's fist. They exchanged a flurry of blows; each clang rang like a bell tolling for justice. His dagger, *Fang*, the soul jar holding Fawkes's soul, and the blaster he'd carried all these years were belted at Decimus's hip. Dracus would reclaim them before this was over.

He feinted left, attacked right, and parried Decimus's counterblow. Stepping backward to invite Decimus's advance, Dracus pivoted, taking an off-angle to expose Decimus's backside. Decimus swiveled, repositioning himself, but something distracted him. His eyes flicked in the direction of the burning ship, just for a moment, but it was enough.

Dracus's tunnel vision didn't allow him to lose focus. He didn't hesitate, lashing out to seize advantage of Decimus's distraction. His blade caught his mentor's pauldron. Decimus staggered backwards, but then Dracus saw what had captured his focus in the first place. Clad in red armor, a figure led the charge of freed Wraith in their direction. Bodies in Order blacks littered the beach in their wake.

Decimus hmphed, lowering his guard as the shouting Wraith bore down on him. "This changes nothing. You may have won this battle, Dracus—" He pointed his sword at the burning ship. "—but King Bohen will not be denied. Order will reign." He dropped his sword to the sand, accepting his fate.

The Wraith, armed with the discarded weapons of Decimus's First Legion, drew nearer, their cries of vengeance growing louder with each footfall. The warrior leading the charge, clad in blood-forged red armor, held a bloody sword before him.

Canton.

Dracus had never seen a more glorious sight.

"Aye," Dracus said, grinning as he advanced on Decimus. He dropped his own sword, taking Fawkes's soul jar, *Fang*, and his blaster from Decimus's hip.

"What are you doing?"

Dracus stepped backwards. "Where there's order, there's justice. Yer life ain't mine to take."

Decimus's jaw hung open as the tide of Wraith washed over him.

Laela

Pain struck like a fork of lightning as the blood artifact sank its prongs into her wrist. Traveling up her arm like a rolling wave of fire, it surged through her. She became pain itself as it enveloped her in its all-consuming wrath. The curse filtered through her veins, stretching up her arm, past her elbow, and beyond. It throbbed with a pulse of life all its own, but it entwined its essence with hers, wanting her—needing her. Its desperation mixed with her own; its fear became hers and hers its.

A blur of visions rushed through her mind's eye accompanied by a gale of emotions not her own. A sealed door separated her from someone she loved, someone in pain. She wanted to help but couldn't.

Laela recognized the medicus's wing in Octarius. *These are Threyna's memories. That's me beyond the door.* She felt Threyna's pain in the blood artifact's embrace. Her fears of being alone, failing those she cared about, being rejected. In a moment, Theodyn's memories flooded in. His fear of being hunted by his brother and father, that it was his duty to fulfill the Purge. His love for her mother. His pain at Arenius's death. His regret as a black wave of death barreled through the Cut to the sound of war drums.

Then the Skeleton King's presence overshadowed all else. The weight of responsibility unwanted. Doubt as hollowed were pinned to trees and burned to crisps. Pressure as a parliament divided. Fatigue after every war was followed by a new one.

He's close. So close.

Blind and deaf to everything else, Laela fell from her perch atop Belrich, wishing she'd just hollowed. She crawled over fallen, soulless bodies in her attempts to get away from the memories flooding her, but more importantly, she needed to escape Belrich. He was still armed, and she wasn't.

Yet she couldn't feel the wound in her stomach. She had retreated somewhere, similar to the way she'd go to her Center of Silence when she fought. All other pains were forgotten in the wake of the blood artifact's bite, but somehow, the red-and-black bracelet clamped onto her wrist knew her injuries needed to be dealt with. The bodies around her seemed to call to her—no, not to her, but it. She took deep gasping breaths, unsure why.

Her ears rang, distorting the cacophony of sounds on the beach. Her vision, spotty and narrow, began to return. Belrich screamed. Steel clashed. A stampede of heartbeats echoed behind her. But the bodies littered around her began to shrink. A cloud of blood hung like a dense fog, ignorant of the swirling sea breeze.

The cloud grew—darker and denser with each rasping breath she took. It moved toward her and the hungry blood artifact, begging for her to do… something.

She drew in a deep breath as she'd seen Threyna do. Flesh and bone obeyed. The shrinking bodies littering the beach desiccated, and the ensuing blood cloud flowed into her. Her flesh stitched back together faster than when she was on the warp in the medicus's quarters. Energy surged back into her; all fatigue melted away as she inhaled the bloody cloud.

Her bracelet *clicked.*

Power surged within her, emanating from her Center of Silence. She sensed a sea of blood begging to be shaped, panicked heartbeats running away, and desperate ones approaching. As intoxicated as she felt with the abilities at her disposal, she felt dwarfed by two greater presences. Within her Center of Silence, she couldn't see them, but she could *feel* them. Two separate vibrations resonated at different amplitudes and frequencies; one was close, its reverberation like a bowstring after loosing an arrow. The other, however, was a deep, quaking throb that threatened to shake the foundation of the world. And it was coming closer.

"Laela!" Threyna called to her.

Laela took in her surroundings. Expecting to find Belrich bearing down on her, she had to search to locate him. Halfway up the dunes, he and a handful of surviving legionaries were running away. Behind her, Canton and the remaining Wraith crashed down on Decimus as Dracus watched the tide roll in. Spinning, she found Threyna standing before the surf, her arms raised as she conjured something vast and bloody in the water.

"Help!" Threyna said over her shoulder. "We're running out of time!"

"What are you doing?" Laela asked, feeling at where the wound in her stomach should have been. Her fingers brushed atop raised flesh—bloody, but intact. She glanced at the blood artifact on her wrist and then over her shoulder to where Aylenia was impaled upon the steppe.

"Laela, I need your help," Threyna said, sparing her a glimpse. Rot spread up and down her arm as she continued to shape something in the water. "The Skeleton King is coming. We need to build a boat. Large enough to take everyone we can and sail away. We don't have much time."

Laela stared at the spear atop the dunes. Aylenia didn't move. She was dead and gone. Anger coursed through her. Loss for a woman she barely knew. The future she'd never even had the chance to long for burned to ash. She didn't want to leave. Belrich was getting away. The Skeleton King was coming. The powerful corruption flowing through her veins didn't want to run. It wanted to fight, to control, to consume.

"Laela, I need you to tap into your Inner Throne. You must focus. Take advantage of spilt blood, conjure your own—picture it in your mind and it will obey your commands." The bloody mass in the water started to take the shape of a ship's hull.

Laela's mind remained rigid, focused on a singular object of desire. Vengeance. Retribution. She wanted to chase Belrich down and impale him. She wanted to face the Skeleton King and destroy him as he had destroyed her home.

Threyna cupped Laela behind the neck, pulling her towards her until their foreheads were practically together. "I'm so sorry. I should have been here. I never should have tried. We never stood a chance..."

Laela pulled away, blinking, not understanding. When she examined Threyna, no longer did she see an insolent, selfish girl hellbent on getting her way. She saw the pain in her eyes, felt the fiery rage that had driven her all these years consume itself until only the sparking embers remained. Within her haunted gaze, Laela saw herself.

Overcoming her anger, releasing her desire to avenge all that was taken from her, she took Threyna's face in her hands. "I'm sorry, too. But we're here now. Together."

"Then help me and let's get out of here."

Sinking into her Center of Silence, she attempted to follow Threyna's instructions. Sensing the blood staining the sand, she called it towards her, beckoning it to congeal and added it toward Threyna's growing blood raft. She felt inefficient and clumsy by comparison to Threyna, and though she was unable to shape it herself, Threyna seemed able to multitask, forming her own conjurations and shaping Laela's contributions.

The blood boat continued to grow and find its form. Laela glanced at the remaining Wraith. There were less than a few dozen of them left, but the survivors had overtaken the legionaries and were finishing off those who had not fled with Belrich. Some wandered over to where she and Threyna formed their vessel of escape, their heartbeats echoing throughout her Center of Silence, singing a song of survival. A rhythm of resilience. They believed. They had faith. But the deep, quaking vibration that threatened to shatter the sanctity of her Center of Silence drew closer.

Rot continued to spread up Threyna's cheek and down towards her fingertips. Dark veins slithered out from the bracelet about Laela's wrist, snaking down the back of her hand, but the boat was not yet large enough for everyone.

Threyna formed a series of ladders along the ship's hull. "Everyone on," she said, voice straining. "We have to get out of here. Now."

Laela didn't need to be told of the urgency of their circumstance. The nearer the quake came, the more she was certain that if it came to a fight, they wouldn't win. Threyna's rhythm emanated so much more power than her own, yet even she was but a drop compared to the approaching downpour.

"Climb in!" Laela ordered. "We're getting out of here, but we need to hurry."

The Wraith trudged through the shallows and crowded around the ladders. Threyna's rot had stopped spreading, despite her continued conjuring. Laela didn't understand how she was doing that, but the boat continued to stretch.

Canton and Dracus were the last to descend the beach and enter the surf. Canton practically had to carry Dracus. He had told her that he was hollowed, but sensing the lack of a heartbeat in his chest stilled her own.

"Don't look at me like that," Dracus said, limping into the shallows. "I'm prime." He grinned at Canton still covered in the blood of the slain. "We're gettin' outta here."

Canton returned Dracus's sentiment as the two made their way toward the ship.

With the ship fully formed and everyone aboard, Laela grabbed a rung and hoisted herself out of the water. She planted her foot and began to climb, but her foot slipped out from underneath her. The excited tenor of the ship's occupants also changed as the waves seemed to sink beneath them.

"No," Threyna said. "No. No. Gory ghosting dammit. No!"

Laela gripped the rung of the ladder tighter and attempted to pull herself up, but she fell, splashing back into the water. Not knowing what had happened, she opened her hand to find it filled with ashes.

The Wraith screamed as the entire boat began to melt into the sea, spilling them into the breaking waves. Again, the hope was swept out from under them. Laela felt her own heart sink into the sea as, on the horizon of the steppe, flying on draconic wings, the quaking presence that disturbed her Center of Silence arrived.

The Skeleton King, haunting even at this distance, pointed at them. "All will bow to the One True God."

Threyna

Despite all the souls ready and waiting to be consumed in her dungeon and all of the Wraith who had aided her efforts thus far, Threyna knew this would be the end. He could disintegrate her conjurations, prevent her from consuming new souls, and worst of all—anything she could do, he could do better.

Consuming souls within her Inner Dungeons to abate the rot in her veins, she glanced at Laela. "Reform the boat… take as many as you can. I'll distract him. Don't wait for me."

Laela protested, but Threyna conjured wings of her own. She chased the crashing waves to the sandy shore and propelled herself into the air. Flapping her wings, she caught a current and sailed low across the beach to meet the Skeleton King for what would be the final time. He descended the dunes, his wings disintegrating and reforming into a long, curved scythe as his feet touched the ground.

"Ripping Corners," Aylenia whispered within Threyna's Inner Throne. *"He's horrible."*

His dark tower blocked out the light filtering through the broken windows of her Inner Throne, its presence a looming nightmare for the Wraith in her throne room. They began to murmur, but Threyna settled them as her own feet touched the sands opposite the Skeleton King.

She allowed her own wings to molt and reform into her double-sided glaive. She'd had every intention of leaving with Laela and the others. But if she couldn't defeat the Skeleton King, there was no way he would let them leave. *For them to leave, I must stay. I must keep his attention on me.* She didn't know if she had enough souls to defend her conjurations from his influence, but if she managed to distract him long enough for Laela to form a ship large enough to carry the rest of the Wraith away, she could hollow knowing she'd done all she could.

The Skeleton King cast her in his ghastly gaze. Lines framed his gaunt features, but they lacked the animosity she felt towards him. The hint of a grin contorted his thin lips; an air of levity adorned his casual stride as he stalked towards her.

"What a cleverly wasteful use of the One True God's gifts," he said, eyeing Laela's attempts to reform the boat Threyna had crafted.

Threyna sneered, approaching cautiously, an idea taking shape in her mind. "You speak of waste." Holding her blood glaive in her left hand, she leveled her right index finger at the Skeleton King as they began to circle one another. "Yet you fight wars you haven't believed in for half a century. How many hollowed? How many shades and darklings have suffered? All because you wanted to prove the One True God wrong, right?"

The Skeleton King's sunken eyes narrowed to slits. "Aye, I held out hope. For Rheynia, for humanity—Bheric's bane, for my people. My sons. Me." His skeletal fingers drummed around the shaft of his scythe. "I suppose I too wasted one of the One True God's most precious gifts: time."

Taking advantage of the conversation to stall for time, Threyna forced a laugh. "Time? That's rich coming from a man with nearly a hundred years to his name. How many souls paid for you to continue your horrific existence?"

"Many. And few."

The darklings encircling the Skeleton King's tower screamed with each revolution, their cries bleeding into her Inner Throne. A song of torment. An existence of hopelessness. Its dread seeped into the essence of the Wraith watching fearfully from within her mind palace.

"Many souls have I taken," the Skeleton King continued. "A small portion of which have I consumed, a practice I sense you have come to learn yourself."

Threyna detached herself of fear, knowing that if she allowed herself to sense it, everyone in her Inner Throne would too. Resigning herself to stoic determination, she inclined her head to look down her nose at her grandfather. "Another waste, in that case."

"It is the only way. To gather the souls of this world will take time, patience. Aid. I would like to end this habit of wastefulness." His scythe dematerialized, raining ashes that were swiftly picked up by the wind to scatter to nothingness. He held out his hand. "I will ask you to join me but once, Granddaughter."

Threyna guffawed, holding fast to her glaive. "Join you?"

"Yes. Join me." The Skeleton King stopped circling her, forcing her to do the same. "The One has shown me; there is a vast world beyond Rheynia. Lands of sand, of ice, expanses of mountains and river valleys, jungles and great geysers. People—innumerable and tortured in the failings of the Creator's so-called Gods. Wars span decades, dividing countries and rending communities. Despite common cause or belief, every faction fractures for some reason or another." He shook his head as if what he'd come to realize after years of rejection was all so clear.

He stalked closer, hand still outstretched. "You seek to end the pain and suffering of Rheynia's people. I know it. I can feel it in you. You blame me because of the half-measures I have taken out of my own fear and rejection of the calling placed on my life. But no longer. There is only one unity, one peace, Granddaughter—the peace under the One True God. Help me unite the world, and together—you, me, your sister—we will end its suffering."

His outstretched hand remained between them. Laela's blood boat was large enough for people to climb aboard, but there wasn't enough room for everyone. In their desperation to escape, the Wraith began pushing and shoving in the surf in an attempt to claim a space for themselves, proving the Skeleton King's point. Even amongst like-minded people, there would always be the haves and have-nots. There would always be division, war, pain, and the heartache left in its wake.

"They will kill each other," the Skeleton King said, pointing toward them. "If not here, out there beyond the veil. They will die true deaths. That is the ultimate waste. But we can stop them from killing each other. We can unite them, give them peace."

But not freedom. Not choice.

Divided, ruin will reign. For so long Threyna thought that meant if they didn't join together and fight, they would lose. But fight or flee, it didn't matter—they were on the same side against the Order's tyranny. They had made that choice. Different in how they approached it, yes, but united in the importance of it. That division was not what would allow ruin to reign. Passivity, giving up on choice to believe the lie that any unity at any cost was a worthy pursuit. She would rather die. Rather suffer knowing she'd tried to resist what she knew was wrong than become part of the problem for the sake of unity. For a liar's version of peace.

"Will you join me, Granddaughter?" her grandfather asked, only an arm's length away.

Threyna met his eyes. She saw her father in them. Even parts of herself. But whatever blood they shared, whatever ties of family, culture, faith, or ideology that could have united them was broken by his willingness to bow to the One True God. She knew what would come next, after she rejected him. He wouldn't waste her; he wouldn't even attempt to kill her. If he wanted to, he could have. He wanted to own her, control her, wield her like a weapon to wage war against humanity for the One True God's version of peace.

"When I deny him, he's going to send darklings into me," Threyna said, addressing the Wraith in her Inner Throne. *"They will invade these walls, but they will not be mine. They will not easily be spirited to the dungeons below. They will fight and stop at nothing to strip me from this throne, take my body, my abilities, and wield them for the Skeleton King and his One True God."*

Many trembled at her words. Most of them were not soldiers of the Underground like her and Aylenia. But what they lacked in a soldier's training, they more than made up for with the spirit of resilience. They had fought together to survive, leaned on one another to keep the hope of escaping alive. She just needed to convince them to hold onto that dream. They needed to believe that together, they could resist.

"I don't know how many he will send," Threyna continued. *"But when they come, I will need your help. I need you to stand with me, fight with me,*

and know that no matter what happens, keep faith that we will sail from these shores. Will you join me?"

Aylenia's lone voice assented. *"Yes!"* The wispy form her soul had taken within her Inner Throne glanced around as if wondering why she was the only one raising her voice. But Threyna understood why.

"I know you do not trust me. An Undergrounder. A saboteur. Many of you likely blame me for why you haven't yet escaped these shores in the first place. And you are right. So I'll ask again—not for you to join me—but for you to stay together, to fight for each other in resisting them. Will you fight for each other? Will you stand together?"

The Wraith nodded, beginning to rally to her words, but Threyna was out of time. The Skeleton King's outstretched hand awaited an answer. She met the man who had single-handedly ruined three generations of Rheynia.

"No, I won't join you. I'd rather hollow in the Gullies, burn in the Scorch Lands, or drown in the Grotto. I'd rather live and fight, try and fail, die and suffer than submit to your idea of *peace*."

The Skeleton King's hand fell to his side. His twisted grin flattened to a hard line. "You will serve."

Darklings poured from his chest and swarmed around her. Scores, hundreds, too many to count or even comprehend. The Skeleton King reforged his wings and scythe and took flight as the world beyond her eyes began to fade away in lieu of the chaos devastating her Inner Throne.

He's going after Laela and the rest of the Wraith.

But there was nothing she could do to help them. Black souls, as dark and twisted as a Dreadroot's vines, zipped around her Inner Throne. The gathered Wraith formed a circle around her throne to defend her from the incoming attack, and though they didn't break, there were too many darklings to stop them all.

A calamity of emotions flooded her Inner Throne as the souls attempted to rip her off her seat of power and seize it for themselves. Threyna sank deeper, inviting their attack. She felt their assault on her emotions, their invasion of her thoughts and memories, but she held up her walls.

Resisting their grasp, she glimpsed their own thoughts, emotions, and memories as they tried and failed to take control of her mind palace. Legionaries who died in service, Justicus who fell to hollowed, hollowed who'd been burned out by Tellers, citizens who'd died of dewskull, starvation, or disease under the Dominion's protection—all presented the same fear, the same desperation to be valued.

"If I deliver her to the Skeleton King, he'll reward me," a former legionary thought.

"Take her. The One True God will spare me. I just have to take her," another believed.

Every soul vying for her body wanted her for the same reasons, not because they wanted to, but because they feared what would happen if they failed. Their fear was brittle in the face of her resolve. Strengthened by the Wraith supporting her, Threyna rebuffed their attempts at control.

"You can't win," Threyna shouted, her words echoing off the walls of her throne room. The swirling souls clawing their way toward her slowed. *"You won't. But let me ask you this… do you even want to?"*

"You will serve!" a Justicus shouted. *"All must serve."*

"That's what the Skeleton King wants," Threyna said. *"That's what his One True God wants. What do you want?"*

Threyna drew the Justicus in closer, connecting herself to his painful past. His family suffered when he was a boy. His parents hollowed. His brother and sister died of dewskull. His uncle trained him to be chosen by the Order so that he could serve and defend the people from the darklings and hollowed that suffered his family. But after he'd perished in his service, he'd been vortexed from his hollowed form and kept in a soul jar. Then he'd been consumed and stored by the Skeleton King and finally learned the truth; he'd never truly served a cause that the Skeleton King couldn't solve himself. His parents hollowed, his siblings died of an ailment that had an easy cure, and he died risking his life to cull the hollowed. A job the Skeleton King could have done across the whole country before the midday rains.

Threyna felt his wants bubble to the surface of his essence. *"You want to see your family again. You want to believe there is an afterlife beyond the curse."*

His soul stilled. His fight left him.

"Instead of fighting me," Threyna continued, *"instead of trying to take control of me for him, join us. Help us leave this place. I don't know what awaits in the afterlife. I don't know if the Savior will bring you to Neutreen, if Neutreen will grant you wings to ascend to Valencia, or if your suffering just ends, but I won't hold you to source my power."*

Even the most aggressive souls vying for control over her Inner Throne slackened at that. As they acquiesced, the black vines wrapping around the columns or climbing the walls of her throne room began to recede. Those who weren't fully convinced could be held in check by Aylenia and the other Wraith.

With her Inner Throne stable, and hundreds more on her side, she sank deeper into her Inner Throne than she ever had before. Power filled her. Flooded her. She opened her eyes to the beach before her. The Skeleton King had once again decimated the blood raft. Belrich and other Order reinforcements were returning to the beach, closing in on the Wraith, but even more were encroaching from Octarius. Bloody spires rose from the surf, ensnaring the rest of the Wraith and dangling them helplessly above the crashing waves. The Skeleton King held his hand out to Laela in much the same way he had to her moments ago.

She won't join him. No one will.

"Aylenia," Threyna said within her Inner Throne, *"empty the dungeons."*

"What? Don't you need them?"

"I do… but I won't use them. Free them."

Aylenia's essence thrummed, pulsing with invigoration. *"Always another fight, eh?"*

With nothing left to lose, the words came easily. *"Always another victory."*

Threyna reconjured her wings and flew towards the Skeleton King, dead set on his demise.

Laela

Laela's conjured escape vessel crumbled to ash only to be tossed by the rolling waves. The Wraith fell into the breakers yet again. Even though they resurfaced, their hopes did not. Further up the beach, the Skeleton King flew towards them on bloodborne wings, leaving Threyna standing motionless in his wake.

The Skeleton King had unleashed an army of darklings on Threyna. *Who could hope to stand against such odds?* Despite all their efforts, their resilience, they had fallen short again.

A tide of black uniforms surged down the steppe and onto the beach as if their defeat wasn't apparent enough. Belrich led at the front of the reinforcements, his presence a harbinger of her doom, and an insult to the injury of her failings.

"Seize hold of yourselves," Laela shouted to the Wraith. Despite the futility of their predicament, they listened, coming close to crowd around her. "This may be our end, but Neutreen is watching. She sees. She knows." Laela wasn't even certain she believed it. But in spite of her doubt, she wanted to believe it more than ever. "Do not forsake her. Do not forsake each other. We will stand. We will fight until the last." She forged a bloody sword to take up arms against the encroaching Skeleton King. "Because if we do not even try, then we have already lost."

She turned to face the Skeleton King, Canton and Dracus coming alongside her. The Skeleton King was close enough that she could see the blue of his deep-set eyes.

"I love you, kid," Dracus said to Canton. "Had a good run, eh?"

"One for the songs," Canton agreed. "Too bad no one will be left to sing it."

"Then we sing it with our dying breath," Laela said. Her throat constricted as the scent of ashes filled her nostrils. The scar across her chest burned with the inevitability of what was about to happen. She gripped her blood-forged sword and leveled it at the approaching Skeleton King.

But her sword point blew away in the wind. Down the bevel of the blade, the length of the sword dematerialized until her fingers curled around empty air.

Tall spires rose around her like twisting trees, seizing Canton, Dracus and the others and thrusting them into the air. Everyone but her hung suspended, screaming. Water dripped from their wet clothes to rain down upon her.

Her breath caught as the Skeleton King drew close. His quaking presence thundered throughout her Center of Silence, shattering any semblance of tranquility. Threyna was right; they never stood a chance. He was absolute in his power, indomitable in his might. She would have been in awe if not for the fear that rattled through her empty fingers.

"Laela Velar..." The Skeleton King's thin lips never moved, but his voice echoed throughout her Center of Silence. *"You and I, we want the same thi—"*

"Do not even try," Laela snapped despite her fear. *Be strong. Be courageous.* She recalled her mother seizing the Dawnshards from Threyna before running toward the Order's Justicus in the bog. *"I will not—we will not join you willingly."* Resolve anchored her tone with each passing word. She would not fall victim to this monster. *"So do what you came here to do. But know this—someone, someday, will stop you. Neutreen take you and your One True God!"*

The Skeleton King treated her with a smile that perhaps once might have been handsome, but his sallow complexion, drawn features, and the skin sloughing off his cheek made his genial expression grotesque. He fixed her with his cruel stare, as if waiting for her to continue, but when she said nothing else, he stalked closer.

"Neutreen is dead."

The quaking reverberations exerted pressure onto her Center of Silence until visions or memories not her own flooded her mind's eye. A blindfolded woman sat before a slightly unbalanced scale with a feather on one side and a cerulean and viridian liquid on the other.

Ghosts... it's Neutreen.

In all of her majesty, the Goddess of Justice prepared to judge an incomplete soul. Neutreen, however, gently pressed her finger down on the feather's side of the scale, balancing the soul's weight versus the feather's.

The tranquility of the moment fractured as the vision rippled. Neutreen had fallen to the floor. Her blindfold had been removed. She stared blankly upwards, eyes wide, mouth agape. The hilt of a red dagger, coursing with forking black lightning similar to the bracelet around Laela's wrist, stuck out of Neutreen's chest.

"No..."

"Yes." The Skeleton King's voice echoed through her Center of Silence. *"Neutreen is dead. Killed in Valencia by the One True God. You may flee this land, and you can search far and wide, but nowhere will she greet you. Nowhere will she bestow you wings to ascend to Valencia. I am your hope for salvation. I am your path to the peace of Valencia."* The Skeleton King spoke softly with a tenderness reserved for a mother to her child.

"You have served Neutreen all your life to help others earn their wings. I am not asking you to do something you do not want. As I said, Laela, we want the same thing—to lead people to peace." There was a pleading earnestness in his tone. He believed what he was saying. But Laela didn't. She refused to accept it. *"Join me. Aid me in delivering others to that peac—"*

A bloody spear erupted through Skeleton King's chest, and he roared in pain. Behind him, Threyna screamed, ripping her glaive free to stab again. The Skeleton King spun, a sickle forming in his hand as he slashed at Threyna. Her glaive fell to ashes, but so too did the Skeleton King's spires constricting the rest of the Wraith, lowering them to the shallow breakers.

"Impossible!" the Skeleton King screamed.

Laela didn't know how, but Threyna had overcome the darklings the Skeleton King had sent into her. Despite being stabbed through the back and out the front of his chest, the Skeleton King's wounds were already restitching themselves. He turned on Threyna, and the two began a dance of ever-conjuring and failing bloodspawns.

Hope restored but with Belrich and Order legionaries storming towards them, Laela was faced with a choice: fight or flee? Many and more legionaries would be sweeping down the steppe and onto the beach, and with Threyna preoccupying the Skeleton King, they might just be able to escape. But if she did, she was forsaking Threyna. Again.

Laela blocked out the battling blood mages, the charging legionaries, and the terrified Wraith to focus deep within her Center of Silence. Rage rumbled with the rhythm of her own heartbeat—a steady, building throb like a war drum's bellow. She sank deeper into that pulse, adding it to the timid heartbeats of the Wraith behind her. *Join me. Fight with me. Fight with her. We fight together. We leave together. Be strong. Be courageous.* She turned to face the Wraith trembling and wet. But from her Center of Silence, she forged blood-spawned blades into each of their hands.

"We fight!" Laela shouted. Canton took up the call, and soon others did too.

Fear remained, but the desire to live and the dream of freedom overcame their fear. It took the same effort of forging a boat large enough to carry them away, but with everyone armed, Laela forged a two-handed great sword of her own.

The Order neared with Belrich leading the charge, hellbent on delivering death. Whether or not the Skeleton King's vision was true, whether Neutreen was still out there or truly gone, Laela took solace in the virtues she'd learned from Neutreen. She would fight for justice. She would die for it.

The war drum of her heartbeat reverberated from her Inner Throne to the people behind her. Laela raised her sword to the gray skies over Rheynia. "For Neutreen!" She charged at Belrich.

Dracus

The salt water invading his open wounds called him to the hollow abyss. If not for Canton's support, the lapping waves and undercurrent would have dragged him to a watery grave, yet here he stood. On the shores of a cursed island with a blood-forged sword in hand, arm in arm with the boy he'd have done anything to save, he stared out to the breakers beyond.

Not yet.

Laela and the others charged ahead to meet Belrich and the Order's reinforcements. Threyna waged war with the Skeleton King a short distance away. Canton cupped his free hand behind Dracus's neck. He was speaking to Dracus. His lips moved with urgency. His eyes darted between Dracus and the battle blossoming around them.

Dracus felt the pain slipping away. The empty numbness held him in its tender grip. The world went dark. He wasn't sure if he'd sunk to the ocean's depths or simply just closed his eyes too long. He should have felt the cold water lapping at his legs, the stinging of steel's kiss, the burning of salt in his cuts.

Nothing.

He should have heard Canton's voice, the clashing steel, the crashing waves.

Nothing.

Apologies, Old Boy. So close.

"Dracus!" Canton's voice felt far away, as if he'd stored a shout in a fatekeeper and it had decayed over time. His shoulders shook. He opened his eyes to find Canton jostling him. Before he knew it, he was being dragged through the water. A blink later and he was on his back, staring at the sky. He didn't even feel the pain left behind by the Vendetta daggers. He was fading. Hollowing.

Let go, my love. Let go and see. Let go the woes and sing high for me.

"Dracus, hold on!" Canton shouted. "Do not let go. Do not!" Tears streaked down the boy's face. He glanced up from Dracus to the battle raging nearby. "Don't give up. There's still hope." He forced something into Dracus's hand and disappeared.

The world went black. Another blink. He wanted to move, wanted to fight, but more than anything, he just wanted to feel. Empty, numb, lost—had he ever felt whole? Had he ever allowed himself to feel anything but guilt and shame?

Canton is fightin' right now. Laela and Threyna, too. Yer jus' lyin' here. The thought should have evoked guilt and shame, but he felt insulated from it, protected by the heavy, paralyzing blanket of hopelessness.

Get up, ya mean bastard.

Lacius took his punishment. Arenius screamed as he burned in Arilette's fires. Rance told them to leave him behind in the tunnels outside of Avengard. Fawkes attempted to caress Dracus's cheek.

"Not here," Fawkes had said in his last moments. *"True death. Out there. Together."*

Pain washed over him. The shame of trying so hard only to fall just short. The guilt of keeping Fawkes trapped inside a soul jar just out of reach of the curse's barrier.

Dracus glanced down at what Canton had shoved into his hands. *Fang.* The simple unadorned dagger that had followed him across Rheynia felt right in his grip. It was meant for traitors.

Belrich. Bohen.

Dracus rolled onto his side and sank into the pain that accompanied the movement. It grounded him in reality, anchoring his soul to his body and purpose to his action. He staggered to his feet, squishing in the wet sand. Laela fought Belrich and a half dozen other legionaries, bodies littering the ground around her. Threyna continued to go toe to toe with the Skeleton King in a storm of blood-conjured weapons. Canton slipped between two legionaries, slashing with a blood-conjured sword in one hand and an Order short sword in the other.

Dracus squeezed *Fang's* hilt, ready to give its blade one last taste of blood. *Not yet, Old Boy. Not yet.* He charged into the fray.

Laela

Blood—sweet, sticky, powerful blood dripped down her fingers after she buried her conjured blade through a legionary's chest. She ripped it free and kicked the failing body away, just in time to deflect Belrich's next thrust.

The shade slipped free of its former shell, but Laela had no time to consider how Threyna went about consuming it to abate the rot. Already, black veins were streaking up her arm to her elbow, but the blood artifact gave no indication of helping her as it had when it healed her wounds after latching on.

She turned aside a stabbing short sword and barely dodged out of the way of a glowing white spear tip. *One of the Underground's reaping spears.* Intent on keeping her soul whole and within her body, she positioned herself to put as many people as possible between her and the spearman. Seeing easier targets, he plunged his spear into the back of the nearest Wraith.

The woman didn't clutch her chest where the spear protruded through; she just fell to the sand—lifeless. Soulless. Fury boiled within Laela. Such technology could have completed the Purge, could have eradicated the hollowed, but instead it was turned on the living—first by the Underground, now by the Order.

Laela seized control of the woman's fallen blood-conjured sword and shaped the scarlet that drenched her light gray tunic. Shaping it into a spear, Laela directed it at the spearman's chest. He ducked. Wrong move. The spear lanced through his face, taking him off his feet.

She spun, sweeping her blood-forged blade in a giant arc to keep the Order's superior numbers at bay. It was difficult to keep her balance on the wet sand as the tides rolled in. The cold seeped into her toes as each wave ripped back out to sea, carrying the sand beneath her feet with it.

Belrich countered at the same time as another legionary struck. Not having time to block both, Laela sank deeper into her Center of Silence and brought up her arm to block. A bloody carapace sprouted along her forearm like an Inquisitor's heavy bracer. Belrich's steel careened off her conjured armor, giving Laela the opportunity to press the legionary. She sliced at the flesh below his armored skirt and above his knee.

With the two-handed sword unwieldy in her one hand, she commanded it to shrink to a short sword. Rearing, she thrust it into the legionary's gut. She drove him back, turning with him to use his body as a dying shield. Belrich chopped down at them both, uncaring who fell in his path.

He just wants the blood artifact.

She shoved the legionary into Belrich and slashed at another, felling him with two short swipes. He dropped with a splash, disappearing into the shallows, but for every one that fell, two more came. And beyond the steppe, more were marching on the beach. As it was, bodies already littered the shoreline as the tide crept in to drag them out to sea. Though many wore Order blacks, too many were her own people. But if they didn't fight, didn't die in battle, they would be impaled in their surrender. Laela ignored the screams of the dying, pushed past the war waging between Threyna and the Skeleton King, and charged between three legionaries surrounding Canton.

She skewered one through the back of the knee, then ripped another down to the ground by the back of his cuirass. Canton stabbed down at the second man, allowing Laela to finish her fallen foe. The third set in on Canton. He twisted to block the first strike, lurched out of the way of the second, but he was in no position to block the third.

Laela jumped forward, closing the distance and slashing upward to catch the legionary's strike before it found Canton. She blocked. Canton repositioned and thrust his blade through the legionary's throat.

Before she could turn, a sinister rhythm within her Center of Silence blared. She ducked. A whoosh slashed just over her head and past her ear. She spun and thrust. But too late.

Belrich's backhanded chop took her in the forearm.

Laela blinked. Crimson, streaked black, filled her vision. Two white bones protruded from her forearm where her hand should have been. It, and the bracelet that had chosen her, fell to the rising tides. Her held sword dissolved to ash as her bloody hand floated in the rolling surf.

Panicked, Laela reached for her disembodied hand, but it was as if her eyes were playing tricks on her. The severed limb and the blood artifact attached to it toppled away and tumbled from sight in a wash of the bloody tide.

Dracus

Dracus drove *Fang* into the neck of a legionary with a reaping spear. With his free hand, he wrestled the spear away and flung it into the chest of another legionary. A scream he never wanted to hear cut through the noise of the battle.

"No!" Canton stabbed at Belrich, but Belrich was faster.

Belrich leaned away and riposted. His thrust took Canton through the chest. But as if something was more important, Belrich abandoned his sword, dropping to his knees to fumble in the bloody tide. Canton stumbled back, clutching the wound in his chest.

Dracus's world fractured around him into a thousand broken dreams.

To dream is to die.

Reaching Sansia, growing old, dying a true death—every hope he'd had for the boy, every future he'd envisioned, they all fell to ashes.

To hope is to lie.

Dracus had lost Canton's hope a decade ago. When Arenius burned in Arilette's fires. When Theodyn declared himself Bherus Fayte and lost. When he'd brought that scared young girl back to Octarius for safety, only to deliver her into the hands of a monster as vicious and manipulative as the Skeleton King. When he'd swallowed that monster's poison...

But despite Dracus's numbed grief, Canton still believed, always daring to dream and fighting for hope. It was never Dracus's hope. He'd never believed Canton's dream was possible. An end to the Order. The defeat of the Skeleton King. But Threyna was standing toe to toe with the undying tyrant. Doomed as they were, outnumbered and overmatched by the Order, if Belrich and the Skeleton King fell, there would still be hope for the future. Perhaps not theirs, but that was Dracus's dream, not Canton's. And Canton's dream was still possible.

Dracus charged at Belrich. Bowling over legionaries, ignoring their swords, and only stopping to deflect reaping spears from his path, Dracus fought through the fray. Belrich disappeared in the rushing tide and mess of legs as he crawled through the surf. Only the Blessing would make him behave in such a way, but Dracus wouldn't let him have it.

Spotting Belrich slapping at the waves in an attempt to locate the blood artifact, Dracus shoved a legionary out of the way and slashed at Belrich's back. Steel cleaved through leather armor, drawing a red comet across his back. Belrich roared, but before he could get up, Dracus thrust his blade through Belrich's spine and deep into the sand, pinning him prone.

Belrich screamed, but the tide rolled in, drowning his cries for help. Dracus plunged *Fang* into his ribs again and again. One for Lacius who'd suffered for standing against tyranny. One for Decimus who had fallen victim to its propaganda. One for the young man Dracus had once been. Again and again, Dracus stabbed until he'd secured a thrust for Arenius, Bherus, Rance, and Canton.

But once he was done, the blood artifact was nowhere to be seen. Dracus cursed himself for letting it get away, but it was too late. *If there's any justice in this world, it will wash out to sea, sink to the abyss, and drown in the deep.*

He abandoned Belrich and the cursed artifact he sought to pick up a fallen blade. Darklings and shades swirled all around, but through bodies and spirits, Dracus found Canton a short distance away. Few Wraith were left standing, but somehow, little remained of the first garrison of the Order's reinforcements. But for as many that had fallen, more were coming.

He staggered through the mess of bodies and the rising tide towards Canton. The surf tossed his weakened body with each wave, but he was still alive, holding his chest. Laela fought with a blood-conjured hand to keep the remaining legionaries at bay.

A wave rolled over Canton, dropping him beneath the surface. Nearing, Dracus dropped to his knees at Canton's side, scooping him out of the wake.

"Hang on, kid." He flipped the switch on his vortex and reached for the soul jar containing Fawkes. "Just hang on."

Laela fought with bloodborne swords, even after losing her hand and the blood artifact. Threyna and the Skeleton King both pulsed with power as they fought with blood-forged weapons. The cries of charging legionaries drew nearer, louder, but the blood leaking from Canton's chest was the most immediate threat.

Canton placed his hand on Dracus's, stopping him halfway through attaching the soul jar to the vortex. "No. Help them."

Dracus didn't believe his ears. He removed Canton's hand from his own, but Canton recovered quickly despite the faraway gaze in his eyes.

Canton shook his head, his face pale, pupils dilated. "Fight. Win. We leave together."

"Cant, we gotta—"

"I won't hollow either," Canton said. "We'll go together. We'll still be together. You, me, Fawkes…"

Dracus blinked, his breath caught. He chewed his mustache, tasting the blood and saltwater, but his mind struggled to process what Canton had said.

"I won't hollow… either."

How did he know? How long has he known?

The thoughts raced through his addled mind, but he couldn't make sense of them.

"We leave together." Canton's weak hands shoved Dracus's vortex away. He pointed toward Threyna and the Skeleton King. "Help her…."

Threyna

Threyna conjured a net and hurled it at the Skeleton King. He caught it in his scythe, but before he could dissolve it to ash, Threyna formed a bloody trident and flung it at him. The trident skewered his stomach, but fell to ashes almost immediately.

Threyna could taste his blood on the air—soiled, rotten, corrupted as it was, it was his, and she had drawn it. While he spent his souls licking his wounds, Threyna called upon the allies of her Inner Throne and the liberated former darklings of her Inner Dungeons. The tower of his seat of power was so close that she could almost reach out and touch it. Atop the tower guarded by circling darklings, a window blinked with the faint glow of radiant light.

His Inner Dungeon—a tower cell under lock and key.

There was only one way to defeat the Skeleton King. She couldn't supplant him from his Inner Throne, but she could liberate his tower prisoners. And if she did, who would source his power?

Within her Inner Throne, Threyna pointed to the Skeleton King's tower. *"Do you wish to escape this cursed land? That there is our weapon. Your people, your countrymen, your families, and friends. They are held prisoner within his tower. I would have them free. Will you join me?"*

Her throne room echoed with the chants of believers as her heart thrummed with the faith of her followers. Through the fractured glass of her stained windows, Threyna led the charge with Aylenia following close behind. The Skeleton King stood before an altar at the base of the tower, but defying all laws of the material world, Threyna flew through the air, over and past him. Absent her bloodborne wings and with hundreds of screaming souls behind her, she ascended the sky, ignoring the Skeleton King and pursuing the souls trapped within his haunting tower.

"Get them!" the Skeleton King roared.

The darklings swarmed, forming a defensive perimeter around the window, but Threyna did not slow, did not bow, and would not break. She bowled through the darklings. They clung to her, attempting to impede her progress, but she cast them off. The candle cares not for the moth, and neither did she for their undying loyalty to the Skeleton King. They were not the ones she sought to save.

Her charging force stampeded over the darklings, and Threyna dove through the tower's open window. While the rest of her souls contended with the Skeleton King's darklings, Threyna and Aylenia prepared for a fight within the tower, but no one waited for them in the circular room. No one, but several wooden shelves. Threyna had never seen so much unrotted wood before, and there were rows of them—each stacked with glass soul jars bathing her in different shades of light. More lined the walls, climbing to the canopied ceiling. Thousands of souls. Each emitted a different hue of light. Some soul jars emitted a radiant white, others a dull gray hum. Some were filled with swirling black darklings begging to get out.

Glass… the first canister before soul jars. How long have these souls been trapped?

"Stop her!" the Skeleton King shouted, his voice rising above the battling souls outside.

He would come for her, so she needed to act quickly. Taking measure of the number of souls in need of freeing, Threyna charged past the shelves erected in the middle of the room, beckoning Aylenia to follow. "Help me free them."

Together, she and the wisp of Aylenia shoved against the last row of shelves housing the glass soul jars. The wooden shelf groaned as it tilted. Glass soul jars rolled from their place on the shelf to crash to the ground, spraying glass across the floor and releasing shades and darklings into the air.

"Push!" Threyna shouted. The shelf fell to lean against the adjacent shelf. Another groan, another shattering of glass. One by one, the shelves fell into one another, releasing hundreds of souls into the tower. There was still another row of shelves, not to mention the ones lining the cylindrical walls, but darklings dove for her.

Their fear overwhelmed her. So long had they been trapped dating back as far as the War of the Seers half a century ago.

"I'm freeing you," she said as they swarmed her. *"So together, we can end him."*

Threyna let down her walls, allowing them access to her thoughts, emotions, and memories, letting them see and know for certain her intentions. It was dangerous, letting them in; at any point, they could turn on her and fight for the Skeleton King, but whether it was her willingness to be vulnerable or their hatred for the Skeleton King, their fears were quelled.

"It's working!" Aylenia said.

The souls slipped away from her, unsure what to do if not intent on violence. Threyna had a job for them. *"Open every soul jar. Let everyone out!"*

She returned to the beach, standing before the Skeleton King. Despite being healed and whole, he screamed as souls erupted out of him. They didn't dive into her as if under his control; they escaped into the air, free at last from their captivity.

The Skeleton King screamed aloud. He set his ghoulish gaze on her. "You meddle for the last time."

He drew in breath to regather the souls she'd freed, but Threyna countered his current. With more souls fueling her power, her draw overcame the Skeleton King's. The freed shades and darklings flowed towards her, practically willingly.

He still had his darklings to fuel him, but she could feel her abilities growing with each and every soul that poured into her. Flashes of their lives and deaths played before her mind's eye. Pain and sorrow inflicted by or because of the Skeleton King's reign made it easy for them to choose which side they were on. They were hers. They were united.

She felt two souls entwine within her Inner Throne.

"You can do this, Little Dove," her father said.

"We can do this!" her mother corrected.

A cathartic flood washed over her, through her. Everything that had been robbed of her ten years ago at the Battle of the Cut, she would have back. She would *take* back.

We can do this.

Threyna attuned to the racing hearts of the bloodlusting legionaries, separating them from the remaining Wraith. She returned to her Inner Throne and sank into her seat of power. With a squeeze of her fist, dozens of hearts exploded, and the men they beat for fell to the sands.

The Skeleton King's scythe returned. Blood-spawned daggers formed around her and dove like a swarm of birds pecking at the last seeds of grain. Threyna seized hold of some conjurations, dissipating them to ash while she conjured a curved shield to defend her other side. The daggers thudded into her shield. She brought it back around just in time to catch the Skeleton King's swinging scythe. A spear rose from the ground to skewer her, but she lurched out of the way.

The Skeleton King continued his reckless advance, but black veins were streaking up from his neck to envelop his ghoulish face in dark rot. Threyna wouldn't allow him to put her on the defensive. She charged in and thrust her glaive at him. He deflected it aside and ripped his scythe towards her. She ducked beneath it, reshaping her glaive and shield into a pair of short swords. Splashing through the bloody water, she stabbed at him. He attempted to make her conjurations fall to ash, but she resisted.

Deflecting the scythe's blade and then a strike with the butt of the shaft, she twisted inside his defenses and stabbed. Her short sword took him through the gut. Not giving him time to counter, she thrust her second blade into his ribs.

He screamed, but as she retracted her first blade to strike again, something in the lapping waves seized her by the ankle. She staggered, but then it wrapped around her knee and twisted. She attempted to free herself, but he conjured grasping tentacles from the bloody water.

Attempting to seize control and make them disintegrate, Threyna met resistance. *He's using everything he has left to stop me.* Threyna reared back to thrust with her short sword, but another tentacle seized her wrist. Then another grabbed her other arm.

The Skeleton King reared back his scythe, his features practically swallowed by the web of black veins. Threyna conjured a floating shield to intercept his strike, but something else made contact with it first.

Laela advanced, charging through the water with a sword raised in a bloody fist. Whatever she'd conjured to snare around the Skeleton King's scythe rained to ashes, but before he could bring it around to strike again, Threyna freed herself from the tentacles and stepped inside the reach of the scythe. With one hand, she beat back the shaft, opening his guard. With the other, she stabbed him a third time, her bloodborne blade piercing his chest.

The Skeleton King staggered back, but Laela was on him. She swiped low at the back of his knees, dropping him to the rising tide. Threyna jabbed her other short sword into his chest, while Laela brought her blade around again to slash down on the space between the Skeleton King's shoulder and neck.

His crown fell from his head, splashing into the sea. He swayed in the tides as his undying body, absent the souls to sustain itself any longer, clung to the last glimpses of life.

"Kill him," Threyna's father said from within her Inner Throne.

"End this," their mother said.

Threyna let her conjured short swords fall to ash and unsheathed *Pure* and *True*. She tossed *True* to Laela. Catching it in her blood-conjured hand, Laela leveled it against the Skeleton King's collarbone. "Divided, ruin will reign."

Threyna placed *Pure* opposite Laela's on the Skeleton King's other shoulder. "Together, tyranny falls."

"This does not end with me," the Skeleton King said through weak, labored breaths. "The One True God does not give up so easily. All will bend. All will bow."

An arcanatek whirred to motion as Dracus limped closer, leveling an irradiator at the Skeleton King. "Not today, darkling. Do it."

Threyna and Laela plunged their daggers down and into the Skeleton King's collarbones. Black blood dripped from torn sinew. His head toppled forwards, dragging his corpse into the tides.

As his darkling rose from his body, Dracus took aim. "Been savin' these charges a long time." The irradiator whined to a crescendo, and Dracus pulled the trigger. White light split the sky and burned a hole through the Skeleton King's darkling, melting it into nothingness.

Cheers erupted within Threyna's Inner Throne. She couldn't believe it herself, but there was no time to process.

"We gotta get Canton beyond the curse," Dracus said, barely able to stand himself.

Threyna never imagined herself leaving Rheynia; she wasn't even sure that she wanted to. But she'd made a promise to the souls that helped her defeat the Skeleton King. That was the only peace they would receive. She owed them that.

"Get Canton," Threyna said to Dracus, looking to the slowly approaching reserves from the battle of Octarius. She nodded at Laela. "Gather whoever is left of the Wraith, anyone still clinging to life. We can at least grant them a true death."

CHAPTER 63

THE ONES WHO MATTER

Dracus XVII

Threyna's bloodborne longboat cut through the water, rising and falling with each wave. Every rhythmic swell beneath them beat like the heart that didn't thud in his chest, but they all served as a sign of the cursed island fading into the distance and the curse's barrier drawing closer.

Watching the Grip disappear into the night, Dracus held Canton to his chest—cold, barely breathing. *Jus' hold on, kid. Little longer.* He wanted to let go too, but not yet. The wounds he'd accumulated over the past ten years were nothing compared to the ones he'd suffered in the past few days. The pain was his constant companion, his stabilizing reminder, but the abyss was as close to him as the churning waters beneath their blood boat.

He closed his eyes, hoping that those churning waters had swallowed the Blessing and buried it at the bottom of the sea. But that was out of his hands. Everything was. He'd done his part—succeeded in some efforts, failed in most. Yet as the end was drawing near, he found himself content, at peace with the notion that he, Fawkes, and Canton would all be together, with whatever awaited them.

He held Canton tighter. *Just a little longer.*

It wasn't hard to block out the boat's other passengers. There were few enough of them as it was. Most were consumed by Threyna, waiting to be released beyond the curse just as he was. Laela had offered to take him, but Dracus refused. He wanted Canton to die a true death, and he didn't want the boy to face it alone.

A wave jarred the boat, and Canton stirred.

"It's alright, kid."

Canton grunted, his eyes barely open. "We did it?"

It wasn't the first time he'd asked. "Yeah, Cant. We got 'em. Dead and gone. Both of 'em." At least he hoped so. Though the Skeleton King was gone for sure, he wasn't certain what fate befell Belrich. He could have hollowed with Dracus's sword through his back and *Fang* in his ribs as the tides rolled in. His shade could have slipped free to wander Rheynia. Or his darkling could have endured. Dracus didn't want to think about it, and he certainly didn't want to burden Canton's conscience with it.

"We did it," Canton said. "You, me, Fawkes… we're leaving. Like you always wanted."

Dracus forced a grin through his pain. It wasn't what he'd always wanted, at least not how he'd pictured it. But those expectations had to die, and out here was as good a time as any to let them. Same as the questions he still had. Like how and when did Canton discover Dracus's condition? Was that why he didn't want to leave—so they could be together? Did he wish to survive in Rheynia with Dracus rather than go to Sansia without him? But just like he had to hold his expectations up to the irradiator, he had to do the same with his soul jar filled with questions.

"Yeah, kid." He patted the soul jar holding Fawkes. "Just like we planned, eh?"

"Not quite." Canton grinned before he sputtered, blood dribbling from his lips. After he wheezed back to the closest thing the dying could have approaching comfort, he sank into Dracus's embrace. "What'd Fawkes leave for you… in his fatekeeper?"

Dracus hmphed. Whatever secret wisdom Fawkes had bestowed in his fatekeeper, Dracus had lost when he opened it to unleash the Blessing. "Dunno. Old Boy can tell us himself on the other side." He chuckled, despite the rattling pain it sent through his ribs.

He gazed at Laela clutching her bloody stump where her hand should have been. It wasn't meant for her. Same way it wasn't meant for Threyna. Now they would both have to bear the curse he'd unleashed on them. There was no telling what it would look like, living with such a condition beyond Rheynia, but he hoped that they would figure it out. Better yet if they could do it together.

"You never wrote me one," Canton said.

Dracus chewed his mustache. "Wrote ya what—fatekeeper?"

"Yeah."

Dracus shrugged, looking to the thinning clouds and the starry sky beyond. "Never wrote one for Fawkes either."

"Why?"

Dracus snorted. In truth, he never knew what to say. *"I love you." "I'm proud." "Why didn'tcha just listen to me, ghost damn ya!"* He shrugged, glad he didn't attempt to, because everything failed to articulate what he wanted to say. "Never had one from my folks. I dunno. Some things words fail to say. Sometimes they say too much and not enough at the same time."

Canton stared at the sky, the stars reflecting in his bleary gaze. "Can you try?" His voice was so weak.

Dracus felt him slipping away. But just ahead, the sky was completely clear. Not a cloud marred the perfect horizon. *It's time.* He repositioned Canton within his grasp and took hold of the soul jar that held Fawkes. He squeezed the switch, unlocking the soul jar. Fawkes's shade slipped free, glowing like the luminescent starlight. The visage of the man he loved in life took shape before him. He stared back at Dracus, a hint of recognition flickering across his eyes.

Hoping Fawkes could hear, Dracus sang to them both. "To dream is to die. To hope is to lie. To live is to lose all we've come by. The lucky, we fall. And the misfortuned, we cry, but forever and ever it is we who survive. Let go, my love. Let go and see. Let go the woes and sing high for me."

When he finished, both Fawkes and Canton stared back at him.

"What's it mean?" Canton asked.

Dracus snorted. "See, pretty words ain't all they're made out to be."

"What's it mean?" Canton asked again, weaker this time.

Dracus took a deep breath, glancing over the bow of the ship at the clear sky ahead. "Means ya can't control much of anythin'. It ain't gonna be pretty. Nothin's gonna go how ya planned. But wherever ya end up, it'll have been worth it if you're with the ones who matter." He returned his gaze to Fawkes's shade and gave Canton a squeeze. Then, all at once, all the pain was gone.

CHAPTER 64

GOLDEN

Threyna XXVIII

The long boat split the seas, carrying the few that remained from Rheynia's shores. Of their dozen occupants, half wouldn't survive the trip. Dracus would never make it beyond the curse. She could feel the life fleeing from Canton with each passing beat of his heart. Others would have been better off if she had just taken their souls to ferry them from Rheynia and release them once past the barrier.

"I want to see the sky," one woman said.

"Lemme die true," another begged, dying on the sands. *"Never truly got to live."*

Threyna understood. As badly as she felt for them, they were the lucky ones. As Rheynia faded into the distance, she didn't look back. She couldn't. Because far fewer were on the boat than on the Grip's beaches or along the Tears' currents. How many more were left along the Spine, fell outside of Aranoc, or never even made it out of Avengard? Too many corpses lay in their wake. And though the souls she'd consumed on the beach and taken from the Skeleton King's possession were celebrating in her Inner Throne, there were many who didn't make it.

Ebrus and Yevon. Rivich and Marius. Even Arilette and Lorath.

There would be no last words. No apologies to ease her conscience. No explanations to be shared to satiate theirs. She would be left with the mysteries that their souls took with them wherever they went after flesh had failed and spirit was spent. Threyna didn't even know if they went anywhere after they were consumed.

Was there an afterlife? A peace past this mortal plane of existence, or a desolation beyond the reach of pain's grasp. What future awaited Aylenia, her mother and father, or any of the other souls she carried? She kept those thoughts locked away from the souls of her Inner Throne. They didn't need her doubt prior to their final voyage. Instead, she clung to the hope that reverberated through the walls of her Inner Throne.

The black rot that had spiraled around the columns in her throne room like corrupted vines had all but burned away in the wash of glowing souls. Their excitement grew the further from Rheynia they sailed. Long-lost souls reconnected, families thought lost reacquainted, and lovers mourned became enraptured in tender embraces once again.

It warmed Threyna's heart to see. But too little. Too late.

She couldn't decide which was a more painful place to be: present in her raucous Inner Throne that would soon be quiet and empty, or upon the sea where Dracus and Canton shared their last words before death took them both. Laela seemed absent, twisting *True*'s hilt within her palm as she stared at the stump where her hand should have been. Perhaps she too retreated into her pontifications to prevent herself from slipping into despondency. Or maybe she was already there.

Goodbyes were coming, something she'd never much enjoyed. But this approaching loneliness was not abandonment. Though it felt the same and brought on the same fears, she knew it was not the case. Not all goodbyes were abandonment. And not all separations were final. She chose to believe that one day she would greet them again in whatever came next. It wouldn't be easy, but it allowed her to believe beyond her doubt—through her skepticism—that there was more to this life than pain and suffering and something more afterwards than the silence of death.

Aylenia approached her within her Inner Throne. *"You did it."*

Threyna stood and hugged her. The embrace felt real, warm—as it had when they were bunkmates in Octarius's barracks. She sank into her friend's arms, wondering if anyone would quite accept her as she was the way Aylenia had.

"We did it," Threyna said. *"Couldn't have done it without you. Without everyone."*

Aylenia grinned, shoving Threyna's shoulder. *"Don't think I'd let you get away with taking all the credit."*

A sad smile parted her lips because this would be the last time she got to share one with Aylenia. She swallowed the knot stuck at the scar on her throat. *"Are you scared?"*

Aylenia pursed her lips before shaking her head. *"No. Not really. Maybe I should be more so."* She shrugged. *"But you should not fear for me."*

Threyna hung her head, unable to meet Aylenia's eyes. *What if I fear for myself?* She kept her thoughts sealed, locked away from Aylenia and the others. She felt selfish for even thinking them as they were about to embark on the voyage of whatever came after, but she couldn't help how she felt.

She didn't know what to say next. She didn't have Ebrus's poetry or Yevon's levity. Nor had she mastered Arilette's matter-of-fact delivery of difficult news. In her pause, Aylenia spoke.

"You've been like a sister to me… And I mean that in a good way. Not in the way you've likely thought about it all these years."

Threyna didn't need an explanation. Despite their differences, Laela had been there when Threyna needed her most, and Threyna had done the same for her. They weren't friends; perhaps they'd never be after all they'd been through. But they were sisters. They had a bond, and maybe that was all they needed. But Aylenia had been the sister she had chosen all these years.

"I never would have survived Octarius without you," Threyna said. *"I never would have survived the Grip without you…"* She struggled not to choke on her words. *How am I going to survive whatever comes next without you?* She couldn't bring herself to say that part.

"You would have found a way," Aylenia said. *"You always do."*

Part of her wanted to ask Aylenia to stay with her, to remain in her Inner Throne so they could face whatever came next together, but she couldn't say that either. Would that she could keep everyone she hadn't had enough time with; it just wasn't how it was supposed to be. To keep them would be to bind them, deprive them of their journey for the sake of comforting herself. Still, she could not stave off the thought of the loneliness that would follow.

Surrounded by hundreds of souls, all she felt was the impending hollow reckoning that would come once they reached the edge of the curse.

Threyna sniffed. *"If you find Eb, Yevon, Daeton, or Rivich out there…"*

Aylenia placed her hand on Threyna's shoulder. *"I'll tell Ebrus you always liked his poems—even the sappy ones. I'll tell Yevon you appreciated his jokes even when you didn't laugh. I'll apologize to Daeton for you, but I already know he's forgiven you. And Rivich… well, there's not much pleasing Rivich, but I know he'll be proud of what we did today."*

Threyna's sad smile returned. *"Ghosts… I miss them all. But I'll miss you most."* She shook her head. *"Is it crazy that I'm jealous of you?"*

"Of course not," Aylenia said, primping her wisps of curly hair. *"There's a lot to be jealous of."* She fixed Threyna with a serious expression, seizing her by both shoulders. *"There's more to life than the past. Whatever Gods I meet—Neutreen, the Corners… ghosts, even the ripping One—I'll pray that they let you live for more than what is behind you. Because there is so much ahead."*

She looked to the starry sky ahead of their blood boat. *"You know, beyond the curse, my mûnta said that the sun rises every day. Like a miracle born on the horizon, it paints everything black in glittering gold."* She stroked the scars along Threyna's arm where the blood artifact had sunk its prongs into her and infected her with the black rot that marred her veins and darkened her soul. *"You're golden, Threyna. You haven't felt the sun yet, but you will. And every day, it will give you something new to live for."*

Tears welled in Threyna's eyes, and she sank back into Aylenia's embrace.

"Looks like I learned something from Ebrus." Aylenia laughed. Even Threyna allowed herself a soft chuckle.

Outside of her Inner Throne, the barrier drew nearer. She was running out of time. Laela stared out at the expanse ahead, a somberness wrinkling her green eyes. *"I think Laela would want to see you... before you go."*

Aylenia gave Threyna one last squeeze before backing away. She nodded in the direction of Threyna's parents as they approached, arm in arm. *"I think you have more goodbyes to make in any case. One day, we'll meet again. Under happier circumstances. But not for a long time yet. There's always another fight ahead."*

"And many more victories." She returned Aylenia's smile, sad that she would have to win them on her own from now on. At her command, Aylenia faded from the marble throne room and passed the short distance across the blood boat from Threyna to Laela. Laela's sullen cheeks suddenly rounded into the fullness of a smile. The sight brought a sorrowful grin to Threyna's lips. She felt the weight of the pouch of Viridite glowstones Aylenia had given her.

"You never know when you'll need a bit of light," Aylenia had said.

Threyna was glad she had them now.

Back within her Inner Throne, her parents approached her.

"Little Dove," her father said, his face whole again, as she remembered him before the Battle of the Cut. He wrapped her in an embrace, the kind she'd longed for since Arilette first told her that he was still alive.

She clung to him as she'd done before the Battle of the Cut ten years ago. Then, she'd thought he'd be coming back. This time, she knew he wouldn't be.

"Father, this wasn't how it was supposed to be."

"I know," he said, not letting her go and squeezing tighter. *"I know. None of this went as it should have. Best-laid plans. Ashes."* He stroked her arm where the prongs had bitten into her. *"I never wanted this for you. I know it doesn't seem like it right now, but there is peace to be found in this*

world." He released her to wrap his arm around her mother. *"Peace, love, hope, purpose. You will find them all."*

The fast-approaching emptiness hollowed out her insides. There was a lifetime of parental wisdom she wanted—needed—for her lonely journey ahead. There were so many questions to ask and not enough time. *"What if I can't find them? Any of them?"*

"You will. But once you do, you can't be afraid to fight for them."

Threyna wrapped her arms around both of them. Soft sobs rattled her ribs. She wasn't ready to let go of them. This was all she had wanted as a girl, for them to be together, and now they were finally united only to be ripped apart again.

Her mother shushed her soothingly. *"You will, Threyna. But it's out there..."* She pointed to the world beyond the stained-glass windows of her throne room. *"In here..."* She placed her hand over Threyna's heart, then shook her head. *"But it's not back where you've been. It's not us. We're sorry you didn't have the childhood you should have. We can't make up for that. But I promise you, Threyna, you will know peace. And in it, I hope you can forgive us our failings."*

Threyna wanted to be angry with Arilette for turning her against her mother, but the spike of rage subsided in the arms of her parents. She imagined what life could have been like if things had been different. If they had sailed on Arenius's ships, if they had made it to Sansia as a family. But wishes and wants wouldn't turn back time, and *what-ifs* were reserved for those trapped in the past.

"I will," Threyna said. She didn't know how or when she'd find this peace her father spoke of. But she wouldn't give up on seeking it. She'd fight for it. She'd run towards it.

The clouds over Rheynia's waters thinned, and just ahead, only clear skies remained.

It's almost time.

Dracus, Canton, and Fawkes's shade nestled together in their final goodbyes. Laela and Aylenia made peace with their truncated future, tears falling from Laela's full cheeks. The others aboard the boat either comforted their loved ones or stared eagerly ahead to the starry sky on the horizon.

"Go forth," her father said. *"Wherever we go, you will be with us, and we will be with you."*

CHAPTER 65

LIVE

Laela XXV

Silence permeated both in and outside her seat of power. She felt the sea sloshing beneath Threyna's conjured boat, the breeze whipping her loose braid, and the throb of phantom pain where her severed hand should have been, but everything else seemed at rest. Not a peaceful, slumbering rest, but a dark disquiet.

Part of her wished the old stories of the carnivorous, shelled Aeritan beasts would hold some truth as they set out from the Grip. Well past Aeritan Bay, no sea monsters had disturbed their passage. Like so many lies she'd been led to believe, it seemed these too held no weight.

Even her father was silent. He had been since the bracelet formed around her wrist. She'd let down her walls. She'd accepted the Blessing. She'd fought. But now the blood artifact was gone. So was her father. And left in their wake, the eerie silence clung to her as tightly as her wet and bloodstained tunic, and as heavily as her broken heart weighed down their supposed victory.

This wasn't the dream she'd pictured when Rance spoke of freedom beyond the curse. This wasn't the celebratory flight from Rheynia's shores her mother had promised. It wasn't anything like the stories where the heroes triumphed over the villains and all lived happily ever after. This was the cost of victory, the price for life in a dark and harrowing world.

Laela alternated between hanging her head and staring into the waiting abyss. She didn't look back, though. Dracus had said the sea swallowed the

Blessing along with Belrich's blood and the Skeleton King's corpse. The Order would be no more. The people would be free to make their choices on whether they stayed and rebuilt or sought to leave.

Once, Laela thought it her purpose to bring people beyond Rheynia's shores, to usher them to safety under Neutreen's wings. She didn't know if what the Skeleton King had shown her was true—that Neutreen was killed at the hands of the One True God. Wherever they were going, Sansia or beyond, there would be no shrines to Neutreen, and she wasn't sure that there should be. There were too few of them to build a new bastion of hope, and even if there were more of them, Laela would still have to be the leader of Neutreen's revival movement.

I lack the faith.

In a more recent dream of the future, she'd imagined her and Aylenia traveling the lands in search of her mûnta. Perhaps it was foolish to even think of. They barely knew each other, yet the prospect of adventuring, seeing the world, being responsible for no one but herself—it was too enticing to deny. To do so with a woman she felt an undeniable connection with, that made it all the more attractive. But that future was gone now too.

Absent the hope of faith, the love of friends and family, what was there to build a life upon? Strength and courage could only get her so far absent hope and love.

She stared at her severed wrist and the black veins snaking up her forearm. She conjured a bloody hand, just to feel whole, but it didn't make her feel any better. Neither did *True*. The dagger Theodyn had given her had seen too many lies to stand for anything solid. They were leaving the curse, doing everything she'd dreamed of. But Redge, Bhen, and Asla were still on the Grip's beaches. Rosler and Taggart were left impaled on pikes. And Aylenia…

She'd failed Rance, lost her mother, betrayed her sister, been betrayed by Tarus, but it was Aylenia's loss she felt most keenly of all. Impaled on the steppe—so far from Sansia, her mûnta, or the dreams she had.

Laela didn't know what became of the souls they'd inhaled. Their curse was a mystery to her. It had served its purpose—she, Threyna, and a clutch of others would arrive on the beaches of Sansia; Dracus, Canton, Fawkes and those bound for the afterlife would receive true deaths beyond the curse. She told herself it was worth it, but despite holding *True* in her remaining hand, she wasn't certain she was being honest with herself.

The waves tossed beneath her, creating more space between her and Rheynia's dread, but the curse would come with her. This painful ordeal, this horrific past would cling to her and flow through her. The bloodborne hand on her severed wrist was proof of that.

She glanced at Threyna, her eyes glazed over, preoccupied with her own inward thoughts. *Maybe we'll find a cure...* She considered that future. The prospect of traveling with Threyna, even after this newfound understanding of each other, wasn't exactly enticing. *She never planned on leaving Rheynia. She never dreamed of rebuilding. All she has known is war, fighting. Would she care about a cure? Would she even want to travel with me?*

They shared blood and trauma, but was that a reason to stay together? Would that bond only serve to grate the wounds between them? Laela didn't know, but the future would soon be upon them.

As the clouds over Rheynia thinned and the starry sky beyond began to abound, a silvery wisp slipped free of Threyna and swirled with the winds toward Laela. A momentary fear startled her, but as the soul slipped into Laela's Center of Silence, the fear became an exposed timidity, then genuine happiness.

A vibrant resonance hummed a sweet song of strength and beauty in the darkness of her Center of Silence, a combination she recognized immediately though she'd never truly known.

"Usually, I offer a girl some Valefyre first..." Aylenia said, her rhythm pleasantly disturbing the quiet through the darkness.

"Aylenia..." The resonance her name made within her Center of Silence was more beautiful than the starry skies beyond the clouds. Their thoughts, emotions, and memories came together but didn't touch, as if

there were an invisible boundary between them. For years, she'd kept her father at a distance, but now, with Aylenia so close, her mother's words returned to her.

"There is strength in knowing when to drop your guard and courage in actually doing so."

A momentary panic filled her at the prospect of such vulnerability, but Laela refused to let anyone keep her hurting. With strength and courage, she allowed herself to submit, releasing hold of the apprehensive walls that she'd put up to protect herself.

No longer separated, their souls entwined. A deep knowing connected them in a way Laela had never experienced before—a level of intimacy she never thought possible. The same wondrous dreams that Laela felt silly for considering flowed through Aylenia's spirit as well.

"I would have enjoyed that future," Aylenia said softly, seeing her dreams of Sansia.

"Can we not still?" Laela asked, not too proud of how desperate she sounded. She didn't care. She didn't want to wander Sansia and the world beyond alone.

Aylenia's essence caressed her own with tender affection. *"Can you think of a greater torture—to be together, but never truly together?"*

She found herself thinking of Aylenia being impaled by the spear atop the steppe.

"Don't think about that," Aylenia said.

Her thoughts turned to what would happen to Aylenia once they crossed the barrier and she released her from the safety of her Center of Silence. *Will she ascend to Valencia? Will she simply cease to be as if she never existed at all?*

"Don't think about that either," Aylenia said, drawing like a salve on her poisonous thoughts. *"Be with me here, now."*

Laela tried to focus, but the moment was too painful. Her mind wandered; her emotions warred, tossing and turning like the breakers along the shore. *"What am I supposed to do, Aylenia?"* She didn't feel strong or courageous. Since departing Rheynia, no swell of pride or sense of accomplishment quelled the rising tides of failure and loss growing within her. *"What am I supposed to do now?"*

Aylenia's rhythm changed until her vibrations opposed Laela's, canceling them out and returning silence to their shared space. A calmness washed over her, a peace she'd seldom felt even at the foot of Neutreen's altar.

"You live," Aylenia said with the assurance of someone who held all the answers. *"You live for those of us who can't."*

"How can you be so calm? What about you?"

Aylenia's thoughts drifted, revealing to Laela stories her mûnta had shared with her about the isles of Palogia. The crystal-clear waters surrounding Kataan's four main islands, the trials held to beseech the Corners's blessings, the Lanaen pirates they all feared—it was so vivid in Aylenia's mind that it became real in Laela's.

"There will always be something to fear, Laela. I've seen enough Gods and learned enough religions to trust that there must be something more. Whatever it is, soon I will meet it. But fearing it won't change it. It'd only change me for the worse. So do not fear what happens next, because I would hate for you to change." Aylenia's rhythm encompassed Laela's to create a harmonious syncopation that steadied her soul.

Outside of her Center of Silence, the clouds had faded in favor of the starry sky. It was time. Dracus's and Canton's souls slipped from their failing bodies. Entwining with Fawkes's shade, the three became orbs of light of different hues. Laela couldn't discern which was which, but they ascended into the sky together, leaving a trail of braided light in their wake.

"See," Aylenia said. *"Don't they look like they have a place to go?"*

The others loaded onto the boat to die beyond the curse fled their flesh to ascend in light to the world beyond the stars.

A tear came to Laela's eyes. *We never needed to earn our wings.* Suddenly, the Four Tenets of Elysianism felt flimsy. Merit, Modesty, Measure, and Moderation—four means to ensure obedience, resource management, dynastic stability, elitism amongst the Dominion, and repression for all that sought to rise above their station. As more souls took to the skies, questions abounded: *Was it always so? Did the Order manipulate the Tenets? Did Neutreen ever grant people their wings?*

As her foundation fractured, so too did her fears. Perhaps Neutreen was gone. Perhaps the One did in fact murder her. But there was still someone, something, watching over all.

Hundreds upon hundreds of souls streamed from Threyna's chest and rose to the stars like the tendrils of smoke Laela once relied on to carry her prayers to Neutreen.

"I hope it's beautiful," Laela said, gazing at the rising lights and the starry sky they ascended to.

"It must be," Aylenia said. *"If it's this stunning from here, how much more so must it be up close?"*

Souls continued to spill from Threyna, some of which began to swirl around Laela before taking their voyage to Valencia. Up close, she saw through their light to the faces they wore in life. Bhen and Asla danced around her prior to taking flight. Redge lingered, swirling atop her shoulders before joining them on the trip to the stars. Lastly, two more souls encircled her. Theodyn, the man who'd loved her as a daughter more than her own father ever could. And her mother. Her light shone so brightly. No longer timid or frail as Laela had seen her in life, she was the epitome of strength and courage. She defied the night, bathing the entire boat in her aura.

Her mother's light came close. "I love you, Laela."

She could have sworn she felt a kiss on her cheek. Real or imagined, she knew what she heard, knew how it made her feel. Watching her mother and Theodyn entwine as they sailed through the sky, Laela began to believe that somehow, some way, eventually, everything would all be fine.

"One day, I'll join you," Laela said to Aylenia.

"Not for a long time yet, I hope." Aylenia slipped free of Laela's Center of Silence, her orb of light shining before her. Tender pressure caressed her cheek. Then, with more force, but no less tender, soft lips pressed against her own. "Farewell, Laela."

And just like that, she too joined the rising lights.

Together, Laela and Threyna stood in awe. As like so many times in their lives before, they watched a thousand embers climb into the sky. But on this occasion, no ashes rained down. No smoke soiled the air as it rose. Only light. And across the horizon, bathed in the glow of the ascending souls, the first glimpse of land jutted out from the sea. A new life. A new home. Hope.

EPILOGUE

Cold rips through me. Soft, supple, beautiful numbness lingers just beyond my grasp, leaving me in lonesome agony. If I could just reach out, if I could but move, all of life's riches would be at my fingertips. But alas, I am left empty-handed in this cold, dark, cruel world.

Wind washes over me, racking me with a chill that starts at the top of my skull and slithers down my spine to follow my ribs' contour. I cough violently, but new pain throttles my existence. I eject whatever foul brine and blood found its way inside my lungs, but it's thrown back in my face by a powerful rush.

I turn from the sound, but too late, and I can't move far enough. Salt burns my eyes and stings my soul as the ocean's wrath lashes out against me only to retreat, carrying with it a distant memory of power's origin. The Blessing and the bloody hand it clung to fell to the surf. It tossed and turned in the waves, suspended between time and space, between destiny and doom. In my mind's eye, I reach for it again, only to be struck in the back. I feel the blade spear me through and through. Before I can lament the irony of falling to the demise of my preferred form of sentencing, I'm met with an onslaught of dagger's kisses. Pecking at me like crows to a corpse, they ensure I will not rise.

I remember watching the tide draw the blood from my body, pulling the very life from me in slow recurring torment. I remember the cries of my men. The screams of my father. I recall losing myself in the abyss as the world went black.

So why am I still here?

I push myself up by pressing my hands into the wet sand of the vicious sea, but I'm impaled anew. Out of the corner of my eye, the hilt protrudes from the center of my back. I curse the world for birthing me to a hollowed mother. I swear by the One that no gift he could bestow would be worth the demands he'd made of me and my family.

I prop myself up to sit on my knees, unsure if I'm alive or hollowed. Staring at the sword point erupting through my stomach, I try to seize the flat of the blade and press it out my back. My trembling fingers are incapable of the task. I try to reach for the hilt by wrenching my arm behind my back, and though I can touch it, I don't have the strength or the angle to pry it free.

I breathe as deeply as my torn flesh will allow, preparing to do what must be done if I am going to survive this newest calamity. I use the tips of my fingers to press the blade's tip back through my torso. My fingers, soft and pruned by the sea, bleed as if I haven't sacrificed enough. I try to clench my chattering teeth through the pain, but my jaw refuses to obey me. Powerless, I persevere. I continue to press into the blade despite the gash along my fingers and the agony of feeling the blade slide out my back.

Yet I have to press deeper. My shaking, bloody fingers slip through the leather of my armor, between the folds of the open wound in my abdomen, and into the warm sinew in an attempt to force the blade free. The touch of my own fingers inside my guts is enough to die for. If that isn't bad enough, the warmth of my blood burns my freezing hands, but I continue. I push. I scream. I endure what my mother must have in bringing me into this world, but once the blade slips free and falls to my heels, I am done.

I fall to my back and stare at the clouds overhead. My body feels afire now like the embers of the Wraith's ship, which only makes me grateful for the cooling tides that climb the sands up to my hips.

I have never been one to count the time, to track the days and weeks, moons and years—it always seemed a fruitless endeavor because Father cared not for time. I believed his immortality would one day become my own, and I too would live and reign forever in service to the One True God. Yet now I stare at the sky and count each moment a blessing.

As I draw in breath, the air fogs before me, but with each labored inhale and every passing wave, I feel the pain lessen. Strength returns. Half-expecting a rageful hunger to consume me as I hollow, or my soul to slip free of this cage of a body, I remain intact. Whole if not for a headache that encircles my scalp. All things considered, I can manage a headache.

As feeling returns to my fingers, I place them to my stomach. They come away bloody, but there is no pain. I poke and prod, knowing now that I must be hollowed, yet I feel only a scar where the blade once was.

My One True God, you have spared me!

I drink in the air, filling my lungs to capacity, simply because I can. To have defied death, to have survived, I am elated. However, it is as ephemeral as mortality. The shoreline is littered with the bodies of my Inquisitors, my legionaries, and, worst of all, my father. I crawl to his side in the light of the smoldering ruin of the ship.

A million times I had pictured this: the Skeleton King dead at my hands. His power becoming mine. His mission, my own. Yet it wasn't supposed to be like this. Not to Bherus's hellhound daughter. Not to a spawn of the Velar brood. And certainly not to Dracus ghosting Alius.

I sink to the sands as I wallow in my miserable failings. There is no telling what will come next in the wake of his death. The stories of the anarchy that ravaged Rheynia following the Disasters ruin my revival from the dead. I am not so young that I do not recall the War of the Seers, yet not so old as to have only watched the Artificers fall. A new war will come, yet for the first time in the better part of a century, there is no blood mage to determine its outcome.

I roll away from my father's corpse, cursing him for letting Bherus make off with what should have been my birthright. Pressing myself to all fours as the tide rolls out beneath me, I feel something flop against my boot.

The ocean ebbs away, leaving a pool in its wake. As the water in the pool stills, I see something I thought lost to me. A pale hand. Five fingers, half closed like a claw. Laughter escapes me as I pluck it from its watery grave. Not because it is still the object of my desire, but because it isn't.

The Blessing is missing from its wrist. It is just a hand. And I am just a man holding it, wishing for more.

The tide rolls in again, and as it retreats, I cast the severed hand out with it. Yet as the water not swallowed by the sea begins to settle, I see my reflection.

Dark veins stretch down my forehead like black lightning. I blink, leaning closer to the pool. I don't believe my eyes, but there it sits. Atop my head rests a red-and-black circlet.

The Blessing… the One True God provides.

My laughter roars to rival rolling thunder. My glee writhes within me like tongues of fire. Purpose blossoms, plans form, and I laugh knowing I will be better than my father ever was, than my brother ever could have been.

"I will unite the world for you. I will be your Champion!"

To be continued in:

A VENGEFUL REALM
Read the completed trilogy now!

ACKNOWLEDGEMENTS

Despite the release date, this was the second story I wrote. I had just finished cutting *The Scales of Balance* from its first draft length of 278,000 words to a much more manageable 125,000. Once that was sent off to my editor, Chersti Nieveen at Writertherapy.com, I, the eager upstart that I am, asked her what I could do in the meantime. I wanted to work on book two in the *A Vengeful Realm* trilogy as I prepared to query book one to agents. She told me I couldn't sell book two if I hadn't sold the first book yet, and to instead work on something new. Something unrelated. A new book one. With that, I decided I was going to start small. A single point-of-view novella—a far cry from the 10+ points of view in the original drafts of *The Scales of Balance*. Threyna, one of the main point-of-view characters cut from that draft, became the main protagonist of that new project. Yet as this new "totally different" and "wholly separate" single point-of-view novella unfolded, I realized two things about myself. One: I am incapable of keeping it short. Two: I won't do anything simple.

Long story short, the novella became something approaching the story you just read. Nowhere close to small, not remotely simple, and certainly not wholly separated from book one. In fact, it not only changed what I wanted to do in book one of AVR, but it altered the trajectory of the trilogy. For that, I could not be more grateful, because it made *A Vengeful Realm* what it is today, but it also made *Ghosts of Rheynia* very difficult to write. Wanting it to serve as a standalone for those who hadn't read AVR and a prequel for those who had, while simultaneously allowing readers to read in either order without significant spoilers, this story needed tremendous amounts of help. Again, I turned to Chersti and her team. I would particularly like to thank Tanner Perkes and Andraea Jones for helping me to wrangle this story into something readable. Your patience, support, and expertise brought this story of undeath to life. I would also like to thank Brian Dooley at Paper Raven Books. While I was working through a bout of depression, worried that this story was too dark to publish, you reminded me that the characters, despite their circumstances, always remained oriented towards hope. Thank you for helping me to see the light through the darkness.

Special shoutouts: Freya from Lunaris Falcon Studio, thank you for another beautiful cover! You are the best at what you do and it is an absolute joy to work with you. Landon Soelberg, the narrator of all of my books thus far, thank you for your creativity and passion. The performances you give are second to none! Mariya Kapitsa, the illustrator for the map of Rheynia, thank you for the heart and soul you put into every detail. You set the tone for the story before page one.

Lastly, I would like to thank the author community for being one of the most uplifting and supportive collectives I've had the pleasure to be part of. Thank you to Nathan Makaryk, Sebastien De Castell, Z.S. Diamanti, John Wells III, SG Blaise, Andy Peloquin, JDL Rosell, Brady Hunsaker, and E.A. Winters.

ABOUT THE AUTHOR

Tim Facciola is the multi-award-winning author of the A Vengeful Realm trilogy. With blue ribbons for the Ozma Award for Fantasy Fiction and the Chanticleer International Best Book of 2023, he continues to write hopeful epic fantasy stories.

When Tim isn't writing, he can often be found in his garage-gym or in the mountains of Arizona where he lives with his wife, Colleen. A virtual fitness professional by trade, he integrates his creative passions into movement, training with maces, clubs, staves, and swords to unlock his inner legionary. To inquire about Gladiator Training, reach out to him at TimFacciolaFit@gmail.com.

More than writing, reading, gaming, playing music, hiking, and paddleboarding, Tim loves story. If he's not working on his own story, he's helping others develop theirs as an author coach. To inquire about Author Coaching services, email Firsttorchbooks@gmail.com.

To listen to Dracus's Lullaby, scan the link below:

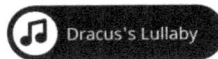

Dracus's Lullaby

www.ingramcontent.com/pod-product-compliance
Lightning Source LLC
LaVergne TN
LVHW040635170125
801529LV00002B/55